THE ANNOTATED

AFRICAN AMERICAN FOLKTALES

---・《》・---

The Annotated Uncle Tom's Cabin
by Harriet Beecher Stowe, edited with an introduction
and notes by Henry Louis Gates Jr. and Hollis Robbins

The Annotated Hans Christian Andersen
translated by Maria Tatar and Julie Allen, with an introduction
and notes by Maria Tatar

The Annotated Secret Garden
by Frances Hodgson Burnett, edited with an introduction
and notes by Gretchen Holbrook Gerzina

The New Annotated Dracula
by Bram Stoker, with an introduction by Neil Gaiman,
edited with a preface and notes by Leslie S. Klinger

The Annotated Wind in the Willows
by Kenneth Grahame, with an introduction by Brian Jacques,
edited with a preface and notes by Annie Gauger

The Annotated Peter Pan
by J. M. Barrie, edited with an introduction and notes by Maria Tatar

The New Annotated H. P. Lovecraft
with an introduction by Alan Moore,
edited with a foreword and notes by Leslie S. Klinger

The New Annotated Frankenstein
by Mary Shelley, with an introduction by Guillermo del Toro
and an afterword by Anne K. Mellor,
edited with a foreword and notes by Leslie S. Klinger

---・《》・---

LIVERIGHT PUBLISHING CORPORATION

A Division of W. W. Norton & Company

Independent Publishers Since 1923

New York • London

THE ANNOTATED

AFRICAN AMERICAN FOLKTALES

EDITED WITH A FOREWORD, INTRODUCTION, AND NOTES BY

HENRY LOUIS GATES JR.
and MARIA TATAR

For information about special discounts for bulk purchases, please contact
W. W. Norton Special Sales at specialsales@wwnorton.com or 800-233-4830

Manufacturing by Transcontinental Printing
Book design by JAM Design
Production manager: Anna Oler

ISBN 978-0-87140-753-5

Liveright Publishing Corporation
500 Fifth Avenue, New York, N.Y. 10110
www.wwnorton.com

W. W. Norton & Company Ltd.
15 Carlisle Street, London W1D 3BS

1 2 3 4 5 6 7 8 9 0

For all those before us who kept these stories alive by
listening to the voices of others:
Talk got us here.

Henry Louis Gates Jr. dedicates this volume to
Eleanor Margaret Gates-Hatley
"L'dor va'dor!"

Maria Tatar dedicates this volume to
Lauren Blum, Daniel Schuker, Jason Blum, Giselle
Barcia, and Roxy Blum

This interlinking of the New World and all countries and ages, by the golden net-work of oral tradition, may supply the moral of our collection.

—WILLIAM WELLS NEWELL,
Games and Songs of American Children

Mouse goes everywhere. She prowls through the houses of the rich, and she visits the poor as well. At night, with her bright little eyes, she watches the doing of secret things, and no treasure chamber is so safe but she can tunnel through and see what is hidden there.

In olden days she wove a story-child from everything she saw, and to each of these she gave a gown of a different color—white, red, blue, or black. The stories became her children and lived in her house and served her because she had no children of her own.

—Nigerian folktale

CONTENTS

AFRICAN AMERICAN TALES

ACKNOWLEDGMENTS

Putting this book together offered the opportunity to stand on the shoulders of giants and geniuses. That did not always imply seeing farther or more clearly, but it did mean the chance to look back, to wade through the tides of time and uncover what remains of robust oral storytelling traditions from a past era. We are both grateful to the vibrant scholarly community in residence at the Hutchins Center for African & African American Research. To the students in our courses at Harvard University, we owe a special debt for turning solitary research into a collective intellectual adventure. Every story in this volume deserves a credit line acknowledging the many students, colleagues, and friends who guided us to sources, shared their wisdom, and contributed generously to the fund of knowledge accumulated over the course of the years dedicated to this volume.

It took the genius of Bob Weil to imagine this book and his powers of persuasion to recruit us to write it. We are grateful to him and Marie Pantojan at Liveright and W. W. Norton, who guided this book through the production process. Doris Sperber provided research materials with lightning speed and solved archival puzzles that were often beyond us. Anne Callahan entered the world of wonderlore and discovered images and stories that had escaped our attention, all the while expertly navigating the world of copyright and permissions.

As for the rest of you, who provided friendship and support, you know who you are, but we can't resist naming some names: Professor Tatar wishes to thank Lauren Blum, Daniel Schuker, Jason Blum, Giselle Barcia, Shirley Blum, John Tatar, Anna Tatar, Steve Tatar, Sanford Kreisberg, Christina Phillips Mattson, Larry Wolff, Perri

Klass, Holly Hutchison, Steve Mitchell, Deborah Foster, Leah Lowthorp, Gregory Nagy, Joseph Nagy, Elizabeth Fox, Katie Kohn, Penelope Laurans, Jack Zipes, Philip Nel, Donald Haase, Cristina Bacchilega, Roger Abrahams, Genesee Johnson, and David Newman.

Professor Gates wishes to thank Kevin Burke, Carra Glatt, Bennett Ashley, David Kuhn, Lauren Sharp, Abby Wolf, Marial Iglesias Utset, Amy Gosdanian, Donald Waters, and Hollis Robbins.

FOREWORD
The Politics of "Negro Folklore"
by Henry Louis Gates Jr.

The Negroes have a wonderfull Art of communicating Intelligence among themselves. It will run severall hundreds of Miles in a Week or Fortnight.

> —John Adams's Diary, September 24, 1775

The American Negroes are rising so rapidly from the condition of ignorance and poverty in which slavery left them, to a position among the cultivated and civilized people of the earth, that the time seems not far distant when they shall have cast off their past entirely, and stand an anomaly among civilized races, as a people having no distinct traditions, beliefs or ideas from which a history of their growth may be traced. If within the next few years care is not taken to collect and preserve all traditions and customs peculiar to the Negroes there will be little to reward the search of the future historian who would trace the history of the African continent through the years of slavery to the position which they will hold a few generations hence.

> —ALICE BACON, Editorial, *Southern Workman*, December 1893

The black man is readily assimilated to his surroundings and the original simple and distinct type is in danger of being lost or outgrown. To my mind, the worst possibility yet is that the so-called educated Negro, under the shadow of this over powering Anglo-Saxon civilization, may become ashamed of his own distinctive features and aspire only to be an imitator of that which can not but impress him as the climax of human greatness, and so all originality, all *sincerity*, all *self*-assertion would be lost to him. What he needs is the inspiration of knowing that his racial inheritance is of interest to others and that when they come to seek his homely songs and sayings and doings, it is not to scoff and sneer, but to study reverently, as an original type of the Creator's handiwork.

—ANNA JULIA COOPER, Letter to the Editor,
Southern Workman, January 1894

I am speaking then, not with regards to the past, but the future, when I say that it is of consequence for the American Negro to retain the recollection of his African origin, and of his American servitude. For the sake of the honor of his race, he should have a clear picture of the mental condition out of which he has emerged: this picture is not now complete, nor will be made so without a record of song, tales, beliefs, which belongs to the stage of culture through which he has passed.

—WILLIAM WELLS NEWELL, "The Importance and Utility of the
Collection of Negro Folk-Lore," *Southern Workman*, July 1894

The field of folklore in general is known to be a battle area, and the Negro front is one of the hottest sectors. One sharply contested point is the problem of the definition of the folk; another that of origins. Allies are known to have fallen out and skirmished behind the lines over such minor matters as identifying John Hardy with John Henry.

—STERLING A. BROWN, "Negro Folk Expression," *Phylon*, 1950

Surely a most interesting volume could be gathered of the traditions, proverbs, sayings, superstitions and folk-lore of the American Negro, and as you suggest, unless this is done immediately—i.e. before the present generation of Negroes pass from the stage, the opportunity will be lost forever. Whatever is done, then, must be done quickly.

—REVEREND WILLIAM V. TUNNELL, King Hall, Washington, D.C.,
Letter to the Editor, *Southern Workman*, December 1893

n July, 1894, the *Southern Workman* magazine published transcripts of two remarkable, indeed historic, speeches delivered on Friday evening, May 25, "at the Hampton Normal School [now Hampton University] under the auspices of the Hampton Folk-Lore Society."[1] The *Southern Workman* was a monthly magazine founded in 1872 by Gen. Samuel Chapman Armstrong, Booker T. Washington's mentor and inspiration, and the founder and first principal of Hampton. It would cease publication in 1939. Though they were delivered second on the program that evening, let's first examine the remarks of Anna Julia Cooper, the pioneering black feminist who had published her powerful manifesto *A Voice from the South* two years earlier, in 1892, and who in the *Southern Workman* was identified as a member of "the Washington Negro Folk-Lore Society." Cooper's argument was, perhaps, the first made by a black feminist intellectual for the importance of Negro folklore, and her remarks proved prescient in defining the terms of the debate about the nature and function of this body of oral lore and its relation to the social progress and political status of an emergent people just twenty-nine years "up from slavery."

Cooper cleverly cast the heart of her argument for preserving Negro folklore in terms of "originality":

> Emancipation from the model is what is needed. Servile copying foredooms mediocrity: it cuts the nerve of soul expression. The American Negro cannot produce an original utterance until he realizes the sanctity of his homely inheritance. It is the simple, common, everyday things of man that God has cleansed. And it is the untaught, spontaneous lispings of the child heart that are fullest of poetry and mystery. . . . [Correggio] felt the quickening of his own self consciousness as he gazed on the marvelous canvasses of the masters. "*I too am a painter*," he cried and the world has vindicated the assertion. Now it is just such a quickening as this that must come to the black man in America, to stimulate his original activities. The creative instinct must be aroused by a wholesome respect for the thoughts that lie nearest. And this to my mind is the vital importance for him of the study of his own folklore. His songs, superstitions, customs, tales, are the legacy left from the imagery of the past. These must catch and hold and work up into the pictures he paints. . . .

1 "Folklore and Ethnology," *Southern Workman* 22, no. 7 (July 1894), 131, https://babel.hathitrust.org/cgi/pt?id=hvd.hngblm;view=1up;seq=535.

The Negro too is a painter. And he who can turn his camera on the last receding views of this people and catch their simple truth and their sympathetic meaning before it is all too late will no less deserve the credit of having revealed a characteristic page in history and of having made an interesting study.[2]

Rarely could a bolder argument for the nature and function of African American folklore have been made, and Cooper was making this argument just less than a year after the appearance of what would become, after its debut in the December 1893 number, a regular column on "Folklore and Ethnology" in the pages of the magazine. Just that November, the first Negro folklore society had been formed at Hampton, under the direction of a far-seeing white administrator there, Alice M. Bacon, as a branch of the American Folklore Society, which itself had launched in 1888. Students and alumni were asked to contribute examples of traditional Negro folklore to the journal, which encouraged them to transcribe tales they remembered or encountered. According to folklorist Alan Dundes, "Not only were students enrolled at Hampton asked to report folklore, but through the notices periodically placed in the *Southern Workman*, past graduates were asked to help the cause."[3] Consequently, the *Southern Workman*, at the turn of the century and well into the twentieth, became a living archive or laboratory of Negro folklore, and its readers became its informants, its documentarians. The collection of black cultural artifacts on a more or less systematic basis had never been attempted before, and we believe that this effort remains unique to this day. In 1983, the historian Donald J. Waters would publish the best of this material in a volume titled *Strange Ways and Sweet Dreams: Afro-American Folklore from the Hampton Institute*, some selections from which we have included in our anthology.

Cooper's advocacy for the crucial importance of collecting Negro folklore may seem at odds with the movement for the "politics of respectability," as the historian Evelyn Brooks Higginbotham has so brilliantly defined it,[4] which emerged in the late nineteenth century as a call to eschew aspects of the slave past (manners, work habits, demeanor, comportment, certain cultural and religious forms and artifacts, and espe-

2 Anna Julia Cooper, "Paper by Miss Anna Julia Cooper," *Southern Workman* 22, no. 7 (July 1894), 133, https://babel.hathitrust.org/cgi/pt?id=hvd.hngblm;view=1up;seq=537.

3 Alan Dundes, *Mother Wit from the Laughing Barrel* (Jackson: University Press of Mississippi, 1990), 251.

4 See Evelyn Brooks Higginbotham, *Righteous Discontent: The Women's Movement in the Black Baptist Church, 1880–1920* (Cambridge, MA: Harvard University Press, 1994).

cially black vernacular spoken English), even as attempts were being made to preserve some selected components of the former slave's cultural heritage. But, as anthropologist Lee D. Baker teaches us, Alice M. Bacon and other key figures in the rise of the Hampton Folklore Society believed that by collecting Negro folklore, they could measure the progress African Americans had achieved, with the aid of institutions like Hampton, since Emancipation, while also preserving the unique traces of a cultural legacy that reached back through enslavement to Africa: how far the freed people— the "Negro American"—had come "up from slavery," in other words, and how they might be related to or different from "the American Negro." "The educators and graduates of Hampton Normal and Agricultural Institute," Baker writes in *Anthropology and the Racial Politics of Culture* (2010), "formed the society to salvage and record cultural practices of rural blacks to demonstrate that industrial education succeeded in fostering the so-called Christian civilization of its graduates—in part by using folklore to evaluate how much African heritage remained to be rooted out."[5] On one hand, then, a certain segment of the African American community saw Negro folklore, like dialect, as a discursive remnant of slavery, a cultural and a social embarrassment, best left behind in the mists of a deeply troubled past, along with the "moonbeam and magnolia" fantasies of slave and master relations on The Old Plantation in the antebellum South. On the other hand, Baker explains, Anna Julia Cooper's comments revealed "that even at the formation of the first black folklore society, some African Americans understood that folklore could provide a positive interpretation of their African heritage or a scientific basis to identify and preserve their distinctive culture."[6]

At the same time, given that "most Hampton graduates did not question their desire to ascend to a civilized state, and even more perhaps loathed any association with Africa," as Baker observes, Cooper's speech at the Hampton Folklore Conference can be read as mocking the aspirations of the culturally "respectable." In her words:

And as the Queen of Sheba sunk under the stupendousness of Solomon's greatness, the children of Africa in America are in danger of paralysis before the splendor of Anglo Saxon achievements. Anglo Saxon ideas, Anglo Saxon standards, Anglo Saxon art, Anglo Saxon literature, Anglo Saxon music—surely this must be to him the

5 Lee D. Baker, *Anthropology and the Racial Politics of Culture* (Durham, NC: Duke University Press, 2010), 33–34.
6 Ibid., 50.

measure of perfection. The whispered little longings of his own soul for utterance must be all a mistake. The simple little croonings that rocked his own cradle must be forgotten and outgrown and only the lullabies after the approved style affected. Nothing else is grammatical, nothing else is orthodox. To write as a white man, to sing as a white man, to swagger as a white man, to bully as a white man—this is achievement, this is success.[7]

Thus, we see that, as early as 1894, the conflict over aesthetics, cultural "authenticity," the relation of American Negroes to their African cultural forebears—which would simmer through the Harlem Renaissance and perhaps reach its zenith in the late 1930s and early 1940s during the famous, heated debate between sociologist E. Franklin Frazier and anthropologist Melville J. Herskovits—was already inscribed in Cooper's essay on the status of Negro folklore.

Of note, Herskovits, in his essay, "The Negro's Americanism," published in Alain Locke's *The New Negro* in 1925,[8] initially maintained that the American Negro was *sui generis*, culturally; that there was no "Africa" remaining in African American cultural and social institutions, because the Middle Passage and slavery had effectively obliterated any remnants of Africa even in African American vernacular culture. But by 1930, he had begun to approach the matter with more nuance, positing what we might think of almost as a sliding scale of Africanism among black peoples in the New World, ranging from "the Bush Negroes of Suriname [*sic*] who exhibit a civilization which is most African," to "a group where, to all intents and purposes, there is nothing of the African tradition left"—Negro Americans in the Northern United States—"who only differ from their white neighbors in the fact that they have pigmentation in their skin." Herskovits argues that evidence for the relation between African and African American culture resides in "folklore, religion, and music."[9] By 1941, he had completely reversed his initial position, and most powerfully so, adopting the stance earlier articulated by his doctoral advisor at New York's Columbia University, Franz Boas, whose disagreement with the seminal University of Chicago sociologist Robert

7 Cooper, "Paper by Miss Anna Julia Cooper," 133.

8 Melville J. Herskovits, "The Negro's Americanism," in *The New Negro*, ed. Alain Locke (New York: Touchstone, 1997), 353–60.

9 Melville J. Herskovits, "The Negro in the New World: The Statement of a Problem," *American Anthropologist* 32.1 (January–March 1930), 149–50, http://www.jstor.org/stable/661054.

E. Park over the presence of African survivals in African American culture was an important precursor to the Herskovits–Frazier debate (Frazier had studied with Park at Chicago before heading up the sociology department at Howard University in Washington, D.C.). In *The Myth of the Negro Past* (1941), Herskovits convincingly demonstrated that the American Negro was an extension of the African Negro, an African people in the New World,[10] and along the way critiqued Frazier's opposite conclusions published in *The Negro Family in the United States* (1939),[11] conclusions quite similar to those expressed in Herskovits's 1925 essay. The two would exchange searching critiques, implicitly and explicitly, in 1942 and 1943, and the debate would continue for many decades.

This dispute over origins had political, as well as cultural implications. As Lee Baker explains, for Park and Frazier, the belief that American Negroes had no authentic culture corresponded to the viewpoint that problems in contemporary African American communities were, in Frazier's phrase, a case of "incomplete assimilation of western culture."[12] Deprived of any cultural inheritance of their own and barred by discrimination from full entry into white America, Negroes were left, in Frazier's view, with what Baker summarizes as a "pathological culture."[13] The solution, for Frazier and his followers, was to advance social welfare and antidiscrimination policies that would end the Negro's "social isolation" and foster the race's assimilation of normative (white) American practices and values. By contrast, those who took the Boasian approach saw in the African roots of Negro folk culture further proof of the inherent equality between the races: for them, an essential precondition for ending discrimination was for society to recognize the Negro as the author and inheritor of a valid, authentic culture. While both groups supported antidiscrimination efforts, Boasian anthropology promoted an attitude of cultural relativism, which was at odds with Park and Frazier's emphasis on cultural pathologies. Though disagreements about the best approach to solving inequalities remain ever with us, the intellectual debate over the strength and endurance of black Americans' African origins was eventually resolved

10 Melville J. Herskovits, *The Myth of the Negro Past* (Boston: Beacon Press, 1990).

11 E. Franklin Frazier, *The Negro Family in the United States* (Notre Dame, IN: University of Notre Dame Press, 1939).

12 E. Franklin Frazier, "Is the Negro Family a Unique Sociological Unit?" *Opportunity* 5 (June 1927), 166.

13 Baker, *Anthropology and the Racial Politics of Culture*, 13.

in favor of cultural continuities, including in the fields of music, vocabulary, linguistic structures, speech patterns, and, of relevance to this volume, folklore, among others.

That debate arose in part from the curious myth that slave ship captains and/or masters of plantations separated their captives from each other by language, in an attempt to prevent them from rebelling. This idea peppers sociolinguistic theory and histories of slavery, and it is very much an urban legend today. For example, Ronald Wardhaugh, in *An Introduction to Sociolinguistics,* drawing on the work of John Rickford and J. L. Dillard, states matter-of-factly that "slave owners deliberately chose slaves from different language backgrounds to discourage rebellion."[14] And the historian Herbert Aptheker, in his classic work, *American Negro Slave Revolts* (1943), noted that "language differences were also in this way introduced which tended to make uprisings and plots more difficult."[15] Aptheker footnotes an essay by Robert E. Park, "The Conflict and Fusion of Cultures with Special Reference to the Negro," published in *The Journal of Negro History* in 1919,[16] and E. Franklin Frazier's same claim from *The Negro Family in the United States* (1939): "In contrast to the situation in the West Indies, African traditions and practices did not take root and survive in the United States."[17] Frazier also footnotes Park's essay, in which he says "as soon as they were landed in this country, slaves were immediately divided and shipped in small numbers, frequently no more than one or two at a time, to different plantations. This was the procedure with the very first Negroes brought to this country. It was found easier to deal with the slaves, if they were separated from their kinsmen."[18] Park goes on to say that subsequent generations of American-born slaves "had already forgotten or only dimly remembered their life in Africa. . . . Everything that marked [newly arrived slaves from Africa] was regarded as ridiculous and barbaric." Moreover, "the memories of Africa which they brought with them were soon lost."[19] Park's source? An anti-abolitionist book published in 1833 by Mrs. A. C. Carmichael, *Domestic Manners and Social Condition of the White, Coloured and Negro Population of the West*

14 Ronald Wardhaugh, *An Introduction to Sociolinguistics* (Malden, MA: Blackwell Publishers, 2010), 79.

15 Herbert Aptheker, *American Negro Slave Revolts* (New York: International Publishers, 1978), 64.

16 Robert E. Park, "The Conflict and Fusion of Cultures with Special Reference to the Negro," *The Journal of Negro History* 4, 2 (April 1919), 117, doi: 10.2307/2713533.

17 Frazier, *The Negro Family in the United States,* 7–8.

18 Park, "The Conflict and Fusion," 117; quoted in Frazier, *The Negro Family in the United States,* 8.

19 Ibid.

Indies,[20] who maintained that "native Africans do not at all like it to be supposed that they retain the customs of their country; and consider themselves wonderfully civilized by their being transplanted from Africa to the West Indies. Creole negroes [those born in the West Indies, not in Africa] invariably consider themselves superior people, and lord it over the native Africans," sentences that Park quotes verbatim for proof of his claim.[21] And there you have it: the genealogy of a most specious claim, authorized by repetition in footnotes, migrating from sociology to anthropology, onto history, and then poured into debates about origins in the fledgling discourse of folklore studies.

This argument, based on nothing but a slavery apologist's claim, would be used as proof that African folktales and African American folktales could not possibly have anything to do with each other. The only problem with these claims is that they are not true. Historically, this sort of ethnic or linguistic separation did not happen, either on the slave ship or on the plantation. And simple reflection helps us to understand why it could not have happened.

When I asked the distinguished historian of the slave trade, David Eltis, to comment on this myth about segregation on the slave ships, this is how he responded: "There's absolutely no evidence of this happening . . . health, age, sex and availability [were] the only determinants of who got put on a slave ship. Thus from Bonny in the Niger Delta, one of the top three embarkation points on the West African coast, two thirds of the people were Igbo, and probably three-quarters could speak Igbo. Yet slave rebellions on these vessels were far fewer than on ships leaving Upper Guinea where the ethnolinguistic mix was far greater." When I asked about the willful separation of African ethnicities on plantations, he said, "This doesn't make sense either. First, after the early years of the slave trade, all slave colonies had majority creole populations," *creole* meaning in this case a person born in the United States, not in Africa. "Second," he continued, "most of the scholarly literature actually argues the very opposite. Many scholars state definitively that planters did have preferences for certain ethnicities. . . . There's certainly no documentary evidence of buyers deliberately mixing language groups to avoid rebellion. The main point is that planters in the Americas only had the dimmest understanding of ethnolinguistic differences. They knew from which part of the African coast a slave ship left, but there's no evidence that they partitioned off lan-

20 A. C. Carmichael, *Domestic Manners and Social Condition of the White, Coloured and Negro Population of the West Indies,* Vol. I. (London: Whittaker and Co, 1834), 251–52.

21 Ibid., 251–52; Park, "The Conflict and Fusion," 117.

guage groups within these regions."[22] As John Adams's 1775 diary entry above makes clear, the slaves had developed what Booker T. Washington (and, much later, Marvin Gaye) would call the grapevine even before the American Revolution. So not only did the captured Africans bring their languages, their music, their gods, and many other salient features of their cultures along with them, they quickly learned to communicate with each other across language barriers not only on their own plantations and other sites of enslavement but across longer distances as well. And the telling and retelling of folktales from Africa, as well as those retold and, in the process, creatively reinvented from African and European sources, along with those invented on the spot, were crucial components of identity-formation and psychic survival under the harshest of circumstances, key aspects in the shaping of an "African American" culture, a culture built on both African and European Old World foundations, yet one original and new. The selections we have chosen for this anthology are examples of each of these three categories of invention, improvisation, and reinvention. Why and how the "originality" and "value" of the myths and tales through which enslaved human beings ordered their lives and amused themselves—like the history of black sacred music forms such as the Spirituals—would play such a key role over such a long period of time in the politics of aesthetics and social science is one of the most fascinating intellectual questions in the history of American race relations. At the heart of the matter was a complex of issues, including the battle over whether, when, and how African Americans could ever become fully integrated and equal "Americans," on a par in every sphere as citizens with every other kind of citizen in the grand American Republic.

Negro folklore, as Sterling A. Brown noted in 1950, was an important front in this battle, and had been since much earlier than most of us had imagined, as we can see in Anna Julia Cooper's reflections, written about nine months before Frederick Douglass died and a little more than a year before Booker T. Washington (who surprisingly supported the efforts to collect and preserve Negro folklore at Hampton) delivered the speech that made him the prophet of social and political accommodation, and the epitome of the politics of respectability. The tension was "always already" there, as Jacques Derrida might put it, embedded in the larger discourse about what being a "black" American actually meant.

22 David Eltis, email to author, August 10, 2016.

In this context, it is quite fascinating to consider the argument that William Wells Newell made in the speech that preceded Anna Julia Cooper's.[23] Newell was for a time a professor of philosophy at Harvard but more importantly, for our purposes, founded the American Folklore Society in 1888. He had been invited to "bless" Hampton's boldly original effort, perhaps with the encouragement of another Harvard professor, Nathaniel S. Shaler, a star pupil of Louis Agassiz, professor of zoology and geology at Harvard and founder of Harvard's Museum of Comparative Zoology, whose extensive writings on polygenesis make him a key thinker in the history of scientific racism. In a Harvard career that stretched from 1864 to his death in 1906, Shaler helped to establish the university's Graduate School of Applied Science and served as professor of paleontology and of geology, and as dean of the Lawrence Scientific School.

Shaler had published an essay on "The Negro Problem" in *The Atlantic Monthly* in November 1884, best summed up in his conclusion that "the inherited qualities of the negroes to a great degree unfit them to carry the burden of our own civilization; . . . that there will naturally be a strong tendency, for many generations to come, for them to revert to their ancestral conditions. . . . They cannot as a race, for many generations, be brought to the level of our own people."[24] In many ways, this essay, and a second essay that Shaler published in *The Atlantic Monthly* in 1890,[25] can be seen as something of a blueprint for the agenda for the role of industrial education within the larger scheme of American social segregation and political disenfranchisement that Booker T. Washington begin outlining in the first half of the 1890s, then articulated as a philosophy and social program in his famous Atlanta Exposition Speech delivered in September 1895. Despite these attitudes, difficult to describe in terms other than racialist, Alice Bacon herself claimed, when she announced the creation of Hampton's Folk-Lore and Ethnology project, that "Prof. Shaler of Harvard, whose article published some years ago in the *Atlantic Monthly*, on Science and the African problem, originally suggested the idea to us."[26] Shaler's influence indicates the complicated motivations behind the creation and activities of the Hampton Folklore Society, which,

23 William Wells Newell, "The Importance and Utility of the Collection of Negro Folk-Lore," *Southern Workman* 22, no.7 (July 1894), 131–32, https://babel.hathitrust.org/cgi/pt?id=mdp.39015080382800;view=1up;seq=82.

24 Nathaniel S. Shaler, "The Negro Problem," *The Atlantic Monthly* 54 (November 1884), 703.

25 Nathaniel S. Shaler, "Science and the African Problem," *The Atlantic Monthly* 66 (July 1890), 36–44.

26 Alice M. Bacon, *Southern Workman* 20, no. 12 (December 1893), 179.

in the words of Lee Baker, combined "a desire for cultural preservation" with a "commitment to espionage and [the] exorcism" of a black cultural inheritance viewed as an obstacle to racial progress.[27]

Having Newell speak at Hampton in 1894 was a major coup, an act of legitimization for a black institution by the nascent but already authoritative American folklore establishment, at the height of the institutionalizations of Jim Crow racial segregation. Newell clearly understood what his presence meant and the stakes involved, and he embraced his task with relish.

Newell saw the collection and analysis of American Negro folklore as a form of historic preservation, providing a *conduit* to the dual past of American slavery and the vast sea of African civilizations that lay far beyond the Atlantic Ocean, in the depths of a submerged antediluvian past—antediluvian in the sense of suggesting antiquity, but also in the sense of being antiquated or primitive. "Folk-lore, then, the mass of racial ideas and habits, is lost in this mental ocean [of the unity of races]; these special forms of life cease to have any continuing existence in fact. Should they therefore possess no further existence in memory? On the contrary. Man is memory," Newell declaimed; "the more memory, the more humanity."[28]

Retrieving folklore, for Newell, was retrieving origins, and in the case of the American Negro, this meant the retrieval and the recuperation of *Africa*, the American Negro's "home"—the complex legacies of their African origins—precisely when so many educated former slaves now seemed to want to leave "Africa"—and, in fact, the experience of enslavement itself—far behind, a process that, Newell is arguing, was necessary for the shaping of American Negroes' status as full and eventually equal stakeholders in their American, and world, cultural citizenship: "I am speaking then, not with regards to the past, but the future, when I say it is of consequence for the American Negro to retain the recollection of his African origin, and of his American servitude." Why? "For the sake of the honor of his race, he should have a clear picture of the mental condition out of which he has emerged: this picture is not now complete, nor will be made so without a record of the songs, tales, beliefs which belongs to the stage of culture through which he has passed."[29]

Far too many African Americans, Newell continues, were embarrassed both by the

27 Baker, *Anthropology and the Racial Politics of Culture,* 47.
28 Newell, "The Importance and Utility of the Collection of Negro Folk-Lore," 132.
29 Ibid.

slave past and the African past: "Too much in haste to appropriate the possessions of the whites, they are not aware that they are obtaining nothing as valuable as what they are surrendering," he observed, specifically in the case of "Negro music in Southern States," which "is a treasure of which any race in the world might be proud. . . . Unhappily, this quality is not sufficiently understood by the Negroes themselves." As with music, so with tales, but "these compositions have their worth, of a somewhat different nature from that which I have claimed for the songs." The fact that Negro folktales— and he points to "the tales of Uncle Remus," "animal folk-tales, which in great part, make their hero the rabbit, [and] celebrate the victory of skill over brute force"—"are by no means solely the possession of Negroes; on the contrary, a good many are nearly cosmopolitan," coming to America by way of multiple routes, including Africa. "Proceeding from some common center, they have traveled about the world, and that by several different routes, meeting in America by the way of Africa, by that of Europe, and it may be, also by that of Asia." Thus, "the universal diffusion of many tales constitutes a striking counterpart to the great diversity of racial customs. We have thus the most striking exhibition of the substantial mental unity of the human race." Moreover, and here he brings home his larger political point, this shared canon of texts demonstrates "not . . . original natural diversity, but [the role] of environment" in creating apparent racial differences, and in this "might be found the strongest possible hope for the future of your own race."[30]

African Americans, Newell concludes, are still very much *African:* "It is the opinion of one of the best qualified observers, not only that the Africans in their own land are in a certain degree in character similar, but that American Negroes still have a great affinity with the race from which they derived." Contrary to Frederick Douglass's famous claim that "genealogical trees did not flourish among slaves,"[31] Newell argues that it is important for African Americans to embrace the study and practice of genealogy: "it will become customary for American Negroes to attend to their genealogical record, and endeavor to discover, so far as they may, from what particular African source their own family was derived." And establishing this relationship *back* to Africa can have an enormous influence on the *future* of Africa: "America, through the American Negro, is destined to exert a mighty influence in the continent

30 Ibid.

31 Frederick Douglass, *Life and Times of Frederick Douglass Written by Himself* (Hartford, CT.: Park Publishing Co., 1882), 25.

of Africa. . . . The United States is the star of hope to the African. What the Negro is becoming, as we hope, that the African and Africa must become." Moreover, he says, this process will end the American Negro's ambivalence or embarrassment about his relationship to Africa, because the discovery "in the so-called Dark Continent" of "Negro civilizations," will be transformative, especially for "the educated Afro-American, who in becoming entirely an American, will be no more ashamed of the continent of his origin, than the Anglo-American is ashamed of England." Understanding the history of "Negro mythology," the term that Alice Bacon used in her call to arms in the *Southern Workman* for the collection of Negro folklore in December 1893 (a statement full of references to the Negro's roots in Africa and the necessity of establishing continuities with those roots) and roots of the American Negro's musical traditions, Newell maintains, on both sides of the Atlantic, can only help the emergent educated American Negro class achieve its most cherished goals of becoming genuinely equal Americans. In language expressing both the essentialism of the times and the condescending attitudes prevalent among whites and blacks about the former slaves still overwhelmingly living in the South, Newell concludes by revealing a most ironic, and most practical, social and political reason for the study of folklore: "all information which it can obtain relative to its antecedents, regarding its primitive and natural way of feeling, will be a weapon in its hand. We must know the truth about the plantation Negro, to deal with the plantation Negro; it is always the truth that makes [us] free."[32] The key to understanding, and to some extent controlling, the Negro, he argues, is knowing the "plantation Negro," and one can best know this enigmatic entity through the cultural artifacts created by what we might think of as the enslaved Negro's mind.

To be sure, Alice Bacon and the students and alumni at Hampton weren't the first to collect Negro folktales or to voice fascination with what we might think of as black vernacular structures of feeling, structures of thought. The songs the slaves sang, their melodies and harmonies, of course, but also the language of their lyrics (their poetic diction), proved to be of enormous interest to Americans early in the nineteenth century. As Bruce Jackson notes in his *The Negro and His Folklore in Nineteenth-Century Periodicals*,[33] an article written by William B. Smith and published in *The Farmer's*

---

32 Newell, "The Importance and Utility of the Collection of Negro Folk-Lore," 132.

33 Bruce Jackson, *The Negro and His Folklore in Nineteenth-Century Periodicals* (Austin: University of Texas Press, 1967).

Register in 1838 describes a "beer-dance" performed by a group of slaves.[34] In 1845, J. Kennard Jr. published an essay titled "Who Are Our National Poets?" in the *Knick-erbocker* commenting on the originality and power of slave music: "These operas are full of negro life," he writes; "there is hardly any thing which might not be learned of negro character, from a complete collection of these original works. A tour through the south, and a year or two of plantation life, would not fail to reward the diligent collector, and his future fame would be as certain as Homer's."[35] Who are America's "national poets?" Kennard answers "our negro slaves, to be sure."[36]

Ten years later, Y. S. Nathanson, writing in *Putnam's Monthly,* observed in an essay on "Negro Minstrelsy: Ancient and Modern" that "every cotton-field teems with melody, and every slave hut, throughout the Southern country, has its little list of genuine ballads, which only need to be known, in order to be received to the heart of a nation."[37] Nathanson is at pains to distinguish between the white minstrel tradition and the Negro folk music tradition that these imitators were mocking: "Why need we groan and grumble under the inflictions of ignorant and self-conceited [white] song-writers," he asks, and "the barefaced and impudent imposition" of white performers and adapters, when the original is, as it were, right beneath our feet"?[38]

The Civil War and the all-too-short period of Reconstruction gave abolitionists and officials working with the Freedmen's Bureau firsthand experience with former slaves and their cultural forms, leading within two years of the end of the war to the first anthology of slave songs, *Slave Songs of the United States,* edited by William Francis Allen, Charles Pickard Ware, and Lucy McKim Garrison, who was the daughter-in-law of the famous and fiery Boston abolitionist newspaper editor, William Lloyd Garrison. Quite fascinating for our purposes is this curious aside in the editors' introduction: "It is often, indeed, no easy matter to persuade them to sing their old songs, even as a curiosity, such is the sense of dignity that has come with freedom. It is earnestly to be desired that some person, who has the opportunity,

---

34 William B. Smith, "The Persimmon Tree and the Beer Dance," in *The Negro and His Folklore in Nineteenth-Century Periodicals*, ed. Bruce Jackson (Austin: University of Texas Press, 1967), 4–9.

35 J. Kennard Jr., "Who Are Our National Poets?" in *The Negro and His Folklore in Nineteenth-Century Periodicals*, ed. Bruce Jackson (Austin: University of Texas Press, 1967), 27.

36 Ibid., 24–25.

37 Y. S. Nathanson, "Negro Minstrelsy: Ancient and Modern," in *The Negro and His Folklore in Nineteenth-Century Periodicals*, ed. Bruce Jackson (Austin: University of Texas Press, 1967), 45.

38 Ibid.

should make a collection of these now, before it is too late."[39] Even by 1867, as this statement reveals, the former slaves exhibited reticence about revealing an aspect of their culture which they wished to remain private, as it were; that they wished to keep their most precious cultural forms from being tampered with, maintaining through silences the integrity of these forms "within the Veil," as W. E. B. Du Bois would put it in his *Souls of Black Folk* just thirty-six years later. (James Baldwin often addressed this matter of what I think of as cultural privacy, a submerged or veiled discourse, a double-voiced discourse, and the reasons why many black people fear unveiling it, as in this observation from *The Fire Next Time* [1963]: "The privacy of [the Negro's] experience, which is only beginning to be recognized in language, and which is denied or ignored in official and popular speech—*hence the Negro idiom*—lends credibility to any system that pretends to clarify it."[40] As Elsie Clews Parsons noted in 1923, "Southern Negroes feel that their stories belong to the part of life, that major part, which they do not share with their white neighbors.")[41] The editors' statement also foreshadows the sense of urgency that we saw in Alice Bacon's manifesto of 1893 calling for the collection of Negro folklore before it is too late, before it disappears, before the elders of the culture take this form and others like it to the next world. The cultural clock was ticking, these writers argued with some desperation, and its tick-tock was heard as early as 1867.

Bruce Jackson charts the transition from attention to black vernacular music to other black vernacular cultural forms, including folklore: "Later, during Reconstruction days, there are several 'discovery' articles—for the first time the Negro is regarded as a bearer of culture, and we are given accounts of his church services, his speech, his superstitions, and, finally, his stories."[42] This is not the place for an analysis of these articles, but a partial list would include Thadden Norris's "Negro Superstitions" published in *Lippincott's Magazine* in 1870,[43] which includes an early version of the canonical "Tar Baby" tale; Robert Lee J. Vance's "Plantation Folklore," in which Vance

39 William Francis Allen, Charles Pickard Ware, and Lucy McKim Garrison, eds., *Slave Songs of the United States* (New York: A. Simpson & Co., 1867), x.

40 James Baldwin, *The Fire Next Time* (New York: Vintage, 1992), 69.

41 Elsie Clews Parsons, *Folk-lore of the Sea Islands, South Carolina* (Cambridge, MA: American Folklore Society, 1921), xiv.

42 Jackson, *The Negro and His Folklore,* xxii–xxiii.

43 Thadden Norris, "Negro Superstitions," in *The Negro and His Folklore in Nineteenth-Century Periodicals*, ed. Bruce Jackson (Austin: University of Texas Press, 1967), 135–43.

says that the earliest reference he could find to African American animal tales was published by an unnamed writer in the November 1868 and 1869 issues of *Riverside Magazine for Young People*;[44] and the first story published by Abigail Mandana Holmes Christiansen, "De Wolf, De Rabbit, and de Tar Baby," in the *Springfield (Mass.) Daily Republican* in 1874.[45] Christensen published more articles in Northern journals throughout the 1870s and 1880s, finally collecting these in *Afro-American Folk-lore: Told Round Cabin Fires on the Sea Islands* in 1892, just a year before Alice Bacon launched Hampton's massive effort to collect folktales. (Christensen, like Allen, Wade, and Garrison, had gathered material in the settlement of newly liberated slaves at Port Royal, and the tales of the Gullah people who lived in the sea islands along the coasts of South Carolina and Georgia proved to be a treasury of black vernacular forms. Christensen was keen to suggest continuities between these tales and their African origins: these "verbatim reports from numerous sable story-tellers of the Sea Islands," she writes, were narrated by "some . . . whose ancestors, two generations back, brought parts of the legends from African forests.")[46]

Joel Chandler Harris introduced the public to his literary conceit, Uncle Remus, in two sketches published in the *Atlanta Constitution* in 1876, followed by *Uncle Remus, His Songs and His Sayings* in 1880,[47] and *Nights with Uncle Remus* in 1883.[48] Harris would publish a total of ten volumes of Uncle Remus stories. The influence of these stories, written in Harris's version of black English vernacular speech, cannot be gainsaid: they were wildly popular and would influence a number of major American authors, including Mark Twain, Charles W. Chesnutt, and William Faulkner.

In 1877, just a year after Harris introduced the American public to Uncle Remus, William Owens published "Folklore of the Southern Negroes" in *Lippincott's Magazine*.[49] *Negro Myths of the Georgia Coast* was published by Charles Colcock Jones Jr., a historian and a former slave-owner, in 1888. Jones pointed to "the swamp region of

---

44 Robert Lee J. Vance, "Plantation Folk Lore," *Open Court* II (1888), 1028–32, 1074–76, 1092–95.

45 Abigail Mandana Holmes Christiansen, "De Wolf, De Rabbit, and de Tar Baby," *Springfield (Mass.) Daily Republican* (June 2, 1874).

46 Christensen, *Afro-American Folk-lore: Told Round Cabin Fires on the Sea Islands* (Boston: J. G. Cupples Company, 1892), xii–xiii.

47 Joel Chandler Harris, *His Songs and His Sayings* (New York: D. Appleton, 1880).

48 Joel Chandler Harris, *Nights with Uncle Remus* (New York: McKinlay, Stone & Mackenzie, 1911).

49 William Owens, "Folklore of the Southern Negroes," in *The Negro and His Folklore in Nineteenth-Century Periodicals*, ed. Bruce Jackson (Austin: University of Texas Press, 1967), 145–56.

Georgia and the Carolinas, where the lingo of the rice-field and the sea-island negroes is *sui generis*," as fecund fields from which to harvest new kinds of black folklore, because they "materially differ from those narrated by the sable dwellers in the interior," the "Middle Georgia," he says, that Harris had plowed.[50]

That same year, 1888, the American Folklore Society was founded and, after extensive debate, and the advocacy of William Wells Newell and the anthropologist Franz Boas (who would influence both Elsie Clews Parsons and Zora Neale Hurston at Columbia), "the folklore of the Southern Negro" was deemed appropriate matter to be "included in the research agenda" of the Society, in fifth place on its list of priorities. And that is how Newell ended up delivering his important address at Hampton six years later, in the late spring of 1894, less than a year after Alice Mabel Bacon organized the Hampton Folk-lore Society, the same year in which Mary Alicia Owen published *Voodoo Tales as Told Among the Negroes of the Southwest*.[51] Newell had been summoned to bless Hampton's endeavor, to give it the legitimacy of a national organization's research agenda. And with that blessing, the quest to collect Negro folklore was on.

Donald J. Waters has masterfully edited and analyzed the best of the folklore collected at Hampton in his important book, *Strange Ways and Sweet Dreams: Afro-American Folklore from the Hampton Institute* (1983).[52] Because of this effort, by the 1920s, collecting Negro folklore had become commonplace, though not without its controversies, controversies that, as we see in Sterling A. Brown's epigraph above, continued long beyond the Harlem Renaissance. But the renaissance saw published several important volumes, including Thomas W. Talley's *Negro Folk Rhymes (Wise and Otherwise)* in 1922 and Elsie Clews Parsons's *Folklore of the Sea Islands* (1923).[53] Clews was a champion for the collection of Negro folklore, commissioning and guest-editing fourteen issues of the *Journal of American Folklore* dedicated to African and African American folklore, in her capacity as the journal's associate editor. In 1925, pioneering black anthropologist Arthur Huff Fauset published "Negro Folk Tales from

50 Charles Colcock Jones Jr., *Negro Myths of the Georgia Coast* (Boston: Houghton-Mifflin, 1888), v–vi.

51 Mary Alicia Owen, *Voodoo Tales as Told Among the Negroes of the Southwest* (Whitefish, MT: Kessinger Publishing, 2007).

52 Donald J. Waters, *Strange Ways and Sweet Dreams: Afro-American Folklore from the Hampton Institute* (New York: ACLS Humanities E-Book, 2008).

53 Thomas W. Talley, *Negro Folk Rhymes (Wise and Otherwise)* (Knoxville: University of Tennessee Press, 1991).

the South (Alabama, Mississippi, Louisiana)" in Alain Locke's manifesto, *The New Negro*,[54] followed in 1931 by *Black Gods of the Metropolis*.[55]

Fauset's essay in *The New Negro* stressed the need for the African American community to preserve a wider and more authentic variety of Negro folklore than the tales popularized—and in part, he argued, distorted—by Joel Chandler Harris. He also compiled a very important bibliography of folk materials for Locke's anthology. Fauset published his essay in the middle of the Harlem Renaissance, the literary politics of which included warring ideas about the forms and content that most appropriately "represented" the race (a year later, in 1926, Du Bois invited writers to participate in a debate about these matters in an ongoing symposium in the pages of *The Crisis*, titled "The Negro in Art: How Shall He Be Portrayed?"). Fauset, keenly aware of the fact that the status of black folklore was a highly charged subject among black critics and writers, argued, first, that Negro folklore was "based upon the original folk tales of the African slaves,"[56] itself a highly contentious claim, a position (as we shall see) fraught with danger for those who were dubious about the status of the cultures created by black people in Africa and who passionately argued that the submerged position of the American Negro in American society was the result of the harmful effects of slavery, having nothing at all to do with the supposedly "debased" place of Africa and Africans on the scale of world civilization. Further, they believed that associations with Africa effectively dragged the position of the American Negro downward: as Tanika JoAnn Beamon writes, "'scientists' in the past had invoked stereotypical notions of 'primitive' Africa as evidence of African American inferiority and as a rationale for social inequality and anti-black discrimination."[57]

Fauset went on to argue for the salient effects of valorizing Negro folklore, precisely at this crucial time when black writers were using culture, especially the verbal arts, written and oral, as prima facie evidence that black people were intellectually equal to white people and hence entitled to the full rights and privileges of American citizenship:

54 Arthur Huff Fauset, "Negro Folk Tales from the South (Alabama, Mississippi, Louisiana)," in *The New Negro,* ed. Alain Locke (New York: Touchstone, 1999), 238–44.

55 Arthur Huff Fauset, *Black Gods of the Metropolis* (Philadelphia: University of Pennsylvania Press, 2002).

56 Fauset, "Negro Folk Tales," 238.

57 Tanika JoAnn Beamon, "A History of African American Folklore Scholarship," PhD diss., University of California, Berkeley (2001), 46.

The great storehouse from which they were gleaned, that treasury of folk lore which the American Negro inherited from his African forefathers, is little known. It rivals in amount as well as in quality that of any people on the face of the globe, and is not confined to stories of the Uncle Remus type, but includes a wide variety of story forms, legends, saga cycles, songs, proverbs and phantastic, almost mythical material. . . . It is not necessary to draw upon sentiment in order to realize the masterful quality of some of the Negro tales: it is simply necessary to read them. . . . The antiquity and the authentic folk lore ancestry of the Negro tale make it the proper subject for the scientific folk-lorist rather than the literary amateur [such as Joel Chandler Harris, whom he cites earlier]. It is the ethnologist, the philologist, and the student of primitive psychology that are most needed for its present investigation.[58]

The last major collection of black folklore during the Harlem Renaissance was Edward C. L. Adams's remarkable *Nigger to Nigger*.[59] Adams, a white physician from South Carolina, presented the words of his subjects without mediation, and included their thoughts on contemporary racial issues. All of these collections seem something of a prelude to the work of Zora Neale Hurston, who published an extended essay, "Hoodoo in America," in the *Journal of American Folklore* in 1931,[60] and whose collection, *Mules and Men*, published in 1935 at the height of the Great Depression,[61] would henceforth define the genre. Hurston's work, including several articles on folklore and her account of her anthropological fieldwork in Jamaica and Haiti in 1936 and 1937, *Tell My Horse: Voodoo and Life in Haiti and Jamaica* (1938),[62] was heavily influenced by her work as a graduate student at Columbia under Franz Boas, who, before his student Melville Herskovits, was a leading proponent of the cultural legitimacy of the African American folk tradition. Hurston's work would be rediscovered in the 1970s, leading both to her canonization in the American literary tradition and to a focus on vernacular language and forms, such as folktales and myths, in black aesthetic

58 Fauset, "Negro Folk Tales," 238–41.

59 E. C. L. Adams, *Nigger to Nigger*, in *Tales of the Congaree* (Chapel Hill: University of North Carolina Press, 1987), 103–302.

60 Zora Neale Hurston, "Hoodoo in America," *Journal of American Folklore* 44 (October–December 1931), 317–417, doi 10.2307/535394.

61 Zora Neale Hurston, *Mules and Men* (New York: HarperPerennial, 2008).

62 Hurston, *Tell My Horse: Voodoo and Life in Haiti and Jamaica* (New York: HarperPerennial, 2008).

theory. Other major collections before the Black Arts era and the birth of Black Studies in the late 1960s include Benjamin Botkin's *Lay My Burden Down: A Folk History of Slavery* (1945),[63] and Langston Hughes and Arna Bontemps's *The Book of Negro Folklore* (1958).[64]

Roger D. Abrahams's *Deep Down in the Jungle: Negro Narrative Folklore from the Streets of Philadelphia* (1964),[65] Bruce Jackson's *The Negro and His Folklore in Nineteenth-Century Periodicals* (1967), Richard M. Dorson's *American Negro Folktales* (1967),[66] and John Mason Brewer's *American Negro Folklore* (1968)[67] were each major interventions in the Black Arts period, providing access to examples of the black vernacular traditions that would heavily inform the shape of black literature for decades to come. Jackson's *Get Your Ass in the Water and Swim Like Me: African American Narrative Poetry from Oral Tradition* (1974),[68] made folklore history by becoming the first text to include an audio disc allowing us to hear the words of his informants, a brilliant innovation. Abrahams's work, and Jackson's collection, provided the raw material for my own theory of African American literary criticism, *The Signifying Monkey* (1988).[69] Harold Courlander's *A Treasury of Afro-American Folklore* (1976),[70] Daryl Cumber Dance's *Shuckin' and Jivin': Folklore from Contemporary Black Americans* (1978),[71] and Dance's more recent *From My People: 400 Years of African American Folklore: An Anthology* (2002)[72] are among the most important collections of African American folklore published in recent decades.

---

63 Benjamin Botkin, *Lay My Burden Down: A Folk History of Slavery* (New York: Delta, 1989).

64 Langston Hughes and Arna Bontemps, *The Book of Negro Folklore* (New York: Dodd Mead, 1983).

65 Roger D. Abrahams, *Deep Down in the Jungle: Negro Narrative Folklore from the Streets of Philadelphia* (New Brunswick, NJ: AldineTransaction, 2009).

66 Richard M. Dorson, *American Negro Folktales* (Mineola, NY: Dover Publications, 2015).

67 J. Mason Brewer, *American Negro Folklore* (New York: Quadrangle, 1968).

68 Bruce Jackson, *Get Your Ass in the Water and Swim Like Me: African American Narrative Poetry from Oral Tradition* (New York: Routledge, 2004).

69 Henry Louis Gates Jr., *The Signifying Monkey* (New York: Oxford University Press, 1988; rpt. 2014).

70 Harold Courlander, *A Treasury of Afro-American Folklore* (New York: Crown Publishing, 1988).

71 Daryl Cumber Dance, *Shuckin' and Jivin': Folklore from Contemporary Black Americans* (Indianapolis: Indiana University Press, 1978).

72 Dance, *From My People: 400 Years of African American Folklore: An Anthology* (New York: Norton, 2003).

> What would you think of whole groups of Negroes who had never heard
> of Brer Rabbit? Or of stories about Monkey and Baboon, Elephant, and
> all the other animals?
>
> —ARTHUR HUFF FAUSET, *Folklore from Nova Scotia*

In an essay published in 1965, titled "Why I Returned," Arna Bontemps points to
the place of African American folklore as a trope and as a placeholder in a larger
battle that had raged within the black middle class about "roots," origins, vernacular
culture, modernism, cultural identity, and social mobility since the politics of respectability debates that, as we have seen, surfaced in the 1890s and continued through the
Harlem Renaissance of the 1920s and well beyond. (The 1926 essay exchange in *The
Nation* between Langston Hughes in "The Negro Artist and the Racial Mountain"[73]
and George Schuyler in "The Negro Art Hokum"[74] is a classic example of the debate
over the form and content of African American literature.) Bontemps is quite eloquent
about the way that diametrically opposed opinions about the life or death of black
vernacular culture could manifest themselves at the dinner table and divide families
into two distinct camps:

> In their opposing attitudes towards roots my father and my great-uncle made me
> aware of a conflict in which every educated American Negro, and some who are not
> educated, must somehow take sides. By implication at least, one group advocates
> embracing the riches of the folk heritage; their opposites demand a clean break
> with the past and all it represents. Had I not gone home summers and hob-nobbed
> with folk-type Negroes, I would have finished college without knowing that any
> Negro other than Paul Laurence Dunbar ever wrote a poem. I would have come
> out imagining that the story of the Negro could be told in two short paragraphs: a
> statement about jungle people in Africa and an equally brief account of the slavery
> issue in American history.[75]

73 Langston Hughes, "The Negro Artist and the Racial Mountain," *The Nation* 122 (June 23, 1926),
692–94.

74 George Schuyler, "The Negro Art Hokum," *The Nation* 122 (June 16, 1926), 662–64.

75 Arna Bontemps, "Why I Returned," in *Black Voices: An Anthology of Afro-American Literature*, ed.
Abraham Chapman (New York: Signet, 2001), 309–10.

In other words, to paraphrase James Weldon Johnson's famous critique of dialect poetry, published in 1922, before he and Langston Hughes and Sterling A. Brown revitalized "dialect" as a resonant and linguistically complex poetic diction, black vernacular cultural forms, especially Negro folklore, in Negro middle-class popular opinion, were trapped between two stereotypical polar oppositions: the jungle and the slave cabin. And both, for different reasons, as we have seen, were—with few but notable exceptions—negative. As James Weldon Johnson put it in 1912, in his novel *Autobiography of an Ex-Colored Man,* referring to the spirituals: "As yet, the Negroes themselves do not fully appreciate these old slave songs. The educated classes are rather ashamed of them and prefer to sing hymns from books. This feeling is natural: they are still too close to the conditions under which the songs were produced: but the day will come when this slave music will be the most treasured heritage of the American Negro."[76] As went the spirituals, so went other vernacular forms, forged—ironically—in the creative crucible of the hell of enslavement.

As far as the black middle class was concerned, all of the black vernacular cultural forms were of a piece: Negro folklore—like the spirituals, like ragtime and the blues, like work songs and the oral tradition of "lying" or tale-telling, like the use of black English or "dialect" in poetry and musical forms—was the linguistic remnant of slavery. And slavery, for many African Americans in the embrace of the politics of respectability at the turn of the century, was best left behind. And so was Africa, the stereotypical portrayals of which had understandably been absorbed uncritically by many African Americans, having had very little, if any, exposure to images of Africa and Africans that were anything other than a negation of "progress," the West, and of "civilization" itself. No, slavery and its cultural artifacts had to be left behind in the residue of history back on the plantation, just as African culture had to be left behind in the jungle. That, as exaggerated as it may sound to us today in an era of recuperation of both the slave past and the African past, summarizes much of the black middle class's attitude to both, as Bontemps frankly confesses. In contrast to the folklorists of the late nineteenth century, who saw themselves as participants in racial uplift efforts dedicated to overcoming the culture of slavery, folklorists of the Harlem Renaissance, such as Fauset and Hurston, dedicated their work to the recovery and preservation of an authentic African and African American inheritance. "Thus," writes Lee D. Baker

76 James Weldon Johnson, *Autobiography of an Ex-Colored Man* (Boston: Sherman, French & Company, 1912), 178.

in *Anthropology and the Racial Politics of Culture,* "the New Negro rationale for collecting folklore in the 1920s was virtually the opposite of the HFS [Hampton Folk-Lore Society] rationale in the 1890s. This one tale was first used to articulate the uplift project, and two decades later it was used to bolster the heritage project."[77]

The game-changer for the fate of black folklore was, for good and for ill, Joel Chandler Harris and his popular sidekick, Uncle Remus. It is safe to say that Uncle Remus remains the most popular black literary character in all of American history. And Joel Chandler Harris's enormous commercial success, if not the way he drew upon and transformed black folktales in his short stories, could not help but draw comment from black writers and readers, and tempt some to try to replicate what he had done, but from within, or out of, what we might think of as a "black aesthetic." No one was more successful at recuperating the Negro folk tradition from "the plantation tradition" than Charles W. Chesnutt, whose stories subverted the tendency among some white folklorists to romanticize antebellum life in the South and render the relations between masters and their slaves in metaphors of consanguinity such as "aunties" and "uncles" (a tendency so persistent that, when I was an undergraduate at Yale in the early 1970s, students nicknamed a history course on the Old South "Moonbeams and Magnolia Blossoms").

Chesnutt burst onto the American literary scene with the publication of his first short story, "The Goophered Grapevine," in *The Atlantic Monthly*, in August 1887,[78] the first black author to appear in those pages, eleven years after Joel Chandler Harris had introduced Uncle Remus to the American reading public in the pages of *The Atlanta Constitution* and seven years after *Uncle Remus: His Songs and His Sayings* was published as a book. Chesnutt was very aware of the relationship of his fictional black character, Julius McAdoo, to Uncle Remus—and of his own relationship to Harris—a relationship of repetition and reversal, or signifying. Uncle Julius is a trickster figure whose Remus-like demeanor fools the white male Northerner who narrates the stories, stories that offer quite realistic depictions of the brutalities of the "slave regime," as Frederick Douglass called it, as well as revelations of ingenious uses of "conjuration" to rescue slaves from those brutalities. Chesnutt collected seven of his stories and published them as *The Conjure Woman* in 1899, to great critical acclaim,

---

77 Baker, *Anthropology and the Racial Politics of Culture,* 35.
78 Charles W. Chesnutt, "The Goophered Grapevine," *The Atlantic Monthly* 60 (August 1887), 259–60.

if not great financial success.[79] Chesnutt was keenly aware of the stakes of his aesthetic project; as he wrote in a fascinating essay, "Superstitions and Folk-lore of the South" (1901), he "embodied into a number of stories" the "old-time belief in what was known as 'conjuration' or 'goopher,'" a set of practices "brought over from the dark continent by the dark people," the African slaves, and "certain features [of which] suggest a distant affinity with Voodooism, or snake worship, a cult which seems to have been indigenous," he concludes erroneously, "to tropical America."[80] Here, quite deftly and at once, Chesnutt has staked a claim for the cultural continuities between continental African and New World African cultures, and valorized the slave experience that fused them together: "In the old plantation days they flourished vigorously, though discouraged by the 'great house,' and their potency was well established among the blacks and the poorer whites."[81] (Chesnutt also wrote about Harris as late as 1931, in his important essay, "Post-Bellum Pre-Harlem.")[82]

If the ghost of enslavement haunted attitudes among the black middle class about black folklore and its related idiomatic forms, the shadows of Joel Chandler Harris (whom the philosopher Alain Locke damned as "a kindly amanuensis for the illiterate Negro peasant")[83] and his equally kindly, and irrepressibly amiable conceit, Uncle Remus, fell over Chesnutt's work (as his silent second text) and over subsequent estimations of the nature and function of African American folklore in general. As Sterling A. Brown put it in 1950, four years after the release of Disney's classic *Song of the South* (in which James Baskett, as Remus, consoles a lonely little white boy, played by Bobby Driscoll, with tales of that wily trickster, Brer Rabbit): "For a long time Uncle Remus and his Brer Rabbit tales stood for the Negro folk and their lore. One thing made clear by the resurrection of Uncle Remus in Walt Disney's *Song of the South* is the degree to which he belonged to white people rather than to the Negro folk."[84] On the other hand, however, Brown is quick to point to the importance of Harris to the preservation of black folklore: "Whether familiarity has bred contempt, or whether there has

---

79 Charles W. Chesnutt, *The Conjure Woman* (Durham, NC: Duke University Press, 1993).

80 Charles W. Chesnutt, "Superstitions and Folk-lore of the South," *Modern Culture* XIII (May 1901), 231.

81 Ibid.

82 Charles W. Chesnutt, "Post-Bellum Pre-Harlem," *Colophon* 2.5 (February 1931).

83 Sterling A. Brown, "Folk Literature," in *A Son's Return* (Boston: Northeastern University Press, 1996), 226.

84 Sterling A. Brown, "Negro Folk Expression," *Phylon* 11.4 (1950), 318.

been too great a sensitivity toward folk expression, Negroes have lagged behind whites in the gathering of folk tales. Without Joel Chandler Harris, it is likely that the Uncle Remus stories, which now belong with the minor masterpieces of American literature, would have been lost."[85] In 1950, Brown lamented the fact that "educated Negroes by and large have not been greatly interested,"[86] despite having concluded in 1941 that "awareness of the importance of a study of the folk is increasing among Negroes, but still slowly."[87] Whether it was the slave experience itself, or its romantic recuperation by apologists for slavery during the post-Reconstruction period—or some combination— Brown honestly reflected on the deeply ambivalent attitudes that middle class African Americans felt toward Southern black folklore just five years before Rosa Parks and the Reverend Dr. Martin Luther King would launch the modern Civil Rights Movement at what had been the symbolic heart of cotton country, Montgomery, Alabama, named the first capital of the Confederate States of America both because of its historic role in cotton production and its location as a major Gulf Coast mercantile port—in other words, at a symbolic center of slave experience and hence the birthplace of Southern Negro folklore itself, rather than in the North, which had long been the home of political activities designed to ameliorate the plight of African Americans, and a growing class of middle class Negroes wary of the merits of preserving or celebrating the culture of the enslaved as depicted in Joel Chandler Harris's writings and in Disney's *Song of the South*.

But the problem with Harris was as much ideological as it was literary: his representation of slavery, through Remus, was part of the larger attempt to reclaim slavery as a golden age in the history of American race relations, a process that unfolded precisely as the effects, insofar as this was possible, of Reconstruction were being rolled back, and Jim Crow segregation was being foisted upon American race relations. In this dreadful process, Negro folklore had been summoned, dressed in the clothes and voiced in the words of the ever-loyal, always-faithful, grateful servant, Uncle Remus, something of a distant family member in blackface, but one never invited to spend the night in the Big House. As Brown puts it, "Harris shows Uncle Remus telling the

85 Brown, "Folk Literature," in *Negro Caravan*, ed. Sterling A. Brown, Arthur Paul Davis, and Ulysses Lee (New York: Dryden Press, 1941), 433.

86 Brown, "Negro Folk Expression," 322.

87 Brown, "Folk Literature," in *Negro Caravan*, ed. Sterling A. Brown, Arthur Paul Davis, and Ulysses Lee (New York: Dryden Press, 1941), 433.

stories for the entertainment of his little white master, and Uncle Remus too often conforms to the [romantic] plantation tradition. Finally, the Uncle Remus stories are considered children's classics," when in fact these were tales that adults told to other adults as well as to children. "The stark and almost cynical qualities of genuine folklore, especially that of rural Negroes, are deleted in favor of gentility and sentiment. A whole school of reminiscent writers gave stories as told by faithful uncles and aunties. But their purpose was more to cast a golden glow over the antebellum South than to set forth authentic Negro folklore."[88]

But, Brown argues, by no means should we allow the denuding of the essence of Negro folklore by apologists for slavery, such as Harris, to deter us from collecting and nourishing the folk tradition. For in these tales, just as in the spirituals, is embedded the first expression of the aesthetic foundation of African American culture:

> Whether laughing at the mishaps of his master or of a fellow slave; whether siding with Brer Rabbit while he checkmates stronger opponents with cunning and deceit, or with the Tar-Baby while he foils Brer Rabbit; whether telling about John Henry defeating the steam drill, or Railroad Bill outshooting the sheriff and his deputies, oral telling of tales has been a favorite occupation of American Negroes. Down by the big gate, at the store or cotton gin, at the end of the row at lunch time, in poolroom, barbershop, fraternal lodge, college dormitory, railroad depot, railroad coach, the Negro has told his tall tales and anecdotes, now sidesplitting, now ironic, now tragic. Though it is an art not likely to die out, it certainly deserves more serious attention than it has received.[89]

For we should never allow ourselves to underestimate the aesthetic merit of black folklore and not fully appreciate its enormous potential as the basis of a great tradition of canonical literature: "Whatever may be the future of the folk Negro," Brown wrote in 1953, "American literature as well as American music is the richer because of his expression. Just as Huckleberry Finn and Tom Sawyer were fascinated by the immense lore of their friend Jim, American authors have been drawn to Negro folk life and character." Moreover, "folk Negroes have themselves bequeathed a wealth of moving song,

88 Brown, "Folk Literature," in *Negro Caravan*, ed. Sterling A. Brown, Arthur Paul Davis, and Ulysses Lee (New York: Dryden Press, 1941), 431.
89 Ibid., 433.

both religious and secular, of pithy folk-say and entertaining and wise folk-tales. They have settled characters in the gallery of American heroes; resourceful Brer Rabbit and Old Jack, and indomitable John Henry. They have told their own story so well that all men should be able to hear it and understand."[90]

In the same pioneering essay, published on the eve of America's entry into World War II, Brown hails the role of Zora Neale Hurston in retrieving Negro folklore from those who would denude it. "The first substantial collection of folk tales by a Negro scholar," he writes, perhaps unaware of Arthur Huff Fauset's work but certainly aware of the noble efforts undertaken at Hampton in the last decade of the nineteenth century, "is *Mules and Men* by Zora Neale Hurston. Miss Hurston is a trained anthropologist, who brings a great zest to both the collecting and the rendering of the 'big old lies' of her native South."[91] In a way, Brown is the link between Zora Neale Hurston and an entire "school" of African American modernists and postmodernists whose work is constructed, in various ways, on the bedrock of black folklore and other vernacular forms, especially the way black people have spoken, and continue to speak, African American versions of American English. I'm thinking especially of Ralph Ellison and Albert Murray, Alice Walker and Toni Morrison, though the list of superb writers in this branch of the African American tradition is long and distinguished, and would have to include Ishmael Reed, Toni Cade Bambara, Leon Forrest, and a host of other brilliant authors. In other words, an entire branch, or school, of African American literature unfolded from the fiction of Zora Neale Hurston and the poetry of Langston Hughes and Sterling A. Brown, themselves indebted to the literary experimentation with black vernacular traditions in the work of James Weldon Johnson, especially *God's Trombones* (1927) and Jean Toomer's modernistic novel, *Cane* (1923).

I think, in part because of Hurston's efforts to collect Negro folklore, in part because of her experiments with folklore in her novels, both Richard Wright and Ralph Ellison (despite having mischievously panned *Their Eyes Were Watching God* in separate book reviews) articulated the fundamental importance of black folklore to defining— and *mining*—a genuine "black aesthetic," a theoretical position that Toni Morrison would also so luxuriously embrace and embody in her fiction. Writing in 1937 from within a Marxist aesthetic but struggling to reconcile it with a nascent cultural nation-

90 Brown, "Negro Folk Expression: Spirituals, Seculars, Ballads and Work Songs," in *A Son's Return* (Boston: Northeastern University Press, 1996), 264.
91 Brown, "Folk Literature," 433.

alism, Richard Wright had this to say: "Negro folklore contains, in a measure that puts to shame more deliberate forms of Negro expression, the collective sense of Negro life in America. Let those who shy at the nationalist implications of Negro life look at this body of folklore, living and powerful, which rose out of a unified sense of common life and a common fate. Here are those vital beginnings of a recognition of value in life as it is *lived*, a recognition that marks the emergence of a new culture in the shell of the old. And at the moment this process starts, at the moment when a people begin to realize a *meaning* in their suffering, the civilization that engenders that suffering is doomed."[92]

However, Wright, whose literary naturalism was at odds both with Hurston's lyrical modernism and Ellison's fiction, which sits on the border of modernism and postmodernism, didn't manage to draw upon the vibrancy of the folk tradition in his fictions. Ellison, on the other hand, successfully did, and refers to the power and importance of black folklore again and again in his critical writings, nowhere more powerfully than in this statement in 1967:

> We have been exiled in our own land and, as for our efforts at writing, we have been little better than silent because we have not been cunning. I find this rather astounding because I feel that Negro American folklore is very powerful, wonderful, and universal. And it became so by expressing a people who were assertive, eclectic, and irreverent before all the oral and written literature that came within its grasp. It took what it needed to express its sense of life and rejected what it could not use . . . What we have achieved in folklore has seldom been achieved in the novel, the short story, or poetry. In the folklore we tell what Negro experience really is. We back away from the chaos of experience and from ourselves, and we depict the humor as well as the horror of living. We project Negro life in a metaphysical perspective and we have seen it with a complexity of vision that seldom gets into our writing.[93]

And though he would have been most reluctant to admit it, Ellison's debt to Hurston's uses of folklore was a considerable one.

Hurston herself collected folklore, using "the spy-glass of Anthropology," theorized

92 Richard Wright, "Blueprint for Negro Writing," in *African American Literary Theory: A Reader,* ed. Winston Napier (New York: New York University Press, 2000), 47–48.
93 Ralph Ellison, "A Very Stern Discipline," *Harper's* 234 (March 1967), 80.

about folklore, and rendered folklore in novels, especially in her classic novel, *Their Eyes Were Watching God* (1937), now solidly part of the American literary canon, which we can think of as the *ur* text in a rich tradition of black women's writing that is still unfolding. In her insightful essay "Characteristics of Negro Expression," Hurston writes: "Negro folklore is not a thing of the past. It is still in the making. Its great variety shows the adaptability of the black man: nothing is too old or too new, domestic or foreign, high or low, for his use. God and the Devil are paired, and are treated no more reverently than Rockefeller and Ford. . . . The automobile is ranged alongside of the oxcart. The angels and the apostles walk and talk like section hands. And through it all walks Jack, the greatest cultural hero of the south; Jack beats them all—even the Devil, who is often smarter than God."[94]

Hurston noted, prophetically, that the folklore invented by African Americans is "still in the making." It is clear that African American folklore is alive and well in one of its principal venues, in the living tradition of African American fiction. Thanks to the brave efforts of pioneering collectors such as Alice Bacon and Arthur Fauset, and the legion of other scholars whose works ours rests upon, the canon of African American folktales was preserved. We hope that our anthology makes even a small contribution to rendering this great tradition of thought and feeling accessible to an even wider audience, both in the classroom and in homes.

94 Zora Neale Hurston, "Characteristics of Negro Expression," in *African American Literary Theory: A Reader*, 36.

INTRODUCTION
Recovering a Cultural Tradition
by Maria Tatar

The stories in this volume have designs on us. They take us out of our comfort zones, shaking us up in the process and sometimes even rewiring our brains. Their wizardry puts us back in touch with lived experience and reconnects us with a history that many have wanted to put behind them. Their expressive intensity enables us to explore the institution of slavery in the United States, the strategies used to survive as well as the ways of managing the complex legacy still with us today. The stories in this volume entered the bloodstream of the vernacular to become communal wisdom in an era when few had access to the instruments of writing and reading. They were meant to entertain, but also to provoke conversation and promote collective problem-solving. Their every word reminds us of the high-wattage power of stories and histories.

Who will tell your story? My story? Or, for that matter, our story? And whose story is "our" story? Those are the questions haunting our culture today, for in our technology-driven world we are quickly learning the value of storytelling as a way to keep the world vital, alive, and human. The past decades have been a time of unprecedented concern with the politics of identity formation in its many different facets. It has also been an era in which cultural memory has been passionately contested, as gender, race, and ethnicity begin to complicate the historical record. What stories do we choose to tell? Which ones have been disavowed and forgotten? Which ones do we want to revive and pass on?

The Annotated African American Folktales aims to capture stories from times past, not autobiographical accounts or biographical narratives so much as collective forms of symbolic expression. Those narratives are part of a heritage that has received scant attention from the gatekeepers and priests of high culture, for they circulated as song and speech, rarely written down and documented since they were part of a vast network of oral storytelling. The time has come to secure a place for them in our history.

Efforts to begin recording these stories began just when what we now call American literature was finding its voice. In 1850, Nathaniel Hawthorne published *The Scarlet Letter,* a novel that D. H. Lawrence was to describe as a perfect work of the American imagination. A year later, Herman Melville's *Moby-Dick*, dedicated to Hawthorne, appeared in print and came to be enshrined as the Great American Novel. Louisa May Alcott wrote *Little Women* (1868), a "girl's book" she did not enjoy writing, but that has been hailed as a vision of the "all-American girl." Walt Whitman's *Leaves of Grass* went into its sixth printing in 1876 and would be distributed to U.S. soldiers marching off to World War II as a symbolic expression of the American Way. In the same year, Mark Twain published *The Adventures of Tom Sawyer* and a decade later *The Adventures of Huckleberry Finn*, two novels that captured boyhood in its quintessential American form. Then came Henry James with *Washington Square* in 1881, just a year after Joel Chandler Harris's *Uncle Remus: His Songs and His Sayings* was rolling from the presses and just a few years before Charles Chesnutt's *The Conjure Woman, and Other Conjure Tales* (1899).

All the works put on parade here are still in the literary canon, with the exception of the Uncle Remus stories. In the past decades, African American folklore has begun to stage a comeback in its less adulterated form, finally earning a deserved place as part of our literary heritage. In this volume, we hope to make its cultural energy more visible and more palpable than ever before.

In the archive—a place for storing print documents, videos, and digital materials— historical memory has been preserved as something seemingly stable, even if it is always also malleable and subject to misreading and reinterpretation. Side by side with what is in the archive exists a repertoire of song, story, dance, spectacle, theater, and other forms of expressive performance that are more fragile and ephemeral, even though they can be committed to memory, internalized, transmitted, and reanimated, sometimes even finding their way into the archive.[1] This is the repertoire that UNESCO (The United Nations Educational, Scientific, and Cultural Organization) is working to preserve by "safeguarding, protecting and revitalizing cultural spaces or forms of cultural expression proclaimed as 'masterpieces of the oral and intangible heritage of humanity.'"[2]

Intangible cultural property has a way of holding its own, containing within itself boundless reserves of expressive energy. But in some cases it is indeed an endangered species, particularly if it is not valued as something worth preserving. That has been the case with African American folklore, which has been regularly anthologized but rarely seen as culturally central to the American imagination and often repudiated because of its associations with slavery. Spirituals and other forms of song and music managed to survive and thrive in the era after the Civil War and were canonized by W. E. B. Du Bois in *The Souls of Black Folk* (1903) and by James Weldon Johnson in his *Book of American Negro Poetry* (1922), as well as in his *Book of Negro Spirituals* (1925). But the tales that circulated among African American slaves and their descendants performed what sometimes feels like a vanishing act. That was the case until writers like Charles Chesnutt and Paul Laurence Dunbar used them as the stuff of their fiction and poetry, while figures like Langston Hughes, Arna Bontemps, Sterling A. Brown, and Zora Neale Hurston collected them and put them between the covers of a book. Unlike the slave narratives which were only salvaged from the archive after great difficulty and since have become an important part of our literary heritage—those written down by Frederick Douglass, William Wells Brown, Solomon Northup, Mary Prince, and Harriet Jacobs immediately come to mind—African American folktales were all too often dismissed by many as vulgar and juvenile, a playfully eccentric mix of mischief and gibberish.

Folk narratives, told in the fields and in cabins, are in many ways a significant part of an American vernacular tradition that preserved collective mother wit and wisdom

1 I borrow the concept of the archive and the repertoire from Diane Taylor's *The Archive and the Repertoire: Performing Cultural Memory in the Americas* (Durham, NC: Duke University Press, 2003). Ruth Finnegan provides a critique of the term *folktale* in her *Oral Literature in Africa* (Cambridge, UK: Open Book Publishers, 2012), 310–11. In oral literature, she emphasizes, "the verbal elaboration, the drama of the performance itself, everything in fact which makes it a truly *aesthetic* product comes from the contemporary teller and his audience and not from the remote past" (311). Her resistance to admitting the repertoire into the archive means that the repertoire will be forever lost.

2 http://unesdoc.unesco.org/images/0012/001205/120546E.pdf.

in the form of story. Sometimes they were heard in snatches of conversation or in other bits and pieces of talk, and sometimes they were performed formally as story—for young and old, rich and poor, men and women, black and white, slaves and masters. They once were what fairy tales like "Cinderella" have become for us today, narratives alive with social energy constantly turning into new versions of themselves as they are repurposed for different audiences. Stunningly dramatic and melodramatic, they stage operas of emotional intensity with "What if?" premises so powerful that we suddenly find ourselves thinking more and thinking harder, not just about a story but also about its terms and how they apply to our own lives. As a quick example, take the tar-baby story, a deceptively simple tale about a mute black figure confronting a thief. As we shall see, it can be read as antic drama on one level, but also as a powerful vehicle for modeling passive resistance and survival skills.

Annotated African American Folktales takes up the challenge of restoring our cultural memory of the African American vernacular. It raids whatever managed to make it into the archive to reconstruct a repertoire that remains alive today and can also still be found in the language rituals of playing the dozens and signifying, the slang of the streets, in the rhythms of rap and hip hop, and in places ranging from barber shops to beauty parlors, Saturday night juke joints to Sunday morning church services, family dinner tables to family reunions, sporting events, restaurants, and family dens or front porches. Lest we forget, many of these stories were preserved precisely because they had once been told, not just in places of leisure, but also at the workplace, at sites of hard labor and dull tasks, where they not only fostered the ability to carry out chores but also to imagine ways out and endure.

ORDERING THE TALES IN THE
AFRICAN AMERICAN UNIVERSE

This volume begins with the African heritage, with stories about Anansi the Spider, patron of storytelling, wisdom, and knowledge—a trickster figure whose philosophy acknowledges duplicity and contradiction as the engines of human intelligence. A selection of African dilemma tales reminds us that folklore operates with shock in order to help us process the unthinkable, provoke debate, and negotiate shared values even in dissent. If dilemma tales engage our mental faculties with cultural contradictions framed as intellectual conundrums (who should marry the beauty, the one who revived her, healed her, or rescued her from a monster?), fairy tales present us with the great counterfactuals. Stimulating the imagination with wonders, they remind us of the perils and possibilities inherent in the human condition. The African fairy tales included here also reveal that the familiar world of European folklore has never been the only source of plots and tropes circulating in tales told in the United States today. Finally, this first section concludes with some sample tales from oral storytelling traditions in African cultures.

From the African prelude, *Annotated African American Tales* moves to its main act, with narratives that emerged among storytelling communities in the New World, improvisations inspired by ritual and myth, meant for the moment and designed to be passed on by word of mouth. Imagine a world without print culture and electronic media, a time when the only conduit for passing on wisdom and knowledge was the spoken word. And then imagine an era—and it is not easy to time-travel back to the United States of the antebellum period, the era before the beginning of the Civil War in 1861—when it took courage for African Americans to speak in public, to tell, to disclose, and to broadcast, if they had the opportunity to say anything at all, especially outside the precincts of the American abolitionist movement. What remains of those narrative circuits? The surviving fragments cannot possibly retain the magic and audacity of the stories in their original form. And yet the glittering remnants also enable us to assemble repertoires, to catch glimpses of performances, and to make some sense of what mattered in another era.

The tales that comprise the first five sections of African American tales turn on language and the transformative power of words—as incantation, spell, charm, or curse. Talk and treachery, silence and strength, seductions good and evil: these are the themes that sound full chords in tales about flying Africans, witches who ride, talking skulls, singing tortoises, tar babies, and devious snakes. The legacy of Legba, the divine linguist, becomes supremely evident in these narratives, tales committed to revealing how words can be our means of bonding and our salvation yet also operate as agents of deception and duplicity. Anansi continues to weave his delicate webs silently in the corners of these narratives, reminding us that our appetites and cravings build the world but can also undermine its fragile beauty.

The next sections of *Annotated African American Folktales* turn to Joel Chandler Harris and Zora Neale Hurston, two collectors who could not have been more different in their approaches. Harris, a white Southerner, published *Uncle Remus: His Songs and His Sayings* in 1880, and the enormous commercial success of the volume affirms Charles Chesnutt's intuition that Northern whites had an endless fascination with Southern black folklore. "Men are always ready to extend their sympathy to those at a distance, than to the suffering ones in their midst."[3] What Chesnutt could not have anticipated but quickly understood as he tracked the enthusiastic response to Harris's work was the appeal to both the North and the South of the Uncle Remus tales, with their deeply confusing universe that invites us in with displays of solidarity (Brer this and Brer that), warmth, and friendship and then kicks us in the head with a show of unbridled appetites, false hospitality, and murderous hostility.

Between Harris and Hurston, there are a host of transitional figures, writers who traffic in local lore and superstition, reacting to Harris's Uncle Remus figure and critiquing him by constructing characters with less stereotypical force and greater psychological depth. There are Charles Chesnutt's complex literary refashionings of folkloric themes and Paul Laurence Dunbar's poetic transformations of African American lore and vernacular language through his "dialect" poetic diction. And there is James Weldon Johnson's canonical "The Creation," which gives us a riff on its antecedents, black creation stories about "how the Negro came to be how he is." There are the poignant and powerful glimpses of talk among African Americans in the work of E. C. L. Adams's *Tales of the Congaree.* But it is in the work of Zora Neale Hurston that we find a restorative rather than a critical turn, with an anthropological mind applying ethnographic knowledge to storytelling sites at sawmills, juke joints, train stations, and porches in order to give us tales and social context.

At times, the rage for order that takes hold of anthologizers vanishes in the face of the entangled histories and kaleidoscopic variations in stories from times past. The final sections of *Annotated African American Folktales* take us into the deep cultural contradictions of slavery, with stories about John and Old Master, tales about obedience and feigned compliance as well as about role reversal and revenge. The *pourquoi* tales that follow are particularly poignant in interrogating the conditions of slavery and how things came to be the way they were. It is here, as in the John and Old Master tales, that humor surfaces as coping mechanism, as weapon, and as a way of shielding against despair.[4] "Laughing to keep from crying," as we hear in the

---

3 Richard H. Brodhead, ed., *The Journals of Charles W. Chesnutt* (Durham, NC: Duke University Press, 1993), 25.

4 Glenda Carpio, *Laughing Fit to Kill: Black Humor in the Fictions of Slavery* (Oxford: Oxford University Press, 2008).

blues. Behind most jokes lurks tragedy, temporary or protracted, and the conditions of slavery offered far too many opportunities for making light of impossible situations or indulging in dark humor.

We have included ballads about heroes and outlaws in large part because they are revealing about collective efforts to enshrine strategies for surviving and enduring as well as transcending and living, in ways both tragic and comic. Sometimes that meant living outside the limitations of slavery and its aftermath, and indeed, sometimes outside the laws of man and the laws of nature in the realm of a mythic discourse. The heroic stories told in the ballads chart forms of rebellion and lawlessness that contrast sharply with what we find in preacher stories, tales about good, law-abiding men of God who are also conmen, masters in the art of using verbal skills to their advantage. Ballads about outlaws and tales about preachers capture opposite poles of the storytelling spectrum, from the mythical and mysterious to the banal and ordinary.

Finally, as a reminder of the big folkloric and mythical picture—the ocean of the stream of stories—we have included folkloric analogs from Caribbean and Latin American cultures as well as fairy tales that resonate with the European canon yet are also inflected in ways that make them culturally distinctive, African American to the core.

In 1957, long after the publication of his classic autobiographical novel *Black Boy*, Richard Wright declared his skepticism about anthologies: "As we all know, anthologists are legion today; to make an anthology requires simply this: Get a big pile of books on a given subject together, a big pot of glue, and a pair of sharp scissors and start clipping and pasting."[5] Cutting and pasting are no longer as laborious a task as in Wright's day, and it could be argued that all you need now is a big pile of books and a scanner. Never mind the challenges of identifying the books, selecting the stories, and creating an organizational logic that navigates and makes sense of the myriad historical, cultural, and social forces at work in what was once a living tradition that carried the shifting weights of entertainment and instruction.

Although writers like Charles Chesnutt, Paul Laurence Dunbar, Langston Hughes, Zora Neale Hurston, Sterling A. Brown, and Arna Bontemps all took a lively interest in African American folklore, there has never been an African American equivalent to the German Brothers Grimm, who popularized stories like "Hansel and Gretel"

5 Richard Wright, "The Literature of the Negro in the United States," in *White Man, Listen!* (Garden City, NY: Doubleday, 1957), 105–6.

and "Snow White," or to the Frenchman Charles Perrault, who gave us our "Sleeping Beauty" and "Cinderella." The challenges of collecting the tales in the Americas are far greater than what the Grimms and Perrault faced. Since the stories spread out from African roots to mix and mingle with other tales and transform themselves into something new in many different regions, efforts to canonize or to create a lineup of authoritative texts can quickly turn reductive, impoverishing rather than enriching the repertoire.

John Updike once remarked that fiction is "very greedy," always demanding more of a writer. The same holds true for every formerly blank page of this book, with its "appetite" for "ever more information, ever more data."[6] And so the challenges of completing a volume like this one are much the same as the ones of beginning it. There is always room for more, but it is our hope that others will build on the foundations laid out here. *Annotated African American Folktales* represents an effort to expand the American literary canon and to let the stories settle in where they belong, as a part of our official cultural heritage.

READING THE AFRICAN AMERICAN REPERTOIRE

Stories are often meant to provide comfort through the consolations of imagination, but the tales in this volume are also confrontational, meant to unsettle and disturb. Readers will take different approaches when they pick up this anthology. Some may decide to select serendipitously, trying out different stories and ignoring the weight of the introductory material and apparatus. They may decide to march through the volume, studying certain types of tales systematically and following the trails indicated in further readings listed. Or they may create their own order by beginning with Joel Chandler Harris's Uncle Remus stories and moving on from there. The introductory comments and running notes elaborate, explain, and provide context, but some readers will prefer to immerse themselves in the wonderful weirdness of each story, unlocking mysteries by reading carefully and using their own knowledge, intuition, and instincts to discover what lies between the lines.

Great stories have a magnetic appeal that transcends generational differences, and *Annotated African American Folktales*, like its counterparts in national folklore collections, is meant for young and old. Its audience is also a "double audience," in the sense

6 Terry Gross, *All I Did Was Ask: Conversations with Writers, Actors, Musicians, and Artists* (New York: Hachette, 2004), 27.

defined by James Weldon Johnson, who drew on W. E. B. Du Bois's concept of "double consciousness" ("this sense of always looking at one's self through the eyes of others") to describe the challenges faced by black writers. "The Afriamerican author faces . . . the problem of the double audience," he wrote. "It is a divided audience, an audience made up of two elements with differing and often opposite and antagonistic points of view. His audience is always both white America and black America."[7] Today, that bifurcation can seem at times just as dramatic. Yet we also live in a multiracial nation whose younger generations have grown up, thanks to *Soul Train* and hip hop, impressively fluent in African American expressive culture. Even literary scholars, after the culture wars of the 1990s, have begun to understand that what they once dismissed as eccentric inventions are narratives symbolically central in the formation of American social and cultural identity.

No one understood more clearly than Ralph Ellison, whose 1952 novel *Invisible Man* jolted the imagination of a nation, just how easy it is to ignore what is right before our eyes. Ellison's invisible man also has an invisible cultural heritage and social history. When teaching a course at New York University on the Harlem Renaissance, Ellison puzzled many of his students by including *The Great Gatsby*. "I find it significant," he noted, "that the character who saw who was driving the 'death car' was a Negro; and yet, some students resist when I tie that in with Tom Buchanan's concern over the rise of the colored races, the scene in which blacks are being driven by a white chauffeur, and the characterization of the Jewish gangster. They miss the broader context of the novel that is revealed in the understated themes of race, class, and social mobility."[8] The reading practices in much of the academy (Howard University was, among a few other institutions, an incandescent exception) rendered African American characters invisible, even when they were present in canonical works of what we call American Literature. But, more important, for a time American literary studies removed the vernacular from the mainstream, pretending that it did not exist, embracing folktales that are German, French, Russian, Italian, or Chinese, anything but African American.

Languishing for decades on what seemed to be the margins, African American

7 James Weldon Johnson, "The Dilemma of the Negro Author," *American Mercury* 15 (December 1928), 477–481.

8 Robert B. Stepto and Michael S. Harper, "Study and Experience: An Interview with Ralph Ellison," in *Conversations with Ralph Ellison*, ed. Maryemma Graham and Amritjit Singh (Jackson: University Press of Mississippi, 1995), 334.

folklore has nonetheless preserved a central, if rarely officially prominent, position in the culture of the Americas. Unlike European immigrants who set down roots in the United States, African slaves lacked the kind of freedom of movement and social mobility that enabled a certain kind of reinvention. However, in a deeply ironic form of compensation they possessed a genius for improvisational freedom and energy, the liberty to express themselves using their own criteria without worrying about standards alien to their own internal aesthetic rules and practices. Ellison tells us that slaves had the chance to be "culturally daring and innovative because the strictures of 'good taste' and 'thou shalt-nots' of tradition were not imposed on them."[9] (To be sure, some of those strictures came to be self-imposed, when middle-class black men and women embraced what the historian Evelyn Brooks Higginbotham has called the politics of respectability.) It is no accident that *Annotated African American Tales* begins with Anansi, the African trickster, master of improvisation, a spider who plots and weaves in scandalous ways, enacting stories that build the human world and make the world human, with all its paradoxes, contradictions, and ambiguities. This book also presents the narrative world of his many accomplices, and it invites readers to join the ranks of his many co-conspirators.

The Canadian novelist Margaret Atwood once observed that all writers must go from *now* to *once upon a time*, that is, they must dig deep into the past and cut through layers of cultural memory to reach some kind of mother lode, a place that she describes as "where the stories are kept."[10] It is not just writers who are duty bound to undertake the journey to that site. "All must commit acts of larceny, or else of reclamation, depending on how you look at it. The dead may guard the treasure, but it's useless treasure unless it can be brought back into the land of the living and allowed to enter time once more—which means to enter the realm of the audience, the realm of readers, the realm of change." It is our hope that this volume may make the journey somewhat less arduous and turn travel into part of the pleasure of discovering a treasure that, once unearthed and brought to light, can not only sustain us but also arouse curiosity rather than awaken fear, promote change rather than foster complacency, and hold out the golden promise of hope.

9 Ibid., 465.

10 Margaret Atwood, *Negotiating with the Dead: A Writer on Writing* (Cambridge, UK: Cambridge University Press, 2002), 178.

THE CONTESTED ORIGINS
OF AFRICAN AMERICAN FOLKLORE

How do you make something from nothing? Or from something that appears to be nothing? African American slaves may not have owned property, but no one could prevent them from storing, remembering, recounting, and, over time, creating and re-creating their own cultural property in the form of songs, stories, and belief systems. They used narratives and other forms of expressive culture not just to strategize and survive, but also to create symbolic and imaginative spaces to which they could escape, almost like an alternate universe, where they could live and breathe. "The entire sacred world of the black slaves," American historian Lawrence Levine writes, "created the necessary space between the slaves and their owners and were the means of preventing legal slavery from becoming spiritual slavery."[11] These were anything but the much-heralded public spaces of freedom that are the signature of democratic societies. Instead, they were private arenas, imaginary playgrounds, secular as well as sacred, in the fields, by the fire, and in cabins. Song and story emerged, often in the form of narratives encoded with symbolic meaning—things made up for the purpose of diverting and entertaining, and also for focusing and concentrating propulsive energies that could not be contained.

Over time, however, our culture has lost touch with many of these improvisations and inventions: "We don't live in places where we can hear . . . stories anymore; parents don't sit around and tell their children those classical, mythological archetypal stories that we heard years ago. But new information has got to get out, and there are several ways to do it," Toni Morrison once remarked.[12] Her strategy was to embed black folklore in the postmodern black novel. Others have made the stories new in a range of creative ways. Or they have laid the groundwork for what we attempt in this volume: collecting, contextualizing, and organizing what remains of stories from times past.

Few have captured more vividly the indestructible energy and resilience of story than Zora Neale Hurston, who documented folklore in action in her 1935 *Mules and Men*, a volume that doubles as autobiography and ethnography. She understood that,

11 Lawrence W. Levine, *Black Culture and Black Consciousness: Afro-American Folk Thought from Slavery to Freedom* (Oxford: Oxford University Press, 1977), 80.

12 Toni Morrison, "Rootedness: The Ancestor as Foundation," in *Black Women Writers (1950–1980): A Critical Evaluation*, ed. Mari Evans (New York: Anchor Press, Doubleday, 1984), 340.

notwithstanding the multiple traumas of the Middle Passage and plantation life, it was impossible to restrain the animating energy of telling tales. In a counternarrative to what Richard Wright, author of *Native Son* and *Black Boy*, reports about the silencing of voices and the damaging losses suffered by slaves, she invokes a tale of survival, one that shows how words, stories, and beliefs made it across the Atlantic and flourished on distant shores. Here is how Hurston works magic with words, reviving stories from times past and bringing to life cultural heroes from faraway lands. High John de Conquer, the mythical trickster and strongman hero of African American lore, was not, as she tells us, a "natural man" in the beginning:

> First off, he was a whisper, a will to hope, a wish to find something worthy of laughter and song. Then the whisper put on flesh. His footsteps sounded across the world in a low but musical rhythm as if the world he walked on was a singing drum. The black folks had an irresistible impulse to laugh. High John de Conquer was a man in full, and had come to live and work on the plantations, and all the slave folks knew him in the flesh.[13]

In this extraordinary scene of animation and embodiment, we are given a cascading sequence of words and phrases that become flesh, a chain of attributes that revive and vivify. High John de Conquer begins as a whisper, transmutes into a wish, and comes alive. His footsteps are attuned to the frequencies of whispers and hopes, amplifying them and turning them into audible laughter and music. The world becomes a "singing drum," sounding in measured, communicative cadences.[14]

In one creative flash, Hurston, who made it her mission to validate and ennoble the African American vernacular, mobilizes High John de Conquer of African American lore to open the possibility for utopian aspirations that defy all the social odds. At a time of scarcity and lack, when everything seems doomed to disappoint, suddenly there is a sign that even those flimsiest of things, whispers and dreams, are more than fugitive and futile acts of imagination. They assert brute presence and material solid-

13 Zora Neale Hurston, "High John de Conquer," *American Mercury* 57 (1943), 450; rpt. in *The Sanctified Church* (Berkeley, CA: Turtle Island Foundation, 1981), 69.

14 Ruth Finnegan writes that the ritual use of drums turns them into "instruments . . . regarded as speaking and their messages consist of words." See *Oral Literature in Africa* (London: Oxford University Press, 1970), 11.

ity, refusing to remain invisible. This is not mere magical thinking; it is words working miracles.

Hurston reveals how the make-believe of folktale, myth, and legend operates in the making of beliefs. Illusion can become so compelling that it rivals material reality, and suddenly the word becomes flesh and phantoms of the mind have substance. It is here that we discover the truth of the maxim that the consolations of imagination are not imaginary consolations. In powerful stories like "And the People Could Fly" (included in this anthology), the enabling force of faith becomes evident. The tale of High John de Conquer gives us the flip side to that story, offering a parable of materialization and empowerment rather than a transcendent vanishing act. But in both stories, passion and desire are so forceful and energetic as to become real.

The transformative energy of bravura moments like the materialization of High John de Conquer is what makes folktales stick and what kept them—and keeps them—from disappearing, even in a culture of material deprivation and physical coercion. Recall the wizardry of Mozart's music in a scene from *The Shawshank Redemption*, a film released in 1994, when the character played by Tim Robbins enraptures the men serving time at Shawshank with song. In a voice-over that comes after the broadcast of a duet from Mozart's opera *Nozze di Figaro*, Morgan Freeman reveals the liberating power, not only of sonic beauty but also of the words used to describe its effects: "It was like some beautiful bird flapped into our drab little cage," Freeman intones (adverting elliptically to Paul Laurence Dunbar's verse about why the caged bird sings), "and made those walls dissolve away, and for the briefest of moments, every last man in Shawshank felt free." Hurston's tale about willing a hero to life reveals the same power of words to summon liberating reserves of strength.

The stories in *Annotated African American Folktales* will offer evidence of High John de Conquer's resurrection in the New World. The volume will begin, as noted, with folklore from African discursive traditions to show how a rich repertoire of stories became powerful source material for a sprawling tangle of tales told by African Americans, which constitute the core of this volume. But rather than rehearsing academic debates about the fate of African cultures in the diaspora, it will lay out the evidence for connections and bonds pointing to a culture that is both of a piece with and distinct from other global traditions. Hurston's survivalist model surely trumps Wright's narrative of cultural obliteration. By embracing it, we can begin to explore how stories migrated and how poetic geniuses made new versions of them in creative bursts that defied efforts to silence and enslave. By borrowing bits and pieces of the old and merging and melding traditions, storytellers in the New World displayed an unparalleled determination to honor ancestral knowledge by preserving the cultural memory encapsulated in stories from times past.

Who wrote these stories down on paper? Not the tellers, who, of course, often lacked access to pen, ink, and paper, but anthropologists, folklorists, and others whose curiosity was piqued by cultural difference and by the desire to create a historical record. To be sure, much was lost in the transition from a performance that emerged organically within a ritualized, communal setting to a formal recitation often aimed to please a scribe putting words down on a page and unconsciously also putting new words into the mouths of the tellers. But all was not lost, much was preserved, and the stories are still here, printed as columns in local newspapers and as features in magazines, embedded in novels and memoirs, collected in anthologies for young and old, invoked in conversations and reminiscences, and still told today. There have been, in short, multiple accomplices in this project of excavating, reclaiming, and anthologizing.

THE LITERATURE OF THE FRONTIER
AND THE POETRY OF THE CABINS

Anyone researching ballads about Stagolee, John Henry, Shine and the *Titanic*, the Signifying Monkey, or Frankie and Johnny will eventually encounter *Mark Twain's America* by the eminent twentieth-century critic Bernard DeVoto. DeVoto emphasizes how Americans are "story-tellers," and he describes and animates the "frontier leisure and frontier realities" that shaped American literature. He evokes with nostalgic joy campfires on the shores of rivers, on the plains, in forests, and on mountains, along with narratives about folk heroes ranging from Mike Fink and Kit Carson to Davy Crockett and "Honest Abe." In passing he mentions Annie Christmas, along with Jim Henry [*sic*] and Frankie and Johnny. He declares these stories to be "the frontier examining itself, recording itself, and entertaining itself." "It is," he observes in a final rhetorical flourish, "a native literature of America."[15]

Frontier leisure? The frontier entertaining itself? How could DeVoto get things so wrong when it came to ballads and folklore? Did he seriously believe that the ballad about John Henry's tragic contest with a machine was born during a rollicking good

---

15 Bernard DeVoto, *Mark Twain's America* (New York: Houghton Mifflin, 1932), 92–93.

time telling stories around blazing campfires? Was he serious when he invoked in a completely untroubled fashion the "rich life of America, and of the common man who composed it"? Of course, DeVoto had a very different tradition in mind, one that flourished in what had already become American literature in its official form. He may have nodded politely in the direction of the legendary Annie Christmas, but he never paid any serious attention to her or to the lives of her folkloric cousins. Nor did it occur to him in the early 1930s to include the slave cabin or the campfires around those cabins in his inventory of storytelling sites. We have "campfires on the shores of lakes and rivers," "taverns, stores, groggeries, and meetinghouses," along with "decks of rafts, scows, flatboats, broadhorns, and steamboats," but no mention of stories told in cultural spaces where black genius manifested itself in the vernacular. For DeVoto, the frontier, an emblem of bold, spirited exploratory energy, was a symbol of the "rugged individualism" prized by American writers. The spirit of storytelling that was to animate American literature for him was overwhelmingly white and male: "wherever frontiersmen met for conversation, this literature flourished."

"I love to sail forbidden seas, and land on barbarous coasts," Ishmael tells us in Herman Melville's epic *Moby-Dick* (1851), and with those words he captured the driving desires of heroes who came to be enshrined in the pantheon of American literature.[16] That longing was already and nowhere more powerfully alive than in the slave cabin, with its songs and stories about breaking loose to freedom. Right alongside the oral tradition described by DeVoto—all those frontier narratives that served as forerunners to the "classics"—was another storytelling culture that had clearly preceded it, one rarely written down because it was kept alive largely by voices. Oppositional and subversive rather than celebrated and enshrined, these were the stories invented by African Americans.

Others have pondered what seems like willful, some might argue institutionalized, blindness to traditions that are visibly present for anyone who takes the time to see them. Houston A. Baker Jr.'s *Long Black Song*, a collection of essays on "Black American Literature and Culture," begins with autobiographical reflections about growing up with books about sports, pioneers, and literary classics with "American" heroes. There came a moment in Baker's postgraduate education when he realized that there were two perspectives on America: one in which the country was seen as a "domain

16 Herman Melville, *Moby-Dick; or, The Whale* (New York: W. W. Norton, 2002), 22.

of boundless frontier," the other as one of "endless slavery." Out of the experience of slavery there emerged what he described as a distinctive body of folk expression: "oral, collectivistic, and repudiative—each of these aspects helps to distinguish black American culture from white American culture."[17]

Writing in the 1960s, at a time of desegregation and racial integration in the United States, Richard Dorson pointed out, in his *Negro Folktales in Michigan,* that black folklore formed a "distinctive repertoire," one that was entirely separate from the narratives of "West Africa, the West Indies, Europe, the British Isles, and white America."[18] He believed that folklore from all of these regions had mixed and mingled with the lived experience of African Americans to produce a unique, independent folk tradition. But in many ways, these stories *are* the indigenous lore of the United States, white and black. In fact, many of the nineteenth-century collections were put together by white men who had heard the stories from black people as children. Unlike the tales of the Brothers Grimm and Charles Perrault, which were imported almost word-for-word from abroad, stories about Brer Rabbit, John Henry, John and Old Master sprang up from native soil. But because their content was associated with slavery and because their language was marked as lacking signs of formal education, they were often publicly disavowed by middle-class, educated blacks and whites alike, even when they constituted a significant part of the nation's collective cultural heritage. These stories were seen, on the one hand, as the linguistic remnants of slavery and, on the other, as signs of ignorance. Those who aspired to join mainstream, middle-class America and who sought social acceptance by embracing the politics of respectability were intent on distancing themselves from what they saw as lowbrow forms of entertainment.

Linked with slavery and conditions that evoke a sense of shame rather than pride, African American folklore was additionally constrained by class pressures, with a middle class firmly opposed to going public. There were also strategic reasons for remaining protective of cultural property that had bored deep into the souls of the enslaved while providing wisdom, sustenance, and diversion over decades of economic subordination. Why let these stories seep out into the public domain, where they could become a fund of knowledge about the "Negro mind" (as white collectors often avowed

17 Houston A. Baker Jr., *Long Black Song: Essays in Black American Literature and Culture* (Charlottesville: University of Virginia Press, 1990), 16.

18 Richard Dorson, *Negro Folktales in Michigan* (Cambridge, MA: Harvard University Press, 1956), 187.

was the case) or, worse yet, a target of derision for those who failed to recognize that black vernacular was a self-conscious invention, crafted and nurtured over time?

As Zora Neale Hurston emphasized, "everything that [the Negro] touches is re-interpreted for his own use." That includes language. But as Charles Joyner points out, black speech was stigmatized and associated with those who worked in the fields, "in contrast to the high prestige of 'proper' English." "In retrospect," he adds, "one should be more impressed with the success of the slaves, a people of diverse linguistic backgrounds and limited opportunities, in creating a creole language and culture than appalled at their 'failure' to adapt it to the language and culture of their masters."[19]

In the introduction to a collection of her short stories, Paule Marshall emphasizes the proprietary and empowering dimensions of storytelling. She reminisces about growing up surrounded by "poets in the kitchen," women who fought back against "invisibility" and "powerlessness" with the spoken word, "the only weapon at their command." "Those late afternoon conversations," she writes, ". . . were a way for them to feel they exercised some measure of control over their lives and the events that shaped them. 'Soully-gal, talk yuh talk!' they were always exhorting each other. 'In this man world you got to take yuh mouth and make a gun!' They were in control, if only verbally and if only for the two hours or so that they remained in our house."[20] This volume captures the voices of poets in the kitchen and in the fields, as well as the storytellers in cabins and around campfires.

"STILL HERE": CAPTURING FOLKTALES
AND PUTTING THEM IN A BOOK

Identifying African cultural traditions and their residues in the diaspora is a compli-cated enterprise. These stories were created and narrated in the only places where it was possible for a black person to speak freely, to have a voice: in the center of a black discursive and culturally private universe, where talking, telling, reporting, and having the freedom to create unfolded within the Veil, as W. E. B. Du Bois so perceptively put it. In his sociobiological analysis of the human condition, E. O. Wilson tells us that the activity of building campfires, constructing nests, and telling stories enabled the con-

19 Charles Joyner, *Down by the Riverside: A South Carolina Slave Community* (Champaign: University of Illinois Press, 1985), 223.

20 Paule Marshall, *Reena and Other Stories* (Old Westbury, NY: Feminist Press, 1981), 7.

quest of the planet.[21] Slave owners may have intuitively understood that talk was not in their interests, for it could promote world-building, communal forms of knowledge, and collective wisdom that could be liberating in every sense of the term. At the same time, they also understood the need for licensed forms of social release, for slavery could endure as an institution only with those outlets. Some encouraged group rituals ranging from religious services with song and dance to cultural celebrations on holidays. Even more important were the spaces that slaves carved out in the interstices of enslavement. How else could they have survived? The "urge to culture" is boundless, irresistible, and, short of death, invincible. Contrary to Hollywood's depictions of slavery as a totalizing institution with power consolidated in the hands of sadistic masters and overseers, the ultimate goal was to "grow" slaves rather than to massacre them, to control them and to kill them only when it was deemed necessary. A labor force of 388,000 slaves shipped to the United States before 1808 grew to become almost four million slaves by 1860. Disciplinary regimes require occasional outlets, even if the social, spiritual, and intellectual capital acquired always brings with it the potential for insurrectionary and emancipatory action. As the philosopher Ernst Bloch put it, once people start telling stories, they dream about the utopian promise of "something better," or a "more colorful and easier somewhere else."[22]

It's "still here," Langston Hughes remarked of the cultural heritage he treasured and put between the covers of *The Book of Negro Folklore*. Perhaps unwittingly, perhaps deliberately, he pointed to how African American folktales are both here and not here, visible yet also hidden from sight. On the one hand, the stories have defied the odds and survived. But "still here" can also imply that silence has descended on the repertoire and that the tales have been imprisoned in something resembling what Walt Disney Studios notionally refers to as the vault. The turbulent cultural energy of the tales may have settled into a motionless calm that has rendered them tame, harmless, and inert.

African American folklore is indeed still here, although not in ways that are immediately self-evident. To be sure, the tales, at the most obvious level, have been repackaged for children, turning them into "harmless" bedtime reading in beautifully produced volumes by Julius Lester, Virginia Hamilton, and others. When Julius Lester,

21 Edward O. Wilson, *The Social Conquest of Earth* (New York: Liveright, 2013).

22 Ernst Bloch, *The Fairytale Moves on Its Own Time: The Utopian Function of Art and Literature. Selected Essays* (Cambridge, MA: MIT Press, 1988).

author of *Look Out, Whitey! Black Power's Gon' Get Your Mama* (1968), decided to retell the tales of Uncle Remus, he published them under the imprint of Dial Books for Young Readers. He hoped to make the tales accessible so that they could be read out loud "in the living rooms of condominiums as well as on front porches in the South." And, in the introduction to the volume, with an unlikely nod in the direction of the politics of respectability from a onetime black nationalist, he reports that he set out to retell the stories with the "same affectionate sense of play and fun as the original, but without evoking associations with slavery."[23] Was this tongue in cheek? Julius Lester surely knew better than anyone else that it is impossible to wipe clean the slate of history and to pretend that the tales had nothing at all to do with the conditions from which they evolved.

Virginia Hamilton had a less sentimental orientation in her large-format, illustrated volume *The People Could Fly: American Black Folktales.* She emphasized that the tales emerged from an "oppressed people" and that they were a "creative" outlet for expressing fears and hopes. "They can be enjoyed by young and old alike," she declared.[24] Yet a quick look at the back cover reveals that the volume has a young audience in mind, or was, at the least, marketed and advertised to them. It was designated as a Notable Children's Book by the American Library Association and as a Notable Children's Trade Book in the Field of Social Studies. And, in addition, the *School Library Journal* and *The Bulletin of the Center for Children's Books* praised the book in reviews.

African American folktales are not just for children. Once part of multigenerational oral traditions that structured and mirrored social rituals no longer with us today, they continue to lead a robust albeit often subterranean afterlife in adult cultural production, as writers rediscovered, repackaged, and reinvented the tropes of lore from times past. It is in the novel that folklore vibrantly lives on in its most obvious manifestations, for narrative—as Richard Wright points out—eagerly absorbs "folk tradition into its thematic structures, its plots, symbolism and rhetoric."[25] But we also often never know exactly how, where, and when folktales will land and come back to life, and they often appear in clever disguises, camouflaged, as we shall see later in this volume.

23 Julius Lester, *The Tales of Uncle Remus* (New York: Dial Books for Young Readers, 1999), viii.

24 Virginia Hamilton, *The People Could Fly* (New York: Knopf, 1985), xii.

25 Ralph Ellison, "Change the Joke and Slip the Yoke," in *Shadow and Act* (New York: Random House, 1995), 58.

Fiction for adults, unlike the tales anthologized in volumes for children, pulls no punches about the tales, recognizing them as repositories of ancestral wisdom, with powerful cultural energy and moral authority. Toni Morrison's *Tar Baby*, for example, engages with a story that has been seen as deeply problematic in its representation of blackness, and although the story is still around, it is a tale unlikely to be read to children today. The trope of the black, sticky figure that traps through its silence and passivity has become radioactive cultural property, hiding behind a big sign reading, Don't touch. Yet Toni Morrison, as we shall see, animates the figure, using it to reimagine ancestral lore while also making it relevant for new generations.

African American folktales are, of course, "still here" for children, even if they are stripped of their rough earthiness. They have also survived in cultural production for adults, where they thrive as they are refashioned and brought up-to-date. But what did the stories look like when they were first told? What can we recover of an oral tradition that was kept off the historical record because it was both ephemeral and transgressive, and because those who created it were not allowed to learn to write? How can we collect stories in ways that ensure that they enter our modern consciousness with a sense of their layered history?

Julius Lester reminds us that putting a tale between the covers of a book does not necessarily sap its vigor or spell the end of its narrative life. "Don't forget," he enjoins his readers. "Your telling the tale will not hurt it. It was here before you; it will be here after you."[26] In other words, print does not fix a text permanently and can instead enable it to survive and give rise to "talk" as it migrates back into the vernacular. There is no way to kill a good story.

Annotated African American Folktales is driven by an expansive collecting impulse, favoring capaciousness rather than giving in to restraining orthodoxies. Gathering multiple variants of a tale, each capturing a different aspect of how it is told, makes it all the easier to get at the narrative core. Talking skulls, singing tortoises, headless hants, flying Africans, and witches that ride—tales with these tropes all pick up bits and pieces of their cultural surround as they move from one continent to another, from one island to another, and from one state to the next. There is no original, just variants and variation, endlessly living, breathing, throbbing variations on *ur*-forms and *ur*-themes.

The stories collected here reach back to the nineteenth century and take us into

26 Julius Lester, *Black Folktales* (New York: Grove Press, 1969), xvi, vii.

our own time, with Zora Neale Hurston, Toni Morrison, and others acting as agents in the process of reclaiming African American folklore. Joel Chandler Harris's *Uncle Remus: His Songs and His Sayings* (1880) and Disney's *Song of the South* (1946), contrary to Alice Walker's view, could not kill African American folklore. Both the anthology and the film have remained cultural reference points with an astonishing impact on white audiences, who embraced them with unexpected fervor. Even if the ghosts of those efforts to memorialize the tales dogged the efforts of later collectors, the stories in Harris's collection gave us a snapshot of one moment in the history of the tales. For many decades, they served, for better or for worse, as authoritative sources for the lore, and even today they remain intriguing in what they conceal and reveal about sources, their audiences, and cultural context. "That's not how I heard it!" or "That's not the right way to tell it!" are not only legitimate responses to Harris's stories and Disney's film, they are also the best responses and the first step toward making the stories your own.

Before turning to some of the foundational themes that animate the stories in this volume, it is important to look at motives. What drove collectors to recognize the value of the stories and then made them feel compelled to document their existence? Many of the first to write down tales from the African American repertoire were outsiders to the culture. Whether we look at collections assembled by missionaries who traveled to Africa in search of tales from "primitive" cultures or consider Joel Chandler Harris's efforts to capture an authentic African American storytelling voice or turn to American and African American folklorists who published anthologies of native lore, we run up against the problem of witnesses observing and recording rather than participants enacting and inscribing their own stories in their own voices for themselves. It was not until the Hampton Institute folklorists settled down to work and not until Zora Neale Hurston published *Mules and Men* (1935) that insiders began to record African American tales in systematic fashion—though Hurston herself recognized that she had become something of an outsider and interloper in her own hometown of Eatonville, Florida.

When there is no deep communal connection to stories heard, something is lost in their recording. Suddenly the letter rules, and the spirit withers under the frosty scrutiny of the collector, who often aims for authenticity, whatever that may be, above all else. There is, in any case, inevitable distortion in the move from improvised performance—with its gestures, asides, and inflections—to written script. How do you represent the oral sign that the spoken black vernacular is? How do you make an adequate transcription of the spoken and performative? Gone also is the give-and-take or call-and-response that structures the telling of a tale and makes of it a collective effort. To be sure, insiders do not necessarily get things right, but they are often attuned to the lived experience of oral tradition and more likely to focus on the spirit rather than the letter of the stories transmitted.

The white missionaries and anthropologists who traveled into African regions and wrote down stories told by Africans were also the first to fret about the fact that they were offering an imperfect record of traditional wisdom. Yet they rarely blamed themselves. Almost all of them worried that the small armies of tellers, transcribers, and translators they had recruited were engaging in forms of self-censorship. They knew that native informants tweaked and edited, spontaneously in some cases, with calculation in others. There was no pleasing everyone who would be looking at the material. These early anthropologists, amateur and professional but nearly always virtuoso by contrast with the arrested development of their contemporaries, were willing to compromise for the sake of getting something on the record. And get it on the record they did, in ways that enable us to find astonishing antecedents for many of the tales later told and anthologized in the United States. Never mind that many of them were motivated by a desire to "read the Negro's mind" or that the tale-tellers may have been determined to foreclose that possibility by giving a mangled version of a story. The stories are on the record and the actions—antic and heroic—of their characters reverberate in African American folklore. In the rich African American repertoire that includes tales about John and Old Master, preachers and parishioners, Brer Rabbit and Brer Fox, Anansi and his son, as well as fairy tales about stolen voices, talking eggs, singing tortoises, and cannibalistic mothers, we find footprints that lead directly back to African sources.

Enter anthropologists and folklorists in the United States, who valued African American tales for providing a window into "the sentiments and habits of the negroes themselves."[27] Or, as one reviewer put it, in more sophisticated and obscure terms, folklore could help "penetrate the mysterious and always vanishing recesses of the ethnological labyrinth."[28] The "curiosities" of African American folklore seemed

27 Robert Hemenway, ed., *Uncle Remus: His Songs and His Sayings* (New York: Penguin, 1982), 14.

28 R. Bruce Bickley, *Critical Essays on Joel Chandler Harris* (Boston: G. K. Hall, 1981), 55.

worth recording, analyzing, and studying largely because it was such a challenge to try to make any sense of them at all. Told in language that was not considered Standard English, these tales seemed more like fractured oddities than purveyors of folk wisdom. What few white collectors realized at the time was that the tales were not only encoded and encrypted, but also deliberately told in the language spoken by the tellers and consumers of the tales, a dialect that functioned as a barrier to outsiders. And, in a self-consciously stylized form, a poetic diction, or a well-studied and well-understood rhetorical structure, as it were, folktales were a performance space within the black community. Still, many collectors, some of whom were professional folklorists, could not miss the fact that the voice of Brer Rabbit might be channeling mythical wisdom for the here and now or that John and Old Master might be reenacting rivalries that reached back to another time and place and were remade to become socially relevant.

What, then, enabled the stories to survive? In many cases, there was a seemingly fatal asymmetry between what collectors were hoping to gather (curiosities) and what storytellers aimed to communicate (wisdom and strategies for survival). How could an African American narrator slip the trap and tell a story straight up to a white outsider without betraying his own community? Charles Chesnutt may have found one answer when he published a story like "The Goophered Grapevine" in a collection called *The Conjure Woman* (1899). In it, as noted earlier, a white man retells a tale from an African American informant (Chesnutt was critiquing the narrative situation in Joel Chandler Harris's work) and thereby discovers the power of stories to challenge, move, and persuade. But for the full answer to the question of how to tell stories with consummate duplicitous finesse, we need to return to Africa.

TRICKSTERS AND PARADOX

In his novel *American Gods,* Neil Gaiman cited a specialist in African American folklore: "One question that has always intrigued me is what happens to demonic beings when immigrants move from their homelands? Irish-Americans remember the fairies, Norwegian-Americans the nisser, Greek-Americans the vrykólakas, but only in relation to events remembered in the Old Country."[29] Gaiman's answer to that question was long and complicated (taking up nearly six hundred pages), but it boiled down to

---

29 Richard Dorson, quoted in Neil Gaiman, *American Gods* (New York: HarperCollins, 2001), epigraph.

the fact that mythical creatures migrate along with the people who have faith in them, although they may manifest themselves in new forms and guises.

The Africans who came to the New World were, of course, not immigrants but enslaved peoples. But in their case too we discover that deities—Esu Elegbara of Yoruba cultures in West Africa, for example—traveled with them, reemerging in the United States, Cuba, and other places where the slave trade flourished. There, like the African Anansi who transformed himself into the Jamaican Aunt Nancy, Esu Elegbara became known by new names, as Exú in Brazil, Echu in Cuba, Papa Legba in Haiti, or Papa La Bas in the Southern United States. As the muse of storytelling, signifying, and interpretation, he was also a messenger of the gods, a figure who stood at the crossroads and who was affiliated with generation and fecundity in both spiritual and biological senses.

Stories migrated right along with the gods into the New World. And those stories were structured by a set of discursive practices associated with Esu Elegbara, the trickster god who mediates between good and evil, truth and lies, revelation and disguise, surfaces and essences, along with all the other contradictions that arise from human social activities. In his magisterial study of the trickster figure, the cultural critic Lewis Hyde noted that Legba, the West African trickster god, works "by means of lies that are really the truth, deceptions that are in fact revelations."[30] Long before the German philosopher Friedrich Nietzsche preached the gospel of indeterminacy in German-speaking lands at the turn of the nineteenth century and undermined stable meanings by emphasizing the primacy of perspective, African mythologies had enshrined those very ideas as guiding truths.

Yoruba mythology encoded the concept of indeterminacy in a foundational cultural story commonly known as "The Two Friends." That story, included in this volume, enacts the principle, showing how perspective changes everything when it comes to the perception and interpretation of reality. In the version recorded by Ayodele Ogundipe in his study of Esu, the Yoruba god wears a hat that is black on one side, white on the other. The friendship of the two men in the title, both farmers, is put to the test by Esu, whose cap becomes a source of dissension, with one of the farmers insisting that it is white, the other adamant in his view that it is black. Each is right, yet also wrong, and both fail to embrace differences in perspective. Insisting on one single

30 Lewis Hyde, *Trickster Makes This World: Mischief, Myth, and Art* (New York: Farrar, Straus and Giroux, 1998), 72.

meaning or truth leads to a destructive undermining of the fragile institutions that we have constructed to keep us human.[31]

West African myths, more powerfully than the lore of other regions in Africa, repeatedly foreground contradiction, paradox, and indeterminacy, to the point of telling stories that at times seem to turn on philosophical principles as much as on figures with real-life struggles and conflicts. Abstractions become the actors in narratives, as in the extraordinary African tale about a man who hates contradictions and discovers the hazards of failing to accept them. Known by the name of Hate-to-Be-Contradicted, he embodies a principle rather than a person, revealing more about mental processes and how our brains work than about human interactions and their consequences.

The tales told in slave cabins were in many instances deceptively simple, seeming to lack the sophistication of their African antecedents. But they are also—and here we return to their African roots—simply deceptive. Deeply enmeshed with African storytelling traditions that privileged double-talk, duplicity, cunning, deception, lies, and artful dodging, African American folktales could also masquerade as harmless confections that were nothing but idle entertainments designed to while away time. On the surface, these stories have what a character in Milan Kundera's *The Unbearable Lightness of Being* calls "an intelligible lie."[32] Beneath lurks "something different, something mysterious or abstract," what could be called an unintelligible truth. The genius of storytelling lies in its double nature as a riveting contrivance revealing as it conceals, feeding our curiosity as it arouses it, and talking to us in order to get us thinking.

TALK AND SILENCE

Two types of African tales are foundational in modeling what is at stake in African American storytelling practices, and each reveals how narrative shuttles between conversation, talk, revelation, and disclosure on the one hand, and silence, reticence, secrecy, and concealment on the other. To illustrate how African American lore is fueled by the self-reflexive strategies of African tales, let us turn for a moment to a story known as "The Talking Skull" and "The Talking Skull Refuses to Talk." We can trace that tale back to multiple sources in Nigeria, Angola, Ghana, and Tanzania, and

---

31 Henry Louis Gates Jr., *The Signifying Monkey* (New York: Oxford University Press, 1988; rpt. 2014), p. 35. Gates relies on Ayodele Ogundipea's recorded tale in *Esu Elegbara, the Yoruba God of Chance and Uncertainty: A Study in Yoruba Mythology*, 2 vols. (PhD diss., Indiana University, 1978), II, 135.

32 Milan Kundera, *The Unbearable Lightness of Being* (New York: Harper Perennial, 2009), 63.

it is also widely disseminated in the United States, with versions recorded in Michigan, Pennsylvania, Arkansas, Mississippi, and other states. Variants of the story, along with tales about a singing tortoise, can be found in this volume, and they document how the compact narrative has remained a vital, urgently present source of wisdom.

In a story that is nothing but "talk," a skull reveals the source of its misfortune: "talking got me here." The fellow who encounters it cannot keep his own mouth shut, and he soon joins the loquacious skull in the dust. By boasting about what he has witnessed, he is branded a liar (the skull refuses to speak to others) and executed. Talk is demonized as frivolous, boastful, and ultimately self-defeating in a medium that consists of nothing but that. In this master narrative of African and African American folklore, we have a densely packed golden nugget of wisdom that remains as relevant in larger communities it was in slave cabins by engaging with questions of speech and silence, deception and straight talk, expression and repression, survival and mortality.

Talking skulls, along with other paradoxical wonders and contradictory concepts, have kept stories alive by inviting us to puzzle out their terms. They tease us, leaving us with a breathless desire to engage in conversation to solve the vexing interpretive problems at their core. Another set of African stories, known as dilemma tales, operates at a more explicit level, posing moral questions and challenging listeners to come up with answers. In one such example, an abusive father boots his son out of the house. A wealthy man adopts the boy and treats him like a beloved son while he raises him. One day, the boy is at a crossroads, given a sword, and told he must slay either his biological father or his adoptive father. Which one should he choose? These tales may not constitute part of the African American folkloric canon, but their commitment to using story as a platform for more talk and more thought informs much of what appears in the New World, especially because so few stories close with the concept of "happily ever after."

Dilemma tales invite listeners to chime in, turning them into chatty collaborators, eager to participate in both the telling of the tale and its interpretation. Told in a communal setting, where values are contested and negotiated (with the understanding that all values are recognized as contingent, partial, and provisional), the stories validate a de-centering of authority and endorse a kind of collective bargaining, even if we are in the realm of the hypothetical and counterfactual.

Dilemma tales, delicate and difficult, resemble haiku forms in their use of narrative shorthand to sketch the main features of their plots. They withhold vital information about interiority—the mix of emotions inside the heads of characters. We know very little about what goes on in the minds of the trio of characters in the dilemma tale that ends with a boy, a sword, and two fathers. Because the characters are standard issue (biological father, adoptive parent, and boy) with virtually no psychological depth (we come to know them only through their actions), we are all the more motivated to fill in the gaps and create textured richness in the story at hand. Folklore gets us talking, thinking, and forming opinions. And, as importantly, it reminds us, in another set of tales, that at times it is also shrewd to hold your tongue.

By oversimplifying and reducing complex situations to their most basic terms and then amplifying them through melodramatic exaggeration, folklore intensifies the conversational stakes, giving us provocations that make it impossible to remain silent. Indeterminacy, the inability to settle on fixed meanings, contradiction, and paradox surface in African American vernacular traditions in ways that challenge us to turn into philosophers, perpetually thinking and rethinking what matters. The stories engage in Signifying, spelled with a capital *S*, to mark a distinction with the ordinary usage of the term. Drawing on humor, play, and self-reflexive irony to express itself, Signifying stands in direct contradiction to straight talk, suggesting that truth often comes through indirection, saying one thing and meaning both that and something else. Unlike literary irony, in which authors say one thing and mean another, Signifying creates its own supplementary meaning. It is the principal weapon in the arsenal of tricksters, those masters of artifice and duplicity who know exactly how to destabilize authority by undermining fixed meanings. They are the mediators who use the trick of mediation to keep us from settling into the status quo. And Signifying also became, in real life, the weapon of the disenfranchised.

LOOTING A CULTURAL HERITAGE: JOEL CHANDLER HARRIS'S STORIES AND WALT DISNEY'S *SONG OF THE SOUTH*

Who owns African American folklore? Does it belong to everyone? Is it the property of black people alone? To whom does black folklore matter? And who has the right to reclaim it, appropriate it, and adapt it? We have seen how, in some mysterious way, like the drumbeat that brought High John de Conquer to life, a canon of various African people's myths and lore survived the Middle Passage to live on as chapter and verse, then mutate and thrive in the New World. The slaves who survived the Middle Passage did not arrive on these shores alone. They brought their culture, their music and dance, their religions and their gods, and their discursive practices with them. The talking skull that once refused to speak to an Ashanti tribal chief in West Africa now fails to talk for Old Master. The trickster Hare has turned into Brer Rabbit. Singing tortoises have become talking turtles, and so on. Traditional tropes, motifs, and rhetorical devices were uprooted and repurposed, mixing and mingling with the new as they took hold on distant shores. Just who is entitled to make proprietary claims on these stories?

Enter Joel Chandler Harris, a nineteenth-century newspaperman who grew up in Georgia listening to stories in slave cabins, and Walt Disney, a twentieth-century entrepreneur and animator who had Harris's retellings read to him as a boy. These two towering figures in the landscape of African American lore were white men who capitalized with unparalleled success on what few others had claimed to own. Appropriating and monetizing traditional tales, both reoriented the stories for an audience of children, smoothing out their jagged surfaces and rough edges while sprucing up their frayed plot lines. Harris and Disney were less invested in preserving and restoring traditions that were steadily eroding than in turning them into a new form of cultural capital that dovetailed neatly with capitalist success.

Joel Chandler Harris's *Uncle Remus: His Songs and His Sayings* (1880) and the many volumes that followed have a monumental quality that makes them impossible to ignore. The first in the series, a landmark in its time, took an African American repertoire and transformed it into entertainment for white children—the "little boy" in the frame listens and learns from his kindly black "Uncle," a man so worn down by his labors that he is content to settle into the stoic role carved out for him by a Southern white journalist. Within months after the publication of the Uncle Remus stories, Joel Chandler Harris became what Mark Twain referred to as "the oracle of the nurseries."

Disney's *Song of the South* selected the best known of Harris's fables for the young and, in a burst of color, sound, and rhythm, lured children into theaters with a beat that was both entertaining and instructive. Suddenly the sinister gave way to the didactic, and the story of the tar baby became less a parable about treachery and entrapment than a cheerful lesson about the importance of staying at home and avoiding "a whole mess o' bran' new troubles."

Thanks to Harris and Disney, many African American tales circulate today, as noted, in the form of "culturally innocent" children's stories and entertainments. Have they, through a process of cultural entropy, turned into cartoon versions of themselves?

Has Brer Rabbit turned into a pale, spindly shadow of the mythical Spider and Hare? Have picture books like John Steptoe's *Mufara's Beautiful Daughters* and Robert Sans Souci's *The Talking Eggs* diluted the power of the stories and consigned them to the nursery?

Harris's 1880 collection, cramped and cautious rather than expansive, uses a "Negro dialect" that the novelist Charles Chesnutt described in the following way: "What we call by the name is the attempt to express, with such a degree of phonetic correctness as to suggest the sound, English pronounced as an ignorant old southern Negro would be supposed to speak it, and at the same time to preserve a sufficient approximation to the correct spelling to make it easy reading."[33] We find this principle, translated onto the big screen, at work in Disney's *Song of the South*, in which Uncle Remus alternately chuckles and furrows his brow as he tells stories to Johnny in language that will be accessible to all children and comforting to theatrical audiences.

At the other end of the spectrum are collectors who cared little for the niceties of decorum and aimed instead for authenticity. In Zora Neale Hurston's *Mules and Men*, African American folklore staged a comeback for adults in the middle of the Great Depression, two years before audiences began to whistle along to songs in Walt Disney's *Snow White and the Seven Dwarfs*. Hurston, a central figure of the Harlem Renaissance, moves us into adult storytelling circles, where she eagerly takes everything in, both as native to the land and anthropological witness. Rejecting the orthodoxies of fieldwork, she listens and relies on memory to record. "How do you learn most of your songs?" an interviewer once asked Hurston. She replied with words that hold true for her method of collecting tales as well: "I just get in the crowd with the people and they singin' and I listen as best I can, then I start a joinin' in with a phrase or two . . . I keep on till I learn all the song, the verses, then I sing them back to the people until they tell me I can sing them just like them. . . . Then I carry it in my memory."[34]

Hurston the anthropologist understood that storytellers use invented languages, idioms based on standard English but refashioned and encoded to become socially relevant. Invested in creating expressive art, they make the language their own, whether through borrowings from the languages of their kinship units, metaphors plucked from

33 *Letters of Charles W. Chesnutt, 1889–1905*, ed. Joseph McElrath Jr. and Robert C. Letiz III (Princeton, NJ: Princeton University Press, 1997), 105.

34 Zora Neale Hurston, "Halimuhfack," recorded by Herbert Halpert, June 18, 1939, Hurston Sound Recordings, American Folk Life Center, Library of Congress, Washington, DC.

their own life experiences, or words communally refashioned for the sake of a cultural heritage that would be their own.

It was, as we shall see, left to Zora Neale Hurston to reclaim African American folklore through an archaeological and anthropological feat that preserved and passed on the tradition by assimilating the vernacular into her own narrative voice. In *Mules and Men*, Zora Neale Hurston did not just collect, but also showed the collective in the heat of folkloric give-and-take in different social settings. We have not just stories but scenes of storytelling that motivate the narratives. Hurston revitalized folklore in her own fiction as well, using vernacular speech to narrate the consciousness of her characters and embedding storytelling rituals into her work in self-reflexive ways. Her major accomplishment was to reveal that folklore can operate in the modern era just as smoothly as it did in times past. The move she made was one that also enabled a succession of literary figures to probe the significance of a cultural heritage that continued to shape social identity in compellingly mysterious ways.

THE AFTERLIFE OF AFRICAN AMERICAN FOLKLORE

To speak of the afterlife of African American folklore implies subscribing to the view that Joel Chandler Harris and Walt Disney inflicted permanent damage upon living traditions. The figures that inhabit tales from times past have never really gone away or expired but, like Snow White, Cinderella, or Jack, they lead a fugitive existence in entertainments for adults, at times shadows of themselves to be sure, but "still there." More important, vernacular traditions served in powerful ways as the foundation for black literary culture, thus establishing a continuity, unprecedentedly robust, between oral traditions and print culture.[35]

African American writers have never shown much reverence for the divide separating oral traditions from print cultures, and there are good reasons why not. They famously—and paradoxically—have chosen to write by engaging with oral traditions. Language is an expressive instrument that captures a shared ethos about how to describe reality, and also how to conceptualize it. Take the term *beautiful-ugly*, which has been invoked as the sign of an African American love of paradox: "The idea that a thing is at the same time its opposite, and that these opposites, these contradictions

35 Gates, *The Signifying Monkey*, xxii.

make up the whole."[36] To move from the vernacular to a purely literary register (one voiced predominately by white writers) would be to lose a heterogeneous idiom rich with ancestral wisdom, cultural truths, and hard-won collective identity.

In cultures with long histories of the literary transmission of knowledge, oral traditions can undergo a process of entropy, shedding their intellectual weight and allure. Once the ability to decode the information in them weakens, the tales themselves begin to be seen as trivial, with no real narrative heft. As one anthropologist team pointed out about folktales: "We often dismiss them as silly or try to reinterpret them with psychobabble."[37] The same might be said about the vernacular in which these tales were told. Yet to give up that linguistic register is to shed a cultural heritage that, once probed, reveals itself to be broad and deep.

As we have already seen, many prominent Anglo-American writers insisted on distancing themselves from oral traditions, seeing in them a lack of sophistication and erudition. By contrast, we find—paradoxically—a disavowal of the vernacular in African American literature along with a self-conscious use of it, a liquidation of the divide between what we hear and what we read or write. Ralph Ellison, who was eager to be embraced by both African American readers and the literary establishment in the United States, once irately accused Zora Neale Hurston of "perpetuating the minstrel tradition" by relying on a spoken idiom as well as on oral storytelling traditions.

In a review of *Their Eyes Were Watching God*, Richard Wright decided to pull no punches and piled onto the critique, accusing Hurston of pandering to white audiences: "Miss Hurston *voluntarily* continues in her novel the tradition which was *forced* upon the Negro in the theatre, that is, the minstrel technique that makes the 'white folks' laugh. Her characters eat and laugh and cry and work and kill; they swing like a pendulum eternally in that safe and narrow orbit in which America likes to see the Negro live: between laughter and tears."[38] "Folklore fiction"—that's what the writer Alain Locke called it, and Hurston was repeatedly accused of creating characters who were caricatures, lacking any real psychological depth.

A rich mix of vernacular styles is, ironically, exactly what became the mark of high modernism in works by writers ranging from James Joyce and Samuel Beckett to John

36 Marshall, *Reena and Other Stories,* 9.

37 Elizabeth Wayland Barber and Paul T. Barber, *When They Severed Earth from Sky: How the Human Mind Shapes Myth* (Princeton, NJ: Princeton University Press, 2004), 2.

38 Richard Wright, "Between Laughter and Tears," *New Masses* (October 5, 1937), 22–23.

Dos Passos and Alfred Döblin. "How good you are in explosion! How farflung is your folkloire and how velktingeling your volupkabulary!" Joyce wrote in *Finnegans Wake* (1939).[39] And who would have thought that in their correspondence T. S. Eliot and Ezra Pound used Brer Rabbit and Old Possum as their monikers?[40] The language and grammar of folklore is attractive not only in its expansive artlessness but also in its restive challenge to the status quo. The Marxist sociologist and philosopher Herbert Marcuse once described how rebellion and insubordination, even when subdued in real life, burst out in the "spiteful and defiant humor" of colloquial speech—"in a vocabulary that calls things by their names: 'head-shrinker' and 'egghead,' 'boob tube,' 'think tank,' 'beat it' and 'dig it,' and 'gone, man, gone.'"[41] Folklore captures the candor of the vernacular, which not only speaks truth to power but can also operate in a vibrantly rich poetic register.

Sometimes folklore asserts its foundational importance with unexpected vehemence. In Ralph Ellison's *Invisible Man*, Brer Rabbit makes a spectacular appearance at a key moment in the narrative. After the Invisible Man's brush with death in a paint factory, he lies in the hospital recovering from an explosion. How is he treated? He is subjected to shock therapy, and, in the aftermath of those jolts, his doctor shows him a series of cards. "WHO WAS YOUR MOTHER?" one asks, in an effort to determine whether his autobiographical memory is intact. Another card bears a startling inscription: "BOY, WHO WAS BRER RABBIT?" In this case, it is Invisible Man's cultural memory that is put to the test, but in a way that demeans the narrator and disparages the folkloric character. Mystified, he asks, "Did they think I was a child?" "I felt like a clown," he declares. But ironically it is the crash course in cultural memory that galvanizes Invisible Man into action, making him determined to be, like his folkloric antecedent, "sly" and "alert."[42]

We could just as well ask, "Who is tar baby?" and Toni Morrison more or less does just that in her classic novel *Tar Baby* (1981). Morrison signifies on Ellison's work, rewriting it with a difference. For Morrison, the tar-baby story is more than "outlaw

39 James Joyce, *Finnegans Wake* (New York: Viking Press, 1967), 419.

40 Michael North, "Old Possum and Brer Rabbit: Pound and Eliot's Racial Masquerade," in *The Dialect of Modernism: Race, Language, and Twentieth-Century Literature* (New York: Oxford University Press, 1994), 77–99.

41 Herbert Marcuse, *One-Dimensional Man: Studies in the Ideology of Advanced Industrial Society*, 2nd ed. (Boston: Beacon Press, 1991).

42 Ralph Ellison, *Invisible Man*, 2nd ed. (New York: Random House, Vintage, 1995).

peasant outwits inventive master with wit and cunning." Folklorists may use that phrase as a classification category, but they flatten out the tale with a univocal message. For Morrison, the tar baby becomes a sticky mediator between master and servant (or plantation owner and slave), an object that aims to "foil and entrap" but also moves "beyond trickery to art." What Morrison does is to breathe new life into the original tale, to take the tropes of the story, remix them, mash them up, and produce something entirely new. She gives us a love story that is also a charged cultural encounter, one that turns allegorical, with its two protagonists—one glamorous and privileged, the other strong-willed and penniless—enacting a conflicted attitude toward African American cultural memory. One heatedly disavows it; the other seeks it out and embraces it.[43]

Jadine, Morrison's heroine, is in some way the tar baby of the novel's title, and it is she who has measured success by the standards of white culture, all the while internalizing its values. An orphan in social terms, she also becomes one in cultural terms. Son, by contrast, the man who challenges her success story, orients himself toward the past, reverting to home and a cultural heritage that refuses to accept conventional notions of accomplishment. It is he who must remind Jadine of the tar baby story and how the two of them are restaging the tale in mysteriously complicated new ways.

Like Sterling A. Brown and Zora Neale Hurston, both Ellison and Morrison deploy the tropes of folktales to shape their plots and to encode their narratives with cultural stories different from the ones found in mainstream literary production. Embracing alterity, they reclaim Brer Rabbit and tar baby as their own, and also start talking to each other in vertiginous moments of intertextual exchange. The point here is that Brer Rabbit and tar baby were never really on life support. They are simply reanimated in ways that are entirely natural and culturally sound, breathing the air of new narrative forms and putting on display the malleability that has enabled them to survive over decades.

Novelists like Ellison and Morrison are supremely well attuned to voices from the past and to ancestral lore, with Morrison in particular deeply committed to honoring ancestors and their stories. The folkloric elements that enter into their fiction are at times front and center, at times part of a subtle register that urges us to go back and heed voices from the past. In *The Grey Album*, the poet and essayist Kevin Young describes his ambition to engage in a project of reclamation, of the need to "rescue

---

43 All quotations are cited from Toni Morrison, *Tar Baby* (New York: Random House, Vintage, 2004), xi–xii.

aspects of black culture abandoned even by black folks, whether it is the blues or home cookin' or broader forms of not just survival but triumph."[44] The pages that follow will capture pictures from life in all its variegated forms, at times harsh and raw, at times elegant and uplifting, along with everything in between.

SOUNDS OF SILENCE: KEEPING QUIET AND TELLING LIES

"Cussing Master" is a story frequently included in collections of African American lore, and it reminds us of how talk can function as a release even in a culture that prohibits expressive outbursts, perhaps especially in that kind of culture. The American folklorist Benjamin Botkin described a version of the story in his "folk history" of slavery, and it features human characters with real names. When the field hand Joe Raines feels outrage about demands made by Master Ed, he goes "'way down in the bottoms where the corn grow high and got a black color." He then "looks east and west and north and south." Seeing no Master Ed, he "pitches into him and gives him the worst cussing a man ever give another man." That is the punch line to a story that begins with Joe's boasts about cursing his master and ends with his failure to mention to his friend Joe Murray, who has taken Joe's advice literally and cursed his master, exactly where he let loose those curses. "Go 'way off somewhere so he can't hear you," Joe cautions, too late to save his friend Joe from a beating.[45] A variant has Joe putting his hands up the dress of the master's wife—the dress, as it turns out, was hanging from a clothesline.

To reclaim by documenting and recording was, as we have seen, a challenge for those whose culture depended largely on oral transmission. Even in the aftermath of Emancipation, such projects were riddled with problems if not doomed, given the impossibility of preserving a vital and nuanced vernacular discourse in print. But more important, cursing, along with other forms of discourse, could be swallowed up in a culture of prohibition against expressive speech. Much was said in places where many might hear. But few could document and record, and some things were held back, especially for an audience of white listeners, by transcribers in acts of self-censorship that required vast reserves of restraint.

We know that slaves "talked back," even if only among themselves and that they

---

44 Kevin Young, *The Grey Album: On the Blackness of Blackness* (Minneapolis: Graywolf Press, 2012), 15.

45 B. A. Botkin, ed., *Lay My Burden Down: A Folk History of Slavery* (Chicago: University of Chicago Press, 1945), 8–9.

defied the imperatives of silence imposed on them by slaveholders. Somehow, like High John de Conquer, talk not only survived but could also remain supple and strong. Narratives were told not just for the purpose of survival but as one small piece of a project for developing a cultural style, a style that enabled enslaved people to fashion their identities and strategize among themselves. Still, the imperative of silence had its own toxic consequences, and manifests itself today in the many ruptures, gaps, and discontinuities that stand in the way of reconstructing a comprehensive history of black Americans before 1865, one that includes a full portrait of folkloric activities.

The talking skull of African American lore reminds us that speech can have fatal consequences and that, in many cases, silence and muteness were logical responses to conditions of enslavement and servitude. Elective muteness can be found in many biographical accounts, fictional and real-life, in a postbellum era. Consider Maya Angelou, an eloquent poet and prolific writer who penned no fewer than seven autobiographies and who was also an abuse survivor who became a selective mute, choosing silence to manage her fears. For Angelou, however, silence was both "a symptom of pain" and a "means of overcoming it" through a period of hibernation from which she emerged with an arsenal of weapons that included words and their poetry.

We have many other inflections of the strategy as well. Read the first pages of Richard Wright's *Black Boy*, and it becomes evident that cultures of silence invaded African American homes in sinister ways. When the eponymous boy's mother speaks in a home that provides little comfort and reassurance, it is to silence: "You stop that yelling" and "You better be quiet" are the phrases that dominate her mode of communication with her sons. And the narrator quickly perpetuates this manner of speaking when he turns to his brother to say, "You shut up."[46]

Yet there are fringe benefits to this repressive regime. The narrator responds to the obligatory muting by building a compensatory world of imaginative wonders. Recall the extraordinary scenes of coruscating beauty that register his responses to nature, among them: "There was the aching glory in masses of clouds burning gold and purple from an invisible sun."[47] He converses with nature, and its expansive beauty becomes the prelude for the boy's first encounters with print culture. It is telling that the young Richard receives his first dose of fairy tales, not from his kin, but from a book read

46 Richard Wright, *Black Boy (American Hunger): A Record of Childhood and Youth* (New York: Harper Perennial, 2004), 3–4.
47 Ibid., 8.

to him on the front porch (the storied site at which tales were exchanged). A school-teacher named Ella reads "Bluebeard and His Seven Wives" (a story about a wealthy serial murderer) to the boy, and the narrator is forever changed by it.

A fairy tale about secrets, forbidden chambers, and raised scimitars makes a direct hit: "I burned to learn to read novels and I tortured my mother into telling me the meaning of every strange word I saw, not because the word had any value, but because it was the gateway to a forbidden and enchanting land." On his own the narrator abandons the punitive world of "Or else!" and enters the searing beauty of "What if?" Tellingly, his grandmother calls the story the "devil's work" and snatches the book away, as if to protect the boy from the harm done by words and stories. What she fails to recognize is how the story opens up the full spectrum of human emotions, creating an alternate universe in which words build worlds that lay bare perils and possibilities.[48]

Wright describes for us how he received his first dose of true lies, the beautiful deceptions and counterfeit truths that do cultural work for us, creating belief systems and symbolic worlds that help us navigate our own. "Lying," Kevin Young tells us, is also known as "storying." It is "the artful dodge, faking it till you make it."[49] Recall Paul Laurence Dunbar's verse about wearing the mask "that grins and lies" as well as Ralph Ellison's description of himself as a "professional liar," and it becomes evident that fabricating fiction is the best antidote to repressive regimes that aim to shut down talk and impose silence. The complicated distortions of fiction are paradoxically a way of getting at straight-up doses of reality.

STRAIGHT TALK: DIALECT, VERNACULAR, AND METAPHORS

This project, then, aims to reclaim, affirm, and reanimate African American folktales. Some had their origins in African cultures and migrated with slaves into the Americas. There they were redesigned in the context of plantation slavery to keep hope alive by enabling talk, talk about everything under the sun: cruelty and compassion, fears and desires, hope and despair. Fueled by all the cultural contradictions that animate storytelling and keep it alive with inventive energy, they are revelatory and sometimes even redemptive, opening up a theater of passions and impulses. There we find rough

---

48 Ibid., 39.
49 Young, *The Grey Album*, 17.

sketches of daily life as well as profound snapshots of the daydreams and nightmares that haunted a people enslaved.

No single volume—or standing library for that matter or even an ocean of free-floating tales—can capture even a small percentage of those stories, but this one will offer a representative sample and attempt to reconstruct some of the cultural surround that shaped African American lives over the centuries and enabled black people to survive the claustrophobic social, cultural, and psychological effects of slavery. "It is important that we talk to our old people before they become ancestors, and get their stories," the novelist Jacqueline Woodson declared at the 2014 National Book Award ceremony.[50] And it is equally important to scour the archive with the hope of restoring stories told over the centuries to canonized cultural memory.

Folklore is shamelessly opportunistic, snatching what is close at hand yet also preserving what was told or made long ago and far away. Drawing on multiple sources, whatever it can get its hands on, the bottom-up, grassroots process of collective story-telling is syncretic, assembling its poetry, wisdom, and beliefs by drawing on multiple sources. African American folklore is no different, and many of the tales in this volume show a deep kinship with tales, not just from Africa but also from India, China, and Europe.

Mediating everyday experience, real and imagined, folklore once gave its listeners straight talk, uninhibited primary process in some cases, carefully constructed narratives in others. Deploying what has been called "folkspeech" and "slanguage," it offered uncensored accounts oriented toward adult audiences rather than toward the children we imagine today as auditors of stories about Brer Rabbit and Brer Fox.[51] These stories developed a style of their own, with sophisticated code words and stylized language that created a template for how to tell a story to an audience eager for knowledge about the past and present as well as for things made up and never written down. They were stylized speech acts, not mere slices of recorded speech indistinguishable from the language of the hearth and home or the language of the field. Works of art and artifice, they were self-reflexive constructs, meditations on language as much as purveyors of social content and cultural wisdom.

50 http://www.newyorker.com/books/page-turner/national-book-awards-ursula-le-guin, accessed January 12, 2015.

51 Gayl Jones, *Liberating Voices: Oral Tradition in African American Literature* (Cambridge, MA: Harvard University Press, 1991).

As is already abundantly clear, there is mischief in these stories. Comforting in some ways, they are also irreverent, told in a scrappy, raw, impertinent manner that may not always seem appropriate for the young. Readers will encounter the terms *Negro* and *nigger, black* and *colored, kaffir* and *Bushman, Afro-American* and *African American*, terms that defined social and cultural identity over various eras and in different regions, at times proudly, at times defiantly, and at times with a queasy sense of discomfort.

Presenting a history of African American folklore means facing down the demons of slavery and anti-black racism that once haunted and still trouble the cultural production of a community. It requires an unflinching look at the evidence preserved by earlier generations and a determination to reveal exactly what the historical record contains. For that reason, the stories have been recorded as they were told, without editing or omitting words that take us out of our comfort zones and that may sound offensive to us today. As Thomas Washington Talley, an African American collector of folklore, put it: "May I be permitted to state that I realize that there are certain terms found in the record such as 'Nigger,' 'Cracker' etc. which are objectionable to us of today. I regret this. But in order to truthfully reproduce the Traditions I had to use the terms, and I know that all will agree that the world ought [to] have the truth."[52] Occasionally a tale has been adapted for the sake of clarity—as is the case with some African tales recorded more than a hundred years ago. In those cases, the original, no-frills translators remained so faithful to the letter that they lost the spirit of the tales and produced stories that flattened out on the page.

One of the challenges, then, of a volume like this one has to do with language. Many of the tales are encoded in a creolized dialect not readily accessible to readers today. They are often told in English-based languages—Gullah, Bahamian Creole, or Jamaican Patois—that require translation. Creole tongues took on some of the characteristics of a secret language, using words in unusual ways, sometimes reversing their meanings, letting them slide into their opposites, or signifying in ways so unusual that the narratives possessed a certain strategic opacity. In addition, there are ways in which the stories overdo stereotypes or indulge in outrageous racial slurs in order to undo those very stereotypes and racist ideologies. In the interest of authenticity and

52 Thomas W. Talley, *The Negro Traditions*, ed. Charles K. Wolfe and Laura C. Jarmon (Knoxville: University of Tennessee Press, 1930), xxv.

historical fidelity, we have remained faithful to the letter and spirit of the stories as they were recorded.

Africanized speech, the vernacular, and eye dialects (in which nonstandard spellings like *de* or *wimmin* are used) were the preferred modes of recording traditional tales that were *told, spoken* rather than read from a page. At one end of the spectrum of that vernacular speech, we find blackface minstrelsy and plantation speech with its deliberate mangling of Standard English. It is the idiom that the great novelist and poet James Weldon Johnson, executive secretary of the NAACP from 1920 to 1931, famously described as moving in only two registers: humor and pathos.[53] And it is this idiom that both Wright and Ellison thought they were critiquing in their evaluation of Zora Neale Hurston's use of black speech in *Their Eyes Were Watching God.* To use it is to evoke stereotypes about the language of slavery (which it was not), with all the invidious cultural associations of ignorance and inferiority left intact. Joel Chandler Harris's tales will form Exhibit A for that particular inflection of black speech. At the other end, however, is a vibrant, self-conscious, creative, and robust idiom that preserves the immediacy of oral storytelling cultures and the lively improvisational style that animated them. In that vernacular—as poetic as it is powerful—we can begin to imagine an original, even if we have nothing more than a distant cousin.

Henry Louis Gates Jr. tells us that dialect can turn language against masters and against authority. A language related to English, but not necessarily subordinated to it, it could also be seen as a strategic idiom, one that created a barrier against outsiders and enabled the transmission of something akin to a secret code. Spoken at a different frequency (a "lower frequency" Ralph Ellison calls it), it could vary and improvise, distort and adorn, preserving cultural memory in a fluid medium not immediately accessible to those outside the group.[54]

Reading always requires collaboration, and its most powerful afterlife comes in the form of conversation. The stories in *Annotated African American Folktales* invite us to renew cultural memory and reimagine the past in ways untainted by sentimental wistfulness and counterfeit nostalgia. They may take us back in evocative ways, but less to stage and reenact than to memorialize the strength of ancestral voices and how they resonate in our culture today. Still, it is tempting to follow the advice of writers

---

53 Jones, *Liberating Voices*, 58.

54 See the discussion of Gates's phrase about dialect turning "metaphor against its master" in Eric Sundquist, *The Hammers of Creation: Folk Culture in Modern African-American Fiction* (Athens: University of Georgia Press, 2006), 60–62.

like John Edgar Wideman, who urges us to give in to the clarion call of imagination and to breathe the air of these stories as well as to investigate the cultural energy they transmit to us today:

> Imagine the situations in which these speech acts occur, the participants' multi-colored voices and faces, the eloquence of nonverbal special effects employed to elaborate and transmit the text. Recall a front stoop, juke joint, funeral, wedding, barbershop, kitchen: the music, noise, communal energy and release. Forget for a while our learned habit of privileging the written over the oral, the mainstream language's hegemony over its competitors when we think "literature." Listen as well as read. Dream. Participate the way you do when you allow a song to transport you, all kinds of songs from hip-hop rap to Bach to Monk, each bearing its different history of sounds and silences.[55]

If we cannot always imagine the sites of storytelling, we can still dream as we read or as we listen to voices from times past.

---

55 John Edgar Wideman, Foreword, *Every Tongue Got to Confess: Negro Folk-tales from the Gulf States*, ed. Carla Kaplan (New York: HarperCollins, 2001), xvii.

AFRICAN
TALES

This gold-covered staff, with Anansi the spider god at its center, was carried by officials within the courts of Akan chiefs in the region once known as the Gold Coast (present-day Ghana). Anansi, who brings wisdom, stories, and weaving to the Akan, is linked to language and becomes the chief linguist at the court. *Gift of the Richard J. Faletti Family, 1986 (1986.475a-c). Image copyright © The Metropolitan Museum of Art. Image source: Art Resource, NY.*

PART I

MAKING SENSE OF THE WORLD WITH ANANSI: STORIES, WISDOM, AND CONTRADICTION

*The wisdom of the spider is greater than
that of all the world put together.*

*Woe to him who would put his trust in Anansi—
a sly, selfish, and greedy fellow.*
—WEST AFRICAN PROVERBS

How fitting that the origins of storytelling begin with Anansi—a figure both human and animal, a creature who weaves webs of beautiful complexity and tells stories about the tangled webs we weave. Anansi stories not only capture the ephemeral—lived sensation and experience—but also provide practical magic and spiritual nourishment. Where there are roadblocks, they tell us about paths forward. Where there are dilemmas, they give us talking points. Where there is darkness, they shine beams of light. They also tell of cunning, deceit, appetite, and greed, encapsulating the story of how humans rose to the top of the food chain and conquered the planet. Anansi never lets us forget, through his antics, that beastliness and beauty coexist and that our capacity to undo all that is good in the world vies with our ability to ennoble and create.

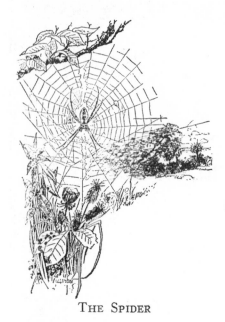

THE SPIDER

This image of a spider and its delicate web illustrates the tale "The Squirrel and the Spider" in *African Myths Together with Proverbs*, an anthology of African folklore collected by historian and teacher Carter G. Woodson.

Anansi tales, sometimes collectively referred to as "Anansem," can be traced back to the Ashanti people of Ghana in Western Africa. *Anansi*, the Akan word for spider, is sometimes written as Ananse. Both spider and man, Anansi is able to communicate with the Sky God, Nyankopon or Nyame. He is husband, father, and everyman, at times selfish and greedy, at times cunning and admirable. The story of how Anansi acquires stories from the Sky God (the tales were once called Nyankonsem or "words of the Sky God") is a foundational myth, revealing how greed, vanity, and stupidity fall victim to the sly Anansi as he acts out the stories and thereby makes them his own, becoming the patron saint of storytelling.

It is no accident that the guardian of stories is embodied in animal form as a spider. Like storytellers, he weaves a fine web of language that captures both the beauty and the horror of human existence. Filmy and fragile, delicate and graceful, Spider's web may be a thing of beauty, but it is also a deathtrap.

Anansi himself is a figure of ambivalence—generous and greedy, amiable and treacherous, courageous and cowardly, magnanimous and selfish. Like language itself, he is an expert in double-dealing, using the self-reflexive nature of the words we speak to show how duplicity can be a creative, life-sustaining strategy and a weapon deadly and destructive.

A bundle of contradictory traits, Anansi embodies paradoxes. As both animal (anansi) and man (Anansi), he bridges the divide between the two, revealing that one is no more

Robert S. Rattray, an anthropologist and British officer in Ghana, employed twelve unnamed West African artists to illustrate *Akan-Ashanti Folk-Tales*, published in 1930. For "How the Spider Got a Bald Head," Anansi is depicted as a hybrid creature with human features and the body of a spider.

" *He could no longer bear it. He threw away the hat and beans* "

ferocious or benevolent than the other. As a boundary crosser and a figure who stands at and guards the crossroads, he is a disruptive presence, constantly challenging the rules of the social order, yet also paradoxically reinforcing and consolidating their hold on us by revealing the scandals that result from testing them.

Ananse returning from the plantation

Ananse and the Cricket

In an illustration for "How Aketekyire, the Cricket, Got His Teeth Burned," Anansi's indifference to suffering becomes evident. For him, survival is everything.

Anansi not only bridges the divide between human and animal. He is also the mediator between the human and the divine, brokering deals with Nyame the Sky God, who has endless tolerance for his bad manners and impertinence. A master of punning, word play, and double entendre, Anansi is the master of direction through indirection, a signifying cultural presence capable of challenging the stability of the linguistic order as well as the social order. "Talking brought me here"—those spooky words, spoken by a skull as a warning against speaking and storytelling, could also be Anansi's motto. Talk is what brings us to life but it also can spell our doom and is itself doomed to vanish.

Closely linked to Anansi are the trickster gods Eshu of Yoruba origins and Legba of the Fon peoples in Benin. Eshu is a deity who revels in ambiguity and conflict: "Sowing dissension is my great delight," he declares in one of the foundational stories about his powers. A master musician, Eshu is often depicted with a flute or whistle, and he is sometimes portrayed as having two mouths, truly a figure who can talk out of both sides of his mouth and an expert in doubletalk. On Brazilian plantations Eshu became an agent of freedom for slaves, killing and poisoning their enemies, if only in the domain of imagination. Legba, also known as the "divine linguist," has the abil-

" While he was laughing, he fell into the fire "

Anansi is presented as a sober, focused figure rather than as an antic trickster in this illustration for *Akan-Ashanti Folk-Tales.*

Anansi is depicted alternately as a man and a spider in these illustrations by Cecilia Sinclair for *West-African Folk-Tales*, compiled by Sinclair and William Henry Barker and published in London in 1917.

ity to speak all languages and is described as an interpreter, facilitating understanding between gods and humans. In his passage to the New World, he was less radical insurgent than an exhausted old man struggling to stay alive. Haitians, who brought the old gods with them from Benin, created Carrefour and Ghede, masters of the crossroads and of language—trickster gods who embody all of Legba's lost vitality.

It seems astonishing to some that Anansi survived the Middle Passage, but the "complete annihilation" of Anansi and his stories would have been "far more remarkable than their preservation" (Gates 1988, 4). Anansi landed in the New World, in places like Jamaica, where he used his wits in conflicts with Tiger rather than the Ashanti Sky-God. In South Carolina Sea Island folklore, he turns up as Miss Nancy, and in Gullah as Aunt Nancy. In Haiti, he is called 'Ti Malice. In this new culture, Anansi was less invested in testing and preserving than in demolishing: "On the Jamaican plantations, Anansi had the potential to serve as the destroyer of an enforced and abhorrent social system rather than challenging the boundaries of a West African society" (E. Marshall 2010, 175). Or he might simply have modeled the art of surviving and winning small battles under the harshest of circumstances.

Walter Jekyll, a folklorist who collected Annancy stories in Jamaica, discovered that the tales—filled with sweetness and cynicism, compassion and outrage, cruelty and concern—produced "peals of laughter." He added: "At the recital of any special piece of knavery on Annancy's part, ordinary means of expression fail and [the listeners] fling themselves on the ground and wriggle in convulsions of merriment" (Jekyll, 1).

What is appealing about Annancy? Here are the words extracted from Jekyll's description of Annancy's attributes: laziness, gluttony, selfishness, treachery, and cruelty. Whatever Annancy can get away with, he does. He reaches for something other than the fulfillment of wishes found in fairy tales. Never satisfied, he incarnates a pleasure principle that gives us all the rough-and-tumble joys of a wild ride through the world.

In the tales that follow, we discover how Anansi stories came to be, in both African settings and in the United States. From there we move to a set of foundational narratives about wisdom, contradiction, and the importance of perspective. The section concludes with questions about justice in a parable about crime, excess, and punishment.

HOW THE SKY GOD'S STORIES CAME TO BE KNOWN AS SPIDER STORIES

"We do not really mean, we do not really mean, that what we are going to say is true."[1]

Kwaku Ananse,[2] or Spider, once went to Nyankopon,[3] the Sky God, in order to buy the Sky God's stories. The Sky God said, "Will you be able to buy them?"

Spider said, "I am sure I will be able to buy them."

The Sky God said, "Great and powerful towns like Kokofu, Bekwai, Asumengya[4] have come, but they were unable to purchase them, and you who are but a mere masterless man, will you really be able to buy them?"

Spider said, "What is the price of the stories?"[5]

The Sky God said, "They cannot be bought for anything except Onini the Python,[6] Osebo the Leopard, Mmoatia the Fairy, and Mmoboro the Hornets."

Spider said, "I will bring some of all these things, and what's more, I'll add my old mother, Nsia, the sixth child, to the lot."

The Sky God said, "Go and bring them then." Spider returned home and told his mother all about what had happened, saying, "I wish to buy the stories of the Sky God, and the Sky God says I must bring Onini the Python, Osebo the Leopard, Mmoatia the Fairy, and Mmoboro the Hornets. And I said I would add you to the lot and give all of you to the Sky God."

Spider consulted his wife Aso, saying, "What is to be done that we may capture Onini the Python?" Aso said to him, "Go cut off the branch of a palm tree and cut some

1 *"We do not really mean, we do not really mean, that what we are going to say is true":* A typical opening line, one that emphatically calls attention to the status of the story as "lie."

2 *Kwaku Ananse:* Ananse is usually referred to as simply Ananse, the Akan word for spider. Here, Kwaku means "father."

3 *Nyankopon:* Nyankopon is one aspect of the triune deity Nyame, with Nyame representing the cosmos, Nyankopon its life-giving force, and Odomankoma, the creative power.

4 *Kokofu, Bekwai, Asumengya:* villages in the Ashanti region of Ghana

5 *"What is the price of the stories?":* Stories are made from mere words, and it seems deeply ironic that we hear about the "buying" and "purchasing" of things that have no material substance. At the same time, nothing is more precious than the stories of a culture, and for that reason the "price" for them is made almost impossible to pay by making a set of challenging demands.

6 *Onini the Python:* The choice of creatures—a python, hornets, a leopard—seems somewhat arbitrary, though each could be seen as incarnating some kind of attribute, e.g., stealth, suffering, swiftness. The Fairy provides the opportunity to stage a version of the tar-baby story. The fact that Ananse throws in his mother for good measure seems astonishing but is treated in matter-of-fact fashion.

"How the Sky God's Stories Came to Be Known as Spider Stories," from R. S. Rattray. ed., *Akan-Ashanti Folk-Tales,*1930. By permission of Oxford University Press.

string-creeper as well, and bring them back." And Spider came back with them. Aso said, "Take them to the stream." So Ananse took them, and, as he was moving along, he said, "It's longer than he is. It's not as long as he is. You lie, it's longer than he is."

Spider said, "There he is, lying over there." Python, who had overheard the imaginary conversation, said, "What's this all about?"

Spider said, "It's my wife Aso, who is arguing with me and telling me that this palm branch is longer than you are, and I say she is a liar."

Onini the Python said, "Bring it over here, and come measure me." Spider took the palm branch and laid it out next to Python's body. He said, "Stretch yourself out."

Python stretched himself out, and Ananse took the rope-creeper and wound it around—the sound of the tying was nwenene! nwenene! nwenene!—until he reached the head. Ananse the Spider said, "You fool! I shall now take you to the Sky God and receive the Sky God's tales in exchange." Ananse took him off to Nyame, and the Sky God said: "My hand has touched it, but there remains what still remains."

Spider returned and told his wife what had happened, saying, "There remain the Hornets." His wife replied, "Look for a gourd, fill it with water, and go off with it."

Spider went along through the bush, when he saw a swarm of Hornets hanging in the air. He poured out some of the water and sprinkled it on the Hornets. Spider then poured the rest on himself and cut a leaf of the plantain[7] and covered his head with it.

7 *plantain:* A major food staple (related to the banana) in parts of Africa, Central America, and the Caribbean Islands.

Then he addressed the Hornets, saying, "Now that it's raining, you should go into the gourd so that the rain won't beat down on you. Can't you see that I've covered myself with a plantain leaf?"

The Hornets replied, "We thank you, Aku, we thank you, Aku." The Hornets all flew into the gourd and disappeared—fom! Father Spider covered its mouth, and he said, "Fools, I have caught you, and I am going to exchange you for the Sky God's stories." And he took the Hornets to the Sky God. The Sky God said, "My hand has touched them, but there remains what still remains."

Spider came back again and said to his wife, "There remains Osebo the Leopard." Aso said, "Go and dig a hole."

Ananse said, "That's enough, I understand." Then Spider went off to look for the Leopard's tracks, and once he found them he dug a very deep pit and covered it. Then he went home. Early the next day, when objects started to become visible, Spider said he would go out, and when he was moving along, lo and behold, a Leopard had landed in the pit. Ananse said, "Little father's child, little mother's child. I told you not to get drunk, and now, just as expected, you have become intoxicated. That's why you fell into the pit. If I were to agree to lift you out, the very next day, if you saw me or any of my children, you would run after them and catch them." The Leopard said, "Oh! I would never do such a thing." Ananse went and cut two sticks, put one here, and one there. He said, "Put one of your paws here, and the other one there." The Leopard placed his paws where he had been told. As he was about to climb up, Ananse lifted up his knife, and in a flash it descended on his head. Gao! was the sound it made. The Leopard landed in the pit and fom! was the sound of the falling. Ananse got a ladder to climb into the pit so that he could pull the Leopard up. He got the Leopard out and went on his way. He said, "Fool, I am taking you to exchange for the stories of the Sky God." He lifted up the Leopard to go and give to Nyame, the Sky God, who said, "My hands have touched it, what remains still remains."

Spider came back and carved an Akua's child. He tapped some sticky fluid from a tree and plastered the doll's body with it.[8] Then he pounded some yams and put them in the doll's hand. He pounded some more yams and placed the doll in a brass basin. He tied some string around the doll's waist and went off with it and put it at the foot of an odum tree, the place where Fairies come to play. And a Fairy came along. She said, "Akua, may I eat a little of this mash?"

8 *plastered the doll's body with it:* Here is the *ur*-form of the tar-baby story, with a doll covered with a sticky substance, an interlocutor insulted by lack of responsiveness, and an aggressive punch that backfires.

Ananse tugged at the string, and the doll nodded her head. The Fairy told one of her sisters, "She says I may eat some." The sister said, "Eat some then." The Fairy finished eating and thanked the doll. But when she thanked her, there was no answer. The Fairy said to her sister, "When I thanked her, there was no answer." The sister of the Fairy said, "Slap her crying-place." And she slapped it, pa! And her hand stuck there. She said to her sister, "My hand is stuck." The sister said, "Take your other hand and slap her crying-place again." And she took it and slapped her, pa!, and this one, too, stuck fast. The Fairy said to her sister, "Both my hands are now stuck." The sister said, "Push it with your stomach." She pushed it with her stomach, and her stomach got stuck too. Ananse came and tied her up, and he said, "Fool, I have got you. I shall take you to the Sky God and exchange you for his stories." And he took her back home with him.

Ananse told his mother, Ya Nsia, the sixth child, "Rise up, let us go, for I am taking you along with the Fairy to exchange you for the Sky God's stories." He lifted them up and went to the place where the Sky God lived. He said, "Sky God, here is a Fairy along with my old mother whom I told you about. She is here too."

Now the Sky God called his elders, the Kontire chiefs, the Oyoko, Ankobea, and

Kyidom. And he put the matter before them, saying, "Great kings have come and were not able to buy the Sky God's stories, but Kwaku Ananse the Spider has been able to pay the price. I received Mmoboro the Hornets from him. I received Mmoatia the Fairy[9] from him. I received Osebo the Leopard from him. I received Onini the Python from him, and, of his own free will, Ananse has added his mother to the lot. All of these things are here."

He said, "Sing his praise." *"Eee!"* they shouted. The Sky god said, "Kwaku Ananse, from today and forever, I take my Sky God's Stories and present them to you. Kose! Kose! Kose! My blessing, my blessing, my blessing. We shall no longer call them the stories of the Sky God and from now on they will be Spider stories."

This is my story,[10] which I have told. If it be sweet or if it be not sweet, take some elsewhere and let some come back to me.[11]

9 *Mmoatia the Fairy:* Mmoatia is also known as Mmotia and Kulparge and Chichiriga, all of whom are mischief-loving fairies and dwarfs.

10 *my story:* The narrator lays claim to the story rather than crediting Ananse with ownership.

11 *let some come back to me:* The story is given an attribute associated with edibles, and the narrator sends it into circulation but hopes to enjoy some returns as well.

SOURCE: Adapted from R. S. Rattray, *Akan-Ashanti Folk-Tales*, 55–58.

Spider is both animal and human, a trickster figure standing betwixt and between, embodying desire in all its excesses along with efforts to measure and contain. On the one hand, we have the expansive, generous wisdom of story and on the other a greedy trapping and acquisition of animals. In this tale, Ananse "buys" the Sky God's stories, and what is the price? Nothing less than all the characters in plots staged by Spider. The Sky God may now own the players, but Spider has created a story about the naming and ownership of stories, a metanarrative that serves a foundational role as charter narrative and that will also be preserved through cultural memory. Note that he would never have succeeded without the specific instructions issued by his wife Aso.

The British captain R. S. Rattray collected this story while in the service of what was then known as the Gold Coast Colony, and it has been adapted here from his version. Rattray established a Department of Anthropology in Kumasi, which gave him the opportunity to devote his full energies to studying Ashanti culture.

RABBIT WANTS MORE SENSE

Rabbit wen' an' asked de Lawd dat he have mo' sense, didn' have sense enough. An' de Lawd said dat he mus' go an' bring home a flock of parridge an' a rattlesnake an' a alligator-tush.[1] An' Rabbit wen'.

He met Rattlesnake firs'. "Good-mornin', Ber Rabbit!"

"Good-mornin', Ber Rattlesnake! Ber Rattlesnake, you grow a big man since I see you las'."

"Man," he say, "I ain't grow so big."

"Oh, yes, man! Le' me measure you by dis stick!" He bring his stick down. Den he tie Rattlesnake tail down to de stick, an' he tie Rattlesnake head down to de stick.

"Man, what you do to me?"

Say, "De oder day[2] dey measure me, short as you see my tail, dey tie um down." Den he kyarry Rattlesnake to de Lawd.

Den he come back. He meet Partridge. "Good-mornin', Partridge!"

"Good-mornin', Rabbit!"

"Partridge, yer fam'ly grow to a big crowd since I see you las'." He had a calabash full o' pease.

Ber Partridge, he said, "I betsh yer you an' all yer fam'ly couldn' jump in dis calabash." An' as dey busy eatin' de pease, Rabbit cover dem down. When dey done eat de pease, dey holler, "House dyark! Ra'[3] done gwine wid dem! House dyark! Ra' done gwine wid dem!"

Ber Rabbit kyarry dem to de Lawd!

Den he come back. Dey goin' now to get Ber Alligator tush. Gone to de riberside wid all de fiddleman to play. Sing,—

> "News come from Santee,
> Pease ripe already."

When dey ax him how he knows pease ripe at Santee, he say 'cause he meet a mess o' pease. Den Alligator holler to him, "Any harm for come sho'?"[4]

"No, suh! No harm for come sho'." Den dey dance. An' after dey come sho', move

1 *alligator-tush:* alligator tooth

2 *De oder day:* the other day

3 *Ra':* refers to Ber Rabbit

4 *Any harm for come sho'?:* Any risk in coming ashore?

his seat higher an' higher from de water, way up f'om de water. An' after dat he kill Alligator, an' pull out he tush an' kyarry *dat* to the Lawd. An' de Lawd drive him away, tell him he got too much sense, wouldn' give him no mo'. An' dat was de en' of him.

SOURCE: Elsie Clews Parsons, *Folk-Lore of the Sea Islands*, 16–17.

In this tale about Rabbit and his desire for "more sense," there is a clear mirroring of the story about Ananse and his wish to make the stories of the world his own, but with the perverse twist that Rabbit is not rewarded, for he is already endowed with sense enough. It quickly becomes evident that African folklore settled comfortably into the New World, transforming itself as all folklore does when it makes itself at home in a new region

HOW WISDOM CAME INTO THE WORLD

There once lived a man named Father Anansi. He possessed all the wisdom in the world. People came to him daily for advice and help.

One day the men of the country made the mistake of offending Father Anansi, who immediately decided to punish them. After much thought, he believed that the most severe punishment he could inflict would be to hide all his wisdom from them. He set to work at once to gather together everything he had already given. Once he succeeded, as he thought, in collecting it, he placed all of it in a great pot[1] and sealed it carefully. He was determined to put it in a spot where no human being could reach it.

Now Father Anansi had a son named Kweku Tsin. This boy began to suspect his father of some secret plan, and he made up his mind to watch him carefully. Next day he saw his father quietly slip out of the house, with his precious pot hung around his neck. Kweku Tsin followed. Father Anansi went through the forest until he left the village far behind. Then, selecting the tallest and most remote tree,[2] he began climbing it. The heavy pot, hanging out in front of him,

1 *placed all of it in a great pot:* Anansi's dreadful instincts are revealed in this tale. He takes offense and punishes, turning wisdom into something material that, like the evils in the story of Pandora, can be stored in a jar. In this version of a foundational story, Anansi is shown to be a punitive hoarder, undone by his own greed. In some variants, Anansi decides to hoard wisdom out of boredom.

2 *the tallest and most remote tree:* Anansi seeks out a spot that is inaccessible, and in a location that

made his ascent almost impossible. Again and again he tried to reach the top of the tree, where he planned to hang the pot. There, he thought, wisdom would indeed be beyond the reach of everyone but himself. But he was unable to carry out his wish. Each time he tried, the pot was in his way.

For some time Kweku Tsin watched his father's hopeless attempts to climb the tree. At last, unable to contain himself any longer, he called out, "Father, why don't you hang the pot across your back? Then you can easily climb the tree."

Father Anansi turned and said, "I thought I had all the world's wisdom in this pot. But now I see that you possess more than I do.[3] All my wisdom was inadequate to show me what to do, yet you have been able to tell me." He was so angry that he threw the pot down to the ground. It struck a great rock and broke into pieces. The wisdom contained in it escaped and spread throughout the world.

SOURCE: Adapted from William Henry Barker and Cecilia Sinclair, *West African Folk-Tales*, 33–34.

connects Earth with the heavens. This "tree of knowledge," unsuccessfully climbed, has interesting connections to other myths about knowledge and transgression and to the biblical narrative about Adam and Eve.

3 *you possess more than I do:* In many folktales, it is the child who speaks truth and wisdom to power. In some variants of the tale, Anansi becomes furious that his son is teaching him a lesson, no matter how valid it may be.

Anansi incarnates the spirit of unruliness, and this tale, told at his expense, reveals his less appealing side. Abstract and constructed from mere words, wisdom is not, as the story asserts, a material substance that can be put into a pot, where it is hoarded and contained. But while wisdom may lack substance, it has a deep pragmatic value, as Anansi discovers while attempting to scale a tree with a pot of wisdom on his belly. Ironically, wisdom eludes the grasp of the one who claims to "possess" it. It is Anansi's son, innocent yet also knowing, whose wisdom is superior to his father's and who enables Anansi to release wisdom into the world.

THE TWO FRIENDS

Everyone knows the story of the two friends who were thwarted in their friendship by Esu. They took vows of eternal friendship to one another, but neither took Esu into consideration. Esu took note of their actions and decided to do something about them.

When the time was ripe, Esu decided to put their friendship to his own little test. He made a cloth cap. The right side was black; the left side was white.

The two friends were out in the fields, tilling their land. One was hoeing on the right side; the other was clearing the bushes to the left. Esu came by on a horse, riding between the two men. The one on the right saw the black side of his hat. The friend on the left noticed the sheer whiteness of Esu's cap.

The two friends took a break for lunch under the cool shade of the trees. Said one friend, "Did you see the man with a white cap who greeted us as we were working? He was very pleasant, wasn't he?"

"Yes, he was charming, but it was a man in a black cap that I recall, not a white one."

"It was a white cap. The man was riding a magnificently caparisoned horse."

"Then it must be the same man. I tell you, his cap was dark—black."

"You must be fatigued or blinded by the hot rays of the sun to take a white cap for a black one."

"I tell you it was a black cap and I am not mistaken. I remember him distinctly."

The two friends fell to fighting. The neighbors came running but the fight was so intense that the neighbors could not stop it. In the midst of this uproar, Esu returned, looking very calm and pretending not to know what was going on.

"What is the cause of all the hullabaloo?" he demanded sternly.

"Two close friends are fighting," was the answer. "They seem intent on killing each other and neither would stop or tell us the reason for the fight. Please do something before they destroy each other."

Esu promptly stopped the fight. "Why do you two lifelong friends make a public spectacle of yourselves in this manner?"

"A man rode through the farm, greeting us as he went by," said the first friend. "He was wearing a black cap, but my friend tells me it was a white cap and that I must have been tired or blind or both."

The second friend insisted that the man had been wearing a white cap. One of them must be mistaken, but it was not he.

"Both of you are right," said Esu.

"How can that be?"

"I am the man who paid the visit over which you now quarrel, and here is the cap that caused the dissension." Esu put his hand in his pocket and brought out the two-colored cap saying, "As you can see, one side is white and the other is black. You each saw one side, and, therefore, are right about what you saw. Are you not the two friends who made vows of friendship? When you vowed to be friends always, to be faithful and true to each other, did you reckon with Esu? Do you know that he who does not put Esu first in all his doings has himself to blame if things misfire?"

And so it is said:

"Esu, do not undo me,

Do not falsify the words of my mouth,

Do not misguide the movements of my feet.

You who translates yesterday's words

Into novel utterances,

Do not undo me,

I bear you sacrifices."

SOURCE: Ayodele Ogundipe, *Esu Elegbara, the Yoruba God of Chance and Uncertainty: A Study in Yoruba Mythology*, II, 133–35.

Esu is often depicted as having two mouths, and he speaks with what has been described as a double-voiced discourse, self-reflexive and also bridging or mediating contradictions. The story of the two friends is probably the best known of all Esu narratives. It survived the Middle Passage and versions of it continued to proliferate in many locations, especially Brazil and Cuba. Ayodele Ogundipe, who recorded this version, tells us that "the conceptualization of Esu's presence as a dynamic principle and his representation as the principle of chance or uncertainty has endured in both the Old and New Worlds" (2012, 207). What Esu reveals is the impossibility of settling on fixed meanings or of creating closure. Meaning is always determined by perspective and the vantage point from which something is seen, as the story of Esu's cloth cap tells us. The fact that the cap is both black and white suggests an embracing of contradictions, and Esu reveals the enrichment that comes with the swerve toward both/and rather than either/or.

HOW IT CAME ABOUT THAT CHILDREN WERE (FIRST) WHIPPED

They say that once upon a time a great famine came over the land and that Father Ananse, the Spider, and his wife Aso, and their children, Ntikuma, Nyiwankonfwea (Thin-shanks), Afudotwedotwe (Belly-like-to-burst), and Tikonokono (Big-big-head), built a little settlement and lived in it. Every day Spider used to bring food home, wild yams, and they boiled and ate them. Now one day, Father Ananse went to the bush. He saw a beautiful dish out there.

"This dish is beautiful!" he said.

The dish replied, "My name is not 'beautiful.'"

Spider said, "What are you called?"

It replied, "I am called 'Fill-up-some-and-eat.'"

Spider said, "Fill up some that I may see."

The dish filled up with palm-oil soup, and Ananse ate it all up. When he was finished, he asked the dish, "What is your taboo?"

The dish replied, "I hate a gun wad[1] and a little gourd cup."

1 *gun wad:* a device used to keep ammunition in place in a gun-barrel

Spider took the dish home, and he put it up on the ceiling. Then Ananse went off to the bush and brought food.

Aso, when she had finished cooking, called Ananse, and he said, "Oh, you need food more than I do. As for me, I am an old man. Why should I have any food when you and the children need it? If you are no longer hungry, then my ears will calm down, for I will not longer hear your complaints."

When they had finished eating, Spider went up to the ceiling where the dish was. He said, "This dish is beautiful!"

The dish replied, "My name is not 'beautiful.'"

Spider said, "What is your name?"

The dish replied, "I am called 'Fill-up-some-and-eat.'"

Spider said, "Fill up some that I may see."

"How It Came About That Children Were (First) Whipped," from R. S. Rattray, ed., *Akan-Ashanti Folk-Tales*, 1930. By permission of Oxford University Press.

And the dish filled up a bowl of ground-nut soup, and Ananse ate. The same thing happened every day.

Now Ntikuma noticed that his father was not growing thin, despite the fact that Ananse was not eating with them. Ntikuma kept an eye on his father and saw that the father had gotten his hands on something. When Ananse went off to the bush, Ntikuma climbed up to the ceiling and discovered the dish. He called his mother and brothers, and they went up there with him.

Ntikuma said, "This dish is beautiful."

The dish replied, "My name is not 'beautiful.'"

Ntikuma said, "What is your name?"

The dish replied, "I am called 'Fill-up-some-and-eat.'"

Ntikuma said, "Fill up a little that I may see."

And the dish filled up to the brim with palm-oil soup. Ntikuma and his mother and brothers ate everything that was in the dish.

And now Ntikuma asked the dish, "What is taboo to you?"

The dish said, "I hate a gun wad and a small gourd cup."

Ntikuma said to Afudotwedotwe, "Go and bring them to me."

And Afudotwedotwe brought them, and he took the gun wad and touched the dish with it. Then he took the little gourd cup and touched the dish with it. Then they all climbed down from the ceiling.

Father Spider, in the meantime, had returned home from the bush with the wild yams. Aso finished cooking them. They called Ananse, and he replied, "You must not have heard what I said. I told you that from this day forward, when I come back home with food, you are the ones who will eat it, for you are the hungry ones." Aso and her children ate. Father Spider washed up. He climbed up to the ceiling and said, "This dish is beautiful." Complete silence! Father Spider said, "It must be because the cloth I am wearing is not beautiful. I shall go and bring the one from the Oyoko[2] tribe and put it on." And he came down from the ceiling and fetched the tartan cloth from the Oyoko tribe and put it on. He put on his sandals. He climbed up there again. He said, "This dish is beautiful." Complete silence! He looked around the room and saw that a gun wad and a little gourd cup were in it.

2 *Oyoko*: a small town in the Ashanti region of Ghana, which gives its name to the resident clan

Ananse said, "It's not one thing, it's not things. There is no doubt that this is the work of Ntikuma."

Ananse smashed the dish and climbed back down. He took off the Oyoko cloth, put it down, and went off to the bush. On the way, he saw a very beautiful thing, a whip called Mpere. He said, "Oh, wonderful! This thing is more beautiful than the last. This whip is beautiful."

The whip said, "I am not called 'beautiful.'"

Spider said, "Then what are you called?"

The whip said, "I am called 'Abiridiabrada' (Swish-and-raise-welts)."

Spider said, "Swish a little for me to see." And the whip fell upon him, "Swish, swish, swish."

Father Spider cried, "Pui! Pui!"

A certain bird perched nearby said to Ananse, "Say Adwobere."[3]

3 *Adwobere:* cool and easy now   And Ananse said, "Adwobere." And the whip stopped beating him.

Ananse brought the whip home. He climbed up to the ceiling and put it there. Aso finishing cooking the food. She said, "Ananse, come and eat."

Ananse replied, "Since you are still here on earth, perhaps you have not heard what I said. I shall not eat."

Ananse climbed up to the ceiling and sat down in a corner quietly. Then he came back down again, and finally he went away and hid off in a corner.

Ntikuma climbed up to the ceiling. He said, "Oh, that father of mine has brought back something else." Ntikuma said, "Mother, Nyiwankonfwea, Afudotwedotwe, come here. What Father has brought this time is even better than what he brought last time." Then all of them climbed up on the ceiling.

Ntikuma said, "This thing is beautiful."

The thing replied, "I am not called 'beautiful.'"

Ntikuma said, "What is your name?"

It replied, "I am called 'Swish-and-raise welts.'"

Ntikuma said, "Swish a little for me to see."

The whip descended upon him and flogged them all severely.

Ananse appeared and shouted, "Lay it on, lay it on, especially on Ntikuma, lay it on him."

Now when Ananse had watched and seen that they were properly flogged, he said, "Adwobere." He took the whip and cut it up into small pieces and scattered them about. That is what made the whip come into the tribe. So it comes about that when you tell your children something, and they will not listen, you whip them.

This is my story, which I have told. If it be sweet or if it be not sweet, take some elsewhere, and let some come back to me.

SOURCE: Adapted from R. S. Rattray, *Akan-Ashanti Folk-Tales*, 63–67.

Whipping children may seem a cruel and unusual punishment, but it has been an astonishingly common practice, one dictated by biblical wisdom and other sources of authority. This version of the tale is transcribed from an oral performance by a collector who prided himself on fidelity to the words of the teller. In a version included by Peggy Appiah in a collection of Ananse tales, it is Ananse who is beaten. His son Ntikuma speaks the words that stop the whip. Ananse then begs his family to forgive him for his greediness. "Each day I have eaten the best food before you came home," he confesses. "Forgive me. You see how I have been punished. Learn from me, my children. Take just what you need, share with others. The pot that helped us has been destroyed. You see what greed has done to your father." As if the point needed driving home, a moral is appended: "That is how Kwaku Ananse was punished for his greed. May you all learn from this lesson, for greed always brings its own punishment" (Appiah 1969, 69).

HOW CONTRADICTION CAME TO THE ASHANTI

Once there was a man called Hate-to-Be-Contradicted, and, because of that, he built a small dwelling all by himself and lived in it alone. A creature called the duiker[1] paid him a visit, and they walked along together for a while and then sat down at the foot of a palm tree. Some of the palm nuts fell down. The duiker said, "Father Hate-to-Be-Contradicted, your palm nuts are ripe."

Hate-to-Be-Contradicted said, "That is the nature of the palm nut. When they ripen, three bunches are ready at once. I cut them down after they have ripened, and

1 *duiker:* Derived from the Dutch word for "diver," the term refers to a small antelope that can leap quickly into the bush.

"How Contradiction Came to the Ashanti," from R. S. Rattray, ed., *Akan-Ashanti Folk-Tales*, 1930. By permission of Oxford University Press.

then I boil them to extract the oil. They make three water pots full of oil. Then I take the oil to Akase to buy an Akase old woman. The Akase old woman comes and gives birth to my grandmother who bears my mother, who in turn gives birth to me. When Mother bears me, I am already standing there."

The duiker said, "As for all that, you are lying."

Hate-to-Be-Contradicted took a stick, hit the duiker on the head, and killed him.

Then along came the little abedee.[2] Hate-to-Be-Contradicted walked for a while with him, and the two sat down under a palm tree, and the same thing happened. And that's how it went with all the animals. Finally, Kawku Ananse, the Spider, went and fetched his cloth and his bag, slung the bag over his shoulders, and went off to visit Hate-to-Be Contradicted's kraal.[3]

2 *abedee:* Ashanti word for antelope

3 *kraal:* an enclosure

4 *Y'aku:* a greeting

He greeted him, "Good morning, Father."

Hate-to-Be-Contradicted replied, "*Y'aku,*[4] and where are you going?"

He replied, "I'm coming to visit you."

And he took his stool and placed it under the palm tree.

Hate-to-Be-Contradicted gave orders, "Cook food for Spider to eat."

While the food was cooking, Ananse and Hate-to-Be-Contradicted sat under the palm tree. Some of the palm nuts fell down, and Ananse took them and put them in his bag. He kept doing that until his bag was full. The food arrived, and Ananse ate. When he had finished eating, more of the ripe palm nuts fell down, and Ananse said, "Father Hate-to-Be-Contradicted, your palm nuts are ripe."

Hate-to-Be-Contradicted said, "It is their nature to ripen like that. When they ripen, three bunches are ready at once. I cut them down after they have ripened, and then I boil them to extract the oil. They make three water pots full of oil. Then I take the oil to Akase to buy an Akase old woman. The Akase old woman comes and gives birth to my grandmother who bears my mother, who in turn gives birth to me. When Mother bears me, I am already standing there."

Spider said, "You are not lying. What you say is true. As for me, I have some okras growing on my farm. When they are ripe, I join seventy-seven long hooked poles in order to reach them to pull them down, but even then I cannot reach them. So I lie on my back and use my penis to pluck them."

Hate-to-Be-Contradicted said, "Oh, I understand. Tomorrow I will come and take a look."

Spider said, "Sure!"

While Spider was on his way home, he chewed the palm nuts that he had gathered and spat them out on the path. The next morning, when you could see things again, Hate-to-Be-Contradicted set out for Spider's village. When Spider had returned home the day before, he said to his children, "A man will come here, and he hates to be contradicted. When he arrives and inquires after me, you must tell him that yesterday I told you that I was going off somewhere. My penis broke in seven places, and I had to take it to the blacksmith for repairs. Since the blacksmith could not finish in time yesterday, I went back to have the work finished."

Not much later, Hate-to-Be-Contradicted came along. He said, "Where is your father?"

The children replied, "Alas, Father went somewhere yesterday, since his penis was broken in seven different places. He took it to a blacksmith, but the man could not finish in time, and Father has left to have it finished. You, Father, didn't you see the blood on the path?"

Hate-to-Be-Contradicted said, "Yes, I saw it." Then he asked, "And where is your mother?"

So they beat Hate-to-be-contradicted so that he died

In this illustration from Robert S. Rattray's compilation *Akan-Ashanti Folk-Tales*, the beating to death of Hate-to-Be-Contradicted undoes in some ways the message of the story.

Spider's child replied, "Mother, too—yesterday she went down to the stream, and her water pot would have fallen and broken if she had not kept it from doing so by catching it at the last moment. But she didn't quite succeed in saving it from falling and returned today to do so." Hate-to-Be-Contradicted did not say a word.

Ananse returned. He said, "Cook some food for Hate-to-Be-Contradicted." While the children were cooking the food, they used only one single little perch but a huge quantity of peppers. They made the stew very hot. When they finished cooking, they set it down before Hate-to-Be-Contradicted. Hate-to-Be-Contradicted ate it. The peppers pained him so much that he wanted to die. He said to one of Ananse's sons, "Ntikuma,[5] bring me some water."

5 *Ntikuma:* a species of spider

Ntikuma said, "There are three different kinds of water in our pot. The water at the top belongs to Father, the part in the middle belongs to my mother's co-wife, and the water at the very bottom of the pot belongs to my mother. I can only draw for you what belongs to my mother, and if I'm not careful while drawing it, I might start a tribal dispute."

Hate-to-Be-Contradicted said, "You little brat! You are lying."

Straightaway Ananse said, "Beat him until he is dead."

Hate-to-Be-Contradicted said, "Why should they beat me to death?"

Spider said, "You say you hate to be contradicted, and yet you have contradicted someone. That is why I am telling them to beat you to death."

So they beat Hate-to-Be-Contradicted to death. Then Ananse cut up his flesh in little pieces and scattered them everywhere.[6]

That is why you can find many people in the tribe today who hate to be contradicted.

SOURCE: Adapted from R. S. Rattray, *Akan-Ashanti Folk-Tales*, 107–9.

6 *Then Ananse cut up his flesh in little pieces:* Many creation myths begin with the dismemberment of some kind of primordial being, and in this case a figure who is deeply opposed to division and self-division leaves bits and pieces of himself in a world that thrives on contradiction and resistance to it.

Hate-to-Be-Contradicted encounters Ananse, the Trickster who loves to be contradicted. As half-man and half-spider, Ananse already incarnates the contradiction of nature and culture. Rejecting the stability and sterility of univocal truths, Ananse embraces division, discord, and the kind of disorder that will lead to higher truths. By contrast, Hate-to-Be-Contradicted lives in near solitary confinement, unable to tolerate difference and alterity. According to Lee Pelton, Ananse possesses a "double doubleness," becoming Love-to-Be-Contradicted, contradicting the contradictor, and negating negation in a way that preserves a permanent state of tension. What Ananse does is to respond to Hate-to-Be-Contradicted in a way that enables him to triumph, not negating his position and confronting him directly, as did the duiker and the abedee, but responding to him "recursively and self-referentially, . . . taking it to such extremes as to nudging it toward destroying itself" (Marks-Tarlow 2008, 173).

PART II

FIGURING IT OUT: FACING COMPLICATIONS WITH DILEMMA TALES

Folktales generate talk. The stories gathered here show how they stimulate conversation and debate, evoking the great "What ifs?" Even when a character resolves the formulated dilemma, or when a narrator steps in to referee or issue a judgment, the audience may still challenge the wisdom of a decision and propose alternative solutions. Some folklorists see dilemma tales as modeling discussion for how to adjudicate disagreements either within the family or in a broader social context. Although these kinds of stories are often associated with African folklore, they can be found in other cultures too, as *adivinanzas* in Spain, as *Fragen* in Germany, and as *choix difficile* or *cas de conscience* in France. In English, they are called "unanswerable riddle stories," "conundrum" and "problem tales," and "folk problems."

The most common dilemma tale in Africa is listed in the standard classification system used by folklorists as "The Rarest Thing in the World" (ATU 653A; Uther I: 359). It is described as follows:

A princess is offered to the one bringing her the rarest thing in the world. Three brothers set out and acquire magic objects: a telescope that shows all that is happening in the world, a carpet (or the like) that transports one at will, and an apple (or an object) that heals or resuscitates. With the telescope it is learned that the princess is dying or dead. With the carpet they go to her immediately and with the apple they cure or restore her to life. They dispute who is to marry her.

There is magic in this tale but it is hardly practical. And whether wisdom can be extracted from the dispute among the brothers is questionable. But what is certain is that the tale makes us reflect on the value of different human aspirations—omniscience, mobility, and the power to heal.

Dilemma tales, as William Bascom has pointed out, fall into two categories: stories that involve a contest and challenge listeners to choose the most skillful of the competitors and tales that require moral or ethical judgments. "The Rarest Thing in the World" gives us an example of the first type, and it invites us also to choose wisely and make a "just" decision. In the second type, an audience is asked to decide questions such as the following: "Who should inherit, the eldest or the youngest son?" "Are sons more desirable than daughters?" "Who is to be saved, a kind adoptive father or a cruel biological father?" These stories draw us into the dark shadows of decision-making, revealing that no decision is "right" or "just" and that there is always a loss of some kind.

"The Cow-Tail Switch," a West African tale collected by Harold Courlander, gives us a wonderful hybrid version. It tells the tale of a warrior who goes out on the hunt and perishes. Three of his sons possess magic powers, but it is not until they are urged on to find their father's remains by a fourth, younger boy that they discover the bones of the missing, forgotten man. One assembles the bones into a skeleton; a second puts flesh on the bones; and a third breathes life into the bones and flesh. The reanimated father returns to the village and decides to give the gift of a cow-tail switch, the emblem of his tribal authority, to the youngest of the four sons, for it was he who honored the memory of his father by refusing to forget that he was gone. These are the tales relevant to developing social and cultural values, as judgments and decisions are weighed and evaluated. Riddles and dilemmas are meant to promote entertaining conversation as much as to stimulate competition. "The enjoyment of a riddle derives from the sharing of it by members of a group rather than from the challenge to the imagination it presents" (Finnegan 426; Messenger 226). The tales that follow include the two different types of dilemma tales, the one raising questions about merit and the other enacting moral inquiries. They take up issues both local and monumental, up close and personal as well as abstract and universal.

WHO SHOULD MARRY THE GIRL?

There was once a beautiful girl who lived with her parents in a certain village. All the young men wanted to marry her. Amongst the most ardent of her admirers were three men: a musician, a hunter, and a swimmer.

One day when the girl went down to the river to wash her clothes, the three men hid nearby and watched her. As she started to do her washing, a crocodile came from the river to stretch himself out in the sun, and he saw the girl doing her washing. He made straight for her, but the poor girl did not notice him, and went on with her work.

The crocodile reached her, opened his mouth and pulled her inside the water.

The musician was the first to see what happened, and he began to play a tune on his harp.

The evil crocodile was so impressed by the music that he sat in amazement with his mouth wide open as he listened. Then the hunter shot the crocodile with an arrow just as he was about to swallow the beautiful girl. The poor girl nearly drowned. At once the swimmer jumped into the river and pulled her out of the water.

The three men were very proud that they had taken part in rescuing her. But the question remained: Who should marry the girl?

What is your judgment?

SOURCE: Gene Baharav, *African Folktales Told in Israel*, III, 22–23.

This story was told by Zenebach Truneh, a student from Ethiopia studying at the International Training Center for Community Services in Israel. A visit to the Israel Folktale Archives inspired the instructor of a course offered there to ask his students to create their own collection of indigenous lore. As Dov Noy well-meaningly put it in his introduction to the tales assembled while the African students were in Israel: "These tales would raise the self-esteem of the story-teller and story-loving people and their trust in their own cultural heritage, used in class with foreign parallels, the stories would prove to young and adult pupils, that man is similar all over the world and that racial and religious differences are artificial and external."

TRACKWELL, DIVEWELL, BREAVEWELL

De man had one daughter. An' dere was t'ree men comin' to see her. Dey was Track-well, Divewell, an' Breavewell. Dey said de man dat had de best right could marry to de daughter. De daughter went an' got lost. After de woman leave de house, she went down to de river. Trackwell track her f'om de house to de aidge of de water. Dat was all Trackwell could do. She went into de river. Divewell went, an' dive until he fin' her. An' after Divewell foun' her, he brought her up on de sho'. An' Breavewell breae his breat' back into her. An' it come a-disputin'. The fader said to de t'ree mens, "Which one of you is entitled to the daughter?" Trackwell said, "I am entitled to the woman, because she was los', an' I track her out." Divewell says, "Your track didn' done no good, because you couldn' fin' her. You track her to the aidge of the water. I had to dive out in dat ocean, take chance of my life, an' hunt until I foun' her." Breavewell said, "All for that what you folk have done, the woman is mine, because she was dead, an' I brough life into her again." So the fader give her to Breavewell.

SOURCE: Elsie Clews Parsons, *Folk-Lore of the Sea Islands, South Carolina*, 75.

This story was told by Henry Bryan, a thirty-five-year-old boatman living on Daufuskie Island off the coast of South Carolina. It gives us a revealing comparison with the African analogue.

A VITAL DECISION

Once there lived a poor man who had three sons and three daughters. He managed to eke out a living by catching rats and selling them as food at the market. In the city there lived a rich man with four hundred slaves and many wives. He had no children. People used to torment him by asking, "Who is going to inherit your fortune?" One day even the king asked him that question. The rich man replied, "I have a son, but he is living in the woods."

"I am going to give him my daughter as his wife," the king replied.

"And I will try to find my son," the man said.

The rich man had two hundred men. But he ordered them to stay where they were, and he alone went out into the forest.

That very day the poor man left home with his sons to go catch rats, and he told them, "If any of you let a rat escape, I will kill you!" They dug around in the ground where rats were living, and suddenly out jumped a rat, and the youngest of the boys couldn't catch it. The father was infuriated, and he took an ax and struck his son with it. Blood poured out from his wounds, and he collapsed.

"Leave him there," the father said. "He is no longer one of us."

They left and before long the rich man came riding by, saw the boy and cleaned his wounds. Since he liked his looks, he dressed him in beautiful clothing and let him ride on his horse with him. At the next village, he sent a messenger to his commander at home and asked him to send all his men along with a horse for his son. Drummers welcomed the rich man back home, and the people shouted, "The rich man has found his son! The rich man has found his son!"

The rich man let his son march at the front with all his men, and the drummers drummed for him alone. The young man greeted the king, and then he was escorted to the rich man's living quarters and was given a beautiful house to live in. Three young slaves came to bathe him and massage his limbs. His father sent him fifty slaves, along with horses, and everything that he could possibly need. The entire city celebrated the discovery of the rich man's son.

Before long the king sent his daughter over with ten slaves. The young woman went to see the rich man's son. She sat down next to him, and the two amused themselves for a while, for the son had no idea what he was supposed to do. But after three days, he married the young woman. The entire city celebrated and before long the young man had become, next to the king, the most beloved and the most powerful man in the kingdom.

In the meantime, the poor man was going everywhere possible to find out if anyone had seen his son. Finally, he found out that his son had married the king's daughter and had become a powerful man. He went to the king and demanded to have his son back.

"Come inside and let's discuss it," the rich man said. "I don't want anyone to hear us talking. Come live here with your entire family, and I will give you land and cattle. But you mustn't say a word to anyone, otherwise I will be mortified."

The poor man was dissatisfied with the offer. He went to his son and asked him, "Why would you want to stay here in the city? We used to get 100 cowries for each rat.

Today they fetch 200. Your brother has already bought three sheep. Come back and live with us in the woods."

The rich man came back and begged the father to leave the young man in peace. But the poor man would not give in, and the rich man finally said, "All right. I will give you back your son and accompany you for a stretch this evening."

In the evening, they departed. First the poor man, then behind him on horseback the rich man, and finally the son. Right in the midst of the bush the rich man stopped and said, "I want to return home."

"That's fine. Farewell," the poor man said. The rich man dismounted and took the young man's hand.

"What do you want," the poor man asked, "now that he has become my son again?"

The rich man drew his sword and gave it to the young man. "If you want to go with your father, then kill me. If you want to stay with me, then kill your father. Unless you come with me, I don't want to return home."

The young man stood between the two men with the sword drawn. Should he kill his father, the man who had raised him but who had also nearly killed him for the sake of a rat? Then people would say that he had killed him for the sake of the money. Or should he kill the rich man, the man who had helped him and made him wealthy, which meant that he would be returning to catching rats? He had no idea what to do, and if the three are not already dead, then they are no doubt still standing there.

SOURCE: Leo Frobenius, *Atlantis: Volksmärchen und Volksdichtungen Afrikas*, IX, 404–6.

Leo Frobenius (1873–1938) was a German archaeologist and ethnographer who set forth the idea of an African Atlantis, a civilization that marked a lost cultural idea. His multivolume collection of African lore was published under the title Atlantis, *the site of which he claimed to have discovered. On January 30, 1911, the* New York Times *reported that "Leo Frobenius, author, leader of the German Inner-African exploring expedition, sends word from the hinterland of Togo . . . that he has discovered indisputable proofs of the existence of Plato's legendary continent of Atlantis. He places Atlantis, which he declares was not an island, in the northwestern section of Africa, in territory lying close to the equator."*

The dilemma tale he included in his collection captures a moment of indecisive paralysis, a recognition that some dilemmas are so intractable that they lead to a dislocating silence rather than to a resolution.

THE STORY OF THE FOUR FOOLS

One day a wizard met a boy who was sitting by the roadside, upset and weeping bitter tears. He asked the reason for his tears, and the boy said, "My father's parrot has flown away. If you can find it, I will give you a reward." The wizard summoned a hunter, a carpenter, and a thief. He told them about the lost parrot and also about the reward for its return. They all agreed to do their best to find the parrot.

"Before we start, let's each demonstrate our special skills," one of the four said. "For the thief: I want you to go and steal an egg from that hen over there without letting the hen know what you have done." The thief went and stole the egg, and the hen did not move at all. The hunter hung the egg up as a target, walked a good distance away from it, and proved his skill by hitting the egg. Then the carpenter showed what he could do by putting the egg back together again. They turned to the wizard, who could see that they each had a special talent.

The wizard decided that it was time to find the parrot, and he invited the four others to board his glass ship. "See that vessel over there?" he asked. "The parrot was stolen by the men on that vessel." The four in the glass boat caught up with the vessel, and the thief boarded it. He caught the parrot, and then he set the table and sat down for a good meal before returning to the glass ship with the parrot.

When the men who had stolen the parrot from the king's son discovered that it was gone, they gave chase to the glass boat. The captain of the vessel summoned a storm and sent rain down on the glass boat, which shattered. But the carpenter mended it, and the hunter fired away at the rain until it stopped.

The captain of the vessel sent down lightning, and it shattered the glass ship again. But the carpenter just mended it again, and the hunter shot at the lightning until it stopped. Eventually the four men reached land and took the parrot to the chief's son and said, "Here is your father's parrot."

The boy was overjoyed to have the parrot back, and he told the four to choose whatever they wanted from his possessions. They could even ask for a wonderful hen that lay jewels, or anything else you might want. They chose the hen and went on their way. But they had not gone very far before the wizard said, "The hen belongs to me, because I told you about the parrot and where it was."

The thief then said, "No, the hen is mine, for I stole the parrot from the vessel."

The carpenter then staked his claim, for he had twice mended the ship in which they were sailing.

Then the hunter said, "It really belongs to me, for I shot at the rain and the lightning."

They argued for a long time and exchanged angry words. Since they could not reach an agreement, they finally did something wildly stupid. They killed the wonderful hen and divided it into four pieces, with each man taking his share. Now which of these four fools should have been given the hen?

This story excited a great amount of discussion. Some argued that this one should have had the hen, and others argued with great conviction that another should have had the hen. Each character had his supporters, but everyone agreed that they were all fools not to share the hen and let it lay jewels for them.

SOURCE: Adapted from John H. Weeks, *Congo Life and Folklore*, 43–45.

The four fools form a fine quartet, with one having magic powers, the second skills in hunting in the wild, the third in building domestic spaces, and the fourth in a lawful form of lawlessness. The coda to their story describes the kind of animated atmosphere fostered by stories that end with an invitation to discuss the terms of the tale.

PART III

ADDING ENCHANTMENT TO WISDOM: FAIRY TALES WORK THEIR MAGIC

African countries have rarely been seen as the source of fairy tales and wonderlore, stories in which magic and metamorphosis feature prominently. For primordial moments of fairy-tale production, folklorists have looked to India, where by the third century BCE a massive set of animal fables had been assembled in a collection known today as *The Panchatantra*. In nineteenth-century Europe, there was a rush to collect fairy tales, before the twin forces of urbanization and industrialization began eradicating their traces. The Brothers Grimm published their *Children's Stories and Household Tales* in two volumes in 1812 and 1815 and succeeded in creating a canon that is still with us today. When the term *fairy tale* is invoked, the associations are with the Grimms, the Frenchman Charles Perrault, the Russian Alexander Afanasev, or with the Dane Hans Christian Andersen more than with Africa.

It is therefore all the more astonishing to find that the characters, motifs, and tropes of European fairy tales appear in kaleidoscopic variation in tales collected in African regions. If Africa has always seemed an outlier when it comes to fairy tales, the narratives printed here tell a different story. Suddenly another continent joins the fairy-tale network, with plots that resemble tales not only from Europe, but also from China, India, and Russia.

Folklorists have advanced two different, although not entirely incompatible, theories to account for the remarkable similarities found among fairy tales of all cultures.

The first, known as the theory of migration or borrowing, proceeds along the assumption that nothing new is ever discovered so long as it is possible to copy. This theory, also known by the name of monogenesis, suggests that one parent tale in a fixed location spawned numerous progeny. The contrasting theory of polygenesis assumes that resemblances among tales can be attributed to independent invention in places unconnected by trade routes or travel. The Russian folklorist Vladimir Propp challenged the truth of monogenesis and diffusion when he asked: "How is one to explain the similarity of the tale about the frog queen in Russia, Germany, France, India, in America among the Indians, and in New Zealand, when the contact of peoples cannot be proven historically?" (Propp 16). It is somehow symptomatic that no African country is represented in his geographical inventory, more than likely because so few anthologies were available to him in twentieth-century Russia.

As Claude Lévi-Strauss tells us, the universe of mythology is "round" and therefore "does not refer back to any necessary starting point" (Lévi-Strauss 13). We cannot fix the origin of "Little Red Riding Hood," which is ultimately about a girl, an animal, and an encounter in the wild any more than we can pinpoint where "Beauty and the Beast," with its alluring bride and grotesque groom, was first told. In the tales that follow, we have full-throated variants of familiar tales, told in ways that make us sit up and take notice and understand how the global story consists of a multitude of local versions.

THE STORY OF DEMANE AND DEMAZANA

Once upon a time there lived a brother and sister, who were twins and orphans. They decided to run away from their relatives because they had been treated so badly.[1] The boy's name was Demane, the girl's Demazana. They discovered a cave with two holes to let in air and light, and that was where they lived. A strong door, fastened from the inside, protected the cave.

Demane went out hunting in the daytime, and he told his sister that she must not roast any meat while he was away. The savory smell might attract cannibals to their dwelling. The girl would have been quite safe if she had done as her brother commanded. But she was wayward, and one day she took some buffalo meat and roasted it over a fire.

A cannibal named Zim smelled the meat and went to the cave, but he found the door shut tight. He tried to imitate Demane's voice and asked to be admitted, but Demazana said, "No, you aren't my brother, your voice is not at all like his."

The cannibal went away, but after a little while he returned. This time he spoke in a different tone of voice: "Do let me in, sister." The girl replied, "Go away, you wicked cannibal, your voice is hoarse, you are not my brother."

The cannibal left, and soon met up with another cannibal, whom he asked, "What do I have to do to obtain what I want?" He was afraid to say exactly what he wanted because he feared that the other cannibal might want a share of the girl. His friend said, "You must burn your throat with a hot iron." He did so, and then he no longer had a hoarse voice.

The cannibal presented himself again at the door to the cave, and this time he succeeded in fooling the girl. She believed that her brother had returned from hunting and was at the door. When she opened it, the cannibal grabbed her.

While the cannibal was carrying her off, the girl dropped some ashes[2] here and there along the path. Not much later, Demane, who had found nothing that day but a swarm of bees, returned and found that his sister was gone. He figured out what had happened, and he also found the ashes and followed the path to Zim's hut. The cannibal's family was out gathering firewood, but he had stayed at home. Demazana was

1 *treated so badly:* The children are not abandoned, as in European analogues, but instead run away.

2 *dropped some ashes:* In "Hansel and Gretel," recorded by the Brothers Grimm in the nineteenth century, Hansel first scatters pebbles on the road to find his way back home, then bread crumbs, which are eaten by birds.

kept prisoner in a big sack, where Zim planned to keep her until the fire was ready. Demane said, "Give me some water, Uncle." Zim replied, "I will, if you promise not to touch this sack." Demane promised. Zim went out to get some water, and while he was gone Demane took his sister out of the sack and put the bees in it. Then they both hid.

When Zim returned with the water, his wife and son and daughter were also back with firewood. Zim said to his daughter, "There's something nice for you in the sack. Go get it."

Zim's daughter opened it, and all at once the bees flew out of the bag[3] and stung her hand. She cried out: "Something's biting me!" Zim sent his son, and after that his wife, but the same thing happened. He was furious and drove everyone out of the hut. He put a block of wood against the door, and he opened the sack for himself. Bees came swarming out and stung his head, aiming at his eyes until he couldn't see anything at all. There was a small opening in the thatched roof, and he forced his way through. Once outside, he began jumping up and down, howling with pain. Then he ran blindly ahead and fell head-

3 *the bees flew out of the bag:* The triple attack of the bees may be the precursor to the story of Brer Rabbit and his Laughing-Place (the site of a hornet's nest).

4 *took all of Zim's possessions:* Like many folkloric siblings, Demane and Demazana become tricksters who outwit the ogre, witch, or monster, not only surviving, but also gaining wealth and power.

long into a pond, where his head stuck fast in the mud. He turned into a block of wood that looked just like the stump of a tree. The bees made their home in the stump. No one could steal their honey, because if anyone stuck a hand in, they would not be able to get it back out again.

Demane and Demazana took all of Zim's possessions,[4] which were great in number, and soon they became wealthy people.

SOURCE: Adapted from "The Story of Demane and Demazana," *The Cape Monthly Magazine* 9 (1874), 248–49.

Described as a "Kafir Nursery Tale" (Kafir, or Kaffir, is now considered a derogatory term for the Xhosa people), this tale was recorded in a monthly magazine published in Cape Town. Its preface elaborated on the cultural context for tales told to children: "Many ancient dames pride themselves upon an extensive knowledge of such stories, and from them little children hear them as soon almost as they begin to lisp. The girls retain them in their memory, and frequently laugh over them in after years, but with the boys it is different. Knowledge derived from a woman—even be that woman his grandmother or mother—is lightly esteemed by a Kafir man, and these stories soon come to be considered by the lads as old women's fables, quite unworthy of their notice." The anonymous collector of the tale selected it for its "reference . . . to cannibals."

Splicing together two different tale types, "The Wolf and the Kids" and "The Household of the Witch," the story moves from capturing to cooking, first telling how a monster gains entrance into the children's home, then how the same monster prepares a feast of human flesh. Note that the monster is a human "cannibal" rather than an animal predator or a supernatural creature.

THE TAIL OF THE PRINCESS ELEPHANT

There once lived a woman who had three sons. They were deeply attached to their mother and always tried to please her. After a time, she grew old and feeble. The boys began to wonder what they could do to make her happy. The eldest promised that he would cut a fine sepulcher in stone after her death. The second said that he would make a beautiful coffin. The youngest said, "I will go and get the tail of the princess elephant and put it in your coffin." This promise was by far the hardest to keep.

Not much later, the mother died. The youngest son set out immediately on his quest, without having an idea of where he would find the tail. After travelling for weeks, he reached a little village. There he met an old woman who seemed surprised to see him. She said that no human had ever been there before. The boy told her why he was searching for the princess elephant. The old woman replied that her village was the home of all the elephants and that the princess slept there every night. She warned him that the animals living there would kill him. The young man begged her to hide him—which she did, in a great pile of wood.

The woman also told him that once the elephants fell asleep, he should get up and go into the far corner of the hut, where he would find the princess. He should walk boldly over to her and cut off her tail. If he acted frightened in any way, the elephants would wake up and catch him.

The animals returned when it was growing dark. The smell of human flesh was in the air, and they asked the old woman about it. She assured them that they were mistaken. Their supper was ready, so they ate it and went to bed.

In the middle of the night the young man got up and walked boldly across to where the princess was sleeping. He cut off her tail. He returned home with it, carrying the tail with great care.

When daylight broke, the elephants woke up. One of them said he had dreamed about the princess's tail and how it had been stolen. The others thrashed him just for imagining such a thing. A second elephant said he had had the same dream, and he was also thrashed. The wisest of all the elephants then suggested that it might be a good idea to see if the dream was true. This they did. They found the princess fast asleep, completely unaware that her tail was gone. They woke her up and sped off to find the young man.

They travelled so fast that in a few hours they were able to make out the young man in the distance. He was terrified when he saw them running after him and cried out to his favorite idol (which he always wore in his hair): "O my juju[1] Depor! What shall I do?"

The juju advised him to throw a branch over his shoulder. He did that, and a huge tree began growing up from it, blocking the path of the elephants. The elephants stopped in front of the tree and started eating it. That took up some time.

1 *juju:* In West African cultures, jujus are amulets and spells used in ritual practices. The juju is usually worn in the hair or on the body, but sometimes it is carried.

Then the elephants began the chase again. The young man cried out, "Oh my juju Depor! What shall I do?" "Throw that corn-cob behind you," answered the juju. The lad did so, and the corncob immediately grew into a vast field of maize.

The elephants ate their way through the maize, but when they arrived on the other side they found that the boy had already reached home. So they gave up the chase and returned to their village. The princess, however, refused to give up, saying, "I will return after I have punished this cheeky boy for stealing my tail." She turned herself into a beautiful maiden, and, taking a calabash cymbal in one hand, she approached the village. Everyone came out to admire this lovely girl.

When the princess arrived in the village, she proclaimed that whoever succeeded in shooting an arrow into the cymbal could marry her. The young men all tried and failed. An old man standing by said, "If only Kwesi—the man who cut the princess elephant's tail—were here. He would be able to hit the cymbal."

"Then Kwesi is the man I shall marry," the maiden said, "whether he hits the cymbal or not."

Kwesi was out ploughing fields, and he was quickly called and told about his good fortune. But he was not at all delighted to hear about it, for he suspected that the maiden had something up her sleeve. Still, he came and shot an arrow, and it struck the center of the cymbal. He and the young woman were married, but all that time she was preparing a punishment for him.

The night after their marriage, the young woman turned back into an elephant while Kwesi was sleeping. She was just about to slay him when Kwesi woke up and shouted, "Oh my juju Depor! Save me!" The juju turned him into a grass mat on the bed, and the princess could not find him anywhere. She was deeply annoyed, and, the next morning, she asked him where he had been all night. "While you were an elephant, I was the mat you were lying on," replied Kwesi. The young woman took all the mats from the bed and burned them.

The next night the princess turned into an elephant again and was just about to slay her husband. This time the juju changed him into a needle, and his wife was unable to find him. In the morning, she asked where he had been. Hearing that the juju had helped him again, she decided to get hold of the idol and destroy it.

The next day Kwesi went to his farm to begin ploughing a field. He told his wife to bring him something to eat at midday. When he finished his food, she said, "Put your head in my lap and go to sleep." Kwesi forgot that the juju was hidden in his hair and did as she said. As soon as he was asleep, she took the juju out of his hair and threw it into a fire she had prepared. Kwesi awoke to find that she had turned back into an elephant. Terrified, he cried out, "Oh my juju Depor! What am I going to do?" The only answer came from out of the flames. "I am burning up. I am burning up. I am burning up." Kwesi called out for help, and the juju replied, "Lift up your arms and pretend that you are going to fly." He lifted his arms and turned into a hawk.

That is why hawks are so often seen flying above the smoke from fires. They are looking for their lost juju.

SOURCE: Adapted from William Henry Barker and Cecilia Sinclair, *West African Folk-Tales*, 123–30.

Both a pourquoi *tale (telling us how something came to be) and a fairy tale, the story of Kwesi and the Elephant Princess features talking animals, the threat of being devoured, and a magical pursuit. The three sons at the beginning of the tale are familiar from the European canon, and not surprisingly the youngest becomes the principal figure in a tale that moves in the mode of Jack and the Beanstalk (with man-eating monsters and a protective female figure), then modulates into a story with a supernatural helper, and includes a classic fairy-tale flight in which obstacles are cast in the path of the villain.*

THE MAIDEN, THE FROG, AND THE CHIEF'S SON

There was once a man who had two wives, and they each had a daughter. He loved one of the two wives and her daughter, but he hated the other one and her daughter.

One day the wife he disliked fell ill, and it was not long before she died. Her daughter was taken in by the other wife, the one he loved. The girl moved into that wife's hut. And there she lived, with no mother of her own, just a father. And every day the woman would push her out of the hut, sending her off to the bush to gather wood. When she returned, she had to pound up the *fura*.[1] Then she had to pound the *tuwo*,[2] and, after that, she had to stir the pot. And then they wouldn't even let her eat the *tuwo*. All she had to eat were the burnt bits at the bottom of the pot. Day after day, things went on like this.

1 *fura:* a kind of gruel, usually eaten in the morning

2 *tuwo:* porridge made of millet or other grain, usually the evening meal

The girl had an older brother, and he invited her to come and eat at his home, which she did. But still, when she returned home from the bush and asked for a drink of water, they would not let her have one. And they would not give her proper food—only the coarsest of what had been scraped from the bottom of the pot. She would take those scrapings and throw them into a pit where there were frogs. They would come out and start eating the scrapings. After they had finished eating, they would return to the water and she too would go back home.

Things went on like that, day after day, until it was time for the Festival. The day before it was to take place, she went with scrapings and coarse leftovers to the pit and

"The Maiden, the Frog, and the Chief's Son," from William Bascom, *Journal of the Folklore Institute* 9 (1972): 56–59. Reprinted with permission of Indiana University Press.

saw a frog squatting there. She realized that he was waiting for her. When she reached the pit, she threw bits of food into it. The frog said: "Young lady, you've always been very kind to us, and now we— Well, just come by here tomorrow morning. That's the morning of the Festival. If you come by then, we will return the favor you have done us." "Fine," she said and returned home.

The next day was the day of the Festival. She was about to go to the pit, just as the frog had told her. But as she was leaving, her half-sister's mother said to her, "Hey— come over here, you good-for-nothing girl! You haven't stirred the *tuwo*, or pounded the *fura*, or fetched the wood or the water." So the girl never left. And the frog spent the entire day waiting for her. As for her, she returned to the compound and set off to fetch wood. Then she fetched water and set about pounding the *tuwo*, which she then stirred and removed from the fire. She was then told to take the scrapings to the pit. She did as she was told and went off to the pit, where the frog was waiting for her. "Tut, tut, girl," he said. "I've been waiting for you since morning, and you never came."

"Old fellow," she said, "I'm a slave and didn't have a choice."

"How come?" he asked.

"Simple," she replied. "My mother died and left me, her only daughter, all alone. I have a brother but he is married and lives in a compound of his own. My father put me in the care of his other wife. He never really loved my mother, and I was moved into the hut of his other wife. As I told you, slavery is my lot. Every morning I go off to the bush to get wood. When I return, I have to pound the *fura*, and then I pound the *tuwo*. I don't get anything to eat, just the scrapings." The frog said, "Give us your hand." And she held it out to him, and both frog and girl leaped into the water.

The frog then picked up the girl and swallowed her. And then he brought her back up. "Good people," he said. "Tell me now, is she straight or is she crooked?"

And they all looked and replied, "She is bent to the left." So he picked her up and swallowed her again and brought her back up. He then asked the same question. "She's quite straight now," they said. "Very good," he replied.

The frog then produced from his mouth all kinds of clothes for her, and bangles, and rings, and a pair of shoes, one of silver and one of gold. "And now," he said, "off you go to the dance." All these things were given to her, and the frog said, "When the dancing is almost over and the dancers begin to leave, you must leave your golden shoe, the right one, there." And the girl replied to the frog: "Very well, old fellow, I understand." And off she went.

Meanwhile the chief's son asked some young men and women to dance for him, and he saw the girl when she joined the dancers. "Well!" said the chief's son. "*There's* a maiden for you, if you like. I'm not going to let her join the dancers. I don't care where she comes from—bring her here!" So the servants of the chief's son went over and came back with her. The chief's son told her to sit down on the couch, and she took her place there.

The two chatted for some time—until the dancers began to leave. Then she said to the chief's son: "I have to leave."

"Oh, are you off?" he asked.

"Yes," she said as she rose to her feet.

"I'll accompany you on your way for a while," he said, and so he did. She, in the meantime, left her right shoe behind. After a while, she said, "Chief's son, you must go back now," and he did so. She returned home on her own.

The frog was sitting by the edge of the water waiting for her. He took her hand, and the two of them jumped into the water. Then he picked her up and swallowed her and brought her back up. There she was, just as she had been before, a sorry sight. And taking her raggedy things, she returned home.

When the girl got back, she said, "Fellow-wife of my mother, I'm not feeling well." And the woman said to her, "You little rascal! You've been up to no good. You have been away and failed to fetch water or wood, failed to pound the *fura* or make the *tuwo*. Very well, then! No food for you today!" And so the girl left for her brother's compound, and there she ate some food and returned home again.

Meanwhile, the chief's son had picked up the shoe and said to his father: "Last night I spoke with a girl who was wearing a pair of shoes, one made of gold, the other of silver. Look, here's the golden one—she left it behind. She's the girl I want to marry. Let all the girls, young and old, gather together. They can each try on the shoe." "Very well," the chief said.

And so it was proclaimed, and all the girls, young and old, gathered in one place. And the chief's son went with the shoe and sat down. Each girl came and tried on the shoe, but it fit no one at all. Then someone said, "Wait a minute! There's that girl in so-and-so's compound, whose mother died some time ago." "Yes, that's right," said another. "Someone should go fetch her." And someone went and fetched her.

The minute the girl arrived to try on the shoe, it ran over to her and slipped itself on her foot. The chief's son said right then and there, "Here's my wife."

At this, the other woman—the girl's father's other wife—said, "The shoe belongs to my daughter. It was she who left it where everyone was dancing, not this good-for-nothing layabout. But the chief's son insisted that the shoe fit the girl who was there. She was the one he wanted to take to his compound in marriage. And so they took her there, and there she spent one night.

The next morning she went out of her hut and walked behind it, and there was the frog. She knelt down respectfully and greeted him, "Welcome, old fellow, welcome." He said, "Tonight we shall be along to bring some things for you." She thanked him and he left.

That night the frog rallied all the other frogs, and all his friends, both great and small, came along. He was their leader, and he said to them, "See here—my daughter is being married. I want every one of you to make a contribution." And each of them went out and fetched what he could afford. Their leader thanked them all, and then regurgitated a silver bed, a brass bed, a copper bed, and an iron bed. And he kept bringing things up for her—woolen blankets, rugs, satins, and velvets.

"Now," he said to the girl, "if your heart is ever troubled, just lie down on this brass bed." And he went on, "And when the chief's son's other wives come to greet you, give them two calabashes of cola-nuts and ten thousand cowrie shells. Then, when his concubines come to greet you, give them one calabash of cola-nuts and five thousand cowries."

"Very well," she said. Then he said, "And when the concubines come to get corn for making *tuwo*, say to them. 'There's a bag full, help yourselves.'" "Very well," she said.

"And," he added, "if your father's wife comes along with her daughter and asks what it is like living in the chief's compound, tell her 'Living in the compound is a tedious business—for they measure out corn there with the shell of a Bambara groundnut.'" [3]

So there she lived until one day her father's favorite wife brought her own daughter along with her at night, took her into the chief's compound, and exchanged the two girls, taking home the one that was not her daughter. The woman said to her: "Oh! I forgot to get you to tell her all about married life in the chief's compound."

3 *Bambara groundnut:* a nut native to West Africa, somewhat like the peanut

"It's a tedious life," the girl said. "How so?" the older woman asked, surprised. "Well, they use the shell of a Bambara groundnut for measuring out corn. Then, if the chief's other wives come to greet you, you reply with a contemptuous 'Pfft.' If the concubines come to greet you, you clear your throat and spit. And if your husband comes into your hut, you yell at him."

"I see," said the woman and she passed all this on to her daughter, who was staying in the compound of the chief's son.

Next morning, when it was light, the wives came to greet her, and she said "Pfft" to them. The concubines came to greet her, and she spat at them. Then when night fell, the chief's son made his way to her hut, and she yelled at him. He was astonished and left, and for two days he pondered the matter.

The chief's son called together his wives and concubines and said to them, "Look now—I've called you together to ask a question. The young woman they brought me is different. How did she treat all of you?" "Hmm—how indeed!" they all exclaimed. "Every morning, when we went to greet her, she would give us cola-nuts, two calabashes full, and cowries, ten thousand of them to buy tobacco flowers. And when the concubines went to greet her, she would give them a calabash of cola-nuts and five thousand cowries to buy tobacco flowers with; and in the evening, corn for *tuwo*. It would be a whole bagful!"

"You see," he said. "As for me, whenever I went to her hut, I found her kneeling respectfully. And she wouldn't get up until I had entered and sat down on the bed."

"Hey," he called out, "Boys, come over here!" And when they came, he went into her hut, took a sword, and chopped her up into little pieces. He had them collected and wrapped up and then sent back to her home.

When the boys reached the house, they found the true wife lying by the hearth. They picked her up and brought her back to her husband.

The next morning, at dawn, the young woman picked up a little gourd water-bottle and went behind her hut. There she saw the frog. "Welcome, welcome, old fellow," she said. She told him that she wanted to build a well. "And then all of you can come live in it and be close to me."

"All right," the frog said. "Tell your husband." And she did.

And the chief's son had a well dug for her, close to the hut. And the frogs came, climbed into the well, and there they lived. That's all. *Kungurus kan kusu.*[4]

4 *Kungurus kan kusu:* formulaic ending for a tale: "Off with the rat's head!"

SOURCE: William Bascom, "Cinderella in Africa," 56–59.

This tale remained a puzzle to twentieth-century folklorists, who encountered the story in a 1911 collection of Hausa folktales. Andrew Lang set the stage for the mystery by asserting, "One thing is plain, a naked and a shoeless race could not have invented Cinderella" (Dundes 1988, 165). Africa could therefore not possibly have served as the source of the tale, despite the fact that our earliest Cinderella is Rhodopis, the Greek courtesan who loses her sandal and marries the ruler of Egypt. That the tale hinges on the motif of a slipper-test rather than on the social elevation of the heroine is a questionable premise. What we have in the tale recorded by Bascom is a Cinderella story that may have sprung up from native soil but that may also have been, like all folktales, inspired by narratives that migrated from one place to another, picking up bits and pieces of the cultural surround as they moved.

ADZANUMEE AND HER MOTHER

There once lived a woman who had one great wish. She longed to have a daughter—but alas! she remained childless. She was never able to feel joy because this one wish remained unfulfilled. Even during feasts the thought would be in her mind, "If only I had a daughter to share this with me."

One day she was gathering yams in the field, and it happened that she pulled one up that was very long and well shaped. "If only this fine yam were a daughter, how happy I would be."

To her astonishment the yam replied, "If I were to be your daughter, would you promise never to scold me for having once been a yam?" The woman agreed at once, and suddenly the yam turned into a beautiful, well-made girl. The woman was overjoyed and was very kind to the girl. She called her Adzanumee. The girl was always useful to her mother. She would make bread, gather yams, and sell them at the market place.

One day Adzanumee was away longer than usual. Her mother grew impatient and angry. "Where can Adzanumee be? She does not deserve such a beautiful name. After all, she is nothing but a yam."

A bird singing nearby heard the mother's words and flew away to the tree under which Adzanumee was sitting. There he began to sing:

Adzanumee! Adzanumee!
Your mother is unkind—she says that you are nothing but a yam.

You do not deserve your name!
Adzanumee! Adzanumee!

The girl heard the bird and returned home weeping. When the woman saw her, she said, "My daughter, my dear daughter! What is the matter?"
Adzanumee replied:

Oh Mother! Dear Mother!
You have scolded me for being a yam.
You said I did not deserve my name.
Oh Mother! Dear Mother!

As she spoke those words, she made her way back to the yam field. Her mother, filled with fear, followed her, wailing,

Adzanumee! Adzanumee!
Do not believe it—do not believe it.
You are my daughter, my dear daughter
Adzanumee!

But it was too late. Her daughter, still singing her sad little song, changed back into a yam. When the woman arrived at the field, the yam was lying on the ground. Nothing she could do or say would give her back the daughter she had so passionately wished for and treated so badly.

SOURCE: William Henry Barker and Cecilia Sinclair, *West African Folk-Tales*, 77–79.

Desire becomes so explosive in this story that it can turn a yam into a child. The mother's failure to keep her promise to protect the girl's origins has tragic consequences. Most European fairy tales with children in them have a cautionary edge, designed to teach a lesson to the child in the story and outside it. By contrast, the parent in this story receives a strong message about preserving an affirmative, loving relationship to her offspring.

THE STORY OF THE CANNIBAL MOTHER AND HER CHILDREN

There once lived a man and a woman with two children, a boy and a girl. The children went to live with their grandfather. Their mother was a cannibal, but not their father.[1]

One day they said to their grandfather, "We have stayed with you long enough. Now we would like very much to go and see our parents."

Their grandfather said: "Ha! Will you be able to return? Don't you realize that your mother is a cannibal?"

After a while the grandfather gave his consent. He said, "You have to plan to arrive there in the evening so that your mother will not be able to see you, only your father."

The boy's name was Hinazinci. He said: "Let us go now, sister."

They left at sunset. When they arrived at their father's hut, they listened outside to find out if their mother was at home. They heard only their father's voice, so they called to him. He came out, and when he saw them he felt bad and said: "Why did you come here, dear children? Don't you know that your mother is a cannibal?"

Just then they heard what sounded like thunder. It was their mother returning home. Their father took them indoors and hid them in a dark corner, where he covered them with skins. Their mother came in with an animal carcass and the body of a man. She said: "There's something in here. What a nice smell it has!"[2]

The woman said to her husband, "Sohinazinci, what can you tell me about the nice smell in the hut? You must tell me whether my children are here."

Her husband replied: "You must be dreaming. They are not here."

The mother went over to the corner where the children were hiding and took the skins away. When she saw them, she said, "Children, I am very sorry that you are here, because I have to eat people up, no matter what."

She cooked the animal she had brought home as a meal for the children and their father, and the dead man she kept for herself. After they had eaten, she went out.

The father said to the children, "When we lie down to go to sleep, you must be watchful. You will hear people dancing, wild beasts roaring, and dogs barking in your

1 *Their mother was a cannibal, but not their father:* As in many European tales about siblings, threat comes from a mother, a mother-in-law, or a witch, each with homicidal drives or a taste for human flesh.

2 *"What a nice smell it has!":* Like the giant in "Jack and the Beanstalk," the mother's appetite is aroused by the presence of humans.

mother's stomach. You will know by those sounds that she is sleeping, and you must then get up at once and leave."

They lay down, but the man and the children only pretended to go to sleep. The children listened for the sounds their father had described. After a while, they heard people dancing, wild beasts roaring, and dogs barking. Then their father shook them and told them they must leave while their mother was still sleeping. They said their farewells and crept out quietly so that their mother would not hear them.

At midnight, the woman woke up, and when she found that the children had left, she took her ax and ran after them. They had already gone a long way on their journey when they saw her in pursuit. They were so tired that they could no longer run. As she came closer, the boy said to the girl, "Sister, sing your beautiful song. Perhaps she will take pity on us when she hears it and return home without hurting us."

The girl replied, "She will not listen to anything now because she needs meat."

Hinazinci said, "Try anyway, sister. It may not be in vain."

So she sang her song, and when the cannibal heard it, she ran backward to her own hut. There she attacked her husband and wanted to chop him up with the ax. Her husband grabbed her arm and said, "Ho! If you kill me, who will be your husband?"

The woman left him and ran after the children again.

The children were now close to their grandfather's village. They were very weak, and their mother soon overtook them. The girl fell down, and the cannibal caught her and swallowed her. The mother ran after her son. He fell down at the entrance to his grandfather's hut, and she picked him up and swallowed him too. She found only the old people and the children of the village at home, all the others being at work in the fields. She ate all the people who were at home and also all the cattle that were there.

Toward evening, she left to return home. There was a deep valley in the way, and when she came to it she saw a beautiful bird.[3] As she approached it, the bird grew larger and larger, until at last, when she was very close to it, it was the size of a hut.

3 *she saw a beautiful bird:* This bird, like the singing bird in "The Juniper Tree" (a tale well-known in European cultures) seeks revenge. Dismemberment becomes the penalty for the mother's excessive appetite, and the bird not only punishes but also rescues the living dead swallowed by the cannibalistic ogre.

The bird began to sing. The woman looked at it, and said to herself, "I shall take this bird home to my husband."

The bird continued its song, and sang:

> I am a pretty bird of the valley,
> And you have brought trouble.

The bird flew slowly toward her, still singing its song. When they met, the bird took the ax from the woman and continued singing.

The cannibal grew fearful.

She said to the bird, "Give me my ax; I don't want your flesh now."

The bird tore one of her arms off.

She said, "I am going away now. Give me what is mine."

The bird would not listen to her and continued its song.

She said again, "Give me my ax and let me go. My husband is at home, and he is very hungry. I want to go and cook some food for him."

The bird sang louder than before and tore one of her legs off.

The woman fell down and cried out, "My master, I am in a hurry to reach home. I do not want anything that belongs to you."

She saw that she was in danger. She said to the bird again, "You don't know how to sing your song nicely. Let me go, and I will sing it for you."

The bird spread its wings and tore open her stomach. Many people came running out, most of them still alive, but some were dead. As they emerged she caught them and swallowed them again. The two children were alive, and they ran away. The woman was dead.

There was great rejoicing in that country. The children returned to their grandfather, and the people came there and made them rulers of the land, because it was through them that the cannibal had met her death.

The girl was married to the son of a great chief, and Hinazinci's wife was the daughter of that great chief.

SOURCE: Adapted from George McCall Theal, *Kaffir Folk-Lore*, 68–71.

This tale offers many challenges, not the least of which has to do with identifying its origins. Is it a European import, a version of "The Juniper Tree"? Or is it an African tale that made its way to Europe? Or were both tales invented independently of each other? Maternal tenderness is here transformed into treachery, with a mother matter-of-factly described as a cannibal. Beauty and song are the two elements that will lead to redemption and resurrection.

TSÉLANÉ AND THE MARIMO

A man had a daughter named Tsélané. One day he set off with his family and his flocks to find fresh pastures. But his daughter refused to go with him. She said to her mother, "I'm not going. Our house is so pretty, with its white and red beads, that I can't leave."

Her mother said, "My child, since you are naughty, you will have to stay here all alone. But shut the door tight in case the Marimos[1] come and want to eat you." With that she went away. But in a few days she came back, bringing food for her daughter.

1 *Marimos:* cannibals

"Tsélané, my child, Tsélané, my child, take this bread, and eat it."

"I can hear my mother, I can hear her. My mother speaks like an *ataga* bird, like the *tsuere* coming out of the woods."

For a long time the mother brought food to Tsélané. One day Tsélané heard a gruff voice saying, "Tsélané, my child, Tsélané, my child, take this bread and eat it." But she laughed and said, "That gruff voice is not my mother's voice. Go away, naughty Marimo." The Marimo went away. He lit a big fire, took an iron hoe, made it red hot, and swallowed it to clear his voice. Then he came back and tried to fool Tsélané again. But he could not, for his voice was still not soft enough. So he heated another hoe, and swallowed it red-hot like the first. Then he came back and said in a still soft voice, "Tsélané, my child, Tsélané, my chee-ild, take this bread and eat it."

Tsélané thought it was her mother's voice and opened the door. The Marimo put her in his sack and walked off. Soon he felt thirsty, and, leaving his sack in the care of some little girls, he went to get some spirits in a village. The girls peeped into the sack, saw Tsélané in it, and ran to tell her mother, who happened to be nearby. The mother let her daughter out of the sack, and stuffed it with a dog, scorpions, vipers, bits of broken pots, and stones.

When the Marimo returned home with his sack, he opened it and was planning to cook and eat Tsélané. The dog and the vipers bit him, the scorpions stung him, the potshards wounded him, and the stones bruised him. He rushed out, threw himself into a mud heap, and was changed into a tree. Bees made honey in its bark, and in the springtime young girls came and gathered the honey for honey-cakes.

SOURCE: James G. Frazer, "A South African Red Riding-Hood," *Folk-Lore Journal* 7 (1889), 167.

This Bechuanan tale from South Africa resembles "The Wolf and the Kids" as well as "Little Red Riding Hood." It was recorded in 1842 by two French missionaries, who, as they stated in the preface to the account of their travels, hoped to "seek out unknown tribes, to open up communication with their chiefs, to mark out plans suitable for missionary stations, to extend the influence of Christianity and civilization" (Arbousset and Daumas 1968, vi). They also wished to give their readers some instances of the "old wives' stories with which mothers put their little ones to sleep, and inculcate betimes the first principles of Bechuana morality,—that is, submission to parental authority, and dread of the Marimos." The story was translated into English by the anthropologist James G. Frazer, author of The Golden Bough, *who published it in the British* Folk-Lore Journal *in 1888.*

Postcard showing a griot, or storyteller, with his calabash harp, an instrument that has as many as twenty-one strings. The photograph was taken by French ethnographer François-Edmond Fortier in Senegal, ca. 1904. *Courtesy of Daniela Moreau / Acervo África, São Paulo, Brazil.*

PART IV

TELLING TALES TODAY: ORAL NARRATIVES FROM AFRICA

In one of several rare instances of twentieth-century fieldwork that tried to capture story and context in an African culture, Mona Fikry-Atallah collected more than one hundred tales from the Wala of Wa (what is now northwestern Ghana). The quartet of tales below from the collection reminds us that passions run high when stories are told, and that the preoccupations of storytellers in Wa are not so very different from those of other cultures. "The Filial Son" stages oedipal dramas; "Men Deceive Women" takes us into the arena of sexual politics; "Know Your Relatives or Else You'll Be Mistaken for a Slave" resonates with the Grimms' story known as "The Goose Girl"; and "Which of the Three Men Was the Most Powerful?" rehearses a conundrum that can be found in many cultures.

For the Wala, tales are divided into *silima* (tales for entertainment) and *lasire* (historical narratives and legends). These narratives, as one elder put it, are "lies" that sound like "actual things." Fikry-Atallah describes the storytelling sessions she attended from 1966 to 1967 as follows: "Children are encouraged to tell tales; yet, invariably, in a group in which many men were present, the men would enthusiastically take over the session. Thus, most of the tales collected have been told by men. The tale sessions were always held in the evening after the men had returned from the farm and had had dinner. Huddled in a group in the center of the compound, men, women, and children (the latter two mainly listening) would tell their tales, one after

Two West African griots are shown with their musical instruments in an illustration from *Travels in the Timannee, Kooranko, and Soolima Countries in Western Africa*, the travel journal of British major Alexander Gordon Laing, published in London in 1825.

the other, for several hours at a stretch, with hardly any interruptions between tales. Tales would almost always begin with the simple phrase *N sinnii be*: 'My story exists, or, this is my story'" (Dorson 1972, 397–98). Many of the tales were interspersed with songs, and occasionally sessions began with riddles. The four tales that follow from Fikry-Atallah's fieldwork show us the mythical power and practical side to tales told at communal gatherings.

"The Filial Son" gives us a focused look at Freud's primal horde in *Totem and Taboo*, revealing the perils of throwing restraint to the winds and casting off the wisdom of tribal elders. Without them, the proverbial truths encapsulated in the coda to the tale would be lost. That wisdom, however, undermines itself by asserting that the tongue, producer of language, divides rather than binding and uniting. The storyteller calls his own words into question with a moral that makes language an instrument of divisiveness and discord.

In "Men Deceive Women" we have both a parable about marriage and a conversation about the terms of the tale told about pairing off. The groom-snake, both seductive and treacherous, captures the perils of marriage for women. Once again there is an emphasis on the double nature of language. In this case a "sweet tongue" has an effect both hypnotic and destructive. Its lies ensnare, entrap, and eventually prove fatal.

"Know Your Relatives or Else You'll Be Mistaken for a Slave" gives us a tale about betrayal and liberation. The hero, like his counterparts in many cultures, falls victim to a servant or slave and frees himself through song or story. By telling his troubles, he reveals the truth about his rival. The trading of items of clothing for the sake of survival is a theme found in Helen Bannerman's *The Story of Little Black Sambo* (1899), set in India, in which the boy gives up his red jacket, blue trousers, purple shoes, and green umbrella to pacify and vanquish a set of ferocious tigers.

Finally, in "Which of the Three Men Was the Most Powerful?" we have an example of a dilemma tale encoded with some social context. Fikry-Atallah reports that she and her assistants believed that the tale had been "badly told," but they decided to preserve it in print because it provided a "rare example of a story in riddle form." That the tale is unmediated and unedited makes it all the more interesting as an example of "authentic" folklore.

Mona Fikry-Atallah gives us story and context in compact form. For more expansive stories with a fuller elaboration of the social world in which the tales are told, Harold Scheub's *African Oral Narratives: Proverbs, Riddles, Poetry and Song* and *The African Storyteller: Stories from African Oral Traditions* are foundational, as are his many other published volumes.

The tales below are all adapted from: Mona Fikry-Atallah, "Wala Oral History and Wa's Social Realities," in *African Folklore*, ed. Richard Dorson, 237–53.

The frontispiece of *African Myths Together with Proverbs*, published in 1923, shows a storytelling audience in an unidentified setting in Africa. Collected and adapted by African American historian Carter G. Woodson, the tales and proverbs in the anthology were intended for American schoolchildren.

THE FILIAL SON

Told by a teacher named Mumuni, about forty years old

Here is my story also. Pay attention here. My story has no songs.

There lived once a wicked chief. Nobody liked him, because of his wickedness. He was wicked to old men and women. By pretending to be kind he tried to be popular with all the young men who lived in that country. When the chief won over the young men, they all liked him. One day, the chief called all the young men and told them, "My friends, don't you see?"

They asked, "What?"

"Don't you see the old men of this country?"

They asked, "What?"

"You should kill all of them. Everyone should kill his father."

Ai! (That they should all kill their fathers!)

As a result, everybody with an old father brought him to be killed. This one went and brought his father to be killed, the other went and brought his father to be killed. They killed all the old men, leaving only one. He was the father of a man who said no.

"Why should the chief kill all the old men and why should I send my old father to be killed?" He got down and went and dug a large hole and concealed it nicely. He sent his father there, where he had dug. He fetched wood and put it across the hole and then covered it with soil, making a small hole for air to pass through. At that time, they had finished killing all the old men. When the chief had executed them all, he called all the young men. "My friends, we have now finished killing all our old men. This is a cow I am giving to you. I am so happy we have got rid of all these old men, so go and kill the cow. When you have killed the cow, cut the best part of the meat and bring it to me. If you don't bring it, you yourselves are not safe." (That is all right!) Eh!

The young men rushed out and slaughtered the cow. Which is the best part of the meat of the cow? They were worried. They went and cut the liver and sent it to him. He asked whether or not that was the best part of the meat. They answered yes. They added part of the bile. He said that wasn't the best part of the meat and that they should go and find it quickly. The people became more worried. Every night the one young man secretly took food to his father. One day he took food to his father, who asked about the news of the town.

He said, "My father, now we are suffering. When we killed all the old men, the chief gave us a cow to go and kill. When we killed the cow, he said we must find both the sweetest and bitterest part of the meat and bring it to him. That if we do not bring them, we are not safe ourselves. This is what is worrying us."

The old man laughed, but asked him if he knew the sweet part of the meat. He said no. He again asked if he did not know the bitterest part. He said no.

"The sweetest and bitterest part is the tongue. When you go, cut the tongue and send it to him and say that the sweetest part of the meat is also the bitterest."

The man rushed home while all the people sat down, undecided about what to do. If something had not happened, they might have thrown the whole meat away and run away.

When the boy arrived, he said, "My friends, take the tongue of the cow in." They cut the tongue for him, and he took it to the chief's palace. He went and threw it down and said, "Chief, see the sweet part of the meat and the bitterest part also."

The chief sat down quietly and finally said, "You did not kill your father. Speak the truth. You have not killed your father."

He said, "It is the truth, I didn't kill him. When all the other young men were killing their fathers, I went and hid mine." He said, "You are the son of a wise old man. The sweetest and bitterest part of man is the tongue. As for that, all these young men are big fools. Why should somebody send his father to be killed? But if you want the sweetest part of the meat, find the tongue. Were it not for your tongue, you would not have an enemy; and it is also because of your tongue that you will not have a friend."

That is the end of my story.

MEN DECEIVE WOMEN

Narrated by Awusara, a young woman about twenty-five years old

Once there was a grown woman, but she refused to marry. She was offered many men, but she refused ("Then she was a prostitute!"), and roamed about. A python ("Woo!")

went and bathed himself and was sparkling like that. He became a black young man and went to her. The young woman said that she had seen her dear husband, yoo! He, too, said that he had also found his dear wife, yoo! They decided to give him water so that he could wash, but he refused and said that he had already washed before coming. They gave him a house to stay in. They went into that house. Soon after, he turned into a python and stretched all around the house. Then he took his mouth and put it at the doorway. Then he went and held the woman's legs. And the woman said, "My mother, my mother! The man spoke lies." (Repeated several times.)

The man swallowed the woman. My mother-in-law! The child is telling a lie. The child is lying, how can a man swallow a woman? And, yet, he was swallowing her. He swallowed her up to her thighs, and she said again, "My mother, my mother! The man spoke lies!"

He kept on swallowing until he reached the stomach. She cried again, "My mother, my mother! The man spoke lies!"

He continued to swallow, and it was not long before he reached the chest. She cried again, "My mother, my mother! The man spoke lies!"

He reached the woman's head, broke it off, and threw it in the house. Then he went out into the yard and kept on crawling, *kpari, kpari,*[1] here and there.

1 *kpari:* a word meant to convey the slithering manner in which a python moves

The following day dawned and the sun was high up, and it became hot, very hot. They called and called and called, but it was for nothing. They opened the door and found only the woman's head there.

And that one ends like that, too.

A conversation followed this tale, concerning its meaning:

A man: What is the meaning of the song?

A woman: As the man wants to marry a woman, he will keep on deceiving her until she's convinced, and as soon as they marry, the man will show his true character.

The man: So sweet that his tongue is able to talk!

Another woman: You keep on giving her promises but as soon as you marry her, you fail to keep them.

The man: Is the woman then foolish (for marrying that man, the python)?

The other woman: Not at all! When a man woos a girl, he tells her sweet words. After marrying her, the man changes.

KNOW YOUR RELATIVES OR ELSE YOU'LL BE MISTAKEN FOR A SLAVE

It is true! A man and his wife went and settled at a place like Kampala.[1] They had a child and a slave child. The man died but his senior brother was living in Wa. The man always used to say, "Hai! Always try to know the difference between your child and the slave boy." Yaa! After his death, his wife sent word to his senior brother in Wa saying that her son and the slave boy were coming. The mother bathed the child. She dressed him in shorts, a smock, and a hat. Then she gave the slave boy water in a gourd to carry.

1 *Kampala:* today the capital and largest city in Uganda

While they were walking, the boy sighed. "Uuhu!" the slave asked, "What?" The boy said he was thirsty. The slave boy said, "Uhuu! If you give me your smock, I will give you water to drink. If you don't then you won't have the water."

The boy took off his smock and gave it to him, and the slave boy, who put it on, gave him the water. They walked until they reached Nodzeli-boo, the valley. The boy said, "Ah! I am thirsty." The slave said, "Aah! Give me your shorts and I will also give you water." When he got the shorts and put them on, the slave boy gave the boy water to drink.

They continued walking until they reached Dr. Faar's house, in Wa. The boy again said, "Ehu!" The slave asked, "What?" The boy said, "I am thirsty." The slave said "Uuh! Take off your hat for me to wear or else I won't give you water to drink."

The boy gave him the hat and got the water. As soon as the boy finished with the water, the slave told him, "Umm! Hold this gourd."

Yaa! When they entered the house of the father's relatives, the child's uncle was sitting down. He told the slave to come and sit by his side, but he pushed away his own brother's son. Hai!

They farmed maize, and partridges would come and peck at the seeds. The following morning, the son was given cold food and a piece of firewood. He put them on his shoulder and went to the farm. As soon as he entered the farm he said, "Haa!" to scare the birds away.

Haa! Haa! Don't eat these things, don't eat!
The day my mother died, yaa!

They turned their real son into a slave, yaa!

But they made the slave their child, yaa!

They turned him into their son!

My father, wo! The day he died, woo! The elephant died.

He made a fire and then climbed up to the top of the shed. Then he took this thing and knocked on it.

Haa! Haa! Don't eat these things, don't eat!

The day my mother died, yaa!

They turned their real son into a slave, yaa!

But they made the slave their child, yaa!

They turned him into their son!

My father, wo! The day he died, woo! The elephant died.

He prepared his food and sat down until evening and then he returned home. The following day he was beaten to get up and he went again to the farm. He was again given cold food, firewood, and told to go. When he got to the farm, he opened his mouth:

Haa! Haa! Don't eat these things, don't eat!

The day my mother died, yaa!

They turned their real son into a slave, yaa!

But they made the slave their child, yaa!

They turned him into their son!

My father, wo! The day he died, woo! The elephant died.

After making his fire, he opened his mouth:

Haa! Haa! Don't eat these things, don't eat!

The day my mother died, yaa!

They turned their real son into a slave, yaa!

But they made the slave their child, yaa!

They turned him into their son!

My father, wo! The day he died, woo! The elephant died.

Hai! An old woman had gone to pick *saalung*[2] and sheanut seeds. When she stopped, she heard the boy. Then she went and told the uncle and his senior brother. She said, "To prove that what I have told you is true, you should wake him up early tomorrow morning, and then one of you should follow him and hide." The next day, yaa! They woke up the boy but only after his uncle had already gone to the farm. As soon as the boy got to the farm, he started his song:

2 *saalung:* vegetables

> Haa! Haa! Don't eat these things, don't eat!
> The day my mother died, yaa!
> They turned their real son into a slave, yaa!
> But they made the slave their child, yaa!
> They turned him into their son!
> My father, wo! The day he died, woo! The elephant died.

He went and made his fire.

> Haa! Haa! Don't eat these things, don't eat!
> The day my mother died, yaa!
> They turned their real son into a slave, yaa!
> But they made the slave their child, yaa!
> They turned him into their son!
> My father, wo! The day he died, woo! The elephant died.

Ei! The senior brother carried him and rushed home. He brought out the slave and beat him up here and there, threw him on the ground, and told him to go to the farm. They took off all his clothes.

Because of this, if you have any relatives somewhere, try to know them; otherwise, one day you will be taken for a slave. ("You are telling lies!"—"It is true!") I have finished; my story is finished.

WHICH OF THE THREE MEN WAS
THE MOST POWERFUL?

This is my riddle. My story! This one does not have a song. There were three young men. They roamed together and were friends. They each had lovers who lived about as far away as Accra. They had to cross water to go and visit them. One of them took a mirror and looked into it. He combed his hair and exclaimed, "Wh! You, my friends, I see our lovers lying there dead." The second one said, "Eh! See? I have this medicine which will be able to take us to our lovers." The third one said that he had medicine, a wisp, that could wake up their lovers. With the aid of the medicine they were able to reach Accra within minutes. Yaa! They had reached it. They pointed the wisp at their lovers and one of them asked them, "What were you doing? Come out and get dressed. Come out! What allowed you to do such mean things to us?"

Which of the three men was the most powerful? The one with the mirror looked into it and saw the girls dead, but could not go to them. The other one had medicine that could wake them up, but he himself couldn't get there. Which of the three was the greatest one? You show the one who was the most powerful. ("But it is the one who owned the medicine." "Ai! The owner of the mirror is powerful because he could see them, but he could not get to them. The owner of the wisp is the one.") Responsibility, Yaa! God says a person is responsible for himself. The Partridge says that it blames its killer more than the one who scared it. The one who saw their lovers was the most powerful. Because of that, the owner of the mirror is the one. Had he not seen them, would they have known that their lovers had died?

AFRICAN AMERICAN TALES

Lots of slaves brought over from Africa could fly. There folks can
fly even now. They tell me them people could do all kinda curious
things. They could even make farm tools work for em just by talkin
to em. And some of em could disappear at will. Wist! And they'd
be gone!!

Ole man Waldburg own slaves, and worked them hard and one
day they was hoein' in the field and the driver come over and two
of em was up under the shade tree and the hoe was working by
itself. The driver say "What's this?" and they say,

Kum Buba Yali
Jum Bumba Tambe,
Kum Kunka Yali, Kum Kuma Tambe

Quick like. Then they rize off the ground and flew back to Africa.
Nobody ever see em no more. My grandmother see that with her
own eyes. Anytime they wanted they would fly back to Africa, then
come back again to the plantation. They'd come back cause they
have chillun who didn't have the power to fly and had to stay on
the plantation.

Artist Carrie Mae Weems, born in 1953, interpreted the legend of the flying Africans in *Sea
Islands Series*, a group of landscape photographs and text panels exploring Gullah cultural
identity. "Untitled (Boone Plantation)" combines a contemporary photograph of slave cabins at
Boone Plantation in South Carolina with a text based on testimony about flying Africans collected
by the Georgia Writers' Project in the 1930s.

PART I

DEFIANCE AND DESIRE: FLYING AFRICANS AND MAGICAL INSTRUMENTS

If you surrendered to the air, you could ride it.
—TONI MORRISON, *Song of Solomon*

Like all charter narratives, tales about flying Africans set down collective beliefs and aspirations, in this case about escaping oppressive conditions, reuniting with kin, and returning home. Stories about literal flight from punishing labor in the fields can be found everywhere in the diaspora, with two different narrative twists on that miraculous feat. In the first, newly arrived Africans take one look at the conditions facing them in the New World and turn their backs on slavery. Dismayed and revolted, they take wing and fly back across the ocean. In the other, an African shaman or some other charismatic figure chants verses to physically depleted slaves laboring in the fields and enables them to fly. Like the lead bird in a migratory formation, he brings them back home.

Some versions of the story give us nuanced variations on the theme. Virginia Hamilton's "The People Could Fly" includes the following preamble before recounting the flight of slaves from a plantation: "They say the people could fly. Say that long ago in Africa, some of the people knew magic. And they would walk up on the air like climbing up on a gate. And they flew like blackbirds over the fields. Black, shiny wings flappin against the blue up there" (Hamilton 1985, 166). Hamilton's slaves, who left

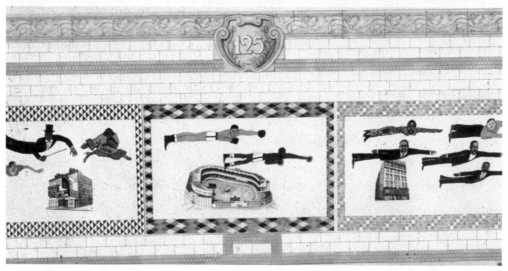

Artist Faith Ringgold, born in 1930, created this glass mosaic for the 125th Street station of the New York City subway. *Flying Home: Harlem Heroes and Heroines (Downtown and Uptown)*, depicts Harlem celebrities flying over city buildings. The title references the song "Flying Home," composed by Lionel Hampton and Benny Goodman, with lyrics written by Sid Robin.

their wings in Africa (the slave ships were too crowded to take them along), recover their power to fly by chanting "magic words" that sound like "whispers and sighs." Language—charged, incantatory, and active—becomes a tool of collective liberation.

Embedded in the notion of flight back to Africa is a double pathway, a realistic route leading to a suicidal plunge into the ocean that separates Old World from New and a mystical one enabling a spiritual journey back home. Legends about flying Africans often capitalize on both possibilities, leaving the question of survival open, perhaps in part because tragic plunge, like redemptive ascent, means release from the punitive labors of slavery. Flight offers a wonderfully compact double meaning, pointing not just to aeronautical activity but also to escape plain and simple. Some tellers are pessimists, revealing that "dey gits drown," while others credit slaves with supernatural powers that enable them to return to their homeland.

In *Rebel Destiny*, Melville and Frances Herskovits published an account foundational for the Dombi clan among the Sarmacca living in the country now known as Suriname. Yankuso, one of the leaders of the clan, told the following story:

> The Dombi Negroes had their man, too. He was Sabaku. He was leaving his people to run away from slavery. He was going into the bush. "If we do not meet again in life, we shall meet in death," he said. He had no boat in which to cross the river, so he went to Yank'o, the buzzard, and he asked him to carry him. "I have no home, O Yank'o," he said to the buzzard, "but I will get on your back, and there my home will be. You who fly high, who fly over water, and over the high bush, carry me to safety." (256–57)

The buzzard spirit hovers over a broad array of sacred and profane cultural practices ranging from blessing and healing to singing and dancing. That same buzzard, invoked and animated by words alone, will have the power to effect material transformations when it appears in the folklore of the Georgia coastal regions, once again carrying a slave back home.

In the 1930s, the Georgia Writers' Project interviewed residents about stories they had heard growing up and published them under the title *Drums and Shadows*. They collected a remarkable set of narratives about flying Africans, some harking back to what the Herskovitses had heard in Africa, some flavored by local customs and even commercial enterprises, including one about a con artist taking down payments for a set of wings. There were also tales about magical hoes and other farm tools that work by themselves, freeing slaves to go Somewhere Else.

In some of these oral accounts, slaves use incantatory language before taking flight; in others, they create a ring formation and run rapidly in circles. That tales about flying animated African American storytelling sessions becomes clear from Toni Morrison's assertion that everyone in her social circles was familiar with the trope of people flying. There may be no living witnesses but there are many true believers. Morrison emphasizes the double meaning of flight as ascent and escape, with escape haunted by the specter of death: "That was always part of the folklore of my life; flying was one of our gifts. . . . It is everywhere—people used to talk about it, it's in the spirituals and gospels. Perhaps it was wishful thinking—escape, death, and all that" (LeClair 1981).

Legends about flying Africans were linked historically to a group of Igbo (Ebo) captives whose faith embraced the notion that the soul returns to ancestral lands after the death of the body. In 1803 about seventy-five slaves were shipped from what is today Nigeria to Savannah, Georgia. The two coastal planters who purchased the slaves loaded them onto a small vessel named the *York* for transport to St. Simon's Island. What happened after that is not entirely clear. The slaves, who had been confined belowdeck, evidently rebelled against their captors, seized control of the ship, and forced the agents into the water. The Igbos then either jumped overboard and drowned or "took to the swamp" and committed suicide collectively. Ebo Landing in Glynn County, Georgia, takes its name from the tragic events that unfolded there. The Igbo mutiny has powerful symbolic importance as an act of resistance and as the first freedom march in African American history. In 2002, the site, which has no historical marker, was consecrated by Chukwuemeka Onyesoh from Nigeria. "I came here to evoke their spirits," Onyesoh movingly declared, "to take them back to Igboland."*

Suicide was not an uncommon practice among captive slaves on ships embarked on the Middle Passage. One chilling document describes a voyage from the coast of West Africa to Trinidad, with 118 survivors of the roughly 250 originally on board. Here is a vivid description of the captain's strategy for preventing slaves from committing suicide:

> Some of the slaves on board the same ship . . . had such an aversion to leaving their
> native places, that they threw themselves overboard, on an idea that they should

---

* http://www.ssiheritagecoalition.org/articles-about-ssaahc.html.

get back to their own country. The captain, in order to obviate this idea, thought of an expedient, viz: to cut off the heads of those who died, intimating to them, that if determined to go, they must return without their heads. The slaves were accordingly brought up to witness the operation. One of them seeing, when on deck, the carpenter, standing with his hatchet up ready to strike off the head of a dead slave, with a violent exertion got loose and flying to the place where the nettings had been unloosed . . . he darted overboard. (*Abstract* 1855, 53–54)

Given the squalid conditions onboard—shackles, darkness, hunger, disease—along with the barbaric behaviors on display, the logic of jumping into the ocean becomes compelling. Fears about the unknown (some captives believed that "these white men with horrible looks, red faces, and loose hair" were driven by cannibalism) as well as the horrors of a lifetime in bondage meant that many resorted to any means possible— hanging, self-starvation, drowning—to escape (Piersen 1977, 147).

Three key figures operate in the narrative logic of flying African tales: the African armed with a "password," the African American Slave as witness or participant, and the white Overseer, generally armed with a whip. As Olivia Smith Storey points out, the three figures each have a different relationship to language, technology, and power (Smith Storey 2004). The African's command of language offers a form of resistance to the Overseer's whip, and both instruments of power contrast with the Slave's utter lack of resources. Lacking access to ritualized forms of language and to the blunt instruments of power, the Slave is left with nothing more than ordinary words to tell this odyssey of withdrawal. Yet those words are not mere breath in the wind but the start of what Zora Neale Hurston called "a whisper," a whisper that transforms itself into hope and into the liberating power of songs and stories that create ancestral solidarity.

Moving and yet without any verbal pyrotechnics, the story "All God's Chillen Had Wings" is told in a terse style that lacks affect but builds up to a crescendo of emotional ferocity. Enriching and expanding reports heard from elders, the story dramatizes hope and elaborates on the liberating forces of faith, imagination, solidarity, or whatever we choose to call the power that enables spiritual levitation and elevation. We become thunderstruck auditors of the poetry describing slaves in flight.

The words used to enable flight resonate with sacred mysteries. "Their talk was strange to him [the Overseer]," we read in "All God's Chillen Had Wings." "*Kum . . . yali, kum buba tambe*," the old man Toby whispers to the young woman carrying a child, and she feels "the magic, the African mystery" in Virginia Hamilton's rendition of the story (169). "Dey gabble, gabble, gabble, an nobody couldn unduhstan um," we learn in Wallace Quarterman's recollections of the tale (*Drums and Shadows*, 159).

"Powerful magical language," Bronislaw Malinowski tells us, "is distinguished by a very high coefficient of weirdness" (220). Substituting performative energy for ordinary meaning, the unfamiliar sounds can take on transformational power, making it seem possible to do things with words, in this case to escape the whip and to become "light as a feather," as we read in one tale variant. The word becomes more powerful than the lash, and the story itself enacts a trope familiar to us today as the pen being mightier than the sword. In real life, of course, all of this was impossible, and yet the lesson about language is more profound than it seems at first sight, for the ability to find the right words, to communicate with passion, and to speak in compelling ways is exactly what enabled change in the postbellum era.

It is not surprising that the story of the flying Africans flashes out to us from the words of a spiritual ("All God's Chillun Got Wings") as well as from novels, films, and musical productions. It has roamed freely, crossing geographical and cultural borders and making itself at home in new media, putting on new disguises, creating fresh moods, and transforming itself into "something else." Toni Morrison's *Song of Solomon* (1997), Paule Marshall's *Praisesong for the Widow* (1984), Richard H. Perry's *Montgomery's Children* (1984), and Gayl Jones's *Song for Anniho* (2000) all rework aspects of the folktale, as do a number of films, ranging from Julie Dash's *Daughters of the Dust* (1991) to Haile Gerimsa's *Sankofa* (1994). Lionel Hampton's "Flying Home," a jazz composition inspired while he was nervously waiting to board a plane for the first time, was recorded in 1939, just a few years before Ralph Ellison published his short story "Flying Home." Maya Angelou brilliantly plays off the title "All God's Chillen Had Wings" in her autobiographical account, *All God's Children Need Traveling Shoes* (1986). And who can forget Robert Hayden's powerful poem "O Daedalus, Fly Away Home," with its line about "weaving a wish and a weariness together to make two wings."

If Jung, Freud, and other psychologists invoke flight as a universal expression of rapturous transcendence, African American writers inflect it differently, as a strategic means of escaping the bodily degradations and spiritual humiliations of slavery and its toxic legacies. Ralph Ellison complicates that point in multiple ways in his short story "Flying Home," which begins when an African American pilot crashes his plane and is found in a rural region by an old farmer and his son (Ellison 1996, 147–73). Drawing on multiple discursive fields—mythical (the stories about Icarus and about the phoenix) and biblical (the fortunate fall and the prodigal son)—Ellison constructs a story that positions flight as an act that can be seen, by turns, as hubristic, predatory, self-destructive, and transcendent. Challenging the idea of univocal meanings or messages, Ellison gives us symbolically charged fields, with a buzzard turning into the avian savior of African lore but also into the lethal force that brings the pilot's plane down.

Ellison's story begins and ends with the sun. Todd, presumably one of the famed Tuskegee Airmen, is blinded by it, unable to tell if the two faces staring at him after his crash are black or white. Jefferson, the old man who comes to his rescue, represents everything that has led Todd to deny his racial identity and cultural heritage, and yet he also becomes the means by which the young pilot reestablishes kinship ties, with a new "current of communication" (172) flowing between the two. As Ellison himself put it, "Todd comes to realize that Jefferson's folk wisdom (his own confabulations about flying) prepares him for a new way of seeing, a way of transcending the internal slavery he has imposed upon himself as well as the actual restrictions that white society places on him." The story ends with the buzzard, a "dark bird" that feeds off prey, gliding into the sun and glowing "like a bird of flaming gold" (173). Todd has secured for himself, through his hard-won understanding of flying as a failed means of self-actualization, a way back home.

In *Song of Solomon,* Toni Morrison writes out of deep conviction that identity is tied to ancestry and community. Milkman Dead, the protagonist of her novel, will not rise from the living dead until he recovers his past, remembering in ways that bring meaning and dignity to the lives of those who came before him. Returning to his ancestral roots, Milkman discovers exactly why he has always had a yearning to fly: "My great-granddaddy could fly . . . ! He didn't need no airplane. . . . He just took off. . . . No more cotton! No more bales! No more orders No more shit! He flew, baby. Lifted his beautiful black ass up in the sky and flew on home" (328). Milkman himself is empowered by the story—whether he will soar like Pegasus or perish like Icarus is not clear—and takes flight. For Morrison, that freedom to soar has a price, and that price falls on children, who experience loss but also find restitution through story: "All the men have left someone, and it is the children who remember it, sing about it, mythologize it, make it a part of their family history" (Taylor-Guthrie 46).

Milkman finally understands the song sung to him by his aunt Pilate (a homonym for *pilot*) about his great-grandfather Solomon, who "cuts across the sky" and flies to freedom. First, he must rid himself of the ballast of all the material things that drag him down, then he must retrace his ancestry, discovering both his personal and cultural heritage. Unaware of the stories told about his great-grandfather, Milkman suddenly understands his own fascination with flight:

> "Why do you call Solomon a flying African?"
>
> "Oh, that's just some old folks' lie they tell around here. Some of those Africans they brought over here as slaves could fly. A lot of them flew back to Africa. The one around here who did was this same Solomon, or Shalimar—I never knew which was right . . ."
>
> "When you say 'flew off' you mean he ran away, don't you? Escaped?"
>
> "No, I mean flew. Oh, it's just foolishness, you know, but according to the story he wasn't running away. He was flying. He flew. You know, just like a bird. Just stood up in the fields one day, ran up some hill, spun around a couple of times, and was lifted up in the air. Went right on back to wherever it was he came from." (322–23)

Song of Solomon is informed by African myths, cosmologies, and cultural practices in powerful ways. The "current of communication" valued by Ellison makes itself felt for Morrison in an even larger ancestral network that connects African Americans to their cultural heritage and to the rites and practices of their enslaved ancestors. Reviving, reworking, and restoring cultural legacies, Morrison drew not only on the lived experience of storytelling in her own social circles and communities but also on the written record of reminiscences in *Drums and Shadows.* Searching far and wide, she remembers not only her own past but reanimates a body of lore, making it new even as she preserves a tradition. Knitting together the vernacular with the literary, Morrison also reinvigorates the tradition of the talking book, the print volume that captures lore and transmits it to future generations. "The novel has to provide the richness of the past as well as suggestions of what the use of it is," she writes. "I try to create a world in which it is comfortable to do both, to listen to the ancestry and to mark out what might be going on sixty or one hundred years from now" (Ruas 1985, 28).

FLYING AFRICANS

THE FLYING MAN

I heard about the flying man up in Arkansas, at Jonesboro. The polices went up to him, and the faster they walked the faster he walked, until he just spread his arms and sailed right on off. And they never did catch him. Said he was faster than the planes. They told about him all through the South, in Alabama, Mississippi, Arkansas.

SOURCE: J. D. Suggs as told to Richard M. Dorson, *American Negro Folktales*, 279.

ALL GOD'S CHILLEN HAD WINGS

Once all Africans could fly like birds; but owing to their many transgressions, their wings were taken away. There remained, here and there, in the sea islands and out-of-the-way places in the low country, some who had been overlooked, and had retained the power of flight, though they looked like other men.

There was a cruel master on one of the sea islands who worked his people till they died. When they died he bought others to take their places. These also he killed with overwork, in the burning summer sun, through the middle hours of the day, although this was against the law.

One day, when all the worn-out Negroes were dead of overwork, he bought, of a broker in the town, a company of native Africans[1] just brought into the country, and put them at once to work in the cotton field.

He drove them hard. They went to work at sunrise and did not stop until dark. They were driven with unsparing harshness all day long, men, women, and children. There

1 *native Africans:* That the slaves are African born becomes an important point, for they have not yet, like the descendants of Africans living in the United States, lost the power to fly.

was no pause for rest during the unendurable heat of the midsummer noon, though trees were plenty and near. But through the hardest hours, when fair plantations gave their Negroes rest, this man's driver pushed the work along without a moment's stop for breath, until all grew weak with heat and thirst.

There was among them one young woman who had lately borne a child. It was her first; she had not fully recovered from bearing, and should not have been sent to the field until her strength had come back. She had her child with her, as the other women had, astraddle on her hip, or piggyback.

The baby cried. She spoke to quiet it. The driver could not understand her words.[2] She took her breast with her hand and threw it over her shoulder that the child might suck and be content. Then she went back to chopping knotgrass; but being very weak, and sick with the great heat, she stumbled, slipped and fell.

2 *The driver could not understand her words:* The slaves are set apart by speech that is incomprehensible and mysterious.

The driver struck her with his lash until she rose and staggered on.

She spoke to an old man near her, the oldest man of them all, tall and strong, with a forked beard. He replied; but the driver could not understand what they said; their talk was strange to him.

She returned to work; but in a little while, she fell again. Again the driver lashed her until she got to her feet. Again she spoke to the old man. But he said, "Not yet, daughter; not yet." So she went on working, though she was very ill.

Soon she stumbled and fell again. But when the driver came running with his lash to drive her on with her work, she turned to the old man and asked: "Is it time yet, daddy?" He answered: "Yes, daughter; the time has come. Go; and peace be with you!" . . . and he stretched out his arms toward her . . . so.

With that she leaped straight up into the air and was gone like a bird, flying over field and wood.

The driver and overseer ran after her as far as the edge of the field; but she was gone, high over their heads, over the fence, and over the top of the woods, gone, with her baby astraddle of her hip, sucking at her breast.

Then the driver hurried the rest to make up for her loss; and the sun was very hot indeed. So hot that soon a man fell down. The overseer himself lashed him to his feet. As he got up from where he had fallen, the old man called to him in an unknown tongue. My grandfather told me the words that he said;[3] but it was a long time ago, and I have forgotten them. But when he had spoken, the man turned and laughed at the overseer, and leaped up into the air, and was gone, like a gull, flying over field and wood.

Soon another man fell. The driver lashed him. He turned to the old man. The old man cried out to him, and stretched out his arms as he had done for the other two; and he, like them, leaped up, and was gone through the air, flying like a bird over field and wood.

Soon another man fell. The driver lashed him. He turned to the old man. The old man cried out to him, and stretched out his arms as he had done for the other two; and he, like them, leaped up, and was gone through the air, flying like a bird over field and wood.

Then the overseer cried to the driver, and the master cried to them both: "Beat the old devil! He is the doer!"

The overseer and the driver ran at the old man with lashes ready; and the master ran too, with a picket pulled from the fence, to beat the life out of the old man who had made those Negroes fly.

But the old man laughed in their faces, and said something loudly to all the Negroes in the field, the new Negroes and the old Negroes.

And as he spoke to them they all remembered what they had forgotten, and recalled the power which once had been theirs. Then all the Negroes, old and new, stood up together; the old man raised his hands; and they all leaped up into the air with a great shout; and in a moment were gone, flying, like a flock of crows, over the field, over the fence, and over the top of the wood; and behind them flew the old man.

The men went clapping their hands; and the women went singing; and those who had children gave them their breasts; and the children laughed and sucked as their mothers flew, and were not afraid.

The master, the overseer, and the driver looked after them as they flew, beyond the wood, beyond the river, miles on miles, until they passed beyond the last rim of the world and disappeared in the sky like a handful of leaves. They were never seen again.

Where they went I do not know; I never was told. Nor what it was that the old man said . . . that I have forgotten. But as he went over the last fence he made a sign in the master's face, and cried "Kuli-ba! Kuli-ba!" I don't know what that means.

But if I could only find the old wood sawyer, he could tell you more; for he was there at the time, and saw the Africans fly away with their women and children. He is an old, old man, over ninety years of age, and remembers a great many strange things.[4]

4 *remembers a great many strange things:* The wood sawyer, or carpenter, is presented as witness and as the repository of cultural memory. The narrator himself is a griot of sorts, telling a tale that has been passed down from one generation to the next.

SOURCE: Told by Caesar Grant of John's Island, carter and laborer. Published in John Bennet's *Doctor to the Dead* (1943–1946), 137–42.

John Bennett (1865–1956) was a writer and illustrator of children's books who moved from Ohio to New York City and finally settled in Charleston, South Carolina. For nearly three decades, he collected stories told at dusk on front porches, sometimes rendering them in Standard English, sometimes in Gullah dialect. His Doctor to the Dead: Grotesque Legends and Folk Tales of Old Charleston *collects twenty-three narratives told by South Carolina storytellers. The excerpt below is from his introduction to the volume, and it reveals something about Caesar Grant, the man who told the story "All God's Chillen Had Wings."*

Forty-five years ago, while a transient resident of the ancient city of Charleston, South Carolina, I chanced upon traces of bizarre legendry, folk story, fable and myth, unobserved by students, unnoted by residents, and untouched by travelers, remnants of a body of folklore already far decayed and rapidly passing out of existence.

These legends and tales differed markedly from the humorous tales of Uncle Remus; yet were hardly less interesting in their revelation of folk mind; yet no one had given them the slightest attention or exhibited the least interest in them. . . .

Sometimes all that remained was the emptied husk of a long-disintegrated tale. Of some only the beginning remained; of others, an end without a beginning. It was often necessary to assemble the fragments of an almost-forgotten story, bit by bit, from spokesmen in widely separated social groups—housemaids, butlers, nurses, washerwomen, coachmen, stable boys, day laborers, and fishermen. . . .

Many were survivals of long-forgotten but actual scandals; such shady reminiscences as are picturesquely referred to by dark-faced storytellers as "jay-bird gossip" or "mockingbird tales." . . .

There emerged from the piebald company a handful of folktales and legends which were more than disreputable scandals, and not merely fanciful fairy tales, but tales having their source in traditions of characters and events once actual, but by primitive superstition and naïve credulity metamorphosed beyond recognition, stories not of things which ever were, but of things which never were, their appeal being not to reason but to unreason. . . .

I regret that I cannot reproduce the scenes in which these stories were set, nor picture my two old black friends, Caesar Grant and Walter Mayrant, sitting on my back porch steps on a moonlit summer evening, smoking their corncob pipes and telling stories for our mutual amusement.

Their telling was simplicity itself. No tale began with a grandiloquent Oriental preamble, "In the name of Allah, the All-Powerful, I, Abou Hussein el Khurassan," but quietly, when their pipes were well lighted and glowing in the dusk: "Now let's we talk about one time, fac' fo' fac' an' true fo' true, lak de Lo'd talk een de Gospel." Or, as once, with the most delightful opening of all: "A long time ago, befo' yestidy was bo'n, an' befo' bygones was uster-bes."

Frequently the end of a tale was simply "that's all." Except when the authenticity of a particularly bizarre tale was affirmed by the statement: "Ah knows dat ter to be a fac', 'cause Ah saw it wid ma own two eye."

ALL GOD'S CHILLUN GOT WINGS

I got a robe
All o' God's chillun got a robe.
When I get to heab'n I'm going to put on my robe
I'm goin' to shout all ovah God's Heab'n
Heab'n, Heab'n
Ev'rybody talkin' 'bout heab'n ain't goin' dere

Heab'n, Heab'n
I'm goin' to shout all ovah God's Heab'n.

I got a-wings, you got-a wings
All o' God's chillun got-a wings.
When I get to heab'n I'm goin' to put on my wings
I'm goin' to fly all ovah God's Heab'n
Heab'n, Heab'n
I'm goin' to fly all ovah God's Heab'n.

I got a harp, you got a harp
All o' God's chillun got a harp.
When I get to heab'n I'm goin' to take my harp
I'm goin' to play all ovah God's Heab'n
Heab'n, Heab'n
Ev'rybody talkin' 'bout heab'n ain't goin' dere
Heab'n, Heab'n
I'm goin' to play all ovah God's Heab'n.

I got shoes, you got shoes
All o' God's chillun got shoes
When I get to heab'n I'm goin' to put on my shoes
I'm goin' to walk all ovah God's Heab'n
Heab'n, Heab'n
Ev'rybody talkin' 'bout heab'n ain't goin' dere.
Heab'n, Heab'n
I'm goin' to walk all ovah God's Heab'n.

This well-known African American spiritual takes up the theme of flight in a Christian setting, turning the destination into Heaven rather than Africa. Its title inspired Eugene O'Neill's 1924 play about an abusive white woman who destroys the career of her black husband.

SWING LOW, SWEET CHARIOT

Swing low, sweet chariot,
Coming for to carry me home,
Swing low, sweet chariot,
Coming for to carry me home.

I looked over Jordan and what did I see
Coming for to carry me home,
A band of angels, coming after me,
Coming for to carry me home.

If you get there before I do,
Coming for to carry me home,
Tell all my friends I'm coming too,
Coming for to carry me home.

Swing low, sweet chariot,
Coming for to carry me home,
Swing low, sweet chariot,
Coming for to carry me home.

*Conceived by Wallis Willis, a Choctaw living in Oklahoma, the words
and melody were transcribed by a minister named Alexander Reid. The
Fisk Jubilee Singers popularized the song when they toured the United
States, and it played an important role in promoting solidarity during
the 1960s Civil Rights Movement.*

NOW LET ME FLY

Way down yonder in de middle o' de fiel',
Angels workin' at de chariot wheel,
Not so partic'lar 'bout workin' at de wheel,
But I jes' wan-a see how de chariot feel.

I got a mother in de Promise Lan',
Ain't goin' to stop till I shake her han',
Not so partic'lar 'bout workin' at de wheel,
But I jes' wan-a get up in de Promise Lan'.

Meet dat Hypocrite on de street,
First thing he do is to show his teeth.
Nex' thing he do is to tell a lie,
An' de bes' thing to do is to pass him by.

Now let me fly,
Now let me fly,
Now let me fly
Into Mount Zion, Lord, Lord.

SOURCE: Langston Hughes and Arna Bontemps, *The Book of Negro Folklore*, 301.

Like "Swing Low, Sweet Chariot," this spiritual holds forth the possibility of returning to the Promised Land, in this case to Mount Zion, which can designate a hill in Jerusalem or the land of Israel. Tropes from the story of Moses, the release of the Israelites from slavery, and the return to the Promised Land became a not so veiled way of talking about liberation from slavery in the United States.

LITTLE BLACK SAMBO FROM GUINEA

A long time ago, before the Negroes were freed, there was a slave named Sambo, owned by a planter whose big house was near Gourdvine Creek in Union County, North Carolina.

Now Sambo was no ordinary slave. Others on the plantation were the sons and daughters of slaves. But this Sambo had been smuggled in by a blackbirder[1] who had captured his cargo in Africa.

This little old Sambo looked wild and afraid at the slave market in Fayetteville where the planter brought him. The old folks who tell the story about Sambo say that the planter was a kindhearted man. He felt sorry for the strange black man from Guinea who had come to a strange land. So he didn't work Sambo as a field hand. He let him work in the big house so Sambo could learn the English language from the white folks.

[1] *Blackbirder:* Blackbirder was a name used to designate men who kidnapped laborers for plantations. The term was associated in particular with the sugar cane industry. It originated in Australia, where *blackbird* is a slang term for indigenous peoples.

When the bobwhite and the whippoorwill and the red fox would talk from the woods, Sambo would answer them in their own language. He'd often ask the white folks where Guinea was. The white man would take a globe map and tell Sambo that the world was round and that Guinea was on the other side of the earth from Gourdvine Creek.

There was a time when the fever struck whites and Negroes, too. Sambo told the white folks that he was sick of the fever. He said he'd seen a dark man at the edge of the woods—and that the dark man was death.

The white man told Sambo that this was a lot of foolishness, but he wiped the tears away from his eyes when Sambo told him he had to die.

Then Sambo asked his master again where Guinea was. "Is it right straight down, Massa?" he asked.

The planter nodded his head.

Then Sambo said, "Mass, dig my grave way out in the woods, and don't let nobody traipse around it. Bury me on my face, because maybe if I look that way sometime, I'll git back to Guinea. If a man yearns for a place maybe he'll get back. Massa, that may take a long time, and that's why I don't want nobody to traipse around my grave."

So when Sambo died the planter had the field hands dig a grave far out into the woods. Then he put out the word that nobody was to traipse around Sambo's grave.

The planter finally died, too, and after freedom came, the planter's family sold the plantation and scattered to the four winds. As the years went by many people forgot that Sambo didn't want anyone to traipse around his grave.

Then strange things began to happen in the woods where Sambo was buried near Gourdvine Creek. The occurrences were told about by fox, coon, and possum hunters. If the hounds chased their quarry into Sambo's woods the dogs would come howling back to their masters, quivering with fear.

Some of the old folks in Union County remembered that they had heard their fathers and grandfathers tell the story about Sambo, who yearned to go back to Guinea. Hunters and hounds feared Sambo's woods for more than a hundred years.

"But today the hounds run fast and free along Gourdvine Creek," said an old man I was talking with recently, who lives near Sambo's woods.

I guess the hounds used to feel Sambo's homesickness. But now, since the hounds run fast and free, I guess Sambo finally got back to Guinea.

SOURCE: J. Mason Brewer, *American Negro Folklore*, 48–49. Told by Heath Thomas.

Born in 1896, J. Mason Brewer received a master's degree from Indiana University, where he studied with the distinguished folklorist Stith Thompson. He was the first African American to be elected to the American Folklore Society, and he taught for many years at Livingstone College in North Carolina. In his preface to the anthology from which this tale is taken, he laments the fact that a "rich strata of Negro folk phenomena still remain undiscovered." "When these are unearthed and brought to light," he added, "they will constitute a meaningful and worthy supplement to the great mass of Negro folk material that already exists." Brewer felt confident that the folktales he had collected were derived from an African culture "that flourished in spite of environmental disadvantages" (ix).

FLYING AFRICANS

Now Sjaki wanted to see the flying slaves. Sjaki had heard of the flying slaves who flew and made an awful noise once a year. And this particular night, Sjaki's brother had explained was the night of the flying slaves, since it was the First of July and Emancipation Day celebration. . . . [Slavery was abolished in Suriname in July 1863.]

"But you don't know it all," said the man-bird. . . . "It was a long time ago, many years before Emancipation, that word had gone round that those of us who could stop eating salt would be able to fly back to Africa. So we all went on a salt-free diet. But our wives and children were forced to eat food in the houses where they worked. So it became clear that it would be mostly us men who would fly back. Our children did not want to lose us. You know what happened next. . . . . Now all we can do is to return every year and shout a warning to our people. We warn them that they cannot fly."

SOURCE: Petronella Breinburg, "Sjaki and the Flying Slaves," in *Legends of Suriname*, 32–38.

> *Salt was associated with diets in white cultures, and eating it implied the loss of the ability to return home. The story of Sjaki offers an explanation for the departure of men and why women and children are left behind.*

MAGIC INSTRUMENTS

Every once in a while, inanimate objects go wild in folktales. Walt Disney's 1940 animated film *Fantasia* popularized the story of "The Sorcerer's Apprentice," in which an apprentice, unable to stop an enchanted broom from fetching water, floods his master's workshop. In the first of the two tales below, a magical hoe migrates from Africa across the Atlantic and makes its way back again in a mysterious allegory of a tool and its enchanted origins.

"The Do-All Ax" begins by invoking the story of flying Africans. As in legends about flying Africans, incantatory language works magic with the hoe, setting it in motion and enabling it to execute agricultural work. Kwako's carelessness and mischief-making lead to a world in which people must labor by the sweat of their brow. Stories about flying Africans deliver a utopian message about nostalgia, solidarity, song, and a collective return home. The tale about the Magical Hoe, by contrast, gives us the dark underside to magic, showing how its invocation can quickly create a form of mad excess that makes matters worse than they were at the start. Magic can always cut two ways.

HOW THE HOE CAME TO ASHANTI

Kwaku Ananse, the Spider, and his children, Tikononkono (Big-big-head), Afudotwedotwe (Belly-like-to-burst), Nyiwankonfwea (Thin-shanks), lived at home along with Kotoko, the Porcupine. When the Porcupine began to work for the first time on a new farm, Kwaku, the Spider, begged for a piece of the farm to cultivate. And Kotoko gave him some. While Kwaku Ananse and his children were hoeing, the Porcupine

"How the Hoe Came to Ashanti," from R. S. Rattray, ed., *Akan-Ashanti Folk-Tales*, 1930. By permission of Oxford University Press.

went home to eat. And when the Porcupine returned, he took up his hoe and began to loosen the ground, raising his voice in song while he worked:

> Gyensaworowa, Kotoko saworowa,
> Gyensaworowa, Kotoko saworowa,
> Gyensaworowa.

The hoe turned over a huge tract of land. Then they all stopped working, left the field, and the Porcupine took the hoe and hid it. Kwaku, the Spider, saw where he had put it. He said, "This hoe that I have seen, tomorrow, very, very early I shall come and take it to do my work." Truly, very, very, very early, the Spider went and got it; he took it to his farm. Now the Spider did not know how to make it stop, and he raised his song:

> Gyensaworowa, Kotoko saworowa,
> Gyensaworowa, Kotoko saworowa,
> Gyensaworowa.

And the hoe continued hoeing and would not stop. And it hoed until it traveled far, far away. Now it reached the Sea-god's water. From there it reached the land of White-men-far, and the white men took it, and looked at it, and made others like it. That is how many European hoes came among the Ashanti. Formerly it was only Kotoko, the Porcupine, who had one.

This, my story, which I have told, if it be sweet, or if it be not sweet, take some elsewhere, and let some come back to me.

SOURCE: R. S. Rattray, ed., *Akan-Ashanti Folk-Tales*, 43.

THE DO-ALL AX

No, don't know as I can tell you anything with magic in it. How you expect I can tell you about magic when they ain't no such thing? Of course, there's two-three exceptions, like those flyin' slaves in the old days. Folks say there was a couple of field hands down around Johnson's Landing who didn't like the way they was bein' treated as slaves, and they just flapped their arms and took off. When last seen they was over the water headed east like a ball of fire.

Then there was the do-all ax. It sure got magic in it, what I mean.

The way it was, in the old days there was a man who had this do-all ax. When it was time to clear the trees off the ground to do some plantin', this man'd take his ax and his rockin' chair and go out and sit down in the shade. Then he'd sing a kind of song:

> Bo kee meeny, dah ko dee,
> Field need plantin', get off my knee.

That ax would just jump off his knee and start choppin' wood without no one holdin' onto the handle or anything. All by itself it went around cuttin' down the timber till the field was cleared. Then it chopped up the trees into stovewood lengths and threw 'em in a pile in the barnyard.

And next thing you know, this ax turn itself into a plow and went to plowin' up the field to make ready for plantin'. And when that's done, the plow turn into a corn planter and plant the corn.

All the time this man who owned it was rockin' back and forth in the shade, fannin' himself with a leaf. Well, that corn was sure-enough magic corn, grew up almost as fast as it went in the ground; little sprouts start to pop out 'fore the sun went down.

'Bout this time the man sing another song:

> Kah bo denny, brukko bay
> Time for dinner, quit this play.

"The Do-All Ax," from Harold Courlander, ed., *Terrapin's Pot of Sense*, 1957. Reprinted by permission of the Emma Courlander Trust.

Then the corn planter turned itself back into an ax and stopped workin'.

Well, three-four days later that corn was tall and ready for hoein'. Man went out with his ax, and it turned into a hoe. It went up and down the rows by itself, hoein' corn till the whole field was done. Next week the man came back and the hoe turn itself into a corn knife to cut all them stalks down. You see, the whole job was done just by this here magic ax.

Other folks used to come around and watch all these goin's-on. Everybody figure if they only had an ax like that, life would be a powerful lot better for them.

There was one man named Kwako who wanted that ax more'n anyone else. Said he reckoned he'd about die if he didn't get that ax. And when there wasn't nobody home one time, this Kwako went in and took it. Figured he'd get his own work done and then bring the ax back and wouldn't nobody know the difference.

He ran home and got his own rockin' chair and went out in the field. Laid the ax across his lap and sang like the other man did:

Bo kee meeny, dah ko dee,
Field need plantin', get off my knee.

Man, that ax went to work. Chopped down all the trees, cut the wood up in stove-wood lengths, and stacked it by the house. Then it turned itself to a plow and plowed the ground. Then it turned to a corn planter and planted corn. 'Bout the time it was done plantin', the corn sprouts was already pokin' through the ground.

Kwako he was mighty pleased when he see all that. He sat rockin' back and forth in the shade enjoyin' himself real good. So when the corn was all planted he hollered, "That's enough for now, come on home." But corn planter didn't pay no attention, just kept jumpin' all around. Kwako hollered, "Didn't you hear what I said? Quit all this foolishness and come on home." Trouble was, he didn't know the song to stop it. He should have said:

Kah bo denny, brukko bay
Time for dinner, quit this play.

But he didn't know the words, and he just kept hollerin', and the corn planter just kept jumpin' around, plantin' corn, every-which-way till the seed was all gone. Then it turned into a hoe and started hoein' up the field. Now that corn wasn't tall enough to be hoed, and it got all chopped to little pieces. Man, that field was a mess. Kwako he ran back and forth tryin' to catch the hoe, but he couldn't make it, hoe moved around too fast. Next thing you know, the hoe turned into a corn knife and started cuttin' in the air. But wasn't no corn to cut. So it went over in the cotton field and started cuttin' down the cotton. Just laid that cotton field low. And then it moved west, cuttin' down everything in the way. And when last seen it was followin' the settin' sun. After that it was gone for good.

Since that time there hasn't ever been a magic do-all ax in this part of the world, and folks has to do their farmin' the hard way.

But get it out of your head that there's magic things roundabout. What I told you is true, but it's an *exception*.

SOURCE: Harold Courlander, ed., *Terrapin's Pot of Sense*, 80–83.

TESTIMONIALS ABOUT FLYING AFRICANS

TESTIMONIALS ABOUT FLYING AFRICANS FROM *DRUMS AND SHADOWS: SURVIVAL STUDIES AMONG THE GEORGIA COASTAL NEGROES*

The names of the informants are followed by the name of the towns in which they resided.

JACK WILSON, OLD FORT

"Muh mothuh use tuh tell me bout slabes jis bring obuh frum Africa wut hab duh supreme magic powuh. Deah wuz a magic pass wud date dey would pass tuh udduhs. Ef dey belieb in dis magic, dey could scape an fly back tuh Africa. I hab a uncle wut could wuk dis magic. He could disappeah lak duh win, jis walk off duh plantation an stay way fuh weeks at a time. One time he git cawnuhed by duh putrolmun an he jis walk up to a tree an he say, 'I tink I go intuh dis tree.' Den he disappeah right in duh tree" (22–23).

ANONYMOUS, SPRINGFIELD

"Ise heahd lots uh stories bout folks wut could fly. Some time back I wuz libin in Woodville wen a man come tru deah. He wuz from Liberty County. Dis man talk lot bout duh story uh duh Africans wut could fly. He say all dis wuz true. He say he wuz takin awduhs fuh wings an dey wuz all yuh need tuh fly. A peah uh wings coss twenty-five dolluhs. Duh man take yuh measure an a five dolluh deposit an say he collec duh bal-

---

"Testimonials About Flying Africans," from Georgia Writers' Project, *Drums and Shadows: Survival Studies among the Georgia Coastal Negroes*, 1940. By permission of University of Georgia Press.

ance wen he delibuh duh wings. Lots uh people gib deah awduh fuh wings, cuz all deah libes dey been heahin bout folks wut could fly. Duh man jis go roun takin awduhs an collectin five dolluhs. Das duh las any ub us ebuh heah uh duh man aw duh wings" (53).

PAUL SINGLETON, TIN CITY

"Muh daddy use tuh tell me all duh time bout folks wut could fly back to Africa. Dey could take wing and jis fly off" (31).

MOSE BROWN, TIN CITY

"My gran use tuh tell me bout folks flyin back tuh Africa. A man an his wife wuz brung from Africa. Wen dey fine out dey wuz slaves an got treat so bahd, dey jis fret an fret. One day dey wuz standin wid some uddah slabes an all ub a sudden dey say, 'We gwine back tuh Africa. So goodie bye, goodie bye.' Den dey flied right out uh sight" (32).

JAMES MOORE, TIN CITY

"Deah's lots uh strange tings dat happen. I seen folks disappeah right fo muh eyes. Jis go right out uh sight. Dey do say dat people brought fum Africa in slabery times could disappeah an fly right back tuh Africa. Frum duh tings I see myself I blieb dat dey could do this" (34).

SERINA HALL, WHITE BLUFF

"Muh ma tell me many times bout a man an his wife wut could wuk conjuh. Anytime dey want tuh dey would fly back tuh Africa and den come back agen tuh duh plantation. Dey come back cuz dey hab some chillun wut didn hab duh powuh tuh fly an hab tuh stay on duh plantation. One uh duh daughtuhs wanted tuh lun fly an wuk cunjuh. Duh faduh tell uh she hab tuh lun duh passwud, den she hab tuh kill a man by conjuh. Attuh dis den she would hab duh powuh. Duh magic passwud mean sumpm like dis, 'Who loss duh key Branzobo?'" (88).

SHAD HALL, SAPELO ISLAND

"Doze folks could fly too. Dey tell me deah's a lot ub um, wut wuz bring heah an dey ain much good. Duh massuh was fixin tuh tie um up tuh whip um. Dey say, 'Massuh, yuh ain gwine lick me,' an wid dat dey runs down tuh duh ribbuh. Duh obuhseeuh [overseer] he sho tought he ketch um wen dey get tuh duh ribbuh. But fo he could git tuh um, dey riz up in duh eah an fly way. Dey fly right back tuh Africa. I tink dat happen on Butler Ilun [Island]" (172).

PRISCILLA MCCULLOUGH, DARIEN

"Duh slabes wuz out in duh fiel wukin. All ub a sudden dey git tuhgedduh an staht tuh moob roun in a ring. Roun dey go fastuhnfastuh. Den one by one dey riz up an take wing an fly lak a bud [bird]. Duh obuhseeuh [overseer] heah duh noise an he come out an he see duh slabes riz up in duh eah and fly back tuh Africa. He run an he ketch duh las one by duh foot jis as he wuz bout tuh fly off. I dohn know ef he wuz neah nuff tuh pull um back down an keep um frum goin off" (158).

WALLACE QUARTERMAN, DARIEN

"I membuhs one boatload uh seben aw eight wut come down frum Savannah. Dat wuz jis a lill befo duh waw. Robbie McQueen wuz African an Katie an ole man Jacob King, dey's all African. I membuhs um all. Ole man King he lib till he ole, lib till I hep bury um. But yuh caahn unduhstan much wut deze people say. Dey caahn unduhstan yo talk an you caahn unduhstan dey talk. Dey go 'quack, quack, quack,' jis as fas as a hawse kin run, an muh pa say, 'Ain' no good tuh lissen tuh um.' Dey git long all right but yuh know dey wuz a lot ub um wut ain stay down yuh. . . .

"Ain yuh heah bout um? Well, at dat time Mr. Blue he wu duh obuhseeuh an Mr. Blue put um in duh fiel, but he couldn do nuttn wid um. Dey gabble, gabble, gabble, an nobody couldn unduhstan um an dey didn know how tuh wuk right. Mr. Blue he go down one mawnin wid a long whip fuh tuh whip um good. . . . Dey's foolish actin. He got tuh whip um, Mr. Blue, he ain hab no choice. Anyways, he whip um good an dey gits tuhgedduh an stick duh hoe in duh fiel an den say 'quack, quack, quack,' an dey riz up in duh sky an tun hesef intuh buzzuds an fly right back tuh Africa. . . . Dey sho lef duh hoe stannin in duh fiel an dey riz right up an fly right back tuh Africa. . . .

"I ain seen um. I bin tuh Skidaway, but I knowed plenty wut did see um, plenty wut wuz right deah in duh fiel wid um an seen duh hoe wut dey lef stickin up attuh dey done fly way" (154–55).

BEN SULLIVAN

"I ain heahd specially bout him [old Alexander] but Ise heahd plenty Africans talk bout flyin. Deah's plenty ub em wut could fly. I sho heahd em talk bout great doins an Ise heahd ole Israel say duh hoe could wuk by itself ef yuh know wut tuh say tuh it. It bin a long time since Ise tought bout tings lak dat, but ef uh studies bout em, dey comes back tuh me" (185).

CARRIE HAMILTON

"I hab heah uh dem people," said this seventy year old woman, who has the tall, heavy frame of a plantation hoe hand. "Muh mudduh use tuh tell me bout em wen we set in du city mahket sellin vegetubbles an fruit. She say dat deah wuz a man an he wife an dey git fooled abode a slabe ship. Fus ting dey know dey wuz sole tuh a plantuh on St. Helena. So one day wen all duh slabe wuz tuhgedduh, dis man and he wife say, 'We gwine back home, goodie bye, goodie bye,' an jis like a bud they flew out uh sight" (42).

TESTIMONIALS ABOUT FLYING AFRICANS FROM MONICA SCHULER, *"ALAS, ALAS, KONGO"*: *A SOCIAL HISTORY OF INDENTURED AFRICAN IMMIGRATION INTO JAMAICA, 1841–1865*, 93–96.

The names of the informants are followed, when available, by the place and date on which they were interviewed.

CHARLES MCKEN, ARCADIA, ST. THOMAS, 3 JULY 1971

"They couldn't go back . . . because they bring down the thing that they call mackerel, herring—a salt—we call mungwa—and after they eat it, they couldn't go back. . . . When the people come a' Jamaica and find out it . . . wasn't so [good] . . . they want to go away back to Africa. Some fly. They fly a' wing—like a dove—and they fly from Jamaica back to Africa."

ISHMAEL WEBSTER, WATERWORKS, WESTMORELAND, 8 AUGUST 1971

"And why you hear they say they fly away . . . they couldn't stand the work when the taskmaster flog them; and they get up and they just sing their language, and they clapping their hands—so—and they just stretch out, and them gone—so—right back. And they *never* come back."

ESTEBAN MONTEJO, CUBA

"They flew through the sky and returned to their own lands. The Musundi Congolese were the ones that flew the most; they disappeared by means of witchcraft. They did the same as the Canary Island witches, but without making a sound. There are those who say the Negroes threw themselves into rivers. This is untrue. The truth is they fastened a chain to their waists which was full of magic. That was where their power came from."

JAMES COLLIER, BROWNVILLE

"I have heard about a magic hoe that folks put in the ground. They speak certain words tuh it; then the hoe goes ahead an cultivates the gahden without anyone touching it. They jist tell it tuh do the wuk and it duz."

PART II

FEARS AND PHOBIAS:
WITCHES, HANTS, AND SPOOKS

Most reports about flying Africans feature heroic men who defy the chains of slavery and take flight. Some accounts describe wise old men, mysterious adepts, shaman figures, or charismatic leaders who, because they control language and know the "password," enable a group of slaves to take wing.

The dark doubles of courageous flying Africans are witches, sinister figures who are predominantly female and specialize in terrifying and torturing the victims they "ride" rather than liberating them. In Mark Twain's *The Adventures of Huckleberry Finn* (1884), Jim is famously the victim of witches, who ride him "all over the world, and tired him most to death, and his back was all over saddle-boils" (8). Affiliated with hoodoo, witches possess a set of ritualized domestic practices designed to assault the senses, inflict bodily pain, and kill desire. Strategies designed to identify witches and ward them off are enumerated in tales told about their powers.

Belief in the existence of witches can be traced back to African myths about creatures that take human form during the day and change into animals at night. Melville Herskovits writes about the Dahomey belief in *azondato*, "dangerous individuals who turn into bats at night . . . and go forth to hold council together or to perform their dark deeds." In Nigeria, witches (*amozu*) and wizards (*ogboma*) are said to take the form of owls, vultures, and night-birds. They can enter houses through the smallest cracks and attack their victims at night (Meek 1970, 79–80).

African American witches did not become a part of the historical record, but they were a vibrant part of oral traditions and turn up in folklore as agents of evil, delighting in inflicting suffering, creating misery, and wreaking havoc. Often they act on their own, but they also stand ready to assist the desperate in exacting revenge, turning tables, or upending the status quo. Unlike the witches of other North American cultures, they are only peripherally affiliated with the devil, who can be invoked in the same breath with them but is rarely connected to them in any kind of meaningful alliance. Because witches offered a compelling explanation for a run of bad luck, they created a booming business for conjurers, who specialized in good-luck charms, talismans, brews, roots, and potions for reversing spells. Witches came to embody countercultural norms and subversive pleasures. Driven by a spirit of unruliness and disorder, they often acted opportunistically, tormenting their victims at random, wherever they could slip in undetected and test their powers.

Both witches and conjurers entered into hoodoo rituals found in the diaspora, in places ranging from Louisiana and Brazil to Puerto Rico and Haiti. Hoodoo is a version of *voodoo* or *voudou*, a term derived from *vodun*, a collective designation for the religious practices from tribes of coastal West Africa. As the dominant source of syncretic religions in the diaspora, it led an underground existence that competed with official faiths authorized by slaveholders in the South. Zora Neale Hurston emphasized the furtive, fugitive nature of the belief system: "Nobody knows for sure how many thousands in America are warmed by the fire of hoodoo, because the worship is bound in secrecy. It is not the accepted theology of the Nation and so believers conceal their faith" (Hurston, *Mules and Men*, 185).

There were many reasons to conceal faith in conjure, and foremost among them was the fact that conjure offered an alternative not only to official faiths but also to dominant ideologies. Lawrence Levine points out that faith in conjure suggested the existence of forces more powerful than what the masters possessed. The whites, he points out, "were neither omnipotent or omniscient"; there were "forces they could not control, areas in which slaves could act with more knowledge and authority than their masters, ways in which the powers of the whites could be muted if not thwarted entirely" (73–74).

Witches had exceptional powers of mobility and could slip through keyholes, cracks, and windows. They had the power to turn sleeping people into their horses ("nightmares") and ride them. As one informant reported: "You can always tell when such witches have been riding you; you feel 'down and out' the next morning" (Puckett 151). Hags could bewitch cattle and keep them from giving milk. And they made "witch balls" from the hides of cows or horses and inflicted injury by throwing them at images of their enemies.

Witches who embarked on nocturnal missions would slip out of their human skins, turn into animals (cats, gnats, horses, and buzzards), and ride their victims to the point of exhaustion. When they returned, they put their skin back on, although there was always the risk that someone might have found it and tampered with it. As was true in West African cultures, sprinkling salt or pepper on the skin—a common apotropaic gesture enacted in most witness accounts—made it impossible for the witch to return to her human form (Dayrell 1910, 11–19).

Professional "witchmasters" put themselves out for hire, and conjure doctors (like African witch doctors) could cure those who had been placed under a spell. Not everyone had to go to such lengths. Brooms placed across a threshold (compelling a witch to count every straw before entering) and sieves hung on the door (every hole had to be counted) stopped witches in their tracks and discouraged them from entering a dwelling. Strewing salt was also an effective deterrent, for witches evidently could not resist examining and counting objects in their path. Any granular material or objects with detail (newspapers, for example!) could slow witches down. The eating of salt is often also blamed for enslaving Africans to whites, whose "skin is white like salt," as one poem tells it (Beier 1966, 56).

The stories below give accounts of witches and their powers to conjure and fly. Newbell Niles Puckett's description of witches and their nocturnal practices suggests that there was great anxiety about a witch appearing in your bedroom and "riding" you, a feat with distinctly sexual overtones, but medical ones as well. In Southern states, sleep paralysis is described as "a witch riding your back." The term *hagridden* goes back to the 1680s, with the meaning of "afflicted by nightmares."

The "Cat-Witch" story and "Skinny, Skinny, Don't You Know Me?" are tales of entrapment and punishment. Sometimes a witch is simply put out of business by fed-up victims, as in Zora Neale Hurston's tale about a witch with thieving ways. "Macie and the Boo Hag" is another witness account, one that reveals the connection between psychological pain and physiological disorders with witches. Macie is haunted by the Boo Hag in adolescence and in old age, phases in the life cycle with disturbing bodily changes and unsettled emotions. Besieged by anxieties, the young Macie responds with a locked jaw and is unable to speak. The older Macie can speak and tell her story, but it is one of loss, the story of an old woman who feels "weak," "down," "fearful," and "tired" in her old age. Macie was seventy-nine when she told the story to Chalmers S. Murray, who was at the Works Progress Administration, a federal agency that hired writers in the 1930s and assigned them to collect folklore and document folkways.

Facing down the evils of ghosts, hants, spirits, and spooks and eluding their stunts and pranks becomes a real challenge for many characters in African American lore. Long-dead ancestors, spouses, friends, and foe are animated in the nocturnal hours, alarming more than harming. "I believe in spirits 'cause I seen them," one tale-teller reports. "I guess they can't hurt you, like shadows" (Dorson 1967, 212). Filmy and flimsy, they often take the form of an animal, usually a dog, a cat, or a rooster. Some seek revenge but others are tortured by the need to divulge information to the living about buried treasure.

The dream of buried treasure was fueled by stories about Native Americans burying ornaments made of silver and gold, pirates entrusting their loot to the safety of the earth, and wealthy farmers storing their profits in underground vaults rather than banks. Plantation owners and their family members most likely buried riches when Union troops arrived. Hence the wealth of tales about the dead, who are haunted by the notion of lost wealth and need to reveal to the living the exact location of what they buried.

Newbell Niles Puckett writes about what he calls "Negro 'Ha'nts'": "In all the squalid lore of mankind there is nothing more ghastly than those unearthly beings who, for the most part, were at one time men. In Negro ghost-lore this hideousness is all the more patent, since the lovable fairy or brownie is completely subordinated to the goblin, incubus, or ogre, who seeks only the harm of mankind" (1926, 116–17). Yet malicious and evil as the "hants" of African American lore may appear, they often befriend the living and bequeath riches on them.

Puckett emphasizes that these specters are often badly mutilated, "forced to live a painful existence in the other world with some of their parts missing. Many are the apparently sincere stories I have heard related," he adds, "about meetings with these headless prowlers of the night" and he relates some memorable examples:

One reputable Negro nurse tells me of driving down the road at night when suddenly the horses shied at the figure of a man dimly outlined in the gloom (horses generally show a great sensitivity to spirits). On looking closely she saw that this silent figure had no head. In another case a murderer chopped a man's head off; to his everlasting horror the head began to talk to him. . . . A wife died, making her husband promise not to sell any of the household furniture. A short time afterwards the unfaithful husband sold a pair of bedsprings and a mattress to a Negress, who, of course, was unaware of the promise he had made. That night she and her sister went to bed, first jamming the ax under the door so that it could not be opened. In the middle of the night they woke up to see the ax mysteriously creeping from under the door. A woman clad in red (the fetish color) walked in. She had a great long neck but no head. There she stood "a-turnin' dat long neck 'bout de room tryin' ter look at us. Us hollered fur us's brudder, he come runnin' in, an' dat ha'nt wuz gone!" Another Vicksburg Negro saw a little man walking across the fields with no legs, while in other cases, headless men, armless men, and dismembered limbs, falling down the chimney one by one, and acting as if they had some real unison, are featured. (127—28)

Langston Hughes and Arna Bontemps offer an inventory of the many ways to conjure ghosts: looking over the left shoulder, peering through a mule's ear, looking into a mirror with someone else, breaking a stick in two, going to the cemetery at noon and calling out a name, or wiping off a rusty nail and putting it in your mouth (1958, 163).

WITCHES

SKINNY, SKINNY, DON'T YOU KNOW ME?

Once there was a woman that could turn into a witch. When the husband would go to bed, she would slip out. . . . While she was gone, the husband missed her and got up. He saw her skin lying by the fire. He got some red pepper and put it inside the skin. Then he locked the door to keep her from coming into the house that night. When she came back, she slipped through the keyhole and went to get into her skin. Every time she went to get in, the pepper would burn her. She would say, "Skinny, skinny, don't you know me?" Then she would try again: it would burn her still. She would say, "Skinny, skinny, don't you know me?" The husband woke up. She got into it, but could not stay. Then she was tarred and burnt to death.

SOURCE: Yvonne P. Chireau, *Black Magic: Religion and the African American Conjuring Tradition*, 87.

SKIN DON'T YOU KNOW ME?

This old witch used to tantalize people out in the country. They didn't know she was a witch; but every day there'd be something missing—diamonds, jewelry. She'd come in through a keyhole, or a crack in the door. So this night she went to a big fine castle. And a man, we'll just call him Mr. John, he's just coming in from a party, about 2:30 a.m. Everybody else is asleep. He looked and he saw a lady standing right at his doorstep.

"I'm just gonna stand here and see what she's gonna do."

First she reaches up, pulls her hat off, lays it down. She pulls off her shoes, and she also lays them down. She undresses, lays the clothes all in the same heap. He seen her hands go up, and her skin begin to move upwards. Up it went, up it went, till it was about five feet in the air. Then it settled back to the ground. Nothing else moved.

"Oh, that's a curious sight." He goes up and examines the clothes. "Huh, this is old Grandma Jane's clothes, what stays over the hill." Then he feels the skin. "Hm, I don't know what this is, but if it's moisture, I know how I'll find out. I'll get some pepper and salt and I'll put them on it." So he eased in the kitchen, gits his red pepper and salt, and sprinkles the hide good all over.

"Now, I'll see what's gonna happen."

In a few minutes he seen the skin begin to work. Next he heard a whistle, and a voice said, "Skin don't you know me?"

The skin was so hot she couldn't get in it. Three times he heard the whistle at the burning, and "Skin don't you know me?"

Next thing the voice said was, "If you will wash this skin with soap and water, I'll give you all the diamonds and jewelry I've stolen from you. This is Grandma Jane." (She had looked and saw him.) Then he obeyed, washed it, and soaped it and greased it good for her. And she was the same old Grandma Jane when she got back into her skin.

Then she restored all their jewelry and became a poor old widowed woman. That salt had taken away all her power of witchcraft.

(They claim that salt kills the power—it holds the dampness, and the witch can't never get power enough to work. Same thing with hyp'tizing—some people got more salt in their blood than others.)

SOURCE: Richard M. Dorson, *Negro Folktales in Michigan*, 145–46.

THE CAT-WITCH

This happened in slavery times, in North Carolina. I've heard my grandmother tell it more than enough.

My grandmother was cook and house-girl for this family of slaveowners—they must have been Bissits, 'cause she was a Bissit. Well, Old Marster had sheep, and he sheared his sheep and put the wool upstairs. And Old Miss accused the cook of stealing her wool. "Every day my wool gets smaller and smaller; somebody's taking my wool." She knowed nobody could get up there handy but the house-girl. So they took her out and tore up her back about the wool, and Old Marster give her a terrible whipping.

When grandma went upstairs to clean up, she'd often see a cat laying in the pile of wool. So she thought the cat laying there packed the wool, and made it look small. And she said to herself, she's going to cut off the cat's head with a butcher's knife, if she catches her again. And sure enough she did. She grabbed the cat by her foot, her front foot, and hacked her foot with the knife, and cut it off. And the cat went running down the stairs, and out.

So she kilt the foot she cut off, and it turned natural, it turned to a hand. And the hand had a gold ring on the finger, with an initial in the ring. My grandmother carried the hand down to her Mistress, and showed it to her. Grandma could not read nor write, but Old Miss could, and she saw the initial on the ring. So it was an outcry; they begin to talk about it, like people do in a neighborhood, and they look around to see who lost her hand. And they found it was this rich white woman, who owned slaves, and was the wife of a young man hadn't been long married. (Witches don't stay long in one place; they travel.) Next morning she wouldn't get up to cook her husband's breakfast, 'cause she didn't have but one hand. And when he heard the talk, and saw the hand with his wife's gold ring, and found her in bed without a hand, he knew she was the cat-witch. And he said he didn't want her no longer.

So it was a custom of killing old witches. They took and fastened her to an iron stake, they staked her, and poured tar around her, and set her afire, and burnt her up.

She had studied witchcraft, and she wanted that wool, and could get places, like the wind, like a hant. She would slip out after her husband was in bed, go through keyholes, if necessary be a rat—they can change—and steal things, and bring them back.

Grandma told that for the truth.

SOURCE: Mary Richardson in *American Negro Folktales*, ed. Richard Dorson, 247–49.

WITCHES WHO RIDE

The chief activity of the witch is riding folks, though occasionally there is that evil succubus who steals wives. One informant regards witches as identical with conjurers: "Dey's who' hoodoos, Marse Newbell, dey sho' is. Dey's done sold deir soul ter de debbil, (the old European view) an' old Satan gi' dem de po'r ter change ter anything dey wants. Mos' gen'ally dey rides you in de shape uv a black cat, an' rides you in de daytime too, well ez de night." You can always tell when such witches have been riding you; you feel "down and out" the next morning, and the bit these evil friends put in your mouth leaves a mark in each corner. When you feel smothered and can not get up, ("jes' lak somebody holdin' you down") right then and there the old witch is taking her midnight gallop. You try to call out, but it is no use; your tongue is mute, your hair crawls out of its braids and your hands and feet tingle. My old mammy was very sick one time. Something heavy was pressing upon her chest. A good woman touched her, the load was lifted, and a dark form floated out through the window. "Hit mus' 'er been a witch." When you find your hair plaited into little stirrups in the morning or when it is all tangled up and your face scratched you may be sure that the witches have been bothering you that night. In Virginia "the hag turns the victim on his or her back. A bit (made by the witch) is then inserted in the mouth of the sleeper and he or she is turned on all-fours and ridden like a horse. Next morning the person is tired out, and finds dirt between the fingers and toes."

There is one Negro song about an old woman who saddles, bridles, boots, and spurs a person, and rides him fox-hunting and down the hillsides, but in general, the Negroes deny that the person ridden is actually changed into a horse. But, horse or not, when a person talks or cries out in his sleep a witch is surely after him. Horses as well as humans are ridden; you can tell when the witches have bothered them by finding "witches' stirrups" (two strands of hair twisted together) in the horses' mane. A person who plaits a horse's mane and leaves it that way is simply inviting the witches to ride, though they will seldom bother the horses except on very dark nights, and even then have a decided preference for very dark horses.

SOURCE: Newbell Niles Puckett, *Folk Beliefs of the Southern Negro*, 151–53.

"Witches Who Ride," from Newbell Niles Puckett, *Folk Beliefs of the Southern Negro*. Copyright © 1926 by the University of North Carolina Press. Used by permission of the publisher.

OUT OF HER SKIN

A white man had a wife. Eve'y night his wife go, but he don' know where his wife go to. He had a servant to wait on dem. So de servant whispered to his master, "Master, don' you know mistress kill all my chil'run?" Say, "Mistress is a hag."—"You think you can prove it? You think you can ketch her?"—"Yes, suh! You let me sleep here one night. I kyan ketch her." So de servant an' his master make de agreement how to ketch 'em. He said to his servan', "Don' you go home to-night. You sleep hyere. I'm goin' away soon in de mornin'." Dey bof (de man an' de wife), dey went to baid, de servan' on de watch. Late in de night de mistress woke up. De servan' watch her. Somet'in' she put on her flesh an' take off her skins. After take off her skins, she roll it up an' put it in her dirty clo'es in de back o' de baid. An' she gone out. After she gone out, de servan' call to her master, said, "Master, mistress is gone. To proof to you dat mistress is a hag, I come now an' show you what she done." She went back ob de baid an' get de clo'es what de skin in, an' bring it to her master, an' say, "Here is mistress skin." An' he said to his servan', "What shall we do wid de skin to ketch her?" She said, "Put black pepper an' salt in de skin on de inside." So de master did dat. So later on de mistress came an' get her skin. An' she 'mence to put it on; an' eve'y time de skin bu'n her so much, she said to de skin, "Skin, skin, you don't know me? 'Tis me." Still she couldn' get it on. So she went to her baid an' wrapped up. Master was out now. She lay down till late. Her husband 'mence to p'ovoke her to get up. Still she won't get up. Jus' keep po'vokin'. All at oncet he snatched off de cover off her, an' dere she was raw like a beef. So he called witnesses to prove. So dey make a kil' of lime an' put her in it, an' bu'n her down. But as much as de fire a-bu'nin', she never holler 'til dey t'row de skin in. De skin 'mence to scream. So dat was de en' of his wife.

SOURCE: Elsie Clews Parsons, *Folk-Lore of the Sea Islands, South Carolina*, 63.

Told by Maria Middleton, a sixty-five-year-old resident of St. Helena, an island off the coast of South Carolina.

MACIE AND THE BOO HAG

I can't get sleep to come to bed with me no more. If and when I do drop off, it don't feel very natural.

I dream that every morning Crow comes into my pea patch and takes every single pea away in his beak. I can see my eats leaving the house with nobody's hands touching them. I see my poor mother; she, so restless in her grave. I see so many things like that. There won't be any snoring good with boo hag[1] all the time riding me!

I was a youngun the first time boo hag rode me. I suspect some jealous girl put the hag up to it. Some young woman didn't like the young men come to court me because I was so pretty. And she wasn't nothing much, too. One boy she liked cared for me best, and so this girl put the hag on me.

One evening, boo hag come to see me. I was ready for bed early, for I was younger then. Halfway up the stairs, this green light comes, *swoosh*! And burst all in my eyes. Then it turns into a red light. I can see this awful, raggedy-looking thing coming up the stairs behind me. The she-thing has a head big as a barrel with bloody-red light shining out of her eyes. My mouth is open to scream, but I can't yell a thing. I moan some, is all I can do. And my dear mother heard me.

She came over to the landing, said to me, "Macie, what's wrong? What's the matter?"

I tried to answer, but something had locked my jaw. Couldn't even turn around to look at her. She knew there was something the matter with me.

"Must've played with bad girls again," she said.

Couldn't say nothing back to her, my mouth was just so closed. That's what boo hag did to me, made me speakless.

And the hag rode me, and I liked to died. I got real thin, she rode me so many late nights. Just like I was some broomstick she rode. Or some skinny night-mare. A whole month of nights, and I couldn't sleep a wink. That's how boo hag did me, and scared me so. And in the night-riding, I see all kinds of bad things. See the devil. See boo daddy, too. And come the dayclean,[2] I'm so sore on my back, like somebody been beating me with a stick.

1 *boo hag:* Boo hags are part of Gullah lore, though they migrated out into other Southern regions. Like vampires, they draw sustenance from their victims, though using their breath instead of their blood for restorative purposes. They often steal the skin of their victims and wear it while they are riding them.

2 *come the dayclean:* at the break of day, or sunrise

My mother said to me, "Macie, I have a mind the hag is riding you, even though you can't say. I got a way to fix the hag, break her spell so she stays fixed, too. You go to sleep now, Macie. And when you wake up, you will feel real better, for true."

Well, I did as my mother said. She gave me a potion, and I slept sound. But it seemed I could hear and see my mother beside me, where she stayed all night. And before the cock crowed, Mother saw me stir and saw me heave as the hag got ready to ride me.

My mother took up this little bottle with a cork in it, set there beside her foot. She took the cork out of the bottle. She held the cork while she put the bottle mouth down on my stomach.

Then, Mother found her some needles. She counted thirty-three, not one more nor less. She lifted the bottle so quick, can't hardly see her hand. She threw one needle in the bottle, fast as lightning. And she corked that bottle, and put thirty-two needles in the cork. This, before boo hag knew what terrible trouble she was in.

And the hag was clean gone. And stayed gone as long as I didn't give that bottle away.

And when I woke up the next dayclean? There was my nerve all back in me. The spell boo hag had over me was melted off me. Oh, did I eat some breakfast? Had me half a loaf of bread and a whole pot of gravy!

For a long time, I was careful as could be. One time, an old woman wanted to borrow some salt, but I talked through the door. Said, "No, ma'am, we all out of salt." I knew it was boo hag come after me again. Scared me to the bones. But you saw how my mother caught that hag spirit in the bottle the way she knew how. You see, she pinned it down in the bottle with that needle. And in case the hag could tear loose, she put those needles through the cork. For it's known that boo hag can't get past some sharp needles all lined up against her.

And if I should give anything to that hag voice on the other side of the door, then she might try hard to get her spirit back out of the bottle, don't you know. And once she had hold of her spirit, boo hag could slip off her skin and fly all over the place, too. Ride you in just the shape of her while her skin hang there behind the door. 'Tis true!

But that's how my dear mother caught the boo hag. Yes, it was. Now, Mother is long in her grave. And now, boo hag comes back in my old age. I don't sleep so good these days. Nowadays, this people generation don't know the tricks, and lack knowing the way my mother knew.

Well, I know how to deal with some ghost. With some ghost, you just throw a hard remark at them, and they vanish. But I tell you, you never have some rest; you always worry about getting weak after the hag has ridden you. And I am down so far these times. I am feeling fearful and tired, all of my days. I wish for my dear mother. I do.

SOURCE: Told to Chalmers S. Murray by a seventy-nine-year-old African American woman for the *South Carolina Writers' Project.*

HANTS AND SPOOKS

THE HEADLESS HANT

A man and his wife was going along the big road. It was cold and the road was muddy and sticky red, and their feet was mighty nigh froze off, and they was hungry, and it got pitch dark before they got where they was going.

'Twan't long before they came to a big fine house with smoke coming outen the chimney and a fire shining through the winder. It was the kind of a house rich folks lives in, so they went round to the back door and knocked on the back porch. Somebody say, "Come in!" They went in, but they didn't see nobody.

They looked up and down and all round, but still they didn't see nobody. They saw the fire on the hearth with the skillets setting in it all ready for supper to be cooked in 'em. They saw there was meat and flour and lard and salsody and a pot of beans smoking and a rabbit a-biling in a covered pot.

Still they didn't see nobody, but they saw everything was ready for somebody. The woman took off her wet shoes and stockings to warm her feet at the fire, and the man took the bucket and lit out for the springhouse to get fresh water for the coffee. They 'lowed they was going to have them brown beans and that molly cottontail and that cornbread and hot coffee in three shakes.

The woman was toasting her feet when right through the shut door in walks a man and he don't have no head. He had on his britches and his shoes and his gallushes and his vest and his coat and his shirt and his collar, but he don't have no head. Jes raw neck and bloody stump.

And he started to tell the woman, without no mouth to tell her with, how come he happened to come in there that a-way. She mighty nigh jumped outen her skin, but she said, "What in the name of the Lord do you want?" So he said he's in awful misery, being dead and buried in two pieces. He said somebody kilt him for his money and took him to the cellar and buried him in two pieces, his head in one place and his corpse in 'nother. He said them robbers dug all round trying to find his money, and when they didn't find it they went off and left him in two pieces, so now he hankers to be put back together so's to get rid of his misery.

Then the hant said some other folks had been there and asked him what he wanted but they didn't say in the name of the Lord, and 'cause she did is how come he could tell her 'bout his misery.

'Bout that time the woman's husband came back from the springhouse with the bucket of water to make the coffee with and set the bucket on the shelf before he saw the hant. Then he saw the hant with the bloody joint of his neck sticking up and he come nigh jumping outen his skin.

Then the wife told the hant who her husband is, and the hant begun at the start and told it all over agin 'bout how come he is the way he is. He told 'em if they'd come down into the cellar and find his head and bury him all in one grave he'd make 'em rich.

They said they would and that they'd get a torch.

The hant said, "Don't need no torch." And he went up to the fire and stuck his front finger in it and it blazed up like a lightwood knot and he led the way down to the cellar by the light.

They went a long way down steps before they came to the cellar. Then the hant say, "Here's where my head's buried and over here's where the rest of me's buried. Now yo' all dig right over yonder where I throw this pot of light and dig till you touch my barrels of gold and silver money."

So they dug and dug and sure 'nough they found the barrels of money he'd covered up with the thick cellar floor. Then they dug up the hant's head and histed the thing on the spade. The hant jes reached over and picked the head offen the spade and put it on his neck. Then he took off his burning finger and stuck it in a candlestick on a box, and still holding on his head, he crawled back into the hole that he had come out of.

And from under the ground they heard him a-saying, "Yo' all can have my land, can have my home, can have all my money and be as rich as I was, 'cause you buried me in one piece together, head and corpse."

Then they took the candlestick blazing with the hant's finger and went back upstairs and washed themselves with lye soap. Then the woman made up the cornbread with the spring water and greased the skillet with hogmeat and put in the hoecake and lifted the lid on with the tongs and put coals of fire on top of the lid and round the edges of the skillet, and cooked the hoecake done. Her man put the coffee and water in the pot and set it on the trivet to boil. Then they et that supper of them beans and that rabbit and that hoecake and hot coffee. And they lived there all their lives and had barrels of money to buy vittels and clothes with. And they never heard no more 'bout the man that came upstairs without no head where his head ought to be.

SOURCE: *Bundle of Troubles, and Other Tarheel Tales, by Workers of the Writers' Program of the Work Projects Administration in the State of North Carolina*, ed. W. C. Hendricks, 98–99. The tale was recorded by Nancy Watkins, and it was told by an African American boy named Dez Foy to the Watkins children at the family's kitchen hearth in Madison, North Carolina.

IN THE NAME OF THE LORD

This little girl (this actually happened), she was living with these people. They was makin' a Cinderella out of her, see, and at night when they get through supper, they use to make her go out on the back porch and wash dishes. And say, every time that she would go out there, something would scare her, and she'd run back in the house. And they'd make her run right back out there. Then she run back—keep on till she get through. So they told the Preacher about it, you know, and he said, "It could be possible the child see something. I'll come over sometime and sit."

And say after they got through with supper, they sent her out on the porch in the dark to wash the dishes, and all at once she screamed and run back in the house, say she saw somethin'. He say, "Now look, daughter, don't get scared now, but whatever it is, when this thing come to you again, say you ask it, 'In the name of the Lord, what do you want?' Say, 'Either speak or leave me alone.'"

So she went back and the thing appeared again. She say, "What in the name of the Lord do you want with me?"

He say, "Take—take a pick and shovel and follow me."

"In the Name of the Lord," from Daryl Cumber Dance, ed., *Shuckin' and Jivin'*, 1978. Reprinted with permission of Indiana University Press.

So she got a shovel and pick and followed him. Say he went on-n-n down—led her down in this little valley like, and say, he say, "Now you dig right here by this tree, and you gonna find a big earthen jar—full of money." He say, "Lil' o' that that runs out, I'm gonna tell you who I want you to give it to, but what stays in there will be yours." And she dug and found it. And they poured it out till it stop runnin' and they left enough in there for her and everybody else. And never did pay her no more visits.

See somebody had buried it and died and they wanted somebody to have it.

SOURCE: Daryl Cumber Dance, *Shuckin' and Jivin': Folklore from Contemporary Black Americans*, 29–30.

THE GIRL AND THE PLAT-EYE

One night in a coast area of the South a young girl went out clamming, but the tide was late going out, and she was very late setting off for home. As she came to a small log bridge, she saw in front of her a huge black cat.

Its eyes were like balls of fire, and its back was arched. Its tail twitched back and forth, and its hair stood on end. It walked across the log in front of her.

The girl said out loud, "I'm not afraid. That ain't no ghost. Ain't no plat-eye.[1] Ain't no nuthin'!"

Then the huge black cat turned around and started toward her.

The girl raised her short clam rake and brought it down, as hard as she could, across the animal's back. If it had been a real cat, she would have pinned it to the log. But the rake went right through it. The cat rose up on its hind legs and pawed the air.

1 *plat-eye:* Spirits who have not been properly buried are called plat-eyes, because they have a single eye dangling from the middle of the forehead. The plat-eye often guards buried treasure.

The girl took off in the other direction.

After running awhile, she had to stop for breath. "Thank you, Lord, for delivering me from that cat," she began, and then she saw the cat. It was as big as a cow, and its eyes burned into her.

She took off again. Just before she reached a clearing, the cat jumped in front of her. This time it was as big as an ox. Suddenly it vanished behind a tree.

The girl's uncle Murphy was a witch doctor. When she told him about the plat-eye in the woods, he gave her some advice: "When you travel in the deep woods where the moss wave low, where Mr. Cooter live and Mr. Moccasin crawl, and the firefly flicker, you carry sulfur and gunpowder mixed in your pocket. Plat-eye can't stand them smells mixed."

From then on, the girl never traveled in the woods at night without loading her pockets with that special mixture, and she never saw a plat-eye again.

SOURCE: James Haskins, ed., *The Headless Haunt*, 70–72.

THE JACK-O'-MY-LANTERN[1]

1 *Jack-o'-My-Lantern:* The Jack-o'-my-Lantern is a variant of the *ignis fatuus*, also known as a will'-o'wisp, Peg-a-lantern, Kitty-candlestick, Jacket-a-wad, as well as by other names. These wandering flames all belong to the recently dead. Their power to lure mortals to their death can be broken by wearing a coat inside out or pockets turned wrongside out. Or they can be dodged by turning your back to them and running for your life.

Jack sold himself to the devil at the crossroads one night at twelve o'clock. For seven years all power was given to him to do as he pleased, but at the end of that period his soul belonged to the devil. Old Satan called for him, but Jack was ready. He had tacked a piece of old shoe sole up above the door, and asked the devil to get it for him. The devil stood in a chair and reached for it, Jack then took a hammer and nailed the devil's hand fast, slipping the chair out from under him. Upon a promise of his freedom, Jack then released old Satan. Finally Jack died. He went up to heaven, but those in charge would not let him in. He went down to hell, but the devil threw a chunk of fire at him and told him he was too smart for hell. Jack, deprived of a dwelling, was forced to pick up the chunk of fire and to spend all his time wandering about the earth luring people into swamps and mud holes at night.

SOURCE: Newbell Niles Puckett, *Folk Beliefs of the Southern Negro*, 135–36.

PART III

SPEECH AND SILENCE: TALKING SKULLS AND SINGING TORTOISES

Stories about talking skulls can be traced to an Ifa divination tale in which Earth seeks to bear a child. Told that her child, a son, shall wear a crown but that she must sacrifice in order to witness his triumph, Earth fails to sacrifice and dies while the child is still a boy. A farmer cultivating yams hears Earth cry out "Ha! Did you chop my head with your hoe?" Hearing this voice, the farmer rushes to tell the king about this strange talking skull. Staking his own life on the truth of the tale, he initiates a cycle of violence in which he fails to win credibility and is decapitated, along with his executioners. The king intervenes directly to make reparations with sacrifices that usher in a new era of proper graveside and burial rituals: "Ifa says that there is a dead person who has not been buried. Ifa says we should hurry and bury this person in fine style, so that it will not draw many people to their death after it." This Ifa tale of respect for the dead and sacrificial rites to ensure human survival is reconfigured in African and diasporic cultures to add a second layer of meaning about reckless boasting and braggadocio. "The Talking Skull" becomes a cautionary tale about telling tales, even as it self-reflexively creates a meaningful narrative that undermines its own message.

Freud tells us in *Totem and Taboo* that we mourn the dead yet also harbor, along with feelings of tenderness, hostility toward them. Those unconscious feelings of hostility manifest themselves in the form of demons, beings projected into the outside world who rejoice in our misfortune and try to murder us. "The Talking Skull" engages with questions of mourning, burial, and coming to terms with the dead, who can haunt us beyond the grave as they seek to coerce the living into joining them.

A variant of "The Talking Skull," but with a vibrantly alive speaker, "The Hunter and the Tortoise" also shows some kinship with folktales about selkies, mermaids, swan maidens, and all those animal brides who leave their natural habitats to live with humans and move from nature to culture. "The Hunter and the Tortoise" is less about ancestors and burial rites than about human indiscretion and lack of reverence for natural beauty.

THE TALKING SKULL

A hunter goes into the bush. He finds an old human skull. The hunter says: "What brought you here?" The skull answers: "Talking brought me here." The hunter runs off. He runs to the king. He tells the king: "I found a dry human skull in the bush. It asks you how its mother and father are."

The king says: "Never since my mother bore me have I heard that a dead skull can speak." The king summons the Alkali, the Saba, and the Degi and asks them if they have ever heard the like. None of the wise men has heard the like, and they decide to send a guard out with the hunter into the bush to find out if his story is true and, if so, to learn the reason for it. The guard accompanies the hunter into the bush with the order to kill him on the spot should he have lied. The guard and the hunter come to the skull. The hunter addresses the skull: "Skull, speak." The skull is silent. The hunter asks as before, "What brought you here?" The skull does not answer. All day long the hunter begs the skull to speak, but it does not answer. In the evening the guard tells the hunter to make the skull speak and when he cannot, they kill him in accordance with the king's command.

After the guard leaves, the skull opens its jaws and asks the dead hunter's head: "What brought you here?" The dead hunter replies: "Talking brought me here."

SOURCE: Leo Frobenius, *African Genesis*, 161–62.

The German archaeologist and ethnologist Leo Frobenius felt it his duty to establish a "science of culture" by exploring zones unknown to Europeans and gathering images and stories to map out the many contact areas among civilizations. He was determined to establish broad networks of knowledge that would establish connections rather than make distinctions. In the version of "The Talking Skull" recorded by him, we can see the remnants of an emphasis on remembering ancestors. The skull is purported to ask the king about its own parents, a reminder to remember the dead.

THE SKULL THAT TALKED BACK

This was uh man. His name was High Walker.[1] He walked into a bone yard with skull-heads and other bones. So he would call them, "Rise up bloody bones[2] and shake yo'self." And de bones would rise up and come together, and shake theirselves and part and lay back down. Then he would say to hisself, "High Walker," and de bones would say, "Be walkin'."

1 *High Walker:* The name is telling in that it points to the mobility of the chief character and contrasts him to the dead, with their bones resting in or on the ground. And "high" of course hints at the arrogance that he puts on display in his encounters with the dead, for whom he fails to display proper reverence.

2 *bloody bones:* "Rawhead and Bloody-Bones" is the name of a bogeyman used to frighten children. The figure can be traced back to England (the earliest mention of the monster in print dates to 1550), from where he migrated to North America, and especially to the U.S. South.

When he'd git off a little way, he'd look back over his shoulder and shake hisself and say, "High Walker and bloody bones," and de bones would shake theirselves. Therefore he knowed he had power.

So uh man sold hisself to de high chief devil. He give 'im his whole soul and body tuh do ez he pleased wid it. He went out in uh drift uh woods and laid down flat on his back beyond all dese skull heads and bloody bones and said, "Go 'way Lawd, and come here Devil and do as you please wid me. Cause Ah want tuh do everything in de world dats wrong and never do nothing right."

And he dried up and died away on doin' wrong. His meat all left his bones and de bones all wuz separated.

And at dat time High Walker walked upon his skull head and kicked and kicked it on ahead of him a many and a many times and said tuh it, "Rise up and shake yo'self. High Walker is here."

Ole skull head wouldn't say nothin'. He looked back over his shoulder cause he heard some noises behind him and said, "Bloody bones you won't say nothin' yet. Rise tuh de power in de flesh."

Den de skull head said, "My mouf brought me here and if you don't mind, you'n will bring you here."

High Walker went on back to his white folks and told de white man dat a dry skull head wuz talkin' in de drift today. White man say he didn't believe it.

"Well, if you don' believe it, come go wid me and Ah'll prove it. And if it don't speak, you kin chop mah head off right where it at."

So de white man and High Walker went back in de drift tuh find dis ole skull head. So when he walked up tuh it, he begin tuh kick and kick de ole skull head, but it wouldn't say nothin'. High Walker looked at de white man and seen 'im whettin' his knife. Whettin' it hard and de sound of it said rick-de-rick, rick-de-rick, rick-de-rick! So High Walker kicked and kicked dat ol skull head and called it many and many uh time, but it never said nothin'. So de white man cut off High Walker's head.

And de ole dry skull head said, "See dat now! Ah told you dat mouf brought me here and if you didn't mind out it'd bring you here."

So de bloody bones riz up and shook they selves seben times and de white man got skeered and said, "What you mean by dis?"

De bloody bones say, "We got High Walker and we all bloody bones now in de drift together."

SOURCE: Zora Neale Hurston, *Mules and Men*, 173–75.

Hurston's inclusion of the tale in her anthology reflects a sense of respect for ancestors and their resting places. That she herself was buried in an unmarked grave is particularly ironic, especially since she wrote to W. E. B. Du Bois in 1945 about a plan to set up a "cemetery for the illustrious Negro dead." "We must assume the responsibility of their graves being known and honored," she added, "since the lack of such a tangible thing allows our people to forget, and their spirits to evaporate" (Kaplan 2002, 18). For her, death rites and reverence for sacred ground enabled the living to carry on and draw sustenance from the lives of ancestors.

DIVIDING SOULS

During the period of slavery time Old Marster always kept one slave that would keep him posted on the others, so that he would know how to deal with them when they got unruly. So this slave was walking around in the moonlight one night. And he heard a noise coming from the cemetery. And it was two slaves counting apples, which they had stole from Old Master's orchard. They couldn't count, so they were exchanging 'em.

"You take dis un and I'll take dat un. Dis un's yours and dat un's mine."

So this slave hear them, and he listened, and he ran back to Old Marster. And running he fell over a skeleton head, and he spoke to the skeleton's head, "What you doing here?"

And the skeleton head said, "Same thing got me here will get you here."

So he told Old Marster when he got to the house that the Devil and the Good Lord was in the cemetery counting out souls. "Dis un's yours and dat un's mine, dis un's yours and dat un's mine."

Old Marster didn't believe him, but he went with him to the cemetery. And Old Marster told him, said, "Now if the Devil and the Good Lord ain't counting out souls, I'm going to cut your head off."

Sure enough the slaves had gone and Old Marster didn't hear anything, and he cut John's head off. Then John's head fell beside the skeleton head. Then the head turned over and said, "I told you something that got me here would get you here. You talk too much."

(That's one my daddy would tell us when we were talking too much.)

SOURCE: Richard M. Dorson, ed., *American Negro Folktales*, 146–47.

A. J. King and Beulah Tate told this tale and "Talking Bones" to the American folklorist Richard Dorson. The first combines a frequently told tale about a man who thinks he hears God and the Devil dividing up souls in a graveyard (usually thieves dividing up loot) with the tale of the talking skull. Both accounts paradoxically use "talk" to warn others about keeping your mouth shut.

TALKING BONES

They used to carry the slaves out in the woods and leave them there. If they killed them—just like dead animals. There wasn't any burying then. It used to be a secret, between one plantation and another, when they beat up their hands and carried them off.

So John was walking out in the woods and seed a skeleton. He says: "This looks like a human. I wonder what he's doing out here." And the skeleton said, "Tongue is the cause of my being here." So John ran back to old Marster and said, "The skeleton at the edge of the woods is talking." Old Marster didn't believe him and went to see. And a great many people came too. They said "Make the bones talk." But the skeleton wouldn't talk. So they beat John to death, and left him there. And then the bones talked. They said, "Tongue brought us here, and tongue brought you here."

SOURCE: Richard M. Dorson, ed., *American Negro Folktales*, 147–48.

This tale gives us the backstory to the appearance of a skull in the woods. An African tale about a talking skull is repurposed here as a means of communicating information about plantation practices and as a cautionary tale.

TALKS TOO MUCH

Man goin' along found skeleton of a man's head. "Ol' Head, how come you here?" – "Mouth brought me here. Mouth's goin' to bring you here." He goes up to de town an' tellin' about de ol' head. A great crowd of people went with him down there. They called on this head to talk to them. The head never said nothin'. They fell on this feller an' beat him. The ol' Head turned an' said, "Didn't I tell you Mouth was goin' to bring you here?"

Elsie Clews Parsons described the tale below as a "second version" of the first.

In slave'y time colored man travellin' 'long came to where dere was a terrapin. Terrapin spoke to him. Said, "One day you shall be free." He done him so much good, he jus' couldn' keep it. Goes up to his master's house, an' says, "A Terrapin spoke to me this mornin'." An' his master say, "What did he say?"—"One day you shall be free."—"I'm goin' down here, an' if this terrapin don't talk to me, I'm goin' to whip you to death." So he called upon de terrapin, an' he went back in his house. He commence whippin' dis colored feller. He near by whipped him to death. So de ol' terrapin raised up on his legs an' says, "It's bad to talk too much."

SOURCE: Elsie Clews Parsons, "Tales from Guilford County, North Carolina," *Journal of American Folklore* 30 (1917), 176–77.

The two tales were told to the folklorist Elsie Clews Parsons by Sam Cruse, a thirty-year-old African American man who had spent time in Ohio and was living in North Carolina. The stories reveal just how closely connected "The Talking Skull" is with "The Hunter and the Tortoise."

THE HUNTER AND THE TORTOISE

A village hunter had one day gone farther afield than usual. Coming to a part of the forest with which he was unacquainted, he was astonished to hear an unfamiliar voice singing. He listened; this was the song:

It is man who forces himself on things,
Not things which force themselves on him.

The singing was accompanied by sweet music—which entirely charmed the hunter's heart.

When the little song was finished, the hunter peeped through the branches to see who the singer could be. Imagine his amazement when he found it was none other than a tortoise, with a tiny harp slung in front of her. Never had he seen such a marvelous thing.

Time after time he returned to the same place in order to listen to this wonderful creature. At last he persuaded her to let him carry her back to his hut, that he might enjoy her singing daily in comfort. This she permitted, only on the understanding that she sang to him alone.

The hunter did not remain content with this arrangement, however. Soon he began to wish that he could show this wonderful tortoise off to all the world, and thereby thought he would gain great honor. He told the secret, first to one, then to another, until finally it reached the ears of the chief himself. The hunter was ordered to come and tell his tale before the Assembly. When he described the tortoise who sang and played on the harp, the people shouted in scorn. They refused to believe him.

At last he said, "If I do not speak truth, I give you leave to kill me. Tomorrow I will bring the tortoise to this place and you may all hear her. If she cannot do as I say, I am willing to die." "Good," replied the people, "and if the tortoise can do as you say, we give you leave to punish us in any way you choose."

The matter being then settled, the hunter returned home, well pleased with the prospect. As soon as the morrow dawned, he carried tortoise and harp down to the Assembly Place—where a table had been placed ready for her. Everyone gathered round to listen. But no song came. The people were very patient, and quite willing to give both tortoise and hunter a chance. Hours went by, and, to the hunter's dismay and shame, the tortoise remained mute. He tried every means in his power to coax her to sing, but in vain. The people at first whispered, then spoke outright, in scorn of the boaster and his claims.

Night came on and brought with it the hunter's doom. As the last ray of the setting sun faded, he was beheaded. The instant this had happened the tortoise spoke. The people looked at one another in troubled wonder: "Our brother spoke truth, then, and we have killed him." The tortoise, however, went on to explain. "He brought his punishment on himself. I led a happy life in the forest, singing my little song. He was not content to come and listen to me. He had to tell my secret (which did not at all concern him) to all the world. Had he not tried to make a show of me this would never have happened."

It is man who forces himself on things,
Not things which force themselves on him.

SOURCE: William Henry Barker and Cecilia Sinclair, *West African Folk-Tales*, 119–21.

This story was recorded in Accra, Ghana, in the early part of the twentieth century.

WHAT THE FROG SAID

Uncle Mooney was a dreamer. Not far from the big house was a tank, or reservoir. He liked to sit beside the tank and think. He hoped some day to be a free man. Some one had told him that animals used to talk, and Uncle Mooney thought that some day some animal might talk to him and tell him how to get his freedom.

Finally, one day while he was seated near the edge of the tank, he saw a big bullfrog at the edge of the water. Uncle Mooney picked up a pebble and threw it at the frog, striking him in the side. As the stone struck the frog, the frog said, "Don' do dat. Le's be frien's."

Uncle Mooney was almost struck dumb when the frog spoke to him, but every morning after that he passed the tank on his way to the field, and the frog would say, "Good mawnin'," and ask Uncle Mooney how he felt. Uncle Mooney always wanted to talk longer, but the frog would only say, "Good mawnin'," and ask how he felt.

One day the thought occurred to Uncle Mooney that a good way to gain his freedom would be to introduce his master to this wonderful talking frog down at the tank. So that evening he called his master and said, "Massa, dere's uh frog down to de tank dat talks."

"Oh, no," said the master, "you know that is not true. If it is, I will give you your freedom, but if it is not true, I am going to give you the worst beating you ever had."

"Aw right, Massa, aw right," said Uncle Mooney, "yuh jes' lemme show yuh."

The next morning the master went with Uncle Mooney to the tank, and, sure enough, there was the frog waiting as usual. "Good mawnin'," said Uncle Mooney to the frog. The frog did not answer. Uncle Mooney, disappointed, spoke again, "Good mawnin'." The frog did not answer. The master then ordered Uncle Mooney back to the house and there gave him a severe whipping.

The next morning Uncle Mooney stopped by the tank again. The frog was waiting for him as usual. "Good mawnin'," said Uncle Mooney.

"Good mawnin'," said the frog.

"How cum yuh didn' say nuffin' yistiddy?" asked Uncle Mooney.

"'Case," said the frog. "Ah tol' yuh de othah day, niggah, yuh talk too much."

"What the Frog Said," from J. Frank Dobie, ed., *Tone the Bell Easy*. University of Texas Press, Austin, TX. *Publications of the Texas Folklore Society* 10 (1932): 48–50.

ADDENDUM TO "WHAT THE FROG SAID"

"Not long ago," writes Mrs. Seb F. Caldwell, of Mt. Pleasant, Texas, to the editor, "I was with a fishing party on Sulphur River. While there we talked with an old Negro man who owns a farm near the river on which he has lived for more than thirty years. He was full of lore about the woods, the river, and animals, and along with other matters he told us of a visionary boy who once upon a time was fishing in the very hole where we were fishing.

"While he was sitting there fishing, the boy noticed a turtle crawling upon on a half-submerged log in the river. The turtle alone was not remarkable, but this turtle had a banjo, and, having made himself comfortable, he began picking it and singing. At the sight of such a marvel the boy jumped up and ran home to tell his family what he had seen. His father was a stern kind of man and he gave the boy a sound thrashing for telling stories. The boy stuck to his tale, however, and finally prevailed upon his father to go down to the river and see the wonderful turtle playing the banjo and singing.

"When they got to the river, nothing was in sight but the quiet water and an empty log. The father began to lecture his son again on telling lies and appeared to be warming up for administering another thrashing. Then, all at once, he and the boy heard musical sounds. They turned and looked, and there on the log was the turtle picking his banjo and singing: 'Live in peace; don't tell all you see. Live in peace; don't tell all you see. Live in peace; don't tell all you see.' Over and over just those words and no others he sang to the picking of his guitar."

SOURCE: J. Frank Dobie, ed., *Tone the Bell Easy*, 48–50.

The two stories present variations of "The Hunter and the Tortoise," with a master-slave pairing in one case, and a father-son combination in the other. Blending elements of "The Hunter and the Tortoise" with "The Talking Skull," the first of these two stories offers a cautionary tale about broadcasting the secret lives of animals. Framed as a tale about a vain effort to secure freedom, "What the Frog Said" pits an animal, conciliatory and friendly, against Uncle Mooney, a "dreamer" whose fantasies about freedom are thwarted. The boy in the appended story has better luck, proving to his father the value of "marvels," "telling stories," and "lies."

PIERRE JEAN'S TORTOISE

A tortoise was crawling along slowly one day when he came to a garden where many birds were eating. It was the garden of a farmer named Pierre John. The turkey, the chicken, the pigeon, the duck, the gris-gris bird,[1] and all the others were there. They invited the tortoise to eat with them. But the tortoise said, "Oh, no. If the farmer who owns this garden should surprise us, you would fly away. But where would I be? He would catch me and beat me."

1 *gris-gris bird:* In Haitian Vodou, the gris-gris is an amulet used to cast spells and secure good luck. It is also used as a way to gain access to the gods.

The birds said, "Don't bother your head about that. We will give you feathers. Then you too can fly." Each of the birds took out some of its feathers and attached them to tortoise, until he looked more like a bird than anything else. So he came and ate with them.

But while they were eating, one of the birds called out: "The farmer is coming! The farmer is coming!" The birds quickly grabbed the feathers they had given the tortoise. They flew away. Tortoise crawled, crawled, crawled, but he was too slow. Pierre John, the farmer, caught him. Pierre John was about to beat him for eating up his garden, but the tortoise began to sing:

> Colico Pierre John oh!
> Colico Pierre John oh!
> If I could I would fly, *enhé*!
> What a tragedy, I have no wings!

The farmer was amazed to hear the tortoise sing. He asked him to sing again. The tortoise sang in his best voice.

"What a curious thing," Pierre John said. "Who ever heard of a singing tortoise?" He took the tortoise home and put him in a box, which he then placed in the rafters

"Pierre Jean's Tortoise," from Harold Courlander, ed., *The Piece of Fire and Other Haitian Tales*, 1964. Reprinted by permission of the Emma Courlander Trust.

for safekeeping. Then he went down to the city. In the marketplace he found a crowd, and he said: "Who ever heard of a singing tortoise?"

The people answered: "There is no such thing."

Pierre Jean took money from his pocket. He said: "Who will bet there is no such thing as a singing tortoise?" Some men bet this, some men bet that. There was much excitement.

While they were talking this way, the President came along in his carriage. He stopped and called out, "What is going on?"

When he heard about Pierre John's singing tortoise, the President said: "This man is a mischief maker. Tortoises don't sing. I will bet one hundred thousand gourdes[2] there is no such thing as a singing tortoise."

But Pierre Jean replied: "My President, I am a poor farmer. Where would I ever get a hundred thousand gourdes?"

The President said: "Pierre John, you are a rascal. You are trying to make mischief. I will bet the hundred thousand gourdes. If a tortoise talks, I will pay you. But if a tortoise doesn't talk, I will have you shot."

This was the way it was in the marketplace. But back in the country Pierre John's wife heard that her husband had a singing tortoise. So she searched the house until she found him. She asked him to sing.

"I can sing only by the edge of the river," the tortoise told her. So she took him to the edge of the river.

"My feet must be wet," the tortoise said. So she placed him in the water by the riverbank. And before she knew what was happening, the tortoise slid into the river and swam away.

Madame Pierre Jean heard the crowd coming up the trail from the marketplace. She was frightened. Her husband's tortoise was gone. She ran home, and on the way she caught a small lizard. She put the lizard in the box where the tortoise had been and closed the lid. When the crowd from the city arrived, Pierre Jean took them to the box. The President said: "Let the singing begin."

Pierre Jean called out, "Sing, tortoise!"

The lizard replied from inside the box, "Crik!"[3]

Pierre Jean called again, "Sing, tortoise, sing!"

And the lizard replied: "Crak!"

2 *gourdes:* Haitian unit of currency.

3 *"Crik!":* Haitian storytellers often announce the beginning of a story by saying "Crick!" to which the listeners reply "Crack!"

The President was angry. He said: "You call that singing? Open the box!" They opened the box. They saw only the small lizard.

The President said: "This man is a vagabond! He thinks we are stupid! Take him down to the river and have him shot!"

So they took Jean Pierre down to the riverbank and stood him against a tree to shoot him. Just at this moment the tortoise stuck his head out of the water and sang:

Colico Pierre John oh!
Colico Pierre John oh!
If I could I would fly, *enhé*!
What a tragedy, I have no wings!

"Ah! That is my tortoise!" Pierre Jean said. "Listen to him sing!"
And the tortoise sang again:

Colico, oh President!
Colico, oh President!
Uncle Pierre John talks too much, *enhé*!
Stupidity doesn't kill a man, but it makes him sweat!

When the President heard that, he laughed. He freed Pierre Jean and paid him the hundred thousand gourdes. The tortoise disappeared. The people went away. But from the tortoise they received the proverb: "Stupidity doesn't kill a man, but it makes him sweat."

SOURCE: Harold Courlander, ed. *The Piece of Fire and Other Haitian Tales*, 29–33.

Harold Courlander recorded this tale in Haiti in the 1960s. He notes in his introduction to the anthology that Haitian stories are for the most part syncretic, pieced together from lore of the Old World (Europe and Africa) and the New (the Americas). This particular tale is clearly inspired by African tales about singing tortoises, but encoded with an indigenous social setting and characters. Among Courlander's informants for Haitian tales were Voluska Saintville, Wilfred Beauchamps, Lydia

Augustin, Libera Borderau, Jean Ravel Pintro, Télisman Charles, Maurice Morancy, and Hector Charles. Courlander does not name the teller of "Jean Pierre's Tortoise."

THE TALKING TURTLE

One time there was a fellow named Lissenbee, and the trouble was that he couldn't keep nothing to himself. Whenever anybody done something that wasn't right, Lissenbee would run and blab it all over town. He didn't tell no lies, he just told the truth, and that's what made it so bad. Because all the people believed whatever Lissenbee said, and there wasn't no way a fellow could laugh it off.

If he seen one of the county officers going to a woman's house when her husband was not home, Lissenbee would tell it right in front of the courthouse, and so there would be hell to pay for two families. Or maybe some citizens liked to play a little poker in the livery barn, but there wasn't no way to keep it quiet, on account of that goddam Lissenbee. And when the Baptist preacher brought some whiskey home, there was Lissenbee a-hollering before the preacher could get the keg out of his buggy. After a while the boys was afraid to swipe a watermelon, for fear old blabbermouth Lissenbee would tell everybody who done it.

The last straw was the time Lissenbee found a turtle in the road. It was bigger than the common kind, so he stopped to look at it. The old turtle winked its red eyes, and it says, "Lissenbee, you talk too damn much." Lissenbee jumped four foot high, and then just stood there with his mouth a-hanging open. He looked all round, but there wasn't anybody in sight. "It must be my ears have went back on me!" says he. "Everybody knows terrapins is dumb." The old turtle winked its red eyes again. "Lissenbee, you talk too damn much," says the turtle. With that Lissenbee spun round like a top, and then he lit out for town.

When Lissenbee come to the tavern and told the people about the turtle that could talk, they just laughed in his face. "You come with me," says he, "and I'll show you!" So the whole crowd went along, but when they got there the old turtle didn't say a word. It looked just like any other turtle, only bigger than the common kind. The people was mad because they had walked away out there in the hot sun for nothing, so they kicked Lissenbee into the ditch and went back to town. Pretty soon Lissenbee set up, and the old turtle winked its red eyes. "Didn't I tell you?" says the turtle. "You talk too damn much."

Some people around here say the whole thing was a joke, because it ain't possible for a turtle to talk. They claim some fellow must have hid in the bushes and throwed his voice, so it just sounded like the turtle was a-talking. Everybody knows that those medicine-show doctors can make a wooden dummy talk good enough to fool almost anybody. There was a boy here in town that tried to learn how out of a book, but he never done no good at it. The folks never found nobody in these parts that could throw his voice like that.

Well, no matter if it was a joke or not, the story sure fixed old blabbermouth Lissenbee. The folks just laughed at his tales after that, and they would say he better go talk to the turtles about it.

SOURCE: Vance Randolph, ed. *The Talking Turtle and Other Ozark Folk Tales*, 3–5.

Vance Randolph began collecting Ozark tales in the 1920s, and he tried to record each story "as accurately as possible, without any polishing or embellishment." He wrote with nostalgia about the Ozark Mountain people, who lack "material wealth" but have inherited "a leisurely way of life." "There is still time for conversation. . . . Every hilltop has its tradition, every hollow is full of tales and legends." The tale about the talking turtle was told by George E. Hastings. "Reports of this story from English-speaking white informants are rare," we learn in the notes to the story added by the folklorist Herbert Halpert. "The story is usually told by Negroes," Halpert adds, "and I believe it is of African origin."

JOHN AND THE BLACKSNAKE

One time John went down to the pond to catch him a few catfish. He put his line in the water, and cause the sun was warm John began to doze off a little. Soon as his head went down a little, he heard someone callin' his name. "John, John," like that. John jerked up his head and looked around, but he didn't see no one. Two-three minutes after that, he heard it again. "John, John." He looked to one side and the other. He looked down at the water and he looked up in the air. And after that he looked behind him and saw a big old blacksnake settin' on a stone pile.

"Who been callin' my name?" says John.

"Me," the blacksnake tell him. "It's me that called you."

John didn't feel too comfortable talkin' to a blacksnake, and he feel mighty uneasy about a blacksnake talkin' to him. He say, "What you want?"

"Just called your name to be sociable," blacksnake tell him.

John look all around to see was anyone else there. "How come you pick me to socialize with?"

"Well," blacksnake say, "you is the only one here, and besides that, John, ain't we both black?"

"Let's get it straight," says John, "they's two kinds of black, yours and mine, and they ain't the same thing."

"Black is black," blacksnake say, "and I been thinkin' on it quite a while. You might say as we is kin."

That was too much for John. He jumped up and sold out, went down the road like the Cannonball Express. And comin' down the road they was a wagon with Old Boss in it. Old Boss stop and wait till John get there. He say, "John, I thought you was down to the pond fishin' for catfish?"

John looked over his shoulder, said, "I was, but I ain't."

Old Boss say, "John, you look mighty scared. What's your hurry?"

John say, "Old Boss, when blacksnakes get to talkin', that's when I get to movin'."

"Now, John," Old Boss say, "you know that blacksnakes don't talk."

"John and the Blacksnake," from Harold Courlander, ed., *A Treasury of Afro-American Folklore*, 1976. Reprinted by permission of the Emma Courlander Trust.

"Indeed I know it," John say, "and that's why, in particular, I'm a-goin', 'cause this here blacksnake is doin' what you say he don't."

"'Pears to me as you been into that liquid corn again," Old Boss say. "I'm disappointed in you, John. You let me down."

"It ain't no liquid corn," John say. "It's worse than liquid corn. It's a big old blacksnake settin' on a rock pile down by the pond."

"Well," Old Boss say, "let's go take a look."

So Old Boss went with John back to the pond, and the blacksnake was still there settin' on the stones.

"Tell him," John said to the blacksnake. "Tell Old Boss what you told me."

But the blacksnake just set there and didn't say a word.

"Just speak up," John say, "tell him what I hear before."

Blacksnake didn't have a word to say, and Old Boss tell John, "John, you got to stay off that corn. I'm mighty disappointed in you. You sure let me down." After that Old Boss got in his wagon and took off.

John looked mean at the blacksnake. He say, "Blacksnake, how come you make me a liar?"

Blacksnake say, "John, you sure let *me* down too. I spoke with you and nobody else. And the first thing you do is go off and tell everything you know to a white man."

SOURCE: Harold Courlander, ed., *A Treasury of Afro-American Folklore*, 441–42.

A variant of tales about talking skulls and singing tortoises, this story meditates on the racial divide, testing loyalties and allegiances, with a blacksnake that insists on solidarity and a slave that disavows color lines and confides in a white Old Boss rather than taking blacksnake in as his confidant. This snake is less treacherous than sociable and trusting, showing his moral superiority by contrast to Old Boss, who brands John a liar.

FARMER MYBROW AND THE FAIRIES

Farmer Mybrow was one day looking about for a suitable piece of land to convert into a field. He wished to grow corn and yams. He discovered a fine spot, close to a great forest—which latter was the home of some fairies. He set to work at once to prepare the field.

Having sharpened his great knife, he began to cut down the bushes. No sooner had he touched one than he heard a voice say, "Who is there, cutting down the bushes?" Mybrow was too much astonished to answer. The question was repeated. This time the farmer realized that it must be one of the fairies, and so replied, "I am Mybrow, come to prepare a field." Fortunately for him the fairies were in great good humor. He heard one say, "Let us all help Farmer Mybrow to cut down the bushes." The rest agreed. To Mybrow's great delight, the bushes were all rapidly cut down—with very little trouble on his part. He returned home, exceedingly well pleased with his day's work, having resolved to keep the field a secret even from his wife.

Early in January, when it was time to burn the dry bush, he set off to his field, one afternoon, with the means of making a fire. Hoping to have the fairies' assistance once more, he intentionally struck the trunk of a tree as he passed. Immediately came the question, "Who is there, striking the stumps?" He promptly replied, "I am Mybrow, come to burn down the bush." Accordingly, the dried bushes were all burned down, and the field left clear in less time than it takes to tell it.

Next day the same thing happened. Mybrow came to chop up the stumps for firewood and clear the field for digging. In a very short time his faggots and firewood were piled ready, while the field was bare.

So it went on. The field was divided into two parts—one for maize and one for yams. In all the preparations—digging, sowing, planting—the fairies gave great assistance. Still, the farmer had managed to keep the whereabouts of this field a secret from his wife and neighbors.

The soil having been so carefully prepared, the crops promised exceedingly well. Mybrow visited them from time to time, and congratulated himself on the splendid harvest he would have.

One day, while maize and yams were still in their green and milky state, Mybrow's wife came to him. She wished to know where his field lay, that she might go and fetch some of the firewood from it. At first he refused to tell her. Being very persistent, however, she finally succeeded in obtaining the information—but on one condition. She must not answer any question that should be asked her. This she readily promised, and set off for the field.

When she arrived there she was utterly amazed at the wealth of the corn and yam. She had never seen such magnificent crops. The maize looked most tempting—being still in the milky state—so she plucked an ear. While doing so she heard a voice say, "Who is there, breaking the corn?" "Who dares ask me such a question?" she replied angrily—quite forgetting her husband's command. Going to the field of yams she plucked one of them also. "Who is there, picking the yams?" came the question again. "It is I, Mybrow's wife. This is my husband's field and I have a right to pick." Out came the fairies. "Let us all help Mybrow's wife to pluck her corn and yams," they said. Before the frightened woman could speak a word, the fairies had all set to work with a will, and the corn and yams lay useless on the ground. Being all green and unripe, the harvest was now utterly spoiled. The farmer's wife wept bitterly, but to no purpose. She returned slowly home, not knowing what to say to her husband about such a terrible catastrophe. She decided to keep silence about the matter.

Accordingly, next day the poor man set off gleefully to his field to see how his fine crops were going on. His anger and dismay may be imagined when he saw his field a complete ruin. All his work and foresight had been absolutely ruined through his wife's forgetfulness of her promise.

SOURCE: William Henry Barker and Cecilia Sinclair, *West African Folk-Tales*, 181–84.

Silence, discretion, and trustworthiness are important values in the universe of the folktale, particularly when it comes to transactions with mysterious, otherworldly creatures. Some readers may be familiar with what folklorists call "The Gifts of the Little People," a story about elves, fairies, or dwarfs who offer help or a reward to a figure in need and then withdraw it or discontinue their services when they are offended in some way. The enigmatic story "The Elves and the Shoemaker," collected by the Brothers Grimm in the nineteenth century, falls into that category.

PART IV

SILENCE AND PASSIVE RESISTANCE: THE TAR-BABY STORY

How is it that tar baby has become taboo? Once among the most widely distributed tales in the world, "The Wonderful Tar-Baby Story" has become an endangered species in the folkloric universe. While variants of fairy tales like "Little Red Riding Hood" and "Sleeping Beauty" seem to proliferate at exponential rates, colonizing new media and settling comfortably into new cultural territory, the tar baby story risks extinction. It has become a sticky subject, especially because of the nexus of associations tied to it, linking blackness with silence and passive-aggressive behavior.

Folklorists have tried to capture the story's essence with the phrase "outlaw peasant outwits inventive master with wit and cunning," but the story resists superficial efforts to pin down its meaning and does its cultural work at a much deeper level than that phrase suggests. Efforts to contain its meaning are doomed, for like many folktales it contains at its core a hermeneutic puzzle, in this case an amorphous mass—mute, passive, and evasive—that invites us to make sense of it and solve its mysteries, if only for our own time and place.

There has been no shortage of critical interventions that read the tar-baby story, rooted in an agrarian culture, as an allegory of slavery, a tale grounded in human passions but with animal actors. Bernard Wolfe, for example, famously read the tar baby story in historical terms as a fable depicting race relationships in the United States, with the tale's central figure as the embodied expression of resistance. "The Negro, in other words, is wily enough to escape from the engulfing pit of blackness, although his opponents, who set the trap, do their level best to keep him imprisoned in it," he wrote (31–41). Lawrence Levine read African American tales like "The Tar Baby" as therapeutic exercises offering "psychic relief" and a "sense of mastery" (Levine 1977, 105). More than expressions of wish-fulfillment, they also broadcast lessons about "the art of surviving and even triumphing in the face of a hostile environment." Both Wolfe and Levine emphasize the therapeutic and strategic value of folklore, all the while keeping their sights trained on the canonical Uncle Remus story.

Over the decades, African Americans made the story of the tar baby their own. They were working within a long and venerable tradition, one that drove Joel Chandler Harris, among others, nearly to distraction. Was the tale of "remote African origin," as Harris speculated, in which case it functioned as "mere amusement"? Or is there something uniquely *American* about Brer Rabbit? "It needs no scientific investigation," Harris wrote, "to show why he [the Negro] selects as his hero the weakest and most harmless of all animals. . . . It is not *virtue* that triumphs, but *helplessness* . . . the parallel between the case of the 'weakest' of all animals, who must, perforce, triumph though his shrewdness, and the humble condition of the slave raconteur, is not without its pathos" (Harris 1880, 158–59). Pathos perhaps, but also anxiety about creatures who do not hesitate to maul and murder, getting revenge as they kill and maim.

Today it seems obvious that the tar-baby story could not possibly have materialized from thin air. Tradition and lore crossed the Atlantic with slaves and were reinvigorated and transmuted to become socially relevant, up close and personal yet also expansive and communal. As we shall see, the tar-baby story has struck deep roots in many cultures. Crucial to understanding its African American incarnations is a look at the broader landscape of the story and the core issues that have given it remarkable staying power.

What quickly becomes evident in combing through a folkloric record that includes hundreds of tar baby stories is the power of the tale's principal trope: a sticky trap that works much like quicksand, perversely drawing its power to ensnare from resistance. Helplessness could not be more vividly evoked. Is it any wonder that the story of the tar baby came to be enshrined as slavery's most ubiquitous narrative, paradoxically capturing both the physical impossibility of liberation as well as the intellectual hope of using words and wit to elude captivity? Brer Rabbit may not be able to use his brawn to escape the grip of the tar baby, but he does cheat a deathtrap through mental agility and the clever use of language.

As we shall see, folklorists have worked hard to describe the story's architecture and its dramatis personae, but they have not drawn up an inventory of the story's binaries, the way in which the plot lines up work against theft, deception against innocence, assault against passive resistance, loquacity against silence, and in some instances male against female as well as human against simulacrum. The story may unfold in an orderly fashion, but it is soon disturbed by disorderly behaviors, drawing listeners and readers into a vortex of cultural oppositions and contradictions. As we try to make sense of the tale, it turns on us, trapping us as we make feints and thrusts to get at its core.

At the mysterious center of the American Brer Rabbit story stands the tar baby— "artfully shaped, black, disturbing, threatening yet inviting" (Morrison 1981, xiii). Enigmatic in its silence, it triangulates the contest between two antagonists and animates the binaries that drive its plot. That figure of blackness anchors the story and represents one of the constitutive features of the tale. But it is just one of many features, and research by folklorists has established many other key components in the tale's structure. Aurelio Espinosa collected well over one hundred versions of the story and set down the following typology:

1. A man or an animal has a garden or orchard, or just food put away somewhere.

2. A certain animal (a jackal, a monkey, a hare or rabbit, etc.) comes night after night to steal the garden produce, the fruit, or the food.

3. The man or animal wishes to catch the thief and sets up a tar-figure, male or female (tar-man, tar-woman, tar-monkey, etc.).

4. A thief approaches to steal and when he sees the tar-figure he tries to engage him in conversation or tells him to get out of the way.

5. Receiving no reply the animal-thief begins to attack, striking first with the right hand or paw.

6. This sticks or is held fast and the animal then begins the dramatic monologue with the usual threats.

7. The dramatic monologue and the attacks continue, and the thief is finally caught fast at four, five, or even six points.

8. The next day the man or animal finds his thief well caught.

9. Although frequently punished the animal-thief escapes alive.

Espinosa enumerates the tale's basic plot moves, yet he too falls into the trap of corralling all stories with the so-called stickfast motif into the tar baby tale type (1930, 129–209).

The origins of "The Wonderful Tar-Baby Story" are deeply contested, in part because its central motif is often taken as the key element. One early study of the tale by the renowned folklorist Joseph Jacobs made the case—on the basis of the stickfast motif as well as the nineteenth-century faith in India as the original home of all folktales— for identifying South Asia as the source. Citing several accounts in the *Jataka*, a literary compilation of episodes from Buddha's previous lives, Jacobs declared India as the tale's point of origin. In one story, Buddha is trapped by a monster called "Sticky-Hair" and persuades the monster to liberate him, though without resorting to reverse psychology. He simply declares his immunity to fear of death (we all die one day anyway), and adds that the story he carries in his body will make mincemeat of anyone who tries to swallow him. Some other experts dispute Jacobs's views and assert French origins, pointing to Reynard the Fox narratives, which could have migrated to the United States with French settlers in the Southern states as well as with slaves from Francophone countries in West Africa (Jacobs, 253–53; Brown 1978, 180–85; Varty 245–67).

A look at African tales with rubber men, tar dolls, and other sticky figures offers compelling evidence that the tale crossed the Atlantic with slaves and was brilliantly mined to create new, socially relevant tales. African tales about sticky images turn on greed, theft, and trickery, and they often feature the unscrupulous Anansi, who is willing to let his children starve before he goes hungry. At times Anansi falls victim to the trap set for him, at times he is the one who ensnares. But what quickly becomes evident in reading accounts about tricksters and traps is the malleability of the tale, which can be used to teach almost anything. In "The Tale of Ntrekuma," for example, Anansi's public humiliation becomes the opportunity to broadcast the message that shame does not require suicidal action. Another variant of the story, however, tells about the origin of theft, born when a man caught by Anansi in the act of stealing was killed and chopped up into small pieces, which were then sown to create a multitude of thieves (shades of Cadmus and other mythological figures).

In some tales, Anansi figures out how to elude his captor; in others, he must rely on his son's ingenuity to liberate him. With each new narrative twist, the tale is reimagined, sometimes with a simple explanatory message, as in the story of Anansi and how spiders ended up in the rafters of houses. That straightforward lesson often masks deeper, less legible truths that require conversation to make sense out of them. "Why the Hare Runs Away," collected from the Ewe-speaking peoples on the west coast of Africa is, on the face of things, an explanatory fable, but it also engages with matters of etiquette and social hierarchies, with a hare who is offended by an image that will not greet him and who subsequently barely escapes with his life from the confrontation with an inert mass of matter. The hare's betrayal of community norms and the consequences for his action make the tale as much a revealing social fable as an explanatory tale telling us about why hares are so jumpy.

Excavating the African past of the tar-baby story reveals much about its African American inflections. The African tales emerged from scenes of storytelling that we can no longer resurrect. But occasionally we come across evocative accounts from the United States, like the one described by the foklorist William J. Faulkner, who grew up with the stories in the South:

> I was a frequent visitor of Simon Brown's during the years he lived in the "downstairs house" next to my family's home. In the center of Simon's house stood a huge brick chimney with two wide fireplaces, one on either side. Simon liked to spend his evenings there, in the warmth and glow of the fire. He'd sit in his homemade cane-bottom rocking chair and tell me stories of his life as a slave in Virginia . . . and how hard it was for our people to live. Or he'd tell me stories out of his imagination or the imagination of others he'd heard around the campfire in the slave quarters years ago. It was a time of great wonder for me. (9, 10)

Simon Brown himself acknowledged that the trickster hero enacted folk wisdom for slaves living in the old South: "Like Brer Rabbit, we had to be deceitful and use our heads to stay alive."

If we will never know all the twists and turns taken by folktales told on long nights around the campfire and hearth, the rough truths encapsulated in them emerge to some extent from the written record. The first recorded version of the African American tar baby tale appeared in 1875 in *Leslie's Comic Almanac*, published in New York (Nickels 364–69). It included both the tar-baby story and a tale about Brudder Wolf feigning death. The excerpt reprinted here includes only the first of the two legends, as they are called. Leslie's prefatory comments suggest that he sees the stories as functioning much the same way as do fairy tales, and he evokes a saccharine scene of storytelling, with a fictitious granny conveying her wisdom to "little wooly heads." The Negro legends are equated with "Little Red Riding Hood" and "Cinderella," as if they belonged to the culture of childhood. Although Leslie concedes that the tales are all about "strategy," he still positions them as harmless, told for amusement rather than instruction, and serving to pass the time more than anything else.

Two years after Leslie published his tar-baby story, William Owens included several African American tales in *Lippincott's Magazine*. Unlike Leslie, who gives a portrait—perhaps real, perhaps imagined—of tales being passed down to the next generation, Owens offers no romantic tableau and no cultural context whatsoever. It is as if he just happened on these tales and decided to write them down. Still, for him, the "fables" recorded furnished a kind of index to the "mental and moral characteristic" of a race. He discovers a near perfect fit between African American "character" and the personal traits of figures in African folklore. The notion of folklore as larger than life, filled with excess and exaggeration, seems to have escaped him. He cheerfully recites an inventory of racial stereotypes, without any awareness whatsoever of the possibility that "many a dark one" might deviate in any way from his model:

> Any one who will take the trouble to analyze the predominant traits of negro character, and to collate them with the predominant traits of African folk-lore will discern the fitness of each to each. On every side he [the reader] will discover evidences of a passion for music and dancing, for visiting and chatting, for fishing and snaring, indeed for any pleasure requiring little exertion of either mind or body; evidences

also of a gentle, pliable and easy temper—of a quick and sincere sympathy with suffering wheresoever seen—of a very low standard of morals, combined with remarkable dexterity in satisfying themselves that it is right to do as they wish. Another trait, strong enough and universal enough to atone for many a dark one, is that, as a rule, there is nothing of the fierce and cruel in their nature, and it is scarcely possible for anything of this kind to be grafted permanently upon them. (748)

Owens fails to realize that the inventory of leisure activities he supplies is not at all unique to one race, although few races had to endure collectively the long days of brute, backbreaking labor to which slaves and sharecroppers were subjected in the southern United States. Less shocking is the ease with which Owens overlooks the "fierce" and "cruel" elements in the stories he has collected, never mind his failure to understand that the stories might be encoded with messages about the social, moral, and economic conditions of slavery.

Those were not Joel Chandler Harris's objections to Owens's stories when he read "Folk-Lore of the Southern Negroes." What bothered him was that Owens had produced versions of the tales that did not at all resonate with his own memories of hearing the stories. Harris was sure that he personally had a hotline to African American folklore and that what he had witnessed as a boy was an authentic storytelling performance rather than a mediated literary production. His tales, told in dialect, would capture the true letter and spirit of the stories. "The Wonderful Tar-Baby Story" recounts Brer Rabbit's capture, while "How Mr. Rabbit Was Too Sharp for Mr. Fox" gives us the famous briar-patch coda to the tale.

In the decades following the publication of Owens's "The Story of Buh Rabbit and the Tar Baby" and Harris's "The Wonderful Tar-Baby Story," the tale became the target of folkloric and anthropological speculations even as it inspired citation, imitation, and reinvention. Julia Collier Harris, the daughter of Joel Chandler Harris, recognized the story's seductive power:

Of all the "Uncle Remus" legends written during twenty-five years and gathered into five separate volumes, the "Tar-Baby" story is perhaps the best loved. Father received letters about this story from every quarter of the civilized world. Missionaries have translated it into the Bengali and African dialects; learned professors in France, England, Austria, and Germany have written, suggesting clues as to its source; it has been used to illustrate points in Parliamentary debates, and has been quoted from pulpits and in the halls of Congress. (Julia Collier Harris, 145)

The simple story about a rabbit, his antagonist, and the simulacrum designed to ensnare him may have once operated as a popular touchstone, but it has lost its cultural traction today. U.S. politicians have repeatedly come under critical fire for using a racial slur by invoking the tale. Writing in *The New Republic*, John McWhorter noted that "those who feel that tar baby's status as slur is patently obvious are judging from the fact that it sounds like a racial slur, because tar is black and baby sounds dismissive."

The nexus of blackness, race, and evil in the cultural imagination was articulated nowhere more clearly than in Paul Laurence Dunbar's short story "The Lynching of Jube Benson," in which the narrator, Dr. Melville, describes his encounter with the victim: "I saw his black face glooming there in the half light, and I could only think of him as a monster. It's tradition. At first I was told that the black man would catch me, and when I got over that, they taught me that the devil was black, and when I recovered from the sickness of that belief, here were Jube and his fellows with faces of menacing blackness. There was only one conclusion: This black man stood for all the powers of evil, the result of whose machinations had been gathering in my mind from childhood up. But this has nothing to do with what happened" (379). The weight of the cultural baggage carried by the white narrator since childhood has, of course, everything to do with what happened, and the disavowal is as telling as the confession. Blackness is connected in his mind with monstrosity and evil, and the tar baby can scarcely evade all those cultural associations.

Even if the reality of the belief that the phrase is a racial slur cannot be refuted, it may be time to reclaim the story, along with the iconic power of the figure at its center. Writers like Toni Morrison have recognized the value of recovering the ancestral past, resurrecting genealogies and histories, along with stories that were once the cultural property of all African Americans. And in a film like *Selma* (2014), directed by Ava DuVernay, ancestors are the spirits inspiring their descendants to determined action.

India, Lithuania, Mexico, Venezuela, Chile, Santo Domingo, Portugal, Jamaica, Mauritius: These are just a few of the sites at which versions of the tar-baby story have been documented. It is in Caribbean cultures that the story still flourishes today, with tellers embroidering on the source material in ways that sometimes make the earlier versions almost unrecognizable. In Antigua, Anansi becomes "Aunt Nancy," a male figure who tries to sweet talk a tar baby into handing over the goods. Jokey, melodramatic, and triumphantly on the side of the trickster, these creolized tales mix and mingle elements, old and new, to refashion, animate, and energize Anansi, Aunt Nancy, Be-Rabbie, and their other folkloric kin.

If Joel Chandler Harris endorsed the African origins of the tale and others insisted that they sprang from the soil of the U.S. South, still others point to Native American versions of the story and European cognates as source material. We have included two Cherokee tales recorded in the mid-nineteenth century as interesting grounds for comparison with other tar baby stories. The competing claims about the exact source for the tale run afoul of all efforts to locate folkloric origins. The lack of documentation in one region is not evidence of the tale's absence in that region. A written record is nothing more than an indicator of one person's desire to document performances that in other places might not have been captured in words. One folklorist cynically identified the underlying nationalist motives for studying a tale's origins: "In each case, the attribution of origin becomes the collector's gift to 'his people'" (Baer 31).

There is much at stake in tracing origins, yet it may make more sense to invoke here the ancient ocean of story, the sea that Salman Rushdie has described as a "liquid tapestry," in which tales are fluid, constantly morphing into new versions of themselves. Elusive and mercurial, they are impossible to pin down to one geographical location or a single era. Far more compelling than the question of origins is the issue of loss. Why is the tar-baby story disappearing from our cultural archive? This creature made up of dark matter is both male and female, mute yet also revelatory, amorphous but also powerfully legible. It challenges us to make the inchoate speak, to attribute meaning to what is presented as dark, mute, and incomprehensible.

Toni Morrison took up the invitation to endow this ancient figure with meaning when she wrote her novel *Tar Baby* (1981). She confronts the enigmatic core to the tale when she asks: "Why a tar figure?" "And why (in the version I was told) is it dressed as a female?" she adds. Her description of the transmission of tales captures how stories are passed down and how they memorialize ancestors and conversations, all the while serving as connective tissue between generations and binding kin together in ways that remind us of how slavery fractured and dismembered African American families.

There were four of us in the room: me, my mother, my grandmother, and my great-grandmother. The oldest one intemperate, brimming with hard, scary wisdom. The youngest, me, a sponge. My mother, gifted, gregarious, burdened with insight. My grandmother a secret treasure whose presence anchored the frightening, enchanted world. Three women and a girl who never stopped listening, watching, seeking their advice, and eager for their praise. All four of us people the writing of *Tar Baby* as witness, as challenge, as judges intent on the uses to which stories are put and the manner of their telling. (2007, xiv)

SPIDER AND THE FARMER

There was a famine in Spider's country, and Spider had nothing to eat. Now Spider had a son, named Kwaku Tyom, and Spider's son used to go to a farm not far away and steal cassavas.[1] And every day when he brought home the cassava roots, his father would ask, "Where did you find these?" Spider's son always answered that he could not say, for if he, Spider, were to go there, some harm might befall him. Spider said, "Oh! You are my own son, and yet you believe that you are more clever than I? Show me the place, and I will make sure that no one sees me." Spider's son still refused to show the place to his father.

1 *cassava:* a starchy, tuberous root from a woody shrub extensively cultivated in tropical regions

Whenever Spider's son went to the farm to dig up cassava roots, he would carry a sack, which he filled up and brought home. Spider played a trick on his son Kwaku Tyom. When night fell and his son was sleeping, Spider put wood ashes into the sack and made a hole in the bottom.

The next morning Spider's son arose and slung the sack around his neck. He left to go to the farm, and, while he was walking, ashes fell on the ground through the hole in the sack and marked the path to the farm. Spider was following his son and saw the road, but he did not go to the farm that day. He returned home and said nothing. In the evening Spider's son returned home with the cassava roots.

The next morning Spider arose early and followed the track left by the ashes. When he reached the farm he saw something there that was made of crossed sticks. It was standing right in the middle of the fields, and there were some snail shells hanging from it. The shells rattled in the breeze.

When Spider was afraid, he greeted whatever it was, saying "Good morning, sir." The whatever it was gave him no answer. Spider was vexed and said, "Oh! Do you want me to shake your hand before you reply?" He put his hand out to whatever it was, and his hand stuck to the sticks. He could not pull it back.

Spider lost his temper and said, "What kind of manners do you have? I was polite enough to shake your hand, and now you are still holding my hand and won't let go." He extended his left hand, and it became stuck as well. "Well, well," said Spider. "What do you want from me? You have both my hands. Did you want a hug from me?" He put his face on the shoulder of whatever it was, and it remained stuck there. He couldn't get his face off the shoulder. He used his feet to kick at the sticks, and they also became stuck.

Spider could not move, and he stayed where he was all day and up until the next morning, when the plantation owner arrived and saw Spider fastened to whatever it was. And the farmer said, "Hello, Father Spider. Are you the one who has been digging up my roots? I have you at last."

Spider's wife and Spider's son Kwaku Tyom knew that Spider had gone over to the farm, for he had not been in the house that night.

The farmer said to Spider, "I have lost about two hundred and fifty cassavas from my farm, and, if you don't pay me, I won't let you go." Spider begged for forgiveness and pleaded with the farmer to let him go. He promised that he would pay him back, and the farmer released him.

Spider told the farmer to come back home with him, and they walked back together. When they arrived at Spider's house, his wife and son were there. The farmer said to Spider's wife, "I saw Spider at my farm this morning. He was stuck in place. I've lost about two hundred and fifty cassavas from my farm. When I asked Spider about them, he confessed that he had taken them. He promised to pay me, and here I am, ready to be paid."

Spider's son said to his father, "I told you not to go to the farm. My mother told me that you put some ashes into my sack when I was asleep, and then you put a hole in the sack. I had no idea that I was spilling ashes on the road. Now, Father, how are you going to manage to pay up?"

Spider answered softly, "Never mind, my son, I will pay him up on the roof."

Spider told the farmer that he wanted to go to the room where he slept, but the farmer said, "No I am not going to let you leave. You are way too tricky." But Spider begged the farmer, saying that he only wanted to go into the room to get the money to pay him, and he said that he would return at once. At last, after a long back and forth, the farmer let Spider go.

When Spider had moved about three steps from where the farmer was sitting, he cried out, "Oh, Oh, daddy farmer. I don't have any money at all for you here, but I will pay you up on the roof top." And he leaped up into the rafters, from where he called out, "I'm not coming back down again."

Since that time, Spider has not come down from the roof, for he owes the farmer too much, and the farmer is still looking for him.

SOURCE: A. B. Ellis, "Evolution in Folklore: Some West African Prototypes of the 'Uncle Remus' Stories." *Appleton's Popular Science Monthly* 48 (1895), 94–96.

The Ewe language is spoken by over three million people in southeastern Ghana and southern Togo. A. B. Ellis's study of Ewe-speaking peoples represents a classic case of anthropology gone wrong, with the researcher imposing Western values on the people observed. The value of the volume lies in its exposure of the nineteenth-century faith in "civilization," with all its tragic blind spots, obtuse thinking, and preposterous "scientific" theories. But thanks to those who also had faith in recording tales as literally as possible, we have a tar-baby story that reveals the African source for African American variants.

Ellis makes the following absurd remarks in his introduction: "The Ewe-speaking peoples of the Slave Coast present the ordinary characteristics of the uncivilized negro. In early life they evince a degree of intelligence which, compared with that of the European child, appears precocious; and they acquire knowledge with facility till they arrive at the age of puberty, when the physical nature masters the intellect, and frequently completely deadens it. This peculiarity, which has been observed amongst others of what are termed the lower races, has been attributed by some physiologists to the early closing of the sutures of the cranium, and it is worthy of note that throughout West Africa it is by no means rare to find skulls without any apparent transverse or longitudinal sutures."

In this version of the tar-baby story, a tale about theft and its punishment is turned into an etiological tale about why spiders weave their webs in rafters. Note that the tale is set in times of famine, the mark of a lack that must be liquidated in some way, to use the terms of the Russian folklorist Vladimir Propp.

TALE OF NTREKUMA

Now it happened that famine came to the land where the family of Anansi was living, and there was little food left in the fields that belonged to Anansi. He decided to pretend to be ill. Calling his children, he told them to hurry and consult a medicine man. Being naturally obedient, they did as they were told. But their father, who had disguised himself as a medicine man, left before they did and was sitting at a crossroads waiting for them. When his children approached him, he asked them why they were in such a hurry. They told him that their father Anansi was ill and that they were on their way to consult a medicine man. Anansi, whom the children did not recognize, said that he was a medicine man. If they wanted, he would help them figure out what was best to do.

The children agreed, and, after consulting his stones and other things, Anansi told his children that their father was going to die and that they must bury him on the farm. They should dig a nice deep grave with one room for the body and then a nice entrance hall. They should not cover it up. At the same time they were told to put plenty of fish, salt, meat, and pepper, along with all kinds of other foods, each day at the entrance hall.

The children, after hearing the sad news, rushed back to the father that they were soon to lose. Unfortunately, they arrived too late and found that Anansi was already dead. There was nothing to be done but to carry out the orders given to them by the elderly gentleman at the crossroads. And so they went out to the fields and dug a nice deep grave with a room and an entrance hall. They brought their father all the food that the medicine man had ordered them to bring. Then they left.

Every night Anansi would get out of his grave and steal enough yams to keep himself well supplied during the day. After a while his son Ntrekuma began to suspect that something was going on, and he had the usual rubber man fashioned and set it up on the farm. He placed plenty of yams that had been cooked and mashed up in front of the figure. That very night Anansi saw the food and begged the rubber man to let him have some of it. The rubber man nodded, and Anansi took that to mean "yes." He leaned down to get some of the food, and one of his arms stuck fast. He flailed with the other, and soon it too was stuck. He kicked his foot, and it was stuck. He butted his head, and it stuck fast in the rubber.

"Tale of Ntrekuma," from Allan Wolsey Cardinall, ed., *Tales Told in Togoland*, 1931. By permission of Oxford University Press.

Anansi had to stay like that until the morning, when his children came into the field. Ntrekuma recognized his father right away, and Anansi shouted: "Go away, go away. I am not your father. I just look like him. Go away! I am full of medicine. Don't come near me! Don't touch me! If you come closer to me, I will turn into your father." The children approached, and Anansi kept shouting: "I shall turn. I shall. I have."

The children walked toward their father, and Ntrekuma scolded him for his trickery. Anansi was ashamed, but because he was a crafty man, he refused to die. And from that day to the present time, many men, although covered with shame, do not go into the bush and kill themselves. At one time everyone did.

A second story runs along similar lines.

Anansi sets a trap. The rubber man catches the farm thief, and Ntrekuma and his father cut the unfortunate fellow up into very small pieces and scatter them all over the place. This was a foolish thing to do, especially since Anansi, as a medicine man, should have known better. The pieces of the thief turned into men and kept the thieving propensities of their forefather. Thus it came about that there are many thieves in the world.

SOURCE: Adapted from Allan Wolsey Cardinall, ed., *Tales Told in Togoland*, 235–37.

Both of these stories take odd turns in their conclusions, with explanations about human nature and cultural practices. Anansi may not do much good in the first story, but—in classic trickster fashion—he commits acts that lead to positive cultural changes. In the second story, he inadvertently makes theft more common than it was before.

TAR BABY

The King had a place with fruit, plantains, and all kinds of other food. But outsiders were stealing the fruit and the food. So the King made them put up a large tar doll in the yard. Now the thief came at night. This was friend Anansi. When he saw the doll he was alarmed. He said, "Father, how are you?" But he did not get a single word in answer. He said, "If you do not answer, I will slap you." The doll did not answer. Anansi struck him a blow. His hand stuck. He said, "If you do not release me, I will hit you with my other hand." Anansi struck with the other hand. But that hand stuck too. He said, "If you do not release me, I will butt you." Anansi butted him. His head stuck. He said, "If you do not release me, I will kick you." So Anansi kicked him. But he could do nothing more because his head, his feet, and his hands were stuck. So he had to remain there until they came and found him. They made an announcement that Anansi was the thief. So the King said he would kill Anansi.

Anansi was about to die, and he sent for his children. He said, "My children, you see I am going to die. But what are you going to do for me?" Each one of his children told him a foolish thing, but the youngest said to him, "Father, you know what I am going to do? I am going to hide on top of a tall tree, where they will put you in order to kill you. Then I will sing:

"They kill Anansi till . . .
They kill Anansi till . . .
The whole country will be flooded;
All the people will die;
The King himself will die.
Anansi alone will remain."

When the King heard the voice singing, he said "What is that?"
Anansi said, "Listen, my King, God himself pleads for me."
The King said, "It is not true. Thieves must be punished."
Anansi said, "My King, you will hear that it is true, because God will plead again for me."
At once they heard the voice:

They kill Anansi till . . .
They kill Anansi till . . .
The whole country will be flooded;
All the people will die;
The King himself will die.
Anansi alone will remain.

Then the King grew alarmed. He was afraid. He freed Anansi.

SOURCE: Melville J. Herskovits and Frances S. Herskovits, *Suriname Folklore*, 167–69.

The American anthropologist Melville J. Herskovits was one of the founding fathers of African and African American studies in the academic world. Rejecting the notion that African Americans lost their cultural heritage when they were enslaved, he showed, in The Myth of the Negro Past, *the many cultural bridges connecting slaves with their past.*

The motif of mimicking a deity by hiding in a tree and chanting words of mercy or retribution is found in many African American tales—further evidence of Herskovits's point. Here it is Anansi's youngest son who proves to be the resourceful one and manages to cheat death for his father. In African American tales, one slave generally recruits another to play God and make pronouncements from the top of a tree.

DE WOLF, DE RABBIT, AND DE TAR BABY

FROM FRANK LESLIE'S INTRODUCTION

The negroes of the South have a literature of their own although, till lately, unwritten and almost unknown. But their lyrics are now becoming famous through the Fisk Jubilee and Hampton Singers. Besides these, there are a great number of fireside legends that have been to them what Cinderella and Red Riding Hood are to us. These are almost all of animals. The negroes, even in common conversation, speak of animals as if they thought, talked, and behaved among themselves like rational beings; and the two animals most prominent in these legends are the wolf and the rabbit. They are represented as enemies, and the rabbit always comes off victorious, through his superior strategy. The following is, I believe, the most powerful of these fireside stories. But to appreciate it, you should see the old grandmother in her blue-checked, home-spun dress, and high red-and-yellow turban, with five or six little wooly heads clustering about her knee before a blazing fire, waiting for the sweet potatoes roasting in the ashes for their supper, and amusing themselves meanwhile with the story of "De Wolf, De Rabbit, and De Tar Baby."

Now de Wolf 'e bery wise man, but 'e not so wise as de Rabbit. De Rabbit, 'e mos' cunnin' man dat go on fo' leg.[1] 'E lib in de brier bush.

Now de Wolf 'e done plant corn one 'ear, but Rabbit, 'e ain't plant nuthin 'tall; 'e lib on Wolf corn all winter. Nex' 'ear, Wolf ain't plant corn, 'e tink corn crop too poor; so 'e plant groun' nut.[2] Rabbit 'e do jus' de same as befo'.

Well, Wolf 'e biggin for tink something wrong. 'E gone out in de mawnin', look at 'e groun' nut patch, look bery hard at Rabbit track, say, "I s'picion somebody ben a tief[3] my groun' nut."

Nex' mawnin', 'e 'gain meet mo' groun' nut gone, say same ting. Den 'e say, "I gwine mek one skeer crow for set up in dis yere groun' nut patch for skeer de tief."

So 'e mek one ole skeer crow, an' set um in de middle ob de groun' nut patch.

Dat night, when Rabbit come wid 'e bag for get groun' nut, 'e see de skeer crow stan' bery white in de moonshine, an' 'e say "Wha' dat?"

Nobody ain't say anyting.

"Wha' dat?" 'e say 'gain. Den nobody ain't say nuthin' an' 'e ain't see nuthin moobe,[4] so 'e gone leetle closer, an' leetle closer, till 'e git closer ter um, den 'e put out 'e paw an' touch de skeer crow. Den 'e say: "You ain't nuthin' but one old bundle o' rag! Wolf tink I gwine 'fraid you? Mus' be fool."

So 'e kick ober de skeer crow an' fill 'e bag wid groun' nut an' gone back home to de brier bush.

Nex' mawnin', Wolf gone out for look at 'e groun' nut patch, an' when 'e meet mo' groun' nut gone and de skeer crow knock down, 'e bery mad. 'E say: "Nebber you min'. I fix ole Rabbit dat done tief all my groun' nut; jus' let me show you."

So 'e mek one baby out o' tar an' set up in 'e groun' nut patch, an' say, "Jus' let ole Rabbit try for knock over dis yere Tar Baby, an' 'e'll see! I jus' want um for to try." Dat night, when Rabbit come 'gain wid 'e bag for get groun' nut an' see de Tar Baby stan' bery black in de moonshine, 'e say "Wha' dat ole Wolf done gone set up nodder skeer crow, mus' be."

So 'e moobe leetle nearer, an' leetle nearer, den 'e stop an' say, "Dis yere enty no skeer crow,[5] dis yere mus' be one gal! I mus' study 'pon dis."

So 'e tun roun' an' spread out 'e bag an' sit down in de middle ob de groun' nut patch an' look hard at de Tar Baby. Bimeby[6] 'e say, "Gal, what you name?"

Gal ain't say anyting.

"Gal, why don't you speak me? What you do dere?"

Den 'e listen long time, ain' hear anyting, 'cept whip-poorwill in 'e swamp. So 'e gone close up ter um, an' say: "Gal, you speak me, you min'! Gal, if you ain't speak me, I knock you! I knock you wid my right paw; den you tink it tunder and lighten too!"[7]

Tar Baby ain't say nuttin', so 'e knock um wid 'e right paw, an' 'e paw stick! Den 'e biggin for ho'ler: "Gal, le' go me; I tell you le' go me; wha' for you hole me?[8] If you don't le' go me, I knock you wid my lef' paw; den you tink it tunder and lighten too!"

So 'e kick um wid 'e right foot, an 'e foot stick! Den 'e say: "Now, gal, if you ain't lef me loose I tell you. If you don't I kick you wid my right foot, den you tink colt kick you."

So 'e kick um wid 'e right foot, an' 'e foot stick! Den 'e say: "Now, gal, if you ain't lef me loose mighty quick I kick you wid my lef' foot; den you tink hoss kick you."

So 'e kick um wid 'e lef' foot, an' 'e lef' foot stick! Den 'e say: "Min' now, gal, I ain't do nuttin' to you, wha' for you hole me? Mebbe you tink I can't do nuttin' to you; ain't you know I can bite you, though? If you ain't lef' me loose, I gwine bite you. Ain't you know my bite worse than snake bite?"

So 'e bite um' an' 'e nose stick!

Nex' mawnin', 'fore sun-up, Wolf gone out to 'e groun' nut patch, for see what 'e kin fin', an' 'e meet poo' Rabbit wid 'e paw an' 'e feet an' 'e nose all farsten on Tar Baby, an' 'e say, "Enty I tole you so? Look a yawnder! I reckon Tar Baby done catch ole Rabbit dis time."

So 'e tuk Rabbit off an' say: "You done tief half my groun' nut, now what I gwine do wid you?"

Den Rabbit biggin for beg,[9] "Oh Maussa Wolf, do le' me go an' I nebber tief groun'-nut no mo'." Wolf say, "No Brudder Rabbit, you ben a tief my corn, las' 'ear, an' you ben a tief my groun'-nut, dis 'ear, an' now I gwine eat you up."

Den Rabbit say, "Oh Maussa Wolf, don't do me so, but le' me beg you. You ma' roas' me, you ma' toas' me, you ma' cut me up, you ma' eat me, but do Maussa Wolf,

6 *Bimeby:* by and by

7 *You tink it tunder and lighten too:* You'll believe that it's thundering and there's lightning too

8 *wha' for you hole me?:* why are you holding me?

9 *biggin for beg:* began to plead

whatebber you do, don't trow me in de brier bush. Ef you trow me in de brier bush I gwine dead!"

So Wolf say, "You ain't want me for trow you in de brier bush, enty? dat jus' what I gwine do wid yaw." So 'e fling um in de bramble bush, an' den Rabbit laugh an' say "Hi! Maussa Wolf, ain't you know I *lib* in de brier bush? ain't yaw know all my fambly barn an' bred in de brier bush? dis jus whar I want you for put me. How you is gwine get me 'gain?"

Den Wolf bery mad 'cause see Rabbit too wise man for him. 'E gone home an' tell 'e wife, "No rabbit-soup for dinner, today," an' dey biggin for contribe,[10] an' dey mek plan for get Rabbit for come to deir house. So one day, Wolf wife call Neighbor Dog an' tell um, "Neighbor Dog, I want you for do one erran' for me. I want you for git on you hoss an' ride fars' as you kin to Rabbit doo' an' tell Brudder Rabbit, Wolf dead, an' 'fo' 'e die he leabe solum word 'e don' want nobody else for lay um out but Brudder Rabbit. An' do, Neighbor Dog, beg um for come ober quick as 'e kin so we all kin hab de funeral, for Wolf say 'e won't hab nobordy for lay um out but Brudder Rabbit."

Rabbit say, "How, Brudder Wolf dead?" "Yes, 'e die las' night an' 'e say 'e ain't want nobordy else for lay um out, an' Sister Wolf beg you for come ober an' lay um out quick as you kin so dey all kin hab de settin' up."

So Rabbit git on 'e hoss an' ride to Wolf doo'; den 'e knock an' say, "How? I yeardy Brudder Wolf dead." Wolf wife say, "Yes, 'e dead for true, an' 'fo' 'e dies 'e leabe solum word 'e ain't want nobordy else for lay um out but Brudder Rabbit."

Den Rabbit say, "Kin I shum?"[11] So Wolf wife tuk um in de bedroom an' show um Wolf lie on de bed cober up wid a sheet. Rabbit lif up de corner ob de sheet an' peep at Wolf.

Wolf nebber wink! So Rabbit took out 'e snuffbox an' drop one leetle grain of snuff on Wolf nose, an' Wolf sneeze!

Den Rabbit say: "Hi! How can *dead* man sneeze?" So 'e git on 'e hoss an' ride home fars' as 'e kin. An' Wolf see Rabbit too wise man for him, an' nebber try for cotch um no mo'.

10 *biggin for contribe:* began to plot

11 *shum:* see him

SOURCE: *The Daily Republican* (Springfield, MA), June 2, 1874. Told in Beaufort, South Carolina.

THE STORY OF BUH RABBIT
AND THE TAR BABY

FROM WILLIAM OWENS'S PREFATORY REMARKS

Of the Buh fables, that which is by all odds the greatest favorite, and which appears in the greatest variety of forms is the "Story of Buh Rabbit and the Tar Baby." Each variation preserves the great landmarks, particularly the closing scene. According to the most thoroughly African version, it runs thus: Buh Rabbit and Buh Wolf are neighbors. In a conversation one day Buh Wolf proposes that the two shall dig a well for their joint benefit, instead of depending upon chance rainfalls or going to distant pools or branches, as they often have to do, to quench their thirst. To this Buh Rabbit, who has no fondness for labor, though willing enough to enjoy its fruits, offers various objections, and finally gives a flat refusal.

"Well," says Buh Wolf, who perfectly understands his neighbor, "if you no help to dig well, you mustn't use de water."

"What for I gwine use de water?" responds Buh Rabbit with affected disdain.

"What use I got for well? In de mornin' I drink de dew, an' in middle o' day I drink from de cow-tracks."

The well is dug by Buh Wolf alone, who after a while perceives that some one besides himself draws from it. He watches, and soon identifies the intruder as Buh Rabbit, who makes his visits by night. "Ebery mornin' he see Buh Rabbit tracks— ebery mornin' Buh Rabbit tracks." Indignant at the intrusion, he resolves to set a trap for his thievish neighbor and to put him to death. Knowing Buh Rabbit's buckish love for the ladies, he fits up a *tar baby*, made to look like a beautiful girl, and sets it near the well. By what magical process this manufacture of an attractive-looking young lady out of treacherous adhesive tar is accomplished we are not informed. But listeners to stories must not be inquisitive about the mysterious parts: they must be content to hear.

Buh Rabbit, emboldened by long impunity, goes to the well as usual after dark, sees this beautiful creature standing there motionless, peeps at it time and again suspiciously; but being satisfied that it is really a young lady, he makes a polite bow and addresses her in gallant language. The young lady makes no reply. This encourages him to ask if he may not come to take a kiss. Still no reply. He sets his water-bucket on the ground, marches up boldly and obtains the kiss, but finds to his surprise that he cannot get away: his lips are held fast by the tar. He struggles and tries to persuade her to let him go. How he is able to speak with his lips sticking fast is another unexplained mystery; but no matter: he does speak, and most eloquently, yet in vain. He now changes his tone, and threatens her with a slap. Still no answer. He administers the slap, and his hand sticks fast. One after the other, both hands and both feet, as well as his mouth, are thus caught, and poor Buh Rabbit remains a prisoner until Buh Wolf comes the next morning to draw water.

"Eh! eh! Buh Rabbit, wah de matter?" exclaims Buh Wolf, affecting the greatest surprise at his neighbor's woeful plight.

Buh Rabbit, who has as little regard for truth as for honesty, replies, attempting to throw all the blame upon the deceitful maiden by whom he has been entrapped, not even suspecting yet—so we are to infer—that she is made of tar instead of living flesh. He declares with all the earnestness of injured innocence that he was passing by, in the sweet, honest moonlight, in pursuit of his lawful business, when this girl *hailed* him, and decoyed him into giving her a kiss, and was now holding him in unlawful durance.

The listener ironically commiserates with his captive neighbor, and proposes to set him free; when suddenly noticing the water-bucket and the tracks by the well, he charges Buh Rabbit with his repeated robberies by night, and concludes by declaring his intention to put him to immediate death.

The case has now become pretty serious and Buh Rabbit is of course woefully troubled at the near approach of the great catastrophe: still, even in this dire extremity, his wits do not cease to cheer him with some hope of escape. Seeing that his captor is preparing to hang him—for the cord is already around his neck and he is being dragged toward an overhanging limb—he expresses the greatest joy by capering, dancing and clapping his hands—so much so that the other curiously inquires, "What for you so glad, Buh Rabbit?"

"Oh," replies the sly hypocrite, "because you gwine hang me and trow me in the brier-bush."

"What for I mustn't trow you in de brier-bush?" inquires Mr. Simpleton Wolf.

"Oh," prays Buh Rabbit with a doleful whimper, "please hang me; please trow me in de water or trow me in de fire, where I die at once. But don't—oh don't—trow me in de brier bush to tear my poor flesh from off my bones."

"I gwine to do 'zactly wah you ax me not to do," returns Wolf in savage tone. Then, going to a neighboring patch of thick, strong briers, he pitches Buh Rabbit headlong in the midst, and says, "Now let's see de flesh come off de bones."

No sooner, however, does the struggling and protesting Buh Rabbit find himself among the briers than he slides gently to the ground, and peeping at his would-be torturer, from a safe place behind the stems, he says, "Tankee, Buh Wolf—a tousand tankee—for *bring me home!* De brier-bush *de berry place where I been born.*"

SOURCE: William Owens, *Lippincott's Magazine of Popular Literature and Science*, 750–51.

THE WONDERFUL TAR-BABY

"Didn't the fox never catch the rabbit, Uncle Remus?" asked the little boy the next evening.

"He come mighty nigh it, honey, sho's[1] you born—Brer Fox did. One day atter Brer Rabbit fool 'im wid dat[2] calamus root, Brer Fox went ter wuk[3] en go 'im some tar, en mix it wid some turkentime,[4] en fix up a contrapshun w'at he call a Tar-Baby, en he tuck dish yer[5] Tar-Baby en he so 'er[6] in de big road, en den he lay off in de bushes fer to see what da news wuz gwine ter be.[7] En he didn't hatter wait long, nudder,[8] kaze bimbeby[9] here come Brer Rabbit pacin' down de road—lippity-clippity, clippity-lippity—dez ez sassy[10] ez a jay-bird. Brer Fox, he lay low. Brer Rabbit come prancin' long twel he spy de Tar-Baby, en den he fotch up on his behime legs like he wuz 'stonished. De Tar Baby, she sot dar, she did, en Brer Fox, he lay low.

"'Mawnin'!' sez Brer Rabbit, sezzee—'nice wedder dis mawnin',' sezee.

1 *sho's:* sure as

2 *fool 'im wid dat:* fool him with that

3 *went ter wuk:* went to work

4 *turkentime:* turpentine

5 *tuck dish yer:* took this here

6 *he so 'er:* he put her

7 *gwine ter be:* was going to be

8 *hatter wait long, nudder:* have to wait long, neither

9 *kaze bimbeby:* because by and by

10 *dez ez sassy:* just as sassy

"Tar-Baby ain't sayin' nuthin', en Brer Fox he lay low.

"'How duz yo' sym'tums seem ter segashuate?'[11] sez Brer Rabbit, sezee.

11 *sym'tums seem ter segashuate:* symptoms seem to sagaciate. "How does your corporosity sagaciate?" was a regional expression, used chiefly in the South, to ask, in an amusing way, how someone was faring. The phrase made it into James Joyce's *Ulysses*, when one of the characters asks: "Your corporosity sagaciating O.K.?"

12 *squall out:* shouted

13 *wunner yo':* one of your

"Brer Fox, he wink his eye slow, en lay low, en de Tar-Baby, she ain't sayin' nuthin'.

"'How you come on, den? Is you deaf?' sez Brer Rabbit sezee. 'Kaze if you is, I kin holler louder,' sezee.

"Tar-Baby stay still, en Brer Fox, he lay low.

"'You er stuck up, dat's w'at you is,' says Brer Rabbit, sezee, 'en I'm gwine ter kyore you, dat's w'at I'm a gwine ter do,' sezee.

"Brer Fox, he sorter chuckle in his stummic, he did, but Tar-Baby ain't sayin' nothin'.

"'I'm gwine ter larn you how ter talk ter 'spectubble folks ef hit's de las' ack,' sez Brer Rabbit, sezee. 'Ef you don't take off dat hat en tell me howdy, I'm gwine ter bus' you wide open,' sezee.

"Tar-Baby stay still, en Brer Fox, he lay low.

"Brer Rabbit keep on axin' 'im, en de Tar-Baby, she keep on sayin' nothin', twel present'y Brer Rabbit draw back wid his fis', he did, en blip he tuck 'er side er de head. Right dar's whar he broke his merlasses jug. His fis' stuck, en he can't pull loose. De tar hilt 'im. But Tar-Baby, she stay still, en Brer Fox, he lay low.

"'Ef you don't lemme loose, I'll knock you agin,' sez Brer Rabbit, sezee, en wid dat he fotch 'er wipe wid de udder han' en dat stuck. Tar-Baby, she ain't sain' nuthin', en Brer Fox he lay low.

"'Tu'n me loose, fo' I kick de natchul stuffin' outen you,' sez Brer Rabbit, sezee, but de Tar-Baby, she ain't sayin' nuthin'. She des hilt on, en de Brer Rabbit lose de use er his feet in de same way. Brer Fox, he lay low. Den Brer Rabbit squall out[12] dat ef de Tar-Baby don't tu'n 'im loose he butt 'er cranksided. En den he butted, en his head got stuck. Den Brer Fox, he sa'ntered for', lookin' dez ez innercent ez wunner yo'[13] mammy's mockin'-birds.

"'Howdy, Brer Rabbit,' sez Brer Fox, sezee. 'You look sorter stuck up dis mawnin',' sezee, en den he rolled on de groun' en laft en laft twel he couldn't laff no mo'. 'I speck you'll take dinner wid me dis time, Brer Rabbit. I don laid in some calamus root, en I ain't gwineter take no skuse,' sez Brer Fox, sezee."

Here Uncle Remus paused, and drew a two-pound yam out of the ashes.

"Did the fox eat the rabbit?" asked the little boy to whom the story had been told.

"Dat's all de fur de tale goes," replied the old man. "He mout, an den agin he moutent. Some say Judge B'ar come 'long en lossed 'im—some say he didn't. I hear Miss Sally callin'. You better run 'long."

SOURCE: Joel Chandler Harris, *Uncle Remus, His Songs and His Sayings: The Folk-Lore of the Old Plantation*, 23–25.

Harris's rendition of the Tar Baby story has become the canonical one, and it is contained within a frame that shows Uncle Remus telling the stories to a "little boy," son of a plantation owner.

The Tar Baby's inability to feel and Brer Rabbit's response to its silence can be seen in symbolic terms as the slave's stoic attitude and the master's inability to take in and validate the silent suffering of a slave. The Tar Baby, an inert being without consciousness or agency, cannot respond and operate within relevant social codes. "It is his being ignored and her being ill-mannered that annoy, then infuriate him," Toni Morrison tells us about Brer Rabbit. Gendered female, the Tar Baby can be seen as a trope for passive resistance, for a refusal to follow the "genteel" codes of Southern manners. Aggression can manifest itself through a form of silence that exaggerates the lack of agency that was the lot of black slaves.

HOW MR. RABBIT WAS TOO SHARP FOR MR. FOX

"Uncle Remus," said the little boy one evening, when he had found the old man with little or nothing to do, "did the fox kill and eat the rabbit when he caught him with the Tar-Baby?"

"Law, honey, ain't I tell you 'bout dat?" replied the old darkey, chuckling slyly. "I 'clar ter grashus I ought er tole you dat, but old man Nod wuz ridin' on my eyelids 'twel a little mo'n I'd a dis'member'd my own name, en den on to dat here come yo' mammy hollerin' atter you.

"W'at I tell you w'en I fus' begin? I tole you Brer Rabbit wuz a monstus soon creetur;[1] leas'ways da's w'at I laid out fer ter tell you. Well, den honey, don't you go en make no udder calkalashuns,[2] kaze in dem days Brer Rabbit en his fambly wuz at de header de gang w'en enny racket wuz on han', en dar dey stayed. Fo' you begins fer ter wip yo' eyes 'bout Brer Rabbit, you wait en see whar'bouts Brer Rabbit gwineter fetch up at. But da's neer yer ner dar.[3]

"W'en Brer Fox fine Brer Rabbit mixt up wid de Tar-Baby, he feel mighty good, en he roll on de groun' en laff. Bimeby he up' say, sezee:

"'Well, I speck I got you dis time, Brer Rabbit,' sezee; 'maybe I ain't but I speck I is. You been runnin' roun' here sassin' atter me a mighty long time, but I speck you done come ter de een' er de row. You bin cuttin' up yo' capers en bouncin' roun' in dis neighborhood ontwel you come ter b'leeve y'se'f de boss er de whole gang.[4] En den youer allers some'rs whar you got no bizness,' sez Brer Fox, sezee. 'Who ax you fer ter come en strike up a 'quaintance wid dish yer Tar-Baby? En who stuck you up dar whar you iz? Nobody in de roun' worl. You des tuck en jam yo'se'f on dat Tar-Baby widout waitin' fer enny invite,' sez Brer Fox, sezee, 'en dar you is, en dar you'll stay twel I fixes up a bresh-pile and fires her up, kaze I'm gwineter bobbycue you[5] dis day, sho',' sez Brer Fox, sezee.

"Den Brer Rabbit talk might 'umble.

"'I don't keer w'at you do wid me, Brer Fox,' sezee, 'so you don't fling me in dat brier-patch.[6] Roas' me, Brer Fox,' sezee, 'but don't fling me in dat brier-patch,' sezee.

"'Hit's so much trouble fer ter kindle a fier,' sez Brer Fox, sezee, 'dat I speck I'll hatter hang you,' sezee.

"'Hang me des ez high as you please, Brer Fox,' sez Brer Rabbit, sezee, 'but do fer de Lord's sake don't fling me in dat brier-patch,' sezee.

"'I ain't got no string,' sez Brer Fox, sezee, 'en now I speck I'll hatter drown you,' sezee.

"'Drown me des ez deep ez you please, Brer Fox,' sez Brer Rabbit, sezee, 'but do don't fling me in dat brier-patch,' sezee.

---

1 *a monstus soon creetur:* a very speedy animal

2 *calkalashuns:* calculations

3 *neer yer ner dar:* neither here nor there

4 *de boss er de whole gang:* Brer Rabbit, as the trickster who always triumphs, is in fact the "boss of the whole gang."

5 *I'm gwineter bobbycue you:* Barbecuing Brer Rabbit is the first in an inventory of tortures that include hanging and dismemberment.

6 *brier-patch:* Brer Rabbit makes himself a home in a thorny environment that provides him protection from predators.

"'Dey ain't no water nigh,' sez Brer Fox, sezee, 'en now I speck I'll hatter skin you,' sezee.

"'Skin me, Brer Fox,' sez Brer Rabbit, sezee, 'snatch out my eyeballs, t'ar out my years by de roots,[7] en cut off my legs,' sezee, 'but do please, Brer Fox, don't fling me in dat brier-patch,' sezee.

"Co'se Brer Fox wanter hurt Brer Rabbit bad ez he kin, so he cotch 'im by de behime legs en slung 'im right in de middle er de brier-patch. Dar wuz a considerbul flutter what Brer Rabbit struck de bushes, en Brer Fox sorter hand 'roun' fer ter see w'at wuz gwineter happen. Bimeby he hear somebody call 'im, en way up de hill he see Brer Rabbit settin' cross-legged on a chinkapin[8] log koamin' de pitch outen his har wid a chip. Den Brer Fox know dat he bin swop off mighty bad. Brer Rabbit wuz bleedzed fer ter fling back some er his sass, en he holler out:

"'Bred en bawn in a brier-patch, Brer Fox—bred en bawn in a brier-patch!' en wid dat he skip out des ez lively ez a cricket in de embers."

7 *t'ar out my years by de roots:* tear my hair out by the roots

8 *chinkapin:* dwarf chestnut

SOURCE: Joel Chandler Harris, *Uncle Remus, His Songs and His Sayings: The Folk-Lore of the Old Plantation,* 29–31.

As Uncle Remus points out, what Brer Fox can't do with his feet, he accomplishes with his head. And in this case Brer Rabbit appeals to Brer Fox's baser instincts, enumerating a host of cruel ways of torturing and killing him and pleading for anything but the briar patch. That site might be considered a perilous outcome for most, but Brer Rabbit has made a career of learning to navigate his way around thorns.

TAR BABY

Dis was a time a dry weather. All de an'mals was press to get water. Dey dug a well an' did reach water. Nancy was not allowed to drink from dis well, 'cause he would not dig. All de people come to drink from dis well, but Nancy was not supposed to come. Still he did come. Dey try all manner a t'ing to cotch Nancy, but dey could not. No matter what dey do, Nancy would get 'way. Dey not able to hol' him.

Dese people decide to fix up a tar baby. Dis was done, an' dey put de tar baby on de water. Each come to drink. None a dese people would touch de tar baby. Dey knew it was a tar baby. In tar baby hand was something sweet to eat. Now hyar come Nancy to steal some a dis water.

When he see de tar baby, t'ink dat it was fine gal. Say, "Hello dere, gal! what dat you got to eat?" De tar baby could not make any reply. When Nancy get his full drink, come to dis gal. "Come on, me fine gal! gi' me some a dat sweet!" he could not persuade dis tar baby. He get fussed, an' say dat he would take de food if she not gi' he some. He reach to get de food; but de tar baby stuck it, an' he not able to pull it off. He get in a rage. Tell de gal dat he will butt. She not move. He in rage for fair. "Mine gal, I gwin' hit you a big butt." An' he gave butt. His head got caught.

"Look out dere! I hit you, gal! Let me go my head! Don' fool me, gal! Loose my head! I hit you one wid dis hand!" He was stick fas'. When tar baby not loose him, he fire wid his one hand. It get stuck fas'.

"What matter you, gal?" he twist an' pullin'. Not able to get hand away. He swipe wid de oder hand. It stuck. "If you play dis way, gal, you will be hurted. Loose me, I say! Now you gwine get boot. Leggo me, 'fore I gi' you dis boot!" She would not. He boot, an' his foot stuck. When she not leggo wid any a him, he try de las' foot. He stuck wid head an' his hands an' his foot too. Nancy was caught in dis way. Dey an'mals come an' find him so.

But Nancy did get away. I don' know how he manage, but dey not smart to hol' him. He get caught; but somet'ing he do, an' dey is fool. Nancy too smart for des an'mals.

SOURCE: John H. Johnson, "Folk-Lore from Antigua, British West Indies," *Journal of American Folklore* (1921), 53.

The informant for "Tar Baby" was George W. Edwards, a native of Antigua, one of the islands in the Lesser Antilles. Edwards was fifty years old at the time that he told the tale in 1920, and he was assisted to some extent by his thirty-year-old wife. Among Antiguans, there is a saying that "if you talk Nancy stories in the day, you will go blind," and as a result the stories Johnson collected in Antigua were recorded at night, in sessions lasting an hour or two. Interestingly, Johnson reports that Nancy is voiced as having nasal speech (he is said to have spent so

much time in conversation with animals that he now talks as they do),
but he "looks like any other man you see."

TAR BABY

Once upon a time, a very good time,
Monkey chew tobacco and spit white lime.

There was once a man name Be-Rabbie and another name Be-Fox.

They use to go in a man field and steal all his things out. Now this man set a tar baby there to catch these thief. Now, when these chap saw this tar girl, Be-Rabbie went to this tar girl. He said "Oh, look, this pretty girl! Oh, my! Let me kiss her." And when he kiss her, his mouth stick; and when his mouth stick, he do all kinds of things to get his mouth off. Then he said, "My father say anybody hold me, I must strike them." And when he struck, his hands stick. And he said, "I bet I kick you." And his foot stick. And he said, "I bet I butt you." And his forehead stick. And when the owner of the place came, he said, "This is the fellow that has been doing the stealing." And he took him off. And they all made up a large fire. And there was a large piece of prickle. And they asked him which one he would go into. And he said, "Don't put me in the prickle, else I will die." And they say, "You don't want to go in the prickle, but I am going to put you there." And when they put him into the prickle, he said, "Oh, you stupid people! This just where I was born!" And he was unharm.

E bo ben.
My story is end.

SOURCE: Elsie Clews Parsons, *Folk-Tales of Andros Island, Bahamas*, 15.

Elsie Clews Parsons describes the inhabitants of Andros as "of mixed
origins and of a mobile habit." She notes that as the islanders migrate
from one place to another, they carry their "ol' storee" with them.
Bahamian tales have formulaic endings and beginnings, and the ending,
in particular, is supposed to connect the story to the occasion of its telling.

Parsons points out that the common Bahamian opening for stories, as in the rhyme that begins the tale above, is closely related to a Scottish and English verse that precedes the telling of a fairy tale:

Once upon a time when pigs spoke rhyme
And monkeys chewed tobacco,
And hens took snuff to make them tough,
And ducks went quack, quack, quack, O!

ANANSI AND THE TAR BABY

Once Mrs. Anansi had a large field. She planted it with peas. Anansi was so lazy he would never do any work. He was afraid that they would give him none of the peas, so he pretended to be sick. After about nine days, he called his wife an' children an' bid them farewell, tell them that he was about to die, an' he ask them this last request, that they bury him in the mids' of the peas-walk, but firs' they mus' make a hole through the head of the coffin an' also in the grave so that he could watch the peas for them while he was lying there. An' one thing more, he said, he would like them to put a pot and a little water there at the head of the grave to scare the thieves away. So he died and was buried.

All this time he was only pretending to be dead, an' every night at twelve o'clock he creep out of the grave, pick a bundle of peas, boil it, and after having a good meal, go back in the grave to rest. Mistress Anansi was surprised to see all her peas being stolen. She could catch the thief no-how. One day her eldest son said to her, "Mother, I bet you it's my father stealing those peas!" At that Mrs. Anansi got into a temper, said, "How could you expect your dead father to rob the peas!"

He said, "Well, mother, I soon prove it to you." He got some tar an' he painted a stump at the head of the grave an' he put a hat on it.

When Anansi came out to have his feast as usual, he saw this thing standing in the groun'. He said, "Good-evening, sir!" but got no reply. Again he said, "Good-evening, sir!" an' still no reply. "If you don' speak to me I'll kick you!" He raise his foot an' kick the stump an' the tar held it there like glue. "Let me go, let me go, sir, or I'll knock you down with my right hand!" That hand stuck fas' all the same. An' he raise his lef' foot an' gave the stump a terrible blow. That foot stuck. Anansi was suspended in air an' had to remain there till morning. Anansi was so ashamed that he climb up beneath the rafters an' there he is to this day.

SOURCE: Martha Warren Beckwith, ed., *Jamaica Anansi Stories*, 25–26.

Martha Beckwith was a student of Franz Boas and collected Jamaican folklore in the 1920s. In her introduction to a volume of Anansi tales told in Jamaica, she points out that folktales are collectively referred to as "Nancy stories." She also emphasizes how Jamaican storytelling is dominated by the trickster figure, whom she describes as follows: "Anansi is the culture hero of the Gold Coast—a kind of god—just as Turtle of the Slave coast and Hare (our own Brier rabbit) of the Bantu people. 'Anansi stories' regularly form the entertainment during wake-nights, and it is difficult not to believe that the vividness with which these animal actors take part in the story springs from the idea that they really represent the dead in the underworld whose spirits have the power, according to the native belief, of taking animal form" (1–2).

THE RABBIT AND THE TAR WOLF

Once there was such a long spell of dry weather that there was no more water in the creeks and springs, and the animals held a council to see what to do about it. They decided to dig a well, and all agreed to help except the Rabbit, who was a lazy fellow, and said, "I don't need to dig for water. The dew on the grass is enough for me." The others did not like this, but they went to work together and dug their well.

They noticed that the Rabbit kept sleek and lively, although it was still dry weather and the water was getting low in the well. They said, "That tricky Rabbit steals our water at night," so they made a wolf of pine gum and tar and set it up by the well to scare the thief. That night the Rabbit came, as he had been coming every night, to drink enough to last him all next day. He saw the queer black thing by the well and said, "Who's there?" but the tar wolf said nothing. He came nearer, but the wolf never moved, so he grew braver and said, "Get out of my way or I'll strike you." Still the wolf never moved and the Rabbit came up and struck it with his paw, but the gum held his foot and it stuck fast. Now he was angry and said, "Let me go or I'll kick you." Still the wolf said nothing. Then the Rabbit struck again with his hind foot, so hard that it was caught in the gum and he could not move, and there he stuck until the animals came for water in the morning. When they found who the thief was they had great sport over him for a while and then got ready to kill him, but as soon as he was unfastened from the tar wolf he managed to get away.

SOURCE: James Mooney, *Myths of the Cherokee*, 272–73.

THE RABBIT AND THE TAR WOLF
(Second Version)

Once upon a time there was such a severe drought that all streams of water and all lakes were dried up. In this emergency the beasts assembled together to devise means to procure water. It was proposed by one to dig a well. All agreed to do so except the hare. She refused because it would soil her tiny paws. The rest, however, dug their well and were fortunate enough to find water. The hare, beginning to suffer and thirst, and having no right to the well, was thrown upon her wits to procure water. She determined, as the easiest way, to steal from the public well. The rest of the animals, surprised to find that the hare was so well supplied with water, asked her where she got it. She replied that she arose betimes in the morning and gathered the dewdrops. However the wolf and the fox suspected her of theft and hit on the following plan to detect her:

They made a wolf of tar and placed it near the well. On the following night the hare came as usual after her supply of water. On seeing the tar wolf she demanded who was there. Receiving no answer she repeated the demand, threatening to kick the wolf if he did not reply. She, receiving no reply kicked the wolf, and by this means adhered to the tar and was caught. When the fox and wolf got hold of her, they consulted what it was best to do with her. One proposed cutting her head off. The hare protested that this would be useless, as it had often been tried without hurting her. Other methods were proposed for dispatching her, all of which she said would be useless. At last it was proposed to let her loose to perish in a thicket. Upon this the hare affected great uneasiness and pleaded hard for her life. Her enemies, however, refused to listen and she was accordingly let loose. As soon, however, as she was out of reach of her enemies she gave a whoop, and bounding away she exclaimed: "This is where I live."

SOURCE: James Mooney, *Myths of the Cherokee*, 273–74

James Mooney collected Cherokee tales from both print sources and living informants. Most of the material in his volume was collected from Cherokee living in the Carolina mountains, for as Mooney points out, "mountaineers guard well the past, and in the secluded forests of Nantahala and Oconaluftee, far away from the main-traveled road of modern progress, the Cherokee priest still treasures the legends and repeats the mystic rituals handed down from his ancestors." The second of the two tales above was published in The Cherokee Advocate *on December 18, 1845, offering evidence that the mythic Hare of Native American lore and Brer Rabbit in African American lore kept company with each other.*

BUH WOLF, BUH RABBIT, AND DE TAR BABY

At las Buh Rabbit tell Buh Wolf: "Don't lick me no mo. Kill me one time. Mek fire an bun me up. Knock me brains out gin de tree." Buh Wolf mek answer: "Ef I bun you up, ef I knock you brains out, you guine dead too quick. Me guine trow you in de brier patch, so de brier kin scratch you life out." Buh Rabbit say, "Do, Buh Wolf, bun me; broke me neck, but don't trow me in de brier patch. Lemme dead one time. Don't terrify me no mo." Buh Wolf yent bin know[1] wuh Buh Rabbit up teh. Eh tink eh bin guine tare Buh Rabbit hide off. So, wuh eh do? Eh loose Buh Rabbit from de sparkleberry bush, and eh tek um by de hine leg, and eh swing um roun, an eh trow um way in de tick brier patch fuh tare eh hide an cratch ey yeye out. De minnit Buh Rabbit drap in de brier patch, eh cock up

1 *yent bin know:* did not know

eh tail, eh jump, an eh holler back to Buh Wolf: "Good bye, Budder! Dis de place me mammy fotch me up—dis de place me mammy fotch me up." An eh gone befo Buh wolf kind ketch um. Buh Rabbit too scheemy.

SOURCE: Charles G. Jones, *Negro Myths from the Georgia Coast: Told in the Vernacular*, 7–10.

After reading Joel Chandler Harris's Uncle Remus stories from "the negroes of Middle Georgia," Charles Jones decided to record stories from coastal regions, "where the lingo of the rice-field and the sea-island negroes is sui generis." He dedicates the book in the following way, completely oblivious to the irony that the "family servants" might not have shared in the comfort and happiness that they evidently gave to the family living on the plantation:

IN MEMORY

OF

MONTE VIDEO PLANTATION

AND OF THE

FAMILY SERVANTS

WHOSE FIDELITY AND AFFECTION CONTRIBUTED SO

MATERIALLY TO ITS COMFORT AND

HAPPINESS

PART V

KINDNESS AND TREACHERY: SLIPPING THE TRAP

Among the many tales about treacherous creatures, the one about a naïve frog and duplicitous scorpion has become something of a cultural meme, adapted and refashioned to suit different social and political circumstances. Often attributed to Aesop and confused with his fable about a frog and a mouse, its origins remain mysterious. The tale has been linked with the Indian collection of animal fables known as the *Panchatantra*, which contains in one of its variant forms a story about a tortoise betrayed by a scorpion. It has, more recently, appeared in cinematic culture, first in Orson Welles's 1954 *Mr. Arkadin*, then in Neil Jordan's 1992 *The Crying Game*. Its main features are outlined below:

> A scorpion meets a frog on a riverbank, and the scorpion asks the frog to let him ride across on its back. The frog worries that the scorpion will sting him, but the scorpion reassures the frog by telling him that he too will die if he stings the frog. Satisfied with that answer, the frog carries him across the river, but in midstream the scorpion stings him. Before he dies, the frog has just enough time to ask "Why?" and the scorpion replies: "It is my nature."

If the tale about the frog and the scorpion takes a fatal turn, resulting in the death of both creatures, there are many stories in which an act of kindness is repaid with a good deed rather than treachery. In "Gratitude," for example, a hunter learns the value of a random act of kindness—even as he is besieged with examples of how humans fail to appreciate the things in their service.

"The Boy and the Crocodile," which appears in Alex Haley's *Roots,* has it both ways, putting on display the capacity for compassion and for cruelty. "No good deed goes unpunished" could be the moral of that tale.

The African American story "Mr. Snake and the Farmer" sends a deeply skeptical message about the transformative power of kindness. It is akin to Aesop's fable about "The Farmer and the Viper," and in many ways the Greek fable appears refashioned by J. D. Suggs, who told the story to the folklorist Richard Dorson in Michigan in 1952. Oscar Brown Jr.'s lyrics for "The Snake" reconfigure the story so that it turns on sexual politics.

GRATITUDE

A hunter went out into the bush. He met an antelope. He killed the antelope. Boaji (the civet) passed by. Boaji said, "Give me some of that meat. I am hungry. I beg you for it. I'll do you a favor some other time." The hunter gave Boaji some of the antelope's meat. Boaji ran off.

The next day the hunter went out into the bush again. He came to a place where the bush was overgrown and it was hard to see where one was going. There, in the middle of the bush, he met a crocodile. The hunter said, "How did you get here? Don't you belong in the water?" The crocodile said, "Last night I went out hunting and now I am far from the river. I cannot find my way back. I beg you, show me the way to the river. If you do, I'll give you five loads of fish." The hunter said, "I'll be glad to help you." The hunter tied a thong around the crocodile's foot and led him to the Niger. At the water's edge, the crocodile said, "Now undo the thong, and I'll go into the water and fetch you your five loads of fish." The hunter freed the crocodile. The crocodile went into the water, and the hunter waited on the bank.

The crocodile came out of the water with a great big fish and put it high on the bank. It slipped back into the water, and he returned with a second load of fish and put it lower on the bank. The hunter climbed down and carried it up higher. The crocodile returned with a third load, which he left at the water's edge. The hunter carried the third load up the riverbank. The crocodile brought a fourth load and put it in the shallow water. The hunter came down, picked the fish up out of the shallow water and carried it high up on the bank. The crocodile returned with a fifth load of fish, which it put on the edge of the deep water. The hunter came down from the bank, waded through the shallow water and came to the edge of the deep water. As he was about to pick up the fish, the crocodile snapped at his foot, caught it fast and dragged the hunter under water.

The crocodile brought the hunter to his brother crocodiles who were lying on a sandbank in midstream. The crocodile called all his friends and said, "We have caught a hunter. We are going to eat him. Come, all of you." The crocodiles came from everywhere and swarmed around the hunter. The hunter said, "Is that fair? This crocodile lost his way in the bush. I brought him back to the river. And now he wants to eat me." The crocodiles said, "We will ask four other people what they think about it."

Down the river floated an Asubi.[1] It was old and torn. The hunter cried "Asubi, help me!" The Asubi said, "What is the matter?" The hunter said, "This crocodile here was lost in the bush, and I brought him back to the river. I saved his life and now he wants to take mine. Is that fair?" The Asubi said, "You are a man. I know humans. When a mat is young and useful, they keep it clean, do not step on it with their feet, roll it up when they have used it and put it carefully to one side. But when a mat is old they forget what it was once like. They throw it away. They toss it into the river. The crocodile will be wise to treat you as people have treated me." The Asubi drifted on. The crocodile said, "Did you hear what the Asubi said?"

A dress, old, torn, and worn came floating down the stream. Someone had thrown it away. The hunter cried, "Dress, help me!" The old dress said, "You are a man. I know humans. So long as a dress is young and beautiful, they wear it everywhere, accept its beauty for their own and say, 'Aren't we lovely?' But it is the dress which is lovely. And the people know that they lie for they fold the dress carefully, smooth out the wrinkles and wrap it up. But as soon as the dress is old they forget what it once was. They throw it in the river. The crocodile will be wise to treat you as people have treated me." The old dress drifted downstream.

The crocodile said, "Did you hear what that old dress said?"

An old mare came down to the river to drink. The mare was old and thin. Her masters had turned her out because she was no longer of any use to them. The hunter cried, "O mare, help me!" The old mare said, "What is the matter?" The hunter said, "I brought this crocodile here, who had lost his way, back to the river. Now he wants to eat me. I saved his life and now he wants to rob me of mine. Is that fair?" The old mare said, "You are a man. I know humans. When a mare is young they build a stall for her. They send out boys to cut her the best grass. They give her the best grain and when she is in foal they give her double of everything. But when a mare is old and cannot foal, when she is weak and ill, they drive her out into the bush and say, 'Take care of yourself as best you can.' Just look at me. The crocodile will be wise to treat you as people have treated me." The mare trotted off.

The crocodile said to the hunter, "You heard what the old mare said?"

Boaji came down to the bank of the Niger to drink. It was the Boaji whom the hunter had helped the day before. The hunter cried: "Boaji, help me!" Boaji said, "What is the matter?" The hunter said, "I brought this crocodile here, who had lost his way in the bush, back to the river. And now he wants to eat me. I saved his life and now he wants to rob me of mine. Is that fair?" Boaji said, "That is difficult to decide. First I must know everything. I do not want to hear only your side of the story but the crocodile's side too—that is, if the crocodile is willing to accept my decision." The crocodile said, "I will tell you." Boaji said, "How did the hunter bring you here?" The crocodile said, "He tied a thong around my foot and dragged me after him." Boaji said, "Did it hurt?" The crocodile said, "Yes, it hurt." The hunter said, "That is not possible." Boaji said, "I cannot decide that until I have seen it. Come ashore here and show me what you did." The crocodile and the hunter went to the shore. Boaji said to the hunter, "Now tie the thong around his foot, just as you did before, so that I can judge whether it hurt him or not." The hunter bound the thong around the crocodile's foot. Boaji said, "Was it like that?" The crocodile said, "Yes, it was like that. And after a while it began to hurt." Boaji said, "I cannot judge that yet. The hunter had better lead you back into the bush. I will come with you." The hunter picked up the thong and led the crocodile into the bush. Finally they came to the place where he and the crocodile had met. The hunter said, "It was here." Boaji said, "Was it here?" The crocodile said, "Yes, it was here. From here on the hunter dragged me behind him to the river." Boaji said, "And you were not satisfied?" The crocodile said, "No, I was not satisfied." Boaji said, "Good. You punished the hunter for his bad treatment of you by grabbing his foot and dragging him to the sandbank. So now the matter is in order. In order to avoid further quarrels of this kind the hunter must unbind the thong and leave you here in the bush. That is my decision."

Boaji and the hunter went off. The crocodile stayed in the bush. The crocodile could not find the way back to the river. The crocodile hungered and thirsted. The hunter thanked Boaji.

There comes a time for every man when he is treated as he has treated others.

SOURCE: Leo Frobenius and Douglas C. Fox, *African Genesis*, 163–70.

AN EXAMPLE OF INGRATITUDE

This is a Hausa tale to explain how *butulu* (ungrateful) came to mean a man who is not thankful.

This is how it came about. There was once a fish called *butulu* swimming around in the water, and one day there came a malam.[1] He put a hook in the water and the fish called *butulu* took it. Feeling the weight, the malam pulled—and there before him was the fish, jumping about and saying to the malam, "Please, please, for the sake of God and the Prophet, let me go, so I can go home. When I get there, if you'll put the hook down again, I'll send my brother. When he comes, pull him up and take him away. Me, I've got too big a family; you couldn't take me away and leave my children orphans." The malam agreed to this and he let the fish go and returned it to the water.

1 *malam:* Muslim cleric

The fish went down into the water and then returned to the surface and saw the malam standing there on the bank. Then says he "There's a bloody stupid malam! What did you go and let me go for, when you'd already caught me? Curse you for a thriftless fellow!" Then the malam pondered in his heart and said to himself "Maybe he's a *butulu*, but there's always tomorrow." So from the next day on, whenever he caught a fish alive, he would beat it to death.

That is the sort of thing we mean by *butulu*—a sort of person who is never thankful, whatever you do for him.

SOURCE: Neil Skinner, ed., *Hausa Tales and Traditions*, II, 448.

THE BOY AND THE CROCODILE

As little as he was, Kunta was already familiar with some of the stories that his own Grandma Yaisa had told to him alone when he had been visiting in her hut. But along with his first-kafo playmates, he felt that the best story-teller of all was the beloved, mysterious, and peculiar old Nyo Boto. . . . Though she acted gruff, the children knew that she loved them as if they were her own, which she claimed they all were.

Surrounded by them, she would growl, "Let me tell a story . . ."

"Please!" the children would chorus, wriggling in anticipation.

And she would begin in the way that all Mandinka story tellers began: "At this certain time, in this certain village, lived this certain person." It was a small boy, she said, of about their rains, who walked to the riverbank one day and found a crocodile trapped in a net.

"Help me!" the crocodile cried out.

"You'll kill me!" cried the boy.

"No! Come nearer!" said the crocodile.

So the boy went up to the crocodile—and instantly was seized by the teeth in that long mouth.

"Is this how you repay my goodness—with badness?" cried the boy.

"Of course," said the crocodile out of the corner of his mouth. "That is the way of the world."

The boy refused to believe that, so the crocodile agreed not to swallow him without getting an opinion from the first three witnesses to pass by. First was an old donkey.

When the boy asked his opinion, the donkey said, "Now that I'm old and can no longer work, my master has driven me out for the leopards to get me!"

"See?" said the crocodile. Next to pass by was an old horse, who had the same opinion.

"See?" said the crocodile. Then along came a plump rabbit who said, "Well, I can't give a good opinion without seeing this matter as it happened from the beginning."

Grumbling, the crocodile opened his mouth to tell him—and the boy jumped out to safety on the riverbank.

"Do you like crocodile meat?" asked the rabbit. The boy said yes. "And do your parents?" He said yes again. "Then here is a crocodile ready for the pot."

The boy ran off and returned with the men of the village, who helped him to kill the crocodile. But they brought with them a wuolo dog, which chased and caught and killed the rabbit, too.

"So the crocodile was right," said Nyo Boto. "It *is* the way of the world that goodness is often repaid with badness. This is what I have told you as my story."

"May you be blessed, have strength and prosper!" said the children gratefully.

SOURCE: Alex Haley, *Roots*, 7–8.

MR. SNAKE AND THE FARMER

Well, you know, a snake, in the wintertime, he goes in the ground and he don't never wake up. When the cold weather gets bad, he never wakes up till the weather warms up.

So the farmer goes out, he's going to break his ground up at the end of February. So he plows up Mr. Snake. "Ain't that something? Here's Mr. Snake."

And Mr. Snake says, "Why I'm just so *cold*. I don't know what I'll do. I just practically froze this winter." He was so stiff, he couldn't move. Said, "Will you put me in your bosom, Mr. Farmer, and let me warm . . . up?"

The farmer says, "No, Mr. Snake, you'll bite me." Said, "I know it."

"No, I wouldn't bite." Said, "Let me tell you, Mr. Farmer, I'm just *cold*. Don't you know I wouldn't bite you after you warmed me up?"

Said, "No. . . . But you a *snake*."

Said, "Mr. Farmer, I won't bite you. Just warm me up, please . . ."

Said, "No. . . . But you a *snake*."

Said, "Mr. Farmer, I won't bite you. Just warm me up, please . . ."

Farmer take him up and unbutton his shirt, put him in his bosom. Oh, he's a *great* big snake. I think he must have been a rattlesnake. . . . And so he plowed along until about nine o'clock. He stopped his mules and unbuttons his bosom, and he pulled it out, like this, you know, and he looks down in there, says, "How you feel, Mr. Snake?"

He says, "Well, I feel a little better. I'm kind of warming up."

"Good, good." Says, "*Gitty-up!*" So he goes around and he plows till about ten thirty. Then, "*Whoa!*" Mules stop. He opens his bosom, and he looked down, and he says, "How you feel, Mr. Snake?"

He says, "Well, I'm feeling pretty good. I'm warming up good."

He says, "Good, good. *Gitty-up!*" Mules started on up, and he plowed and he plowed till about eleven thirty. And so he could feel the snake kind of twisting, you know, and he just stopped, you know. Pulled his . . . shirt out and looks in his bosom again.

"How you feel, Mr. Snake?"

Says, "Oh, I'm feeling a whole lot better. I'm warming up. You feel me moving?"

Said, "Yeah! I *thought* you was doing better."

"Yes, I'm feeling a whole *lot* better."

"Well," farmer says, "Well, I'll be out plowing awhile longer, and I'll quit and go to dinner, then I'm going to get my dinner and put him out at the end."

So he plowed till about fifteen minutes till twelve. He pulled out his shirt and he looked down there again. He said, "Well how are you, Mr. Snake?"

Says, "Oh, I'm warm. I'm just feeling good."

He says, "Good." Says, "Well, I'll go a round or two, and then when I get ready to go to dinner, I'll put you out at the end." So he plowed around, and when he got near about back, Snake didn't wait for him to open his shirt. He done stuck his head out, twitching away out between the shirt buttons, and looking at him in his face and licking out his tongue. Well, a snake's angry. Every time he see you and go to licking out his tongue, he's mad. And the farmer *knew* he's going to bite then.

He said, "Now, Mr. Snake." Said, "Now you told me you wouldn't bite me after I warmed you."

"Yeah. But you knowed that I's a *snake*."

He said, "Yeah. But . . . don't do that, don't bite me. Please."

"You see, I'm a snake. I'm *supposed* to bite you."

He said, "Yeah, but you told me you wasn't going to bite me."

"Yeah, but you know I's a *snake* before. I'm supposed to bite you, and you know that." So he all went on and bit the farmer, right in the mouth. His face begin to swell, so he goes to the house, running. He didn't take time to take his mules out of there. Went in.

Wife says, "Well, what the matter?"

He said, "Well, Mr. Snake. I seen him out there in the field. I plowed him up, and he said he was so cold he was stiff. And if I would warm him up, he would not bite me." And said, "After I got him warm, he bit me in the face." And said, "Let me tell you one lesson. Don't care when you see a snake, don't never warm him, put him in your bosom, put him up, cause when he gets warm, he's sure going to bite you."

Then he laid down and died.

And that's why he left word with his wife, "Don't never fool with a snake."

SOURCE: Carl Lindahl, ed. *American Folktales from the Collections of the Library of Congress*, 191–93.

THE TORTOISE AND THE TOAD

A lot of her stories were lies, but some might have been true. Well, let's say I thought they were lies, though the others thought they were the truth. Heaven help anyone who tried to tell one of those old women she was wrong!

I remember the story of the tortoise and the toad; she must have told it to me a hundred times. The tortoise and the toad had this big feud going for years, and the toad used to deceive the tortoise because he was frightened of her and thought she was stronger than him. One day the toad got hold of a big bowl of food and presented it to the tortoise, setting it down right under her nose, almost in her mouth. When the tortoise saw the bowl she took a fancy to it and gobbled it so fast she choked. It never even crossed her mind that the toad had put it there for a reason. She was very simple-minded, and so it was easy to trick her. After that, feeling full and satisfied, she started wandering through the forest in search of the toad, who had hidden himself in a cave. When the toad saw her in the distance, he called out, "Here I am, tortoise, look." She looked but couldn't see him, and after a while she got tired and went away til she came across a heap of dry straw and lay down to sleep. The toad seized her while she was asleep and poisoned her by peeing over her, and she didn't even wake up because she had eaten so heavily. The moral of this story is that people shouldn't be greedy, and you should trust no one. An enemy might offer you a meal merely to trick you.

SOURCE: Esteban Montejo, *The Autobiography of a Runaway Slave*, 183–84.

In the celebrated story of his life, the Cuban runaway slave Esteban Montejo describes hearing Ma Lucia tell stories about life in Africa. He begins with a meditation on the stories as "lies" and ends by extracting a moral from one tale told to him.

PART VI

JOEL CHANDLER HARRIS AND THE UNCLE REMUS TALES

As far as I'm concerned, he stole a good part of my heritage.
—ALICE WALKER, "The Dummy in the Window: Joel
Chandler Harris and the Invention of Uncle Remus"

Joel Chandler Harris once declared that he was not really the creative genius behind the Uncle Remus tales. All he had done was to channel and write down the words of a mysterious second self. "As for myself—though you could hardly call me a real, sure enough author—I never have anything but the vaguest ideas of what I am going to write; but when I take pen in my hand, the rust clears away and the 'other fellow' takes charge" (Julia Collier Harris 345). In a sense, neither Harris nor Uncle Remus wrote down the tales. Instead they are penned by an elusive figure who stands in between, listening and retelling. That raconteur is a mix of Harris, the Southern journalist, with nostalgic views about plantation life in the Old South, and Uncle Remus, the embodied presence of a fierce storytelling tradition that was itself divided, doubly coded, and fiercely committed to speaking truth to power through indirection.

Harris's literary renown and his role in undertaking the first large-scale effort to collect African American lore challenge us to think hard about the minstrel aspects of the Uncle Remus Stories. As Robert Hemenway points out, Harris had a "deep need to imagine himself as Uncle Remus" (1982, 16). He impersonated as he appro-

This portrait of Harris was the frontispiece for his fictionalized memoir *On the Plantation*, published in 1892.

priated, mimicking black speech and priding himself on his fine ear for dialect. He often referred to himself as Uncle Remus and signed letters using that name. And he was flattered that the president of the United States referred to him as Uncle Remus. The assertion that the "other fellow" writes the stories collapses under the pressure of telling moments in real life. The "other fellow" is in fact Joel Chandler Harris performing Uncle Remus in classic minstrel fashion.

"Presidents may come and presidents may go," Theodore Roosevelt once said at a White House dinner, "but Uncle Remus stays put" (Bickley 1978, 58). Roosevelt's wife Edith told Harris that she read his stories to "the little folk" on "nearly every night" of her life. For Mark Twain, Harris was the "oracle of the nursery," and children in the United States grew up with tales about Brer Rabbit and Brer Fox, stories about Laughing Places and Aunt Nancy's House, as well as fables about Tar Babies and Squinch Owls. What was once part of a living oral tradition of adaptation and improvisation was put into fixed letters on the printed page. And a vibrant storytelling culture for adults began its long migration from campfires and slave cabins into the nursery. The move to turn the tales into harmless entertainments for the young had its beginnings in Atlanta, Georgia, in 1880.

As spokesman for what has been called the "Arcadian South of Aunt Jemima [and] Uncle Ben," Joel Chandler Harris and his stories have come under heavy fire in the past decades (Cartwright 2002, 129). The author of the Uncle Remus stories famously extolled the virtues of the antebellum South in an essay called "The Old Plantation," in which he mourned the demise of a culture that had "passed away" but that retained "the sweet suggestions of poetry and romance—memorials that neither death nor decay can destroy" (1877, 2). Books like Thomas Nelson Page's *Social Life in Old Virginia before the War* continued to extol plantation life as late as 1897: "The peace of it all was only emphasized by the sounds that broke upon it; the call of ploughers to their teams; the shrill shouts of children; the chant of women over their work. . . . Far off, in the fields, the white-shirted 'ploughers' followed singing their slow teams in the fresh furrows, wagons rattled, and oxcarts crawled along . . . loud shouts and peals of laughter, mellowed by the distance, floating up from time to time, telling that the heart was light and the toil not too heavy" (1897, 27–28). We do not hear these sounds: "The lashes given a slave during a flogging might be ten or fifty or two hundred—or at least there is evidence to that effect. Of course two hundred blows usually meant a death sentence if administered at one time, so such a sentence was nearly always meted out twenty-five or fifty blows on different dates" (Saxon 234).

Any value attached to Joel Chandler Harris's attention to vernacular performance and his insistence on the African origins of the tales (scholars looked to India, to Native American cultures, and to Europe—anywhere but Africa—for prototypes) has been tarnished not only by the minstrel aspects of the project but also by the collection's frame narrative. In this utopian depiction of Southern plantation life as one community, deep bonds of affection join slave cabins to "big houses" and mansions. And yet the narrative frame that gives us Uncle Remus in conversation with the little boy also exposes—perhaps unwittingly through the "other fellow"—the cruel contradictions of an economic and social nexus that created a vast system of dislocation, exploitation, and disenfranchisement.

The voice of the "other fellow" was one that Alice Walker, born, like Joel Chandler Harris, in Eatonton, Georgia, could not tolerate. For her, Disney's *Song of the South*, inspired by the Uncle Remus stories, "killed" the stories she had heard as a child. "We no longer listened to them," she declared with mournful outrage. Walker describes a childhood enlivened by the stories both parents told, blending their voices together to produce a narrative. Poverty could not diminish the poetry of these tales: "Both of my parents were excellent storytellers, and wherever we lived, no matter how poor the house, we had fireplaces and a front porch. It was around the fireplaces and on the porch that I first heard, from my parents' lips—my mother filling in my father's pauses, and he filling in hers—the stories that I later learned were Uncle Remus stories."

When did Alice Walker learn that Uncle Remus was the "source" of those stories? She went to the movies with her parents and watched *Song of the South*. That event, which took place in a segregated theater, was a double insult. Not only were black children and their parents in the "colored section," but those same children and parents were obliged to witness their cultural property transferred to white children: "Uncle Remus in the movie saw fit largely to ignore his own children and grandchildren in order to pass on our heritage—indeed, our birthright—to patronizing white children, who seemed to regard him as a kind of talking teddy bear" (1981, 29–31).

Disney's *Song of the South* did more than appropriate African American lore, transferring it from the intimacy of the porch, the fireside, and other close-knit communal settings to the big screen. With one stroke, the local became the global. Improvisation, banter, chitchat, and small talk were turned into monolithic forms, cartoon images set in celluloid frames and words frozen into a sound track. Italo Calvino once shrewdly observed that "folktales remain merely dumb until you realize that you are required to complete them yourself, to fill in your own particulars" (Parr and Campbell 2012, 127). Now Brer Rabbit, Brer Fox, Brer Bear, and Tar-Baby were imagined for audiences, with no gaps left and few windows of opportunity for conversation and debate. The stories themselves were turned into cartoon versions of themselves, banished to the nursery as comic entertainments for the young.

Still, why let Joel Chandler Harris or *Song of the South* kill Brer Rabbit? As Robert Bone tells us in a meditation on Uncle Remus and the oral tradition: "To neglect the Brer Rabbit tales because a white man was the first to write them down is to betray the black man's folk tradition" (Bickley 1981, 135). Joel Chandler Harris may have been an interloper and intruder in the cabins where he went to eavesdrop and collect. He may also have created a grotesquely distorted picture of plantation life as serene and untroubled. "What days they were—those days on the old plantation!" he declared in all seriousness. But he did create a record of sorts, one that allows us to see, if only through a glass darkly, evening diversions in an era lacking not only electronic entertainments but also nearly every form of art requiring more than the human voice. Brer Rabbit has been around for far longer than Joel Chandler Harris, who took what he found from an oral tradition of African American storytellers and worked hard to avoid "cooking" the tales, as he put it.

If any collection evokes the hushed-up paradoxes of African American folklore, it is Joel Chandler Harris's Uncle Remus stories. With a powerfully dissonant relationship between the romance of the frame and the ferocity of the tales, *Uncle Remus: His Songs and His Sayings* (originally entitled *Uncle Remus's Folk-Lore*), like the volumes that followed it, will not let us forget that beneath the thin veneer of polite affability in the social world there is a turbulent mix of toxic rivalries and murderous hostility. The frame features a scene of hospitality, with Uncle Remus telling tales and the little boy periodically bringing ginger cookies and mince pie to his host. But the tales themselves alert listeners to the dangers of rolling out the welcome mat. The characters in them are constantly violating the rules of hospitality, with both hosts and guests refusing to mind their manners, especially at mealtime (Keenan 1984, 59). Alarm bells rightly go off at the mention of supper. The appetites may be animal and the passions may play out among beasts, but the beasts become our curved mirrors, looking-glasses that reflect back to us not only who we are but how we relate to each other across racial boundaries (Sundquist 1993, 344).

Bernard Wolfe famously described Uncle Remus as the Negro "grinner-giver," a figure who is kept subservient through threats and fear and who must all the while appear amiable and eager to please. Paul Laurence Dunbar also called attention to the perpetual masquerade of "grins and lies" performed by blacks over the centuries in his poem "We Wear the Mask." Uncle Remus's "beaming countenance" and his "mellow" voice, always "cheerful" and "good-humored," delight the young master's son, who sits on Remus's knee and "nestles" in his lap. The two bond over the stories, and, save for an occasional reprimand, there appears to be nothing but love and affection coursing between the two, as the boy listens with wide-eyed wonder to the wisdom and wit of the old man. No racial or generational conflicts enter into this idyllic scene. Nothing of the stand-off between a "proud and insolent" youth facing down a "dark and sinister" foe, as in J. M. Barrie's *Peter Pan*, another work that features the trope of the *puer/ senex* pairing. What we have is not even close to the complex and nuanced Huck and Jim friendship in Mark Twain's 1884 novel, a work that may have been influenced by Harris's frame narrative. Instead Joel Chandler Harris gives us, as in *Uncle Tom's Cabin*, a study in contrasts, pure and simple, a young, innocent white child and a decrepit and aging, but wise and loving "old time darky."

Uncle Remus is a literary construct, animated by Harris's fantasies about plantation life and the quasi-paternal affection between a black man and a white boy. Brer Rabbit by contrast, and his confrères, are all rough-and-tumble communal creations, figures brought to life by collective cultural work. It is precisely the friction between the two that makes sparks fly. On the one hand, we have the quiet dignity of a bearded and bespectacled figure who passes on wisdom and experience; on the other the antics of an outlaw with dreadful manners—a crafty beast who is anything but a good example for the young.

Just who was Uncle Remus? Joel Chandler Harris tells us that he was not an invention of his own, but a "human syndicate." One member of that syndicate was surely Harriet Beecher Stowe's Uncle Tom, who seems to have migrated effortlessly into Harris's frame from the Shelby plantation. Caught in an idyllic eternal present with the

Little Boy, Uncle Remus reenacts every evening a scene of doting tenderness and loving storytelling. Without giving us the history behind the "rough, weather-beaten face" that "beams" kindly on the little boy, Harris lures us into an immersive drama that enraptures rather than arouses. Unlike Harriet Beecher Stowe, who let the scenes that unfold in Uncle Tom's cabin move readers to protest and intervention, Joel Chandler Harris was content to replay the fantasy of the "beauty" and "tenderness" of "the old plantation as we remember it" (Bernstein 2011, 139–40).

Literary influences played a role in making Uncle Remus who he was. But Harris also acknowledged the role of real-life informants. He admitted to creating the "human syndicate" of Uncle Remus from "three or four old darkies whom I knew." The process is described with singularly aggressive force: "I just walloped them together into one person and called him 'Uncle Remus.'"

Harris's daughter provides a more gentle scene of origins, depicting her father and his boyhood chums basking in the warm glow of a fire while entertained by stories told by adult "companions." "When the work and play of the day were ended and the glow of the lightwood knot could be seen in the negro cabins, Joel and the Turner children would steal away from the house and visit their friends in the slave quarters. Old Harbert and Uncle George Terrell were Joel's favorite companions, and from a nook in their chimney corners he listened to the legends handed down from their African ancestors—the lore of animals and birds so dear to every plantation negro." Harris's daughter fails to take note of but betrays through her words the disturbances in this idyllic scene. The talk of "work and play of the day," "African ancestors," the "plantation negro," the "negro cabins," and the "slave quarters" all give the lie to the notion of "friends" and "companions" (Julia Collier Harris 1918, 33–34). It may be true that the bond between Harris and Old Harbert and Uncle George Terrell was solidified by Harris's role in helping a runaway slave, and it was said about the two elderly men that "there was nothing they were not ready to do for him at any time of day or night" (Hemenway 1982, 12). But even that episode is nothing but another stark reminder of the power asymmetries between black men in slave cabins and white boys in "the house."

Uncle Remus is "venerable enough to have lived during the period he describes," Harris tells us. And, in a jaw-dropping statement that has led many readers to rub their eyes in disbelief, he adds that Uncle Remus is a man who has "nothing but pleasant memories of the discipline of slavery" (Harris 1955, xxvii). Hardly a trace of resentment, ill will, or antipathy mars his relationship to the adoring young white boy. Indeed, Harris often invoked the romance of the plantation, describing how the "new dispensation" had "hushed into silence" the poetry of the past, the stories and "songs of the negroes" (Bickley 1981, 110). He went even further in "Observations from New England" when he described slavery as "an institution which, under Providence, grew into a university in which millions of savages served an apprenticeship to religion and civilization" (Julia Collier Harris 1918, 166).

Did Harris ever stop to wonder why the tales Uncle Remus tells are so full of malice, greed, envy, hatred, and murder? They stand in so emphatically dissonant a relationship to the pastoral frame that it defies credibility to think that Harris could not detect trouble in his folkloric paradise. Brer Rabbit decapitates Fox, brings the head to Mrs. Fox, drops it into her cooking pot as "nice beef," and lets the son discover his father's head. Who can forget the inventory of possible executions (barbecuing, roasting, hanging, drowning, skinning,

This photograph of George Terrell was probably taken in the late 1800s. Harris credited "Uncle George Terrell" and "Old Harbert," enslaved workers on the Turnwold Plantation, as sources for the tales in the Uncle Remus books and as models for the Uncle Remus character. *Joel Chandler Harris Papers, Stuart A. Rose Manuscript, Archives, and Rare Book Library, Emory University.*

snatching out eyeballs) recited in "The Wonderful Tar-Baby Story"? Brer Rabbit scalds Wolf to death, calls a secret grove full of hornets his "laughing place," and sets Possum on fire. When Brer Wolf screams "Ow-ow! I'm a-burnin'," Brer Rabbit responds by dumping more leaves to fuel the fire where he has trapped Brer Wolf. He prides himself on the ability to lie, cheat, and steal in the competition for food and women. Although Harris

This group portrait is part of a collection of early-twentieth-century snapshots of the Turnwold Plantation, where Joel Chandler Harris worked as a printer's apprentice and heard stories he would later use in the Uncle Remus books. The subjects of the photograph are identified in a caption as "The negro descendants of the Turner slaves," the setting as the "Last of the Negro cabins at the Turner plantation." *Joel Chandler Harris Papers, Stuart A. Rose Manuscript, Archives, and Rare Book Library, Emory University.*

at one point tells us that the tales depict nothing more than the "roaring comedy of animal life," his preface to the collection tells us otherwise. "It needs no scientific investigation," he asserts, "to show why he, the negro, selects as his hero the weakest and most harmless of all animals and brings him out victorious in contests with the bear, the wolf, and the fox. It is not virtue that triumphs, but helplessness. It is not malice but mischievousness. Indeed, the parallel between the case of all animals who must, perforce, triumph through his shrewdness and the humble condition of the slave raconteur is not without its pathos and poetry" (Julia Collier Harris 1918, 158). That Harris acknowledged the tales as allegories of enslavement makes it all the more troubling that he framed them as children's fare.

Uncle Remus himself disavows the notion that humor might be the chief ingredient in his tales. Why does he never smile? Tempy asks him. And he replies "with unusual emphasis": "Well, I tell you dis, Sis Tempy . . . ef deze yer tales wuz des fun, fun, fun, en giggle, giggle, giggle, I let you know I'd done drapt um long ago. Yasser, w'en it come down ter gigglin' you kin des count old Remus out" (Harris 1955, 331). In other words, humor is not his accomplice but his sworn enemy.

What is it if not deadly malice—rather than light-hearted mischievousness—that leads Brer Rabbit to betray Brer Fox to a farmer and stand by while he is beaten to death? The help-lessness emphasized in Harris's introduction rarely produces the triumphant scenes of revenge we witness in one tale after another. Nature is red in tooth and claw in these stories, and so is human nature, the tales imply, even if almost all we see are animal actors. Unlike Aesop's fables, which stage morality plays in the animal kingdom, these stories send the message that vice works best in a hostile world full of predators and false friends. Hypocrisy trumps almost every other trait, for it cre-ates an advantage by lulling opponents into a feeling that all is well in the world. We

Joel Chandler Harris continued to publish Uncle Remus stories in Georgia newspapers, among them *The Sunny South*, which printed two Thanksgiving stories, "signed" by Harris.

may cheer Brer Rabbit on as he rides up the well in a bucket and sends Brer Fox to his doom, but we recognize that fortunes shift quickly—Brer Rabbit tells us as much—and every victory is merely temporary in these dog-eat-dog adventures.

Joel Chandler Harris was a newspaper man, beginning his career as a printer's devil, and working his way up to editorial writer at the *Atlanta Constitution*, where the Uncle Remus stories first appeared. Born in 1848, his father, an Irish railroad laborer, abandoned mother and child shortly after his son was born. (Many have speculated that Uncle Remus may be invested with all the paternal affection Joel Chandler Harris had missed out on as a boy.) Mary Harris, who kept her maiden name, settled in Eatonton, Georgia, with her mother and worked as a seamstress. Her son attended school until age thirteen, when he took an apprenticeship in the printing trade at the Turner plantation. It was at that plantation, called Turnwold, that the young Joel Chandler Harris heard the tales that would later enter the pages of the multiple volumes of the Uncle Remus stories.

The immediate catalyst for collecting the tales can be traced to Harris's review of an 1877 article by William Owens entitled "Folklore of the Southern Negroes." There he came to the conclusion that the piece was "remarkable for what it omits rather than for what it contains" (Harris 1877, 2). Owens, he believed, lacked an understanding of the deep, lived experience and profound wisdom in the tales, and he also had no connection whatsoever to the dialect in which the tales were told. How could he possibly refer to Brer Rabbit as Buh Rabbit? There were already far too many "literary" treatments of these stories, along with shoddy versions distorted by presentations on the "minstrel stage." In one of the deep ironies that marks the history of collecting African American folklore, Joel Chandler Harris felt compelled to respond with hard evidence about the true nature of these stories.

Harris didn't rely only on his own childhood memories. Like the Brothers Grimm before him in a very different cultural climate, he issued an appeal to friends, family, and colleagues for recollections of stories from the oral tradition. In a newspaper ad placed in 1879, he solicited "Negro fables and legends" along with any "quaint myths" that were "popular on plantations." We do not know much about the response, but we do know that Harris was deeply committed to oral storytelling, to the *told* tale rather than the one written down. Precisely because he was producing a work that would be an anthem to folkloric authenticity, he did not write the tales down verbatim at the site of the telling. Pen and pad would have had an inhibiting effect. Instead he relied on his own long-term and short-term memory, as well as the recollections of others. Over time his standards relaxed somewhat, but his resourcefulness remained compelling. When he met with reluctance to tell tales, he began reciting the stories out loud to validate their value: "I have found few negros who will acknowledge to a stranger that they know anything of these legends, and yet to relate one of the stories is the surest way to their confidence and esteem. In this way, and in this way only, I have been enabled to collect and verify the folk-lore included in this volume." At one point, he sent out his children to collect stories from teenage boys, perhaps in part because he had such vivid memories of stories told to him at that age (Baer 1980, 22).

In all he wrote down 263 tales, with nearly half featuring Brer Rabbit. There may be much to condemn and criticize not only in a frame narrative that turns African American tales into a white child's cultural heritage but also in what can be seen as Harris's own minstrel-like performance of a black voice. Harris insisted that he had done his best to remain faithful to the sources. On the tales in his collection, he noted: "Not one of them is cooked, and not one nor any part of one is an invention of mine. They are all genuine folk-tales" (Brookes 1950, 26). And part of that authenticity required capturing the rhythms and inflections of the language in which they were told. Ironically, the more authentic he tried to make the collection, the more troubling the entire project became.

As artificial and constructed as the voice of Uncle Remus may be, the use of that voice still pays tribute to the power of performance and to the importance of *how* a tale is told as well as the actual source for the tale. That the masquerade was too complete is revealed by Mark Twain's report that New Orleans schoolchildren were deeply disappointed when they welcomed Harris to their city: "Why, he's white!" they intoned in chorus. It was Twain who believed that only one white person had mastered the "negro dialect," and that was Joel Chandler Harris (Bickley 1981, 53). In his own defense of the use of black vernacular speech, Harris wrote that "old man Chaucer was one of the earliest dialect writers" (Brasch 2000, 153). Keith Cartwright has argued persuasively that *Nights with Uncle Remus*, the second installment to the tales, shows that Harris's storytelling style evolved in ways that revealed a new thoughtfulness about the performance elements to the tales and a nuanced understanding of different dialects that allowed different voices to emerge, including the Gullah-speaking African Jack (2002, 115).

Both Uncle Remus and Joel Chandler Harris have their defenders. "Remus's innocence is more strategic than pastoral; he is never as guileless as he seems," one critic asserted. Another critic raised the ante by concluding in his analysis of the collection that "Brer Rabbit is a trickster disguise for Remus, who in turn is a trickster disguise for Harris himself." A third agreed, adding that Harris's strategies as a writer are much like those used by Uncle Remus and Brer Rabbit: "Each presents himself as a benign figure in full compliance with expected mannerisms and behaviors. . . . Meanwhile,

BY THE SAME AUTHOR.

UNCLE REMUS: His Songs and His Sayings. The Folk-Lore of the Old Plantation. With Illustrations by F. S. Church and J. H. Moser, of Georgia. 12mo. Cloth, $1.50.

"The volume is a most readable one, whether it be regarded as a humorous book merely, or as a contribution to the literature of folk-lore."—*New York World.*

"A thoroughly amusing book, and much the best humorous compilation that has been put before the American public for many a day."—*Philadelphia Telegraph.*

"The idea of preserving and publishing these legends in the form in which the old plantation negroes actually tell them, is altogether one of the happiest literary conceptions of the day. And very admirably is the work done."—*London Spectator.*

"Mr. Harris's book may be looked on in a double light—either as a pleasant volume recounting the stories told by a typical old colored man to a child, or as a valuable contribution to our somewhat meager folk-lore. To Northern readers the story of Brer (brother, brudder) Rabbit may be novel. To those familiar with plantation life, who have listened to these quaint old stories, who have still tender reminiscences of some good old mauma who told these wondrous adventures to them when they were children, Brer Rabbit, the Tar Baby, and Brer Fox come back again with all the past pleasures of younger days."—*New York Times.*

"Uncle Remus's sayings on current happenings are very shrewd and bright, and the plantation and revival songs are choice specimens of their sort."—*Boston Journal.*

New York: D. APPLETON & CO., Publishers.

Joel Chandler Harris's *On the Plantation: A Story of a Georgia Boy's Adventures during the War* (1892) was dedicated to Joseph Addison Turner, who owned the Turnwold Plantation. Harris described the account as a "mixture of fact and fiction." The volume included an advertisement for the Uncle Remus stories.

behind the smiles, the same threesome busies itself, each on his own level, with the exposure and demolition of . . . stereotypes" (Hedin 1982, 84; Sundquist 1993, 343; Cochran 2004, 22).

Harris deserves some credit for his efforts to validate the vernacular and to offer stories that complicate lore, putting us into a dizzying hall of mirrors that creates indeterminacy when it comes to meaning. Who can decide what anyone *really* thinks, when the narrator, Uncle Remus, and Brer Rabbit are all world-class experts in trickery? Harris can also be commended for acknowledging early on the African origins of the tales, in a move that was at the time contested by many folklorists. While some scholars believed that "Negro tales" were "borrowings" from North American Indians, others thought that they came from Europe, and only a few, like Harris, were persuaded that they were related to African prototypes (at least half of the tales derive from African sources according to one folklorist [Roberts 1990, 107]).

The distinguished folklorist Alan Dundes declared some years ago that the time for guesswork was over: "There are a limited number of possibilities" about the origins of African American tales, he stated. "(1) The tale came from Africa. (2) The tale came from Europe. (3) The tale came from American Indian tradition. (4) The tale arose in the New World as a result of the Afro-American experience there" (1965, 207). Dundes neglects to mention a fifth possibility, which would be all of the above, and Harris himself recognized a certain syncretic quality to his collection, which drew on multiple sources, traditions, and experiences, while retaining a strong African core.

After publishing the first volume of Uncle Remus stories, Harris found himself the recipient of letters from all over the world. "Fellows of this and professors of that, to say nothing of doctors of the others" wrote to make inquiries about matters

In the early 1930s, the Coca-Cola Company produced a children's cutout inspired by A. B. Frost's illustrations for the Uncle Remus stories. Harris's widow sued the company for copyright infringement, and the courts ruled in favor of Coca-Cola, which had negotiated the rights to the illustrations with Appleton, the publisher of the stories. *Coca-Cola Archives.*

philological, linguistic, and folkloristic. Harris had become an instant authority not only on "negro dialect" but also in the field of folklore, and he signed up to become a charter member of the *American Folklore Society* and subscribed to the British *Folk-Lore Journal.* But he quickly became disillusioned with the scientific approach to storytelling. In a work of fiction called *Wally Walderoon and His Story-Telling Machine,* Harris had one character make the following pronouncement, one that he no doubt endorsed: "It was one of the principles taught in the university where I graduated that a story amounts to nothing and less than nothing, if it is not of scientific value. I would like to tell the story first, and then give you my idea of its relation to oral literature, and its special relation to the unity of the human races" (1903, 180).

One of the ironies of Joel Chandler Harris's project is that it paradoxically both preserved and destroyed the stories. To understand exactly how Uncle Remus "killed" African American folklore, it is important to return to Alice Walker and the disappointments of *Song of the South*, a film that expanded Harris's frame to include a narrative about crisis in a white family and planted Uncle Remus squarely in an Arcadian South. It was also the film that transformed Remus's stories into cartoonish versions of themselves, with a grim undercurrent to be sure.

"I'm just a worn out old man what don't do nothin' but tell stories," Uncle Remus tells the boy Johnny in *Song of the South*, and that is exactly how he is portrayed. Bearing little resemblance to the West African Griot, who is the keeper of cultural knowledge in a community, Remus has been reduced to a lumbering fellow who takes in and nurtures young Johnny at a time when his family is experienc-

Brer Rabbit's name has come to be associated with various products, but at no time more frequently than with molasses. This 1920 magazine advertisement presents a romantic image of Southern plantation life where young boys glimpse farm labor from the field's edge, while the masters of the house enjoy food served by a figure reminiscent of Uncle Remus.

ing some mysterious domestic disturbances. (He is no longer "the busiest person on the plantation," as Joel Chandler Harris described him.) His storytelling voice has transmogrified into a cartoon that gives us a top-down, mass-produced corporate version of Brer Rabbit's antics. No longer an active storyteller, he gains an iconic significance as a comforting mediator, a garrulous and harmless presence that bears little resemblance to the characters in the cartoons.

Set in the Reconstruction era, Disney's *Song of the South* was released in 1946. "Ever since I have had anything to do with the making of motion pictures, I have wanted to bring the Uncle Remus stories to the screen," Walt Disney reported. The books came out in print when he was a boy, and the young Walt read every single one of them. These tales were "the greatest American folk stuff there is." When the Golden Books edition of *Walt Disney's Uncle Remus* appeared, the preface explained that Disney had made a film about Harris's stories because of their "universal appeal . . . and their place in the heritage of this country" (Russo 1992, 20). Before making the film, Walt paid a visit to Wren's Nest, Harris's home, "to get an authentic feeling of Uncle Remus country so we can do as faithful a job as possible to these stories" (Watts 1997, 273; Gabler 2007, 433).

Song of the South is hardly "faithful" to its source material, nor does it offer historical authenticity. Brer Rabbit is no longer a complex and vexatious mythical trickster figure, but what Walt Disney called "the naïve, happy-go-lucky little hero of the Tales—protagonist of the human race, actually—who stumbles into one kind of trouble after another, always managing through belated thought, courage and a bit of 'footswork' to squeak through" (Brasch 2000, 275–76). And the frame narrative gives a romantic portrayal of the Reconstruction era, with African Americans singing mellifluous melodies ("I'm going to stay right here in the home I know") on their way to the cotton fields and back again.

"I think Remus is a great character, a strong character. He is the dominant force in the story. There is no reason for Negroes to take offence," Disney declared at the same time that he worried about making "booboos" (Rapf 1999, 130). At the 1946 premiere in Atlanta, a segregated city, James Baskett, who had played Uncle Remus, was absent, because, like Hattie

The U.S. Post Office memorialized Joel Chandler Harris on a postage stamp for his one hundredth birthday in 1948.

McDaniel and other African American cast members, he would not have been able to book a room in any of the nearby hotels. In addition, he would have had to sit in the balcony, had he attended. At theaters in New York, Los Angeles, and San Francisco, the National Negro Congress staged demonstrations, with protesters chanting, "Disney tells, Disney tells / Lies about the South. / We've heard those lies before / Right out of Bilbo's mouth." (Theodore Bilbo had been governor of Mississippi and later worked hard as a senator against voting rights for African Americans.) At the New York premiere in Times Square, demonstrators emphasized just how insulting the film was to African Americans returning from service in World War II: "We fought for Uncle Sam, not Uncle Tom" (Snead 1994, 92).

Disney's 2007 decision not to rerelease the film was applauded by the Los Angeles Urban Policy Roundtable on the grounds that "the film depicts blacks as happy-go-lucky, submissive, storytelling servants and helpmates." Or as Sterling A. Brown put it more generally about cultural products like *Song of the South*: "the grown-up slaves were contented, the pickaninnies were frolicking, the steamboat was hooting around the bend, God was in his heaven, and all was right with the world" (1969, 18). Maurice Rapf, who was hired to work on the screenplay, had already set off alarm bells about Uncle Remus as a condescending stereotype, a black man who is able "to forgive all the injustices of slavery in his Christian forbearance, and not only love his white masters, but remain eager to please them" (I. Thomas 2012, 223).

Disney gives us a dehistoricized South, "not your time, not my time, but sometime." Its opening titles about how the tales of Uncle Remus have come out of a "humble cabin, out of the singing heart of the Old South" and how the stories are "rich in simple truths, forever fresh and new" underscores the determination to create a South untouched by the suffering of slaves and unscarred by a destructive Civil War. Black children frolic around a wagon that pulls up to the mansion, and the melodies of spirituals create a sense of utopian plenitude at evening campfires. Bosley Crowther of the *New York Times* called the film "the most meretricious sort of slush" and denounced an Uncle Remus who is depicted as "just the sweetest most wistful darky slave that ever stepped out of a sublimely unreconstructed fancy of the Old South" (1946). Crowther, like many other viewers, was unaware that the film was set in the Reconstruction Era, most likely because the film is encoded with scenes of field hands singing on their return from work with loads of cotton on their backs. They cook, drive wagons, hoe, and engage in labor that enables the lavish life style of the white grandmother in the film. *Ebony* magazine expressed outrage at the "Uncle Tom–Aunt Jemima caricature" in the film, "complete with all the fawning standard equipment thereof—the toothy smile, battered hat, gray beard, and a profusion of 'dis' and 'dat' talk" (Cohen 1997, 61). The NAACP noted that the production helped to "perpetuate a dangerously glorified picture of slavery." The film was condemned for its exploitation of African American folklore, which was instrumentalized to give the "impression of an idyllic master-slave relationship." As the actress Fredi Washington wrote in the *People's Voice*, the film "perpetuates the idea that Negroes throughout American history have been illiterate, docile, and quite happy to be treated as children—without even the average child's ambition and without thought of tomorrow" (Cohen 1997, 60–61; Washington 1946).

Song of the South begins with a melody about the music of Dixie and how it weaves a "magic spell." Its visual evocation of a bleached-out landscape (cottonwoods / moonlight / field of white) is remarkable, disrupted chromatically only by a cabin door:

> Song of the South, I see
> The scenes I know so well.
> Cottonwoods in blossom
> over my cabin door.
> Pale moonlight on a field of white.

The suggestive melody effaces the historical record, substituting sentimental scenes of communal labors for the backbreaking work carried out by men, women, and children. We do not see the large sacks, weighing up to one hundred pounds when full, that they dragged behind them. We do not see hands bloodied from the sharp spikes on the cotton plant. All is well in this still pastoral setting, awash in soft moonlight, melodies, and fragrances.

Joel Chandler Harris put Uncle Remus up front and center, but *Song of the South* subordinates the source of storytelling to a nostalgic vision of plantation life, a white-washed vision that serves as a powerful defense against harsh historical realities. In this faux South, Uncle Remus will play the very real domestic role historically taken on by house slaves, rescuing and healing Johnny, the white child traumatized by the departure of his father while the family is staying at the impressive estate of his grandmother. We never learn much about the exact nature of the domestic disturbances in the family, but Uncle Remus steps in as surrogate parent, telling Johnny stories that are cheerfully didactic as well as diverting. The first story he tells the boy, for instance, is designed to deter him from running away from home. After all, when Brer Rabbit left "his old troubles behind," it turned out that he was just "headin' straight for a whole mess o' bran' new troubles."

With one stroke of the Disney wand, African American folktales, which were encoded with complex cultural signs and functioned as carriers of wisdom and tradition, were transformed, much like their European counterparts, into "simple truths" designed to teach children morals and lessons. Never mind that Brer Rabbit has to endure capture and dangle from a trap set by Brer Fox or that Brer Bear is tricked by Brer Rabbit into taking his place in the trap, this first story is flattened out into a cautionary tale about the perils of running away from home. Uncle Remus's stories are reduced to innocuous fare for children.

Even the "Wonderful Tar-Baby Story" becomes a tutorial for Johnny, who learns to use reverse psychology on the boys who are trying to reclaim their puppy. "Ain't dat what Brer Rabbit did to Brer Fox?" the African American Toby asks Johnny, the boy who has been put in his charge for the duration of his visit (both are the same age yet one takes care of the other). And Johnny reveals his powers to abstract a larger lesson from the tale: "Sh, Sh! Bein' little an' without much strength, we s'posed to use our heads instead of our foots," mimicking Toby's speech with creepy precociousness. The appropriation is complete, with the white boy instructing his black counterpart about the wisdom embedded in the tales and later trying to comfort his friend Ginny with a story about the "bodacious" Brer Rabbit. Brer Rabbit seems fully tamed, domesticated, and appropriated.

Johnny's mother feels sure that Uncle Remus's stories are making it "difficult" to bring Johnny up to be "obedient and truthful," and she places a moratorium on his storytelling, one that is violated almost immediately when Uncle Remus, who cannot stop himself from dispensing wisdom, tells the story about Brer Rabbit's Laughing Place to comfort Johnny's friend, Ginny.

Brer Rabbit, up until this moment, seems fully assimilated to the culture of child-hood, until we hear a story about the Laughing Place—the most violent of all the tales—with Brer Fox determined to barbecue Brer Rabbit for dinner and getting his comeuppance when he is chased out of Brer Rabbit's Laughing Place by a swarm of bees. The Laughing Place, as it turns out, is a trap designed to torture everyone but Brer Rabbit. His gleeful laughter becomes tainted by sadism in unsettling ways, espe-cially when we see Brer Rabbit's grinning face dissolve into Uncle Remus's chuckling features. The film at first disavows the violence of the cartoon sequence in Johnny's realization that his "Laughing Place" is Uncle Remus's cabin. But Disney then pulls out all the stops to suggest that Uncle Remus's Laughing Place may be just as perilous as Brer Rabbit's. Distraught that Uncle Remus has been "sent away" by his mother, Johnny races across an enclosed field to keep him from leaving. He is gored by an enraged bull. Only the healing hymns of the field hands and the soothing voice of Uncle Remus (never mind that he was the immediate cause of the accident) reciting a tale to the boy revive him from his delirious state.

The happy ending to *Song of the South* reconstitutes the white family, but at a price. Crucial to the successful reconciliation of the parents and the rescue of the child is another family, one that stays fragmented and dismembered. Uncle Remus, Aunt Tempy, and Toby might be said to mirror the trio of Johnny and his parents but these three figures all play supporting roles, independently of one another—roles that enable the white nuclear family to stay intact as a unit. Despite a faint whiff of romance in Uncle Remus's love of Aunt Tempy's cooking, the two live under sepa-rate roofs, standing in no kinship relation to each other. Toby, moreover, assigned to care for Johnny, has no parents at all to look out for him. And both Remus and Tempy worry far more about Johnny than they do about Toby, who is constantly marginalized, even by the film's sightlines. In the film, the actor who plays Toby even appears "somewhat annoyed at his systematic exclusion," as one critic points out (Snead 1994, 98).

The film not only dismembers the black family but also renders Uncle Remus superfluous. In its musical coda, Johnny leads his friends Ginny and Toby, as they skip down the road and are greeted by Brer Rabbit, who is joined by other woodland creatures. He can now conjure the African narratives out of his own imagination. "As he romps up the hill," James Snead writes, "we see that he has learned to 'tell Uncle Remus Stories'—an art defined in the film as the ability to conjure up cartoons— without blacks" (Snead 1994, 96). Uncle Remus has been "made obsolete" and "Johnny can now bring the cartoon animals to life *independently*."

The film becomes a self-reflexive allegory of cultural appropriation, with Johnny as a kind of stand-in for Joel Chandler Harris, who listened to tales as a boy, wrote them down, and published them under his name (to be sure with a title that attributes them to an "Uncle Remus" who, in the final analysis, received neither real credit nor royalty checks).

Is it any wonder then, to return to Alice Walker, that the tales told by Uncle Remus become, in their new form, less a source of communal pride than a badge of shame. "The worst part of being in an oppressed culture is that the oppressive culture—primarily because it controls the production and dispersal of images in the media—can so easily make us feel ashamed of ourselves, of our sayings, our doings, and our ways. And it doesn't matter whether these sayings, doings, or ways are good or bad. What is bad about them, and, therefore, worthy of shame, is that they belong to us" (*Dummy in the Window*, 32).

Joel Chandler Harris himself never understood how his appropriation of the tales might have done violence to stories that, with astonishing economy, encapsulated folk wisdom with a vital social and cultural function. For him, the goal was to "preserve the legends themselves in their original simplicity, and to wed them permanently to the quaint dialect . . . through the medium of which they have become part of the domestic history of every Southern family." It never occurred to him that the tales might have emotive weight as the simple expression of complex thought. Perhaps Uncle Remus's "quaint dialect" preserves mysteries that are not necessarily the cultural property of "every Southern family."

Today, *Song of the South* has been placed in the Disney vault, yet it continues to have a robust afterlife in the theme park attraction Splash Mountain, which features a flume ride. Uncle Remus has disappeared, and all that is left are the animated characters of Brer Rabbit, Brer Fox, and Brer Bear, along with a host of cartoon characters from the bayou. The chirpy melody "Zip-a-Dee-Doo-Dah" fills the air as visitors reach the end of the ride. By fragmenting the narrative line of the film into bits and pieces and removing all reference to its frame, Splash Mountain provides visceral thrills that culminate in a "fall" mimicking Brer Rabbit's drop into the briar patch, followed by an upbeat serenade of happily-ever-after. Uncle Remus is gone, Tar Baby has been turned into a pot of honey, and the cinematic inspiration has been transformed into a garish pantomime featuring "critters" that chase Brer Rabbit only to be outsmarted by him.

Ripe for parody, Uncle Remus's name comes up in popular television entertainments (in *The Office* one of the workers refers to Stanley as "Uncle Remus"), in novels (Jason Bourne plays Brer Rabbit to a character named Uncle Remus in Robert Ludlum's *The Bourne Connection*), and in films. The 1989 *Fletch Lives* reveals that Uncle Remus and his tales have been pretty much "killed" for everyone, black and white. In it, I. M. Fletcher, played by Chevy Chase, falls asleep on an airplane and dreams about the Louisiana plantation he has just inherited. Chase is surrounded by white field hands and servants who serenade him and are about to dance for him, when he announces "Dance for me? Why I'll dance for them!" "Zip-A-Dee-Do-Dah" is the song to which he and field hands dance and sing. Defamiliarizing the conditions of slavery with white "slaves" dressed in elaborate white costumes and serving a white master, the film makes a mockery of the Disney tune by literally whitewashing plantation life.

Alice Walker describes the "vastly alienating" effects of the "second interpretation of our folklore" in *Song of the South*: "Our whole town turned out for this movie, black children and their parents in the colored section, white children and their parents in the white section." The film was "vastly alienating" in two ways: "not only from the likes of Uncle Remus—in whom I saw aspects of my father, my mother, in fact all black people I knew who told these stories—but also from the stories themselves, which, passed into the context of white people's creation, the same white people who, in my real everyday life, would not let a black person eat in a restaurant or through their front door, I perceived as meaningless" (*Dummy in the Window*, 31–32). The road to respectability would be a long one for African American folklore, and many of the figures that took center stage, thanks to the work of Joel Chandler Harris and Walt Disney, are now still impatiently waiting for their second acts.

UNCLE REMUS INITIATES THE LITTLE BOY[1]

1 *initiates:* Initiation suggests a rite of passage in which the old man serves as mentor for the little boy. The two occupy a space that is removed from reality yet also planted squarely in it. To modern ears, the term sounds odd, for it has overtones that challenge the innocent tenderness of the interactions between the two.

2 *Bimeby:* by and by

3 *he ain't mo'n got de wuds out'n his mouf twel:* he had hardly got the words out of his mouth when

4 *Moggin hoss:* Morgan horse (often used to draw carriages)

5 *confab:* conversation

6 *jubously:* dubiously

7 *'pen' on you:* depend on you

One evening recently, the lady whom Uncle Remus calls "Miss Sally" missed her little seven-year-old boy. Making search for him through the house and through the yard, she heard the sound of voices in the old man's cabin, and, looking through the window, saw the child sitting by Uncle Remus. His head rested against the old man's arm, and he was gazing with an expression of the most intense interest into the rough, weather-beaten face, that beamed so kindly upon him. This is what "Miss Sally" heard:

"Bimeby,[2] one day, arter Brer Fox bin doin' all dat he could fer ter ketch Brer Rabbit, en Brer Rabbit bin doin' all he could fer to keep 'im fum it, Brer Fox say to hisse'f dat he'd put up a game on Brer Rabbit, en he ain't mo'n got de wuds out'n his mouf twel[3] Brer Rabbit come a lopin' up de big road, lookin' des ez plump, en ez fat, en ez sassy ez a Moggin hoss[4] in a barley-patch.

"'Hol' on dar, Brer Rabbit,' sez Brer Fox, sezee.

"'I ain't got time, Brer Fox,' sez Brer Rabbit, sezee, sorter mendin' his licks.

"'I wanter have some confab[5] wid you, Brer Rabbit,' sez Brer Fox, sezee.

"'All right, Brer Fox, but you better holler fum whar you stan'. I'm monstus full er fleas dis mawnin',' sez Brer Rabbit, sezee.

"'I seed Brer B'ar yistiddy,' sez Brer Fox, sezee, 'en he sorter rake me over de coals kaze you en me ain't make frens en live naberly, en I told 'im dat I'd see you.'

Den Brer Rabbit scratch one year wid his off hinefoot sorter jubously,[6] en den he ups en sez, sezee:

"'All a settin', Brer Fox. Spose'n you drap roun' termorrer en take dinner wid me. We ain't got no great doin's at our house, but I speck de old 'oman en de chilluns kin sorter scramble roun' en git up sump'n fer ter stay yo' stummuck.'

"'I'm 'gree'ble, Brer Rabbit,' sez Brer Fox, sezee.

"'Den I'll 'pen' on you,'[7] sez Brer Rabbit, sezee.

"Nex' day, Mr. Rabbit an' Miss Rabbit got up soon, 'fo' day, en raided on a gyarden like Miss Sally's out dar, en got some cabbiges, en some roas'n-years,[8] en some sparrer-grass,[9] en dey fix up a smashin' dinner. Bimeby one er de little Rabbits, playin' out in de backyard, come runnin' in hollerin', 'Oh, ma! oh, ma! I seed Mr. Fox a comin'!' En den Brer Rabbit he tuck de chilluns by der years en make um set down, en den him and Miss Rabbit sorter dally roun' waitin' for Brer Fox. En dey keep on waitin', but no Brer Fox ain't come. Atter 'while Brer Rabbit goes to de do', easy like, en peep out, en dar, stickin' fum behime de cornder,[10] wuz de tip-een' er Brer Fox tail. Den Brer Rabbit shot de do' en sot down, en put his paws behime his years en begin fer ter sing:

8 *roas'n-years:* roasting ears (of corn)

9 *sparrer-grass:* asparagus

10 *de cornder:* the corner

> *"De place wharbouts you spill de grease,*
> *Right dar youer boun' ter slide,*
> *An' whar you fine a bunch er ha'r,*
> *You'll sholy fine de hide.'*

"Nex' day. Brer Fox sont word by Mr. Mink, en skuze hisse'f kaze he wuz too sick fer ter come, en he ax Brer Rabbit fer to come en take dinner wid him, en Brer Rabbit say he wuz 'gree'ble.

"Bimeby, w'en de shadders wuz at der shortes', Brer Rabbit he sorter brush up en sa'nter down ter Brer Fox's house, en w'en he got dar, he hear somebody groanin', en he look in de do' en dar he see Brer Fox settin' up in a rockin' cheer all wrop up wid flannil, en he look mighty weak. Brer Rabbit look all 'roun', he did, but he ain't see no dinner. De dishpan wuz settin' on de table, en close by wuz a kyarvin' knife.

"'Look like you gwineter have chicken fer dinner, Brer Fox,' sez Brer Rabbit, sezee.

"'Yes, Brer Rabbit, dey er nice, en fresh, en tender,' sez Brer Fox, sezee.

A. B. Frost's illustrations for *Uncle Remus and His Friends* (1892) and *Uncle Remus: His Songs and His Sayings* (1921) became the best-known representations of the characters in Harris's tales.

"Den Brer Rabbit sorter pull his mustarsh, en say: 'You ain't got no calamus root,[11] is you, Brer Fox? I done got so now dat I can't eat no chicken ceppin' she's seasoned up wid calamus root.' En wid dat Brer Rabbit lipt out er de do' and dodge 'mong de bushes, en sot dar watchin' fer Brer Fox; en he ain't watch long, nudder, kaze Brer Fox flung off de flannil en crope out er de house en got whar he could cloze in on Brer Rabbit, en bimeby Brer Rabbit holler out: 'Oh, Brer Fox! I'll des put yo' calamus root out yer on dish yer stump. Better come git it while hit's fresh,' and wid dat Brer Rabbit gallop off home. En Brer Fox ain't never kotch 'im yit, en w'at's mo', honey, he ain't gwine'ter."

11 *calamus root:* The calamus is a perennial plant that has been used for medicinal purposes and as a substitute for ginger, cinnamon, and nutmeg.

In the tale that opens the cycle, we are introduced to a trio that functions as a family, with Remus as a "kindly," paternal storyteller, an appreciative little boy, and an approving mother. We have here an ode to plantation life, an idealized, romantic version of evenings in the old

A. B. Frost.

South. The phrase "bimeby" (by and by) operates like the "once upon a time" of fairy tales, and the story ends with reassuring words about Brer Rabbit's ability to survive any of Brer Fox's traps. In the tale, murderous hostility masquerades as friendship, and we quickly learn that Brer Rabbit's chief strategy for survival is to feign being "agreeable," a fact that immediately destabilizes the tender relationship between Uncle Remus and the little boy in the frame narrative.

This introductory tale introduces the paradox of what the philosopher Jacques Derrida calls "hostipitality," a term that reminds us of the contradictory impulses embedded in hospitality and friendship.

1 *breff:* breath

2 *fier:* fire

3 *tuck'n s'ply:* went and supplied

4 *bimeby:* by and by

THE SAD FATE OF MR. FOX

"Now, den," said Uncle Remus, with unusual gravity, as soon as the little boy, by taking his seat, announced that he was ready for the evening's entertainment to begin; "now, den, dish yer tale w'at I'm agwine ter gin you is de las' row er stumps, sho. Dish yer's whar ole Brer Fox los' his breff,[1] en he ain't fin' it no mo' down ter dis day."

"Did he kill himself, Uncle Remus?" the little boy asked, with a curious air of concern.

"Hol' on dar, honey!" the old man exclaimed, with a great affectation of alarm; "hol' on dar! Wait! Gimme room! I don't wanter tell you no story, en ef you keep shovin' me forerd, I mout git some er de facks mix up 'mong deyse'f. You gotter gimme room en you gotter gimme time."

The little boy had no other premature questions to ask, and, after a pause, Uncle Remus resumed:

"Well, den, one day Brer Rabbit go ter Brer Fox house, he did, en he put up mighty po' mouf. He say his ole 'oman sick, en his chilluns col', en de fier[2] done gone out. Brer Fox, he feel bad 'bout dis, en he tuck'n s'ply[3] Brer Rabbit widder chunk er fier. Brer Rabbit see Brer Fox cookin' some nice beef, en his mouf 'gun ter water, but he take de fier, he did, en he put out to'rds home; but present'y yer he come back, en he say de fier done gone out. Brer Fox 'low dat he want er invite to dinner, but he don't say nuthin', en bimeby[4] Brer Rabbit he up'n say, sezee:

A. B. Frost.

"'Brer Fox, whar you git so much nice beef?' sezee, en den Brer Fox he up'n 'spon', sezee:

"'You come ter my house termorrer ef yo' fokes ain't too sick, en I kin show you whar you kin git plenty beef mo' nicer dan dish yer,' sezee.

"Well, sho nuff, de nex' day fotch Brer Rabbit, en Brer Fox say, sezee:

"'Der's a man down yander by Miss Meadows's w'at got heap er fine cattle, en he gotter cow name Bookay,' sezee, 'en you des go en say *Bookay*, en she'll open her mouf, en you kin jump in en git des as much meat ez you kin tote,' sez Brer Fox, sezee.

"'Well, I'll go 'long,' sez Brer Rabbit, sezee, 'en you kin jump fus' en den I'll come follerin' atter,' sezee.

"Wid dat dey put out, en dey went promernadin' 'roun' 'mong de cattle, dey did, twel bimeby dey struck up wid de one dey wuz atter.[5] Brer Fox, he up, he did, en holler *Bookay*, en de cow flung 'er mouf wide open. Sho nuff, in dey jump, en w'en dey got dar, Brer Fox, he say, sezee:

5 *wid de one dey wuz atter:* with the one they were after

"'You kin cut mos' ennywheres, Brer Rabbit, but don't cut 'round' de haslett,'[6] sezee.

"Den Brer Rabbit, he holler back, he did: 'I'm a gitten me out a roas'n'-piece,' sezee.

"'Roas'n', er bakin', er fryin',' sez Brer Fox, sezee, 'don't git too nigh de haslett,' sezee.

"Dey cut en dey kyarved, en dey kyarv'd en dey cut, en w'iles dey wuz cuttin' en kyarvin', en slashin' 'way, Brer Rabbit, he tuck'n hacked inter de haslett, en wid dat down fell de cow dead.

"'Now, den,' sez Brer Fox, 'we er gone, sho,' sezee.

"'W'at we gwine do?' sez Brer Rabbit, sezee.

"'I'll git in de maul,'[7] sez Brer Fox, 'en you'll jump in de gall,' sezee.

"Nex' mawnin' yer cum de man w'at de cow b'long ter, and he ax who kill Bookay. Nobody don't say nuthin'. Den de man say he'll cut 'er open en see, en den he whirl in, en 'twa'n't no time 'fo' he had 'er intruls[8] spread out. Brer Rabbit, he crope out'n de gall, en say, sezee:

"'Mister Man! Oh, Mister Man! I'll tell you who kill yo' cow. You look in de maul, en dar you'll fin' 'im,' sezee.

"Wid dat de man tuck a stick and lam down on de maul so hard dat he kill Brer Fox stone-dead. W'en Brer Rabbit see Brer Fox wuz laid out fer good, he make like he mighty sorry, en he up'n ax de man fer Brer Fox head. Man say he ain't keerin', en den Brer Rabbit tuck'n bring it ter Brer Fox house. Dar he see ole Miss Fox, en he tell 'er dat he done fotch her some nice beef w'at 'er ole man sont[9] 'er, but she ain't gotter look at it twel she go ter eat it.

"Brer Fox son wuz name Tobe, en Brer Rabbit tell Tobe fer ter keep still w'iles his mammy cook de nice beef w'at his daddy sont 'im. Tobe he wuz mighty hongry, en he look in de pot he did w'iles de cookin' wuz gwine on, en dar he see his daddy head, en wid dat he sot up a howl en tole his mammy. Miss Fox, she git mighty mad w'en she fin' she cookin' her ole man head, en she call up de dogs, she did, en sickt em on Brer Rabbit; en ole Miss Fox en Tobe en de dogs, dey push Brer Rabbit so close dat he hatter take a holler tree. Miss Fox, she tell Tobe fer ter stay dar en min' Brer Rabbit, w'ile she goes en git de ax, en w'en she gone, Brer Rabbit, he tole Tobe ef he go ter de branch en git 'im a drink er water dat he'll gin' 'im a dollar. Tobe, he put out, he did, en bring some water in his hat, but by de time he got back Brer Rabbit done out en gone. Ole Miss Fox, she cut and cut twel down come de tree, but no Brer Rabbit dar. Den she lay

6 *haslett:* the edible innards of an animal, including the heart, liver, and lungs

7 *maul:* stomach lining

8 *intruls:* entrails

9 *sont:* sent

de blame on Tobe, en she say she gwine ter lash 'im, en Tobe, he put out en run, de ole 'oman atter 'im. Bimeby, he come up wid Brer Rabbit, en sot down fer to tell 'im how 'twuz, en w'iles dey wuz a settin' dar, yer come ole Miss Fox a slippin' up en grab um bofe. Den she tell um w'at she gwine do. Brer Rabbit she gwine ter kill, en Tobe she gwine ter lam ef its de las' ack. Den Brer Rabbit sez, sezee:

"'Ef you please, ma'am, Miss Fox, lay me on de grinestone en groun' off my nose so I can't smell no mo' when I'm dead.'

"Miss Fox, she tuck dis ter be a good idee, en she fotch bofe un um[10] ter de grine-stone, en set um up on it so dat she could groun' off Brer Rabbit nose. Den Brer Rabbit, he up'n say, sezee:

"'Ef you please, ma'am, Miss Fox, Tobe he kin turn de handle w'iles you goes atter some water fer ter wet de grine-stone,' sezee.

"Co'se,[11] soon'z Brer Rabbit see Miss Fox go atter de water, he jump down en put out, en dis time he git clean away."

"And was that the last of the Rabbit, too, Uncle Remus?" the little boy asked, with something like a sigh.

"Don't push me too close, honey," responded the old man; "don't shove me up in no cornder.[12] I don't wanter tell you no stories. Some say dat Brer Rabbit's ole 'oman died fum eatin' some pizen-weed,[13] en dat Brer Rabbit married ole Miss Fox,[14] en some say not. Some tells one tale en some tells nudder; some say dat fum dat time forerd de Rabbits en de Foxes make fre'n's en stay so; some say dey kep on quollin'. Hit look like it mixt. Let dem tell you what knows. Dat what I years you gits it straight like I yeard it."

There was a long pause, which was finally broken by the old man:

"Hit's 'gin de rules fer you ter be noddin' yer, honey. Bimeby you'll drap off en I'll hatter tote you up ter de big 'ouse. I hear dat baby cryin', en bimeby Miss Sally'll fly up en be a holler'n atter you."

"Oh, I wasn't asleep," the little boy replied. "I was just thinking."

"Well, dat's diffunt," said the old man. "Ef you'll clime up on my back," he continued, speaking softly, "I speck I ain't too ole fer ter be yo' hoss fum yer to de house. Many en many's de time dat I toted yo' Unk Jeems dat away, en Mars Jeems wuz heavier sot[15] dan what you is."

10 *fotch bofe un um:* took both of them

11 *Co'se:* Because you see

12 *cornder:* corner

13 *eatin' some pizen-weed:* Kwaku Tse tells Spider in the African version of this tale that his mother died by poison.

14 *Brer Rabbit married ole Miss Fox:* In some African tales, the trickster hero kills the partner and then marries his surviving widow.

15 *sot:* sort

A. B. Frost.

*"Sad Fate" wildly understates what happens to Brer Fox. The tale
lulls us into the usual sense of faith in harmonious solidarity among
animals as they struggle to survive. It quickly takes a bad turn that
leads to captivity, betrayal, murder, and near cannibalism. Despite the
efforts of European folklorists to relate the tale to "Tom Thumb" (who
lands in the stomach of a cow), to "The Juniper Tree" (in which a father
devours the remains of his son after they are cooked up by his wife
in a stew), or "Open Sesame" (use of a password to enter a forbidden
space), the tale's main features point to African sources. In one African
analogue, summarized by the folklorist T. F. Crane, Elephant and
Tortoise quarrel. Elephant is determined to kill Tortoise and asks:
"Little Tortoise, shall I chew you or swallow you down?" Tortoise asks
to be swallowed, enters Elephant's body, chews up his vital organs,*

and emerges from the carcass, alive and mobile. In another African variant (included in this volume), Spider and Kwaku Tse cut the meat from inside two cows to provide an endless supply of nourishment for a king. As Alan Dundes observed, "This African/Afro-American tale type has an identity of its own."

What does it mean to magically enter another beast and feed surreptitiously on its innards? Why choose such an unappetizing way to acquire food? Brer Fox and Brer Rabbit indulge in an orgy of cutting, carving, slashing, and hacking away, more as if they were at war with the cow than in search of nourishment. The phrase feeding frenzy *acquires a new depth of meaning here, almost as if frenzy trumps feeding. If Brer Fox is punished for his invasive actions by nearly being served up to his wife and children for a cannibalistic feast, Brer Rabbit goes free. Perhaps the initial lack of charity and generosity dooms Brer Fox. But is there an actual moral calculus in the tale, or is it instead a grotesque mélange of ritualized violence aimed at one of the perpetrators but mainly at the innocent cow, a female animal that provides a nurturing substance to humans?*

HOW SPIDER AND KWAKU TSE KILLED THE KING'S COWS AND TOOK HIS WIVES

(Africa)

There was a certain king who had two fine cows, and these two cows were in the same town with the king. In this town people often could not get meat to eat, but the king always had meat to eat from the two cows, for they used to void meat every morning.[1]

Now, Spider and Kwaku Tse came to that town as strangers,[2] and when they came the people had no meat to eat; they had nothing but plantains and *dokonno*;[3] so Spider and Kwaku Tse asked the master of the house in which they lodged, since he had no meat to give them, to show them the house of the king.

1 *void meat every morning:* Much like the table that sets itself in European folklore, these cows are the source of an endless supply of nourishment.

2 *as strangers:* Spider and his family can take on human form, and, as humans, they are spider-like, lean and hairy.

3 *dokonno:* a kind of boiled maize bread

Then Spider and Kwaku Tse went to the king, and said to him: "We are strangers who have come to your town, and tomorrow we will go on our way. We can find no meat to eat, but on the way here, we saw two fine cows." The king replied: "The cows belong to me, and they are not to be killed." Spider asked, "Why can't the cows be killed?" and the king answered, "They supply me with meat." Then Spider and Kwaku Tse asked the king if he could not give them just a small piece of meat, and the king refused.

Spider and Kwaku Tse departed and returned to the house in which they were lodging, and they told the owner of the house everything they had said to the king, and how the king had refused to give them even a small piece of meat. They said to the man, "The king said that his two cows supplied him with beef, and that therefore he could not kill them." Spider said, "My name is Spider, and this man is my namesake Kwaku. Never before have I seen a cow that could supply meat and yet live. I was only passing through here and going on my way, but now I will stay here for a while to see how cows can supply the king with meat."

The owner of the house answered, "You won't be able to see that, for they do it in the king's private yard." Spider said, "I am he who is called Kwaku Anansi, and any-thing in this world that I want to see or want to do and that I am not able to see or do, I have not yet found." He said, "These two cows of the king. I will kill them, and I will take their heads. I will do that with my friend. We will each kill one, and, as for the heads of the cows, the king will cut them off and give them to us."

The owner of the house marveled greatly to hear these words from Spider, and he ran and called his neighbor and said to him, "Come and listen, for the strangers who have come to lodge with me are about to bring great trouble down on me." When the neighbor arrived, the owner of the house told him, in the presence of Spider, what Spider had said, and Spider gave them a proverb, saying, "If the load on your head is heavy, and it is something to eat, while you are eating it, you are lightening it." Then Kawku Tse said, "We have said this in your house. It is of no concern to anyone else."

Then Spider and Kwaku Tse told the owner of the house that they were going out to see if they could get the heads of the two cows and bring them back. And they left and went to the king's yard, and it was night time, and they found the place where the cows used to sleep. They had with them a leaf that made people sneeze when they smelled it, and they rubbed the leaf on the noses of the two cows. The cows looked at once as if they were about to sneeze. They opened their mouths wide, and Spider and Kwaku Tse made themselves very small, and each one jumped into the mouth of a cow. And the cows swallowed them up. Then they cut meat from the insides of the cows, but the cows did not die.

The next morning the king went to his cows to get meat, and the cows voided meat for the king, but this time the meat was not as fresh as usual, because Spider and Kwaku Tse had cut it and left it inside all night. The king said, "I wonder why the meat is not as fresh as usual?" He sent for a medicine man to see if he could cure the cows, for he thought that they were sick. When the medicine man came, he said that the cows must have eaten a bad leaf, and he poured medicine down their throats. Then the medicine purged them, and they voided more meat, but it was all stinking.

When the king and the medicine man left, and there was nobody left with the cows, Kwaku Tse came out and went into the other cow. When he got there, he found that Spider had done the same thing as he, Kwaku Tse, had done in the other cow. He said to Spider, "I do not know why we cannot make these two cows die. We have cut all the meat inside them. I am going back to my cow, and after I have gone inside, I will cut its belly right through with a knife."

Spider answered, "No, do not do that. When you go in, you may cut neither the belly nor the heart." Kwaku Tse asked, "Why not?" and Spider said, "Because if we kill the cows while we are still inside, we will not be able to get out again, and what will we do then?" Kwaku Tse asked, "Why wouldn't we be able to come out?" Then Spider said, "Your mother is dead, isn't she?" and Kwaku Tse answered, "She died by poison." Spider said, "When she was dead, didn't a medicine man come and try to make her sneeze or open her mouth. And did he not fail? You must know that if the cows die while we are still inside them, we will not be able to get out. But we can hide and that is what we will do. The king will rip open their bellies to discover the cause of their death. You must chop the meat on one side into small pieces so that they will think that the cows received a blow and died of it. When the king rips open the cow, hide in the stomach, and if you see that they are about to search around there, you must run into the bowels and hide. When you go back into the cow now, after you have chopped the side as I told you, you must look for the heart and cut it down. When you have cut down the heart, the cow will die. And then be careful where you hide so that you escape the knife which they use to open the belly. But before you do this, first run to the man in whose house we are staying and tell him that we are going to the water side to wash up."

Then Kwaku Tse went to the house-master and told him, and returned into the belly of the cow, and chopped the side and cut the heart down, and the cow died. And Spider did the same in his cow, and both cows were dead.

SOURCE: Adapted from A. B. Ellis, "Evolution in Folklore: Some West African Prototypes of the 'Uncle Remus' Stories," 93–104.

In a November 1895 Popular Science Monthly, *a Colonel A. B. Ellis reported that he had found West African variants of tales collected by Joel Chandler Harris. He published them with the hope of showing how folklore is affected by "change of environment," an extraordinary euphemism for a move from tribal life on the Gold Coast to enslaved conditions in the Southern States. Ellis tells us nothing about his collecting practices. The story above is the first half of a longer narrative that also includes tricks played by Spider and Kwaku Tse to secure for themselves the king's wives.*

MR. RABBIT GROSSLY DECEIVES MR. FOX

One evening when the little boy, whose nights with Uncle Remus were as entertaining as those Arabian ones of blessed memory,[1] had finished supper and hurried out to sit with his venerable patron, he found the old man in great glee. Indeed, Uncle Remus was talking and laughing to himself at such a rate that the little boy was afraid he had company. The truth is, Uncle Remus had heard the child coming, and, when the rosy-cheeked chap put his head in at the door, was engaged in a monologue, the burden of which seemed to be—

> *"Ole Molly Har',*
> *W'at you doin' dar,*
> *Settin' in de cornder*
> *Smokin' yo' seegyar?"*[2]

1 *Arabian ones of blessed memory:* The narrator is referring to *The Thousand and One Nights*, a collection that also has a frame narrative, one in which Scheherazade tells King Shahriyar a story every night, and breaks off the tale midway in order to pique the curiosity of the king, who delays her execution by one more day.

2 *seegyar:* cigar

As a matter of course this vague allusion reminded the little boy of the fact that the wicked Fox was still in pursuit of the Rabbit, and he immediately put his curiosity[3] in the shape of a question.

3 *his curiosity:* The little boy's curiosity parallels that of King Shahriyar in *The Thousand and One Nights*.

4 *Miss Meadows en de gals:* The phrase is used generically to designate womenfolk in the tales, and, with male animals playing the main roles in Uncle Remus's tales, the women in general are conspicuous by their absence.

5 *bimeby:* by and by

"Uncle Remus, did the Rabbit have to go clean away when he got loose from the Tar-Baby?"

"Bless gracious, honey, dat he didn't. Who? Him? You dunno nuthin' 'tall 'bout Brer Rabbit ef dat's de way you puttin' 'im down. W'at he gwine 'way fer? He moughter stayed sorter close twel de pitch rub off'n his ha'r, but twern't menny days 'fo' he wuz lopin' up en down de neighborhood same ez ever, en I dunno ef he wern't mo' sassier dan befo'.

"Seem like dat de tale 'bout how he got mixt up wid de Tar-Baby got 'roun' 'mongst de neighbors. Leas'ways, Miss Meadows en de gals[4] got win' un' it, en de nex' time Brer Rabbit paid um a visit Miss Meadows tackled 'im 'bout it, en de gals sot up a monstus gigglement. Brer Rabbit, he sot up des ez cool ez a cowcumber, he did, en let 'em run on."

"Who was Miss Meadows, Uncle Remus?" inquired the little boy.

"Don't ax me, honey. She wuz in de tale, Miss Meadows en de gals wuz, en de tale I give you like hit wer' gun ter me. Brer Rabbit, he sot dar, he did, sorter lam' like, en den bimeby[5] he cross his legs, he did, and wink his eye slow, en up and say, sezee:

'Ladies, Brer Fox wuz my daddy's ridin'-hoss fer thirty year; maybe mo', but thirty year dat I knows un,' sezee; en den he paid um his 'specks, en tip his beaver, en march off, he did, des ez stiff en ez stuck up ez a fier-stick.

"Nex' day, Brer Fox cum a callin', and w'en he 'gun fer ter laugh 'bout Brer Rabbit, Miss Meadows en de gals, dey ups en tells 'im 'bout w'at Brer Rabbit say. Den Brer Fox grit his

A. B. Frost.

tushes[6] sho' nuff, he did, en he look mighty dumpy, but w'en he riz fer ter go he up en say, sezee:

"'Ladies, I ain't 'sputin'[7] w'at you say, but I'll make Brer Rabbit chaw up his words en spit um out right yer whar you kin see 'im,' sezee, en wid dat off Brer Fox put.

"En w'en he got in de big road, he shuck de dew off'n his tail, en made a straight shoot fer Brer Rabbit's house. W'en he got dar, Brer Rabbit wuz spectin' un 'im, en de do' wuz shet fas'. Brer Fox knock. Nobody ain't ans'er. Brer Fox knock. Nobody ans'er. Den he knock agin—blam! blam! Den Brer Rabbit holler out mighty weak:

"'Is dat you, Brer Fox? I want you ter run en fetch de doctor. Dat bait er pusly[8] w'at I e't dis mawnin' is gittin' 'way wid me. Do, please, Brer Fox, run quick,' sez Brer Rabbit, sezee.

"'I come atter you, Brer Rabbit,' sez Brer Fox, sezee. 'Dar's gwine ter be a party up at Miss Meadows's,' sezee. 'All de gals'll be dere, en I promus' dat I'd fetch you. De gals, dey 'lowed dat hit wouldn't be no party ceppin' I fotch you,' sez Brer Fox, sezee.

"Den Brer Rabbit say he wuz too sick, en Brer Fox say he wuzzent, en dar dey had it up and down, 'sputin' en contendin'. Brer Rabbit say he can't walk. Brer Fox say he tote 'im. Brer Rabbit say how? Brer Fox say in his arms. Brer Rabbit say he drap 'im. Brer Fox 'low he won't. Bimeby Brer Rabbit say he go ef Brer Fox tote 'im on his back. Brer Fox say he would. Brer Rabbit say he can't ride widout a saddle. Brer Fox say he git de saddle. Brer Rabbit say he can't set in saddles less he have bridle fer ter hol' by. Brer Fox say he git de bridle. Brer Rabbit say he can't ride widout blin' bridle,[9] kaze Brer Fox be shyin' at stumps 'long de road, en fling 'im off. Brer Fox say he git blin' bridle. Den Brer Rabbit say he go. Den Brer Fox say he ride Brer Rabbit mos' up ter Miss Meadows's, en den he could git down en walk de balance er de way. Brer Rabbit 'greed, en den Brer Fox lipt out atter de saddle en de bridle.

"Co'se Brer Rabbit know de game dat Brer Fox wuz fixin' fer ter play, en he 'termin' fer ter outdo 'im, en by de time he koam his ha'r en twis' his mustarsh, en sorter rig up, yer come Brer Fox, saddle en bridle on, en lookin' ez peart ez a circus pony. He trot up ter de do' en stan' dar pawin' de ground en chompin' de bit same like sho' nuff hoss, en Brer Rabbit he mount, he did, en dey amble off. Brer Fox can't see behime wid de blin' bridle on, but bimeby he feel Brer Rabbit raise one er his foots.

"'W'at you doin' now, Brer Rabbit?' sezee.

6 *tushes:* teeth

7 *'sputin':* disputing

8 *Dat bait er pusly:* That bite of parsley

9 *widout blin' bridle:* without a bridle with blinders

"'Short'nin' de lef stir'p, Brer Fox,' sezee.

"Bimeby Brer Rabbit raise up de udder foot.

"'W'at you doin' now, Brer Rabbit?' sezee.

"'Pullin' down my pants, Brer Fox,' sezee.

"All de time, bless grashus, honey, Brer Rabbit wer' puttin' on his spurrers, en w'en dey got close to Miss Meadows's, whar Brer Rabbit wuz to git off, en Brer Fox made a motion fer ter stan' still, Brer Rabbit slap de spurrers inter Brer Fox flanks, en you better b'lieve he got over groun'. W'en dey got ter de house, Miss Meadows en all de gals wuz settin' on de peazzer,[10] en stidder stoppin'[11] at de gate, Brer Rabbit rid on by, he did, en den come gallopin' down de road en up ter de hoss-rack, w'ich he hitch Brer Fox at, en den he sa'nter inter de house, he did, en shake han's wid de gals, en set dar, smokin' his seegyar same ez a town man. Bimeby he draw in a long puff, en den let hit out in a cloud, en squar hisse'f back en holler out, he did:

10 *peazzer:* porch

11 *en stidder stoppin':* instead of stopping

"'Ladies, ain't I done tell you Brer Fox wuz de ridin'-hoss fer our fambly? He sorter losin' his gait now, but I speck I kin fetch 'im all right in a mont' er so,' sezee.

A. B. Frost.

"En den Brer Rabbit sorter grin, he did, en de gals giggle, en Miss Meadows, she praise up de pony, en dar wuz Brer Fox hitch fas' ter de rack, en couldn't he'p hisse'f."

"Is that all, Uncle Remus?" asked the little boy as the old man paused.

"Dat ain't all, honey, but 'twon't do fer ter give out too much cloff fer ter cut one pa'r pants," replied the old man sententiously.

Brer Rabbit is a survivor, and he quickly recovers from the tar-baby trap set by Brer Fox and quietly plots his revenge on his enemy. Uncle Remus's introductory melody suggests that solitary activities ("sitting in the corner") have some kind of active component ("What you doing there?"), and in fact Brer Rabbit's retreat from social activities signals the beginning of a new plot. In this case, he does more than turn the tables, for he makes a public spectacle of Brer Fox's subjugation, humiliating him before an audience of women (Miss Meadows and the gals). The "grossly deceives" of the title reveals just how complete Brer Rabbit's revenge is. The little boy's closing question "Is that all, Uncle Remus?" and Uncle Remus's reply about the importance of economy are reminders that the narrative style remains compact, leaving plenty of narrative gaps to provoke conversation about the story.

RABBIT MAKES WOLF HIS HORSE

(South Sea Islands)

Dey gave a ball, a party like, an' inwite all de animals—Wolf an' Rabbit an' ev'y bit. An' Wolf was payin' 'dress dis young girl, an' Rabbit was payin' 'dress to um. An' all was goin' to de party. An' Rabbit was tellin' de girl dat Wolf couldn' go to de party, 'cause he was his saddle-horse. So Wolf wen' to Brer Rabbit, an' say, "How you tell dem girls I you' saddle-horse? I like fo' you to prove it."—"I sick."—"I'll kyarry you half way."— "Man, I kyan' go 'less you le' me put de saddle on you."—"Put him on."—"I'll hide him in de bush." Gets de spur. Go t'rough a little swamp. Rabbit lick his spur in Ber Wolf side. Lick him in de head. Sunday, too, all dem girls out. Rabbit ride up to de house.

Say, "Whoa! Didn' I tell yer, girl, dis my fader ridin'-horse? Boy, take dat saddle off an' feed him for me."

SOURCE: Elsie Clews Parsons, *Folk-Lore of the Sea Islands, South Carolina*, 53–54.

The folklorist Elsie Clews Parsons recorded this short, snappy version of what Joel Chandler Harris called "Mr. Rabbit Grossly Deceives Mr. Fox." She gives us the story, which exists in many different versions, in Gullah dialect.

BROTHER RABBIT'S LOVE-CHARM

The Ashanti tale in which Anansi wants all stories known by his name or seeks a monopoly on wisdom can be found in many variant forms in the New World, and some have been included in the first section of this volume. In most versions, the trickster figure wants wisdom or power, but in some cases he is looking for a wife, a child, two extra legs, or a long tail. To earn his prize, he must obtain one or more objects or is required to measure something, often a snake (a boa, python, or rattlesnake, depending on the region). In some instances, he must capture a wild animal—lions, hyenas, alligators, or jackals. And in others he must fill a gourd with birds or insects. And, finally, occasionally he must come up with the milk of a deer, buffalo, cow, or the tears of a lion or elephant. William Bascom provides summaries of more than eighty variants of what he calls "Trickster Seeks Endowments" in African Folktales in the New World. He discredits the theory that the tale originated with Native Americans and documents its origins in African storytelling cultures.

African Jack's insistence on telling the tale—he interrupts Uncle Remus—points to Harris's awareness of the African origins of the tale. The African herbalist and root doctor is a source of power in Senegambian traditions, as Keith Cartwright points out, and he is more likely to reward Rabbit than God or the Sky God, who often dismisses Rabbit or punishes him. In "Buh Rabbit and the Conjur Man," Rabbit traps yellow jackets in a calabash and fetches a live rattlesnake. The Conjure Man tells him: "Buh Rabbit, you is suttenly de smartest ob all de animal, an you sense shill git mo and mo ebry day. Mo na dat, me gwine pit white spot on you forrud, so ebrybody kind see you had de best sense een you head" (113).

"Dey wuz one time," said Uncle Remus one night, as they all sat around the wide hearth—Daddy Jack, Aunt Tempy, and the little boy in their accustomed places—"dey wuz one time w'en de t'er[1] creeturs push Brer Rabbit so close dat he tuck up a kinder idee dat may be he wa'n't ez smart ez he mought be, en he study 'bout dis plum' twel he git humble[2] ez de nex' man. 'Las' he 'low ter hisse'f[3] dat he better make inquirements—."

"Ki!" exclaimed Daddy Jack, raising both hands and grinning excitedly, "wut tale dis? I bin yerry de tale[4] wun I is bin wean't[5] fum me mammy."

"Well, den, Brer Jack," said Uncle Remus, with instinctive deference to the rules of hospitality. "I 'speck you des better whirl in yer en spin 'er out. Ef you git 'er mix up anywhars I ull des slip in front er you en ketch holt whar you lef' off."

With that, Daddy Jack proceeded:

"One tam, B'er Rabbit is bin lub one noung leddy."

"Miss Meadows, I 'speck," suggested Uncle Remus, as the old African paused to rub his chin.

"'E no lub Miss Meadows nuttin' 't all!" exclaimed Daddy Jack, emphatically. "'E bin lub turrer noung leddy fum dat. 'E is bin lub werry nice young leddy. 'E lub 'um hard, 'e lub 'um long, un 'e is gwan try fer mek dem noung leddy marry wit' 'im. Noung leddy seem lak 'e no look 'pon B'er Rabbit, un dis is bin-a mek B'er Rabbit feel werry bad all da day long. 'E moof 'way off by 'ese'f; 'e lose 'e fat, un 'e heer is bin-a come out.[6] Bumbye,[7] 'e see one ole Affiky mans wut is bin-a hunt in da fiel' fer root en yerrub fer mek 'e met'cine truck. 'E see um, un he go toze um, Affiky mans open 'e y-eye big; 'e 'stonish'. 'E say:

"'Ki, B'er Rabbit! You' he'lt'[8] is bin-a-gone; 'e bin-a gone un lef' you. Wut mekky you is look so puny lak dis? Who is bin hu't-a you' feelin'?'"

1 *t'er:* other

2 *he study 'bout dis plum' twel he git humble:* he thought about this so hard that he grew humble

3 *'Las' he 'low ter hisse'f:* Finally, he admitted to himself

4 *I bin yerry de tale:* I heard that tale

5 *wean't:* weaned

6 *'e heer is bin-a come out:* his hair is falling out

7 *Bumbye:* by and by

8 *he'lt':* health

"B'er Rabbit lahf wit' dry grins. 'E say:

"'Shoo! I bin got well. Ef you is see me wun I sick fer true, 'twill mekky you heer[9] stan' up, I skeer you so.'

"Affiky mans, 'e mek B'er Rabbit stick out 'e tongue; 'e is count B'er Rabbit pulse. 'E shekky 'e head; 'e do say:

"'Hi, B'er Rabbit! Wut all dis? You is bin ketch-a da gal-fever, un 'e strak in 'pon you' gizzud.'

"Den B'er Rabbit, 'e is tell-a da Affiky mans 'bout dem noung leddy wut no look toze 'im, un da Affiky mans, 'e do say 'e bin know gal sem[10] lak dat, 'e is bin shum[11] befo'. 'E say 'e kin fix all dem noung leddy lak dat. B'er Rabbit, 'e is feel so good, 'e jump up high; 'e is bin crack 'e heel; 'e shekky da Affiky mans by de han'.

"Affiky mans, 'e say B'er Rabbit no kin git da gal 'cep' 'e is mek 'im one cha'm-bag. 'E say 'e mus' git one el'phan' tush,[12] un 'e mus' git one 'gater toof, un 'e mus' git one rice-bud bill.[13] B'er Rabbit werry glad 'bout dis, un 'e hop way fum dey-dey.[14]

"'E hop, 'e run, 'e jump all nex' day night, un bumbye 'e see one great big el'phan' come breakin' 'e way troo da woots. B'er Rabbit, 'e say:

"'Ki! Oona[15] big fer true! I bin-a yeddy talk[16] 'bout dis in me y-own countree. Oona big fer true; too big fer be strong.'

"El'phan' say: 'See dis!'

"'E tek pine tree in 'e snout; 'e pull um by da roots; 'e toss um way off. B'er Rabbit say:

"'Hi! dem tree come 'cause you bin high; 'e no come 'cause you bin strong.'

"El'phan' say: 'See dis!'

"'E rush troo da woots; 'e fair teer um down. B'er Rabbit say:

"'Hoo! dem is bin-a saplin wey you 'stroy. See da big pine? Oona no kin 'stroy dem.'

"El'phan' say: 'See dis!'

"'E run 'pon da big pine; da big pine is bin too tough. El'phan' tush stick in deer fer true; da big pine hol' um fas'. B'er Rabbit git-a dem tush; 'e fetch um wey da Affiky mans lif. Affiky mans say el'phan' is bin too big fer be sma't. 'E say 'e mus' haf one 'gater toof fer go wit el'phan' tush.

9 *heer:* hair

10 *sem:* some

11 *shum:* seen

12 *tush:* tusk

13 *rice-bud bill:* rice-bird's bill, or bobolink's bill

14 *dey-dey:* down there

15 *Oona:* you

16 *yeddy talk:* heard

"B'er Rabbit, 'e do crack 'e heel; 'e do far fly fum dey-dey.[17] 'E go long, 'e go 'long. Bumbye 'e come 'pon 'gater. Da sun shiun hot; da 'gater do 'joy 'ese'f. B'er Rabbit say:

"'Dis road, 'e werry bad; less we mek good one by da crickside.'

"'Gater lak dat. 'E wek 'ese'f up fum 'e head to 'e tail. Dey sta't fer clean da road. 'Gater, 'e do teer da bush wit' 'e toof; 'e sweep-a da trash way wit' 'e tail. B'er Rabbit, 'e do beat-a da bush down wit' 'e cane. 'E hit lef', 'e hit right; 'e hit up, 'e hit down; 'e hit all 'roun'. 'E hit un 'e hit, tell bumbye 'e hit 'gater in 'e mout' un knock-a da toof out. 'E grab um up; 'e gone fum dey-dey. 'E fetch-a da 'gater toof wey[18] da Affiky mans lif.[19] Affiky mans say:

"'Gater is bin-a got sha'p toof fer true. Go fetch-a me one rice-bud bill.'

"B'er Rabbit gone! 'E go 'long, 'e go 'long, tell 'e see rice-bud swingin' on bush. 'E ahx um kin 'e fly.

"Rice-bud say: 'See dis!'

"'E wissle, 'e 'sing, 'e shek 'e wing; 'e fly all 'roun' un 'roun'.

"B'er Rabbit say rice-bud kin fly wey da win' is bin blow, but 'e no kin fly wey no win blow.

"Rice-bud say, 'Enty!'[20]

"'E wait fer win' stop blowin'; 'e wait, un 'e fly all 'roun' un 'roun'.

"B'er Rabbit say rice-bud yent[21] kin fly in house wey dey no win'.

"Rice-bud say, 'Enty!'

"'E fly in house, 'e fly all 'roun' un 'roun'. B'er Rabbit pull de do' shed; 'e look at dem rice-bud; 'e say, 'Enty!'

"'E ketch dem rice-bud; 'e do git um bill, 'e fetch um wey da Affiky mans lif. Affiky mans says dem rice-bud bill slick fer true. 'E tekky da el'phan' tush, 'e tekky da 'gater toof, 'e tekky da rice-bud bill, he pit um in lil bag; 'e swing dem bag 'pon B'er Rabbit neck. Den B'er Rabbit kin marry dem noung gal. Enty!"

Here Daddy Jack paused and flung a glance of feeble tenderness upon 'Tildy. Uncle Remus smiled contemptuously, seeing which 'Tildy straightened herself, tossed her head, and closed her eyes with an air of indescribable scorn.

"I dunner w'at Brer Rabbit moughter done," she exclaimed; "but I lay ef dey's any

17 *fum dey-dey:* from there

18 *wey:* where

19 *lif:* live

20 *Enty!:* can't he! (an expression of astonishment)

21 *yent:* ain't

ole nigger man totin' a cunjer-bag in dis neighborhood, he'll git mighty tired un it 'fo' it do 'im any good—I lay dat!"

Daddy Jack chuckled heartily at this, and dropped off to sleep so suddenly that the little boy thought he was playing possum.

BROTHER RABBIT'S LAUGHING-PLACE

This new little boy was intensely practical. He had imagination, but it was unaccompanied by any of the ancient illusions that make the memory of childhood so delightful. Young as he was he had a contempt for those who believed in Santa Claus. He believed only in things that his mother considered valid and vital, and his training had been of such a character as to leave out all the beautiful romances of childhood.

Thus when Uncle Remus mentioned something about Brother Rabbit's laughing-place, he pictured it forth in his mind as a sure-enough place that the four-footed creatures had found necessary for their comfort and convenience. This way of looking at things was, in some measure, a great help; it cut off long explanations, and stopped many an embarrassing question.

On one occasion when the two were together, the little boy referred to Brother Rabbit's laughing-place and talked about it in much the same way that he would have talked about Atlanta. If Uncle Remus was unprepared for such literalness he displayed no astonishment, and for all the child knew, he had talked the matter over with hundreds of other little boys.

1 *spang:* directly, squarely

"Uncle Remus," said the lad, "when was the last time you went to Brother Rabbit's laughing-place?"

"To tell you de trufe, honey, I dunno ez I ever been dar," the old man responded.

"Now, I think that is very queer," remarked the little boy.

Uncle Remus reflected a moment before committing himself. "I dunno ez I yever went right spang[1] ter de place an' put my han' on it. I speck I could a gone dar wid mighty little trouble, but I wuz so use ter hearin' 'bout it dat de idee er gwine dar ain't never got in my head. It's sorter like ol' Mr. Grissom's house. Dey say he lives in a quare little shanty not fur fum de mill. I know right whar de shanty is, yit I ain't never been dar, an' I ain't never seed it.

"It's de same way wid Brer Rabbit's laughin'-place. Dem what tol' me 'bout it had likely been dar, but I ain't never had no 'casion fer ter go dar myse'f. Yit if I could walk fifteen er sixty mile a day, like I use ter, I boun' you I could go right now an' put my han' on de place. Dey wuz one time—but dat's a tale, an', goodness knows, you done hear nuff tales er one kin' an' anudder fer to make a hoss sick—dey ain't no two ways 'bout dat."

Uncle Remus paused and sighed, and then closed his eyes with a groan, as though he were sadly exercised in spirit; but his eyes were not shut so tight that he could not observe the face of the child. It was a preternaturally grave little face that the old man saw and whether this was the result of the youngster's environment, or his training, or his temperament, it would have been difficult to say. But there it was, the gravity that was only infrequently disturbed by laughter. Uncle Remus perhaps had seen more laughter in that little face than any one else. Occasionally the things that the child laughed at were those that would have convulsed other children, but more frequently, as it seemed, his smiles were the result of his own reflections and mental comparisons.

"I tell you what, honey," said Uncle Remus, opening wide his eyes, "dat's de ve'y thing you oughter have."

"What is it?" the child inquired, though apparently he had no interest in the matter.

"What you want is a laughin'-place, whar you kin go an' tickle yo'se'f an' laugh whedder you wanter laugh er no. I boun' ef you had a laughin'-place, you'd gain flesh, an' when yo' pa comes down fum 'Lantamatantarum,[2] he wouldn't skacely know you."

"But I don't want father not to know me," the child answered. "If he didn't know me, I should feel as if I were some one else."

[2] 'Lantamatantarum: A fanciful name for Atlanta.

"Oh, he'd know you bimeby," said Uncle Remus, "an' he'd be all de gladder fer ter see you lookin' like somebody."

"Do I look like nobody?" asked the little boy.

"When you fust come down here," Uncle Remus answered, "you look like nothin' 'tall, but since you been ramblin' 'roun' wid me, you done 'gun ter look like somebody—mos' like um."

"I reckon that's because I have a laughing-place," said the child. "You didn't know I had one, did you? I have one, but you are the first person in the world that I have told about it."

"Well, suh!" Uncle Remus exclaimed with his well-feigned astonishment; "an' you been settin' here lis'nin' at me, an' all de time you got a laughin'-place er yo' own! I never would a b'lieved it uv you. Wharabouts is dish yer place?"

"It is right here where you are," said the little boy with a winning smile.

"Honey, you don't tell me!" exclaimed the old man, looking all around. "Ef you kin see it, you see mo' dan I does—dey ain't no two ways 'bout dat."

"Why, you are my laughing-place," cried the little lad with an extraordinary burst of enthusiasm.

"Well, I thank my stars!" said Uncle Remus with emotion. "You sho does need ter laugh lots mo' dan what you does. But what make you laugh at me, honey? Is my britches too big, er is I too big fer my britches? You neen'ter laugh at dis coat, kaze it's one dat yo' granddaddy use ter have. It's mighty nigh new, kaze I ain't wo'd it mo' dan 'lev'm year. It may look shiny in places, but when you see a coat look shiny, it's a sign dat it's des ez good ez new. You can't laugh at my shoes, kaze I made um myse'f, an' ef dey lack shape dat's kaze I made um fer ter fit my rheumatism[3] an' my foots bofe."

"Why, I never laughed at you!" exclaimed the child, blushing at the very idea. "I laugh at what you say, and at the stories you tell."

"La, honey! You sho dunno nothin'; you oughter hearn me tell tales when I could tell um. I boun' you'd a busted de buttons off'n yo' whatchermacollums. Yo' pa use ter set right whar you er settin' an' laugh twel he can't laugh no mo'. But dem wuz laughin' times, an' it look like dey ain't never comin' back. Dat 'uz 'fo' eve'ybody wuz rushin' 'roun' trying fer ter git money[4] what don't b'long ter um by good rights."

"I was thinking to myself," remarked the child, "that if Brother Rabbit had a laughing-place I had a better one."

"Honey, hush!" exclaimed Uncle Remus with a laugh. "You'll have me gwine 'roun' here wid my head in de a'r, an' feelin' so biggity dat I won't look at my own se'f in de lookin'-glass. I ain't too ol' fer dat kinder talk ter spile me."

"Didn't you say there was a tale about Brother Rabbit's laughing-place?" inquired the little boy, when Uncle Remus ceased to admire himself.

"I dunner whedder you kin call it a tale," replied the old man. "It's mighty funny 'bout tales," he went on. "Tell um ez you may an' whence you may, some'll say 'tain't no tale, an' den ag'in som'll say dat it's a fine tale. Dey ain't no tellin'. Dat de reason I don't like ter tell no tale ter grown folks, speshually ef dey er white folks. Dey'll take it an' put it by de side er some yuther tale what dey got in der min' an' dey'll take on dat slonchidickler[5] grin what allers say, 'Go way, nigger man! You dunner what a tale is!' An' I don't—I'll say dat much fer ter keep some un else fum sayin' it.

"Now, 'bout dat laughin' place—it seems like dat one time de creeturs got ter 'sputin' 'mongs' deyselves ez ter which un kin laugh de loudest. One word fotch on an'er twel[6] it look like dey wuz gwine ter be a free fight, a rumpus an' a riot. Dey show'd der claws an' tushes,[7] an' shuck der horns, an' rattle der hoof. Dey had der bristles up, an' it look like der eyes wuz runnin' blood, dey got so red.

"Des 'bout de time when it looks like you can't keep um 'part, little Miss Squinch Owl flew'd up a tree an' 'low, 'You all dunner what laughin' is—ha-ha-ha-ha! You can't laugh when you try ter laugh—ha-ha-ha-haha!' De creeturs wuz 'stonisht. Here wuz a little fowl not much bigger dan a jay-bird laughin' herse'f blin' when dey wa'n't a thing in de roun' worl' fer ter laugh at. Dey stop der quollin' atter dat an' look at one an'er. Brer Bull say, 'Is anybody ever hear de beat er dat? Who mought de lady be?' Dey all say dey dunno, an' dey got a mighty good reason fer der sesso,[8] kaze Miss Squinch Owl, she flies at night wid de bats an' de Betsy Bugs.

"Well, dey quit der quollin', de creeturs did, but dey still had der 'spute; de comin' er Miss Squinch Owl ain't settle dat. So dey 'gree dat dey'd meet som'ers when de wedder got better, an' try der han' at laughin' fer ter see which un kin outdo de yuther." Observing that the little boy was laughing very heartily, Uncle Remus paused long enough to inquire what had hit him on his funny-bone.

"I was laughing because you said the animals were going to meet an' try their hand at laughing,"[9] replied the lad when he could get breath enough to talk.

Uncle Remus regarded the child with a benevolent smile of admiration. "You er long ways ahead er me—you sho is. Dey ain't na'er an'er chap in the worl' what'd a cotch on so quick. You put me in min' er de peerch, what grab de bait 'fo' it hit the water. Well, dat's what de creeturs done. Dey say dey wuz gwine ter make trial fer ter see which un is de out-laughin'est er de whole caboodle, an' dey name de day, an' all prommus fer ter be dar, ceppin' Brer Rabbit, an' he 'low dat he kin laugh well nuff fer ter suit hise'f an' his fambly, 'sides dat, he don't keer 'bout laughin' less'n dey's sump'n'

5 *slonchidickler:* oblique, ironic

6 *fotch on an'er twel:* fetched or led to another twelve

7 *Tushes:* teeth

8 *sesso:* say so

9 *try their hand at laughing:* The little boy tries to show his wisdom by laughing at the notion that animals can laugh but he quickly learns to suspend disbelief.

fer ter laugh at. De yuther creeturs dey beg'm fer ter come, but he shake his head an' wiggle his mustash, an' say dat when he wanter laugh, he got a laughin'-place fer ter go ter, whar he won't be pestered by de balance er creation. He say he kin go dar an' laugh his fill, an' den go on 'bout his business, ef he got any business, and ef he ain't got none, he kin go ter play.

"De yuther creeturs ain't know what ter make er all dis, an' dey wonder an' wonder how Brer Rabbit kin have a laughin'-place an' dey ain't got none. When dey ax 'im 'bout it, he 'spon', he did, dat he speck 'twuz des de diffunce 'twix' one creetur an' an'er. He ax um fer ter look at folks, how diffunt dey wuz, let 'lone de creeturs. One man'd be rich an' an'er man po', an' he ax how come dat.

"Well, suh, dey des natchally can't tell 'im what make de diffunce 'twix' folks no mo' dan dey kin tell 'im de diffunce 'twix' de creeturs. Dey wuz stumped; dey done fergit all 'bout de trial what wuz ter come off, but Brer Rabbit fotch um back ter it. He say dey ain't no needs fer ter see which kin outdo all de balance un um in de laughin' business, kaze anybody what got any sense know dat de monkey is a natchal laugher, same as Brer Coon is a natchal pacer.

"Brer B'ar look at Brer Wolf, an' Brer Wolf look at Brer Fox, an' den dey all look at one an'er. Brer Bull, he say, 'Well, well, well!' an' den he groan; Brer B'ar say, 'Who'd a thunk it?' an' den he growl; an' Brer Wolf say 'Gracious me!' an' den he howl. Atter dat, dey ain't say much, kaze dey ain't much fer ter say. Dey des stan' 'roun' an' look kinder sheepish. Dey ain't 'spute wid Brer Rabbit, dough dey'd a like ter a done it, but dey sot about an' make marks in de san' des like you see folks do where dey er tryin' fer ter git der thinkin' machine ter work.

"Well, suh, dar dey sot an' dar dey stood. Dey ax Brer Rabbit how he know how ter fin' his laughin'-place, an' how he know it wuz a laughin'-place atter he got dar. He tap hisse'f on de head, he did, an' 'low dat dey wuz a heap mo' und' his hat dan what you could git out wid a fine-toof comb. Den dey ax ef dey kin see his laughin'-place, an' he say he'd take de idee ter bed wid 'im, an' study 'pon it, but he kin say dis much right den, dat if he did let um see it, dey'd hatter go dar one at a time, an' dey'd hatter do des like he say: ef dey don't dey'll git de notion dat it's a cryin'-place.

"Dey 'gree ter dis, de creeturs did, an' Brer Rabbit say dat while dey er all der tergedder, dey better choosen 'mongs' dyse'f which un uv um wuz gwine fus', an' he'd choosen de res' when de time come. Dey jower'd an' jower'd, an' bimeby, dey hatter leave it all ter Brer Rabbit. Brer Rabbit, he put his han' ter his head, an' shot his eye-balls an' do like he studyin'. He say 'De mo' I think 'bout who shill be de fus' one, de mo' I git de idee dat it oughter be Brer Fox. He been here long ez anybody, an' he's purty well thunk uv by de neighbors—I ain't never hear nobody breave a breff ag'in 'im.'

"Dey all say dat dey had Brer Fox in min' all de time, but somehow dey can't come right out with his name, an' dey vow dat ef dey had 'greed on somebody, dat somebody would sho a been Brer Fox. Den, atter dat, 'twuz all plain sailin'. Brer Rabbit say he'd meet Brer Fox at sech an' sech a place, at sech an' sech a time, an' atter dat dey wan'n't no mo' ter be said. De creeturs all went ter de place what dey live at, an' done des like dey allers done.

A. B. Frost.

"Brer Rabbit make a soon start fer ter go ter de p'int whar he promus ter meet Brer Fox, but soon ez he wuz, Brer Fox wuz dar befo' 'im. It seem like he wuz so much in de habits er bein' outdone by Brer Rabbit dat he can't do widout it. Brer Rabbit bow, he did, an' pass de time er day wid Brer Fox, an' ax 'im how his fambly wuz. Brer Fox say dey wuz peart ez kin be, an' den he 'low dat he ready an' a-waitin' fer ter go an' see dat great laughin'-place what Brer Rabbit been talkin' 'bout.

"Brer Rabbit say dat suit him ter a gnat's heel, an' off dey put. Bimeby dey come ter one er deze here cle'r places dat you sometimes see in de middle uv a pine thicket. You may ax yo'se'f how come dey don't no trees grow dar when dey's trees all round, but you ain't gwine ter git no answer, an' needer is dey anybody what kin tell you. Dey got dar, dey did, an' den Brer Rabbit make a halt. Brer Fox 'low, 'Is dis de place? I don't feel no mo' like laughin' now dan I did 'fo' I come.'

"Brer Rabbit, he say, 'Des keep yo' jacket on, Brer Fox; ef you git in too big a hurry

A. B. Frost.

10 *a-projickin':* fooling

it might come off. We done come mighty nigh ter de place, an' ef you wanter do some ol' time laughin', you'll hatter do des like I tell you; ef you don't wanter laugh, I'll des show you de place, an' we'll go on back whar we come fum, kaze dis is one er de days dat I ain't got much time ter was'e laughin' er cryin'.' Brer Fox 'low dat he ain't so mighty greedy ter laugh, an' wid dat, Brer Rabbit whirl 'roun', he did, an' make out he gwine on back whar he live at. Brer Fox holler at 'im; he say, 'Come on back, Brer Rabbit; I'm des a-projickin'[10] wid you.'

"'Ef you wanter projick, Brer Fox, you'll hatter go home an' projick wid dem what wanter be projicked wid. I ain't here kaze I wanter be here. You ax me fer ter show you my laughin'-place, an' I 'greed. I speck we better be gwine on back.' Brer Fox say he come fer ter see Brer Rabbit's laughin'-place, an' he ain't gwine ter be satchify twel he see it. Brer Rabbit 'low dat ef dat de case, den he mus' ac' de gentermun all de way thoo, an' quit his behavishness. Brer Fox say he'll do de best he kin, an' den Brer Rabbit show 'im a place whar de bamboo briars, an'

A. B. Frost.

de blackberry bushes, an' de honeysuckles done start ter come in de pine thicket, an' can't come no furder.

"Twa'n't no thick place; 'twuz des what de swamp at de foot er de hill peter'd out in tryin' ter come ter dry lan'. De bushes an' vines wuz thin an' scanty, an' ef dey could a talked dey'd a hollered loud fer water.

"Brer Rabbit show Brer Fox de place, an' den tell 'im dat de game is fer ter run full tilt thoo de vines an' bushes, an' den run back, an' thoo um ag'in an' back, an' he say he'd bet a plug er terbacker 'g'in a ginger cake dat by de time Brer Fox done dis he'd be dat tickled dat he can't stan' up fer laughin'. Brer Fox shuck his head; he ain't nigh b'lieve it, but fer all dat, he make up his min' fer to do what Brer Rabbit say, spite er de fac' dat his ol' 'oman done tell 'im 'fo' he lef' home dat he better keep his eye open, kaze Brer Rabbit gwine ter run a rig on 'im.

"He tuck a runnin' start, he did, an' he went thoo de bushes an' de vines like he wuz runnin' a race. He run an' he come back a-runnin', an' he run back, an' dat time he struck sump'n' wid his head. He try ter dodge it, but he seed it too late, an' he wuz gwine too fas'. He struck it, he did, an' time he do dat, he fetched a howl dat you might a hearn a mile, an' atter dat, he holler'd yap, yap, yap, an' ouch, ouch, ouch

A. B. Frost.

an' yow, yow, yow, an' whiles dis wuz gwine on Brer Rabbit wuz thumpin' de ground wid his behime foot, an' laughin' fit ter kill. Brer Fox run 'roun' an' 'roun', an' kep' on snappin' at hisse'f an' doin' like he wuz tryin' fer ter t'ar his hide off. He run, an' he roll, an' wallow, an' holler, an' fall, an' squall twel it look like he wuz havin' forty-lev'm duck fits.

"He got still atter while, but de mo' stiller he got, de wuss he looked. His head wuz all swell up, an' he look like he been run over in de road by a fo'-mule waggin.[11] Brer Rabbit 'low, 'I'm glad you had sech a good time, Brer Fox; I'll hatter fetch you out ag'in. You sho done like you was havin' fun.' Brer Fox ain't say a word; he wuz too mad fer ter talk. He des sot aroun' and lick hisse'f an' try ter git his ha'r straight. Brer Rabbit 'low, 'You ripped aroun' in dar twel I wuz skeer'd you wuz gwine ter hurt yo'se'f, an' I b'lieve in my soul you done gone an' bump yo' head ag'in' a tree, kaze it's all swell up. You better go home, Brer Fox, an' let yo' ol' 'oman poultice you up.'

11 *fo'-mule waggin:* four-mule wagon

"Brer Fox show his tushes, an' say, 'You said dis wuz a laughin'-place.' Brer Rabbit 'low, 'I said 'twuz my laughin'-place, an' I'll say it ag'in. What you reckon I been doin' all dis time? Ain't you hear me laughin'? An' what you been doin'? I hear you makin' a mighty fuss in dar, an' I say ter myse'f dat Brer Fox is havin' a mighty big time.'

"'I let you know dat I ain't been laughin',' sez Brer Fox, sezee."

Uncle Remus paused, and waited to be questioned. "What was the matter with the Fox, if he wasn't laughing?" the child asked after a thoughtful moment.

Uncle Remus flung his head back, and cried out in a sing-song tone,

"He run ter de Eas', an' he run ter de Wes'
An' jammed his head in a hornets' nes'!"

Once again, perspective is everything in African American folklore. In this case Brer Rabbit's laughing-place becomes a site of torture for Brer Fox. Cruelty triumphs in this tale, and it can hardly be said to send a message appropriate for children. But it does serve to put a smile on the "grave little face" of the boy to whom Uncle Remus tells the story.

BROTHER RABBIT DOESN'T GO TO SEE AUNT NANCY

1 *to patch an old waistcoat:* Uncle Remus's needle and thread connect him to Aunt Nancy, who spins and weaves, with one telling yarns and the other inspiring a story that is told to Brer Rabbit, and in turn to the young boy. That Uncle Remus has to patch despite his advanced age—he has trouble threading a needle—is another sign of the social divide between old man and young boy.

Uncle Remus, one day, was doing his best to patch an old waistcoat.[1] The little boy was interested in this work mainly because it became necessary once and again for the old man to thread the large needle with which he was doing his work. Sometimes he tried to place the thread in the sharp end, where there was no eye, and even when he held it correctly, it required several attempts before he succeeded. He watched the little boy closely at each effort, expecting him to laugh at his failures, but the youngster was as solemn as could be desired.

"I wuz des a-wonderin'," Uncle Remus declared in the midst of his mending, "ef you had de strenk fer ter go on a long journey." "On the wagon, or in the train?" inquired the little boy. Uncle Remus chuckled, "No, honey; ef we go we'll hatter set right whar we is an' let time take us. You know how de birds does—de peckerwoods, an' de swallers, an' de bee-martins; dey'll ketch bugs roun' here de whole blessed summer, an' den, 'fo' fros' comes, dey'll h'ist up an' fly off some'rs, I dunner whar. Dey has der seasons an' der reason fer comin' an' gwine.[2] Well, des ez de birds does now, des dat-a-way de creeturs done twel Brer Rabbit tuck an' broke it up. It seem like dat when de time come, dey 'gun ter feel ticklish; dey had dat creepy feelin' runnin' up an' down der backbones like folks does when a possum runs cross der grave."[3]

Uncle Remus looked hard at the little boy[4] to observe what effect his last statement would have, but beyond moving uneasily in his seat, the lad gave no sign of mental disturbance.

"It seem like," Uncle Remus went on, "dat all de creeturs, big an' little, long-tail, bob-tail, an' no-tail, hatter go once a year fer ter make der peace wid ol' Aunt Nancy."

"But who was Aunt Nancy?" the child asked.

"It seem like," the old man responded, "dat she was de granny er Mammy-Bammy-Big-Money[5]—dat's de way dey han' it out ter me. Her rule went furder dan whar she live at, an' when she went ter call de creeturs, all she hatter do wuz ter fling her head back an' kinder suck in her bref an' all de creeturs would have a little chill, an' know dat she wuz a-callin' un um. But ol' Brer Rabbit, he got over havin' de chill,[6] an' he say he wa'n't gwine trapesin' way off ter de fur country fer ter see no Aunt Nancy. De creeturs all tell 'im dat he better come on an' go, but he say he done been an' seed, an' he wa'n't gwine no mo'. He 'low, 'when you-all git whar you gwine des ax Aunt Nancy fer ter shake han's wid you, an' den you'll see what I done seed.'

"De yuther creeturs shuck der heads, but went on an' lef' Brer Rabbit smokin' his corn-cob pipe an' chawin' his cud. Dey went on, an' bimeby dey come ter Aunt Nancy's house. Ef you'd a' seed it, honey, you'd 'a' said it look des like a big

2 *Dey has der seasons an' der reason fer comin' an' gwine:* Shanna Greene Benjamin points out that Remus uses folklore "to teach the young boy about the seasonal movement of animals," and he creates a text "with textile qualities that enmeshes the young boy and readers alike in an enticing story line" (45–46). He also appears to be offering the boy a tutorial on the great existential mysteries, as part of the avowed "initiation" process.

3 *when a possum runs cross der grave:* "Someone is walking over my grave" is an odd phrase for a living person to use, but it is the equivalent of the Southern expression about a possum running across your (future) grave and giving you the shivers.

4 *looked hard at the little boy:* Uncle Remus seems here to do what many adults do when telling stories to children: monitoring effects to ensure that a story is not too much for a child.

5 *de granny er Mammy-Bammy-Big-Money:* In his introduction to *Nights with Uncle Remus*, Harris writes about how "the Rabbit seeks out Mammy-Bammy Big-Money, the old Witch-Rabbit." "It may be mentioned here," he adds, "that the various branches of the Algonkian [*sic*] family of Indians, allude to the Great White Rabbit as their common ancestor. All inquiries among the negroes, as to the origin and personality of Mammy-Bammy Big-Money, elicit but two replies. Some know, or even pretend to know, nothing about her. The rest say, with entire unanimity, 'Hit's des de old Witch-Rabbit w'at you done year'd talk un 'fo' now.' Mrs. Prioleau, of Memphis, sent the writer a negro story in which the name 'Big-Money' was vaguely used. It was some time before that story could be verified. In conversation one day with a negro, casual allusion was made to 'Big-Money.' 'Aha!' said the negro, 'Now I know. You talkin' 'bout ole Mammy-Bammy Big-Money,' and then he went on to tell, not only the story which Mrs. Prioleau had kindly sent, but the story of Brother Rabbit's visit to the old Witch-Rabbit."

6 *But ol' Brer Rabbit, he got over havin' de chill:* It is, of course, supremely ironic that Brer Rabbit, who is an African American incarnation of Anansi, would be the first to express irreverence for a rival, female incarnation of Anansi.

7 *it look des like a big chunk er fog:* Aunt Nancy's home is shrouded in mystery, and the "fog" conceals the webs that could function as a death trap.

8 *sont:* sent

9 *work her jaws like she chawin' sump'n' good:* Aunt Nancy's chewing recalls Brer Rabbit' "chawin' his cud" at the first convocation of the animals. And the chewing activity is invoked at the end of the tale as well.

10 *half 'oman an' half spider:* Aunt Nancy, who is both human and beast, spins her web in a space that unites earth and sky. Like Anansi, she occupies a liminal space but one that keeps her isolated and away from the social world.

chunk er fog.[7] I speck 'twuz ez bi ez dis house, but it kinder wavied in de win' des like de fog you see on de two-mile branch.

"Ol' Brer B'ar, he hailed de house, an' den ol' Aunt Nancy, she come out wid a big long cloak on her an' sot down on a pine stump. She look roun', she did, an' her eyeballs sparkle red des like dey wuz afire. 'I hope all un you is here,' se' she, 'an' I speck you is, but I'm agwine ter count you an' call de roll.'

"Eve'y count she made, she'd nod her head, an' de creetur dat she nodded at an' had her red eye on, would dodge and duck his head. Well, she count an' count, an' when she git thoo, she say, 'I done counted, an' ef dey ain't one un you missin', I'm might much mistooken.' She helt Brer Fox with her red eye, an' he up an' say, 'I speck 'tain't nobody in de roun' worl' but Brer Rabbit.'

"Aunt Nancy say, se' she, 'I'll Brer him! Is he sont[8] any skuse?'

"An' Brer Wolf, he tuck up de tail, an' say, 'No, ma'am, not ez I knows un.'

"Den ol' Brer B'ar, he say, 'Brer Rabbit sont word fer ter tell you howdy, an' he ax us fer ter tell you ter shake han's wid us, an' 'member him in yo' dreams.'

"Aunt Nancy roll her red eye an' work her jaws like she chawin' sump'n' good.[9] She say, se' she, 'Is dat what he tell you? Well you des tell 'im, dat ef he'll come ter dis place I'll shake han's wid 'im, an' ef he don't come ez hard ez his legs'll fetch 'im, I'll go an' shake han's wid 'im whar he lives at.'

"Ol Brer B'ar, he up an' say, 'How come you don't shake han's wid we-all, when we come so fur fer ter se you?'

"Aunt Nancy roll her red eyes an' work her jaws. She got up fum whar she was settin' at, an' try fer ter pull de cloak close 'roun' her, but it slipped off a little way, an' de creeturs what wuz watchin' un her, seed wid der own eyes that she wuz half 'oman an' half spider.[10] She had sev'm arms an' no han's. When dey see all dis, de creeturs tuck ter de woods, an' got away fum dar des ez hard ez dey kin. An' dat de reason de house look like it 'uz made out'n fog. It 'uz wovened out'n web;[11] 'twuz web fum top ter bottom. De creeturs went back an' tol' Brer Rabbit what dey done seed, an' he jump up an' crack his heels tergedder, an' holler 'Ah-yi!' an' den he went on chawin' his cud like nothin' ain't happen."

11 *It 'uz wovened out'n web:* Aunt Nancy's abode is constructed from the same kinds of threads Uncle Remus uses to patch his coat. It can be connected with weaving and storytelling but it is also, like spiderwebs, a place of dread and death.

This tale remained in the Joel Chandler Harris Memorial Collection of Emory University until 1948, when it was published with six others to celebrate the centennial of Harris's birth. The male archetypes of the Yoruba trickster Esu Elegbara and Anansi the Spider are replaced in this tale by a mysterious female figure who is connected with threads, webs, and spinning and who demands that her subjects pay tribute to her with an annual visit. Unlike Esu Elegbara and Anansi, she inspires more dread than reverence and admiration.

THE ADVENTURES OF SIMON AND SUSANNA

"I got one tale on my min'," said Uncle Remus to the little boy one night. "I got one tale on my min' dat I ain't ne'er tell you; I dunner how come; I speck it des kaze I git mixt up in my idees. Deze is busy times, mon, en de mo' you does de mo' you hatter do, en w'en dat de case, it ain't ter be 'spected dat one ole broke-down nigger kin 'member 'bout eve'ything."

"What is the story, Uncle Remus?" the little boy asked.

"Well, honey," said the old man, wiping his spectacles, "hit sorter run dis away: One time dey wuz a man w'at had a mighty likely daughter."

"Was he a white man or a black man?" the little boy asked.

"I 'clar' ter gracious, honey!" exclaimed the old man, "you er pushin' me mos' too close. Fer all I kin tell you, de man mout er bin ez w'ite ez de driven snow, er he mout er bin de blackes' Affi'kin[1] er de whole kit en b'ilin'. I'm des tellin' you de tale, en you kin take en take de man en w'itewash 'im, er you kin black 'im up des ez you please. Dat's de way I looks at it.

1 *Affi'kin:* African

"Well, one time dey wuz a man, en dish yer man he had a mighty likely daughter. She wuz so purty dat she had mo' beaus[2] den w'at you got fingers en toes. But de gal daddy, he got his spishuns[3] 'bout all un um, en he won't let um come 'roun' de house. But dey kep' on pesterin' 'im so, dat bimeby he give word out dat de man w'at kin clear up six acres er lan' en roll up de logs, en pile up de bresh in one day, dat man kin marry his daughter.

2 *beaus:* suitors

3 *spishuns:* suspicions

4 *sparrer-nes':* sparrow nest

5 *bleege:* obliged

6 *borry de ax:* borrow the ax

"In co'se, dis look like it unpossible, en all de beaus drap off 'ceppin' one, en he wuz a great big strappin' chap w'at look like he kin knock a steer down. Dis chap he wuz name Simon, en de gal, she wuz name Susanna. Simon, he love Susanna, en Susanna, she love Simon, en dar it went.

"Well, sir, Simon, he went ter de gal daddy, he did, en he say dat ef anybody kin clear up dat lan', he de one kin do it, least'ways he say he gwine try mighty hard. De ole man, he grin en rub his han's terge'er, he did, en tole Simon ter start in de mornin'. Susanna, she makes out she wuz fixin' sumpin in de cubberd, but she tuck 'n kiss ter hen' at Simon, en nod 'er head. Dis all Simon want, en he went out er dar des ez happy ez a jay-bird atter he done robbed a sparrer-nes'.[4]

"Now, den," Uncle Remus continued, settling himself more comfortably in his chair, "dish yer man wuz a witch."

"Why, I thought a witch was a woman," said the little boy.

The old man frowned and looked into the fire.

"Well, sir," he remarked with some emphasis, "ef you er gwine ter tu'n de man inter a 'oman, den dey won't be no tale, kaze dey's bleege[5] ter be a man right dar whar I put dis un. Hit's des like I tole you 'bout de color er de man. Black 'im er whitewash 'im des ez you please, en ef you want ter put a frock on 'im ter boot, hit ain't none er my business; but I'm gwine ter 'low he wuz a man ef it's de las' ac'."

The little boy remained silent, and Uncle Remus went on:

"Now, den, dish yer man was a witch. He could cunjer folks, mo' 'speshually dem folks w'at ain't got no rabbit foot. He bin at his cunjerments so long, dat Susanna done learn mos' all his tricks. So de nex' mornin' w'en Simon come by de house fer ter borry de ax,[6] Susanna she run en got it fer 'im. She got it, she did, en den she sprinkles some black san' on it, en say, 'Ax, cut; cut, ax.' Den she rub 'er ha'r 'cross it, en give it ter Simon. He tuck de ax, he did, en den Susanna say:

"'Go down by de branch, git sev'n w'ite pebbles, put um in dis little cloth bag, en whenever you want the ax ter cut, shake um up.'

"Simon, he went off in de woods, en started in ter clearin' up de six acres. Well, sir, dem pebbles en dat ax, dey done de work—dey did dat. Simon could'a' bin done by de time de dinner-horn blowed, but he hung back kaze he ain't want de man fer ter know dat he doin' it by cunjerments.

"When he shuck de pebbles de ax 'ud cut, en de trees 'ud fall, en de lim's 'ud drap off, en de logs 'ud roll up terge'er, en de bresh 'ud pile itself up. Hit went on dis away twel by de time it wuz two hours b' sun, de whole six acres wuz done cleaned up.

"'Bout dat time de man come 'roun', he did, fer ter see how de work gittin' on, en, mon! he wuz 'stonish'. He ain't know w'at ter do er say. He ain't want ter give up his daughter, en yit he ain't know how ter git out'n it. He walk 'roun' en 'roun', en study, en study, en study how he gwine rue de bargain. At las' he walk up ter Simon, he did, en he say:

"'Look like you sort er forehanded[7] wid your work.'

"Simon, he 'low: 'Yasser, w'en I starts in on a job I'm mighty restless twel I gits it done. Some er dis timber is rough en tough, but I bin had wuss[8] jobs den dis in my time.'

"De man say ter hisse'f: 'W'at kind er folks is dis chap?' Den he say out loud: 'Well, sence you er so spry, dey's two mo' acres 'cross de branch dar. Ef you'll clear dem up 'fo' supper you kin come up ter de house en git de gal.'

"Simon sorter scratch his head, kaze he dunner whedder de pebbles gwine ter hol' out, yit he put on a bol' front en he tell de man dat he'll go 'cross dar en clean up de two acres soon ez he res' a little.

"De man he went off home, en soon's he git out er sight, Simon went 'cross de branch en shook de pebbles at de two acres er woods, en t'want no time skacely 'fo' de trees wuz all cut down en pile up.

"De man, he went home, he did, en call up Susanna, en say:

"'Daughter, dat man look like he gwine git you, sho'.'

"Susanna, she hang 'er head, en look like she fretted, en den she say she don't keer nuthin' fer Simon, nohow."

"Why, I thought she wanted to marry him," said the little boy.

"Well, honey, w'en you git growed up, en git whiskers on yo' chin, en den atter de whiskers git gray like mine, you'll fin' out sump'n 'n'er 'bout de wimmin folks. Dey ain't

7 *forehanded:* looking to the future

8 *wuss:* worse

ne'er say 'zackly w'at dey mean, none er um, mo' 'speshually w'en dey er gwine on 'bout gittin' married.

"Now, dar wuz dat gal Susanna what I'm a-tellin' you 'bout. She mighty nigh 'stracted 'bout Simon, en yit she make 'er daddy b'lieve dat she 'spize 'im. I ain't blamin' Susanna," Uncle Remus went on with a judicial air, "kase she know dat 'er daddy wuz a witch en a mighty mean one in de bargain.

"Well, atter Susanna done make 'er daddy b'lieve dat she ain't keerin' nothin' 'tall 'bout Simon, he 'gun ter set his traps en fix his tricks. He up'n tell Susanna dat atter 'er en Simon git married dey mus' go upsta'rs in de front room, en den he tell 'er dat she mus' make Simon go ter bed fus'. Den de man went upsta'rs en tuck'n tuck all de slats out'n de bedstid ceppin' one at de head en one at de foot. Atter dat he tuck'n put some foot-valances 'roun' de bottom er de bed—des like dem w'at you bin see on yo' gran'ma bed. Den he tuck'n sawed out de floor und' de bed, en dar wuz de trap all ready.

"Well, sir, Simon come up ter de house, en de man make like he mighty glad fer ter see 'im, but Susanna, she look like she mighty shy. No matter 'bout dat; atter supper Simon en Susanna got married. Hit ain't in de tale wedder dey sont fer a preacher er wedder dey wuz a squire browsin' 'roun' in de neighborhoods, but dey had cake wid reezins in it, en some er dish yer silly-bug w'at got mo' foam in it den dey is dram,[9] en

dey had a mighty happy time.

9 *dram:* something to drink

"W'en bedtime come, Simon en Susanna went upsta'rs, en w'en dey got in de room, Susanna kotch 'im by de han', en helt up her finger. Den she whisper en tell 'im dat ef dey don't run away fum dar dey bofe gwine ter be kil't. Simon ax 'er how come, en she say dat 'er daddy want ter kill 'im kaze he sech a nice man. Dis make Simon grin; yit he wuz sorter restless 'bout gittin' 'way fum dar. But Susanna, she say wait. She say:

"'Pick up yo' hat en button up yo' coat. Now, den, take dat stick er wood dar en hol' it 'bove yo' head.'

"W'iles he stan'in' dar, Susanna got a hen egg out'n a basket, den she got a meal-bag, en a skillet. She 'low:

"'Now, den, drap de wood on de bed.'

"Simon done des like she say, en time de wood struck de bed de tick en de mattruss went a-tumblin' thoo de floor. Den Susanna tuck Simon by de han' en dey run out de back way ez hard ez dey kin go.

"De man, he woz down dar waitin' fer de bed ter drap. He had a big long knife in he han', en time de bed drapped, he lit on it, he did, en stobbed it scan'lous. He des natchully ripped de tick up, en w'en he look, bless gracious, dey ain't no Simon dar. I lay dat man wuz mad den. He snorted 'roun' dar twel blue smoke come out'n his nose, en his eye look red like varmint eye in de dark. Den he run upsta'rs en dey ain't no Simon dar, en nudder wuz dey any Susanna.

"Gentermens! den he git madder. He rush out, he did, en look 'roun', en 'way off yander he see Simon en Susanna des a-runnin', en a-holdin' one nudder's han'."

"Why, Uncle Remus," said the little boy, "I thought you said it was night?"

Edward Windsor Kemble, famous for illustrating Mark Twain's *The Adventures of Huckleberry Finn*, created the illustrations for "The Adventures of Simon and Susanna" and the other tales in Harris's *Daddy Jake: The Runaway*. Kemble was criticized by the Hampton Camera Club for creating caricatures of African Americans.

"Dat w'at I said, honey, en I'll stan' by it. Yit, how many times dis blessid night is I got ter tell you dat de man wuz a witch? En bein' a witch, co'se he kin see in de dark.

"Well, dish yer witch-man, he look off en he see Simon en Susanna runnin' ez hard ez dey kin. He put out atter um, he did, wid his knife in his han', an' he kep' on a gainin' on um. Bimeby, he got so close dat Susanna say ter Simon:

"'Fling down yo' coat.'

"Time de coat tech de groun', a big thick woods sprung up whar it fell. But de man, he cut his way thoo it wid de knife, en kep' on a-pursuin' atter um.

"Bimeby, he got so close dat Susanna drap de egg on de groun', en time it fell a big fog riz up fum de groun', en a little mo' en de man would a got los'. But atter so long a time fog got blowed away by de win', en de man kep' on a-pursuin' atter um.

"Bimeby, he got so close dat Susanna drap de meal-sack, en a great big pon' er water kivered de groun' whar it fell. De man wuz in sech a big hurry dat he tried ter drink it dry, but he ain't kin do dis, so he sot on de bank en blow'd on de water wid he hot breff, en atter so long a time de water made hits disappearance, en den he kep' on a-pursuin' atter um.

"Simon en Susanna wuz des a-runnin', but run ez dey would, de man kep' a-gainin' on um, en he got so close dat Susanna drapped de skillet. Den a big bank er darkness fell down, en de man ain't know which away ter go. But atter so long a time de darkness lif' up, en de man kep' on a-pursuin' atter um. Mon, he made up fer los' time, en he got so close dat Susanna say ter Simon:

"'Drap a pebble.'

"Time Simon do dis a high hill riz up, but de man clum it en kep' on atter um. Den Susanna say ter Simon:

"'Drap nudder pebble.'

"Time Simon drap de pebble, a high mountain growed up, but de man crawled up it en kep' on atter um. Den Susanna say:

"'Drap de bigges' pebble.'

"No sooner is he drap it den a big rock wall riz up, en hit wuz so high dat de witch-man can't git over. He run up en down, but he can't find no end, en den, atter so long a time, he turn 'roun' en go home.

"On de yuther side er dis high wall, Susanna tuck Simon by de han', en say:

"'Now we kin res'.'

10 *said the old man slyly:* whether the "old man" refers to Susanna's father or Uncle Remus is not entirely clear, and "slyly" adds a clever twist to the ending.

"En I reckon," said the old man slyly,[10] "dat we all better res'."

Radically different from other tales in the collection, this story from Harris's third installment of Uncle Remus tales, Daddy Jake, the Runaway *(1889), is closer to European lore, which is full of impossible challenges as well as stories about magic flight. Harris added a note about the source: "This story was told to one of my little boys three years ago by a Negro named John Holder. I have since found a variant (or perhaps the original) in Theal's* Kaffir Folktales." *Theal's Kaffir folktales are themselves a curious mix of European and Africa lore and thus not a reliable source of unadulterated African tales. Simon and Susanna are, of course, common names in the Southern United States.*

PART VII

FOLKLORE FROM THE *SOUTHERN WORKMAN* AND THE *JOURNAL OF AMERICAN FOLKLORE*

In 1893 Alice Mabel Bacon (1858–1918) went to the Hampton Institute in Virginia to teach and serve as an administrator. The Hampton Institute, now known as Hampton University, is a private, historically black, school founded by leaders of the American Missionary Association. Booker T. Washington was one of its earliest students. The school's mission was to train and educate teachers, and it was located at a site that had once been a refuge for slaves fleeing the Confederacy.

The daughter of a New Haven, Connecticut, white abolitionist minister, Alice Bacon quickly grew into a new role at an institution where her sister was serving as assistant principal. Bacon became the editor of the *Southern Workman*, the journal of the Hampton Institute, and she launched a Folklore and Ethnology Department for the purpose of building bridges between educated blacks and those they had left behind in the rural South. Folklore constituted for her a body of knowledge passed down from generation to generation and included folktales, customs, autobiographical accounts, survivals of African traditions, ceremonies and superstitions, proverbs and sayings, and songs both sacred and secular.

Bacon declared that members of the group would "collect and preserve all traditions and customs peculiar to the Negroes." She recognized that the work could not be done by "white people," but rather by "intelligent and educated colored people who are at work all through the South among the more ignorant of their own race." In 1893,

Winona Lodge   Virginia Hall   Memorial Chapel   Academic Hall.   Huntington Industrial Works

(Water front about half a mile.)

Hampton Normal and Agricultural Institute.

HAMPTON VIRGINIA.

The Hampton Normal and Agricultural Institute buildings, from the December 1893 cover of the *Southern Workman*, the Hampton Institute's monthly journal.

A current events class at the Hampton Normal and Agricultural Institute photographed by Frances Benjamin Johnston in 1899. Commissioned by the Hampton Institute administration, Johnston's photographs of daily activities at the Hampton Institute were exhibited at the 1900 Paris Exposition and widely published in promotional materials. They became iconic representations of the Hampton Institute, cited as visual evidence of its success.

the Hampton Folklore Society, composed mainly of African American members, was founded. It met regularly for six years and published monthly columns in the Folklore and Ethnology section of the *Southern Workman.* By the time Alice Bacon left the Institute in 1899, a rich repertoire had been put together and documented in the columns of the Hampton Institute's monthly publication.

The Hampton folklorists believed that what they were collecting contained "the beginnings of all arts and sciences, and ceremonies and religion." Foundational and fundamental to understanding a culture, folktales had been passed down from one generation to the next as a verbal tradition that was poetic rather than scientific, abounding in "metaphors, figures, similes, imaginative flights, humorous designations, saws and sayings" (*Southern Workman,* 23 [1894]: 191). Still, the students were to engage with folklore "in a spirit of scientific inquiry" and take a critical view of the superstitions, songs, lore, and wisdom that constituted folk traditions of a rural population.

Robert Russa Moton, ca. 1907. Moton, a Hampton Institute administrator later named principal of Tuskegee Institute, was an active member of the Hampton Folklore Society. He represented the Hampton Institute at the 1894 annual meeting of the American Folklore Society.

Alice Mabel Bacon, ca. 1893. Bacon, editor of the *Southern Workman*, set up the Hampton Institute Folklore Society in a December 1893 column urging readers to submit notes and observations about "traditions and customs peculiar to the Negroes."

Anna Julia Cooper in her master's gown, ca. 1923. Cooper, a scholar and activist, supported and contributed to the work of the Hampton Folklore Society, providing an important critical perspective on scientific modes of studying folklore. Cooper delivered an address at the 1894 Hampton Folklore Conference and served as interim editor of the *Southern Workman*, overseeing the Folklore and Ethnology section.

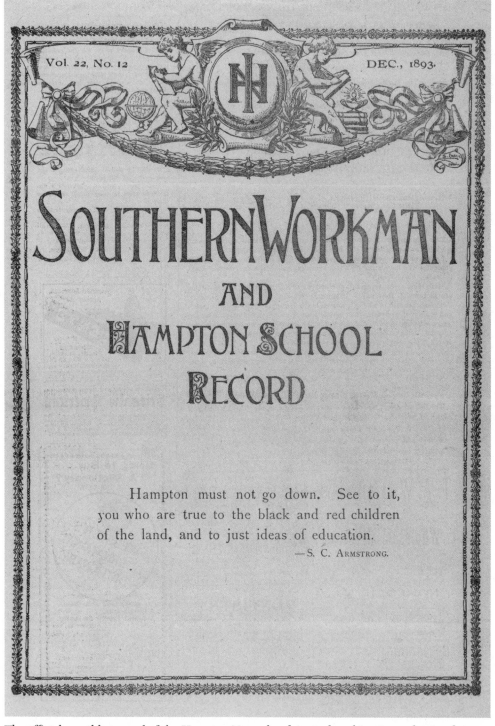

Vol. 22, No. 12   DEC., 1893.

SOUTHERN WORKMAN

AND

HAMPTON SCHOOL RECORD

Hampton must not go down. See to it, you who are true to the black and red children of the land, and to just ideas of education.

—S. C. ARMSTRONG.

The Folk-lore and Ethnology column first appeared in the December 1893 issue of the *Southern Workman.* Readers were urged to submit notes and observations about "traditions and customs peculiar to the Negroes" before modern schooling succeeded in "eradicating the old and planting the seeds of the new." Seven subject categories were listed as a guide for contributors: customs, "Traditions of ancestry in Africa," "African words surviving in speech or song," superstitions, proverbs, and song lyrics and music.

The official monthly journal of the Hampton Normal and Agricultural Institute, the *Southern Workman,* was published from 1872 to 1939. Its content was designed to appeal to students, alumni, and benefactors of the school, as well as politically sympathetic general readers.

WORKMAN. Dec., 1893.

ered of the traditions, proverbs, sayings, superstitions and folk-lore of the American Negro, and as you suggest, unless this is done immediately—i. e. before the present generation of Negroes pass from the stage, the opportunity will be lost forever. Whatever is done, then, must be done quickly.

You can rely upon my doing all that is possible to me in my limited sphere to aid you in such accumulation, not only by collecting what I can, but by enlisting the sympathy and co-operation of my friends, many of whom are in possession of, or are accessible to, such data.

Hoping that the issue may be a substantial contribution to our literature, believe me,

Yours very truly,
WILLIAM V. TUNNELL."

With this encouragement from leading men of both races we have decided to open in the SOUTHERN WORKMAN a Department of Folk-Lore and Ethnology, where we shall print, from month to month, reports from observers in the field. Our graduates resident at the school have already formed a Folk-Lore Society among themselves, and we hope that other local societies will be formed in correspondence with the WORKMAN. Then, when the time comes, we hope to follow out Mr. Newell's suggestion and form them all into a Negro Branch of the American Folk-Lore Society. Whether our plan works successfully or not, readers of the WORKMAN will discover, as they look in the Folk-Lore corner from month to month. If any readers desire extra copies of the circular letter for distribution, they can be obtained on application to A. M. Bacon, SOUTHERN WORKMAN Office, Hampton, Va.

Folk-Lore and Ethnology.

To Graduates of the Hampton Normal School and others who may be interested.

Dear Friends:

The American Negroes are rising so rapidly from the condition of ignorance and poverty in which slavery left them, to a position among the cultivated and civilized people of the earth, that the time seems not far distant when they shall have cast off their past entirely, and stand an anomaly among civilized races, as a people having no distinct traditions, beliefs or ideas from which a history of their growth may be traced. If within the next few years care is not taken to collect and preserve all traditions and customs peculiar to the Negroes, there will be little to reward the search of the future historian who would trace the history of the African continent through the years of slavery to the position which they will hold a few generations hence. Even now the children are growing up with little knowledge of what their ancestors have thought, or felt, or suffered. The common-school system with its teachings is eradicating the old and planting the seeds of the new, and the transition period is likely to be a short one. The old people, however, still have their thoughts on the past, and believe and think and do much as they have for generations. From them and from the younger ones whose thoughts have been moulded by them in regions where the school is, as yet, imperfectly established, much may be gathered that will, when put together and printed, be of great value as material for history and ethnology.

But, if this material is to be obtained, it must be gathered soon and by many intelligent observers stationed in different places. It must be done by observers who enter into the homes and lives of the more ignorant colored people and who see in their beliefs and customs no occasion for scorn, or contempt, or laughter, but only the showing forth of the first child-like, but still reasoning philosophy of a race, reaching after some interpretation of its surroundings and its antecedents. To such observers, every custom, belief or superstition, foolish and empty to others, will be of value and will be worth careful preservation. The work cannot be done by white people, much as many of them would enjoy the opportunity of doing it, but must be done by the intelligent and educated colored people who are at work all through the South among the more ignorant of their own race, teaching, preaching, practising medicine, carrying on business of any kind that brings them into close contact with the simple, old-time ways of their own people. We want to get all such persons interested in this work, and to get them to note down their observations along certain lines and send them in to the Editor of the SOUTHERN

Dec., 1893 SOUTHERN WORKMAN. 181

WORKMAN. We hope sooner or later to join all such contributors together into a Folk-Lore Society and to make our work of value to the whole world, but our beginning will be in a corner of the SOUTHERN WORKMAN and we have liberty to establish there a department of Folk-Lore Ethnology.

Notes and observations on any or all of the following subjects will be welcomed.

1. Folk-tales—The animal tales about Brer. Fox and Brer. Rabbit and the others have been well told by many white writers as taken down from the lips of Negroes. Some of them have been already traced back to Africa; many are found existing, with slight variations, among Negroes and Indians of South as well as North America. These, with other stories relating to deluges, the colors of different races and natural phenomna of various kinds, form an important body of Negro mythology. Any additions to those already written out and printed, or variations on those already obtained would be of great value.

2. Customs, especially in connection with birth, marriage and death, that are different from those of the whites. Old customs cling longest about such occasions. The old nurse, who first takes the little baby in her arms, has great store of old-fashioned learning about what to do and what not to do, to start the child auspiciously upon the voyage of life. The bride receives many warnings and injunctions upon passing through the gates of matrimony, and the customs that follow death and burial tend to change but little from age to age. What was once regarded as an honor to the dead, or a propitiation of his spirit, must not be neglected lest the dead seem dishonored, or the spirit,—about which which we know so little after all—wander forlorn and lonely, or work us ill because we failed to do some little thing that was needful for its rest. And so the old ways linger on about those events of our lives, and through them we may trace back the thoughts and beliefs of our ancestors for generations.

3. Traditions of ancestry in Africa, or of transportation to America. Rev. Dr. Crummell, in his eulogy of Henry Highland Garnett, says of that great man, "He was born in slavery. His father before him was born in the same condition. His grandfather, however, was born a free man in Africa. He was a Mandingo chieftain and warrior, and, having been taken prisoner in a tribal fight, was sold to slave traders, and then brought as a slave to America." If this tradition was preserved for three generations, may there not be others that have been handed from father to son, or from mother to daughter through longer descents? The slavery system as it existed in the United States tended to obscure pedigrees and blot them out entirely by its brutal breaking up of all family ties, but even if only here and there such traditions are still found, they are worth preserving as tending to throw light upon the derivation of the American Negroes.

4. African words surviving in speech or song. Here and there some African word has crept into common use, as *goober* for peanut, which is manifestly the same as n'gooba, the universal African designation for the same article of food. Are there not other words less common which are African? Do not children sing songs, or count out in their games with words which we may have taken for nonsense, but which really form links in the chain that connects the American with the African Negro? Do not the old people when they tell stories use expressions sometimes that are not English and that you have passed over as nonsense? Are there songs sung by the fireside, at the camp-meeting, or at work, or play, that contain words, apparently nonsensical, that make a refrain or chorus? If there are, note them down, spelling them so as to give as nearly their exact sound as possible and send them in with a note of how they are used.

5. Ceremonies and superstitions—Under this head may be included all beliefs in regard to the influence of the moon or other heavenly bodies; superstitions in regard to animals of various kinds and their powers for good or evil, as well as all ideas about the medical or magical properties of different plants or stones. Here also may be noted all that can be learned about beliefs in ghosts, witches, hags, and how to overcome supernatural influences. How to cork up a hag in a bottle so that she cannot disturb your slumbers, how to keep her at work all night threading the meshes of a sifter hung up in the doorway and so escape her influence, how to detect or avoid conjuring, or magic in any form, how to escape the bad luck that must come if you turn back to get something you have forgotten, or if a crow flies over the house, or if your eye twitches, or if any of the thousand and one things occur which, in the minds of the ignorant and superstitious, will bring bad luck if the right thing is not done at once to avert the evil influence.

6. Proverbs and sayings—From the time of King Solomon until now there have always been embodied in proverbs many bits of sound wisdom that show the philosophy of the common people. The form that the proverbs and sayings take depends largely upon the habits and modes of thought of the people who make them. Thus a collection of the proverbs of any people shows their race characteristics and the circumstances of life which surround them. Joel Chandler Harris in his "Uncle Remus's Songs and Sayings" has given a series of Plantation Proverbs that show the quaint humor, the real philosophy and the homely surroundings of the plantation Negroes. A few specimens from his list may call attention to what we mean. "Better de gravy dan no grease 'tall." "Tattlin' 'oman can't make de bread rise." "Mighty po' bee dat don't make mo' honey dan he want." "Rooster make mo' racket dan de hin w'at lay de aig." In Mr. Harris's book the Georgia Negro dialect is carefully preserved, but that is not necessary for our work, though adding to its value where it can be done well.

7. Songs, words or music or both. The Hampton School has been at some pains to note down and preserve many of the "spirituals" which are probably the best expression so far attained of the religious and musical feeling of the race, but there are innumerable songs of other kinds which have never been taken down here. One of the earliest methods of recording and preserving historical or other knowledge is through the medium of rhythmic and musical utterance. The Iliad of Homer, the great historical psalms of the Hebrew poets, the Norse sagas, the Scotch, English and Spanish ballads were but the histories of the various races moulded into forms in which they could be sung and remembered by the people. In the absence of written records, or of a general knowledge of the art of reading, songs are the ordinary vehicle of popular knowledge. A few years ago, I was listening to the singing of some of our night students. The song was new to me, and at first seemed to consist mainly of dates, but I found as it went along and interpreted, itself that it was a long and fully detailed account of the Charleston earthquake, in which the events of successive days were enumerated, the year being repeated with great fervency again and again in the chorus. Are there not other songs of a similar character that take up older events? Are there not old war songs that would be of permanent value? Are there not songs that take up the condition and events of slavery from other than the religious side? Are there any songs that go back to Africa, or the conditions of life there? What are your people singing about—for they are always singing—at their work or their play, by the fireside, or in social gatherings? Find out and write it down, for there must be much of their real life and thought in these as yet uncollected and unwritten songs.

There are many other lines along which observation would be of value for the purpose of gaining a thorough knowledge of the condition—past and present, of the American Negro. Are there any survivors of the later importations from Africa, or are there any Negroes who can say to-day, "My father or my mother was a native African?" If there are, talk with them, learn of them all they can tell you and note it down. Are there any families of Negroes, apparently of pure blood, characterized by straight or nearly straight hair? If there are, do they account for it in any way? What proportion of the colored people in the district where you live are of mixed blood? Give the number of pure and mixed blood. What proportion having white blood have kept any traditions of their white and Negro ancestry so that they know the exact proportion of white to Negro blood? How many have traditions of Indian ancestry? Reports on all these subjects would be in the line of our work.

And now, having shown as fully as is possible within the limits here set down what it is that the Hampton School desires to do through its graduates and all other intelligent Negroes who are interested in the history and origin of their own race, we would say, in closing, that we should be glad to enter into correspondence with any persons who wish to help in this work, and to receive contributions from all who have made or who can make, observations along the proposed lines of investigation. Correspondence with prominent men of both races, leads us to believe that we have the possibility ahead of us of valuable scientific study, that in this age when it is hard to open up a new line of research, or add anything to the knowledge of men and manners and beliefs that the world already possesses, we, if we labor earnestly and patiently, may contribute much that shall be of real and permanent value in spreading among men the understanding of their fellowmen as well as in furnishing material for the future historian of the American Negro. Is not this worth doing?

Correspondence in regard to this matter may be addressed to Miss A. M. Bacon, SOUTHERN WORKMAN Office, Hampton, Va.

The author of the column, likely Alice Mabel Bacon, editor of the *Southern Workman* and founder of the Hampton Folklore Society, stated that the work of collecting folklore "cannot be done by white people, much as they would enjoy the opportunity of doing it, but must be done by the intelligent and educated colored people who are at work all through the South . . . carrying on business of any kind that brings them into close contact with the simple, old-time ways of their own people."

BRER RABBIT'S BOX, WITH APOLOGIES TO JOEL CHANDLER HARRIS

Southern Workman 28 (1899), 25–26

T. J. Bolden submitted the story below, with its brilliant punch line that undermines the value and values of the Uncle Remus stories.

BRER RABBIT'S BOX

With Apologies to Joel Chandler Harris
by T. J. BOLDEN (*Class '99*)

"One time while Brer Rabbit was off at school, Thanksgivin' cum 'roun', en he got a box from home."

"I didn't know the rabbit ever went to school, Uncle Remus," said the little boy.

"Co'se Brer Rabbit went to school," said the old man indignantly. "How yo' spec's he goin' ter know how to do all dem smart things what he done widout he went to school. How some never, if yo' doan wanter hear dis story, den yo' ken say he didn't went to school, dat's all I'se got to say 'bout it."

The little boy saw his mistake and urged Uncle Remus to go on with the story.

"Ez I was sayin'," proceeded the old man, "Brer Rabbit got a gre't big box from home, full ob de nices' tings yo' ever laid eyes on. Dyar wuz spyar ribs, sweet 'taters, chitlins, cracklin' bread, turkey and cake in dis yer box, en w'en Brer Rabbit opened it he smack his mouf w'en he thought 'bout how he gwine to eat 'em all en not gi' Brer Fox en Brer Wolf none.

"Brer Fox done see Brer Rabbit w'en he kyar de box to his room so he holler out:

"'Hey, Brer Rabbit, w'at dat yo' got dar?'

"'Taint nuttin' but a box er ol' papers whar Miss 'Oman jes' done gin me,' en Brer Rabbit mek 'ase to git to he room fo' Brer Fox ker ketch up wid 'im.

"Brer Fox wuz mighty s'prised w'en he heah Brer Rabbit talk 'bout de box ob ol' papers, kase he know dat Brer Rabbit aint never kear so much 'bout paper dat he got to kyar ol' ones to he room, so arter he scratch he haid en fleck[1] for some time, he rive

---

1 *scratch he haid en fleck*: scratched his head and reflected

at de conclusion dat Brer Rabbit mus' did have somefin' better'n ol' papers in dat air box en dat he better 'vestigate de mattah.

"So bimeby, 'fo' Brer Rabbit done got thoo lookin' at de nice tings in de box he heah sumpin' 'Bim! Bim!' on de do'. Co'se he know 'tis Brer Fox so he slip de box under de baid en grab he his'ry en mek preten' like he studden. Presin'ly anudder knock come: 'Bap! Bap!' 'Come in!' holler Brer Rabbit, en Brer Fox walk in. Brer Rabbit busy studden he hist'ry. ''Pears to be so mighty taken up wid yer box ob ol' papers, yo' cyarnt hear nobody w'en dey knocks on yo' do',' sez Brer Fox sezee. 'O!' sez Brer Rabbit, kinder innercent like, 'I'se jes studden my history.' But all de time Brer Rabbit thinkin' 'bout how he gwine sarcumwent[2] Brer Fox. Bimeby he shet up de his'try and turnin' to Brer Fox he sez: 'Brer Fox yo' ain't nevah is had no simmon beer is yo'?' Brer Fox kinder sot he ears up w'en he hear dat questum kase he allers hankerin' arter sumpin' good, so he sez: 'Naw Brer Rabbit, I ain't nevah is had much es I want,' and wid dat Brer Rabbit went to de box en got out a mejium size bottle whar he done fin' in dar. Co'se he aint tell Brer Fox what else he got in dar.

2 *sarcumwent:* circumvent

"Now Brer Rabbit allers hear dat if yo' drink simmon beer on de increase ob de moon, yo' is bound to swell up, en if yo' drinks nuff yo' is bound to bus' open, but Brer Fox is so greedy he ain't thinkin' 'bout whedder de moon increasin' or decreasin' so he jes' tek de bottle en turn it up to he haid en dreen every drap. But Brer Fox wa'nt hahdly thoo smackin' he lips en wishin' for mo', w'en he 'gin to swell up. W'en he see he sides 'gin to stick out en de mis'ry 'gin to run thoo him, he 'gin to git skeered, en he eyes gin to stick out like stack racks. Brer Rabbit he know dat Brer Fox ain't drink nuff to bus' him open, but he jes' want skeer Brer Fox, so he hollers out: 'Lawdy Brer Fox, w'at's de mattah wid yo'? W'at yo' want drink all dat simmon beer for? 'Pears like harf un it would ha' bin nuff for any gemman, but, aw naw, yo's got to drink all in de bottle. Now jes' see w'at's done happen to yo'.' Brer Fox ain't wait to hear no mo'. He jes' bolt outen dat room en nex' thing Brer Rabbit hear, Brer Fox sick in de hospital. Brer Rabbit kinder smile w'en de folks tell 'im 'bout de diffunt things w'at de mattah wid Brer Fox, kase he is de only one wha' know de right thing, but he ve'y well satisfied kase Brer Fox ain't git none ob his odder good things."

The old man cleared his throat and looking intently at the ceiling slowly remarked: "Brer Rabbit mighty like some people in dis yer day en time. Dey allers wants de bestes' fer demselves en don't nevah think dat ol' cullud gemmens like to eat cake an turkey ez well ez tell 'bout Brer Rabbit."

This thrust had its effect. The little boy slipped away and soon returned with a basketful of the choicest things from his mother's table.

The old man looked affectionately at him and said, "Bless yo' soul honey, yo' is allers a good little boy—sometimes."

THE DONKEY, THE DOG, THE CAT AND THE ROOSTER

Southern Workman 23 (1894), 150

Much like the German story about the musicians from Bremen, this tale about mistreated animals banding together to find a home is especially resonant in the context of slavery.

THE DONKEY, THE DOG, THE CAT AND THE ROOSTER

Once upon a time there was a man who owned a donkey, a dog, a cat and a rooster. They became discontented for some reason. The man was a cruel master, he worked the donkey very hard from before sunrise until long after sunset. The donkey got mad and very discontented and said that if this continued, he would leave. It was continued, and so one morning when the man got up the donkey had gone. This made the man mad and he kicked the dog and he ran away into the woods. The next morning the cat was sitting in front of the fire and the man told it to get out of his way, so the cat ran off and did not come back.

The man used to get up very early but the next morning he got up a little later than usual which made him mad and he said the rooster was to blame because he didn't crow at the right time, so he flogged the rooster and the rooster got mad and ran away.

After a while as the donkey was wandering about in the wood looking for something to eat he met the dog. "Hello what are you doing here," he said. "Oh I ran away," answered the dog. "Master kicked me, so I couldn't stand it." "Well, let us go together," said the donkey.

After a while they met the cat. "What are you doing here?" said they to her. "What are you both doing here?" she replied. "Oh the old man flogged us and we left." "Well, we will all three go together and get our living." As they were searching about for something to eat they ran across the rooster. "Well! What are you doing here?" they exclaimed. The rooster told his story, and then they decided to live together. If they were going to live together they must first have a house. The rooster said he knew of an old deserted house he had seen as he was coming down the road. "Now we will go there and take possession of it."

When they got there they found the door fastened and a little smoke was coming out the chimney and they could smell something good to eat. There was no roof on the house. The rooster said "We must see what is inside. Now let the donkey stand close to the wall, the dog on his back, the cat on the dog's back and then I'll get on the cat's back and look over and tell you what I see." When the rooster looked over he saw some gamblers sitting about the fire cooking their supper. This frightened the rooster and he fell in and scared the men so that they all ran off.

Then the donkey, the dog and the cat came inside. They said "These men ran off but they will come back again, what shall we do?" The rooster, who seemed to be wiser than the others, said "I'll tell you what to do. Let the donkey go down by the gate, the dog lie at the door, the cat at the hearth and I will go as usual to the roof. If the spy comes back he will come to the fire to make a light, then let the cat touch him; when he goes to the door the dog can touch him and as he leaves the gate the donkey can strike him and I will give the alarm."

By and by the spy did come, but soon ran back to his companions crying that the house was haunted! For, he said, when I went to take a light something slapped me on the face; then I ran out of the door and something cut me on the leg and when I got to the gate something gave me an awful blow on the back with a stick and then the ghost cried—"Hand him up here to touch! Hand him up here to touch!"

JACK AND THE KING

Southern Workman 28 (1899), 232–33

Written down by W. G. Anderson, this trickster tale resembles some of the European "master-thief" narratives, in which numbskulls get the better of innkeepers, kings, and others of high social rank by engaging in farcical pranks.

JACK AND THE KING

In days of old a king lived in his kingdom with his family and he had a man working for him by the name of Jack. He was very bright, but tricky and careless. The king said one morning when he had been setting things wrong that if he was going to be a rogue he ought to go to school and be a professional. So Jack went off for two or three years and then came back, and as he was going along whistling loudly he met the king out walking. "Oh, there you are!" said the king. "Well, I suppose you are now a trained professional rogue." Jack said he was. The king said he had twelve horses that he thought a great deal of, and that if Jack could get them away from the keepers he could have them. So Jack goes off and gets a gallon of tar, then he goes to his wife and says he wants a feather bed. He smears the tar all over himself, and rolls in the feather bed, then goes and gets up on the stone wall around the stables. When the keeper lets the horses out to the trough to drink, Jack gets on to the gate post and frightens the keeper, who runs back to the stables leaving the gate open and the horses in Jack's hands. Jack mounts the leader and gallops off, and all the rest follow him. When the king sees his horses are gone he sends for Jack and says "I suppose you got my horses." "Yes sir," said Jack. The king said, "I have a set of fine gold and silver ware for my table and if you can get it you can have it." Jack found out through one of the servants that the set was only used on Sunday. The family went to church except the oldest girl who expected a friend to call, and pretended to be busy with the household work. Jack managed to get into the house near the dining room; he saw the butler take the set out and put it on the table but he did not see any way of getting away with it, and then the butler locked the door and went off. Jack went into the room where the girl and her friend were and passed as some stranger who was there by mistake, and talked to them until the king drove up to the door, and the lover was forced to hide under the sofa; Jack didn't know what else to do, so he got under the sofa too. The family sat down to dinner in the next room. By and by Jack thought of singing an old song which he said he had not sung since he was a boy, so he told the man he didn't care, he wanted to sing. The man said, "Oh, don't sing!" but Jack said he must. The man said he would give him $100 if he wouldn't and Jack said "all right" and took the money. Pretty soon he said "I've got to sing that song," and the man said "O take my ring and watch but don't sing, please don't sing." So Jack took the ring and the watch, but pretty soon he said "I've got to sing that song." The man said "I'll give you all my clothes if you don't sing that song." When they had changed clothes Jack raised a shout and the king and others rushed out to see what it was and Jack doubled up the table cloth and walked off with it. The poor man who was hiding cut and run, but was caught and put to death. When the king found what had really happened he said, "That's one of Jack's tricks." He sent for Jack and said, "Did you get my gold and silver set?" and Jack said he did. "Well," said the king, "I have a solid gold wedge worth $50,000 in my house, if you can get that I won't kill you and you can have it." He wanted to catch Jack after all that he had done. Jack saw that the house was lighted from a shaft, for he stood in with one of the servants as I told you. The king brought his wedge into his wife's room and said "Jack is after this wedge and I want you to take it and put it away where no one will get it." So she took it away and put it away.

As Jack was going along the road thinking how he could get the wedge, he went by the house of an old colored preacher who was singing "I am gwine to heaven, if any one wants to go, come along, come along." Presently the old man came out of his house and Jack said to him, "You come along to this house with me and you'll go right through the pearly gates straight into heaven." The old man went with him; Jack took him up on top of the house, tied a rope around his body and let him down the shaft. The king heard him coming and thinking it was Jack opened his door and grabbed him and without noticing what he was told the servant to take him out and behead him. While the king was busy with the old minister, Jack dressed up in some of the king's clothes and skipped into his wife's room and said, "Where is that wedge? I am afraid Jack will get it." So she got it and gave it to him and he went off. Pretty soon the king came in and asked the same question. "Where is the wedge? I am afraid Jack will get it." "Why I just gave it to you," his wife said, and then the king knew that Jack had it.

The next morning the king called up Jack and said "I am going to have you beheaded for stealing my wedge," and Jack said "I am going to have you beheaded for killing your daughter's sweetheart and the old colored minister." The king begged him not to do that, and said "If you don't, I'll move out and you can move in," which they did.

W. G. ANDERSON

PLANTATION COURTSHIP

Southern Workman 24 (1895), 14–15

The American slave's life was a desert of suffering certainly, but in it there were oases whose shades and springs yielded comforts whose delights were all the keener for their infrequency.

He had his holidays and his social seasons, and there were hours when, his day's task done, he poured his story of admiration and love into the ears of some dusky maiden whose presence brought to him a joy as sweet, perhaps sweeter, than that which his smart young master felt in the society of the free women whom he loved and honored.

The slave girl had to be won as surely as did her fair young mistress, and her black fellow in slavery who aspired to her hand had to prove his worthiness to receive it.

Instances were not a few where the black knight laid down his life in defence of the honor of his lady-love, but of course milder proofs of worthiness were the rule.

Among the slaves there were regular forms of "courtship," and almost every large plantation had an experienced old slave who instructed young gallants in the way in which they should go in the delicate matter of winning the girls of their choice.

I have distinct recollection of "Uncle Gilbert," a bald, little dark man, who carried his spectacles on his forehead the most of the time.

"Uncle Gilbert" was the shoemaker on a plantation where there were a hundred slaves, whose good young master, "Pete," allowed them to receive company Sundays and some evenings in the week from all the surrounding neighborhood.

What gay times there were on that plantation in the days befo' de wah!

"Uncle Gilbert" was very learned in the art of "courtship," and it was to his shop the slave lads went for instruction in "courtship's words and ways."

The old man had served a half dozen masters, had won and buried as many wives, and had traveled much. It was therefore conceded by the people of all the neighborhood that nobody thereabouts was a greater authority on wooing than he.

"Uncle Gilbert" held the very generally accepted opinion that "courtin' is a mighty ticklish bizness," and that he who would "git a gal wuth havin, mus' know how to talk fur her."

I never had the honor of being one of "the old man's" pupils, being too young when I knew him to make inquiry along the courtship line, but I tracked many young men to Uncle Gilbert's shop in the interest of general gossip.

The courtship idea, of course, belongs to people of every clime and race. People only differ in expressing it.

The American slave courtship words and forms are the result of his attempt at imitating the gushingly elegant manners and speech of his master.

Uncle Gilbert's rule of courtship was that a "young man mus' tes' an' prove a gal befo' offerin' her his han'. Ef er gal gives a man as good anser as he gives her question, den she is all right in min'. Ef she can look him squar in de face when she talks to him, den she kin be trusted; and ef her patches is on straight, an' her close clean, den she is gwine ter keep de house straight and yer britches mended. Sich er ooman is wuth havin'."

ECHOES FROM A PLANTATION PARTY

Southern Workman 28 (1899), 59

by Daniel Webster Davis

The natural tendency of the day is to forget the black history of the past; and so the younger generation seldom speak of the days of yore, with all of their lights and shadows. It is surprising to know the difficulty I have experienced in gathering the facts of this article. I have approached many old fathers and mothers and each confessed that he had forgotten the old plays. I recalled them to their memory and I have seen many an eye, dimmed by the withering blast of old age begin to twinkle and glow as memory brought again pictures of the days that are no more and ever and anon, a silent tear would steal down a faded cheek, as these reminiscences would conjure up visions of departed happiness, and of faces that once engaged in the old "ring plays," and are now covered with mold, awaiting the trumpet blast that shall awake the sleeping dead.

It is indeed true that the "greatest study of mankind is man," and this study need not be confined to his darker musings, and deeper thoughts, but in the province of his pleasures may be found many things to entertain and instruct, and from which we can better understand the peculiarities and idiosyncracies of this people.

The darker side of slave life had its silver lining. There is never a sorrow, but has its corresponding joy, never a midnight without its dawning, never a tear without its smile. God has wisely so decreed, or else this life would be to many unbearable, and every breath a prayer for deliverance from the body of this death. Slavery was no exception to this rule, and while some who understand the mazes of the cauliflower, the poetry of the waltz, the beauty of the lanciers, and the peculiar pleasure found in the modern party methods, now dignified by higher sounding titles, may smile at the strange modes of entertaining in those old days, yet to them it gave the most exquisite enjoyment.

The slaves worked in the summer from daybreak to sundown, and in winter, those who worked in the house would frequently be kept until ten o'clock at night, carding, knitting, spinning, weaving and sometimes getting "rations" ready for the hands the next day. The field-hands would gather most any night in the "quarters," and shuffle around to the sound of a banjo, or if that was not forthcoming, to the beating of a tin pan, that furnished music not so classical, and yet served the purpose admirably well.

The great times for enjoyment would be on Saturday and Sunday nights, when all were comparatively free from labor. Sunday nights did not constitute any bar to the playing of the ordinary "ring plays," as they were not considered dancing: in fact, nothing was considered dancing unless you "crossed your feet."

Dancing, and the more elaborate ring plays were left to "sinnuz," as non-members of the church were denominated, and of which there were a large number. This fact is not surprising, when it is considered what a laborious process "getting religion" was. The "travels" to be had, the amount of praying to be done, the long experience to be told, and the length of time it was considered proper for one to "seek" before "coming through" made the process so tedious that when a convert once got "through," he would seldom go back to the "beggarly elements of the world." Singing a song, dancing, etc. were considered mortal sins, while other things mentioned in the decalogue were passed by in comparative silence.

But it was at a regular "party" that the old time belles and beaux could be seen at their best. These were frequently given with a practical object in view. Bed quiltings were often had, where the people from the plantations around would gather to quilt a spread used for the bed, with which many of the colored people were often well supplied. The rags from the "great house" were carefully kept until such time as sufficient were gathered to make the much-to-be-desired quilt.

"Molasses stews" were frequent, at which time the great brass kettle of black molasses was put on the fire to stew. In a given time it was taken off, the hands of the merrymakers scrupulously washed, and then the pulling would begin. The candy would be pulled until almost white, large quantities, set apart for "marster; mistis, and de whi' chillun," and the rest consumed by the "pullers."

When the corn for the winter had been gathered in, many indulgent masters would allow the slaves to have a "corn shucking." The master might kill an old steer, now past the possibility of work, and prepare a big supper. Spirited races would sometimes take place between rival shuckers, and happy was the man who would come out ahead. Again it would be a "husking bee," when the same process would be gone through, only this time it would be for the purpose of getting the corn off the husk that it might be carried to the mill and ground into meal for the slaves.

In the summer "Watermelon Feasts" would be the order of the day. On the plantations too far removed from the city to carry them to market to be sold, they were raised for home use only. In some portions of Hanover County, the large, luscious melons were raised in such numbers that quantities of them were fed to the hogs. Frequently, in the height of the season, permission would be granted the servants to have a grand feast to which the slaves for miles around were invited. These were glorious times, and the memory of those pleasant events still lingers fondly with many of our fathers and mothers.

Dress did not play a conspicuous part in the enjoyment of the party of the past. The dress of the field hands was exceedingly monotonous, the linsey-woolsey dress and bed-ticking pantaloons being the chief styles. For days before the party the hair of the females was tightly wrapped with white strings to be unloosed on this momentous occasion, when it would show itself in the most beautiful "waves."

House servants were the observed of all observers. They would come attired in the cast-off finery of an indulgent mistress, and would be resplendent in ribbons representing all the hues of the rainbow. Sometimes an especially favored lady's maid might be seen dressed in the cast-off silk that had done duty on many a "state occasion" for the lady of the "great house." The extravagance would excite many a jealous pang in the breast of less-favored damsels. The swains would look askance at these expensively bedecked damsels until all would become cosmopolitan in the mazes of the country dance. Not infrequently the young master and mistresses would grace the occasion with their presence, which however was rather a check upon the exuberant spirits of the participants.

Persons coming from a distance to these parties would be expected to have a pass. When the master did not feel disposed to supply this, it made but little difference to the party-goer, as he would go anyway and take the chances on not being found out. Some sharper than the rest would scratch a few marks on a piece of paper and feel secure, as the patrolmen, or "patter rollers" as they were called, would sometimes scarcely look at the pass and even if they did it was not an unusual occurrence to meet with one that could not read, and these crudely made marks could easily pass muster.

These parties began late, since supper must be served, dishes washed, and the children tucked snugly in bed before the servants were free to get ready for this happy event.

The party would start off with a general greeting and conversation. Telling tales, some of them calculated to "freeze the young blood, and cause each particular hair to stand on end like quills upon the fretful porcupine" was a common mode of entertaining. Next would come the guessing of riddles propounded by the more erudite portion of the company or "pulling handkerchiefs" for kisses. "Fruit in the Basket," "Walking the Lonesome Road," "I'm in the Well," and "Fishing," were devices for getting a kiss from some fair one. In the play "I'm in the Well," a gentleman would make the startling announcement that he was in the well. Some sympathizing friend would ask, "How many feet deep?" and it is surprising how many feet a fellow could get in the well, if some pretty girl asked the question. He would then be asked, "Who will you have to pull you out?" He would answer, "Miss so and so," and the lady mentioned would be expected to kiss him as many times as he was feet deep in the well. This was certainly a most pleasant way to be rescued from drowning. By this effort the lady would get into the well herself and have to be rescued in like manner. The plays I have mentioned, "Buff" and many others are similar in character. In lieu of what we call the Grand March there was a play known as "Walk Old John the Blind Man." Now as to what this meant I must plead my entire ignorance, nor have I found a single old person able to enlighten me. The ladies and gentlemen would lock arms, march around the room and sing,

"Walk old John the Blind Man, so long fare you well.
Walk old John the Blind Man, so long fare you well.
How you know he's a blind man? so long fare you well.
'Cause he ain't got but one eye, so long fare you well."

To make a variation in the march they would sometimes have one in front without a partner, form a line and sing,

"Come all ye young men in your youthful days,
Come look to the Lord in your sinful ways,
You will be happy, you will be happy,
While we are growing old."

At this each lady would "let go" the arm of her escort, and take that of the next gentleman in front. Thus the odd fellow would get a partner, and leave some other fellow odd to take his chances at the next go 'round.

Strange to state while many of these plays by their wording show their historical connections, but few show any marks of the plays of our mother country.

HAGS AND THEIR WAYS / THE CONQUEST OF A HAG

Southern Workman 23 (1894), 26–27

The Folk-Lore Society held a special session on dream signs and hag stories on January 8, 1894. For the column on "Folk-Lore and Ethnology," a summary of the discussion was included with a story about how to defeat a hag.

FOLK-LORE AND ETHNOLOGY
Hags and Their Ways

The regular meeting of the Folk-Lore Society was held on Monday evening, January 8th. The subject appointed for study and discussion was "Dream-Signs and Hag Stories," although a few questions came up in regard to other matters. During the month preceding, an effort had been made to get hold of any strange words used in games or elsewhere, and "Hully gully," "Oli ola" and "Coonjine" had been gathered as a nucleus for further study. Any person reading this report who can throw light upon the meaning or origin of these expressions, will be conferring a favor by writing to the *Workman* in regard to them. Comparison of notes among members of the society developed the information that "coonjine" is used on the Mississippi River for a peculiar motion of the body used apparently to lighten or hasten the labor of loading and unloading. "Hully-gully," or "Hull da gull" as it appears in a report from Kentucky, is a phrase used in a game. The player holds up a handful of grain or parched corn, shakes it before his opponent and says "Hully gully how many?" A guess is then made by the player and in some cases, in the reply, the expression, "Oli ola" is used, though some members of the society had never heard it though familiar with the rest of the game. Another set of words used in playing the same game is as follows:

1st. Player. "Jack in the bush."
2nd. Player. "Cut him down."
1st. Player. "How many licks?"
to which the second player responds with a guess.

Letters were received from Mr. Geo. W. Cable, Mrs. A. J. Cooper and Miss Mary Alicia Owen, all most encouraging to the infant society and after that the work of the evening began. Of dream signs, the following were brought in.

To dream of the dead is a sign of rain.

To dream of seeing a dead friend dressed in white is a sign that that friend is happy, but if he appears in black, he is unhappy.

To dream of eggs is a sign of a quarrel.

To dream of a wedding is a sign of death; of a funeral is a sign of a wedding.

> Friday night dream
> Sat'day morning told,
> Comes to behold
> Before nine days old.

To dream of silver money is a sign of a quarrel, but it means good luck if you dream of paper money.

To dream of your teeth's falling out is a sign of death.

The hag in Negro folk-lore is the very essence of nightmare, about whose personality gather all the morbid fancies of distempered dreams. She oozes in at your key hole, pervades your room with her malicious but invisible presence, rides you in your sleep, and is so persistent in her persecutions of her victims that they sometimes pine away and die after a year or two of her nightly visitations. Many devices are resorted to to keep her out of the house, or to catch her after she gets in. You may know of her presence by noticing the uneasy moaning and twitching of your dog as he sleeps before the fire. The hag is riding him now, but will seek nobler prey when you have lain down for your night's rest. Or you may hear her oozing in at your key-hole with a peculiar whizzing, gurgling sound that you can feel as well as hear as you lie in your bed, and you know that she has left her skin upon your doorstep and is moving in a semi-fluid and wholly horrible condition toward her seat upon your chest. There she will perch and ride the whole night through, unless by some means you can delay her progress or catch her and hold her till the morning dawns. But the hag has a weakness, and she may be detained from her evil work by anyone who knows her ways. She must pick over and count any small things she may find along her path as she moves through the house; corn scattered near the door by which she must enter will keep her at work; a sifter hung over the keyhole may detain her all night, for she must count the meshes before she leaves it. An open book placed at the head of the bed will surely keep her out of mischief, for she must count every letter in every word before making her attack upon her victim. A wool card or two will serve the same purpose, though not so effectively, for she must count the teeth and may be delayed until the approach of dawn warns her to flee lest she become visible and be recognized. There are also many ways of catching a hag, although when caught she may change her form, and is exceedingly hard to kill. There are ways by which she may be coaxed into a bottle with nine new needles and nine new pins, or her victim may gain possession of the tormentor's skin and sprinkle it with pepper and salt, so that it can not be used. A story is told of a hag who finds her skin on the doorstep thus doctored, and after trying it on several times and finding it smart and burn, she dances wildly about crying "O Skinny, Skinny, Skinny, don't you know me?" She may be caught in a sifter, when you can detect a sort of web clinging to it, cut this web and the hag will appear in her true shape. Other ways there are undoubtedly by which she may be trapped, and further information on this subject from any source will be most welcome. The following hag story, told in full at the Folk-Lore meeting, shows the midnight terror in all its uncanny habits. Hundreds of such stories are told about the cabin fires still, and we wish to get hold of as many of them as possible, for the hag is an interesting psychological development out of the mental and physical surroundings of the Negroes in the South.

THE CONQUEST OF A HAG

There was a poor woman who had been ridden by a hag night after night until she had grown thin and weak from the horror of her nightly visitations. Feeling that she must die as others had died before her, from the torment of this unseen enemy, she resolved to be rid of her at any cost. She went to a hag catcher, who told her how to trap and conquer her tormentor. That night, before she went to bed she stopped every keyhole in the house except one, for the hag enters only by keyholes. She can not come in by the window even if that is left open and the keyholes all stopped. Directly inside of the door with the open keyhole, the woman scattered a quantity of wheat. Then she went to bed, to lie awake and listen for the approach of her enemy. Soon she felt the hag coming and heard at the keyhole the peculiar whizzing sound that told her that dreadful visitor had laid her skin upon the doorstep and was oozing into the house. She lay still and listened. Soon the gurgling noise ceased and she heard the hag utter a strange imprecation when she saw the scattered wheat upon the floor. She might well be disappointed; for she must collect and count every grain of that wheat before she could begin her ride. The listener in the bed heard her pick and pick at the wheat as she laboriously counted it grain by grain. Once, when it was all counted and collected, the hag by an accidental kick, destroyed her own work and scattered the wheat far and wide, and so it happened that she was detained at the door until the day began to break. At dawn her victim arose and went out to see if she had caught the hag, but she saw only a white chicken picking at the wheat on the floor. The woman had been warned that the hag, if caught, would take the form of some animal, so she spoke to the chicken, saying "I know you, Aunt Jane, but I don't know what harm I have ever done you, that you should torment me so." The chicken made no reply nor did she turn back to her true shape.

Then the woman caught the chicken and fastened it up in a coop, and ran around to the door-step to find the hag's skin. There it lay on the step just where it had been left by its owner the night before. She took up the skin, peppered and salted it, and put it safely away, then went back to look for her chicken, but it had worked its way out of the coop and was gone. Then she knew that she had really caught a hag.

Her next step was to go down and visit her neighbor, Aunt Jane, whom she had all along believed to be her persecutor. She found that Aunt Jane was very ill and would see no one, but kept herself so closely covered in bed that not even the top of her head was visible. Aunt Jane's husband, the only person who had seen her that day, had made the horrible discovery in the early morning that his wife had lost her skin, but he had told no one of the fact.

All that day the hag remained in bed, skinless and writhing in agony,—all day the skin, peppered and salted, remained in possession of her victim. When night fell, a reformed and penitent hag oozed through the keyhole of her conqueror's door, solemnly promising that she would never ride again if she might only be given her skin. The promise given, the woman who had taken it, washed the skin carefully and thoroughly and returned it once more to its owner, who put it on, thenceforth cured of her trick of riding her neighbors.

WHY THE CLAY IS RED

Southern Workman 27 (1898), 36–37

Masquerading as a pourquoi *tale about origins, this story about grotesque maternal cruelty contains the motif of the magical flight often found in European fairy tales.*

WHY THE CLAY IS RED

Once upon a time there lived an old lady who had two sons: one was named Jimbore, and the other was named John. One evening just at sunset she sent the boys to the spring with a sifter to get water for the night. They staid very long, because every time they dipped the water it ran out. They soon heard their mother calling, "You Jimbore! You John! Come here." They replied, "Oh, Mother! Every time we dip the water it runs out." She became very much vexed with them and ran to the spring with a long switch to whip them. At the first stroke the boys jumped into the well and turned into little ducks. She threw at them until they flew out and lit on a tree, but she soon cut the tree down and they flew into the river. She continued to follow them and when she came to the river she said, "Look out, river, I will swallow you," and jumped into it with great speed. In the meantime the little ducks flew out and hid themselves in a thick cluster of briars. The mother did not drown, but she came out quite slowly and went to the cluster of briars and said, "Look out briars, I will eat you up," and she jumped in with great speed, but reached her fate. She burst and the red clay that you see was stained by her blood.

C. H. HERBERT

FISH STORIES

Southern Workman 26 (1897), 229–30

We give this month two variants of the same story, brought in by two members of the Hampton Folk-Lore Society. The story is evidently manufactured with the high moral purpose of securing a careful observance of the Sabbath on the part of the younger people on the plantations.

1. Our first version comes from Farmville, Va.

There was once a slave who spent most of his Sundays on the river bank at a certain famous fishing hole, fishing. This was, of course, against the advice and wishes of his fellow slaves, who assured him that sooner or later, some very bad luck would befall him. First they told him that he could not catch any fish on Sunday, "'cause they wouldn't bite." This prediction, however, proved futile, for Sambo was a very successful fisherman and caught large quantities of fish every Sunday. Sambo's friends then predicted that the fish would kill him if he ate them, but this prophecy failed also, and Sambo still found himself as strong and as healthy as any of his master's slaves. After using every means of persuasion to prevent Sambo's fishing on Sunday, his friends finally decided to apply to their master to stop him, but the master seemed rather indifferent, and said that Sambo had a right to fish on Sunday if he so desired, and that that was Sambo's own business.

Finally the young people came to the conclusion that there was no such thing as bad luck, because Sambo was just as lucky as they were, if not more so, but the old people still clung to the idea that "bad luck would sure come to Sambo." Time went on and Sambo's wicked conduct continued. The old people would have nothing to do with such a sinner, while the young people, on the other hand, rather admired him, partly because he was daring, and partly because he had apparently proved that the various bad luck theories of the old people were "fogeyisms."

But one Sunday, when Sambo was fishing in his usual way, he sat for hours and hours and had not a single bite. He finally noticed a slight quiver of his cork and then he had a real bite. He pulled with all his might, and found it difficult to get the fish to the surface. When at last he pulled it out, he discovered that he had caught an animal such as he had never before seen. It had a head like a duck, wings like a bird, and tail like a fish, and worse than all, he had a voice like a human being, and sang the words it uttered. Sambo was frightened and dropped hook, lines, animal, and everything, and started for the house as fast as his legs could carry him. But the animal sang after him these words:

> "Come back, Sambo,
> Come back, Sambo,
> Domie ninky head, Sambo,"
> > and Sambo came back.

Then the animal sang:—

> "Pick me up, Sambo,
> Pick me up, Sambo,
> Domie ninky head, Sambo."
> > Sambo picked him up.

Then he sang:—

> "Carry me home, Sambo,
> Carry me home, Sambo,
> Domie ninky head, Sambo."
> > Sambo carried him to the house.

Then he sang:—

> "Clean and cook me, Sambo,
> Clean and cook me, Sambo,
> Domie ninky head, Sambo."
> > Sambo cleaned him and put him on to cook,

supposing that after he was in the pot he would stop singing commands to him, but he had no such good luck as that, for as soon as Sambo's fish was sufficiently cooked he piped up from the pot in his old musical voice,

> "Now take me off, Sambo,
> Take me off, Sambo,
> Domie ninky head, Sambo."
> > Sambo took him off.

Then he sang:—

> "Eat me up, Sambo,
> Eat me up, Sambo,
> Domie ninky head, Sambo."
> > Sambo began to eat him up, as he was commanded,

but one can not imagine Sambo as being very hungry under such circumstances, so Sambo ate a mouthful or two and then stopped, but his dinner sang:—

> "Eat me all, Sambo,
> Eat me all, Sambo,
> Domie ninky head, Sambo."
> > Sambo ate him all, as he was told.

By this time the slaves from several plantations had gathered, and great consternation and excitement prevailed among the Negroes and white people alike. The old colored people sang and shouted, and many of them said, "I knowed it would come, I knowed it would; case de Bible said so."

In the meantime, Sambo had swollen to enormous proportions, and he continued to swell till he burst open and the animal came out whole and alive, as he was when caught. He went back to the river singing:—

> "Don't fish on Sunday,
> Don't fish on Sunday,
> Domie ninky head, Sambo."

In a few minutes after the animal came out, Sambo died.

2. Our second version comes from Danville, Va.

Simon went fishing on Sunday and pulled out a big black animal as large as a pig. It frightened him so, that he dropped his hook and ran. The animal fell back into the water, saying, "Come pull me out, Simon, come pull me out, out Simon, for Mollie's got to go home ho! hey! Mollie's got to go home ho! hey!"

Simon went back and pulled him out. "Now carry me home, Simon. Now carry me home Simon, for Mollie's got to go home, ho! hey! Mollie's got to go home ho! hey!"

"Now kill me Simon, now kill me Simon, for Mollie's got to go home, ho! hey! Mollie's got to go home ho! hey!"

"Now wash me, Simon, now wash me, Simon, for Mollie's got to go home, ho! hey! Mollie's got to go home ho! hey!"

"Now salt me, Simon, now salt me Simon, for Mollie's got to go home, ho! hey! Mollie's got to go home ho! hey!"

"Now put me on, Simon, now put me on, Simon, for Mollie's got to go home, ho! hey! Mollie's got to go home ho! hey!"

"I am done enough, Simon, I am done enough, Simon, for Mollie's got to go home, ho! hey! Mollie's got to go home ho! hey!"

TWO GHOST STORIES

Southern Workman 26 (1897), 122–23

Both stories were told by informants who had grown up in Virginia, and the ending to each tale suggests a possible link with stories about flying Africans.

The two stories that we give this month are rather unusual in their denouement and seem to be worth the preserving. Both come from the same section of Virginia.

1. There were two slaves who used to pass an old barn at night when they went to visit their wives on a neighboring plantation. The barn seemed to be unused, except that whenever they passed it they saw a young heifer standing outside of it. This heifer, which was apparently a yearling, did not seem to grow any larger as the weeks went

by, but it was nice and fat. At last Gibbie, one of the men, made up his mind that if the yearling was not taken by the time they passed the barn again, they would kill her and take the meat home. The next time they went by, there stood the heifer, and Gibbie went up to her and took her by the horns, calling to his chum to help him. The heifer pulled and twisted, so Gibbie jumped up on her back and tried to hold her. Yearling got jumping and jumped up off the ground. "Hold her, Gibbie," shouted his chum. "I got her," answered Gibbie, and held on. The heifer went on up until she got as high as the roof of the barn. "Hold her, Gibbie," called out the man below. "I got her," answered Gibbie. The heifer kept on going up until she was nearly out of sight. "Hold her, Gibbie," shouted the other man, as Gibbie sailed off into the clouds. "I got her, she got me, one," called Gibbie, as he disappeared entirely from view. That was the last that was ever seen or heard of Gibbie or the heifer.

2. Before railroads were built in Virginia, goods were carried from one inland town to another on wagons. There were a great many men who did this kind of work from one end of the year to the other. One of them, "Uncle Jeter," tells the following story.

A number of wagons were traveling together one afternoon in December. It was extremely cold and about the middle of the afternoon began to snow. They soon came to an abandoned settlement by the roadside, and decided it would be a good place to camp out of the storm, as there were stalls for their horses and an old dwelling house in which they, themselves, could stay. When they had nearly finished unhooking their horses a man came along and said that he was the owner of the place and that the men were welcome to stay there as long as they wanted to, but that the house was haunted, and not a single person had staid in it alive for twenty-five years. On hearing this the men immediately moved their camp to a body of woods about one-half mile further up the road. One of them whose name was Tabb, and who was braver than the rest, said that he was not afraid of haunts, and that he did not mean to take himself and horses into the woods to perish in the snow, but that he'd stay where he was.

So Tabb staid in the house. He built a big fire, cooked and ate his supper, and rested well through the night without being disturbed. About day-break he awoke and said, "What fools those other fellows are to have staid in the woods when they might have staid in here, and have been as warm as I am." Just as he had finished speaking he looked up to the ceiling, and there was a large man dressed in white clothes just stretched out under the ceiling and sticking up to it. Before he could get from under the man, the man fell right down upon him, and then commenced a great tussel between Tabb and the man. They made so much noise that the men in the woods heard it and ran to see what was going on. When they looked in at the window and saw the struggle, first Tabb was on top and then the other man. One of them cried, "Hold him, Tabb, hold him!" "You can bet your soul I got him," said Tabb. Soon the man got Tabb out of the window. "Hold him Tabb, hold him," one of the men shouted. "You can bet your life I got him," came from Tabb. Soon the man got Tabb upon the roof of the house. "Hold him, Tabb, hold him," said one of the men. "You can bet your boots I got him," answered Tabb. Finally the man got Tabb up off the roof into the air. "Hold him, Tabb, hold him," shouted one of the men. "I got him and he got me, too," said Tabb. The man, which was a ghost, carried Tabb straight up into the air until they were both out of sight. Nothing was ever seen of him again.

HAUNTED HOUSE, BURIED TREASURE, THE SIX WITCHES

Journal of American Folklore 35 (1922), 289, 290–91, 286–87

For a special issue of the Journal of American Folklore, *Elsie Clews Parsons and Alice Bacon included tales like the ones below about haunted houses, buried treasure, and witchcraft. In the last of the trio of tales, the theme of levitation is sounded once again, with witches who sing a siren song.*

HAUNTED HOUSE

There was a traveling preacher who was looking for a place to stay just for one night. He went to a very rich family and ask them, if they had room, would they let him stay until morning. They told him that they did not have a room there, but there was an old house that sat over there in the field, it was very haunty, and "If you can stay, you are welcome to it, for several men have been there, but did not come out again." The preacher went over there to the old house, opened the door, and went upstairs, made himself a good fire in the fireplace, and sat there reading his Bible until twelve o'clock. He heard the dishes and pans rattling, and the chairs moving about, and some one scuffling around the floor. He said to himself, "I did not know that there were another family in here." He did not pay any attention to that, he went on reading his Bible. After a while he heard some one come scuffling up the stairs. They said to him, "Mr. White said come down and have supper."—"Tell him that I am not at all hungry, I have just been to supper." The second time he sent a cat. It scratched on the door and said, "Mr. White says please come down and have supper."—"Tell him that I do not care for anything. I have just been to supper." The third time he said, "Mr. White says, if you don't come down, you wish you had." The preacher began to feel frighten', and said, "I will be down there in a minute." The preacher went down there to supper. There was a table all set with pretty dishes and plenty to eat. All the chairs around the table were filled with people except one, and that was for the preacher. When he sat down, they ask him if he would bless the table. He said, "Yes, I will." This is the blessing that he said: "Good Lord, make us thankful for what we are about to receive, for Christ sake. Amen." When he raised his head up, everybody was gone, and he was left there in the dark. He had to feel his way back up to his room. This was the only man ever lived there that did not get killed or ran away before morning. The next morning the preacher left the house, and thanked the people for letting him stay there.

Written by ELSIE JOHNSON.

HAUNTED HOUSE

Once upon a time was a family of people who were different from all the people around them. They had very nice stock around them, a large orchard, all kinds of poultry, and a beautiful flower-yard. When one of the family died, they that remained buried the one that was dead. When all of them died but one, he became very lonely and died very soon. There was not any one to bury him, so he lay on his bed and decayed. After his death the house was said to be haunted, and no one could go inside of it. The next year after the last one of this family died, the fruit-trees bore a tremendous quantity of fruit but no one came to get it.

When people rode along the road which was near the house, they were often tempted to take some of the fruit that hung over the road; but when they put their hands to get the fruit, some one would speak to them and frighten them, so that they would forget the fruit. One day an old man who was a thief came by the house, and saw all the fruit and the poultry, and a large number of eggs lying under the flowers. He asked the people around why they did not get some of those things that were wasting there. The people answered by telling him if he could get any of them, he might have them. "Very well," replied the old man, "I will have some of those things before I sleep tonight." So he laid his coat that had his arms down just a little ways from the house, and stopped there until night came. As soon as it was a little dark, the man arose and went inside of the orchard, and tied eight hens which were up a large apple-tree to roost. When he had tied the eight, he discovered a light somewhere, he did not know where. He looked down on the ground, and there were two large dogs with lamps on their heads, which were giving him a good light. When he saw this, he became so frightened that he turned the hens loose and fell backwards out of the tree. The dogs jumped after him just as soon as he got to the ground. The man jumped up and began to run as fast as he could, with the dogs right behind him. His home was about four miles, and he ran every step of it. When he got to his house, he fell in the door speechless, and lay speechless for a long time. When he came to his senses, he told his wife and family about what had happened to him. After that there was not a man in the community that was any more honest than he was. He had been a rogue all of his life up to this time. After this happened he always worked for what he got.

Informant, DUNCAN. *Recorded by* A. M. BACON.

BURIED TREASURE

It is said once a very rich man died, and his store was haunted; and his brother wanted some one to stay there at night, but everybody was afraid. Then he said that he would give fifty dollars to any man to stay there one night. A doctor said that he would stay there that night; and he went in and closed the door, and took his newspaper to read. Now everybody was quiet, and he was reading away, he heard something walking on the doorsteps. Then he raised up his head, and the door flew open and in came a cow with no head; and he jumped up and ran out the other door. When the owner of the store heard this, he said, "I will give five hundred dollars to any one that will stay here the next night." Then a preacher said, "I will stay"; and the preacher went in and closed the door, and took his Bible to read. He said to himself, "I will go upstairs," and away he went. When all the town was still, he heard something coming in; he read on, then he heard it coming upstairs; read on, it came to him; then he looked up and saw four men without a head, with a coffin. Brought it to him, sat it down, and started toward him. The preacher left, and told the news; and when the owner heard this, he said, "I will give five thousand dollars to any one that will stay here one night." Then a poor man said, "I will stay." He went in and closed the door, and in a few minutes he heard something coming in at the door. He was very much afraid; but he said, "I will not run, but I will ask it what it wants here." At this moment the door flew open, and in came a man without head and arms. The poor man said, "What do you want here?" Then he said, "That is what I have been coming here for, for some one to ask me that. Sir, my money is down the hill; and if you come with me, I will show it to you, and you may have two thousand dollars of it, and I want you to divide the rest with my brothers." And he did so.

Informant, JONAS MCPHERSON. *Recorded by* A. M. BACON.

THE SIX WITCHES

Once upon a time there was a house which was scarcely noticed, that stood just outside of a very famous little village. In this house lived an old lady and her five daughters. The house looked terribly bad outside; but if any one had gone inside of it, they would have found it very different from the outside. The old lady and her five daughters were witches, and it is said that they got all they wanted from the village stores. One afternoon two travelers happened by this house just about sunset, and asked if they might stay all night. The old lady told them they could if they would be satisfied with the place she would give them, as she was not a rich person. The men told her it was all right, just so they were not out of doors. She asked them to come and sit down, she would have them something to eat in a few minutes. So she did. And the two men ate, and then went to bed very soon, for they were very tired from walking so hard. One of them went to sleep very soon after he got into bed; but the other one would not go to sleep, because he thought the old lady and her daughters were up to something. Just as soon as the old lady and her family thought the men were asleep, they reached up the chimney and (each) got an old greasy horn, and put it to their mouths, then said a few words, and was gone. The man that was not asleep grew very much frightened for a while, but soon got over it. As soon as he got over his fright, he got up and put on his clothes, and looked for the horns that the old lady and the five daughters used. He succeeded in finding the horns[1] up the chimney. And as soon as he got them, he put one of them in his mouth and said a few words,[2] and out he went. When he stopped, he was in a man's store in the village, where he found, to his surprise, the old lady and her daughters. He did not know how he got in the store; so he went up to the old lady and began to talk with her, but she gave him no answer. The old lady looked at her daughters, and said a few words which the man could not understand; and out they went, and left the man alone in the store. The man said as near as he could the same things that the old lady said, but could not get out. He would rise up as far as the ceiling of the store and strike his head, but could not get out. When day came, the poor man was so afraid, that he did not know what to do. The clerk of the store came down very soon, and unlocked the door. "I have been missing things out of my store for a long time," replied the clerk, thinking that the man had hidden himself in the store before he closed it the night before. "Oh, no!" replied the man. "If you will allow me a chance, I will tell you just how I happened to be here." So he told the clerk all about it, and also took the clerk to the old lady's house, where his partner was. When the clerk entered the old lady's house, he saw several things that he knew he had in his store and had missed them. So he went back to the village, and sent the sheriff after the old lady and her daughters, and let the man go free. When the old lady and her daughters were brought to trial, they were guarded; and when they got ready to pass the sentence on them, they began to sing a little song, which every one wanted to hear. They sang for about fifteen minutes; and as they sang, they began to move directly upwards until they got so far up in the air that a person could hardly see them, and then disappeared. Those that were guards began to quarrel with each other because one did not shoot and the other did not shoot. So they got mad, and began shooting each other.

Written in 1903 by W. S. BURRELL. *Recorded by* A. M. BACON.

1. *Variant*: Gourd.

2. *Variant*: "Flute, I'm gone." The other witches respond, "I'm after you."

THE WITCH CATS

Southern Workman 24 (1895), 49–50

THE WITCH CATS

There was an old grist mill, used by witches for a meeting place. Some thought it was haunted; no one could spend the night there; one after another tried but disappeared before morning. Finally an old preacher offered to try, a slave of the owner of the mill, who promised the man his freedom if he succeeded. He took his Bible and a sword and went to the mill early in the evening. He built a fire on the hearth, placed a lighted candle on the table and sat down to read his Bible. At twelve o'clock a spotted cat came in through the cat hole and lay down by the fire. It was a rainy night, and the water from the cat's body, as it lay before the fire came near putting the fire out, but the old preacher built it up again before it was quite extinguished. After the cat had departed quite dried before the blaze, immediately a second cat appeared, a yellow one even wetter than the first, and lay down and dried itself, but this time the fire grew very low indeed before the cat departed. Again the old man replenished it, and again it was nearly extinguished by a third cat that came and went like its predecessors. A fourth and fifth followed, no two alike among the strange visitors; finally a sixth entered, a coal black animal with water running from its fur in such streams as to put out the fire completely, leaving the poor old man too frightened to rekindle it and not knowing what might happen next. A few minutes passed and then a snow white cat entered, and walking to the hearth, looked at the dead fire and then at the terrified preacher. Then she leaped lightly on the table and lifted one paw toward the candle, when suddenly the old man raised his sword and with one blow struck off the paw. The cat jumped down and ran whimpering away. The rest of the night passed quietly enough but just after sunrise the old man, glancing at the table was horrified to see that the paw of the white cat was gone and in its place was a human finger with a gold ring on it. Presently the master appeared, to find out what had happened to the old slave, and when the preacher told the tale of the night's adventure and at its close showed him the finger with the ring, the master recognized the finger, but told the old man, to say nothing about the matter, and took the finger home. He found his wife sick in bed, and this strengthened his suspicions, which soon became certainty when he saw that one of her fingers was missing. After that the mill was no longer haunted, for with the discovery the nightly gathering of the witch cats had been broken up.

THE BOY AND THE GHOST

Southern Workman 27 (1897), 57

THE BOY AND THE GHOST

Once there was a very rich family of people and they all died. Everybody was afraid to go there. Finally someone set up a sign board which said "Anyone who will go to this house and stay over night can have the house and all that is in it."

A poor boy came along and read it. "I will go," he said, and he went at sunset. He found all he wanted and went to work to cook his supper. Just as he was ready to eat it he heard a voice from the top of the chimney. He looked up and saw a leg. The leg said, "I am going to drop." "I don't keer," said the boy, "jes' so's you don' drap in my soup."

The leg jumped down on a chair, and another leg came and said, "I am going to drop." "I don't keer," said the boy, "jes' so's you don' drap in my soup."

The leg jumped down on a chair, and another leg came and said, "I am going to drop." "I don't keer," said the boy, "so you don' drap in my soup." One after another all the members of a man came down in this way.

The little boy said, "Will you have some supper? Will you have some supper?" They gave him no answer. "Oh," said the little boy, "I save my supper and manners too." He ate his supper and made up his bed. "Will you have some bedroom? Will you have some bedroom?" said the little boy. No answer. "Oh," said the little boy, "I save my bedroom and my manners too," and he went to bed.

Soon after he went to bed, the legs pulled him under the house and showed him a chest of money. The little boy grew rich and married.

MR. CLAYTOR'S STORY *AND*
MRS. SPENNIE'S STORY

Southern Workman 23 (1894), 179–80

Both raconteurs remind their audiences that there is more to folklore than animal stories. A note appended to the two tales points out that it is impossible to reproduce the "dialect and intonations" that made the narratives "unique specimens."

MR. CLAYTOR'S STORY

"As I have been sitting here listening to these other stories, quite a collection of stories have come back to me that I had once known and almost forgotten. As you have already had stories concerning animals you will be interested, I think, in one of a different nature.

"I remember hearing my mother tell the story of a man who seemed to be in a bad way. Once upon a time he went out hunting. While he was out hunting some one invited him into his house.

"So he went with that person, who seemed in some way unnatural, and when he got to the place it didn't seem like a real place, but when he got there this strange person showed him everything in the house, there were many things and lots of money.

"The man had told him he would give him money if he would go to his home. So he gave him some money, and when he had spent it he felt in his pocket, and found he had the same money.

"The spirit said before he left 'Don't you want to live with me?' The man said, 'no, not now.' 'Would you like to come back in seven years from to-day?' 'I don't know.' 'Well I think you must come in seven years.'

"After he got home he half forgot about it and yet it seemed as if he had a feeling that he still owed something to that man. At the end of seven years, this boy said to his mother, 'don't you see those large cats?' 'No; I don't see them,' his mother said, 'make them go away!'

"'They are just as black as a coal but their eyes sparkle like fire! Can't you drive them out and make them go away?' he said. But his mother couldn't see them. Finally he said 'Don't you remember I promised a man I would go with him after seven years, now he is going to take me?' Then he screamed and said the cats had jumped on him. The people in the room could see where the cats scratched him but couldn't see the cats. Finally he went off no one knew where he had gone, but they thought the devil got him."

The next story teller was Mrs. Spennie of the Hampton Folk-Lore Society.

MRS. SPENNIE'S STORY

There have been so many animal stories that I will tell you one about an old man who was very disfigured and who had all kinds of marks on his face. Once we children asked him to tell us why he was so ugly. "None of your business," he said at first, but after awhile he called us to him and said, "I tell you children what made me so ugly. Once on a time long ago, I was a mighty bad boy. I remember one night when I was livin' in de country I went to town. I had mighty good time, as I allus did and was late gittin' home. It was awful late, de road was dark and lonely an' I was a leedle scared, but I had to be home early in de mornin' to work. I knowed men's sperits walk round about that time an' hour. I felt a little uneasy as if things warent jes rite. Pretty soon I stumbled around something small. I looked around and saw a little cat. I swore at it and kicked it. Then that cat got mad and in a minute it grew to be as big as a dozen cats. Children, ye better believe me! I never seed anything to grow quite so fast as that thing did in all my life. I didn't think to ask 'In de name of the Father, Son an' Holy Ghos' wa't de yer want?' but I went to cussin at it jess as hard as I could; dat made de thing madder an' it began to grow bigger still. I began to feel pretty scared an' as I turned to cut an' run, dat thing got me down and broke dis arm, and broke dis leg, an' made dis yer mark yee an' scratched my face an' when I got home in de mornin' my ole master said I'd had a pretty big frolic.

"Now, I tells yur chillen, if yes ever out at night an' meets any strange thing be sure to say, 'In the name of the Father, Son and Holy Ghos', what you want,' else you get disfigured jest as I is."

PLAYING GODFATHER, FLOWER OF DEW, *AND* SOUL OR SOLE

Journal of American Folklore 35 (1922), 325–27

Alice Bacon and Elsie Clews Parsons contributed the story about Sister Weasel, which had been told to them by Gladys Stewart from Phoebus, Virginia. The "Flower of Dew," recorded by Alice Bacon, closely resembles "Jorinde and Joringel," a tale in the Brothers Grimm collection. And "Soul or Sole," written down by William Herbert, is a reminder of how word play is an important feature of folklore

PLAYING GODFATHER
(Version b)

One day Bro' 'Possum gathered a large kittle of pease and put them in a kittle to cook. In the meantime he ask' Sister Weasel to come over and help him work in the garden and have dinner with him. Sister Weasel came; and, as she couldn't leave her three little babies home, she brought them along, too.

Bro' 'Possum had told Sister Weasel abou' the pease he had on cooking; and the whole time she was working, she was thinking of how she could get into the house to eat them befo' Bro' 'Possum did. At last the thought came to her mind that she would tell Bro' 'Possum to let her go into the house to name one of her babies. When she thought the pease were done, she said, "Bro' 'Possum, got to go into de house to name one ob my babies. Won't be gone long."—"All right, Sis' Weasel! Don't stay long!"

Sister Weasel went into the house, and found the pease nice and done. So she ate the top off and ran back to work. "What did you name your baby, Sister Weasel?" asked Bro' 'Possum. "Top-Off," answered Sister Weasel, working all the time. In a few minutes Sister Weasel felt hungry again; and she said to Bro' 'Possum, "Bro' 'Possum, I got go in and name my second baby,"—"All right, Sister Weasel! but don't stay long!" said Bro' 'Possum.

Sister Weasel went in this time and ate half of the pease. This time, when she came out, Bro' 'Possum asked, "Well, Sister Weasel, what did you name this one?"—"Half-Gone," said Sister Weasel, and away she went chopping in the garden. Pretty soon she felt hungry again; for, once she had tasted those pease, she couldn't stop until she had eaten them. So she said, "Bro' 'Possum, let me go in now and name my last baby, and I won't bother you any more." Bro' 'Possum gave his consent. This time Sister Weasel cleaned the kettle, and came running out agin. "What did you name this baby, Sister Weasel?" asked Bro' 'Possum. "All-Gone," said Sister Weasel, and went hard at her work. Pretty soon Bro' 'Possum noticed that Sister Weasel was getting sluggish on the job, and he thought that she was hungry. So he said, "Come, Sister Weasel, let's eat the kittle of pease, and we will feel more like working."—"All right!" said Sister Weasel. When Bro' 'Possum went into the house and found that the pease had gone, he became very angry, and told Sister Weasel that she had eaten all his pease. "Now, Bro' 'Possum, I haven't eaten your pease," said Sister Weasel. "You have eaten my pease, Sister Weasel, and I am going to eat you for my dinner." When Sister Weasel heard this, she became frightened, for she well knew that Bro' 'Possum would eat her up with little trouble. But what was she to do? Bro' 'Possum's garden, which she loved dearly, was a long ways from the house, but one with a keen eye could see all over the garden. Sister Weasel knew that Bro' 'Possum could not do this, on account of his poor sight. So she said, "O Bro' 'Possum! just look how the Wren children are stealing your crop!" At this Bro' 'Possum forgot all about his pease, an' ran down to his garden. In the mean time Sister Weasel grabbed her babies and ran as fast as she could to the woods and hid. After she got herself hidden, she laughed to herself of how she had fooled Bro' 'Possum.

Written by GLADYS STEWART OF PHOEBUS.

FLOWER OF DEW

Once there was an old woman who staid in the wood. She was a witch. A man and his young wife were out in the woods. The old witch saw the young woman, and she changed her to a nightingale. The man wept a great deal, and he began to seek some way to get his wife. He was out walking, and he found a crimson flower with dew in the middle. He pulled the flower and went to the witch's house, and went to the cage of his wife; and she came out, and they went home.

Recorded by A. M. BACON.

SOUL OR SOLE

Once upon a time there lived a girl. She wanted to know any kind of dance, and sing any kind of song. One day while she was alone, a man stood before her. He said, "You are always thinking about dancing and singing." He said, "If you want to, I will make you so as long as you want to. You must give your soul to my master when your time is up."—"I should like to be with him for twenty-eight years," she said. The time rolled by quickly. When her time was up, she heard a loud noise, saying, "I am coming! I am coming! I am coming after you! According to your word, I am coming after you!" The master had come after her soul. She did not want to give him her real soul. She took up an old shoe-sole and threw it at him. The ugly, man-like thing did not know the difference, and he was contented.

Written by WILLIAM HERBERT.

The Brownies' Book

MARCH, 1920

BROWNIES LAND.

One Dollar and a Half a Year   Fifteen Cents a Copy

This cover illustration by Albert Alex Smith shows a young girl welcomed into "Brownies Land," a fantastical world of gnomes, fairies, sprites, and outsized plant life that served as a visual metaphor for the magazine's content.

PART VIII

FOLKTALES FROM *THE BROWNIES' BOOK*

*T*he Brownies' Book was a monthly magazine that ran from January 1920 until December 1921. It was designed for "the children of the sun," and intended for "all children, but especially for *ours*." The dedication in the first issue read:

> To Children, who with eager look
> Scanned vainly library shelf and nook,
> For History or Song or Story
> That told of Colored Peoples' glory,-
> We dedicate THE BROWNIES' BOOK.

Edited by W. E. B. Du Bois, with assistance from Augustus Granville Dill and Jessie Fauset, the magazine published a rich assemblage of folktales, poetry, stories, games, puzzles, essays, letters, biographies, and photographs for young readers, with a monthly column from Du Bois, "As the Crow flies." It aimed to be "a thing of Joy and Beauty, dealing in Happiness, Laughter and Emulation" for children from the ages of six to sixteen.

The Brownies' Book built on proposals made in an NAACP column written by Carrie W. Clifford and entitled "Our Children." Clifford looked both to the present and past as a source of content. On the one hand, she wanted to publish "stories, drawings, charades, puzzles, etc." from children and grownups, but she was equally invested

W. E. B. Du Bois in the editorial office of *The Crisis*, New York, ca. 1920

in the notion of gathering and preserving "folk-tales of the race" in order to "awaken in the children race consciousness and race pride" (Clifford 1917, 306–7).

What Du Bois wanted above all was a showcase for what he called the "Talented Tenth" (the group of African Americans most gifted and best positioned to serve in leadership positions). *The Brownies' Book* sought to promote racial pride and excellence in education as well as to teach "Universal Love and Brotherhood for all little folk—black and brown and yellow and white." It soon became a venue for publishing the work of children who aspired to be writers. Langston Hughes was a contributor, publishing both fiction and nonfiction in the magazine. *The Brownies' Book* recruited about five thousand subscribers, not enough to enable it to remain financially viable, and the magazine was forced to shut down in 1921.

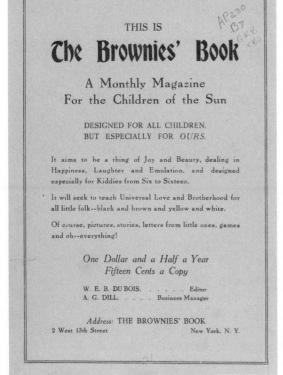

The front covers of *The Brownies' Book* featured images of children with whom readers could identify. The cover of the first issue featured a portrait of a girl in a playful pose taken by Cornelius Marion Battey, head of the Photographic Division at the Tuskegee Institute. Battey's portraits of black activists, scholars, and performers often appeared on the covers of *The Crisis*.

The April 1921 *Brownies' Book* cover is an artistic photographic double portrait of Yvette Keelan, granddaughter of lecturer and activist Mary Burnett Talbert. Talbert hosted the first meeting of the Niagara movement, forerunner of the National Association for the Advancement of Colored People, in her Buffalo, New York, home in 1905.

W. E. B. Du Bois identified the intended audience for *The Brownies' Book* on the inside front cover of the first issue: "Designed for all children, but especially for *ours*."

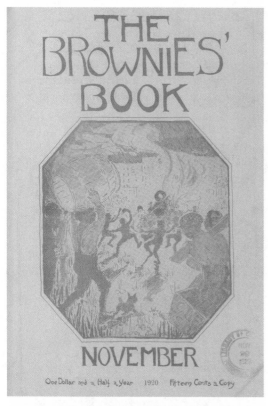

For the November 1920 issue, illustrator Laura Wheeler Waring depicted a lively scene of young people gathering fuel for a celebratory Election Day bonfire.

An illustration by Albert Alex Smith for an Anansi tale in *The Brownies' Book*, March 1920.

Cornelius Marion Battey photographed this scene of Uncle Remus posing with a young boy, which appeared as the frontispiece in the November 1920 issue of *The Brownies' Book*. The camera in the boy's hand suggests an unexpected relationship between the two figures: the boy as photographer, Uncle Remus as his subject.

THE STORY OF "CREASUS"

Told by Katie Jones Harvell

Submitted by a reader of The Brownies' Book, *this tale resonates with European folklore, with its many tales about ogres being outwitted by numbskulls and ne'er-do-wells. Uncle Parker bears a faint resemblance to Uncle Remus, with his expansive narrative tone and willingness to tell tales in exchange for a gourd of water and the promise of cake. But he is also a more erudite figure, one familiar with mythical and biblical figures, with a repertoire of scary stories as well.*

Grandfather was in the yard under a large shade tree, with the back of his old, leather-bottomed chair leaning against the trunk.

"Hello, Uncle Parker," the boys yelled as they came up.

"Howdy, boys, howdy. What does you want today?"

"These boys been tellin' stories," said Frank. "But I tell 'em you're the only one can tell tales."

"That's right, tell us a sho' 'nough tale, Uncle Parker," said Bob.

"Yes, tell us a tale," they all said as they drew closer to Uncle Parker.

"If you will, I'll git mama to give you a big piece of her chocolate cake tomorrow," Teddy added.

"I know y'all wants water, so run ter de well end git yer a cool drink end bring me some; den I guess I'll have ter tell you one."

Off they ran to the well and soon returned with a gourd of water for Uncle Parker. When they had seated themselves around him, he began his story.

"When I'se see folks gwine 'bout in de woods huntin', hit makes me think o' a tale my ol' daddy tol' me way back, fo' de war, 'bout a young man name Creasus.

"You mout heard tell o' dat rich man Creasus, dat libed 'way, long time ago,—'bout ol' King Solomon's time.

"Once Creasus wus po' as Job's turkey—"

"How did he ever git so rich?" Teddy asked.

"Well, ain't I fixin' t' tell you, now?

"Well, in dem days deer skins wus pow'ful high. Now dar wus a forest whar a lot o' deers libed, but witches libed dar, too, and mighty few folks dat went out dar ever got back. Now dis man Creasus wus po' as Job's turkey, is I done fo' said, but he had a mighty big mind; so he got two other men end dey up end went out huntin' deers.

"Dey didn't had no hosses, so dey had ter walk. When dey got dar, dey found mo' deers den dey could shake a stick at. Dey kilt end kilt end kilt, till 'bout dark when hit commenced ter drizzle rain, end dey didn't had no tents ter stay in.

"Dey wus huntin' 'round fer some limbs ter make a bresh house when one o' em found a path end looked 'way up de way hit led end seed a little house wid a light in hit. Creasus 'lowed dat he's gwine ter dat house end ef witches libed dar, he didn't kere, 'cause he ruther stay in a house den out doze, 'cause dat rain wus wet, end cold wid hit. De other two didn't wanter go, but dey seed he wus bent on gwine, so dey went wid him.

"When dey got dar end knocked, a ol' man come ter de do'. Dey told him dey 'stress. He says, 'Mens, dis place 'round my house is a graveyard. I'se sorry I ain't got no room in my house fer you, but I'll give you de keys ter de tool house. Hits got a fireplace and some dry wood end cheers ter set in.'

"Dey took de keys, thanked him, end went down ter de tool house.

"De ol' man walked a piece de way wid 'em end told 'em dat dar wus a ol' 'oman dat wus a witch end dat she loaped 'bout de graveyard ter kill folks end rob 'em, end fer dem ter watch out fer her. When dey got dar, dey put deir skins in a corner end went out ter kill some meat for dey supper.

"De youngest one wus fust ter git back; after he built a fire, he put his rabbit on ter cook; he sot down ter smoke whilse hit cooked. In a few minutes somebuddy knocked at de do'.

"'Who dat?' he asked.

"'I'se a ol' 'oman kotched out in de rain end dark. Kin I stay in dar wid you till mornin'?'

"'You kin come in end wait till de others come, end see whut dey say,' he said, end let her in.

"'You cookin', I see,' she said.

"'Yes'm; me end my two buddies got kotched in de rain, too,' he said.

"'Is you got any salt on yo' meat?' she axed.

"'No'm,' 'lowed de man.

"'I make hit a habit ter ca' salt 'bout wid me,' de 'oman said, as she handed him some salt out a lil' bag she had.

"He tuck his rabbit off, sprinkled de salt on hit, end 'gin ter eat. Two minutes after he tuck de fust swaller, he keeled over end died fum de pisen he done put on his meat.

"She den got offen him whut wus wuf gittin', —got all de deer skins, drug him end tuck other things off end hid 'em,—end come back 'bout time de next man wus cookin' his rabbit. She said perzactly de same things ter him dat she said ter de other fellow, end handed him salt end drug him out de same way.

"By end by, Creasus he come back wid two rabbits, 'cause he wus a mighty big fool 'bout his eatin'.

"He seed de fire end rabbit hair end wonder whar his buddies went after dey et.

"Trectly long come dat same ol' 'oman agin. She knocked.

"'Who dat?' Creasus 'lowed.

"'I'se a po' ol' 'oman kotched out in de rain end dark,' she says. 'Kin I set in dar wid you till daybreak?'

"'Ef yo' face clean, you kin come in; ef it ain't, you kin stay out, 'cause I'se cookin' end don' want no dirty face folks hangin' 'round.'

"She say her face was clean; so he let her in. She wus tryin' ter shiver, makin' out she wus cold. She sot dar a while watchin' him cook end 'lowed,

"'Got any salt on yo' rabbit?'

"'Naw, end don' want none,' Creasus say.

"'Dat rabbit tase mighty good wid salt on hit. I got some. I ca's salt wid me all de time.' She got up end started ter sprinkle some on de rabbits, but Creasus pushed her back end say,

"'I tol' you I didn't want none o' yo' salt; don' you put none on dat meat neither, or I'll split yo' haid open wid my gun. I don' 'low nobody ter fool 'round whut I got ter eat. If you wanter stay in here, set down end 'have yo'self, or I'll kick yer out doze.'

"She went back end set down, but jes' is Creasus turned 'round ter git some bread out his coat pocket, she slipped up end tried ter put salt on de rabbit anyhow; but he wus 'spicious end had kep' his eyes on her, 'cause he thunk she wus de ol' witch 'oman dat sexton tol' him 'bout.

"When he seed her, he wheeled 'round, grabbed up his gun, end knocked her up aginst de wall wid de butt end o' hit.

"She jes' hollered, 'Please don' kill me! Please don' kill me! Would you do a po' 'ol 'oman dis a way?'

"'Naw, I wouldn't. Ef you wus a sho' 'nough 'oman, I wouldn't hit you, but youse a witch end I knows hit and I ain't skeered o' you, neither. You been killin' a heap o' folks, but ter night *you* goter die.'

"'Ef you don' kill me, I won't never bother you no mo' end I give you a magic treasure wot'll help you out in mighty tight places.'

"He ax whut hit was, 'cause ef hit looked lak a bargain ter him, he'd let her off. She tuck a red flannel rag out o' her bosom and showed him a little bottle wid three draps o' water in hit end said, "'Dis is magic water; ef you drap hit on de ground end say, "Grow, water, grow," in two minutes atter, a riber will rise,—so long you can't go 'round hit, so wide you can't swim over, so deep you can't wade across. Den here is a grain o' corn; if you drap hit on de ground end say, "Grow, corn, grow"; a field o' corn will spring up in two minutes,—so long you can't go 'round hit, so thick you can't go through. End here is a clod o' mud; ef you drap hit on de ground end say, "Grow, clay, grow," a mountain will spring up,—so long you can't go 'round hit, so steep you can't climb up hit. Den here is a acorn; ef you drap hit on de ground end say, "Grow, acorn, grow," in two minutes a oak tree will grow dat will mind de one dat planted hit, but nobody else; hit'll do anything you say but git up end walk, 'cause hit can't walk. Now ain't dat wuf havin'?' she say.

"Creasus 'cided he mout make good use o' dat, so tuck de bargain, end let her go."

"I wouldn'ter let her went if I'd been him," interrupted Frank.

"Me neither," Bob said.

"Couldn't she have killed him anyway?" Teddy asked.

"Well, she mout, end agin she mout not, least ways she didn't," Uncle Parker said. "Creasus was a mighty good hand on tellin' de truth, so he didn't kill her lak he promised.

"Nex' morning he found his two buddies behind de house. Him end de sexton dug graves end put 'em in 'em; den Creasus went on feelin' mighty lonesome by hisse'f. By end by he got los' in de thick woods. He kep' blundering 'round till he blundered upon a nother man, los' in de woods lak him. Dey kep' on till dey come to a little house in de woods. When dey knocked, a lil' ol' 'oman come ter de do' end ax' em in. Dey ax her whut road ter take ter git ter de city. She 'lowed dat two o' her sons gwine ter de city in de morning, end dey better spend de night end have company de next day. Dey 'cided ter stay.

"By end by another los' man drapped by, and he 'cided ter stay, too.

"After supper dat night, de ol' 'oman say dey all had ter sleep in de same bed, end her three sons would sleep in de same room in another bed, 'cause she didn't have much room.

"Now when dey went in ter go ter bed, dese men got very 'spicious end 'cided ter change beds; so dey make out de bed wus too soft, end made dem other men change beds wid 'em; but while dey wus changing, Creasus noticed dat dey had red night caps, whilse dem other mens had on green uns.

"When ever'body else wus sleep, he crep' up, he did, end tuck all dey caps off end put 'em on dem other men; den he put de men's caps on 'em. But he wan't saterfied yit; so he woke his mens up, end dey stuffed de pillers in dey caps end put 'em in de bed lak dey was dem; den dey hid in de room, 'cause de do's end windows wus locked end dey couldn't git out.

"Trectly de ol' 'oman eased in, tipped ter de bed whar de green caps wus, end seed dey wus sleep. Den she went ter de bed whar de red caps wus, pulled a great, long knife, dat looked lak a sword, out fum under her apron; den she give one good lick on each neck end whacked 'em clean off. She went den ter t' other bed, shook 'em end say,

"'Git up fum dar, you lazy bones. Do you think I hired you ter lay up end sleep? Well, I didn't. I hired you ter he'p me; so git up end ca' dese mens out o' here.'

"Dey wouldn't git up; so she snatched de cover off ov 'em.

"Lo end come behold, twon't nothin' dar but pillers. She run ter de other bed end seed she done kilt her hired men.

"'Bout dat time Creasus end 'em jumped out on her, end dey had a time, I tell you, tryin' ter tie her; but dey done hit.

"Dey lit in den, sarching de house, Dey found gold, silver, rubies, diamonds, end all kinds o' jewl'ry; deer hides; silk, end a lot o' fine hosses end camels; end mos' ever'thing under de sun dat had any wuf ter hit, end dat didn't had no wuf, 'cause dey found a big graveyard in de garden, wid three open graves made fer 'em.

"Dey got all dey could ca' end put de ol' 'oman in a hole she had made fer 'em; den dey lef' her in dar.

"Fo' dey could git started off wid dey hosses end things, dey spied de ol' witch done got loose, end wus comin' atter 'em. Dey jumped on a hoss end lit out. De 'oman jumped on one end lit out atter 'em.

"Creasus wus leading dat race, bless yo' life. De ol' witch kotched one man and whilse she stopped ter kill him, de others wus makin' time. Trectly she kotched t' other man. Whilse she stopped ter kill him, Creasus wus most nigh flying; but when he looked back, she wus in twenty feet o' him. He thunk he was done fer den, but he jes' thunk o' his lil' red bag. He tuck de grain o' corn out, drapped hit on de ground, end tol' hit ter grow. He felt sompen push him down end shove him on; he thunk sho' de whole jig wus up den, but hit wus jes' de field o' corn pushin' him out de way so hit could grow.

"De witch wus s'prised ter see de corn end tried ter ride through, but hit wus too thick; she tried ter go 'round, but hit wus too long end wide; so she went back home fer er ax ter cut hit down. Whilse she was doing dat, Creasus wus makin' time; but she was pretty swif' end hit didn't take her long.

"Creasus looked back end seed her, 'bout fifteen feet o' him. His heart jumped in his mouf, but he thunk o' his lil' red bag. He drapped—"

"Uncle Parker, how did she cut all dat corn dat quick?" asked Bob.

"She didn't cut 't all,—she had mens ter he'p her, maybe; she jes' cut a path through hit."

"Where did she git the men from?" Teddy asked.

"Look a here, now, if I'se tellin' dis, you let me tell hit, 'dout being pestered. My ol' mammy always teached me not ter cross-talk folks when dey wus talkin', 'specially ol' folks. When my pa wus tellin' me dat story, I sot quiet end lis'ened, end didn't think 'bout sich fool questions; 'sides dat, I wan't dar, end don' know no mo' den he tol' me.

"Is I afo'said,—Creasus drapped de draps er water on de ground end made de riber come. De ol' witch tried ter swim over on her hoss, but hit wus too wide ter swim end too deep ter wade. She tried ter go 'round, but couldn't find de end, so she went back end got a whole lot o' hosses, cows, end camels ter come drink de water up; den she went on after Creasus.

"When he looked back, he seed her 'bout ten feet o' him, wid her knife drawed back. His hair riz up on his haid, 'cause he wus so tired he couldn't go fas'; but he thunk o' his lil' red bag, end drapped de ball o' mud on de ground.

"De witch throwed de knife at Creasus, but hit stuck in de side o' de mountain dat riz 'tween him end her. She wus mighty s'prised ter see all dem things, but she 'termined she wus gwine ter kill Creasus."

"Wus she de same witch dat wus at de graveyard?" asked Bob.

"Naw," said Uncle Parker; "boy, if I'd axed questions, lak y' all chilluns do now, in my days de ol' folks woulder gin me a lick side my knot; now if you want me ter finish dis, you jes' keep yo' mouf shet.

"Now here's whar I lef off, 'bout when de mountain riz up. Well, she tried ter go over, but hit wus too steep; she tried ter go 'round hit, but couldn't find de end; so she went home, got mens end shovels, end dug a hole through hit.

"When she come out on t' other side, Creasus wus so weak end tired end hongry, end his hoss done died. Dat made him set down ter res', end he hadn't run a bit.

"When he seed her comin', he drapped his acorn on de ground, made de tree grow, end climb up hit. De ol' 'oman come up end ax him fer ter come down, but he say he wan't gwine do hit. She shook de tree, but he wouldn't fall, so she tuck her big ol' knife end commenced chopping on de tree.

"De tree commenced ter shake end de chips begin ter fly. Jes, 'bout time de tree wus ready ter fall, Creasus said,

"'Ol' tree, who made you?'

"De tree said, 'Creasus.'

"'Well, obey Creasus, chips, end fly back ter yo' places,' de man said.

"De witch wus mighty s'prised ter see de chips jump up offer de ground end git back in de tree, jes' lak dey ain't been cut. She cut hit some two er three times, but ever time Creasus made de chips fly back ter dey places.

Illustration by Laura Wheeler Waring for "The Story of Creasus." *The Brownies' Book*, February 1920.

"De ol' witch got so mad she begin ter throw rocks up de tree, but de leaves wus so thick she couldn't hit Creasus; den she lit in cuttin' agin: when she cut till de tree wus mos' ready ter fall. Creasus said,

"'Ol' tree, who made you?'

"'Creasus,' de tree said.

"'Well, I want you ter fall, end fall on de one dat chopped you down.'

"When de witch heard dat, she broke end run; but de tip top o' de tree kotched her end fell right on her neck.

"De fall didn't hurt Creasus much, 'cause de leaves end limbs made de fall kind o' easy. Creasus scrambled out from 'mong de limbs right quick, grabbed up de big knife, pulled de limbs back so he could find de ol' 'oman, den he whacked her haid off. Creasus waited end seed dat she wus sho' 'nough dead, den he got on her hoss end rid back ter her house.

"When de mens dar seed him comin' on de ol' witch's hoss dey knowed dat she must be dead; so dey all lit out, for fear Creasus mout kill 'em.

"Creasus had de whole house ter hisse'f den, so he went ter huntin' end ramblin'. He brung out ever'thing he wanted ter eat or ca' off. He loaded de fine hosses end mules end camels wid finery, put em in de road, end started off drivin' 'em lak folks drive a herd o' cattle. He didn't know de way ter de city, but he knowed dat road led ter somewhar, so he jes' went on.

"Hit wus way atter de full moon done sot when 'bout daybreak, Creasus seed dat he done come ter a city. He looked all about him, end nearly shouted when he found out dat he wus in de city whar he lived.

"Atter a few days Creasus moved fum dat little house, he been livin' in, ter a big, fine house wid big barns end stables, end nobody in de world, at dat time, had much is Creasus."

Uncle Parker locked his hands behind his head and leaned back in his chair as he finished his story.

"Dat's all I know 'bout Creasus end his richness, boys."

The boys moved about, stretched their tired limbs, and rubbed their sleepy eyes.

"Is that the truth?" asked Teddy.

"I don' know; my pa tol' me. I wan't dar when hit happened."

"Tell us another, please," said Bob.

Full-page photograph accompanying "The Story of 'Creasus'" capturing story hour at a library in Tennessee and showing how the tales in *The Brownies' Book* were used. *The Brownies' Book*, February 1920.

"Now hit's gittin' dark, end you lil' boys better run 'long home, fo' yo' ma's be callen' er sendin' fo' you. I mout tell you one tomorrow night or evenin', ef I feels lak hit."

The boys obeyed and began to get their hats and buckets.

"What will the other one be about?" James asked as he started off.

"Lemme see," said Uncle Parker, as he rubbed his hand across his face.

"Well, 'bout Jack o' Lantern, I reckon."

THE TWIN HEROES

An African Myth
adapted by Alphonso O. Stafford

In that far-off time when the world was young, there lived in a town of a powerful king, a widow whose name was Isokah, and whose husband, a brave warrior, had fallen in battle.

She had two baby sons, called Mansur and Luembur. They were twins, with bodies round and shapely, the color of dull gold. At their birth an old man, known for his gift of prophecy, had said, "Twins are a gift of Anambia, the Great Spirit, and they have been sent to us for a special work."

Everyone in that town, knowing how true were the sayings of the old man, believed thereafter that the twin babes of Isokah would grow into manhood and become warriors of note and possibly heroes of great renown.

When they were six weeks old, their mother planted in her garden, a short distance apart, two seeds. With great care she watered the earth about and when the seeds sprouted and became tiny plants, her care for them did not cease.

As the years passed, Isokah's two sons grew tall, strong, and pleasing to the eye, like the graceful pine trees around their home. In play, in the hunt, and in deeds of daring, these two boys always took first place among their companions. Meanwhile, the two plants grew into fine trees with beautiful spreading foliage. When Mansur and Luembur were old enough to understand, Isokah took each of them to one of the trees, and said,

"This, my son, is your life tree. As it thrives, withers, or dies, so you will grow, be in peril, or perish."

After that day, Mansur and Luembur [each] watched his own tree with increasing interest and felt for it a loving tenderness when resting under its spreading branches during the heat of the day, or in the cool of the evening, while listening to the strange cries in the jungle; or gazing with wonder at the clear sky with its brilliant stars, and the silver crescent changing nightly into a great golden ball.

How happy was Isokah as she watched her boys grow into early manhood, and the life trees thrive in strength and beauty with them.

During this time, Mansur had many strange dreams—dreams of great perils in the jungle, dreams of different lands—but more often he had visions of Yuah, the daughter of Zambay, who was Old Mother Earth, the first daughter of the first father.

Yuah was said to be beautiful. Her beauty was like the dusk at twilight, when the stars begin to twinkle in the afterglow of the Western sky.

One day, after Mansur had passed his twentieth year, he said to his mother, "The time has come for me to marry and I am going in search of Yuah, the daughter of Old Mother Earth."

Though her sorrow was great when she heard these words, Isokah knew that she could not always keep her son near her. So she called upon Muzimu, a wizard of strange power, and asked him for some magic to help her son, Mansur, in his quest.

When this was given, she returned and gave it to him, saying, "My son, this is your magic. I shall guard your life tree while you are away and Luembur, your brother, will watch over me."

Mansur then put his strong arms around his mother's shoulders, bowed his head upon her cheek, and gave her his farewell kiss. Then, taking from her the magic, he touched some grass he had plucked from the ground. One blade was changed into a horn, another into a knife, and still another into a spear.

Before leaving, he called Luembur, saying, "Brother, be ever near mother Isokah, and let no harm befall her."

For days and days Mansur travelled. What a picture of natural beauty met his eye everywhere! How verdant was the foliage of the trees, shrubs, and plants of the African plains and highlands; how sparkling the streams that foamed over rocky beds of granite and sandstone, how beautiful was the coloring of the flowers, how gay was the plumage of the birds, how graceful and striking in size were the animals that fled before him as he pushed his way onward to the land of Zambay, the mother of his desired Yuah. When overcome by hunger, Mansur called upon his magic for food.

At last, the far country of Zambay was reached. Whenever a stranger entered it, he was escorted at once to Zambay, the queen, the all powerful ruler of that land. The usual custom followed, when Mansur was seen striding forward with his spear in hand, horn across shoulder, and knife at side.

Standing near her mother, Yuah saw the stranger—saw him in his strength and in his early manhood, so lithe in movement and so fearless in bearing. Straightway her heart warmed to him. How happy was Mansur when he beheld this dream-girl as a reality and saw in her eyes, a look of friendly interest that passed into admiration when he recited the story of his travels and the purpose of his visit.

Three days later, they were married. A fine feast was held, followed by joyous singing and a merry dance. The finest house in the town was given to the bride and groom, where for many months their happiness was complete.

One day, while idling in his new home, Mansur opened the door of a strange room which he had never noticed. In it were many mirrors, each covered so that the glass could not be seen. Calling Yuah, he asked her to remove the covers so that he might examine them. She took him to one, uncovered it, and Mansur immediately saw a perfect likeness of his native town; then to another, and he saw his mother and his brother, Luembur, sitting in peace beneath his life tree. In each mirror he saw something that carried his memory back to his past life and the country of his birth.

Coming to the last mirror, larger than the others, Mansur was filled with a strange foreboding. Yuah did not uncover it. "Why not let me look into it, Yuah?" asked Mansur.

"Because, my beloved one, in it you will see reflected the land of Never Return—from it none returns who wanders there."

Now this remark made Mansur very curious, and he longed, as never before, to see this mirror that would picture so strange a land or so mysterious a scene.

"Do let me see it," urged Mansur. Yielding at last to his entreaties, Yuah uncovered the mirror, and her young husband saw reflected therein that dread land of the lower world—that unsought place of cruel King Kalungo, of which all men had heard. Mansur looked in the mirror a long time, then he said,

"I must go there; I must leave you, my dear."

"Nay, you will never return; please do not go, my beloved one," pleaded Yuah.

"Have no fear," answered Mansur. "The magic of Muzimu will be my protection. Should any harm befall me, my twin brother, Luembur, will come to my rescue."

Now this made Yuah cry and she was very, very sad, but her tears did not move Mansur from his desire and his purpose.

In a few hours he had departed for the Land of Never Return.

After travelling many days, Mansur came upon a weird old woman working in the fields. In her eyes, there was mystery; in her presence, there came to him a feeling of awe. Though he knew not then, she was the never sleeping spirit that guarded the secrets of the Land of Never Return.

Approaching her, Mansur said, "My good woman, please show me the road to the land whence no man returns who wanders there."

The old woman, pausing in her work, looked at him as he stood there, so tall and straight. A smile passed over her wrinkled face as she recognized in Mansur one of the true heroes for whose coming she had waited many years.

Much to his surprise, the old woman, after a long and deep gaze, said, "Mansur. I know you and I shall direct your way, though the task before you is one of peril. Go down that hill to your right, take the narrow path, and avoid the wide one. After an hour's travel, you will come to the dread home of Kalungo, the Land of Never Return. Before reaching his abode, you must pass a fierce dog that guards his gate, fight the great serpent of seven heads within the courtyard, and destroy the mighty crocodile that sleeps in the pool."

These impending dangers did not frighten Mansur. Following the narrow path, he came within a short time to a deep ravine. Through this he walked, head erect, eyes alert, and spear uplifted. Suddenly he observed the outer gate of the Land of Never Return.

By means of his magic, he passed the fierce dog, and after a severe battle he succeeded in destroying the serpent, that seven-headed monster. Near the pool, he saw the mighty crocodile resting on its bank, and rushed forward to strike him. Then, by accident, Mansur's magic fell upon the ground, and immediately he was seized by the crocodile and disappeared within his terrible mouth.

At home, his mother, Isokah, and brother, Luembur, noticed with fear that the life tree of Mansur had suddenly withered.

"Mother, my brother is in danger. I must go at once in search of him," cried Luembur.

Rushing to Muzimu, the wizard, Isokah procured some more magic, returned home and gave it to Luembur and besought him to go immediately in search of his twin brother.

As he departed, a great weakness seized her, and supporting herself for a while against the trunk of Luembur's life tree, she slowly sank to the ground, with a foreboding that she would never again see her sons.

When Luembur reached the town of Zambay, Yuah was much struck with the resemblance he bore to his brother, and she was overjoyed that he had come to go in search of Mansur. She noticed with pleasure that Luembur also carried the same kind of spear, horn, and knife that Mansur had.

Yuah showed him the magic mirrors, reserving for the last the fateful one that had caused Mansur to depart for the Land of Never Return.

After resting awhile, Luembur continued his journey and, as in the case of his brother, came after many days to the weird old woman working in the fields.

The story of his quest was soon told. After it was finished, she said, "I know you, also, Luembur." She then gave him the same directions.

When he reached the gates of the Land of Kalungo, the fierce dog fell before the magic spear of Luembur. Then rushing to the bank of the pool where the mighty crocodile was dozing in the sun, Luembur with one great blow of his spear slew him. Then taking his knife he cut along the under side of the dead crocodile and, strange to state, Mansur jumped out, well and happy.

Swift as the wind, the twin brothers left the gates of the dread Land of Never Return and travelled upward to the place where the weird old woman worked in the field, under the rays of the glinting sun.

When she beheld them, she stood erect, a deeper mystery flashed into her age-old eyes, and in her presence, there returned to the brothers, that same feeling of awe, but now more intense.

Finally she spoke, "Brothers, by slaying the fierce dog, the terrible serpent, and the mighty crocodile, you have released the spirits of the brave, the wise, and the good, who were prisoners in the realm of cruel Kalungo. They may now return to Mother Earth when they desire, and visit the abode of their mortal existence. Your task here below is now finished.

"You, Mansur, shall be Lightning, that mortals may ever see your swift spear as it darts through the clouds; and you, Luembur, shall be Thunder, that mortals may ever hear and know the power of that flashing spear."

With these words, the sleepless spirit of the Land of Never Return touched each of the brothers, and Mansur went to the East and became the swift, darting lightning; and Luembur went to the West and became the loud, pealing thunder.

In the land of Zambay, when Yuah, through her magic mirror, saw what had happened to the brothers, she cried with much grief. Neither by day nor by night would she be comforted.

At last her mother, Zambay, said in a gentle and sad voice, "My daughter, when your husband, Mansur, and his brother, Luembur, are angry in their home, amid the clouds, and have frightened men and beasts, here in my land, your beauty and your smile will

Illustration by Albert Alex Smith for "The Twin Heroes: An African Myth." *The Brownies' Book*, April 1920.

bring them joy. At such times, your body clothed with many colors, will bend and touch me, your Mother Earth. Go hence, and live with them."

With these words, Yuah went away from the home of her mother, and we see her now as the beautiful Rainbow, after the storm clouds of Mansur and Luembur have passed on their way to the home of The All Father, the Great Sky-Spirit, Anambia.

Illustration by Laura Wheeler Waring for "Chronicles of Br'er Rabbit." *The Brownies' Book*, October 1920.

CHRONICLES OF BR'ER RABBIT

Julia Price Burrell

Br'er Rabbit and Br'er Pa'tridge went hunting. They brought in a fine little sheep.

"Now," said Br'er Rabbit, "who will go get some fire to cook our meat?"

"You shall go, for you are larger than I, and you can carry more," declared the little Partridge.

Said Br'er Rabbit, "You shall go, Br'er Pa'tridge, for you can fly more swiftly than I can run, and we will not wait so long for our feast."

Br'er Pa'tridge set off; soon as he was out of sight, Br'er Rabbit fell to work tearing the flesh into pieces convenient for him to carry off—and when Br'er Pa'tridge returned with the fire he found only a few scraggly pieces left. He fairly gasped: "Well! WHERE is our meat, Br'er Rabbit?"

Br'er Rabbit scratched his chin with his right forepaw—he stared hard at the spot where the meat had been—then with a sudden upward jerk of his naughty head he said:

"Why, Br'er Pa'tridge, I just turned my eyes towards a queer sound I heard in yonder brush and 'fore I turned me round again that meat been gone! Oh, what shall we do, Br'er Pa'tridge?"

But without seeming to notice the greedy Rabbit, Br'er Pa'tridge lifted his head and in answer to his call, "Bob-White!" a score of hungry partridges flew to him and they all ate the miserable fragments which Br'er Rabbit had not been able to steal away. As they all flopped over onto the ground, Br'er Pa'tridge cried, "O, Br'er Rabbit, that meat was surely poison. See, all my brothers dying!"

"Poison meat won't do for me!" thought Br'er Rabbit. "Let me go fetch that meat I hid away!" and he bounded over the ground, returning with the tender meat which he had meant to eat alone. When he had brought it all, Br'er Pa'tridge said quietly, "Now, Br'er Rabbit, let's divide equally!"

And they did.

BR'ER RABBIT WINS THE REWARD

Br'er Fox and Br'er Wolf were hired by the King to work in a certain field. Now because the mosquitoes were so many and stung so hard in this hay field the King had had great difficulty in securing workers, so as a spur to the laborers he promised to him who should work longest without heeding the mosquitoes a special reward.

All three, Br'er Rabbit, Br'er Fox, Br'er Wolf, set to work, each determined to win the reward. How those mosquitoes did bite! Every half minute Br'er Wolf stopped to slap one! Every five minutes Br'er Fox stopped to swat at the troublesome pests!

What of Br'er Rabbit? Oh, they were not sparing him either, but that little animal is a "schemy" creature! He worked away, and as he worked he talked. Said he, "My old Dad, he haves a plough horse; he black here and here," and as he said "here" each time he slapped his stinging legs where the mosquitoes were biting—"and," he went on, "he white all here"—slapping again at the enemy!

So he continued talking and slapping and working. It never occurred to the King that Br'er Rabbit was killing mosquitoes. It appeared to those who looked that Br'er Rabbit was not bothered.

He won the reward.

BR'ER RABBIT LEARNS WHAT TROUBLE IS

Br'er Rabbit approached the King. "O, King," he began, "teach me what is trouble. I hear the people talk of trouble, but I have never seen it."

Then the King said thoughtfully, "Br'er Rabbit, if you would always be happy, give up this desire of yours to know trouble—for it brings tears and much weeping. Return to the brier patch and be a good rabbit child."

But Br'er Rabbit was not so to be put off—and seeing that he was determined, the King slowly brought forth a small tightly covered box.

"Do not open it until you have almost reached the further end of the open field near the brier patch. There is trouble in this box," cautioned the King.

"As Br'er Rabbit ran down the path he thought of his box—he ran faster; as his pace increase, so did his curiosity. He paused a second and held the box to his ear—what

Illustration by Laura Wheeler Waring for "The Chronicles of Br'er Rabbit." *The Brownies' Book*, October 1920.

was it he heard? he thought. It must be a baby crying. "Hush, baby!" he said, but as the racket continued he thought he would take just the merest peep inside. He turned just to see if anyone were watching. The King was following him.

"Don't you open that box, Br'er Rabbit!" he cried.

"Oh, no! no! no!" Br'er Rabbit prevaricated. "I just only looked to see how close behind me you were!"

Br'er Rabbit ran on—again he paused to listen—and to peep—again the King shouted and Br'er Rabbit refrained. He had run now as long as he could— his curiosity burned him past endurance. He would raise the top and peep inside so quickly that even the King, as he followed, should not notice. His little paw scarcely moved the cover. Oh, wow! if you will excuse me for saying so. "Br-r-r! Bow-wow-wow-wow!!" and "B-r-r-r!" Two hungry hounds burst out and upon poor little Br'er Rabbit, giving him a pretty chase over the fields until he finally reached the welcome brier-patch, worn and breathless. The dogs did not catch Br'er Rabbit—but to this day just the sight of a dog means *trouble* to Br'er Rabbit.

HOW MR. CROCODILE GOT HIS ROUGH BACK

Julian Elihu Bagley

It was a bleak November afternoon in New York City. To be more exact it was in Harlem. The snow was falling fast, and between the long row of high dwellings on 135th Street thousands of flakes were whirling, swirling about much the same as goose feathers would whirl if dumped from some high building into a rushing wind. The sun had long since hid his face, while the white fleecy clouds of the morning were fast changing into a cold, cold gray. It was too cold for the kiddies to go out. So in the high windows dozens of them could be seen watching the grown-ups hurrying along the street below. Occasionally some one tripped on the sidewalk. Then the youngsters could be seen tumbling back into their houses in an uproar of laughter.

Among these children was a little curly headed boy named Cless. But Cless had a different purpose from the other boys and girls. He was looking for the letter carrier. For every day Cless received some pretty post card from his father who was then working in a hotel at Palm Beach, Florida.

How Mr. Crocodile Got His Rough Back
by
Julian Elihu Bagley

Illustration by Laura Wheeler Waring for "How Mr. Crocodile Got His Rough Back." *The Brownies' Book*, November 1920.

"What will it be today, and why doesn't the mail man come on?" thought Cless. Finally the postman turned into 135th Street and made his way to the entrance of the building in which the little boy lived. Cless ran down to meet him. The postman handed him a card. On one side was Cless' address, on the other a picture of a little colored boy riding a big crocodile. Cless was both disappointed and frightened.

"Oo-ee! what an ugly thing this is," he shouted as he turned and walked into the elevator.

"Let me see?" asked the elevator boy.

Cless handed him the card.

"Sure is ugly! And that's the thing that eats little colored boys. See all them rough bumps on his back? Well, they are the toes of little colored babies sticking up under his skin. That's Mister Crocodile," concluded the elevator boy. "He used to have a smooth back before he began to eat little colored babies, but now it's rough."

Little Cless was very much frightened, and as soon as the elevator reached his floor he dashed out and went running to his apartment crying: "Granny! Granny! oh Granny, look what daddy sent me today—a big ugly crocodile! And I hear he eats little colored babies. Granny, is it true? Is it true, Granny?"

"Why certainly not, Cless. Who in the world told Granny's little man such a story?"

"Elevator boy, Granny—elevator boy," answered little Cless between sobs. And a little later he stopped crying and told his grandmother the story just as the elevator boy had told him.

"It's no such a thing, it's no such a thing," said Granny. "Why don't you know frogs were the real cause of crocodiles having rough backs?"

"How's that, Granny? Please tell me—tell me quick, Granny please," begged little Cless.

"All right, I'll tell you," promised Granny, "for I certainly don't want my little man scared to pieces with such ugly stories." Now little Cless felt relieved. He hopped into Granny's lap, huddled up close to her side and listened to her story of how the crocodile got his rough back.

"A long, long time ago," she said, "in Africa, down on the River Nile there lived a fierce old crocodile. And this was the first crocodile in the world. Before him there was no others. Now this crocodile lived in a cluster of very thick brush, and, although there were many other animals in the swamp larger than he, he was king of them all. Every day some poor creature was seized and crushed to death between this cruel monster's jaws. He was especially fond of frogs and used to crush dozens of them to death every

Illustration by Laura Wheeler Waring for "How Mr. Crocodile Got His Rough Back." *The Brownies' Book*, November 1920.

day. Now the frogs could hop faster than the crocodile could run and he never caught them in a fair race. But he always got the best of them by hiding in the mud until some poor frog came paddling along and then he would nab him and crush him to death between his big saw-teeth. Of course this was easy, for at that time Mister Crocodile had a smooth, black back, and it was so much like the mud that the frogs could never tell where he was.

"But one day a happy thought struck Mister Bull Frog who was king of all the frogs in that swamp. He thought it would be a good idea to pile some lumps of mud on the crocodile's back, and then the frogs could always tell where he was. This plan was gladly accepted by all the frogs in the swamp. So the next time the crocodile crawled into the mud to take his winter nap, Mister Bull Frog and all the other frogs went to the place where the monster lay and daubed a thousand little piles of mud on his back. And when they had finished they could see him from almost any part of the swamp. Now they knew they were safe. How happy they were! They all joined hands, formed a big circle around the sleeping crocodile, and while Mister Bull Frog beat time on his knee the others shouted this jingle so hard that their little throats puffed out like a rubber ball:

"'Ho, Mister Crocodile, king of the Nile,
We got you fixed for a long, long while.
Deedle dum, dum, deedle dum day,
Makes no difference what you say!'

"They shouted this jingle over and over again. And the last time they sang it Mister Bull Frog got so happy he stopped beating time, jumped up in the air, cut a step or two, then joined in the chorus with his big heavy voice:

"'Honkey-tonkey tunk, tunk, tink tunk tunk!
Honkey-tonkey, tunk, tunk, tink tunk tunk!'

"And when all the singing and dancing were over the little frogs went home.

"But Mister Bull Frog chose to stay and watch the crocodile. All winter long the crocodile lay in the mud. Nevertheless the Bull Frog kept close watch over him. Each day the lumps of mud that the frog had stuck on his back were growing harder and harder.

"At last spring came. The sleepy creature awoke and immediately began to shake his back and flop his tail. But the more he did this the madder he became. Finally he was just whirling 'round and 'round in the mud, biting himself on the tail and groaning, 'Honk! honk! honk!' But the lumps of mud had done their work. They were there to stay. And finding it of no use to wiggle he crawled out on the bank of the river and began to look for something to eat. Nothing could be found on the shore, however, so he slipped back into the muddy water to see if he could catch some frogs. In this he failed, for no longer could he hide himself. No matter how much his skin looked like the mud, the little frogs could always tell where he lay by his rough back.

"So ever since that day little frogs have lived in perfect safety along the banks of the River Nile or any other place so far as crocodiles are concerned. And as for Mister Crocodile himself, he has gone on and on even down to this day with his rough scaly back. And this is how he got it, Cless," ended Granny, "and not by eating little colored babies."

Little Cless had followed every word of Granny's with eager interest. Now he smiled a smile of relief, thanked her for the story, jumped from her lap and skipped out to join the happy group of little children who were still peeping into the street from their windows. Here Cless showed his crocodile to as many children as were close enough to see it. And to those who were nearest he told the story over and over again of how the crocodile got his rough back.

The pourquoi *tale told here has a cathartic effect, purging the fears and anxieties of Cless about carnivorous crocodiles. Granny not only creates a new "origins tale" but also stages it in a way that reveals how sharp wits can defeat brute physical strength.*

Illustration by Laura Wheeler Waring for "How Br'er Possum Learned to Play Dead." *The Brownies' Book*, January 1921.

HOW BR'ER POSSUM LEARNED TO PLAY DEAD

Julian Elihu Bagley

Little Cless had just returned to his apartment from an excursion to the famous Bronx Park in New York City. At last his wish to see the many wonderful animals in the zoo had come to pass. But somehow they didn't interest him quite as much as he expected. Perhaps this was due to the fact that there were countless other holiday attractions, or perhaps it was because Granny couldn't go along to tell him the wonderful stories that she knew about them. But this was no grown-ups' outing—this trip. It was a holiday excursion conducted by Cless' teacher—and for kiddies only! So poor Granny had to stay at home. However, as soon as Cless began his dinner he commenced to tell Granny all about the strange animals he had seen at the park. And what do you think he imagined the funniest creature in the whole zoo?—Br'er Possum!

"Oh, Granny! You just ought to see him," shouted Cless. "He's the cutest little thing in the whole zoo. And every time you go near his cage he just stretches out and plays dead. Granny, what makes him do that—was he born that way?"

"Why, of course not, Cless. Haven't you ever heard how Mister Tortoise taught Br'er Possum that trick? Well," added Granny quickly—she knew Cless hadn't heard this tale—"guess I'll have to tell you—but after dinner, honey."

"Now understand, Cless," explained Granny as she began, "this was many years ago, long before you were born—or even Granny. Br'er Possum was living away down in old Virginia in the hollow of a cypress tree in Chuckatuck swamp. And on the side of this same swamp, away down in a dark, crooked hole, there lived Mister Tortoise. Now Br'er Possum was a particular friend of Mister Tortoise, and used to visit him every night to get some of the delicious carrots and beets and turnips that he kept in his hole. This made life very easy for Br'er Possum, so instead of working he just cuddled up in his hollow every day and slept till night. But one day a strange storm blew up. Big, rolling clouds hid the sun and after a while there was a heavy downpour of a mixture of sleet and snow. For three days and three nights this sleet and snow poured down so hard that neither Br'er Possum nor Mister Tortoise could go out.

"Now, Mister Tortoise was all prepared for this weather. He had already stored up his carrots and beets and turnips for his winter food, so the storm only stopped him from going fishing. Br'er Possum was not so lucky. He didn't have one bite in his hollow, so it wasn't long before he began to squeal desperately for something to eat. Naturally, just as soon as the storm lulled he crawled out of his hollow and went dragging over to Mister Tortoise's den to get something. He was hungry and weak and was therefore compelled to travel very slowly, and when he got there Mister Tortoise had just crawled out of his hole and toddled on down to the river a-fishin'. Br'er Possum wondered what to do. Should he go on down to the river and help his friend fish? He thought a while and then decided to go down to the river. But he had not gone long on his way before he met Br'er Fox.

"'Hello there, Br'er Possum,' says Br'er Fox. 'How you do this morning, and where you going so early?'

"Br'er Possum replied that he was feeling pretty hungry and was going to the river to fish with Mister Tortoise, his friend.

"'Why,' says Br'er Fox, 'I've just come from the river a-fishin' with Mister Tortoise myself, and he's caught just one little minnow fish.'

"Then Br'er Fox went on to tell Br'er Possum how Mister Tortoise had been fishing since sunrise and how he had threatened to keep on fishing till sundown if he didn't catch a big fish. Furthermore, he told Br'er Possum that Mister Tortoise had promised him some carrots and beets and turnips if he'd stay and help him fish. 'But,' said he, 'it was too cold down there for me I just couldn't stand it.'

"Nevertheless, he had promised to go back to the river that afternoon and carry Mister Tortoise home on his back. But, of course, he didn't mean to go back to the river at all. What he really meant to do was to find Mister Tortoise's hole and rob it of the carrots and beets and turnips. So after throwing one or two hints at Br'er Possum, Br'er Fox came right out and said: 'Seems like you ought to know where Mister Tortoise lives, Br'er Possum—he's your friend.'

"'I do,' says Br'er Possum.

"'And you claim you pretty hungry?' asked Br'er Fox.

"'Yes, hungry as I can be.'

"'Well, would you listen to a scheme to get something to eat?'

"'Maybe I would,' says Br'er Possum. 'What is it?'

"'Would you go and help me rob Mister Tortoise's hole while he's at the river?'

"'Oh no! no! no!' exclaimed Br'er Possum as he wolloped his big, rough tail on the ground. 'I could never do that. He's my best friend.'

"'But how's he going to know it?' argued Br'er Fox. 'How's he going to know it when he's at the river a-fishin'?'

"Well, Br'er Fox kept on asking this question and saying, 'And yet you claim you so hungry!' till Br'er Possum got the notion of going. So he said, 'Wait here, Br'er Fox, till I go home and get a basket and we'll go and rob Mister Tortoise.'

"Of course, Br'er Fox agreed to wait, so Br'er Possum started off to get the basket. But on his way home he began to think of the many kind things that Mister Tortoise had done for him. Now this worried Br'er Possum so much that before he got to his hollow he had completely changed his mind. So instead of going right back to Br'er Fox with the basket he took a short cut through the swamp to see if Mister Tortoise was still fishing at the river. And sure enough what did he see but a great big tortoise with his head chucked through the ice and his feet away up in the air, just a-going 'flippey-te floppey-te!' He was struggling to catch a fish. Br'er Possum sneaked up behind Mister Tortoise, grabbed him by the hind legs and snatched him out of the ice.

"'Spe—u!' whistled Mister Tortoise as the cold water gushed from his mouth. 'My gracious alive, Br'er Possum, you liked to scared me to death—I thought you were Br'er Fox. Where in the world did you pop up from any way?'

"'Just from Chuckatuck Hill,' says Br'er Possum, 'and I met Br'er Fox up there.'

"'Sure enough!—what did he say?' asked Mister Tortoise.

"'Said he'd been down here a-fishin' with you all morning. Said you'd just caught one little minnow and—!'

"Right here is where Mister Tortoise cut Br'er Possum right short and asked: 'Did he say I promised him something to eat?'

"'Yes,' said Br'er Possum, 'and you better watch him too 'cause he's just been trying to get me to go with him to your hole and steal all you got.'

"'A low-down scamp!' says Mister Tortoise. 'How can we get him, Br'er Possum?'

"'Just you get on my back,' says Br'er Possum, 'and let me take you to your hole. Then I'll go back and get Br'er Fox and bring him there to pretend like I'm going to steal your carrots and beets and turnips, and when he comes down in your hole you just grab him and choke him to death.'

"Now both of them agreed to this trick and as soon as Br'er Possum had gulped down the little fish to give him enough strength to run, he took Mister Tortoise on his back and started to his hole by a round about way through the swamp. In about ten minutes they were home. Mister Tortoise slid off Br'er Possum's back and scrambled on down in his hole to wait for Br'er Fox. Now Br'er Possum started back in the same round about way to meet Br'er Fox. When he got back Br'er Fox was very angry and asked why he had stayed so long. Br'er Possum told him that he couldn't find the basket.

"'Well,' says Br'er Fox to Br'er Possum, 'how come you panting so hard like you been running a long ways?'

"'Oh, that's because I'm hungry,' says Br'er Possum, 'I didn't run a step.'

"'Hush up your mouth, Br'er Possum,' says Br'er Fox, 'didn't I hear you way through the swamp running *bookiter! bookiter! bookiter!* Who you fooling? And how come your breath smells so much like fresh fish?'

"Of course, all this was enough to make Br'er Fox suspicious, but he was so hungry and Br'er Possum played so innocent that he still thought he would take a chance in Mister Tortoise's hole. So the two hungry creatures started out. But as soon as they came to Mister Tortoise's hole and saw all the fresh tracks around it, Br'er Fox balked and declared that he would never take the chance. Well, they stood in front of the hole and fussed and argued, and argued and fussed till Br'er Possum was sure Mister Tortoise heard all they said. Then he hollered right out loud: 'Oh pshaw! Get out the way, Br'er Fox, you too scared to do anything! Get out the way! I'll go down; you stay up here and fill the basket as I bring the food up.'

"To be sure, Br'er Fox didn't object to this, so Br'er Possum crawled into the hole and slid on down to the bottom. Soon as he got down there he met Mister Tortoise and told him that they would have to think up a better trick to catch Br'er Fox.

"'Heard every word you spoke,' said Mister Tortoise. 'Just you leave it to me, and when I tell you to squeal,—*squeal loud*. And when I tell you to lie down and play dead, don't squeal at all!—Do you understand?' Br'er Possum said he did. Now Mister Tortoise grabbed him by the back and pretended that there was a mighty scuffling going on. My, there was such a-squealing and a-squealing and a-grunting and a-groaning that poor Br'er Fox way at the top of the hole was just shaking with fright. Finally there was a sudden hush. Then Mister Tortoise gave Br'er Possum a butcher knife and told him to go over in the corner and lie down just like he was dead. Br'er Possum obeyed. And about that time Br'er Fox thought everything was over, so he poked his head in the hole and hollered: 'Hello there, Mister Tortoise.'

"'Who's that darkening this hole?' says Mister Tortoise.

"'It's me—Br'er Fox—come for the carrots and beets and turnips you promised me this morning at the river.'

"'Oh sure! sure!—come on down,' says Mister Tortoise. 'You're the very one I'm looking for. I've just killed a great big possum. Come on down and help me skin him and I'll give you a piece.'

"Br'er Fox went down and sure enough there was Br'er Possum all stretched out just like he was dead. Now Br'er Fox was just as tickled as he could be. He began to strut about and say, 'Oh, what a fine supper I'll have tonight!' But his fun did not last long, for as soon as he turned his back, Mister Tortoise jumped on him, grabbed him by his throat so he couldn't squeal, and then hollered for Br'er Possum to come with his butcher knife. Br'er Possum came. And while Mister Tortoise held Br'er Fox by his long mouth, Br'er Possum cut Br'er Fox's head clean off. That same night they skinned him and baked him and ate him for their supper. And after supper they talked much of this trick of playing dead. Br'er Possum liked it so well that he took it up, played it once or twice on Br'er Rabbit, and since that day he has played it on everybody but Mister Tortoise."

Granny's tale was finished. She tickled little Cless under his chin and asked him if he thought he could tell the story of how Br'er Possum learned to play dead. He assured her that he could. So now she pressed his little round face close to hers and literally smothered him with soft kisses. Then she slipped him from her lap and told him that he might join the romping holiday kiddies out in the street below.

*Br'er Possum and Br'er Tortoise, accomplices in duplicity and violence,
stand in sharp contrast to Little Cless and Granny, who showers the boy
with affection and seeks to pass on stories from times past, justifying
them as mere fables about the origins of animal practices and craft.*

The Brownies' Book, May 1921.

YADA: A TRUE AFRICAN STORY

Frederica Bado Brown

Kamala hi, Kamala hi,
Yru bah yah, yru,
Kamala wa na gbo ti,
Te ya ya ya!
Te—ya—ya—ya! ! !

As the last sound died away over the sleepy African village, little Yada rose from her position in the doorway of the hut and went out into the night. She was to meet her small playmates at the banana grove near the village when the toot of the horn of the High Priest told them that he had offered up the sacrifices for the night. Little girls and boys were not allowed out of doors during the ceremony.

This was to be her last evening with her friends, for tomorrow the big brown man that lived in the queer circular hut across the road from her house, was to claim her for his wife.

Yada had thought about this thing, in fact she had thought of it lots more than little African girls are supposed to think about anything at all. Somehow it did seem to her that since she had to marry that her parents would have picked out some one more suited to her. She inwardly rebelled, but finally she decided that she need not think any longer, tonight she was going to have her fun, she was going to enjoy this last opportunity for all too soon her childhood was to be taken away from her.

Yet on the way to the grove many things again came into her mind. Did not this man have six wives already? What could possibly be her position in his home? She would certainly have to be the burden-bearer of the household.

What was it that the missionary lady had told them that day she came to the town to read about the funny Jesus-man that loved everyone? That made her think—could she—? But of course that was too silly for her to think of doing. She had never heard of a little African girl rebelling and running away from her fate. But it was nice to think of it even though she knew she could not do it. She could never find her way to the missionary lady, but if she did would they try to get her back and beat her as they had done that time when she refused to bow to the great idol in the temple?

Te—ya—ya—ya!!!

No, she could not do it tonight for the children were having such a nice time and she wanted to join them in their play, but maybe in the morning she could if—in the meantime she must go and play and act as if nothing was happening inside of her, for no one must suspect anything.

Wasn't that funny last night when she had made faces in the dark at the big brown man? He couldn't see very well, but he was sort of nice anyway. He would be lots nicer if he didn't try to be nice. Last night he had brought her some bracelets for her legs, they were very beautiful, they jangled when she walked and all the other girls would be envious of her. She wished that she could take them with her tomorrow, but maybe since she was leaving him she had better not take either that, or the heads and the engagement straw that he had put in her hair, when her parents consented for her to marry him.

The hoot of the owl told her that she would have to hurry as it was getting late. Already her mother was standing in the doorway calling to her.

"Yada, what a strange child you are! Why don't you hurry and meet the children? They are all playing without you," said her mother.

"Yes, mother, I am going now," said Yada.

The next morning as soon as her mother left the hut for the farm and Yada knew that her father had gone to the men's Palaver or Council she stole away in the direction of the big woods.

Fear clutched at her heart, but she remembered that the missionary lady had said that the great God would take care of all the little ones and she was one of those surely. Anyway she would have a whole day's walk ahead of anyone who might follow to take her back to the village.

She thought of the stories that her mother had told of the spirits that lived in the trees, the grass, and the flowers and so she began to talk aloud to them so that they might help her in her journey. She tried to walk around the grass and to keep from plucking the flowers so as not to offend the spirits. She knew all about them. Everything had a spirit and she had only to be real good and they would not harm her. Probably they would forgive her the disgrace that she was bringing on her family, for the whole village would point to them in scorn as people who had failed to keep their promise. Oh well she couldn't help that now she was too far away to turn back, it was too late now to do that; she was going on to the end.

Pretty soon the sun was so hot that it made Yada thirsty and she stopped to look for some water. She found a nice clear spring and she stooped and drank, then she got out her little lunch of cassava and fish and ate. A deer or two came out of the woods to drink, but they became frightened on seeing her and ran away. She was not afraid though for she had seen many wild animals when she went on hunting trips with her father and the men. She nestled down in the hollow place of the tree and thought of home, oh dear she was afraid that she was going to sleep, she hoped that she wasn't, as that would just spoil everything, but how was a little girl going to keep awake—maybe her mother was worrying.

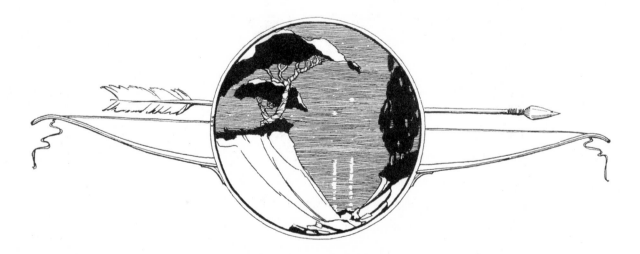

The Brownies' Book, May 1921.

When Yada awoke she found herself on her own little mat in her own little hut and all her own dear folks standing over her. There were mother and father, and the old medicine man of the village who drove away the evil spirits that caused sickness. Maybe she was sick and he was going to stick the red hot needle into her to drive away the pain. It must be nearly time to begin putting on the clay for the marriage ceremony.

But what was that her father was saying to the medicine man? She could just make out. The Big Brown Man-had-been-found-dead-and-he-guess-that-Yada-was-free. Why the spirits had helped her, hadn't they? She was so happy now over the idea of her rescue, she believed that she would go out in the banana grove and play with the children. They were playing the same little game that they had played last night when she joined them, for she could hear one little girl's voice as it led the others in shouting:

Kamala hi, Kamala hi,
Yru bah yah, yru,
Kamala wa na gbo ti,
Te ya ya ya!
Te ya ya ya! ! !

Yada's story provides an interesting mélange of cultural values, with native customs, missionary preachings, medicine men, and High Priests. The placement of the story in The Brownies' Book *comes as something of a surprise, but the editors for the magazine were anything but predictable in their choice of subject matter.*

PART IX

ZORA NEALE HURSTON COLLECTS AFRICAN AMERICAN FOLKLORE

"How *can* any deny themselves the pleasure of my company! It's beyond me," Zora Neale Hurston once declared (Wall 1995, 829). That was not a question but an expression of bewilderment. Growing up in Eatonville, Florida, the fifth in a family of eight children, Hurston lost her mother—the woman who urged her to "jump at de sun"—when she was just thirteen years old. "Bare and boney of comfort and love," she left a home life fractured by the addition of a stepmother who deeply resented her. She made her way into the world, working a series of menial jobs, restarting school, and finally landing at Howard University. She went on to Barnard College, where she was the only African American student ("I am a dark rock surged upon, overswept by a creamy sea," she recalled of her time there [Wall 1995, 828]). After earning a BA in anthropology, she went on to two years of postgraduate work at Columbia University with Franz Boas, the preeminent anthropologist of his time.

Scholar, storyteller, and literary luminary, Hurston was precocious as a child, adventurous as an adolescent, and fearless as an adult. Living a life of unusual mobility, she was, as a writer, to double-duty bound, committed to preserving stories from times past even as she used the sorcery of words to create her own narratives. But why the passion for collecting from someone who was so expert in making things up and writing them down? In retrospect, the answer seems obvious. Stories fired her imagination at a young age. She read them on her own, but she also heard them on the

Zora Neale Hurston at a recording site in Belle Glade, Florida, in 1935. *Lomax Collection, Prints and Photographs Division, Library of Congress.*

front porch of Joe Clark's Eatonville store, where adults engaged in "double talk" during "lying sessions" (Wall 1995, 600). There must have come a time when she wondered why the stories told on the porch—tales in which "God, Devil, Brer Rabbit, Brer Fox, Sis Cat, Brer Bear, Lion, Tiger, Buzzard, and all the wood folk walked and talked like natural men"—never made it onto the printed page.

The stories Zora Neale Hurston encountered as a child in books were uplifting yet also oddly disabling. "I was exalted by [the myth of Pluto and Persephone]," she wrote. Yet reading gave her "great anguish," she later conceded. "My soul was with the gods and my body in the village" (Wall 1995, 583). At the same time, a love of reading became Hurston's passport to educational opportunity. When the fifth-grader read out loud in class for two white visitors, they rewarded her with a roll of shiny new pennies and boxes of books (among them Norse tales and the Grimms' fairy tales) along with dresses and other clothing. "I acted as if books would run away," she confessed. At Barnard, Hurston used fairy-tale metaphors to describe the lack of magic in her own life and to capture the sluggish pace of her progress: "Oh, if you knew my dreams! . . . How I constantly live in fancy in seven league boots, taking mighty strides across the world." Desperately feeling the need for wings, she found herself forever riding "on tortoise back" (Boyd 2003, 111).

Happily, home-grown tales somehow lacked the dispiriting effects of myth and fairy tale. "Life took on a bigger perimeter by expanding on these things," she recollected. "I picked up glints and gleams out of what I heard and stored it away to turn it to my own uses." Yet there was a downside there too, for when the young Hurston made up her own stories (one in which fish greeted her as she walked across the waters of a lake), her grandmother responded to her confabulations with a face that looked "like open-faced hell." Only the protective intervention of her mother ("she's just playing") prevented the child from receiving a "handful of peach hickories on her back-side" (Boyd 2003, 40).

The porch of Joe Clark's store in Eatonville, Florida. *By permission of Temple University Press. © 2005 by Temple University. All rights reserved.*

Hurston, like many of her contemporaries, including the young Richard Wright, faced a culture of silencing, the legacy of a world in which it had always been wise to keep your mouth shut and your thoughts to yourself. Hurston referred once to the "muteness of slavery," a time before the "black mouth" could become "vocal" (Wall 1995, 905). Letting your imagination run wild was risky business, and expressiveness was rarely affirmed.

There is a palpable sense of relief in the first sentence of *Mules and Men*, when Hurston's desire to connect with the world she abandoned and to collect the stories she heard as a child is validated. "I was very glad when somebody told me, 'You may go and collect Negro folklore.'" It feels odd to us today to think that Zora Neale Hurston required official approval from an academic authority for her mission, yet her words are also a sober reminder that it took a real act of will to put together *Mules and Men*. Constantly forced to scrape together living expenses and dependent on the demands of academic mentors (Boas complained that Hurston's approach was too journalistic), benefactors, and publishers, Hurston kept her dignity even as she never lost her defiant edge.

Mules and Men is divided into two parts, with the first containing about seventy tales and the second, called "Hoodoo," collecting conjure tales as well as information about the origins and rituals of the mystical practice. Hurston serves as visible narrator throughout, providing context, commentary, and information about the performative aspects of telling and healing. The yoking of the two activities reveals the hidden differences and consonances between them, with the one dominated by men, the other by women. Hoodoo practices serve multiple purposes, but in the main they focus on healing, securing power over adversaries, and creating love potions or spells. If there is a more powerful dose of magic in them, it is in part because African American folktales told in the Deep South had a gritty realism and cynical wisdom that often dispensed with magic as the source of solutions.

Hurston's informants for the folktales were for the most part "menfolk" who gathered in social spaces to swap stories or tell what they called "big old lies." Rather than observing them from the margins and using a "scientific" method to collect the tales, Hurston became part of the conversation, actively engaging in the exchanges, participant as well as witness, being open all the while about what she was up to. One of her informants was skeptical about her project: "Who you reckon want to read all them old-time tales about Brer Rabbit and Brer Bear?" Hurston was telling "de biggest lie first thing" when she asserted that others would pay attention to these yarns. "We want to set them down before it's too late. . . . Before everybody forgets all of 'em" (Wall 1995, 14), Hurston replied, with language that echoes the anxieties of many folklorists and ethnographers working in an age of transition from oral storytelling to print cultures.

Hurston's determination to collect African American folktales, whether authorized or not, shines through in her meditations on the decision to head south. Did she really need the blessing of Franz Boas? Possibly not, for she tells us: "I want to collect like a new broom" (Kaplan 2002, 116). She also reports: "I am using the vacuum method, grabbing everything I see" (Kaplan 2002, 129). These are odd metaphors, to be sure, signaling intense physical and emotional engagement with the task at hand, and at the same time linking the writing down of the tales with women's work, with the myriad oppressive domestic chores that can wear you down. At the same time, Hurston recognizes that collecting also implies appropriation and violation. Sweeping and vacuuming up, she may also be engaging in an operation that implies eradicating even as it attempts to preserve.

More than Boas's approval, Hurston needed financial resources, and she found help in a wealthy New York patron, Charlotte Osgood Mason, an eccentric woman who had supported Langston Hughes, Alain Locke, Aaron Douglas, and other members of the Harlem Renaissance. Unlike Boas, whose concept of cultural relativism discredited theories about racial superiority, Mason reveled in the possibility of cultural renewal through the vital emotional and sensual power of "primitive" races. She charged Hurston with the task of collecting "all information possible, both written and oral, concerning the music, poetry, folk-lore, literature, hoodoo, conjure, manifestations of art and kindred subjects relating to and existing among North American Negroes" (Kaplan 2002, xxvi). The support was invaluable, but the price for it was

Zora Neale Hurston sits with Rochelle French and Gabriel Brown on a porch in Eatonville, Florida. The photograph, taken by Alan Lomax in 1935, shows her listening to stories and songs. *Lomax Collection, Prints and Photographs Division, Library of Congress.*

high. Not only was Hurston obliged to turn over all her findings to Mason, she also had to accept edits from her white patron. "She says the dirty words must be toned down," Hurston wrote with an almost audible sigh. Yet she also added, "Of course I knew that. But first I wanted to collect them as they are" (xxvii).

Hurston was both insider and outsider, a Southerner returning home with the map of Dixie "on her tongue," as she put it, but also an educated woman from up North who planned to train "the spyglass of Anthropology" on her informants. Betwixt and between, she found herself positioned as an outsider in her own hometown: "Very little was said directly to me and when I tried to be friendly there was a noticeable disposition to *fend* me off." In what she saw as a "rich field for folk-lore," there was Zora Neale Hurston, "starving to death in the midst of plenty" (*Mules and Men*, 60). How did she solve the problem? By hinting that she was neither detective nor revenue officer (as her shiny gray Chevrolet implied) but rather a "fugitive from justice"—a fabrication that enabled her to listen to what one informant called "lies above suspicion."

Being an outsider had its advantages. Hurston grew up with the capers of Brer Rabbit as well as with the wisdom of Squinch Owl, but those stories fit her like "a tight chemise": "I couldn't see it for wearing it." It was only when she left home that she could see herself "like somebody else and stand off and look at my garment." She was now the Columbia-trained anthropologist (*Mules and Men*, 1).

Collecting African American folklore posed special challenges. It was "not as easy to collect as it sounds," Hurston observed. "The best source is where there are the least outside influences, and these people, being usually under-privileged, are the shyest." She captured the exact nature of the challenges in words that remind us of her own ambiguous status as outsider and insider, alternating between "the Negro" and "we" in her description of what she famously called "feather bed resistance":

> And the Negro, in spite of his open faced laughter, his seeming acquiescence, is particularly evasive. You see we are a polite people and we do not say to our questioners, "Get out of here!" We smile and tell him or her something that satisfies the white person because, knowing so little about us, he doesn't know what he is missing. The Indian resists curiosity by a stony silence. The Negro offers a feather bed resistance, that is, we let the probe enter, but it never comes out. It gets smothered under a lot of laughter and pleasantries. (*Mules and Men*, 2–3)

J. R. R. Tolkien once referred to the "Cauldron of Story," and Hurston had her own metaphor, one that emphasized the nourishing aspects of tales. The stories we tell are passed around on "a great, big, old serving-platter." "Whatever is on the plate," she added, "must come out of the platter, but each plate has a flavor of its own because the people take the universal stuff and season it to suit themselves on the plate. And this local flavor is what is known as originality" (Wall 1995, 875). For Hurston, folklore is like the fabled table that sets itself. You can help yourself from the platter, but it will never empty, no matter how large the appetite.

Like Tolkien and others who used gastronomical metaphors to capture how stories are as vital to our well-being as the food we eat and the air we breathe, Hurston understood that stories permeate daily lives. Their punchlines are encapsulated in pithy folk truths; they circulate in the form of neighborhood gossip; they animate conversations in their imaginative forms; and they remind us of the importance of "talk."

"I have tried to be as exact as possible," Hurston wrote to Langston Hughes. "Keep

Jitterbuggers in a juke joint in 1939 in Clarksdale, Mississippi, the kind of site described in Zora Neale Hurston's *Mules and Men. Farm Security Administration, Prints and Photographs Division, LIbrary of Congress.*

to the exact dialect as closely as I could, having the story teller to tell it to me word for word as I write it. This after it has been told to me off hand until I know it myself." The technique of writing down "from the lips" was designed to keep Hurston from letting herself "creep in unconsciously" (Hemenway 1980, 128). It was a strategy that refused to scorn "to do or be anything Negro." (Wall 1995, 838–39). She wanted the exact words of the storyteller and nothing else would do. But she also added local color, creating a collection unique in its presentation of the social context for oral storytelling traditions. The folktales, as she put it, were "done over and put back in their natural juices." Interestingly, Hurston explained to Franz Boas that she had inserted the "between-story conversation and business" for pragmatic reasons: "without it, every publisher said it was too monotonous" (Boyd 2003, 253, 259).

Using words alone to capture the performance of a story has many shortcomings, all of which Hurston understood. It seems all the more likely that her strategy for

Men wait for a sawmill motor to cool off in this photograph taken by Marion Post Wolcott in Childs, Florida, in 1939. Hurston collected folklore at sawmill and turpentine camps in in neighboring Polk County, Florida, in 1928. *Farm Security Administration, Prints and Photographs Division, Library of Congress.*

collecting was somewhat less "exact" and "word for word" than she had claimed. What she manages so successfully is to produce a "speakerly text," words that sound spontaneous and conversational even as they are crafted and constructed with a literary sensibility. Mediating between "a profoundly lyrical, densely metaphorical, and quasi-musical, privileged black oral tradition on the one hand, and a received but not yet fully appropriated standard English literary tradition on the other," Zora Neale Hurston brilliantly mimics, repeats, and revises, creating the "Talking Book" so prized by African American writers (Gates 1989, 174, 198).

Mules and Men did not meet with unanimous critical acclaim. Sterling A. Brown, a fellow collector, complained that the book seemed "singularly *incomplete*." Hurston's informants are depicted as "naïve, quaint, complaisant, bad enough to kill each other in jooks, but meek otherwise, socially unconscious." If the book were "more bitter," he added, it would be "nearer the total truth" (Y. Taylor 2012, 275). Hurston's response can be predicted from what she once wrote in an essay entitled "How It Feels to Be Colored Me": "I do not belong to the sobbing school of Negrohood who hold that nature somehow has given them a lowdown dirty deal and whose feelings are all hurt about it. . . . No, I do not weep at the world—I am too busy sharpening my oyster knife" (Wall 1995, 827). But the full answer to Brown's critique is more complicated, as Hurston would also have noted. Valerie Boyd, for instance, speculates in her biography of the writer that Hurston believed that it was just as important to celebrate "the verbal agility of her people as it was to rail against white racism and southern injustice" (282).

Other reviewers were far more benighted, with Lewis Gannett writing in the *New York Herald Tribune Weekly Book Review* that he could not remember "anything better since *Uncle Remus*." In *The New Republic*, Henry Lee Moon praised the volume as "more than a collection of folklore" and admired its "valuable picture of the life of the unsophisticated Negro in the small towns and backwoods of Florida." The condescending tone of H. I. Brock's review in the *New York Times* could not have escaped Hurston's attention: "A young Negro woman with a college education has invited the outside world to listen in while her own people are being as natural as they can never

Zora Neale Hurston at the New York Times Book Fair in 1937, reading from a book entitled *American Stuff*, an anthology of works produced by the Federal Writers' Project. *Zora Neale Hurston Papers, George A. Smathers Libraries, University of Florida.*

be when white folks are literally present . . . when Negroes are having a good gregarious time, dancing, singing, fishing, and . . . incessantly talking" (King 2008, 110–12).

More importantly, Hurston was pragmatic and strategic in her life and her art. She was writing at a time when magazines routinely produced instructions for their contributors, putting constraints on African American writers with rules, regulations, and restrictions. To be sure, she was not about to rattle her mentors and patrons with tales of bitterness, resentment, and exploitation, but still she spoke the truth in her own way. Sterling Brown failed to recognize how Zora Neale Hurston practiced a form of "signifying" that is broadcast in the book's very title. *Mules and Men* may have signaled to some readers that the tales collected included lore about animals and men, but it also effectively equated the men of its title with beasts of burden, underscoring Southern culture in all its dehumanizing aspects even as it acknowledged the stubborn, disrespectful, laboring mule as brother and kin to the black man. The title is something of a trap set for readers, and Brown, like many critics, fell right into it. As Trudier Harris points out, under slavery mules and men were "interchangeable." "Hurston's title might therefore have been transformed to an equation: 'mules are men' or 'men are mules' (17)."

In *Mules and Men*, Hurston redefined the relationship between the spoken and the written word, capturing the poetry of folk wisdom (what she famously called the "will to adorn") and elevating the vernacular (what Hurston called the "Negro's poetical flow of language") to reveal its textured complexities. The tellers, like the author, sometimes speak in tongues, channeling folk wisdom through the ages, but they also employ a discourse that both conceals and reveals, lies and speaks the truth, offers straight talk yet also misrepresents. Specializing in lies as well as in the lives of the folk raconteurs who told them, Hurston furnished her readers with the higher truths of fiction even as she struggled with the question of whether to reveal and publish or conceal and protect what one critic has called "cultural secrets of the vernacular tradition" (Ladd 2007, 109). The prodigal daughter became, through *Mules and Men* as well as in her other writing, what Alice Walker put on the tombstone erected many decades after Hurston's death: "Novelist, Folklorist, Anthropologist" and also "A Genius of the South."

FRANZ BOAS, PREFACE TO *MULES AND MEN*

Boas was the founding father of American anthropology, and, at Columbia University, he chaired the first PhD program in anthropology in the United States. A firm advocate of cultural relativism, he was deeply committed to understanding human diversity in all its manifestations and rejected evolutionary approaches that created false hierarchies. Below he declares his faith in Hurston's ethnographic research, noting that she could operate as both insider and outsider to the culture she explores. Boas's comments about Hurston and the "charm of a loveable personality" read as dismissive to us, suggesting that he does not fully appreciate the seriousness of his student's research. Contrary to his belief that Hurston's recorded stories will reveal the "true inner life" of her observed subjects, Hurston herself famously pointed out the impossibility of reading minds through words spoken or written: "He can read my writing but he sho' can't read my mind."

Ever since the time of Uncle Remus, Negro folklore has exerted a strong attraction upon the imagination of the American public. Negro tales, songs and sayings without end, as well as descriptions of Negro magic and voodoo, have appeared; but in all of them the intimate setting in the social life of the Negro has been given very inadequately.

It is the great merit of Miss Hurston's work that she entered into the homely life of the southern Negro as one of them and was fully accepted as such by the companions of her childhood. Thus she has been able to penetrate through that affected demeanor by which the Negro excludes the White observer effectively from participating in his true inner life. Miss Hurston has been equally successful in gaining the confidence of the voodoo doctors and she gives us much that throws a new light upon the much discussed voodoo beliefs and practices. Added to all this is the charm of a loveable personality and of a revealing style which makes Miss Hurston's work an unusual contribution to our knowledge of the true inner life of the Negro.

To the student of cultural history the material presented is valuable not only by giving the Negro's reaction to everyday events, to his emotional life, his humor and passions, but it throws into relief also the peculiar amalgamation of African and European tradition which is so important for understanding historically the character of American Negro life, with its strong African background in the West Indies, the importance of which diminishes with increasing distance from the south.

FROM ZORA NEALE HURSTON, WORKS-IN-PROGRESS FOR *THE FLORIDA NEGRO*

Folklore is the boiled-down juice of human living. It does not belong to any special time, place, nor people. No country is so primitive that it has no lore, and no country has yet become so civilized that no folklore is being made within its boundaries. . . .

In folklore, as in everything else that people create, the world is a great, big, old serving-platter, and all the local places are like eating-plates. Whatever is on the plate must come out of the platter, but each plate has a flavor of its own because the people take the universal stuff and season it to suit themselves on the plate. And this local flavor is what is known as originality. So when we speak of Florida folklore, we are talking about that Florida flavor that the story- and song-makers have given to the great mass of material that has accumulated in this sort of culture delta. And Florida *is* lush in material because the State attracts such a variety of workers to its industries. . . .

[Art] is a series of discoveries, perhaps intended in the first instance to stave off boredom.

SOURCE: Cheryl A. Wall, ed., *Zora Neale Hurston: Folklore, Memoirs, and Other Writings*, 825–26.

FROM ZORA NEALE HURSTON, "NEGRO FOLKLORE"

Negro Folklore is not a thing of the past. It is still in the making. Its great variety shows the adaptability of the black man: nothing is too old or too new, domestic or foreign, high or low, for his use. God and the Devil are paired, and are treated no more reverently than Rockefeller and Ford. Both of these men are prominent in folklore, Ford being particularly strong, and they talk and act like good-natured stevedores or millhands. Ole Massa is sometimes a smart man and often a fool. The automobile is ranged alongside of the ox-cart. The angels and the apostles walk and talk like section hands. And through it all walks Jack, the greatest culture hero of the South; Jack beats them all—even the Devil, who is often smarter than God.

SOURCE: Cheryl A. Wall, ed., *Zora Neale Hurston: Folklore, Memoirs, and Other Writings*, 836.

FROM ZORA NEALE HURSTON, "CULTURE HEROES"

The Devil is next to Jack as a culture hero. He can outsmart everyone but Jack. God is absolutely no match for him. He is good-natured and full of humour. The sort of person one may count on to help out in any difficulty.

Peter the Apostle is third in importance. . . . Now of all the apostles Peter is the most active. When the other ten fell back trembling in the garden, Peter wielded the blade on the posse. Peter first and foremost in all action. . . .

The rabbit, the bear, the lion, the buzzard, the fox are culture heroes from the animal world. The rabbit is far in the lead of all the others and is blood brother to Jack. In short, the trickster-hero of West Africa has been transplanted to America.

John Henry is a culture hero in song, but no more so than Stacker Lee, Smokey Joe or Brad Lazarus. There are many, many Negroes who have never heard of any of the song heroes, but none who do not know John (Jack) and the rabbit.

SOURCE: Cheryl A. Wall, ed., *Zora Neale Hurston: Folklore, Memoirs, and Other Writings*, 836–37.

FROM ZORA NEALE HURSTON, "RESEARCH"

Research is formalized curiosity. It is poking and prying with a purpose. It is a seeking that he who wishes may know the cosmic secrets of the world and they that dwell therein.

Two weeks before I graduated from Barnard College, Dr. Boas had arranged a fellowship for me. I was to go south and do research in folk-lore.

I was extremely proud that Papa Franz felt like sending me. As is well known, Dr. Franz Boas of the Department of Anthropology of Columbia University, is the greatest Anthropologist alive for two reasons. The first is his insatiable hunger for knowledge and then more knowledge; and the second is his genius for pure objectivity. He has no pet wishes to prove. His instructions are to go out and find what is there. He outlines his theory, but if the facts do not agree with it, he would not warp a jot or dot of the findings to save his theory. So knowing all this, I was proud that he trusted me. I went off in a vehicle made out of Corona stuff.

SOURCE: Cheryl A. Wall, ed., *Zora Neale Hurston: Folklore, Memoirs, and Other Writings*, 687.

HOW THE CAT GOT NINE LIVES

1 *a large gar:* A slow-moving fish found in shallow, brackish areas of rivers, lakes, and bayous. Known as voracious predators, they catch their prey with needle-like teeth. Their unusual green bones make them less appetizing than other fish.

2 *spit white lime:* A variant reads "Brer Monkey chew opium, and give a good rhyme."

3 *this was a man dat had a wife and five chillun, and a dog and a cat:* The family unit is configured as one in which the wife and child are subordinated through their roles to the "man." Dog and cat are included in a way that suggests that they too are family members.

Cliff hauled away and landed a large gar[1] on the grass.

"See, Ah told you, Gran'pa. Don't you worry. Ah'm gointer ketch you mo' fish than you kin eat. Plenty for Mama and Gran'ma too. Less take dis gar-fish home to de cat."

"Yeah," said Jim Presley. "Y' take de cat a fish, too. They love it better than God loves Gabriel—and dat's His best angel."

"He sho do and dat's how cats got into a mess of trouble 'bout eatin' fish," added Jim Presley.

"How was dat? I done forgot if Ah ever knowed."

"If, if, if," mocked Jim Allen. "Office Richardson, youse always iffin'! If a frog had wings he wouldn't bump his rump so much."

"Grand'pa is right in wid de cats," Cliff teased. "He's so skeered he ain't gointer git all de fish he kin eat, he's just like a watch-dog when de folks is at de table. He'll bite anybody then. Think they cheatin' 'im outa his vittles."

Jim Presley spat in the lake and began:

> Once upon a time was a good ole time
>> Monkey chew tobacco and spit white lime.[2]
> Well, this was a man dat had a wife and five chillun, and a dog and a cat.[3]

"How the Cat Got Nine Lives," from Zora Neale Hurston, *Mules and Men*. Copyright 1935 by Zora Neale Hurston; renewed © 1963 by John C. Hurston and Joel Hurston. Reprinted by permission of HarperCollins Publishers.

Well, de hungry times caught 'em. Hard times every-where. Nobody didn't have no mo' than jus' enough to keep 'em alive. First they had a long dry spell dat parched up de crops, then de river rose and drowned out everything.[4] You could count anybody's ribs. De white folks all got faces look lak blue-John[5] and de niggers had de white mouf.[6]

So dis man laid in de bed one night and consulted with his piller.[7] Dat means he talked it over wid his wife. And he told her, "Tomorrow less git our pole and go to de lake and see kin we ketch a mess of fish. Dat's our last chance. De fish done got so skeerce and educated[8] they's hard to ketch, but we kin try."

They was at de lake bright and soon de next day. De man took de fishin' pole hisself 'cause he was skeered to trust his wife er de chillun wid it. It was they last chance to get some grub.

So de man fished all day long till he caught seven fishes. Not no great big trouts nor mud-cats but li'l perches and brims. So he tole 'em, "Now, Ah got a fish apiece for all of us, but Ah'm gointer keep on till Ah ketch one apiece for our dog and our cat."[9]

So he fished on till sundown and caught a fish for the dog and de cat, and then they went on home and cooked de fish.

After de fish was all cooked and ready de woman said: "We got to have some drinkin' water. Less go down to de spring to git some. You better come help me tote it 'cause Ah feel too weak to bring it by myself."

So de husband got de water bucket off de shelf and went to de spring wid his wife. But 'fore he went, he told de chillun, "Now, y'all watch out and keep de cat off de fish. She'll steal it sho if she kin."

De chillun tole him, "Yessuh," but they got to foolin' round and playin' and forgot all about de cat, and she jumped up on de table and et all de fish but one. She was so full she jus' couldn't hold another mouthful without bustin' wide open.

When de old folks come back and seen what de cat had done they bust out cryin'. They knowed dat one li'l fish divided up wouldn't save their lives. They knowed they had to starve to death. De man looked at de cat and he knowed dat one mo' fish would kill her so he said, "Ah'm gointer make her greedy gut kill her." So he made

4 *de river rose and drowned out everything:* Like many folktales, this one begins with famine, hunger, and the threat of starvation. First comes a drought and lack, then a flood and excess, wiping out crops and the possibility of finding sustenance.

5 *blue-John:* skimmed milk

6 *white mouf:* one symptom of starvation is ash-gray skin around the mouth

7 *piller:* pillow

8 *skeerce and educated:* Animals are humanized and described in terms usually applied to humans.

9 *for our dog and our cat:* The fisherman may be hungry and exhausted, but he finds the strength to keep fishing to enable the dog and cat to survive.

de cat eat dat other fish[10] and de man and his wife and chillun and de dog and cat all died.[11]

De cat died first so's he was already in Heben when de rest of the family got there. So when God put de man's soul on de scales to weigh it, de cat come up and was lookin' at de man, and de man was lookin' at de cat.

God seen how they eye-balled one 'nother so he ast de man, "Man, what is between you and dis cat?"

So de man said, "God, dat cat's got all our nine lives in her belly." And he told God about de fish.

God looked hard at dat cat for a hundred years, but it seem lak a minute.

Then he said, "Gabriel, Peter, Rayfield,[12] John and Michael, all y'all ketch dat cat, and throw him outa Heben."

So they did and he was fallin' for nine days, and there ain't been no cats in Heben since. But he still got dem nine lives in his belly and you got to kill him nine times befo' he'll stay dead.[13]

Stepped on a pin, de pin bent
and dat's de way de story went.

"Dat may be so, Presley," commented Jim Allen, "but if Ah ketch one messin' 'round *my* fish, Ah bet Ah kin knock dat man and woman and dem five chillun, de dog *and* de cat outa any cat Ah ever seen wid one lick."

"Dat's one something. Ah ain't never gointer kill," announced Willard forcefully. "It's dead bad luck."

"Me neither," assented Sack Daddy. "Everybody know it's nine years hard luck. Ah shot a man once up in West Florida, killed him dead for bull-dozin' me in a skin game, and got clean away. Ah got down in de phosphate mines around Mulberry and was doin' fine till Ah shacked up wid a woman dat had a great big ole black cat wid a white star in his bosom. He had a habit of jumpin' up on de bed all durin' de night time. One night Ah woke up and he was on my chest wid his nose right to mine, suckin' my breath.

10 *So he made de cat eat dat other fish:* Even if the last fish could not have saved the entire family, it could have saved one member. That the man chooses revenge over one life is telling.

11 *de man and his wife and chillun and de dog and cat all died:* The sobering deaths of all in the family echo the endings of what folklorists call cumulative tales, or chain tales, stories like "The Gingerbread Man" or "The Cock and the Hen," with spare plots that build up to a disastrous ending.

12 *Rayfield:* Raphael

13 *you got to kill him nine times befo' he'll stay dead:* The origins of a cat's proverbial nine lives are unclear. The fact that they survive falls and other situations that would be fatal to humans most likely gave rise to the proverb that "a cat has nine lives" and "For three he plays, for three he strays, and for the last three he stays."

Ah got so mad Ah grabbed dat sucker by de tail and bust his brains out against a stanchion.[14] My woman cried and carried on 'bout de cat and she tole me Ah was gointer to have back luck. Man, you know it wasn't two weeks befo' Sheriff Joe Brown laid his hand on my shoulder and tole me, 'Le's go.' Ah made five years for dat at Raiford. Killin' cats is bad luck."[15]

SOURCE: Zora Neale Hurston, *Mules and Men*, 121–23.

14 *stanchion:* an upright supporting fixture

15 *Killin' cats is bad luck:* From the notion of cats having nine lives, the tale expands outward to the bad luck that comes from killing cats. Proverbs and superstitions often provide the pretext for a story whose truth can rarely be captured in a one-liner.

In Mules and Men, *Zora Neale Hurston shows us folklore in action, giving us stories with their cultural surround. What appears to be a straightforward explanatory tale about "How the Cat Got Nine Lives" turns out to be a rich site of interpretive activity, with Jim Presley the teller showing us the motivation for the story and his audience chiming in at the end of the tale, demonstrating its relevance to their own lives. The story is introduced through a chain of associative banter and is then processed through improvisational talk. Hurston's "spyglass of anthropology" enables her to zoom in on both teller and audience, watching what leads up to the tale and enabling us to witness its afterlife in a community.*

"BLOOD IS THICKER THAN WATER" *AND* BUTTERFLIES

"Take for instance de time they had de gopher up in court.

"De gopher come in and looked all around de place. De judge was a turtle, de lawyers was turtles, de witnesses was turtles and they had turtles for jurymen.

"So de gopher ast de judge to excuse his case and let him come back some other time. De judge ast him how come he wanted to put off his case and de gopher looked all around de room and said, 'Blood is thicker than water,' and escused hisself from de place."

"Yeah," said Floyd Thomas, "but even God ain't satisfied wid some of de things He makes and changes 'em Hisself."

Jim Presley wanted to know what God ever changed, to Floyd's knowledge.

Well, He made butterflies after de world wuz all finished and thru. You know de Lawd seen so much bare ground till He got sick and tired lookin' at it. So God tole 'm to fetch 'im his prunin' shears and trimmed up de trees and made grass and flowers and throwed 'em all over de clearin's and dey growed dere from memorial days.

Way after while de flowers said, "Wese put heah to keep de world comp'ny but wese lonesome ourselves." So God said, "A world is somethin' ain't never finished. Soon's you make one thing you got to make somethin' else to go wid it. Gimme dem li'l tee-ninchy[1] shears."

1 *tee-ninchy:* small

So he went 'round clippin' li'l pieces offa everything—de sky, de trees, de flower, de earth, de varmints and every one of dem li'l clippin's flew off. When folks seen all them li'l scraps fallin' from God's scissors and flutterin' they called 'em flutter-bys. But you know how it is wid de brother in black. He got a big mouf and a stumbling tongue. So he got it all mixed up and said, "butter-fly" and folks been calling 'em dat ever since. Dat's how come we got butterflies of every color and kind and dat's why dey hangs 'round de flowers. Dey wuz made to keep de flowers company.

SOURCE: Zora Neale Hurston, *Mules and Men*, 119–20.

The tales in Mules and Men *are set off visually from Hurston's description of conversations among the tellers. But occasionally a story is told in the narrative frame itself and gives rise to a new tale, creating a sense that human exchanges are driven by story itself. The cynical tale about a gopher who declines to bring his case to court on the grounds that the courtroom is packed with turtles is juxtaposed to a vignette about beauty and social bonding in the natural order. Butterflies and flowers, unlike gophers and turtles, mix and mingle freely for their mutual benefit.*

WHEN GOD FIRST PUT FOLKS ON EARTH *AND* WHY WOMEN ALWAYS TAKE ADVANTAGE OF MEN

Below are two versions of the same folktale, one told to Hurston by a male informant, the other by a woman.

WHEN GOD FIRST PUT FOLKS ON EARTH

When God first put folks on earth there wasn't no difference between men and women. They was all alike. They did de same work and everything. De man got tired uh fussin' 'bout who gointer do this and who gointer do that.

So he went up tuh God and ast him tuh give him power over de woman so dat he could rule her and stop all dat arguin'.

He ast Hum tuh give him a lil mo' strength and he'd do de heavy work and let de woman jus' take orders from him whut to do. He told Him he wouldn't mind doing de heavy [work] if he could jus' boss de job. So de Lawd done all he ast Him and he went on back home—and right off he started tuh bossin' de woman uh-round.

So de woman didn't lak dat a-tall. So she went up tuh God and ast Him how come He give man all de power and didn't leave her none. So He tole her, "You never ast Me for none. I thought you was satisfied."

She says, "Well, I ain't, wid de man bossin' me round lak he took tuh doin' since you give him all de power. I wants half uh his power. Take it away and give it tuh me."

De Lawd shook His head. He tole her, "I never takes nothin' back after I done give it out. It's too bad since you don't like it, but you shoulda come up wid him, then I woulda 'vided it half and half!"

De woman was so mad she left dere spittin' lak a cat. She went straight to duh devil. He tole her: "I'll tell you whut to do. You go right back up tuh God and ast Him tuh give you dat bunch uh keys hangin' by de mantle shelf; den bring 'em here tuh me and I'll tell you whut to do wid' em, and you kin have mo' power than man."

So she did and God give 'em tuh her thout uh word and she took 'em back to de devil. They was three keys on dat ring. So de devil tole her whut they was. One was de key to de bedroom and one was de key to de cradle and de other was de kitchen key. He tole her not tuh go home and start no fuss, jus' take de keys and lock up everything an' wait till de man come in—and she could have her way. So she did. De man tried tuh ack stubborn at first. But he couldn't git no peace in de bed and nothin' tuh eat, an' he couldn't make no generations tuh follow him unless he use his power tuh suit de woman. It wasn't doin' him no good tuh have de power cause she wouldn't let 'im use it lak he wanted tuh. So he tried tuh dicker wid her. He said he'd give her half de power if she would let him keep de keys half de time.

De devil popped right up and tole her naw, jus' keep whut she got and let him keep whut he got. So de man went back up tuh God, but He tole him jus' lak he done de woman.

So he ast God jus' tuh give him part de key tuh de cradle so's he could know and be sure who was de father of chillun, but God shook His head and tole him: "You have tuh ast de woman and take her word. She got de keys and I never take back whut I give out."

So de man come on back and done lak de woman tole him for de sake of peace in de bed. And thass how come women got de power over mens today.

SOURCE: Zora Neale Hurston, *Every Tongue Got to Confess*, 7–9. Told by "Old Man Drummond."

WHY WOMEN ALWAYS TAKE ADVANTAGE OF MEN

"Whut ole black advantage is y'll got?" B. Moseley asked indignantly. "We got all de strength and all de law and all de money and you can't git a thing but whut we jes' take pity on you and give you."

"And dat's jus' de point," said Mathilda triumphantly. "You *do* give it to us, but how come you do it?" And without waiting for an answer Mathilda began to tell why women always take advantage of men:

You see in de very first days, God made a man and a woman and put 'em in a house together to live. 'Way back in them days de woman was just as strong as de man and both of 'em did de same things. They useter get to fussin 'bout who gointer do this and that and sometime they'd fight, but they was even balanced and neither one could whip de other one.

One day de man said to hisself, "B'lieve Ah'm gointer go see God and ast Him for a li'l mo' strength so Ah kin whip dis 'oman and make her mind. Ah'm tired of de way things is." So he went on up to God.

"Good mawnin', Ole Father."

"Howdy man. Whut you doin' 'round my throne so soon dis mawnin'?"

"Ah'm troubled in mind, and nobody can't ease mah spirit 'ceptin' you."

God said: "Put yo' plea in de right form and Ah'll hear and answer."

"Ole Maker, wid de mawnin' stars glitterin' in yo' shinin' crown, wid de dust from yo' footsteps makin' worlds upon worlds, wid de blazin' bird we call de sun flyin' out of yo' right hand in de mawnin' and consumin' all day de flesh and blood of stump-black darkness, and comes flyin' home every evenin' to rest on yo' left hand, and never once in yo' eternal years, mistood de left hand for de right, Ah ast you *please* to give me mo' strength than dat woman you give me, so Ah kin make her mind. Ah know you don't want to be always comin' down way past de moon and stars to be straightenin' her out and it's got to be done. So give me a li'l mo' strength, Ole Maker and Ah'll do it."

"All right, Man, you got mo' strength than woman."

So de man run all de way down de stairs from Heben till he got home. He was so anxious to try his strength on de woman dat he couldn't take his time. Soon's he got in de house he hollered "Woman! Here's yo' boss. God done tole me to handle you in which ever way Ah please. A'm yo' boss."

De woman flew to fightin' 'im right off. She fought 'im frightenin' but he beat her. She got her wind and tried 'im agin but he whipped her agin. She got herself together and made de third try on him vigorous but he beat her every time. He was so proud he could whip 'er at last, dat he just crowed over her and made her do a lot of things she didn't like. He told her, "Long as you obey me, Ah'll be good to yuh, but every time yuh rear up Ah'm gointer put plenty wood on yo' back and plenty water in yo' eyes."

De woman was so mad she went straight up to Heben and stood befo' de Lawd. She didn't waste no words. She said, "Lawd, Ah come befo' you mighty mad t'day. Ah want back my strength and power Ah useter have."

"Woman, you got de same power you had since de beginnin'."

"Why is it then, dat de man kin beat me now and he useter couldn't do it?"

"He got mo' strength than he useter have, He come and ast me for it and Ah give it to 'im. Ah gives to them that ast, and you ain't never ast me for no mo' power."

"Please suh, God, Ah'm astin' you for it now. Jus' gimme de same as you give him."

God shook his head. "It's too late now, woman. Whut Ah give, Ah never take back. Ah give him mo' strength than you and no matter how much Ah give you, he'll have mo'."

De woman was so mad she wheeled around and went on off. She went straight to de devil and told him what had happened.

He said, "Don't be dis-incouraged, woman. You listen to me and you'll come out mo' than conqueror. Take dem frowns out yo' face and turn round and go right on back to Heben and ast God to give you dat bunch of keys hangin' by de mantel-piece. Then you bring 'em and Ah'll show you what to do wid 'em."

So de woman climbed back up to Heben agin. She was mighty tired but she was more out-done than she was tired so she climbed all night long and got back up to Heben agin. When she got befo' de throne, butter wouldn't melt in her mouf.

"O Lawd and Master of de rainbow, Ah know yo' power. You never make two mountains without you put a valley in between. Ah know you kin hit a straight lick wid a crooked stick."

"Ast for whut you want, woman."

"God, gimme dat bunch of keys hangin' by yo' mantel-piece."

"Take 'em."

So de woman took de keys and hurried on back to de devil wid 'em. There was three keys on de bunch. Devil say, "See dese three keys? They got mo' power in 'em than all de strength de man kin ever git if you handle 'em right. Now dis first big key is to de do' of de kitchen, and you know a man always favors his stomach. Dis second one is de key to de bedroom and he don't like to be shut out from dat neither and dis last key is de key to de cradle and he don't want to be cut off from his generations at all. So now you take dese keys and go lock up everything and wait till he come to you. Then don't you unlock nothin' until he use his strength for yo' benefit and yo' desires."

De woman thanked 'im and tole 'im, "If it wasn't for you, Lawd knows whut us po' women folks would do."

She started off but de devil halted her. "Jus' one mo' thing: don't go home braggin' 'bout yo' keys. Jus' lock up everything and say nothin' until you git asked. And then don't talk too much."

De woman went on home and did like de devil tole her. When de man come home from work she was settin' on de porch singin' some song 'bout "Peck on de wood make de bed go good."

When de man found de three doors fastened what useter stand wide open he swelled up like pine lumber after a rain. First thing he tried to break in cause he figgered his strength would overcome all obstacles. When he saw he couldn't do it, he ast de woman, "Who locked dis do'?"

She tole 'im, "Me."

"Where did you git de key from?"

"God give it to me."

He run up to God and said, "God, woman got me locked 'way from my vittles, my bed and my generations, and she say you give her the keys."

God said, "I did, Man, Ah give her de keys, but de devil showed her how to use 'em!"

"Well, Ole Maker, please gimme some keys jus' lak 'em so she can't git de full control."

"No, Man, what Ah give Ah give. Woman got de key."

"How kin Ah know 'bout my generations?"

"Ast de woman."

So de man come on back and submitted hisself to de woman and she opened de doors.

He wasn't satisfied but he had to give in. 'Way after while he said to de woman, "Le's us divide up. Ah'll give you half of my strength if you lemme hold de keys in my hands."

De woman thought dat over so de devil popped and tol her, "Tell 'im, naw. Let 'im keep his strength and you keep yo' keys."

So de woman wouldn't trade wid 'im and de man had to mortgage his strength to her to live. And dat's why de man makes and de woman takes. You men is still braggin' 'bout yo' strength and de women is sittin' on de keys and lettin' you blow off till she git ready to put de bridle on you.

B. Moseley looked over at Mathilda and said, "You just like a hen in de barnyard. You cackle so much you give de rooster de blues." Mathilda looked over at him archly and quoted:

> Stepped on a pin, de pin bent
> And dat's de way de story went

"Y'all lady people ain't smarter *than* all men folks. You got plow lines on some of us, but some of us is too smart for you. We go past you jus' like lightnin' thru de trees," Willie Sewell boasted. "And what make it so cool, we close enough to you to have a scronchous[1] time, but never no halter on our necks. Ah know they won't git none on dis last neck of mine."

1 *scronchous:* exciting

SOURCE: Zora Neale Hurston, *Mules and Men*, 31–34.

In both these tales the foundational question of the gendered division of labor and responsibility is taken up, with additional refinements and embellishments on the theme coming out in the second story through conversational banter. The story of Adam and Eve and their expulsion from the Garden of Eden takes us into the same territory as these two tales. The battle between brawn and brains is a central preoccupation of folktales, and here it is not depicted as a struggle between a lumbering giant and a smaller, quick-witted and fleet-footed adversary but between men and women. Stories like these take us into a circle that includes men and women. Their provocations and overstated claims ensure that there will always be something to talk about and debate.

WHY DE PORPOISE'S TAIL IS ON CROSSWISE
AND ROCKEFELLER AND FORD

WHY DE PORPOISE'S TAIL IS ON CROSSWISE[1]

Now, I want to tell you 'bout de porpoise. God had done made de world and everything. He set de moon and de stars in de sky. He got de fishes of de sea, and de fowls of de air completed.

He made de sun and hung it up. Then He made a nice gold track[2] for it to run on. Then He said, "Now, Sun, I got everything made but Time. That's up to you. I want you to start out and go round de world on dis track just as fast as you kin make it. And de time it takes you to go and come, I'm going to call day and night." De Sun went zooming' on cross de elements. Now, de porpoise was hanging round there and heard God what he tole de Sun, so he decided he'd take dat trip round de world hisself. He looked up and saw de Sun kytin' along,[3] so he lit out too, him and dat Sun!

So de porpoise beat de Sun round the world by one hour and three minutes. So God said, "Aw, naw, this aint gointer do! I didn't mean for nothin' to be faster than de Sun!" so God run dat porpoise for three days before he run him down and caught him, and took his tail off and put it on crossways[4] to slow him up. Still he's de fastest thing in de water.[5]

And dat's why de porpoise got his tail on crossways.

ROCKEFELLER AND FORD

Once John D. Rockefeller and Henry Ford was woofing at each other.[1] Rockefeller told Henry Ford he could build a solid gold road round the world. Henry Ford told him if he

1 *"Why de Porpoise's Tail Is On Crosswise":* What folklorists call *pourquoi* tales, or etiological stories explain the origins of animals as well as of their characteristics. See Part XI, How in the World? *Pourquoi* Tales.

2 *He made a nice gold track:* The track made for the sun anticipates the "gold road round the world" in the story of Rockefeller and Ford.

3 *kytin' along:* moving fast as a kite

4 *put it on crossways:* The triangular-shaped tail of the porpoise is at a right-angle to its body.

5 *de fastest thing in de water:* Porpoises are small cetaceans, but the fastest in a group that includes dolphins and whales.

1 *woofing at each other:* speaking in an aggressive manner with each other but with no real malice or intent to harm

2 *tin lizzies:* The Ford Model T or Tin Lizzie was manufactured efficiently with assembly line production in Henry Ford's plant and became the first affordable automobile in the United States.

would he would look at it and see if he liked it, and if he did he would buy it and put one of his tin lizzies[2] on it.

SOURCE: Zora Neale Hurston, *Folklore, Memoirs, and Other Writings,* 837.

Included in Hurston's "Characteristics of Negro Expression," the two stories above mirror each other, revealing that drives manifested at the beginning of the world shape desires in the contemporary world. A competitive spirit rules in both the natural order and in a capitalist social order. The can-do attitude of Ford with his Tin Lizzie contrasts with the imperious Rockefeller, who produces the same kind of golden road constructed in the first tale by God.

ANANSI AND THE FROG

Inside the room the old ones kept the duppy entertained with Anansi stories. Now and then they sang a little. A short squirt of song and then another story would come. Its syllables would behave like tambour tones under the obligato[1] of the singing out-

1 *obligato:* a musical line that is not to be omitted

2 *Grassquit:* a type of bird

side. It fitted together beautifully because Anansi stories are partly sung anyway. So rhythmic and musical is the Jamaican dialect that the tale drifts naturally from words to chant and from chant to song unconsciously. There was Brer Anansi and Brer Grassquit;[2] Brer Anansi and the Chatting Pot; Brer Frog's dissatisfaction with his flat behind and Anansi's effort to teach him how to make stiffening for it. And how all the labor was lost on account of Brer Frog's boasting and ingratitude. "So Frog don't learn how to make him behind stick out like other animals. Him still have round behind with no shape because him don't know how to make the stiffening." A great burst of laughter. This is the best-liked tale and it is told more than once.

SOURCE: *Tell My Horse,* in Zora Neale Hurston, *Folklore, Memoirs, and Other Writings,* 319.

While doing fieldwork in Jamaica, Zora Neale Hurston took part in a séance that conjured what Jamaicans call a "duppy," a term of African origin meaning a ghost or spirit. The evening is filled with song and storytelling, as relatives of the duppy try to appease the spirit of the dead man.

THE ORPHAN BOY AND GIRL AND THE WITCHES

An orphan boy and girl lived in the house with their grandmother, and one day she had to go on a journey and left them there alone. The little girl was sick and the boy went to search for food for them both.

After he was gone, the girl felt stronger so she got out of bed. She was walking in the house when he came back.

"Why do you get out of bed?" he asked her.

She said that she got out of bed because she smelt the witches about. He laughed at her and persuaded her to eat some yams. While they were eating, sure enough in came three witches.

The witches wanted to eat them at once, but they begged to be spared until their grandmother returned at sundown. The witches didn't want to wait, so they said that they would not eat them if they would go and get some water from the spring. The children gladly said that they would go.

The witches gave them a sieve to fill with water, and told them that if they did not return at once with it, they would be eaten immediately.

The boy and girl went to the spring for the water and dipped and dipped to try to fill the sieve, but the water always ran out faster than they could fill it. At last they saw the witches coming. Their teeth were far longer than their lips.

The boy and girl were terribly frightened. He seized her and said, "Let us run. Let us go across the deep river."

The children ran as fast as they could. They saw the witches behind them coming so fast that they made a great cloud of dust that darkened the sun. The little girl stumbled and the witches gained ground so fast that they saw they could not reach the river before the witches, and so climbed a great tree.

The witches came to the foot of the tree and smelt their blood. They came with a broad-ax and began to chop down the tree. The little girl said: "Block eye, chip, block eye chip!" and the pieces that the witches chopped off would fly back into the witches' eyes and blind them.

The boy called his dogs. [Chant] "Hail Counter! Hail Jack! Hail Counter! Hail Jack!"

The witches at the foot of the tree chopping away said, [chant]: "O-ooo! Whyncher, whyncher! O-ooo! Whyncher, whyncher!" [Here it is understood that each actor in the drama is speaking, or chanting his lines without further indications.]

"Hail Counter, Hail Jack!"

"O-ooo! Whyncher, whyncher!"

"Block eye chip, block eye chip!"

The Tree was toppling and the children was so scared but the boy kept on calling: "Hail Counter, Hail Jack!"

"Block eye chip, block eye chip!"

"O-ooo! Whyncher, whyncher!"

The little girl asked her brother: "Do you see the dogs coming yet?"

He said, "Not yet. Hail Counter! Hail Jack!" He didn't see the dogs coming and he began to sing: "I'm a little fellow here by myself for an hour."

The dogs was tied at home. They heard his voice and wanted to come, but they were tied. The grandmother was asleep. She was very tired from her journey. She wondered where her grandchildren were. She did not hear the dogs whining to go to the aid of the boy. But a black fast-running snake heard the boy and ran to the house and struck the grandmother across the face with his tail and woke her, and she loosed the dogs.

"I'm a little fellow here by myself for an hour."

"Block eye, chip, block eye, chip!"

"Hail Counter, hail Jack!"

"O-oooo! Whyncher, whyncher!"

By that time here come the dogs. The tree was falling. The boy and girl was so glad to see the dogs. He told one dog: "Kill 'em!" He told another one, "Suck their blood!" He told the last one, "Eat the bones!"

By that time I left.

SOURCE: Zora Neale Hurston, *Every Tongue Got to Confess*, 66–68, told by Hattie Reeves, born on the Island of Grand Command.

The breathless pace of this tale about a witch, a grandmother, and her two orphaned grandchildren makes tales like "Little Red Riding Hood" feel tame. The orphaned children find protective forces in the natural world rather than in the human one. Snakes and dogs come to their rescue, and they also use language in the form of charms to ward off cannibalistic witches. Closer to the fairy-tale canon than many of the folktales collected by Hurston, this story contains many tropes familiar from European tales, from the (grand)mother who leaves the children home alone to the magical pursuit by demons.

JACK AND THE DEVIL

A man had two sons. One was name Jack and de other one was name Frank. So they got grown and their father called 'em one day and says, "Now, y'all are grown. Here's five hundred dollars a piece. Go out for yourself."

Frank took his and went and bought him a farm and settled down.

Jack took his and went on down de road. He got into a crap game and bet his five hundred dollars and won. He bet five hundred more and won agin.

He went walking on down de road and met a man. "Good morning, my boy, what might be your name?"

"My name is Jack. Who are you?"

"Lie-a-road to ketch meddlers."

Jack says, "I speck youse de man I'm looking for to play me some five-up."

"All right, let's go."

So they set down and played and Jack lost. "I got five hundred more that says I'll win." They played and Jack lost agin. "Well," he says, "I got five hundred more." He lost dat.

Den de man says, "I'll tell you what I'll do. I'll play you a game for your life against all the money."

Jack lost again. So the man he says, "My name is the devil. My home is across the Atlantic ocean.[1] If you gets there before this sun rises and goes down again I'll save your life. If not, you'll have to die."

Jack was down by de road crying and a ole mast ast him, "What are you crying for?"

Jack says, "I played five-up wid de devil and he have won my life. He's gone back across the Atlantic Ocean. He told me if I'm not there before the sun rises and goes down again he's bound to take my life. I don't see no chance of getting there."

Old man says, "Youse in a pretty bad fix, all right. There's only one thing can cross the ocean in twelve hours. That's a bald eagle. She comes here every morning and dips herself in de ocean and walks out and plucks off her dead feathers. Now you be here tomorrow morning with a bull yearling; when she get through plucking her feathers she'll be ready to go. You mount her back wid dis bull yearling and every time she hollers, you put a piece of meat in her mouf and she'll carry you straight across the ocean by nine o'clock."

Jack was there nex' morning wid de bull yearling and saw de eagle when she dipped herself in de ocean and come out on shore to pick off her dead feathers. She dipped herself the second time and shook herself. When she rocked herself and made ready to mount the sky, Jack mounted her back wid his yearling.

After while she hollered, "Hah-ah! One quarter cross de ocean. I don't see nothing but blue water." Jack tore off one de hams of dat yearling and stuck it in her mouf and she flew on.

After a while, "Hah-ah! Half way cross de ocean—don't see nothing but blue water, Hah!" He gave her de rest and pretty soon she landed. Jack hopped off and met an old black man with red eyes and ast him if he knew where de devil live at. He told him, "Yeah, he live in de first little house down de road."

He knocked on de door and de devil opened it. "Well, you made it, didn't you? Come in and have breakfast with me."

After breakfast he says to Jack, "I got a lil job for you to do and if you do it, you can have my youngest daughter; but if you fail I'll hafta take yo' life. I got seventy-five acres of new ground—never a bush cut on it. Every bush, every tree, every stump got to be cut and piled up and burnt before twelve o'clock."

1 *across the Atlantic ocean:* A possible allusion to Africa, where souls return after death.

Jack went on down there and went to work; then he begin to cry and de devil's youngest daughter come down wid his breakfast. She says, "Whut's de matter, Jack?"

"Your father gimme a hard task. I can't clean all dis off by twelve o'clock."

"Eat yo' breakfast, Jack, and lay yo' head in my lap and go to sleep."[2]

Jack done so, and when he woke up every bush, every tree, every stump was cut and piled up and burnt. So Jack went on back to de house.

"I get one more little hard task for you to do. If you do, you kin have my daughter; if you don't, I'll hafta take yo' life. I got a well three thousand feet deep—I want every drop of water dipped out and bring me whut you find on the bottom."

Jack went to dipping the water out de well, but it run in faster than he could dip it out; so he set down and went to crying. Here come de devil's daughter and ast him: "Whut's de matter, Jack?"

"Your father have give me another hard task. I can't do this work."

"Lay down and put your head in my lap and go to sleep."

Jack done so and after while she woke him up and hand him a ring and tole him: "Heah, take dis to papa. That's whut he want. Mama was walking out here de other day and lost her ring."

Devil say, "I got one more task for you to do and you kin have my youngest daughter. If you don't, I'll hafta take your life." De devil had some coconut palms three hundred fifty feet high. He tole Jack, "You kill these two geeses and go up dat palm tree and pick 'em and bring me back every feather."

Jack took de geeses and went on up de tree and de wind was blowing so strong he couldn't hardly stay up there. Jack started to cry. Pretty soon here come de devil's daughter. "Whut's de matter, Jack?"

"Your father have given me too hard a task. I can't do it."

"Just lay your head on my lap and go to sleep."

Jack done so and she caught the feathers that had got away from Jack and when he woke up she hand him every feather and de geese and says: "Heah, take 'em to papa and let's get married."

So de devil give them a house to start housekeeping in.

2 *lay yo' head in my lap and go to sleep:* It is not unusual for a heroine to accomplish impossible tasks while the hero sleeps, though often it is an animal bride who works the magic.

That night the girl woke up and says: "Jack, father is coming after us. He's got two horses out in the barn and a bull. You hitch up de horses and turn their heads to us."

He hitched up de horses and she got in and they went. De devil misses 'em and run to git his horses. He seen they was gone, so he hitched up his bull. De horses could leap one thousand miles at every jump and de bull could jump five hundred. Jack was whipping up dem horses but de devil was coming fast behind them and de horses could hear his voice one thousand miles away. One of 'em was named Hallowed-Be-Thy-Name and the other one Thy-Kingdom-Come.

De devil could call, "Oh, Hallowed-Be-Thy-Name, Thy-Kingdom-Come! don't you hear your Master calling you? Jump Bull, jump five hundred miles." Every time he'd holler de horses would fall to their knees and de bull would gain on 'em.

De girl says, "Jack, get out de buggy and drag your heel nine steps backward[3] and throw dirt over your left shoulder and git back in and let's go."

3 *drag your heel nine steps backward:* The devil's daughter seems familiar with the techniques of conjure.

They did this three times before de horses got so far off they couldn't hear their master's voice. After dat they went so fast they got clean away. De devil kept right on coming and so he passed an old man and ast: "Did you see a girl black as coal, with eyes of fire, wid a young man in a buckboa'd?" He tole him yeah. "Where did you hear 'em say they were going?"

"On de mountain."

"I know 'tain't no use now, I can't ketch 'em. [Chant] Turn, bull, turn clean around, turn bull, turn clean around."

De bull turnt so short till he throwed de devil out and kilt him and broke his own neck.

That's why they say, "Jack beat the devil."

SOURCE: Zora Neale Hurston, *Every Tongue Got to Confess*, 47–51. Told by Jerry Bennett.

Connected with stories about a man who sends his sons out into the world as well as with tales about winning the devil's treasures, this particular narrative also takes up bargains with the devil. Impossible tasks figure prominently in many folktales, and in this case, it is the heroine who takes up the challenge of carrying them out.

KING OF THE WORLD

"Y'all been tellin' and lyin' 'bout all dese varmints but you ain't yet spoke about de high chief boss of all de world which is de lion," Sack Daddy commented.

"He's de King of de Beasts, but he ain't no King of de World, now Sack," Dad Boykin spoke up. "He thought he was de King till John give him a straightenin'."

"Don't put dat lie out!" Sack Daddy contended. "De lion won't stand no straightenin'."

"Course I 'gree wid you dat everybody can't show de lion no deep point, but John showed it to him. Oh, yeah, John not only straightened him out, he showed dat ole lion where in."

"When did he do all of dis, Dad? Ah ain't never heard tell of it." Dad spoke up:

Oh, dis was befo' yo' time. Ah don't recolleck myself. De old folks told me about John and de lion. Well, John was ridin' long one day straddle of his horse when de grizzly bear come pranchin'[1] out in de middle of de road and hollered: "Hold on a minute! They tell me you goin' 'round strowin' it[2] dat youse de King of de World."

John stopped his horse: "Whoa! Yeah, Ah'm de King of de World, don't you b'lieve it?" John told him.

"Naw, you ain't no king. Ah'm de King of de world. You can't be no King till you whip me. Git down and fight."

John hit de ground and de fight started. First, John grabbed him a rough-dried brick and started to work de fat offa de bear's head. De bear just fumbled 'round till he got a good holt, then he begin to squeeze and squeeze. John knowed he couldn't stand dat much longer, so he'd be jus' another man wid his breath done give out. So he reached into his pocket and got out his razor and slipped it between dat bear's ribs. De bear turnt loose and reeled on over in de bushes to lay down. He had enough of dat fight.

John got back on his horse and rode on off.

De lion smelt the bear's blood and come runnin' to where de grizzly was layin' and started to lappin' his blood.

1 *pranchin':* variant of prancing

2 *strowin' it:* broadcasting it (*strow* is an archaic form of *strew*)

De bear was skeered de lion was gointer eat him while he was all cut and bleedin' nearly to death, so he hollered and said: "*Please* don't touch me, Brer Lion. Ah done met de King of de World and he done cut me all up."

De lion got his bristles all up and clashed down at de bear. "Don't you lay there and tell me you done met the King of de World and not be talk 'bout me! Ah'll tear you to pieces!"

"Oh, don't tetch me, Brer Lion! Please lemme alone so Ah kin get well."

"Well, don't you call nobody no King of de World but me."

"But Brer Lion, Ah done *met* de King sho' nuff. Wait till you see him and you'll say Ah'm right."

"Naw, ah won't neither. Show him to me and Ah'll show you how much King he is."

"All right, Brer Lion, you jus' have a seat right behind dese bushes. He'll be by here befo' long."

Lion squatted down by de bear and waited. Fust person he saw goin' up de road was a old man. Lion jumped up and ast de bear, "Is dat him?"

Bear say, "Naw, dat's Uncle Yistiddy, he's a useter-be!"

After while a li'l boy passed down de road. De lion seen him and jumped up agin. "Is dat him?" he ast de bear.

Bear told him, "Naw, dat's li'l tomorrow, he's a gointer-be, you jus' lay quiet. Ah'll let you know when he gits here."

Sho nuff after while here come John on his horse but he had done got his gun. Lion jumped up agin and ask, "Is dat him?"

Bear say: "Yeah, dat's him! Dat's de King of de World."

Lion reared up and crack his tail back and forwards like a bull whip. He 'lowed, "You wait till Ah git thru wid him and you won't be call' him no King no mo'."

He took and galloped out in de middle of de road right in front of John's horse and laid his years back. His tail was crackin' like torpedoes.

"Stop!" de lion hollered at John. "They tell me you goes for de King of de World!"

John looked him dead in de ball of his eye and told him, "Yeah, Ah'm de King. Don't you like it, don't you take it. Here's mah collar, come and shake it!"

De lion and John eye-balled one another for a minute or two, den de lion sprung on John.

Talk about fighting! Man, you ain't seen no sich fightin' and wrasslin' since de mornin' stars sung together. De lion clawed and bit John and John bit him right back.

Way after while John got to his rifle and he up wid de muzzle right in old lion's face and pulled de trigger. Long, slim black feller, snatch 'er back and hear 'er beller! Dog damn! Dat was too much for de lion. He turnt go of John and wheeled to run to de woods. John leveled down on him agin and let him have another load, right in his hindquarters.

Dat ole lion give John de book: de bookity book.[3] He hauled de fast mail[4] back into de woods where de bear was laid up.

"Move over," he told de bear. "Ah wanta lay down too."

"How come!" de bear ast him.

"Ah done met de King of de World, and he done ruint me."

"Brer Lion, how you know you done met de King?"

"'Cause he made lightnin' in my face and thunder in my hips. Ah know Ah done met de King, move over."

SOURCE: Zora Neale Hurston, *Mules and Men*, 131–34.

3 *de bookity book:* "Bookity-book" means quickly, and the phrase has been thought to imitate the sound of feet running.

4 *hauled de fast mail:* "Hauling the mail" and "toting the mail" both mean "to run away quickly."

Who is the master of the world when it comes to a contest between the king of the beasts and a man named John? When John "got his gun," the playing field is no longer quite level, and, despite efforts to naturalize gunshot as thunder and lightning, it is clear that firearms are decisive when it comes to naming the King of the World.

PART X

LESSONS IN LAUGHTER: TALES ABOUT JOHN AND OLD MASTER

In the earthy realism of tales about John and Old Master, we do not have the mythical depth found in some stories about High John the Conquer. Like his folkloric cousins (the British Jack, the Russian Ivan, the French Jean, or the German Hans), John is a kind of Everyman. A comic, folkloric spinoff of the mythical John referred to by Zora Neale Hurston as a "hope-bringer," he uses his wit and imagination to model survival skills. Still, it is not entirely clear that John of the Old Master tales is related structurally to High John the Conquer. The two figures may, despite Zora Neale Hurston's insistence on their identity, have developed from entirely different traditions, one connected with tricksters, the other with heroic redeemers. But they are united by their resourcefulness and ability to "conquer," as it were, in the face of circumstances that were designed to vanquish body and soul.

John and Old Master serve as constants in the stories that follow, and their relationship remains enduringly transactional rather than transformative. Conflict is the motor of these plots, and the recurring situational struggle never resolves itself but is destined to repeat itself endlessly. Each story begins with the violation of a taboo—failure to follow orders, theft, impersonation, cursing, and so on. John and Old Master are constantly sparring with each other, with John seeking the advantages that his Master enjoys, and Old Master doing everything he can to obstruct John's plans. This set of stories was less invested in revealing something about character than in modeling the

John Rose's watercolor *The Old Plantation* was most likely painted in the late eighteenth century. It is thought to represent a marriage ceremony (with the ritual of jumping the broom), but it may also represent a form of dance in African cultures. It is remarkable in its effort to depict a joyful, self-contained episode in the lives of enslaved people. *The Colonial Williamsburg Foundation. Gift of Abby Rockefeller.*

"skillful handling of varieties of settings by actors in a given social relationship" (Dickson 1974, 428). How well matched (or *equal*) master and slave are becomes evident from the fact that a rough tally of the recorded tales reveals "a draw in the contest of wits" (Dorson 1959, 86).

Still, John and Old Master are not by any stretch of the imagination social equals. John works on the plantation, plowing, planting, cutting wood, toting water, milking cows, keeping records, and undertaking almost the entire range of labors customarily carried out by slaves. More of a house slave than a field hand (he is rarely shown picking cotton), he enjoys a special relationship with Old Master (sometimes called Massa, Marster, Marse, or Old Boss in the postbellum era), a man who can be harsh and demanding, but also indulgent and kind when it comes to John (who sometimes appears with a generic name for a male slave).

John himself is the classic numbskull, a figure both nimble and quick-witted but often under the guise of stupidity. "Are they stolidly stupid," one female slave owner wondered, "or wiser than we are, silent and strong, biding their time?" (Litwack 1980, 4). Her observation is revealing in its failure to recognize that slaves were wise to play "stolidly stupid" and that "silent and strong" was one of the few strategies available under the plantation system for avoiding punishment. Is it any wonder that John is constantly learning from chatty skulls and loquacious animals about the perils of talking too much? Or that John's victories depend on the capriciousness of his master, who shows varying degrees of tolerance for being duped?

Slavery was a social system based on asymmetrical power relationships riven by conflict and violence. Yet stories about John and Old Master often, if not always, offer up a peaceful resolution of differences, one in which wagers, contests, disagreements, and the violation of taboos are resolved or smoothed over through good-natured exchanges capped by displays of exceptional wit or strength. John and his master are often portrayed as friendly rivals rather than hardened enemies, and John's challenges to the master's authority are rarely punished severely. Nor are his periodic thefts of chickens and pigs viewed as anything more than mild transgressions, only mildly annoying. Despite plots with realistic settings and plausible circumstances, these tales could be seen as moving in the mode of the counterfactual, giving us high fantasy by suggesting an impossible fraternal friendliness between master and slave and a denial of the hierarchical nature of their relationship. Still, one historian reads the tales optimistically, finding in them "symbolic denials of white Southerners' claims to any kind of inherent superiority over blacks." And in this way, he adds, John did get the best of Old Master "all the time" (Dickson 1974, 429).

JOHN DE FIRST COLORED MAN

De first colored man what was brought to dis country was name John. He didn't know nothin' mo' than you told him and he never forgot nothin' you told him either. So he was sold to a white man.

Things he didn't know he would ask about. They went to a house and John never seen a house so he asked what it was. Ole Massa tole him it was his kingdom. So dey goes on into de house and dere was the fireplace. He asked what was that. Ole Massa told him it was his flame 'vaperator.

The cat was settin' dere. He asked what it was. Ole Massa told him it was his round head.

So dey went upstairs. When he got on de stair steps he asked what dey was. Ole Massa told him it was his Jacob ladder. So when they got up stairs he had a roller foot bed. John asked what was dat. Ole Mass told him it was his flowery-bed-of-ease. So dey came down an went out to de lot. He had a barn. John asked what was dat. Ole Massa told him, dat was his mound. So he had a Jack in the stable, too. John asked, "What in de world is dat?" Ole Massa said: "Dat's July, de God dam."

So de next day Ole Massa was up stairs sleep and John was smokin'. It flamed de 'vaperator and de cat was settin' dere and it got set afire. The cat goes to de barn where Ole Massa had lots of hay and fodder in de barn. So de cat set it on fire. John watched de Jack kicking up hay and fodder. He would see de hay and fodder go up and come down but he thought de Jack was eatin' de hay and fodder.

So he goes upstairs and called Ole Massa and told him to get up off'n his flowery-bed-of-ease and come down on his Jacob ladder. He said: "I done flamed the 'vaperator and it caught de round head and set him on fire. He's gone to de mound and set it on fire, and July the God dam is eatin' up everything he kin git his mouf on."

Massa turned over in de bed and ask, "What dat you say, John?"

John tole 'im agin. Massa was still sleepy so he ast John agin what he say. John was gittin' tired so he say, "Aw, you better git up out dat bed and come on down stairs. Ah done set dat ole cat afire and he run out to de barn and set it afire and dat ole Jackass is eatin' up everything he git his mouf on."

SOURCE: Zora Neale Hurston, *Mules and Men*, 79–80.

> *This is a tale about language—who controls it and how. The story begins in almost biblical fashion, with John as the first man to be sold as a slave in the New World. His Master names objects for him, in an inventory that suggests the limited nature of John's world. More importantly, the names are all manipulative, deceptive, or nonsensical, made-up language designed for a man who will not be able to use language as a tool for communication. It takes an emergency for all the illusions to drop, for the rituals of deception to collapse. John has had access to meaningful language all along; he has simply played along, following orders about how to speak all the while watching, listening, and learning.*

"'MEMBER YOUSE A NIGGER!"

Ole John was a slave, you know. Ole Massa and Ole Missy and de two li' children—a girl and a boy.

Well, John was workin' in de field and he seen de children out on de lak in a boat, just a hollerin'. They had done lost they oars and was 'bout to turn over. So then he went and told Ole Massa and Ole Missy.

Well, Ole Missy, she hollered and said: "It's so sad to lose these 'cause Ah ain't never goin' to have no more children." Ole Massa made her hush and they went down to de water and follered de shore on 'round till they found 'em. John pulled off his shoes and hopped in and swum out and got in de boat wid de children and brought 'em to shore.

Well, Massa and John take 'em to de house. So they was all so glad 'cause de children got saved. So Massa told 'im to make a good crop dat year and fill up de barn, and den when he lay by de crops nex' year, he was going to set him free.

So John raised so much crop dat year he filled de barn and put some of it in de house.

So Friday come, and Massa said, "Well, de day done come that I said I'd set you free. I hate to do it, but I don't like to make myself out a lie. I hate to git rid of a good nigger lak you."

So he went in de house and give John one of his old suits of clothes to put on. So John put it on and come in to shake hands and tell 'em goodbye. De children they cry, and Old Missy she cry. Didn't want to see John go. So John took his bundle and put it on his stick and hung it crost his shoulder.

Well, Ole John started on down de road. Well, Ole Massa said, "John, de children love yuh."

"Yassuh."

"John, I love yuh."

"Yassuh."

"And Missy *like* yuh!"

"Yassuh."

"But 'member, John, youse a nigger."

"Yassuh."

Fur as John could hear 'im down the road he wuz hollerin', "John, Oh John! De children loves you. And I love you. De Missy *like* you!"

John would holler back, "Yassuh."

"But 'member youse a nigger, tho!"

Ole Massa kept callin' 'im and his voice was pitiful. But John kept right on steppin' to Canada. He answered Old Massa every time he called 'im, but he consumed on wid his bag.

SOURCE: Zora Neale Hurston, *Mules and Men*, 89–90.

In this tale, John plays the role of what Zora Neale Hurston called the "Pet Negro," a black man in whom the white man takes special "pride and pleasure." And Ole Massa has good reason to treasure John, who not only saves his children but also brings in his crops. The contrast between John's unwavering loyalty and Missy's callousness as well as Ole Massa's hypocrisy could not be more pointed. The deep ambivalence of plantation owners toward slaves emerges in Ole Massa's alternating declarations of affection and arrogance.

CATCHING JOHN

He had one, do call him John, and it come a traveler and stayed all night. Old Master pointed out John and said, "He ain't never told me a lie in his life." The traveler bet Master a hundred dollars 'gainst four bits he'd catch John in a lie 'fore he left. Next morning at the table the mice was pretty bad, so the traveler caught one by the tail and put him inside a coverlid dish what was setting there on the table, and he told Old Master tell John he could eat something out of every dish after they got through but that coverlid one, and not to take the cover offen it. And John said, "No, sir, I won't." But John just naturally had to see what was in that dish, so he raise the lid and out hopped the mouse. Then here come Old Master and asked John iffen he done what he told him not to do, and John 'nied it. Then the traveler look in the dish and the mouse wasn't there, and he said, "See there, John been lying to you all the time, you just ain't knowed it." And reckon he right, 'cause us had to lie.

SOURCE: B. A. Botkin, *Lay My Burden Down*, 3.

This story turns on a motif prominent in folktales from many cultures: a forbidden container, dish, pot, or door. The traveler's hunch that John will succumb to the temptation to look at the forbidden dish comes true. What makes this tale unique is the generalization built into the ending, which does not warn about the perils of curiosity (at times snakes and scorpions inhabit the dish) but instead explains the need for deceptive practices. This particular story, another "true lie," justifies John's behavior, less because it represents human fallibility, than because he lives in a culture that requires disobeying orders and using deception.

THE MOJO

There was always the time when the white man been ahead of the colored man. In slavery times John had done got to a place where the Marster whipped him all the time. Someone told him, "Get you a mojo, it'll get you out of the whipping, won't nobody whip you then."

John went down to the corner of his Boss-man's farm, where the mojo-man stayed, and asked him what he had. The mojo-man said, "I got a pretty good one and a very good one and a damn good one." The colored fellow asked him, "What can the pretty good one do?" "I'll tell you what it can do. It can turn you into a rabbit, and it can turn you to a quail, and after that it can turn you to a snake." So John said he'd take it.

Next morning John sleeps late. About nine o'clock the white man comes after him, calls him: "John, come on, get up there and go to work. Plow the taters and milk the cow and then you can go back home—it's Sunday morning." John says to him, "Get on out from my door, don't say nothing to me. Ain't gonna do nothing." Boss-man says, "Don't you know who this is? It's your Boss." "Yes, I know—I'm not working for you any more." "All right, John, just wait till I go home; I'm coming back and whip you."

White man went back and got his pistol, and told his wife, "John is sassy, he won't do nothing I tell him, I'm gonna whip him." He goes back to John, and calls, "John, get up there." John yells out, "Go on away from that door and quit worrying me. I told you once, I ain't going to work."

Well, then the white man he falls against the door and broke it open. And John said to his mojo, "Skip-skip-skip-skip." He turned to a rabbit, and run slap out the door by Old Marster. And he's running son of a gun, that rabbit was. Boss-man say to his mojo, "I'll turn to a greyhound." You know that greyhound got running so fast his paws were just reaching the grass under the rabbit's feet.

Then John thinks, "I got to get away from here." He turns to a quail. And he begins sailing fast through the air—he really thought he was going. But the Boss-man says, "I will turn to a chicken hawk." That chicken hawk sails through the sky like a bullet, and catches right up to that quail.

Then John says, "Well, I'm going to turn to a snake." He hit the ground and begin to crawl; that old snake was natchally getting on his way. Boss-man says, "I'll turn to a stick and I'll beat your ass."

SOURCE: Richard Dorson, ed., *American Negro Folktales*, 141–42. Told by Abraham Taylor.

A mojo is an amulet used in African American hoodoo practices. The amulet, also known as a "prayer in a bag," is kept in a small flannel bag. The custom goes back to West African belief systems that used mojo to cast spells, bring good fortune, and to drive away evil spirits. In this tale, both John and the Boss-man use mojo in a story that is an adaptation of what folklorists call a "transformation combat" tale. The two antagonists use magic to shape-shift and gain an advantage over each other. In the end, John seems to have lost his bid to escape a whipping, for he will get an equally severe beating as a snake.

HOW?

It was said that this large plantation owner had many slaves, and for one reason or another the Devil appeared to him one day and said that he was going to take the man's slave whose name was John.

And the plantation owner said, "Why John?"

He said, "Well, it's just John's time."

He said, "Please don't take *John*."

And the Devil said, "Well, what's so special about *John*?"

He said, "Well, John is my record keeper." Says, "I don't keep any records. I keep no books whatsoever. John has a memory that's *fantastic*, and he just doesn't forget *anything*. I can ask him about my crops and what I made last year, and all I have to do is tell him and I call him back and ask him what I made and how many bushels of corn and what have you, and John has the answer just like that."

So say the Devil said, "That's unbelievable. Are you sure about that?"

He said, "I'm positive."

"How?," from Daryl Cumber Dance, ed., *Shuckin' and Jivin': Folklore from Contemporary Black Americans*, 1978. Reprinted with permission of Indiana University Press.

So the Devil said, "Well, will you call John up here? I want to talk to John—I want to test him out now. If he doesn't prove you're right, I'm going to have to take John."

So the Master called John up, and he said, "Now, Mr. Devil, you can ask him anything you want."

So the Devil said to John, say, "John, do you like eggs?"

And John said, "Yes, sir," and immediately the Devil disappeared.

Well, it was two years to the day and John was in the cornfield plowing the corn, laying beside the corn, and it was a hot day. John had stopped the mule and sat under a tree. He had his old straw hat just fanning himself, you know. The Devil pops out of the ground, and he says one word to John; he says, "How?"

John says, "Scrambled."

SOURCE: Daryl Cumber Dance, ed. *Shuckin' and Jivin': Folklore from Contemporary Black Americans*, 203–4. Collected in 1974 in Charles City, Virginia.

"Test of memory" is the folkloric motif on display in this tale. John not only works the fields but also keeps flawless records. Stories about the strength of memory were particularly important in a culture that did not keep written records, and John, as the keeper of memory, could serve not only his own master but also his community. As importantly, he is a man who will never forget.

JOHN OUTWITS MR. BERKELEY

This story begins with a very covetous man, Mr. Berkeley, who was a very rich and a very selfish man, too. Everything he saw, he wanted. One day, he met an old woman who had a fine cow she was taking to market. He knew it was worth about a hundred dollars, but he said to the woman, "You don't want to take that cow all the way to the market. I will give you five dollars for it right here." Not knowing much about the value of anything, the old woman thought that five dollars was a lot of money, so Mr. Berkeley got the cow.

"John Outwits Mr. Berkeley," from Elsie Clews Parsons. *Folk-Lore of the Antilles, French and English*, 1933–43. Reprinted with permission of Indiana University Press.

When she got home, she told her only son, whose name was John, what she had done, and he said, "Damn! Mommy, Mr. Berkeley really paid you nothing close to what that cow was worth. But I'm going to make Mr. Berkeley really do a flying dance for what he has done to us." So he made a plan. His mother had a nice bucket in the house filled with some good-looking sugar. John went and got some cow manure and other shit and put it into the bottom of a pan, and then covered that over with the sugar. He carried it down that same road that his mother was taking the cow earlier, knowing that was where Mr. Berkeley passed all of the time.

When Mr. Berkeley saw John and all that nice sugar, he asked him, "John, what do you have on your shoulder there?" John said, "Sugar, Mr. Berkeley, some nice sugar to sell at the market." Mr. Berkeley came over to him and said, "Well, that's pretty good-looking sugar. Why don't you sell it to me instead of carrying it all the way to the market?" John said, "Well, I want five hundred dollars for it." Well, Mr. Berkeley, when he saw something that he really liked, he just had to have it. So he paid him the five hundred dollars for the panful.

He carried it on home and invited all his friends to come and have tea with him so they could taste this wonderful sugar that he had found. They came and thought the sugar was just wonderful in their tea. After using the sugar for a few days, though, Mr. Berkeley dipped in his spoon and it came up smelling awful! He said, "Good God, I'm going to beat that John when I catch up with him." And he took off for John's house right away.

Well, John had thought out the whole plan. He had taken a large copper boiling pot that they use for making sugar, filled it with yams and potatoes and other provisions from the garden. He balanced the whole thing on three stones and built a large fire under the pot, and began to boil the whole thing down. But there was one spot where the fire was so hot it showed through the covering of ashes, which he covered over with fresh dirt.

As soon as Mr. Berkeley got there, he called out to John, and John answered, "I'm in here, Mr. Berkeley." And before Mr. Berkeley could say anything, John said, "Mr. Berkeley, Mr. Berkeley, come and see this pot that cooks food by itself." He hit the kettle as hard as he could with a whip, and he said, "Mr. Berkeley, just listen to that." Sure enough, the kettle was boiling. He hit it again, and the kettle seemed to boil even harder. Mr. Berkeley didn't have to hear the third crack of the whip when he said, "You have to sell me that pot that cooks food by just lashing it." John said, "Well, I have to have five hundred dollars for the pot and another five hundred for the special whip." So Mr. Berkeley gave it to him, five hundred for the pot and five hundred for the whip.

So he took it to this large field, put the pot on these stones, and brought lots of food to put into it. Then he invited all his friends to a great big cook-up, to show them how he was going to boil food without any fire. So all the friends came bright and early, before they had eaten their food at home, even, expecting to have a big feast at Mr. Berkeley's. Well, when they got there, they saw Mr. Berkeley taking this whip and hitting the pot, *Whop!* He gave it a hard lash but nothing happened. He hit it a second time, but the food stayed just as cold as when he put it in. He gave the pot a hundred lashes, and still the water stayed as cold as before. He was disappointed and getting mad now. And all his friends left, hungry and laughing at the same time.

Now, John went on to the next part of his plan. He killed a goat and took out its heart and had his mother put it inside of her dress, right on top of where her own heart was. He told her to play dead when he touched it with a knife. As soon as he saw Mr. Berkeley coming to him, as vexed as he could be, he took out a knife and he stabbed his mother right in the goat's heart, and she fell over. Now Mr. Berkeley supposed she was dead. Mr. Berkeley said, "John, you have killed your mother." He was scared, you know, with the knife in John's hand and the blood all around. John said, "Oh, Mr. Berkeley, Mama will raise herself up once more, you'll see." So he took up this shell and he blew on it *pouu-uu.* His mother stirred a little. He blew it again, *pouu-uu*; his mother opened her eyes. The third time he blew she sat up, and the fourth time she got up and started to walk around.

Mr. Berkeley was astonished. He asked, "John, what do you want for a knife that cuts like that? John said, "Well I have to have five hundred dollars." So he gave John the money, and five hundred more for the shell.

Now he went home, got all his servants, his wife and his children, and put them all in a row. Again he invited all his friends over to see how he was going to kill all these people and then bring them back to life again. He took the knife and stabbed his wife and she fell dead. He took all the servants and killed them, and the rest of his family. They were all dead on the ground in front of him, so he blew on the shell, *pouu-uu,* and nothing happened. He blew again and again, from morning to night, but nobody came back to life. He looked around and said, "All right, I am going to kill John with just one stab, too, for God's sake."

This time, John had no other tricks, so Mr. Berkeley tied him up, wanting to shame John like John had shamed him in front of all his friends. He brought him up to the bay side, to the rum shop there, and started to have a drink with all his friends while they laughed at John, all tied up there. But another man, whose name was Wolf, passed by there. He saw John crying, and said to him, "Friend John, how did you get yourself in this fix?" John said, "I have discovered this huge gold field under the water on Mr. Berkeley's property, and you know how he is, being so selfish, so he has tied me up until he can get all that gold and split it up between us." Wolf said, "But it seems so cruel that you should be tied." And John said, "It is, it is, but you know Mr. Berkeley. He must have his gold. Maybe, if I told you where the gold is, you would want to have my half of it." Wolf said, "Would you do that?" And John said, "Yes, because he is making so much fun of me in front of his friends." So Wolf unloosened the ropes, and they exchanged clothes, and John tied him up just as tightly as he had been tied. So John went away and left Wolf there in his place; and when Mr. Berkeley came out of the rum shop later, he just picked up Wolf without looking and carried him out to his boat and went out on the open sea and shoved Wolf over and drowned him.

About three months later, Mr. Berkeley saw John coming toward him in the carriage he had taken when he changed places with Mr. Wolf. He said, "Is that you, John?" and John said, "Oh yes, Mr. Berkeley." He asked, "Well, how did you come back to life and get such a fine carriage?" John said, "Well, you remember when you threw me into the sea? Well, I fell right into a gold field itself!" Mr. Berkeley said to John, "You have to show me where this gold field is. Will you do that for me?" John said, "Yes, but you must give me something in return." Mr. Berkeley said he would give him anything he wanted. John said, "But you know it is deep in the ocean, and you must put weights on your body so you can get down to it." So John tied Mr. Berkeley as tightly as Mr. Berkeley had tied him, put some stones on his body and put him in the boat, went out on the open sea, and shoved him over. That's the gold mine Mr. Berkeley wanted, but now John had all the things that Mr. Berkeley had, and John was alive, too.

That's the reason why an envious and covetous man always loses when he tries to get too much.

SOURCE: Elsie Clews Parsons, *Folk-Lore of the Antilles, French and English*, III, 48–58. Told in Trinidad.

The tale about John and Mr. Berkeley gives us a kaleidoscopic twist on John and Old Master stories, pitting a clever young man against a man who is "covetous," "rich," "envious," and "selfish." Although John and Mr. Berkeley are not in a master-slave relationship, their conflicts, with an escalating series of punishments, repeat what is seen in John and Old Master tales. The scenes of revenge are, in this case, not at all realistic and recall some of the antics of Brer Rabbit as well as of European tricksters and swindlers. The tale's origins can be traced to "fatal deception" tales in Africa, as well as to stories about two farmers, one rich and dim-witted, the other poor and resourceful.

OLD BOSS AND JOHN AT THE PRAYING TREE

This also happened back in the old days too. It was one year on a plantation when the crops were bad. There wasn't enough food for all the slave hands, no flour at all, all they had to eat was fatback and cornbread. John and his buddy was the only slickers on the farm. They would have two kinds of meat in the house, all the lard they could use, plenty flour and plenty sugar, biscuits every morning for breakfast. (They was rogues.) The Boss kept a-missing meat, but they was too slick for him to catch 'em at it.

Every morning, he'd ask John, "How are you getting along over there with your family?" John said, "Well, I'm doing all right, Old Marster. (*High-pitched whiny*) I'm fair's a middling and spick as a ham, coffee in the kittle, bread on the fire, if that ain't living I hope I die."

The Old Boss checked on John. And he saw his hams and lard and biscuits all laid up in John's place. (In those days people branded their hams with their own name.) He said, "John, I can see why you're living so high. You got all my hams and things up there." "Oh, no," John told him. "those ain't none of your 'am. Boss, God give me them ham, God is good, just like you, and God been looking out for me, because I pray every night."

Boss said, "I'm still going to kill you John, because I know that's my meat."

Old John was real slick. He asked his Marster, "Tonight meet me at the old 'simmon tree. I'm going to show you God is good to me. I'm going to have some of your same ham, some of your same lard, and some of your same flour."

So that night about eight o'clock (it was dark by then in the winter), John went for his partner. They get everything all set up in the tree before John goes for Old Boss. They go out to the tree. Old Boss brings along his double-barreled shotgun, and he tells John, "Now if you don't get my flour and stuff, just like you said you would, you will never leave this tree."

So John gets down on his knees and begins to pray. "Now, Lord, I never axed you for nothing that I didn't get. You know Old Marster here is about to kill me, thinking I'm stealing. Not a child of yours would steal, would he, Lord?" He says, "Now I'm going to pat on this three times. And I want you to rain down persimmons." John patted on the tree three times and his partner shook down all the persimmons all over Old Boss. Boss shakes himself and says, "John, Old Boss is so good to you, why don't you have God send my meat down?"

John said, "Don't get impatient: I'm going to talk to him a little while longer for you." So John prayed, "Now Lord, you know me and I know you. Throw me down one of Old Boss's hams with his same brand on it."

Just at that time the ham hit down on top of Old Boss's head. Old Boss grabbed the ham, and said, "John, I spec you better not pray no more." (Old Boss done got scared.) But John kept on praying and the flour fell. Old Boss told John, "Come on John, don't pray no more." "I just want to show you I'm a child of God," John tells him, and he prays again. "Send me down a sack of Old Boss's sugar, the same weight and the same name like on all his sacks."

"John, if you pray any more no telling what might happen to us," Boss said. "I'll give you a forty-acre farm and a team of mules if you don't pray no more." John didn't pay no attention; he prayed some more. "Now God, I want you to do me a personal favor. That's to hop down out of the tree and horsewhip the hell out of Old Boss." So his buddy jumped out with a white sheet and laid it on Old Boss.

Boss said, "You see what you gone done, John; you got God down on me. From now on you can go free."

SOURCE: Richard M. Dorson, ed., *American Negro Tales*, 131–32. Told by Tommy Carter.

Drawing on the folkloric motif of "man behind statue (tree) speaks and pretends to be God (spirit)," this tale shows John in a position of abject prayer and supplication, yet still able to get the better of Old Boss and win his freedom by staging a pantomime in which another slave "lords" it over a double-barreled-shotgun-toting master.

OLD MASTER AND OKRA

Old Master had to go down to New Orleans on business, and he left his number-one slave named Okra in charge of things. Okra declared to himself he goin' to have a good time whilst Old Master was away, and the thing he did the very first mornin' was to go out and tell the other slaves, "Now you get on with your affairs. Old Master gone to New Orleans and we got to keep things goin'."

Then Okra went in the kitchen to cook himself up some food, and in the process of doin' so he got ruffled and spilled the bacon grease on top of the stove. It burst up into a big fire, and next thing you know that house was goin' up in flame and smoke. Okra he went out the window and stood off a ways, lookin' real sorry. By the time the other hands got there, wasn't nothin' else to do *but* look sorry. They was so busy with lookin' that they never noticed that the sparks lit in the wood lot and set it afire too. Well, Okra ordered everybody out to the wood lot to save it, but by then the grass was sizzlin' and poppin', a regular old prairie fire roarin' across the fields, burnin' up the cotton and everything else. They run over there with wet bags to beat it out, but next thing they knowed, the pasture was afire and all Old Master's cattle was a-goin', throttle out and racin' for the Texas Badlands.

Okra went to the barn for the horses, but soon's he opened the door they bolted and was gone. "If'n I can get that ox team hitched," Okra said, "I'll go on down to Colonel Thatcher's place and get some help." Well, minute he started to put the yoke on them oxen, the left-hand ox lit out and was gone. The right-hand ox went after him, and the both of 'em just left Okra holdin' the ox yoke up in the air. When Old Master's huntin' dog see them oxen go off that way, he figured something was wrong, and he sold out, barkin' and snappin' at their heels.

'Bout that time Okra looked around and found all the slaves had took off, too, headin' North and leavin' no tracks. He was alone, and he had to digest all that misery by himself.

Week or two went by, and Okra went down to meet the boat Old Master comin' back on. Old Master got off feelin' pretty good. Told Okra to carry his stuff and say, "Well, Okra, how'd things go while I was away?"

"Old Master and Okra," from Harold Courlander, ed., *Terrapin's Pot of Sense*, 1957. Reprinted by permission of the Emma Courlander Trust.

"Fine, just fine," Okra say. "I notice they're fixin' the bridge over Black Creek. Ain't that good?"

"Yeah," Old Master say, "that's fine, Okra, just fine. Soon's we get home I'm goin' to change my clothes and do some quail shootin'."

"Captain," Okra say, hangin' his head, "I got a little bad news for you."

"What's that?" Old Master say.

"You ain't neither goin' qual huntin'," Okra say, "your huntin' dog run away."

Old Master took it pretty good. He say, "Well, don't worry about it none, he'll come back. How'd he happen to run away?"

"Chasin' after the right-hand ox," Okra say. "That ox just lit out one mornin'."

"Where to?" Old Master say.

"I don't know where to," Okra say. "He was tryin' to catch up with the left-hand ox."

Old Master began to frown now, and he say to Okra, "You mean the whole ox team is gone? How come?"

"I was yokin' em up to go after Colonel Thatcher, after the horses bolted," Okra say.

"How come the horses bolted?" Old Boss say.

"Smoke from the pasture grass. That's what scared all your livestock and made 'em break down the fence and run for the swamp."

"You mean all my livestock is gone? Okra, I goin' to skin you. How'd that pasture get on fire?"

Okra he just stood there lookin' foolish, scratchin' his head. "Reckon the fire just came across from the cotton field, Captain," he say.

"You mean my cotton's burned!" Old Master holler. "How'd that happen?"

"Couldn't put it out, Captain. Soon as we see it come over there from the wood lot, we went down with wet bags but we couldn't handle it. Man, that was sure a pretty cotton field before the fire got there."

Right now Old Master was lookin' pretty sick. He talk kind of weak. "Okra, you tryin' to tell me the wood lot's gone too?"

"I hate to tell you, Captain, but you guessed it," Okra say, kind of sad. "Imagine, all them trees gone, just 'cause of one lonesome spark."

Old Master couldn't hardly talk at all now. He just whisperin'. "Okra," he say, "Okra, where'd that spark come from?"

"Wind blew it right from the house," Okra say. "It was when the big timbers gave and came down. Man, sparks flew in the air a mile or more."

"You mean the house burned up?" Old Master say.

"Oh, yeah, didn't I tell you?" Okra reply. "Didn't burn *up*, though, as much as it burned *down*."

By now Old Master was a miserable sight, pale as a ghost and shakin' all over.

"Okra, Okra," Old Master say, "let's go get the field hands together and do somethin'!"

"Can't do that," Okra say, "I forget to tell you, they's all sold out for Michigan."

Old Master just set there shakin' his head back and forth. "Okra," he say, "why didn't you come right out with it? Why you tell me everything was fine?"

"Captain, I'm sorry if I didn't tell it right," Okra say. "Just wanted to break it to you easy."

SOURCE: Harold Courlander, ed., *Terrapin's Pot of Sense*, 76–79.

In fairy tales, the survivors generally live happily ever after, but folktales can pile on disasters in ways that are so excessive that they become tragicomic rather than catastrophic. Okra decides to have a "good time" after Old Master leaves, and he touches off a chain of events that leads to the loss of everything the slaveholder owns, including the slaves, who flee North. Fractured by irony, the tale turns the "good time" into a "bad time" for Old Master. The exchanges between Okra and Old Master cleverly disguise a sense of triumph in the liberation of slaves who "leave no tracks," only the loss and destruction of property.

A LAUGH THAT MEANT FREEDOM

There were some slaves who had a reputation for keeping out of work because of their wit and humor. These slaves kept their masters laughing most of the time, and were able, if not to keep from working altogether, at least to draw the lighter tasks.

Nehemiah was a clever slave, and no master who had owned him had ever been able to keep him at work, or succeeded in getting him to do heavy work. He would always have some funny story to tell or some humorous remark to make in response

"A Laugh That Meant Freedom," from J. Frank Dobie, ed., *Tone the Bell Easy*. University of Texas Press, Austin, TX. *Publications of the Texas Folklore Society* 10 (1932): 14–15.

"...ef yuh tole ez big uh lie ez Ah did."

The illustrator Rue Knapp sketched this portrait of Nehemiah and his master for the story "A Laugh That Meant Freedom." Reproduced from *Encyclopedia of Black Folklore and Humor* by Henry D. Spalding. Illustrated by Rue Knapp. *By arrangement with Jonathan David Publishers, Inc., www .jdbooks.com.*

to the master's questioning or scolding. Because of this faculty for avoiding work, Nehemiah was constantly being transferred from one master to another. As soon as an owner found out that Nehemiah was outwitting him, he sold Nehemiah to some other slaveholder. One day, David Wharton, known as the most cruel slave master in Southwest Texas, heard about him.

"I bet I can make that rascal work," said David Wharton, and he went to Nehemiah's master and bargained to buy him.

The morning of the first day of his purchase, David Wharton walked over to where Nehemiah was standing and said, "Now you are going to work, you understand. You are going to pick four hundred pounds of cotton today."

"Wal, Massa, dat's aw right," answered Nehemiah, "but ef Ah meks you laff, won' yuh lemme off fo' terday?"

"Well," said David Wharton, who had never been known to laugh, "if you make me laugh, I won't only let you off for today, but I'll give you your freedom."

"Ah decl', Boss," said Nehemiah, "yuh sho' is uh goodlookin' man."

"I am sorry I can't say the same thing about you," retorted David Wharton.

"Oh, yes, Boss, yuh could," Nehemiah laughed out, "yuh could, if yuh tole ez big uh lie ez Ah did."

David Wharton could not help laughing at this; he laughed before he thought. Nehemiah got his freedom.

SOURCE: J. Frank Dobie, ed., *Tone the Bell Easy*, 14–15.

This tale broadcasts the advantages of lying, showing how it enables one slave to win his freedom. Wit and humor rarely sufficed in real life to lighten assigned labors, but here they appear capable of softening even the "most cruel" master. The use of nonstereotypical names and real places gives the story an aura of authenticity, even as it remains one of the tallest of tales in suggesting that laughter can be liberating in a literal sense.

HOW BUCK WON HIS FREEDOM

Buck was the shrewdest slave on the big Washington plantation. He could steal things almost in front of his master's eyes without being detected. Finally, after having had his chickens and pigs stolen until he was sick, Master Harry Washington called Buck to him one day and said, "Buck, how do you manage to steal without getting caught?"

"Dat's easy, Massa," replied Buck, "dat's easy. Ah kin steal yo' clo'es right tonight, wid you a-guardin' 'em."

"No, no," said the master, "you may be a slick thief, but you can't do that. I will make a proposition to you: If you steal my suit of clothes tonight, I will give you your freedom, and if you fail to steal them, then you will stop stealing my chickens."

"Aw right, Massa, aw right," Buck agreed. "Dat's uh go!"

That night about nine o'clock the master called his wife into the bedroom, got on his Sunday suit of clothes, laid it out on the table, and told his wife about the proposition he had made with Buck. He got on one side of the table and had his wife get on the other side, and they waited. Pretty soon, through a window that was open, the master heard the mules and horses in the stable lot running as if someone were after them.

"Here, wife," said he, "you take this gun and keep an eye on this suit. I'm going to see what's the matter with those animals."

Buck, who had been out to the horse lot and started the stampede to attract the master's attention, now approached the open window. He called out, "Ol' lady, ol' lady, ol' lady, you better hand me that suit. That damn thief might steal it while I'm gone."

"How Buck Won His Freedom," from J. Frank Dobie, ed., *Tone the Bell Easy*. University of Texas Press, Austin, TX. *Publications of the Texas Folklore Society* 10 (1932): 15–16.

The master's wife, thinking that it was her husband asking for the suit, took it from the table and handed it out the window to Jack. This is how Buck won his freedom.

SOURCE: J. Frank Dobie, ed., *Tone the Bell Easy*, 15–16.

The "master thief" tale is a familiar one in many cultures, with a young man from a poor family as the expert in theft. He steals everything from horses and dogs to bedcovers and wedding rings, and, in the end, he is banished from his native land, pardoned, and in some cases, as in this one, rewarded.

VOICES IN THE GRAVEYARD

One night two slaves on the Byars plantation entered the potato house of the master and stole a sack of sweet potatoes. They decided that the best place to divide them would be down in the graveyard, where they would not be disturbed. So they went down there and started dividing the potatoes.

Another slave, Isom, who had been visiting a neighboring plantation, happened to be passing that way on the road home, and, hearing voices in the graveyard, he decided to stop and overhear what was being said. It was too dark for him to see, but when he stopped he heard one of the thieves saying in a sing-song voice, "Ah'll take dis un, an' yuh can take dat un. Ah'll take dis un, an' yuh can take dat un."

"Lawd, ha' mercy," said Isom to himself. "Ah b'lieve dat Gawd an' de debbil am down hyeah dividin' up souls. Ah's gwine an' tell ol' Massa."

Isom ran as fast as he could up to the master's house and said, "Massa, Massa, Ah's passin' tho'oo de graveya'd jes' now, an' what yuh reckon Ah heerd? Gawd an' de debbil's down dar dividin' up souls. Ah sho' b'lieves de Day oh Judgment am come."

"You don't know what you are talking about," said the master. "That's foolish talk. You know you are not telling the truth."

"Yas, sah, Massa, yas, sah, Ah is. Ef yuh don' b'lieve hit, cum go down dar yo'se'f."

"Voices in the Graveyard," from J. Frank Dobie, ed., *Tone the Bell Easy*. University of Texas Press, Austin, TX. *Publications of the Texas Folklore Society* 10 (1932): 39–40.

"All right," said the master. "And if you are lying to me, I am going to whip you good tomorrow."

"Aw right, Massa," said Isom, "'case Gawd an' de debbil sho' am down dere."

Sure enough, when Isom and the master got near the graveyard, they heard the sing-song voice saying, "Yuh take dis un, an' Ah'll take dat un. Yuh take dis un, an' Ah'll take dat un."

"See dar, didn' Ah tell yuh, Massa?" said Isom.

In the meantime, the two darkies had almost finished the division of the potatoes, but remembered they had dropped two over by the fence—where Isom and the master were standing out of sight. Finally, when they had only two potatoes left, the one who was counting said, "Ah'll take dese two an' yuh take dem two over dere by de fence."

Upon hearing this, Isom and the master ran home as fast as they could go. After this the master never doubted Isom's word about what he saw or heard.

SOURCE: J. Frank Dobie, ed., *Tone the Bell Easy*, 39–40.

There are many versions of this tale about dividing up souls in the graveyard, and the story belongs to a tale type known as "the murderer's house." In that international tale type, two young men see the owner of a house take a knife and hear him say, "No matter how young they are they have to die." The owner is referring to domestic animals, but the two men believe that they are the targets. The tale can be traced back to a British source from the sixth century about dividing souls on Judgment Day.

SWAPPING DREAMS

Master Jim Turner, an unusually good-natured master, had a fondness for telling long stories woven out of what he claimed to be his dreams, and especially did he like to "swap" dreams with Ike, a witty slave who was a house servant. Every morning he would set Ike to telling about what he had dreamed the night before. It always seemed,

"Swapping Dreams," from J. Frank Dobie, ed., *Tone the Bell Easy*. University of Texas Press, Austin, TX. *Publications of the Texas Folklore Society* 10 (1932): 18–19.

however, that the master could tell the best dream tale, and Ike had to admit that he was beaten most of the time.

One morning, when Ike entered the master's room to clean it, he found the master just preparing to get out of bed. "Ike," he said, "I certainly did have a strange dream last night."

"Says you did, Massa, says you did?" answered Ike. "Lemme hear it."

"All right," replied the master, "it was like this: I dreamed I went to Nigger Heaven last night, and saw there a lot of garbage, some old torn-down houses, a few old broken-down, rotten fences, the muddiest, sloppiest streets I ever saw, and a big bunch of ragged, dirty niggers walking around."

"Umph, umph, Massa," said Ike, "you sho musta et de same t'ing I did las' ight, 'case I dreamed I went up to de white man's paradise, an' de streets was all of gol' an' silver, and dey was lots o' milk an' honey dere, an' putty pearly gates, but dey wasn't a soul in de whole place."

SOURCE: J. Frank Dobie, ed., *Tone the Bell Easy*, 18–19.

This tale sounds full chords and succinctly captures a contrast that no doubt never made it to the ears of the masters on plantations.

HOW JOHN STOPPED HIS BOSS-MAN FROM DREAMING

John had just finished eating his Sunday dinner and was seated on the steps of his cabin whittling with his pocket knife on a piece of the lumber left over from the new barn that had been built on Colonel Clemons' plantation that week, when he looked up and saw the Colonel walking across the cotton fields toward his cabin. John knew that the Colonel was on his way to make his regular Sunday afternoon call in order to fuss at him about something or to see what Mariah had cooked for dinner. Colonel Clemons was not satisfied at mistreating the hands all week but he even meddled around the cabins and worried them on Sundays.

"How John Stopped His Boss-Man from Dreaming," from J. Mason Brewer. *Mexican Border Ballads and Other Lore*, pp. 89–90. Austin: Texas Folklore Society, 1946.

While John was wondering what the Colonel was going to fuss about this time, Colonel Clemons walked up, spoke to John and sat down beside him on the steps. "John," he said, "I'll tell you what—let's make a bargain; we both dream a lot, so let's agree that everything I dream you'll see to it that I get it and everything you dream I will see to it that you get it."

"Awright," said John. "Dat suits me."

Next morning before daybreak John was down at the Colonel's house knocking on the door.

"What you want, you fool," yelled the Colonel, "come waking me up at this time of morning."

"Boss," replied John, "you know what Ah dreamed last night? Ah dreamed yuh gimme forty acres an' a mule."

"All right," replied the Colonel, cursing John. "Go and take them, and don't come down here again so early in the morning."

When the next day came, however, the Colonel was down at John's cabin before daybreak. When John heard him knock, he jumped out of bed and ran to the door. The Colonel was standing on the doorsteps.

"John," he said, "I dreamed last night that you gave me that mule and that forty acres back."

"Awright," said John. "Go on an' take 'em."

But the next morning John was down at the Colonel's house again before sunup knocking on his door. The Colonel rushed to the door and said, "Didn't I tell you not to wake me up this early in the morning?"

"Sho, Boss, sho," replied John, "but Ah wanted to tell yuh da dream Ah had before it slipped muh remembrance; Ah dreamed yuh gimme dat mule an' dat forty acres back an' forty acres more."

"All right," said the Colonel, slamming the door in John's face and stamping on the floor, "go on and take them."

The next morning before sunrise, however, John heard somebody rapping on his door again. Before he could open it, he heard the Colonel yelling, "John, John, wake up; you know what I dreamed last night? I dreamed that you gave me back all that I gave you yesterday and that we didn't dream no more."

And this is how John stopped Colonel Clemons from dreaming.

SOURCE: J. Mason Brewer, "John Tales," in *Mexican Border Ballads and Other Lore*, ed. Mody C. Boatright, 90–91.

"Forty acres and a mule" was a concept developed as part of agrarian reform in the United States following the Civil War. As this story makes clear, plantation owners resisted even this most modest form of reparations. Judging from the folkloric record, plantation owners seem obsessed with making bets, wagers, and bargains with their subordinates. John is positioned in the beginning of the tale as a laborer (part of the workforce building Colonel Clemons's new barn) and as an artisan (whittling something from leftover scraps). The punch line to the tale is charged with deep cynicism, for Colonel Clemons has no need to "dream," while John's wish for "forty acres and a mule" will remain forever unfulfilled.

JOHN AND THE CONSTABLE

There were not only a large number of rabbits, possums, and squirrels in the stretches of woods on the Southern plantations but also deer.

There was no law against killing the other wild animals, but at a certain season of the year it was against the law to kill a deer. If anyone killed a deer at this time, he was arrested and taken to jail; then he was tried and fined twenty-five dollars.

Most of the plantations had woods filled with deer, but Colonel Clemons had cut down most of the trees on his plantation and planted cotton, sugar cane, and corn on the land. Directly across the road from the Colonel's plantation, however, was a large forest owned by the Colonel's brother; so John went with McGruder every year during this season of the year to Colonel's brother's farm to hunt and kill deer.

McGruder would kill the deer and John would sell them. Then they would divide

"John and the Constable," from J. Mason Brewer. *Mexican Border Ballads and Other Lore*, pp. 102–4. Austin: Texas Folklore Society, 1946.

the money. John knew exactly how to sell them. He was well acquainted with all the sheriffs and constables in that part of the country. He also knew the men who came out to the plantation every year to buy the deer that McGruder killed. Consequently, he and McGruder had never been caught. They had regular customers.

This went on for four years.

One Saturday, John, McGruder, and John's little boys went to hunt deer. Just as John and McGruder were about to get through the barbed-wire fence and go into the Colonel's brother's thickly wooded forest, the little boys looked up and saw a white man driving a pot-bellied horse to an old wobbly buggy coming towards them. John's first impulse was to move on, but as they had not been able to sell many deer that year, he decided to wait and see whether the man might be one of their customers.

But as the man came nearer they realized that he was a stranger, so John decided to let him pass without speaking to him. But the man stopped, got out of his buggy and walked over to where John, McGruder, and the little boys were standing.

Singling John out, he asked, "Do you know where I can buy a deer?"

John hesitated at first, but finally he said, "Sho, boss, sho. Ah don' have none now but Ah kin git you one in 'bout a houah."

John was all smiles; he saw five dollars apiece in sight now for him and McGruder— their luck was coming back.

"How do you know you can?" asked the stranger, while John was grinning over the almost certain sale of the deer.

"'Cause," replied John, "me an' mah pardner jes' kilt one yistiddy down in dat stretch o' woods 'cross de road."

"You did?" said the stranger. "And do you know who I am?"

"Naw suh, naw suh," replied John. "Who is yuh?"

"Well," answered the stranger pulling back his coat and showing a badge. "I'm the biggest constable in the South."

"Says yuh is, Bos, says yuh is," replied John. "Well, know who Ah is? Ah's de biggest liar in de South."

SOURCE: J. Mason Brewer, "John Tales," in *Mexican Border Ballads and Other Lore*, ed. Mody C. Boatright, 102–4.

> *If tales about talking skulls warn of the dangers of broadcasting and*
> *bragging, stories that end with confessions about lying have the same*

cautionary edge. To be sure, declaring oneself to be a world-class liar is a fine way of undermining the assertion made.

OLD JOHN AND THE MASTER

The three tales below were told by Dr. Van Allen Little, a professor of Entomology at what was then Texas A&M College. Little grew up in northeast Texas, and the tales were written down by his son, William. "The Onion Thief" shows John recruiting an animal to trick his Master. "Old John and the Panther" and "Old John and the Bear" exist in many variants. Both take up the conflict between man and beast, with different outcomes, but always with the expectation that the slave's life can be sacrificed to the beast.

THE ONION THIEF

Old John liked onions and had been stealing them from the Master's garden at night. The Master became aware that somebody had been taking onions and asked John to catch the thief. John caught a skunk which he said was the thief. Old John further said that if Master didn't believe him, he could smell the skunk's breath.

OLD JOHN AND THE PANTHER

Master's children went to a one-room country school near home. To reach the school-house, they had to go through a wooded area where a panther was lurking and scaring them. Master told John to take his gun and kill the panther. John flushed the panther, shot and missed. When the panther started after John, he dropped his gun and ran for the schoolhouse nearby. John was running for dear life, but the panther was gaining. John ran up the doorstep just as the panther sprang. John slipped and fell, and the panther, which had overshot its mark, skidded into the schoolhouse. Quick as a flash, John jumped up and slammed the door shut. He had the panther trapped in the schoolhouse. When he went home and proudly told Master that he had caught the panther and put him in the schoolhouse, Master didn't believe him. John said, "If you go with me, I'll show you." And he took Master and showed him. The panther was looking through the windows as they approached the schoolhouse. Master said, "John, since you are a man so mighty as to be able to catch a panther with your bare hands, I want to see if you can take him out." John replied that that was not the agreement. "Getting him out is your job," John said.

OLD JOHN AND THE BEAR

A bear had been eating up Master's roasting ears in the cornfield. Master sent John to kill the bear. When John shot and wounded the animal, it attacked him. In the scuffle that followed, John succeeded in grabbing the bear by the tail and jerking him around to keep the bear's head away from him. By jerking the bear first one way and then another, John was able to prevent the bear from reaching around and biting him. This continued until John's strength waned. The bear finally got the upper hand and mauled and killed John. That was the end of the faithful old slave.

SOURCE: John Q. Anderson, *Southern Folklore Quarterly* 35 (1961), 195–97.

PART XI

HOW IN THE WORLD?
POURQUOI TALES

*P*ourquoi tales, also called etiological stories, tell how things came to be the way they are. At times they do nothing more than explain physical characteristics (spots, a long tail, a cracked shell); at times they reveal the origins of behavioral traits (greed, sloth, fearfulness). Unlike creation myths, which form sacred charter narratives, *pourquoi* tales tend to be irreverent yet also have a whiff of the didactic, channeling messages about the consequences of certain actions in a comic mode.

Pourquoi tales gained cultural relevance in African American communities by focusing on differences in status between whites and blacks. They sought to explain asymmetrical power relationships and show why social circumstances were what they were, often through racial binaries that position black characters as shortchanged—sometimes through no fault of their own but sometimes owing to stereotypical shortcomings—as they compete for various favors doled out by a capricious and irrational God. Using the strategy of exaggerating and overdoing in order to undo stereotypes, these narratives are shot through with satire that is both poignant and unsettling.

WHY WE SEE ANTS CARRYING BUNDLES AS BIG AS THEMSELVES

Kweku Anansi and Kweku Tsin—his son—were both very clever farmers. Generally, they succeeded in getting fine harvests from each of their farms. One year, however, they were very unfortunate. They had sown their seeds as usual, but no rain had fallen for more than a month after and it looked as if the seeds would be unable to sprout.

Kweku Tsin was walking sadly through his fields one day looking at the bare, dry ground, and wondering what he and his family would do for food, if they were unable to get any harvests. To his surprise he saw a tiny dwarf seated by the roadside. The little hunchback asked the reason for his sadness, and Kweku Tsin told him. The dwarf promised to help him by bringing rain on the farm. He asked Kweku to fetch two small sticks and to tap him lightly on the hump, while he sang:

"O water, go up, O water, go up,
And let rain fall, and let rain fall."

To Kweku's great joy rain immediately began to fall, and continued till the ground was thoroughly well soaked. In the days following, the seeds germinated and the crops began to do well.

Anansi soon heard how well Kweku's crops were growing—while his own were still bare and hard. He went straightway to his son and demanded to know the reason. Kweku Tsin, being an honest fellow, at once told him what had happened.

Anansi quickly made up his mind to get his farm watered in the same way, and accordingly set out toward it. As he went, he cut two big, strong sticks, thinking, "My son made the dwarf work with little sticks. I will make him do twice as much work with my big ones." He carefully hid the big sticks, however, when he saw the dwarf coming toward him. As before, the hunchback asked what the trouble was, and Anansi told him. "Take two small sticks, and beat me lightly on the hump," said the dwarf. "I will get rain for you."

But Anansi took his big sticks and beat so hard that the dwarf fell down dead. The greedy fellow was now thoroughly frightened, for he knew that the dwarf was jester to the King of the country, and a very great favorite of his. He wondered how he could fix the blame on someone else. He picked up the dwarf's dead body and carried it to a kola-tree. There he laid it on one of the top branches and sat down under the tree to watch.

By and by Kweku Tsin came along to see if his father had succeeded in getting rain for his crops. "Did you see the dwarf, father?" he asked, when he saw the old man sitting alone. "Oh, yes!" replied Anansi; "but he has climbed this tree to pick kola. I am now waiting for him." "I will go up and fetch him," said the young man—and immediately he began climbing. As soon as his head touched the dwarf's body, the dwarf fell to the ground. "Oh! What have you done, you wicked fellow!" cried his father. "You have killed the King's jester!" "That is all right," the son replied quietly (for he had seen that this was one of Anansi's tricks). "The King is very angry with him and promised a bag of money to anyone who killed him. I will now go and get the reward." "No! No! No!" Anansi shouted. "The reward is mine. I killed him with two big sticks. *I* will take him to the King." "Very well!" the son replied. "Since you were the one who killed him, you can take him."

Anansi set off, quite pleased with the prospect of getting a reward. He reached the King's court only to find the King very angry at the death of his favorite. The body of the jester was shut up in a great box, and Anansi was condemned—as a punishment—to carry it on his head forever. The King enchanted the box so that it could never be set down on the ground. The only way that Anansi could ever get rid of it was by getting some other man to put it on his head. Of course, no one was willing to do that.

At last, one day, when Anansi was almost worn out with his heavy burden, he met Ant. "Will you hold this box for me while I go to market and buy some things I need really badly?" Anansi asked Mr. Ant.

"I know your tricks, Anansi," Ant replied. "You want to be rid of it."

"Oh, no, indeed, Mr. Ant," protested Anansi. "I will come back for it. I promise."

Mr. Ant, who was an honest fellow and always kept his own promises, believed him. He put the box on his head, and Anansi hurried off. Needless to say, the sly fellow did not have any intention of keeping his word. Mr. Ant waited in vain for his return and was obliged to wander all the rest of his life with the box on his head. That is the reason we so often see ants carrying great bundles as they hurry along.

SOURCE: Adapted from William Henry Barker and Cecilia Sinclair, *West African Folk-Tales*, 63–67.

The motivation for this tale (explaining why ants carry heavy burdens) has almost nothing to do with the terms of the plot, which turn on Anansi's multiple betrayals of his son and the dwarf who helps them both. Anansi's greed, lack of gratitude, and treachery take a murderous turn, but Anansi himself is off the hook, with an innocent ant shouldering the burden which he had been condemned to carry. The tale may explain why ants carry a burden, but it fails to explain anything at all about the moral calculus at work in Anansi's machinations. It is almost as if the explanation aims to sweep away the listener's objections to the amoral antics described in the tale.

WHY THE HARE RUNS AWAY

This is the story of the hare and the other animals.

The weather was drying up the earth into hardness. There was no dew. Even the creatures of the water were suffering from thirst. Soon famine came, and the animals, having nothing to eat, assembled in council.

"What shall we do," they said, "to keep from dying of thirst?" And they deliberated a long time.

At last they decided that each animal should cut off the tips of its ears and extract the fat from them. Then all the fat would be collected and sold, and with the money they would get for the fat, they would buy a hoe and dig a well so as to get some water.

And all cried, "It is good. Let us cut off the tips of our ears."

They did so, but when it came the turn of the hare to cut off the tips of his ears, he refused.

The other animals were astonished, but they said nothing. They took up the ears, extracted the fat, went and sold all, and bought a hoe with the money.

They brought back the hoe and began to dig a well in the dry bed of a lagoon. "Ha! At last some water! Now we can slake our thirst a little."

The hare was not there, but when the sun was in the middle of the sky, he took a calabash and went towards the well.

1 *gañ-gañ:* a drum

As he walked along, the calabash dragged on the ground and made a great noise. It said—"Chan-gañ-gañ-gañ.[1]"

The animals, who were watching by the lagoon, heard

the noise. They were frightened. They asked each other, "What is it?" Then as the noise kept coming closer, they ran away.

Reaching home, they said there was something terrible at the lagoon that had forced the watchers by the lagoon to flee.

Then all the animals by the lagoon were gone. The hare drew up water without any interference at all. Then he went down into the well and bathed so that the water was muddied.

The next day, all the animals ran to get water, and they found it muddied.

"Oh," they cried, "who spoiled our well?"

They went and made an image. Then they made bird-lime and smeared it all over the image.

When the sun was again in the middle of the sky, all the animals went and hid in the bush near the well.

The hare came. His calabash cried, "Chan-gañ-gañ-gañ, Chan-gañ-gañ-gañ." He approached the image. He never suspected that all the animals were hiding in the bush.

The hare greeted the image. The image said nothing. He greeted it again, and still the image said nothing.

"Watch out," said the hare, "or I will give you a slap."

He gave a slap, and his right hand remained stuck in the bird-lime. He slapped with his left hand, and it remained stuck also.

"Oh! Oh!" he cried, "I must kick with my feet."

He kicked with his feet, and they remained stuck, and the hare could not get away.

Then the animals ran out of the bush and came to see the hare and his calabash.

"Shame on you, oh! hare," they cried out together. "Didn't you also agree to cut off the tips of your ears, and, when it came to your turn, you then refused? What! you refused, and yet you come to muddy our water?"

They took whips, they fell upon the hare, and they beat him. They beat him until they nearly killed him.

"We ought to kill you, accursed hare," they said. "But, no—run."

They let him go, and the hare fled. Since then, he does not leave the grass.

SOURCE: A. B. Ellis, *The Ewe-Speaking Peoples of the Slave Coast of West Africa*, 275–77.

A variant of the tar-baby story, this African tale shows how the hare undermines collaboration with his self-centered behavior. Not only does he fail to cut off the tips of his ears (thus creating a second implicit pourquoi story about why the hare has such long ears), he also dirties the water for the other animals. The tale seems to turn less on why hares stay in the grass or run away than on the question of survival through cooperation and group problem-solving or through self-interested behavior. In a sense, we have more of a dilemma tale—a provocation that gets listeners to respond and talk—than an etiological fable.

TORTOISE AND THE YAMS

1 *alo:* The term is used to designate a story, but the literal meaning of the word is riddle, something invented, with twists and turns.

My *alo*[1] is about Tortoise.

There was once a famine in the land, and food was not to be found anywhere.

One day, Lizard was on a plantation searching for something to eat, when he discovered a large boulder with yams in it. Here's how it happened.

Lizard saw a plantation owner and heard him shout, "Rock, open," and the boulder before him opened up. The man went in, took some yams, and came back out again. Then he said, "Rock, shut," and the boulder closed up.

Lizard watched all of this. He heard what the man said, and he went back home.

The next morning, once the rooster had crowed, Lizard went back to the boulder. He said, "Rock, open," and the boulder opened. He went inside and picked out some yams to take home and eat. Then he said, "Rock, shut," and the boulder closed back up again. The Lizard did this every day.

One day Tortoise, the bald-headed elf, met Lizard on the road and saw that he was carrying yams. He asked, "Where did you find all those yams, my friend?"

Lizard said, "If I were to tell you and take you to the place where I found them, I might be killed." The bald-headed elf answered, "I will not say a word to anyone. Please show me the place." And Lizard said, "Very well, then. Come and find me tomorrow morning when the cock crows, and we will go there together."

The next morning, long before the rooster began crowing, Tortoise arrived at Lizard's house. He stood outside and cried, "Cock-a-doodle-do." A second time he called out, "Cock-a-doodle-do." Then he went in and woke Lizard. "The cock has crowed, and it's time to go," he said.

"Let me sleep a while longer," Lizard said. "The cock has not yet crowed."

"All right," said Tortoise. And they both went back to sleep until dawn.

After Lizard woke up, the two left to find the yams. As soon as they reached the boulder, Lizard said, "Rock, open," and the rock opened. Lizard went in, took some yams, and came out again.

He said to Tortoise, "It is time to go. Take your yams and let's go."

"Wait a minute," said Tortoise.

"All right," said Lizard. "Rock, shut." And he left without his friend.

Tortoise, the bald-headed elf, helped himself to more yams. He put yams on his back and yams on his head; he put yams on his arms and yams on his legs.

Lizard arrived home and lit a fire. Then he lay on his back with his feet in the air, as if he were dead. And he stayed like that all day long.

When Tortoise, the bald-headed elf, was ready to leave, he wanted to make the boulder open up again. But he could not remember what he was supposed to say. He tried one word after another[2] but never found the right words, and the boulder remained shut.

Before long the plantation owner came by. He ordered the boulder to open up and found Tortoise inside. He grabbed hold of him and beat him. He beat him hard.

"Who brought you here?" asked the man.

"It was Lizard who brought me here," Tortoise replied.

The man took a piece of string and tied it around Tortoise's neck, and then he went over to where Lizard was living.

When they arrived, the man found Lizard lying on his back, with his feet in the air, as if he were dead. He starting shaking him. Then he said, "This bald-headed elf claims it was you who took him to my plantation and showed him the yams I stored up."

"Me?" said Lizard. "You can see for yourself that that's not possible. I am not in a condition to go out. I have been sick for three months, lying flat on my back. I have no idea where your plantation is."

The man picked Tortoise up and smashed him to the ground. Poor Tortoise, groaning and moaning, said in a pathetic voice, "Cockroach, come and mend me. Ant, come and mend me."

And Cockroach and Ant came and mended him. And you can still see the places where they mended him, for those are the parts of Tortoise's shell which are rough.

2 *He tried one word after another:* Like the brother of Ali Baba in the tale from *The Thousand and One Nights* about the forty thieves, Tortoise is unable to recall the correct magical password.

SOURCE: Adapted from A. B. Ellis, *The Yoruba-Speaking Peoples of the Slave Coast of West Africa*, 271–74.

Folklorists have identified a motif known as "mountain opens to magical formula," and in this story, crafty Lizard manages to trap Tortoise by counting on his flawed memory. But in the final analysis, it is Tortoise's greed that does him in. In some versions of the tale about how the tortoise came to have his shell marked, the mended spots are seen as decorative designs that ennoble and embellish rather than as unsightly scars.

WHAT MAKES BRER WASP HAVE A SHORT PATIENCE

Creatures don't all stay just the way God made them. No, sir. With the mistakes made, and accidents, and natural debilitation, and one thing or another, they become different as time goes on, until sometime later they are hardly the same thing at all.

At one time, Brer Wasp looked very different from the way he does today. He was big on company, and he loved to talk, and joke, and cut the fool. He was one person that had to have his laugh.

One day, he was walking on a path, and he met up with Brer Mosquito. Now, Brer Mosquito and his whole family weren't very big at all, but they took themselves mighty seriously. Brer Mosquito and his pa planted a little patch of ground together, but they always called it the plantation. They talked so big about their crops and land and everything that you would have thought that they had a twenty-mile place. Now, Brer Wasp loved to draw Brer Mosquito out on the subject.

That same week, there had been a heavy frost, and all the sweet-potato vines died and turned black and everybody was forced to dig for the early potatoes. And Brer Wasp, after he had passed the time of day with Brer Mosquito, and inquired about his family, asked him about his pa's health and how he had made out with his crop. "We made out fine, Brer Wasp," Brer Mosquito said; "just too fine. We had the biggest crop you ever have seen!" "The potatoes were big, then?" "I tell you, sir! They were huge! You have never seen such potatoes!" "How big are they, Brer Mosquito?" Brer Wasp questioned him. "My friend," Brer Mosquito said, puffing out his chest and reaching down and pulling his little britches tight around his little leg. "Most of our crop came up bigger than the calf of my leg!"

Well, sir! Brer Wasp looked at Brer Mosquito's poor little leg, and as he thought about those "huge potatoes," he had to laugh to himself. Now, he tried to mind his manners, but his chest and face swelled up, and his eye water ran out of his eyes, and he burst out laughing right in Brer Mosquito's face. He laughed and he laughed till his sides hurt him. Whenever he thought he would stop, he looked at that ridiculous leg that stood there like a toothpick, and he laughed more than ever. His sides hurt him so much he had to hold them in with both his hands and rock himself back and forth.

"What makes you have to do that?" Brer Mosquito asked him. "You had better explain yourself. That is, if you can act sensible!" Brer Wasp gasped out, "Good lord, Brer Mosquito, looking for the biggest part of your leg is like hunting for the heaviest part of a hair! How big those huge potatoes must be, if you say they are as big as that!" And he laughed again till his sides hurt so bad that it wasn't enough just to press them—he had to grab them in both his hands and squeeze.

Brer Mosquito was so annoyed that he felt like fighting Brer Wasp right on the spot. But then he remembered that Brer Wasp was kind of nasty when he got in a row. So he just drew himself up, and stuck out his mouth, and said, "Laugh, you no-mannered devil! Laugh! But take care that the day doesn't come when somebody laughs at you the same no-mannered way!" And he went away so blistering mad that his two little coattails stuck straight out behind him.

But that didn't stop Brer Wasp. All the way to his house he had been laughing so hard that he had to stop now and catch his breath. At last he got home and started to laugh some more and tell his family about Brer Mosquito.

Just then his wife got a good look at him, and she hollered out, "For crying-out-loud, Brer Wasp! What's happened to your stomach?" Brer Wasp looked down where his waist had been, and he saw how much he had shrunk up, and he was afraid to so much as sneeze.

Then he remembered what Brer Mosquito had said to him. He remembered all those people he had been joking about and laughing at so hard and for such a long time and he thought about how now the others were going to have their turn to laugh at that little waist he had now. He got so that he couldn't get that shameful thing out of his mind. And that is why he has such a short patience! Everywhere he goes he thinks

THE ANNOTATED AFRICAN AMERICAN FOLKTALES

somebody is ready to laugh at him. If anyone so much as looks at him, he gets so mad that he is ready to fight.

And that isn't the worst, because from that day to this day, he can't laugh anymore, because if he does, he will burst in two!

SOURCE: Samuel Gaillard Shelby and Gertrude Matthews, *Black Genesis: A Chronicle*, 81–84.

The story of Brer Wasp and his thin waist sends a clear message about the consequences of rudeness and cruelty. Brer Wasp's mocking laughter has physical effects and is turned against him—he becomes vulnerable and testy as a result of his intolerance. Only rarely do African American folktales transmit a message so clearly moral and instructive, without the usual complications about the multiple ambiguities and unintended consequences of human behavior.

DE REASON WHY DE 'GATOR STAN' SO

De Rabbit an' de Alligator was to hab a dance an' dey invited all de gals to come to de dance dat night, an' de Alligator was to come out de ribber to meet de Rabbit.

So arfter dey all was come into de dancin' room dey all biggin for say, "Big so, an' big so anudder"—dat was de chune[1] dey dance by.

Well, Br'er Rabbit biggin for tink Br'er Alligator ben kiss de gals tummuch. So 'e git behin' de doo' wid a club in 'e han', an' as Br'er Alligator come dancin' by 'e hit um ober de eye, an' dat what mek de knobs ober de 'Gator eye dat we all see stan' so tel dis day.

1 *chune:* tune

2 *yeardy:* heard

3 *for come sho':* to come ashore

Br'er Alligator neber know what struck um; 'e run clean out de house down to de ribber side.

Well, one day, Br'er Rabbit was walkin' 'long de ribber sho' feedin' an' 'e yeardy[2] Br'er Alligator da fetch long groan,—same like we year um groan sometime now in de pon'. So 'e call um for come sho'[3] an Alligator come sho', an' 'e say, "Br'er Alligator, what mek dem knob ober you eye?"

386 ◆

Br'er Alligator say, "Dat mek I hab to gib sich long groan, 'cause something ben knock me in de eye." So Br'er Rabbit tell um *him* ben mek dat knob on 'e eye, an' arfter dat dey biggin for mek peace. An' whiles dey ben a talk, Br'er Alligator say, "Br'er Rabbit, you know wha' trubble is?"

Rabbit tell um, "Br'er Alligator, when de win' blow to de Norderwes' you mus' go in de broom grass[4] an' lay down, an' ef you le' me know de day you gwine I'll le' you know wha' trubble is."

An de Alligator went one day an' lie down in de broomgrass, an' de win' was blowin' from de Norderwes', blowin' bery brisk dat day when de Alligator went right out an' lay down in de broom grass, an' 'e tell Br'er Rabbit 'e was gwine dere.

So while him gone in de grass lie down, Rabbit gone set de broom grass on fire all roun' while 'Gator ben sleepin'.

An' whiles de win' ben catch de fire, blow um right on alligator; when 'e git 'bout ten feet 'Gator biggin for wake up.

Rabbit stan' leetle way off, da whoop! An' while de fire da blaze up, 'Gator aint know wha' for do. 'E dance an' de fire da blaze. At lars' 'e couldn't do no better, had to jump right in de fire for git out. 'E run right t'ru' de fire an' run on tel 'e jump in de water, an' by dat de fire bu'n um so tel 'e back ben all cober ober wid scale an' barnacle, same like you allers shum[5] de Alligator back to dis day.

4 *broom grass:* a type of tall grass

5 *shum:* see

SOURCE: A. M. H. Christensen, *Afro-American Folk Lore, Told Round Cabin Fires on the Sea Islands of South Carolina,* 54–57.

Told in Gullah dialect, this tale was collected by Abigail Christensen, who heard it from a man of sixty or seventy named Baskin, who in turn had the stories from his grandfather, who came to the United States on a slave ship. The story neatly enacts the hazards of asking for trouble, and it shows Br'er Rabbit as a vengeful figure who cannot get enough when it comes to inflicting punishments.

WHY THE NIGGER IS SO MESSED UP

When the Creator made man, He was making the white man first, and all of the scrap pieces, the ends of the fingernails and the toes and the backsides, and what have you, He said, "Well, I don't know what I'm gon' do with all of these ends. I'll throw them over here in the corner, and when I get time, I'll decide what to do with them."

And, ALL OF A SUDDEN, something popped out of the corner, say, "Lawd, here me!"

And He turned around and it was a nigger—he made himself. He say, "Since you so smart, now, you stay like that."

And that's why the nigger is so messed up. He couldn't wait until the Lord fixed him right. He had to make himself.

SOURCE: Daryl Cumber Dance, *Shuckin' and Jivin': Folklore from Contemporary Black Americans*, 7.

In this creation tale, the black man brings himself to life, from scraps and remnants. Creative genius and improvisational verve backfire, for the man made of remnants appears to be not quite complete—"messed up." A strength is turned into a weakness, even as it is used to mock notions of racial inferiority. Daryl Dance recorded the story in Richmond, Virginia, in 1975 as it was told to him by a fifty-year-old woman.

TWO BUNDLES

"Don't never worry about work," says Jim Presley. "There's more work in de world than there is anything else. God made de world and de white folks made work."

"Why the Nigger Is So Messed Up," Daryl Cumber Dance, ed., *Shuckin' and Jivin': Folklore from Contemporary Black Americans*, 1978. Reprinted with permission of Indiana University Press. "Two Bundles," from Zora Neale Hurston, *Mules and Men*. Copyright 1935 by Zora Neale Hurston; renewed ©1963 by John C. Hurston and Joel Hurston. Reprinted by permission of HarperCollins Publishers.

"Yeah, dey made work but they didn't make us do it," Joe Willard put in. "We brought dat on ourselves."

"Oh, yes, de white folks did put us to work too," says Jim Allen.

Know how it happened? After God got thru makin' de world and de varmints and de folks, he made up a great big bundle and let it down in de middle of de road. It laid dere for thousands of years, then Ole Missus said to Ole Massa: "Go pick up that box, Ah want to see whu's in it." Ole Massa look at de box and it look so heavy dat he says to de nigger: "Go fetch me dat big old box out dere in de road." De nigger been stumblin' over de box a long time so he tell his wife:[1]

"'Oman, go git dat box." So de nigger 'oman she returned to git de box. She says:

"Ah always lak to open up a big box[2] 'cause there's nearly always something good in great big boxes." So she run and grabbed a-hold of de box and opened it up and it was full of hard work.

Dat's de reason de sister in black works harder[3] than anybody else in de world. De white man tells de nigger to work and he takes and tells his wife.

"Aw, now, dat ain't de reason niggers is working so hard," Jim Presley objected.

Dis is de way *dat* was.

God let down two bundles 'bout five miles down de road. So de white man and de nigger raced to see who would git there first. Well, de nigger out-run de white man and grabbed de biggest bundle. He was so skeered de white man would git it away from him he fell on top of de bundle and hollered back: "Oh, Ah got here first and dis biggest bundle is mine." De white man says: "All right, Ah'll take yo' leavings," and picked up de li'l tee-ninchy[4] bundle layin' in the road. When de nigger opened up his bundle he found a

1 *he tell his wife:* In *Tell My Horse*, Hurston describes the roles assigned to Caribbean black women and how they occupy the lowest rung on the social totem pole, more akin to beasts than humans. "If she is of no particular family, poor and black, she is in a bad way indeed. . . . She had better pray to the Lord to turn her into a donkey and be done with the thing. It is assumed that God made poor black females for beasts of burden" (58).

2 *Ah always lak to open up a big box:* The woman's desire to know what is in the box finds parallels with the curiosity of the mythical Pandora and the biblical Eve.

3 *De sister in black works harder:* In the story of Adam and Eve, Adam and Eve are condemned to labor by the sweat of their brows, while Eve must also suffer the pains of childbirth.

4 *tee-ninchy:* tiny, and sometimes expressed as "little-tee-ninchy"

5 *chop-axe:* This term, like "writin'-pen," which appears right after it, is what Hurston called the "double descriptive," a noun that has action added to it. As Hurston put it: "Everything illustrated. So we can say the white man thinks in a written language and the Negro thinks in hieroglyphics," an insight relevant to the ending of this tale.

6 *usin' his tools:* The tools of the agricultural worker, who labors under the "hot sun," and the white man's writing instrument, used to determine the distribution of wealth, take on powerful symbolic importance, and the writing down of a tale that circulates in conversations marks a powerful rupture with the past. Hurston has taken possession of the "writin'-pen."

7 *ought's a ought: Aught* and *ought* are the opposite of *naught* and *nought,* and can mean *anything* or *all.* But in common usage, ought is used as a synonym for *zero.*

pick and shovel and a hoe and a plow and chop-axe[5] and then de white man opened up his bundle and found a writin'-pen and ink. So ever since then de nigger been out in de hot sun, usin' his tools[6] and de white man been sittin' up figgerin', ought's a ought,[7] figger's a figger; all for de white man, none for de nigger.

SOURCE: Zora Neale Hurston, *Mules and Men,* 74–76.

Framed by conversations about bad weather leading to a day off from work, these two stories take up the gendered division of labor as well as a racial division of labor. They enact the folk wisdom that good things come in small packages, while also sending a warning about the hazards of greed.

COMPAIR LAPIN AND MADAME CARENCRO

Do you know why buzzards are bald? No? Well, I am going to tell you.

Once upon a time Mme Carencro[1] was sitting on her nest on an oak tree. Her husband was a good-for-nothing fellow, and she was always starving. At the foot of the tree there was a big hole in which a rabbit lived. Compair Lapin was big and fat, and every time Mme Carencro saw him she wanted to eat him. One day while Compair Lapin was sleeping, she took some moss and bricks and closed up the hole in the tree. Compair Lapin would never be able to get out, and he would die of hunger.

1 *carencro:* a term for buzzards

When Compair Lapin woke up and he found out that he was shut up in the hole, he begged Mme Carencro to let him out, but she replied each time: "I am hungry and I must eat the flesh on your bones."

When Compair Lapin realized that begging was of no use, he stopped trying. Mme Carencro was so happy to have caught Compair Lapin that she licked her lips as she thought of the good dinner she would be having. When she did not hear Compair Lapin moving, she was sure that he must be dead, smothered, and she removed the moss and the bricks that closed the hole. She started to go in through the opening, but just then Compair Lapin made a single leap and escaped. When he was at some distance, he said: "You see, it is you who are caught, and not I."

Compair Lapin ran away and went to stay at the house of one of his friends, because he was afraid to go back into the oak tree near Mme Carencro. Some days later Mme Carencro, who had forgotten Compair Lapin, went to take a walk with her children, who had all come out of their shells. She passed near the house of Compair Lapin's friend. Compair Lapin was glad, because it made him think about how he could get revenge on Mme Carencro. He ran into the kitchen and fetched a large tin pan full of burning embers and hot ashes. When Mme Carencro and her children passed nearby, he threw everything in the tin pan down on them in order to burn them. But buzzards, as you know, have thick feathers everywhere except on the top of their heads. They shook off the embers and ashes but not quickly enough to prevent the feathers on their heads from burning down to the skin.

That is why buzzards are bald and never eat the bones of rabbits.

SOURCE: Adapted from Alcée Fortier, *Louisiana Folk-Tales*, 22–23.

Compair Lapin may not always win in the first contest of wits, but he almost always wins in the end. Compair Lapin and Compair Bouki (bouki means hyena in Wollof) are the clever rabbit and the stupid fool in tales collected by Fortier, who was president of the American Folklore Society and dean of Foreign Languages at Tulane University.

JOHN HENRY, THE STEEL DRIVING MAN

John Henry was a railroad man.
  He worked from six 'till five,
"Raise 'em up bullies and let 'em drop down,
  I'll beat you to the bottom or die."

John Henry said to his captain:
  "You are nothing but a common man,
Before that steam drill shall beat me down,
  I'll die with my hammer in my hand."

John Henry said to the Shakers:
  'You must listen to my call,
Before that steam drill shall beat me down,
  I'll jar these mountains till they fall."

John Henry's captain said to him:
  "I believe these mountains are caving in "
John Henry said to his captain: "Oh Lord !"
  "That's my hammer you hear in the wind."

John Henry he said to his captain:
  "Your money is getting mighty slim,'
When I hammer through this old mountain,
  Oh Captain will you walk in?"

John Henry's captain came to him
  With fifty dollars in his hand,
He laid his hand on his shoulder and said:
  "This belongs to a steel driving man."

John Henry was hammering on the right side,
  The big steam drill on the left,
Before that steam drill could beat him down,
  He hammered his fool self to death.

They carried John Henry to the mountains,
  From his shoulder his hammer would ring,
She caught on fire by a little blue blaze
  I believe these old mountains are caving in.

John Henry was lying on his death bed,
  He turned over on his side,
And these were the last words John Henry said
  "Bring me a cool drink of water before I die."

John Henry had a little woman,
  Her name was Pollie Ann,
He hugged and kissed her just before he died,
  Saying, "Pollie, do the very best you can."

John Henry's woman heard he was dead,
  She could not rest on her bed,
She got up at midnight, caught that No. 4 train,
  "I am going where John Henry fell dead."

They carried John Henry to that new burying ground
  His wife all dressed in blue,
She laid her hand on John Henry's cold face,
"John Henry I've been true to you."

Price 5 Cents   W. T. BLANKENSHIP.

A printed broadside of "John Henry, the Steel Driving Man" dating to the late nineteenth or early twentieth century.

PART XII

BALLADS: HEROES, OUTLAWS, AND MONKEY BUSINESS

Song and story have always helped to pass time while carrying out repetitive chores. Whether spinning yarn, harvesting crops, sewing garments, mending tools, or rolling cigars, laborers have depended on chants, melodies, and plots to pass time, lighten workloads, and also to create a sense of group solidarity by building collective memories. For the grueling work of picking cotton, carried out from dawn to dusk, song provided the only distraction from the exhaustion produced by merciless heat and humidity, aching backs, bleeding fingers, and irksome insects.

Work songs in the fields often took the form of "hollers," echoing calls that once resounded in West African savannah regions. In *The Cotton Kingdom*, Frederick Law Olmsted describes hearing one of these "hoolies" or "hollers," which sonically bonded farmhands, muleskinners, plantation workers, and railroad teams. At midnight, he is awakened and observes a "gang of negroes" around the fire, enjoying a meal together: "Suddenly one raised such a sound as I had never heard before, a long, loud, musical shout rising and falling and breaking into falsetto, his voice ringing through the woods in the clear, frosty night air, like a bugle call. As he finished, the melody was caught up by another, and then another, and then by several in chorus" (164). When the workers rolled bales of cotton up an embankment, the same sounds filled the air.

Expressive culture builds social ties, personal connections, and communal solidarity. Through a process of signaling, stories and lyrics encode news, values, and behaviors in symbolic forms that create a cohesive group identity. Their words envision perils and possibilities, test hypotheses and speculations, model successful relationships and failed partnerships, and build a collective spirit of inquiry.

In the 1920s, the young Ralph Ellison was jealous of classmates who left school to work in the fields with their parents during the cotton-picking season. "Those trips to the cotton path seemed to me an enviable experience, because the kids came back with such wonderful stories," he wrote. "And it wasn't the hard work which they stressed, but the communion, the playing, the eating, the dancing and the singing. And they brought back jokes, *our* Negro jokes—not those told about Negroes by whites—and they always returned with Negro folk stories which I'd never heard before and which couldn't be found in any books I knew about. This was something to affirm and I felt there was a richness in it" (1995, 7). Ellison reminds us that storytelling was once an immersive experience and that it flourished in communal spaces, not only at sites of labor but also of leisure:

> The places where a rich oral literature was truly functional were the churches, the schoolyards, the barbershops, the cotton-picking camps; places where folklore and gossip thrived. The drug store where I worked was such a place, where on days of bad weather the older men would sit with their pipes and tell tall tales, hunting yarns and homely versions of the classics. It was here that I heard stories of searching for buried treasure and of headless horsemen, which I was told were my own father's versions told long before. There were even recitals of popular verse, "the shooting of Dan McGrew," and, along with these, stories of Jesse James, of negro outlaws and black United States marshals, of slaves who became the chiefs of Indian tribes and of the exploits of negro cowboys. There was both truth and fantasy in this, intermingled in the mysterious fashion of literature. (157)

Bad men, renegades, and outlaws figure prominently in the ballad tradition, and these rebels, who were in a state of constant conflict with the law, had a certain heroic bravado in their antagonism toward the social order. Self-destructive, antisocial, and solitary, they were less invested in justice and revenge than in displays of strength and terror. By contrast with stoic cultural heroes like John Henry, they refused to play by the rules. They exist perhaps because the John Henrys, who challenge stereotypes and are models of strength and fortitude, perish before their time, leaving a legacy of suffering and endurance rather than agency and action. Stagolee, Frankie, Annie Christmas, and others like them do not fare much better, but they stage their deaths as exercises in willful self-determination and are remembered for reckless audacity, even if, in the end, it is self-defeating.

---

pound of iron on stone, the sound of men's voices rising strong, rough, but tuneful, carving melody out of toil and blackness, mining and bringing to the light the rich ore of art which to the creative spirit lies hidden in even the dull facts and the routine of daily existence.

To have lost art out of the life of the worker is one of the most deadening blights of commercial civilization. Wherever still possible, humanity should hold fast to its God-given power of weaving some beauty of its own fashioning, some thread of personal interest through self-expression, into the woof of labor. For work, all work, is one of the great rhythms of life, and this the Negro exemplifies in his song. See how individual is the Negro's rhythmic invention in even such a simple chant as this one, built around a pounding hammer; and note how typical of the black man's sense of syncopation is the scanning of verses shown in the line-division and accentuation of the shouted phrases.

The folk-poems of these work-songs, mirroring as they do the daily life of black laborers, are gems in the literature of the United States, valuable both for their intrinsic interest—historically, poetically, socially—and for their worth as "human documents." They are alive; and the spirit of song that gave them birth should continue to live, not alone in the Negro's contribution to American letters, but in all the work of the race, from the humblest to the highest.

HAMMERIN' SONG

Boss is call-in'—huh!*
Let her drive, boys—huh!*
　　Foller me—huh!*
　　Foller me—huh!*

I been hammer-in'—huh!
In dis moun-tain—huh!
　　Four long year—huh!
　　Four long year—huh!

Ain't no ham-mer—huh!
In dis moun-tain—huh!
　　Ring like mine—huh!
　　Ring like mine—huh!

Capt'n tol'-me—huh!
Heard ma ham-mer—huh!
　　Forty-nine mile—huh!
　　Forty-nine mile—huh!

*Hammer falls here, while the men expel their breath with a sharp ejaculation.

[24]

Everybo-dy—huh!
What talks 'bout hammer-in'—huh!
　　Don't know how—huh!
　　Don't know how—huh!

Hammer' man, you—huh!
Can't beat me—huh!
　　I'll go down—huh!
　　I'll go down—huh!

Ef I beat you—huh!
To de bot-tom—huh!
　　Don't git mad—huh!
　　Don't git mad—huh!

Ef I leads yer—huh!
O my part-ner—huh!
　　Don't git mad—huh!
　　Don't git mad—huh!

Hammerin' man, don't—huh!
Hammer so hard—huh!
　　You'll break down—huh!
　　You'll break down—huh!

Dis ol' ham-mer—huh!
Keep on ring-'in—huh!
　　Roun' ma hade[1]—huh!
　　Roun' ma hade—huh!

Dese ol' rocks in—huh!
Dis yere moun-tain—huh!
　　Hu'ts[2] my side—huh!
　　Hu'ts my side—huh!

Ain't no use ter—huh!
Sen' fer de doc-ter—huh!
　　Water-boy's dade[3]—huh!
　　Water-boy's dade—huh!

[1]Head.
[2]Hurts.
[3]Dead.

[25]

The four-part *Hampton Series Negro Folk-Songs*, published in 1918–1919, includes nineteen songs transcribed and notated by folklorist Natalie Curtis Burlin, based on recordings made at the Hampton Institute in Virginia. "Hammerin' Song" and "Cott'n Pickin' Song" appear in Book IV, *Work- and Play-Songs*. In the description preceding "Hammerin' Song," Curtis Burlin extols—without a touch of irony—the moral value of work and the inventiveness of the black worker who transformed work's "great rhythms" into song. The names of the singers, all Hampton students, are listed together with their singing parts and courses of study: "Ira Godwin (Lead) Agriculture, Joseph Barnes (Tenor) Tinsmith, William Cooper (Baritone) Schoolteacher, Timothy Carper (Bass) Bricklayer."

COTT'N-PICKIN' SONG

Dis cott'n want a-pickin'
                so bad,
Dis cott'n want a-pickin'
                so bad,
Dis cott'n want a-pickin'
                so bad,
        Gwine clean all ober dis farm.

One twenties[1] of May mo'nin'
Under dat barnyard tree,
Dem Yankees read dem papers
An' sot dem darkies free.

Dis cott'n want a-pickin'
                so bad,
Dis cott'n want a-pickin'
                so bad,
Dis cott'n want a-pickin'
                so bad,
        Gwine clean all ober dis farm.

I's been workin' in er contract
Eber since dat day,
An' jes' found out dis yur[2]
Why hit[3] didn't pay.

Dis cott'n want a-pickin'
                so bad,
Dis cott'n want a-pickin'
                so bad,
Dis cott'n want a-pickin'
                so bad,
        Gwine clean all ober dis farm.

When Boss sol' dat cott'n
I ask fo' ma half.
He tol' me I chopped out
Ma half wid de grass.

NOTE:—Some singers omit the word "gwine" from the last line of the chorus.

[1] Twentieth. [2] Year. [3] It.

[11]

From *Hampton Series Negro Folk-Songs* by Natalie Curtis Burlin (1918–1919).

This eight-foot-tall bronze statue of John Henry stands next to two tunnels, one of which he helped build in 1872, the other was completed in 1930. Sculpted by Charles Cooper, the statue was unveiled in 1972 on the hundredth anniversary of the completion of the first tunnel. *Photograph by Chris Dorst*, Charleston Gazette-Mail.

JOHN HENRY

When John Henry was a little fellow,
You could hold him in the palm of your hand.
He said to his pa, "When I grow up
I'm gonna be a steel-driving man.
Gonna be a steel-driving man."

When John Henry was a little baby,
Setting on his mammy's knee,
He said "The Big Bend Tunnel[1] on the C. & O. Road
Is gonna be the death of me,
Gonna be the death of me."

1 *Big Bend Tunnel:* The tunnel, which is also referenced in the last stanza, is located in West Virginia.

One day his captain told him,

How he had bet a man

That John Henry would beat his steam-drill down,

Cause John Henry was the best in the land,

John Henry was the best in the land.

John Henry kissed his hammer,

White man turned on steam,

2 *shaker:* the worker who holds the chisel or drill for the man who hammers holes into rock.

Shaker[2] held John Henry's trusty steel,

Was the biggest race the world had ever seen,

Lord, biggest race the world ever seen.

John Henry on the right side

The steam drill on the left,

"Before I'll let your steam drill beat me down,

I'll hammer my fool self to death,

Hammer my fool self to death."

John Henry walked in the tunnel,

His captain by his side,

The mountain so tall, John Henry so small,

He laid down his hammer and he cried,

Laid down his hammer and he cried.

Captain heard a mighty rumbling,

Said "The mountain must be caving in."

John Henry said to the captain,

"It's my hammer swinging in de wind,

My hammer swinging in de wind."

John Henry said to his shaker,

"Shaker, you'd better pray;

for if ever I miss this piece of steel,

tomorrow'll be your burial day,

tomorrow'll be your burial day."

John Henry said to his shaker,
"Lord, shake it while I sing.
I'm pulling my hammer from my shoulders down,
Great Gawdamighty, how she ring,
Great Gawdamighty, how she ring!"

John Henry said to his captain,
"Before I ever leave town,
Gimme one mo' drink of dat tom-cat gin,
And I'll hammer dat steam driver down,
I'll hammer dat steam driver down."

John Henry said to his captain,
"Before I ever leave town,
Gimme a twelve-pound hammer wid a whale-bone handle,
And I'll hammer dat steam driver down,
I'll hammer dat steam driver down."

John Henry said to his captain,
"A man ain't nothin' but a man.
But before I'll let dat steam drill beat me down,
I'll die wid my hammer in my hand,
Die wid my hammer in my hand."

The man that invented the steam drill
He thought he was mighty fine,
John Henry drove down fourteen feet,
While the steam drill only made nine,
Steam drill only made nine.

"Oh, lookaway over yonder, captain.
You can't see like me."
He gave a long and loud and lonesome cry,
"Lawd, a hammer be the death of me,
A hammer be the death of me!"

John Henry had a little woman,
Her name was Polly Ann,
John Henry took sick, she took his hammer,
She hammered like a natural man,
Lawd, she hammered like a natural man.

John Henry hammering on the mountain
As the whistle blew for half-past two,
The last words his captain heard him say,
"I've done hammered my insides in two,
Lawd, I've hammered my insides in two."

The hammer that John Henry swung
It weighed over twelve pound.
He broke a rib in his left hand side
And his intrels[3] fell on the ground,
And his intrels fell on the ground.

3 *intrels:* entrails

John Henry, O, John Henry,
His blood is running red.
Fell right down with his hammer to the ground,
Said, "I beat him to the bottom but I'm dead,
Lawd, beat him to the bottom but I'm dead."

When John Henry was lying there dying,
The people all by his side,
The very last words they heard him say,
"Give me a cool drink of water 'fore I die,
Cool drink of water 'fore I die."

John Henry had a little woman,
The dress she wore was red,
She went down the track, and she never looked back,
Going where her man fell dead,
Going where her man fell dead.

John Henry had a little woman,
The dress she wore was blue,
De very last words she said to him,
"John Henry, I'll be true to you,
John Henry, I'll be true to you."

"Who's gonna shoes yo' little feet,
Who's gonna glove yo' hand,
Who's gonna kiss yo' pretty, pretty cheek,
Now you done lost yo' man?
Now you done lost yo' man?"

"My mammy's gonna shoes my little feet,
Pappy gonna glove my hand,
My sister's gonna kiss my pretty, pretty cheek,
Now I done lost my man,
Now I done lost my man."

They carried him down by the river,
And buried him in the sand.
And everybody that passed that way,
Said, "There lies that steel-driving man,
There lies a steel-driving man."

They took John Henry to the river,
And buried him in the sand,
And every locomotive come a-roaring by,
Says "There lies that steel-drivin' man,
Lawd, there lies a steel-drivin' man."

Some say he came from Georgia,
And some from Alabam,
But it's wrote on the rock at the Big Bend Tunnel,
That he was an East Virginia man,
Lord, Lord, an East Virginia man.

SOURCE: *Norton Anthology of African-American Literature*, 31–34.

John Henry, the "steel-driving man," is celebrated in song and story as the victor in a race against a machine: the steam-powered hammer. According to legend, John Henry's heart gave out after his triumph, and he died, hammer in hand. The mythical John Henry has driven railroad spikes but also hammered holes for dynamite charges. Various historical figures have been proposed as the source for the legend, among them an African American named John William Henry, from Talcott, West Virginia, who worked on the Chesapeake and Ohio Railroad Line. In the city of Leeds, Alabama, citizens claim that the contest took place at the Coosa Mountain Tunnel of the Columbus and Western Railway in 1887. The John Henry in that contest was born a slave named Henry in 1850. Although there are many claims of eyewitness accounts to the contest as well as efforts to identify the man, no one has established with certainty that the story is factual rather than the stuff of legends, tall tales, and myths, all pieced together from various sources.

"The Ballad of John Henry" begins with John's early premonition of his death and moves swiftly to the contest with the steam-powered hammer, then on to his death and burial, and, finally, to the reaction of his wife. The so-called hammer songs that shadow the ballad—and most likely emerged before it—set the pace for work on the railroads. Those songs were rhythmic chants more than melodies, and they synchronized the efforts of the hammer man and the man who rotated the drill, while also ensuring that exertions did not exceed what was physically possible for the men in the group.

John Henry became not only a folk hero but also a powerful symbol of muscle for labor movements as well as for the Civil Rights Movement. Embodying strength and endurance, he represented the dignity of the working man who labored on despite capitalist exploitation and the threat of being replaced by machines. Beyond that, he has been seen as a towering figure of heroic struggle in general. The celebrated author Julius Lester writes: "I'm not certain what the connection is between

John Henry and [Martin Luther] King. However, I suspect it is the connection all of us feel to both figures—namely, to have the courage to hammer until our hearts break and to leave our mourners smiling in their tears" (1994).

There are many John Henrys. For Southern millworkers, he was a model of strength and integrity. For coal miners, he became a symbol of endurance under the harshest of working conditions. For Communist organizers, he became "the hero of the greatest proletarian epic ever

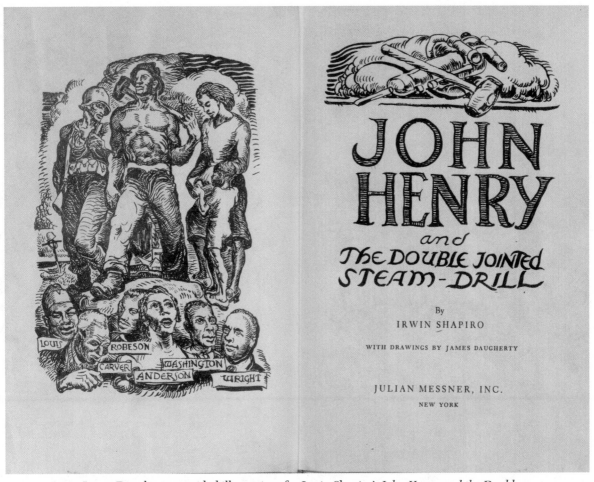

Artist James Daugherty provided illustrations for Irwin Shapiro's *John Henry and the Double-Jointed Steam-Drill*, published in 1945. The frontispiece shows the hero, together with a soldier and a mother and child, as originators of a legacy inherited by celebrated African American athletes, activists, performers, and scientists.

created" (Nelson 2006, 157). *In one version of the song, John Henry becomes too ill to work, and his wife takes over:*

> *Well they called John Henry's woman*
> *Yes they called for Julie-Anne*
> *Well she picked up the hammer where John Henry lay*
> *And she drove that steel like a man, Great God!*
> *And she drove that steel just like a man.*

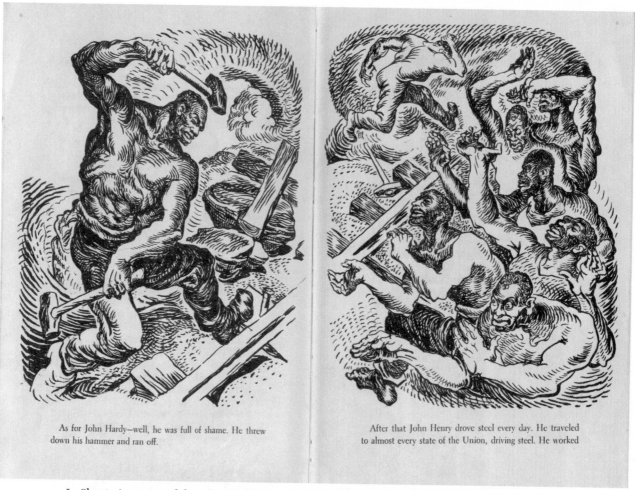

As for John Hardy—well, he was full of shame. He threw down his hammer and ran off.

After that John Henry drove steel every day. He traveled to almost every state of the Union, driving steel. He worked

In Shapiro's version of the tale, John Henry competes with John Hardy in tests of strength and endurance. Here, John Henry bests John Hardy at driving steel railroad spikes.

John Henry shuffled over to the piano, feeling sad. He played a few chords and began to sing the weary blues:

> I beat the steam drill, but see what it did to me,
> Beat the ol' steam drill, but look what it did to me,
> John Henry ain't the man he used to be.

He was still at it when Pollie Ann came back.

She took one look at him and burst out, "You, John Henry —you get back in your bed! No need to sing the blues. Just lay back easy while I fix you a snack. You'll fatten up and soon you'll be back on the mountain again."

"But what are we goin' to do? How we goin' to live?" asked John Henry.

"Well," said Pollie Ann, "I can't drive steel on the mountain. But I reckon I can drive steel where they're layin' track. I'll get me a job till you're on your feet again."

And that's just what she did. While John Henry lay on his bed, Pollie Ann drove steel like a man. As soon as she got home she'd fix John Henry a snack of hog jowls, chittlin's, cracklin's, corn pone, side meat, and greens. And John Henry began to fatten up. He began to get his strength back, too. Every day he tried to lift his hammer, and each day he could raise it a little more. And one day he found he could give it a full swing—not the way he used to, maybe, but better than anybody he knew.

"Just need a little practice," he thought.

John Henry's wife is able to drive steel "like a man" even as she nurses her husband back to health.

The song exists in over two hundred recorded versions, as part of the blues but also as one of the first documented country songs. It has been performed by many artists, among them Leadbelly, Paul Robeson, Harry Belafonte, Woody Guthrie, Pete Seeger, Van Morrison, Johnny Cash, and Bruce Springsteen. The figure of John Henry has also inspired novels, films, and plays and has an enduring presence in popular culture in the root sense of the term—in being of the people, by the people, and for the people.

ANNIE CHRISTMAS

Oldtimers say that the Negro longshoremen and all life on the riverfront are not what they used to be. It's gone soft now, say they. In other days men were really men, yet the toughest of them all was a woman.

Her name was Annie Christmas. She was six feet, eight inches tall and she weighed more than two hundred and fifty pounds. She wore a neat mustache and had a voice as loud and as deep as a foghorn on the river. The tough keelboatmen, terrors of the river in other days, stood in awe of her, and there wasn't a hulking giant of a stevedore who didn't jump when Annie snapped her black fingers. She could lick a dozen of them with one arm tied behind her back, and they knew it.

Most of the time Annie dressed like a man and worked as a man. Often she worked as a longshoreman, pulled a sweep[1] or hauled a cordelle.[2] She would carry a barrel of flour under each arm and another balanced on her head. Once she towed a keelboat from New Orleans to Natchez on a dead run, and never got out of breath.

1 *pulled a sweep:* conduct a search by towing a drag under water

2 *cordelle:* a heavy rope once used for towing boats

Annie could outdrink any man in the South. She would put down a barrel of beer and chase it with ten quarts of whiskey, without stopping. Men used to buy her whiskey just to see her drink. Sometimes she got mad in a barroom, beat up every man in the place and wrecked the joint. Sometimes she did it for fun.

Then, every once in a while, Annie would get into a feminine mood. When this happened she was really all of two hundred fifty pounds of coal-black female, really seductive and enticing in a super sort of way. At these times Annie would rent a barge, fill it with the best fancy women in New Orleans and operate a floating brothel up and down the Mississippi, catering to keelboatmen and stevedores, river pirates and longshoremen. She would always stage contests, and offer a hundred dollars cash to the women entertaining the most men satisfactorily in a given period of time. Of course, Annie was as magnificent amorously as she was as a fighter and drinker and she always won her own first prize.

She would really dress up for these occasions, wearing red satin gowns and scarlet plumes in her woolly hair. She always wore a commemorative necklace containing beads for all the eyes, ears and noses she had gouged from men, a bead for each one. The necklace was only thirty feet long, but then she only counted white men; there would not have been enough beads in New Orleans if she had counted Negroes.

Annie had twelve coal-black sons, each seven feet tall, all born at the same time. She had plenty of other babies, too, but these were her favorites. Whenever she got ready to have a baby, she drank a quart of whiskey and lay down somewhere. Afterward she had another quart and went straight back to work.

Finally, Annie met a man who could lick her and then she fell in love for the first time in her life. But the man didn't want her, so Annie bedecked herself in all her finery and her famous necklace and committed suicide.

Her funeral was appropriately elaborate. Her body was placed in a coal-black coffin and driven to the wharf in a coal-black hearse, drawn by six coal-black horses. Six on each side, marched her coal-black sons, dressed in coal-black suits. At the riverfront the coffin was placed on a coal-black barge, and that coal-black night, with no moon shining, her dozen coal-black sons floated on it with the coal-black coffin out to sea and vanished forever.

SOURCE: Lyle Saxon, Robert Tallant, and Edward Dreyer, eds., *Gumbo Ya-Ya*, 376–77. *For other versions of "Annie Christmas," see Virginia Hamilton,* Her Stories, *84–89, and "Annie Christmas," in Richard and Judy Dockrey Young,* African-American Folktales for Young Readers, *130–32.*

The female counterpart to such figures as Mike Fink, Paul Bunyan, and John Henry, Annie Christmas is legendary for her feats of physical strength. Although there are no print versions of ballads sung about her, she is included here as a female folk figure who is talked about in much the same way as the subjects of ballads.

The first print version of an Annie Christmas story appeared in Gumbo Ya-Ya, *an anthology of Louisiana folktales published in 1945 under the auspices of the Federal Writers' Project, a branch of Franklin Delano Roosevelt's Works Progress Administration designed to combat the economic effects of the Depression. Lyle Saxon, who served as head of* the Louisiana Writers' Project and who co-edited Gumbo Ya-Ya, *claimed that he and a friend made Annie up over drinks in New Orleans—she "floated up out of the whiskey-and-soda glasses" of the two men. Saxon suggested that they authenticate Annie's folkloric origins as a river lady by "discovering" manuscripts. At first the two wanted to call her "Mary Christmas," but Saxon decided, "Nobody would believe that. Call her Annie Christmas."*

Still, Annie's origins are contested. Is her story an example of pure fakelore, the confabulation of two intoxicated pals? Or is she firmly rooted in communal storytelling cultures? And does it matter? The road between literature and folklore has always been heavily traveled, and figures migrate back and forth with astonishing ease. Should we feel a need to begin patrolling the border between two different sources?

When Richard and Judy Young put together an anthology of African American folktales for "young readers," they saw Annie Christmas as a John Henry figure—"most probably a real person" and "so popular in folklore that many different kinds of people claim her as their heroine." They point out that the story has "grown" over the years, as it is told and retold.

Virginia Hamilton, renowned for her collections of African American folklore, sorts out the evidence and comes to the following conclusion: "'Annie Christmas' is one of the hometown stories of New Orleans. She is as common to southern Louisiana as is the Gumbo, the French patois *spoken by some American blacks and Creoles." She too sees in Annie Christmas a female John Henry, "larger than life" and "fashioned after someone who actually lived" and discredits the view that two New Orleans journalists "created" Annie Christmas. "It's possible that they did make up a story about a white Annie Christmas. But tales about black Annie have been around for longer than anyone can remember. It's more than likely that they will continue to be told and added to" (1994, 88–89).*

STAGOLEE

Stackalee

It was in the year of eighteen hundred and sixty-one
In St. Louis on Market Street where Stackalee was born.
Everybody's talking about Stackalee.
It was on one cold and frosty night
When Stackalee and Billy Lyons had one awful fight,
Stackalee got his gun. Boy, he got it fast!
He shot poor Billy through and through;
Bullet broke a lookin glass.
Lord, O Lord, O Lord!
Stackalee shot Billy once; his body fell to the floor.
He cried out, Oh, please Stack, please don't shoot me no more.

The White Elephant Barrel House was wrecked that night;
Gutters full of beer and whiskey; it was an awful sight.
Jewelry and rings of the purest solid gold
Scattered over the dance and gambling hall.
The can-can dancers they rushed for the door
When Billy cried, Oh, please, Stack, don't shoot me no more.
Have mercy, Billy groaned, Oh, please spare my life;

Stack says, God bless your children, damn your wife!
You stole my magic Stetson; I'm gonna steal your life.
But, says Billy, I always treated you like a man.
'Tain't nothing to that old Stetson but the greasy band.
He shot poor Billy once, he shot him twice,
And the third time Billy pleaded, please go tell my wife.
Yes, Stackalee, the gambler, everybody knowed his name;
Made his livin hollerin high, low, jack and the game.

Meantime the sergeant strapped on his big forty-five,
Says now we'll bring in this bad man, dead or alive.

And brass-buttoned policemen tall dressed in blue

Came down the sidewalk marchin two by two.

Sent for the wagon and it hurried and come

Loaded with pistols and a big gatlin gun.[1]

1 *gatlin gun:* The Gatling gun is a rapid-fire weapon said to be a forerunner of the machine gun.

At midnight on that stormy night there came an awful wail

Billy Lyons and a graveyard ghost outside the city jail.

Jailer, jailer, says Stack, I can't sleep,

For around my bedside poor Billy Lyons still creeps.

He comes in shape of a lion with a blue steel in his hand,

For he knows I'll stand and fight if he comes in the shape of a man.

Stackalee went to sleep that night by the city clock bell,

Dreaming the devil had come all the way up from hell.

Red devil was sayin, you better hunt your hole;

I've hurried here from hell just to get your soul.

Stackalee told him yes, maybe you're right,

But I'll give even you one hell of a fight.

When they got into the scuffle, I heard the devil shout,

The next time I seed the devil he was scramblin up the wall,

Yellin, come and get this bad man fore he mops up with us all.

II

Then here come Stack's woman runnin, says, daddy, I love you true;

See what beer, whiskey, and smoking hop[2] has brought you to.

But before I'll let you lay in there, I'll put my life in pawn.

She hurried and got Stackalee out on a five thousand dollar bond.

When they take me away, babe, I leave you behind.

But the woman he really loved was a voodoo queen

From Creole French market, way down in New Orleans.

2 *smoking hop:* Hops are in the same family as cannabis and can be used as an alternative to marijuana.

He laid down at home that night, took a good night's rest,

Arrived in court at nine o'clock to hear the coroner's inquest.

Crowds jammed the sidewalk, far as you could see,

Tryin to get a good look at tough Stackalee.

Over the cold, dead body Stackalee he did bend,

Then he turned and faced those twelve jury men.

The judge says, Stackalee, I would spare your life,

But I know you're a bad man; I can see it in your red eyes.

The jury heard the witnesses, and they didn't say no more;

They crowded into the jury room, and the messenger closed the door.

The jury came to agreement, the clerk he wrote it down,

And everybody was whisperin, he's penitentiary bound.

When the jury walked out, Stackalee didn't budge,

They wrapped the verdict and passed it to the judge.

Judge looked over his glasses, says, Mr. Bad Man Stackalee,

The jury finds you guilty of murder in the first degree.

Now the trial's come to an end, how the folks gave cheers;

Bad Stackalee was sent down to Jefferson pen for seventy-five years.

Now late at night you can hear him in his cell,

Arguin with the devil to keep from goin to hell.

And the other convicts whisper, whatcha know about that?

Gonna burn in hell forever over an old Stetson hat!

Everybody's talking bout Stackalee.

That bad man, Stackalee!

SOURCE: Onah L. Spencer, "Stackalee," *Direction* 4 (1941), 14–17.

Stackolee

One dark and dusty day

I was strolling down the street.

I thought I heard some old dog bark,

But it warn't nothing but Stackolee gambling in the dark.

Stackolee threw seven.

Billy said, It ain't that way.

You better go home and come back another day.

Stackolee shot Billy four times in the head

And left that fool on the floor damn near dead.

Stackolee decided he'd go up to Sister Lou's.

Said, Sister Lou! Sister Lou, guess what I done done?

I just shot and killed Billy, your big-head son.

Sister Lou said, Stackolee, that can't be true!

You and Billy been friends for a year or two.

Stackolee said, Woman, if you don't believe what I said,

Go count the bullet holes in that son-of-a-gun's head.

Sister Lou got frantic and all in a rage,

Like a tea hound dame on some frantic gage.

She got on the phone, Sheriff, Sheriff, I want you to help poor me.

I want you to catch that bad son-of-a-gun they call Stackolee.

Sheriff said, My name might begin with an *s* and end with an *f*

But if you want that bad Stackolee you got to get him yourself.

So Stackolee left, he went walking down the New Haven track.

A train come along and flattened him on his back.

He went up in the air and when he fell

Stackolee landed right down in hell.

He said, Devil, devil, put your fork up on the shelf

'Cause I'm gonna run this devilish place myself.

There came a rumbling on the earth and a tumbling on the ground,

That bad son-of-a-gun Stackolee, was turning hell around.

He ran across one of his ex-girl friends down there.

She was Chock-full-o'-nuts and had pony-tail hair.

She said, Stackolee, Stackolee, wait for me.

I'm trying to please you, can't you see?

She said, I'm going around the corner but I'll be right back.

I'm gonna see if I can't stack my sack.

Stackolee said, Susie Belle, go on and stack your sack.

But I just might not be here when you get back.

Meanwhile, Stackolee went with the devil's wife and with his girl friend, too.

Winked at the devil and said, I'll go with you.

The devil turned around to hit him a lick.

Stackolee knocked the devil down with a big black stick.

Now, to end this story, so I heard tell,

Stackolee, all by his self, is running hell.

Stagolee (also known as Stackolee, Stacker Lee, Staggerlee) represents the antihero, the Badman who lives outside the law, defies authority, and knows no social boundaries. He is far removed from cabins and fields and emerges from an urban setting of gambling, drinking, womanizing, and exchanging fire. His badge of courage has more to do with violating accepted codes of conduct than conforming to them. Unlike the "noble robber" or "good outlaw" of Western culture (the Robin Hood figure who rights wrongs and steals from the rich to give to the poor), the Badman is cruel and vengeful. Historian Lawrence Levine sees the figure's origins in "the most oppressed and deprived strata" and describes how he operates apart from and above the law in a celebration of self-destructive bravado. Within the social circumstances of the Badman's world, "to assert any power at all is a triumph" (1977, 418).

The legend of Stagolee began with the blues in the 1890s. But it has also been traced to a field holler among slaves and a tune from Southern prisons, where it was sung to the rhythms of hard labor. Charles Haffner of Mississippi claimed to have sung about Stagolee as early as 1895, while Will Starks, another Mississippi resident, stated that he learned the song in a labor camp near St. Louis (Levine, 1977, 413). The folklorist Howard Odum reports that the song was widely known throughout the South by 1910.

In 1911, Odum published two versions of "Stacker Lee." Both recount the murder of Billy Lyons, after he and Stacker Lee quarrel about a Stetson hat while gambling. Longer versions offer details on Stacker Lee's arrest and execution. Over time, the ballad was encoded with spiritual and superstitious markers, with Stacker Lee telling Satan that he is planning to usurp his role and "rule hell by myself." Stacker Lee's affiliation with the blues and the "dens of iniquity" in which they were played, suggests that his story emphatically links the secular music of the blues (as opposed to sacred spirituals) with corrupt practices that are all the devil's work.

Since 1911, Stagolee has been the subject of toasts, songs, raps, and tales. Richard Wright, James Baldwin, and Gwendolyn Brooks wrote prose and poetry inspired by his story. Duke Ellington performed a version of the song, and artists ranging from James Brown and Wilson Pickett to Bob Dylan and the Grateful Dead have made recordings of it. The poet Carl Sandburg evidently loved the tune. Cultural critic Greil Marcus tells us that the "black American has never tired of hearing and never stopped living out" the legend of Stagolee (66). According to novelist and historian Cecil Brown, the ballad of Stagolee did not emerge until 1895, when a man named Lee Shelton shot another St. Louis resident named William Lyons (2003). But others have asserted that Stacker Lee was a Confederate cavalry officer, and still others claim that he was the son of the Lee family of Memphis, who owned steamers that moved up and down the Mississippi. What becomes clear in surveying the vast literature on the Badman is that he has been pieced together from fragments of histories and stories to produce a figure larger than life and twice as unnatural—an outlaw who tests limits and serves as cautionary example as much as cultural hero.

FRANKIE AND JOHNNY

Frankie and Johnny were lovers, O Lordy, how they could love.
Swore to be true to each other, true as the stars above;
He was her man, but he done her wrong.

Frankie she was a good woman, just like everyone knows.
She spent a hundred dollars for a suit of Johnny's clothes.
He was her man, but he done her wrong.

Frankie and Johnny went walking, Johnny in a brand-new suit,
"Oh, good Lord," says Frankie, "but don't my Johnny look cute?"
He was her man, but he done her wrong.

Frankie went down to Memphis, she went on the evening train.
She paid one hundred dollars for Johnny's watch and chain.
He was her man, but he done her wrong.

Frankie lived in the crib house, crib house had only two doors;
Gave all her money to Johnny, he spent it on those call-house whores.
He was her man, but he done her wrong.

Johnny's mother told him, and she was mighty wise,
"Don't spend Frankie's money on that parlor Alice Pry.
You're Frankie's man, and you're doing her wrong."

Frankie and Johnny were lovers, they had a quarrel one day,
Johnny he up and told Frankie, "Bye-bye, babe, I'm going away.
I was your man, but I'm just gone."

Frankie went down to the corner to buy a glass of beer.
Says to the fat bartender, "Has my lovingest man been here?
He was my man, but he's doing me wrong."

"Ain't going to tell you no story, ain't going to tell you no lie,
I seen your man 'bout an hour ago with a girl named Alice Pry.
If he's your man, he's doing you wrong."

Frankie went down to the pawnshop, she didn't go there for fun;
She hocked all of her jewelry, bought a pearl-handled forty-four gun
For to get her man who was doing her wrong.

Frankie she went down Broadway, with her gun in her hand,
Sayin', "Stand back, all you livin' women, I'm a-looking for my gambolin' man.
For he's my man, won't treat me right."

Frankie went down to the hotel, looked in the window so high,
There she saw her loving Johnny a-loving up Alice Pry.
Damn his soul, he was mining in coal.

Frankie went down to the hotel, she rang that hotel bell.
"Stand back, all of you chippies, or I'll blow you all to hell.
I want my man, who's doing me wrong."

Frankie threw back her kimono, she took out her forty-four,
Root-a-toot-toot three times she shot right through that hotel door.
She was after her man who was doing her wrong.

Johnny grabbed off his Stetson, "Oh, good Lord, Frankie, don't shoot!"
But Frankie pulled the trigger and the gun went root-a-toot-toot.
He was her man, but she shot him down.

Johnny he mounted the staircase, crying, "Oh, Frankie, don't you shoot!"
Three times she pulled that forty-four-a-root-a-toot-toot-toot-toot.
She shot her man who threw her down.

First time she shot him he staggered, second time she shot him he fell,
Third time she shot him, O Lordy, there was a new man's face in hell.
She killed her man who had done her wrong.

"Roll me over easy, roll me over slow,
Roll me over on my left side for the bullet hurt me so.
I was her man, but I done her wrong.

"Oh my baby, kiss me, one before I go.
Turn me over on my right side, the bullet hurt me so.
I was your man, but I done you wrong."

Johnny he was a gambler, he gambled for the gain,
The very last words that Johnny said were, "High-low Jack and the game."
He was her man, but he done her wrong.

Frankie heard a rumbling away down in the ground.
Maybe it was Johnny where she had shot him down.
He was her man and she done him wrong.

Oh, bring on your rubber-tired hearses, bring on your rubber-tired hacks,
They're taking Johnny to the cemetery and they ain't a-bringing him back.
He was her man, but he done her wrong.

Eleven macks a-riding to the graveyard, all in a rubber-tired hack,
Eleven macks a-riding to the graveyard, only ten a-coming back.
He was her man, but he done her wrong.

Frankie went to the coffin, she looked down on Johnny's face,
She said, "Oh, Lord, have mercy on me. I wish I could take his place.
He was my man and I done him wrong."

One of the most popular of all ballads in the United States tells the story of Frankie Baker's shooting of her boyfriend Allen, or Albert, Britt, in 1899. In the tradition of the murder ballad, which recounts events leading up to a killing, the song tells about passions running high after Johnny abandons Frankie. The refrain of most versions—"He was my man, but he done me wrong"—sides with Frankie, although in some variants she shows remorse about her wrongdoing: "He was my man and I done him wrong."

Frankie Baker was born in 1876 in St. Louis and was twenty-two years old when she met the seventeen-year-old Albert. As a teenager, Frankie had suffered severe facial wounds inflicted by the knife-wielding girlfriend of a waiter she was seeing. One evening, soon after meeting Frankie, Albert Britt entered and won first prize in a dance contest with a woman named Alice Pryor. When the pair met up later after the contest, Frankie claimed that Albert threatened her with a knife. It was only in self-defense, she claimed, that she pulled a gun from under her pillow and shot Albert. The jury ruled the killing justifiable homicide and accepted the plea of self-defense.

"Frankie and Al" became popular just a few months after Albert's

death, but Albert Britt's father was evidently so incensed by the ballad that the title was changed to "Frankie and Johnny." The first published version of the ballad appeared in 1904. Frankie herself spent a good part of her life defending her name and bringing lawsuits against motion picture companies for damaging her reputation. "Frankie Baker wants to appropriate for her own use, one of the finest ballads of American folklore," the defense claimed. "Don't make her a rich woman, because forty years ago, she shot a little boy here in St. Louis" (Brown 2006, I, 465). She died in 1952 in Oregon, after being declared mentally ill.

The ballad, which some musicologists claim predates the murder of Albert Britt and may simply have been based on a made-up story, has inspired several films, two made in the 1930s, as well as Frankie and Johnny *starring Elvis Presley and directed by Frederick de Cordova (1966), and* Frankie and Johnny *starring Al Pacino and Michelle Pfeiffer and directed by Garry Marshall (1991).*

RAILROAD BILL

Railroad Bill

Some one went home an' tole my wife
All about—well, my pas' life,
It was that bad Railroad Bill.

Railroad Bill, Railroad Bill,
He never work, an' he never will,
Well, it's that bad Railroad Bill.

Railroad Bill so mean an' so bad,
Till he tuk ev'ything that farmer had,
It's that bad Railroad Bill.

I'm goin' home an' tell my wife,
Railroad Bill try to take my life,
It's that bad Railroad Bill.

Railroad Bill so desp'rate an' so bad,
He take ev'ything po' womens had,
An' it's that bad Railroad Bill.

Railroad Bill

Railroad Bill mighty bad man,
Shoot dem lights out o' de brakeman's han'.
It's lookin' fer Railroad Bill.

Railroad Bill mighty bad man,
Shoot the lamps all off the stan',
An it's lookin' fer Railroad Bill.

First on table, nex' on wall,
Ole corn whiskey cause of it all,
It's lookin' fer Railroad Bill.

Ole McMillan had a special train,
When he got there wus a shower of rain.
Wus lookin' fer Railroad Bill.

Ev'ybody tole him he better turn back,
Railroad Bill wus goin' down track.
An it's lookin' fer Railroad Bill.

Well, the policemen all dressed in blue,
Comin' down sidewalk two by two,
Wus lookin' fer Railroad Bill.

Railroad Bill had no wife,
Always lookin' fer somebody's life,
An it's lookin' fer Railroad Bill.

Railroad Bill was the worst ole coon,
Killed McMillan by de light o' de moon,
It's lookin' fer Railroad Bill.

Ole Culpepper went up on Number Five,
Goin' bring him back, dead or alive,
Wus lookin' fer Railroad Bill.

Standin' on corner didn't mean no harm,
Policeman grab me by my arm,
Wus lookin' fer Railroad Bill.

SOURCE: Howard W. Odum, "Folk-Song and Folk-Poetry as Found in the Secular Songs of the Southern Negroes," *Journal of American Folklore*, 289–91.

Fragments of what later became known as the Railroad Bill ballad were collected by folklorists in the early part of the twentieth century. They range from humorous doggerel to deadly serious pronouncements: "Talk about yer five er yer ten dollar bill; / Ain't no bill like de Railroad Bill" and "Railroad Bill cut a mighty big dash; / He killed Bill Johnson with a lightning-flash." Over time, Railroad Bill came to be connected with Morris Slater, a turpentine worker from Alabama, who killed a police officer and fled town on a freight train. He evidently made a living by selling canned goods stolen from freight trains to African Americans living near the tracks. In 1895 he shot and killed Sheriff E. S. McMillan, who had made a campaign promise to hunt down Railroad Bill. With a twelve hundred dollar bounty on his head, Railroad Bill realized that his days were numbered, and, just a year later, two men gunned him down at a store in Alabama. The ballads that emerged over the course of the twentieth century are only loosely connected to the story of Morris Slater, and they are often improvised and cobbled together rather than driven by one man's history.

THE *TITANIC*

THE TITANIC SHIP

Carolina Slim is a poet, a wandering black minstrel, who sings of his own prowess constantly, as longshoreman, fighter and lover. Slim has a favorite composition, though; this one is about his girl, Agnes, he vows, but Agnes is not mentioned throughout the song, only *The Titanic Ship*, the title of the epic. This song he sings most tenderly, most passionately.

"It's a long story," Carolina says. "When the *Titanic* sunk me and my baby was fightin'. When the word come that the ship was down, she told me she didn't want me no more. Then after she gone and left me, I thunk up *The Titanic Ship*. It goes like this:

> I always did hear that the fif' of May was a wonderful day,
> You believe me, everybody had somethin' to say,
> Telephone and telegraphs to all parts of town,
> That the great *Titanic* ship was a-goin' down.
>
> The captain and the mate was standin' on deck havin' a few words,
> 'Fore they know it, the *Titanic* had done hit a big iceberg.
> Had a colored guy on there call Shine, who come down from below,
> And hollered, "Water is comin' in the fireroom do'!"
>
> Shine jumped off that ship and begun to swim,
> Thousands of white folks watchin' him.
> Shine say, "Fish in the ocean and fish in the sea,
> This is one time you white folks ain't gonna fool me!"

There is lots more. Carolina Slim can sing a dozen or two verses. The hero, Shine, reaches land, and

THE ANNOTATED AFRICAN AMERICAN FOLKTALES

There was thousands of people waitin' to shake his hand.
Shine said, "Push back, stand there and hear my pedigree.
I don't want nobody messin' with me.
"My pillow was an alligator and a boa-constrictor was in my den.
I lived on the water and I didn't have to pay no rent.
And I don't owe nobody a damn red cent.
When the great *Titanic* in the river sank."

Carolina Slim calls himself a "roamin' longshoreman," but he is more a hobo than a worker. He boasts that he has the strength of three men, can do the work of three men. Most of the time he gets his money from women and he always invests it quickly—in crap games. The women don't really mean anything to him, because he's always thinking about Agnes. He says he "jest cain't stay put for long," so he is a wandering minstrel.

SOURCE: Lyle Saxon, Edward Dreyer, and Robert Tallant, eds., *Gumbo Ya-Ya*, 373–74.

SINKING OF THE *TITANIC*

It was 1912 when the awful news got around
That the great *Titanic* was sinking down.
Shine came running up on deck, told the Captain, "Please,
The water in the boiler room is up to my knees."

Captain said, "Take your black self on back down there!
I got a hundred-fifty pumps to keep the boiler room clear."
Shine went back in the hole, started shoveling coal,
Singing, "Lord, have mercy, Lord, on my soul!"

Just then half the ocean jumped across the boiler room deck.
Shine yelled to the Captain, "The water's 'round my neck!"
Captain said, "Go back! Neither fear nor doubt!
I got a hundred more pumps to keep the water out."

"Your words sound happy and your words sound true,

But this is one time, Cap, your words won't do.

I don't like chicken and I don't like ham—

And I don't believe your pumps is worth a damn!"

The old *Titanic* was beginning to sink.

Shine pulled off his clothes and jumped in the brink.

He said, "Little fish, big fish, and shark fishes, too,

Get out of my way because I'm coming through."

Captain on bridge hollered, "Shine, Shine, save poor me,

And I'm make you as rich as any man can be."

Shine said, "There's more gold on land than there is on the sea."

And he swimmed on.

When all them white folks went to heaven,

Shine was in Sugar Ray's Bar drinking Seagram's Seven.

SOURCE: Langston Hughes and Arna Bontemps, *The Book of American Negro Folklore*, 366–67.

Why did the Titanic *figure so prominently in the African American imagination? No doubt in part because it provided an allegory of seemingly divine punishment for the excesses of the opulent lifestyle that contrasted so sharply with the economic circumstances of most African Americans, who would have been denied passage on the ship even if they could afford a ticket. The story of Shine is included here because he has become something of a survivor and folk hero. When the* Titanic *sank in 1912, two stories circulated about African Americans on board, both apocryphal. In fact, there were no African Americans on the ship, and the only two people of color were a Haitian engineer and an Italian-Egyptian man who was employed as a personal secretary to an industrialist. But there was much talk about a heavyweight boxing champion named Jack Johnson being denied passage, as well as about a fellow named Shine, who allegedly worked in the ship's boiler room. Shine survived, not by jumping into a lifeboat, but by swimming ashore. The first version above was told by an African American man living in Louisiana around 1945, and it is framed by commentary from the tale's collector. The second was published in a 1958 anthology of African American lore.*

There are many ballads, toasts, and jokes about the sinking of the Titanic, *and some of the off-color versions can be found in Roger D. Abrahams's* Deep Down in the Jungle . . . : Negro Narrative Folklore from the Streets of Philadelphia, *published in 1963, and Bruce Jackson's* Get Your Ass in the Water and Swim Like Me, *published in 2004.*

THE SIGNIFYING MONKEY

The Monkey and the Lion
Got to talking one day.
Monkey looked down and said, Lion,
I hear you's king in every way.
But I know somebody
Who do not think that is true—
He told me he could whip
The living daylights out of you.
Lion said, Who?
Monkey said, Lion,
He talked about your mama
And talked about your grandma, too,
And I'm too polite[1] to tell you
What he said about you.
Lion said Who said what? Who?
Monkey in the tree,
Lion on the ground.

1 *I'm too polite:* Everything Monkey says is open to doubt, and by prefacing his statements with phrases such as this one, Monkey both praises himself and maligns Elephant.

Monkey kept on signifying
But he didn't come down.
Monkey said, His name is elephant—
He stone sure is not your friend.
Lion said, He don't need to be
Because today will be his end.
Lion took off through the jungle
Lickity-split,
Meaning to grab Elephant
And tear him bit to bit. Period!
He come across Elephant copping a righteous nod
Under a fine cool shady tree.
Lion said, You big old no-good so-and-so,
It's either you or me.
Lion let out a solid roar
And bopped Elephant with his paw.
Elephant just took his trunk
And busted old Lion's jaw.
Lion let out another roar,
Reared up six feet tall.
Elephant just kicked him in the belly
And laughed to see him drop and fall.
Lion rolled over,
Copped Elephant by the throat.
Elephant just shook him loose
And butted him like a goat.
Then he tromped him and he stomped him
Till the Lion yelled, Oh, no!
And it was near-nigh sunset
When Elephant let Lion go.
The signifying Monkey
Was still setting in his tree
When he looked down and saw the Lion.

Said, Why, Lion, who can that there be?

Lion said, It's me.

Monkey rapped, Why, Lion,

You look more dead than alive!

Lion said, Monkey, I don't want

To hear your jive-end jive.

Monkey just kept on signifying,

Lion, you for sure caught hell—

Mister Elephant's done whipped you

To a fare-thee-well!

Why, Lion, you look to me

You been in the precinct station

And had the third-degree,

Else you look like

You been high on gage[2]

And done got caught

In a monkey cage!

You ain't no king to me.

Facts, I don't think that you

Can even as much as roar—

And if you try I'm liable

To come down out of this tree and

Whip your tail some more.

The Monkey started laughing

And jumping up and down.

But he jumped so hard the limb broke

And he landed—*bam!*—on the ground.

When he went to run, his foot slipped

And he fell flat down.

Grrr-rrr-rr-r! The Lion was on him

With his front feet and his hind.

Monkey hollered, Ow!

I didn't mean it,[3] Mister Lion!

2 *gage:* marijuana

3 *I didn't mean it:* The Monkey alternates between saying what he means and not meaning what he says, forever walking a fine line between speaking the truth and telling lies—or, to put it succinctly, signifying.

Lion said, You little flea-bag you!
Why, I'll eat you up alive.
I wouldn't a-been in this fix a-tall
Wasn't for your signifying jive.
Please, said Monkey, Mister Lion,
If you'll just let me go,
I got something to tell you, *please*,
I think you ought to know—
Lion let the Monkey loose.
To see what his tale could be—
And Monkey jumped right back on up
Into his tree.
What I was gonna tell you, said Monkey,
Is you square old so-and-so,
If you fool with me I'll get
Elephant to whip your head some more.
Monkey, said the Lion,
Beat to his unbooted knees,
You and all your signifying children
Better stay up in them trees.
Which is why today
Monkey does his signifying
A-way-up out of the way.

SOURCE: Langston Hughes and Arna Bontemps, *The Book of American Negro Folklore*, 363–66.

The African American vernacular usage of the term signifying *uncannily captures the linguistic distinction between* signifier *(a word or linguistic sign) and* signified *(the thing to which a word refers). In conversation,* signifying *is used to designate a range of verbal practices, from insult, innuendo, and abuse to parody, pastiche, and homage. The foundational story about Signifying, or the clever use of double talk, appears in "The Signifying Monkey," which exists in many variant forms, often filled with obscene language. It reflects on the power of language to deceive and misrepresent, to create multiple meanings and messages that can be contradictory. By taking advantage of the gap in all languages between the thing signified and the signifier, this verbal practice creates meaning and also undermines it.*

PART XIII

ARTISTS, PRO AND CON: PREACHER TALES

"The Preacher is the most unique personality developed on American soil. A leader, a politician, an orator, a 'boss,' and idealist—all these he is, and ever, too, the center of a group of men," W. E. B. Du Bois wrote in *The Souls of Black Folks* (1903). Charismatic and eloquent, black preachers exercised their influence in both the sacred and secular spheres, shaping domestic arrangements as well as spiritual matters. Charged with managing ritualized ceremonies such as baptisms, weddings, and funerals, preachers relied on oral traditions, blending together local religious practices with African beliefs in a uniquely African American style. The result might be seen as a syncretic faith that remained outwardly Christian, even as it developed a robust performance style of its own.

Heading an institution that had no serious official rivals within African American communities (there were, to be sure, surreptitious practices such as hoodoo and conjuring), preachers played a key role in setting social and political agendas. The church became, as Du Bois put it, "the center of amusements, of what little spontaneous economic activity remained, of education and of all social intercourse." Often released from hard labor, preachers were able to devote their energies to activities that could quickly arouse suspicion unless managed in a spirit of accommodation with slavery. Still, from the antebellum era on into the present, preachers have played a central leadership role in African American communities, serving as agents of political and social change both during and after slavery. They played a vital role in creating the space for an expressive culture, ephemeral to be sure, but captured in part through spirituals, sermons, institutional practices and traditions, and even tales handed down across generations about their own ways.

One expert has described the unique performative style of black preachers as characterized by the use of "vivid imageries and innovative metaphors, storytelling, signifying, humor, and a kinetic style referred to as 'stylin' out,' which involves innovative vocal techniques such as moaning, shouting, and uses of rhythmic repetitions that rouse congregations to ecstatic and frenzied emotional states." Black preachers were revered for their oratorical skills, verbal wizardry, and aesthetic vitality. They occupied an unparalleled position of power in the community. It is no accident that Martin Luther King Jr., the most acclaimed African American spiritual and political leader, served first as a pastor, at the Dexter Avenue Baptist Church in Montgomery, Alabama. But it could also be said that countless "aesthetic tributaries" flow from the figure of the preacher and include dancers, actors, comedians, storytellers, as well as performers of jazz, blues, hip hop, soul, rhythm and blues, and funk (Rabaka, *Greenwood Encyclopedia*, II, 1015).

If many preachers were true artists, gifted with verbal and performative skills that stirred emotions and inflamed passions, some were also con artists, opportunistic men less invested in saving souls than in capitalizing on the respect and remuneration bestowed on them by members of their congregations. Or so African American preacher tales imply, with a host of clergymen who are greedy, deceitful, promiscuous, and dishonest. Their pranks range from wolfing down all the food on the table while no one is looking to seducing wives while their husbands are at work in the fields. No form of authority is sacred when it comes to folklore and storytelling.

HOW THE BROTHER WAS CALLED TO PREACH

"Aw, Ah don't pay all dese ole preachers no rabbit-foot,[1]" said Ellis Jones. "Some of 'em is all right but everybody dats up in de pulpit whoopin' and hollerin' ain't called to preach."

"They ain't no different from nobody else," added B. Moseley. "They mouth is cut cross ways, ain't it? Well, long as you don't see no man wid they mouth cut up and down, you know they'll all lie[2] jus' like de rest of us."

"Yeah; and hard work in de hot sun done called many a man to preach," said a woman called Gold, for no evident reason. "Ah heard about one man out clearin' off some new ground. De sun was so hot till a grindstone melted and run off in de shade to cool off. De man was so tired till he went and sit down on a log. 'Work, work, work! Everywhere Ah go de boss say hurry, de cap' say run. Ah got a durn good notion not to do nary one. Wisht Ah was one of dese preachers wid a whole lot of folks makin' my support for me.' He looked back over his shoulder and seen a narrer li'l strip of shade along side of de log, so he got over dere and laid down right close up to de log in de shade and said, 'Now, Lawd, if you don't pick me up and chink me on de other side of dis log, Ah know you done called me to preach.'

"You know God never picked 'im up, so he went off and tol' everybody dat he was called to preach."

"There's many a one been called just lak dat,"[3] Ellis corroborated. "Ah knowed a man dat was called by a mule."[4]

"A mule, Ellis? All dem b'lieve dat, stand on they head," said Little Ida.

"Yeah, a mule did call a man to preach. Ah'll show you how it was done, if you'll stand a straightenin'."

"Now, Ellis, don't mislay de truth. Sense us into dis mule-callin' business."

1 *rabbit-foot:* Hurston glosses this sentence as meaning, "Ignore these preachers."

2 *they'll all lie:* For Hurston, the term *lying* conflates misrepresentation and swindling with storytelling and higher truths.

3 *"There's many a one been called just lak dat":* These tales are presented as a verbal sparring match. The second "lie" is told to outshine the first by painting an even more ridiculous portrait of a man called to preach. It is likely that Hurston constructed this scene, perhaps from reminiscences of similar interactions, because the stories appear separately in her original manuscript, later published as *Every Tongue Got to Confess.*

4 *called by a mule:* Ellis decides to top the story told by the woman named Gold. He illustrates how storytelling sessions turn into competitions.

———

Ellis: These was two brothers and one of 'em was a big preacher and had good collections every Sunday. He didn't pastor nothin' but big charges. De other brother decided he wanted to preach so he went way down in de swamp behind a big plantation to de place they call de prayin' ground, and got down on his knees.

"O Lawd, Ah wants to preach. Ah feel lak Ah got a message. If you done called me to preach, gimme a sign."

Just 'bout dat time he heard a voice, "Wanh, uh wanh! Go preach, go preach, go preach!"

He went and tol' everybody, but look lak he never could git no big charge. All he ever got called was on some saw-mill, half-pint church or some turpentine still. He knocked around lak dat for ten years and then he seen his brother. De big preacher says, "Brother, you don't look like you gittin' holt of much."

"You tellin' dat right, brother. Groceries is scarce. Ah ain't dirtied a plate today."

"Whut's de matter? Don't you git no support from your church?"

"Yeah, Ah gits it such as it is, but Ah ain't never pastored no big church. Ah don't git called to nothin' but saw-mill camps and turpentine stills."

De big preacher reared back and thought a while, then he ast de other one, "Is you sure you was called to preach? Maybe you ain't cut out for no preacher."

"Oh, yeah," he told him. "Ah *know* Ah been called to de ministry. A voice spoke and tol' me so."

"Well, seem lak if God called you He is mighty slow in puttin' yo' foot on de ladder. If Ah was you Ah'd go back and ast 'im agin."

So de po' man went on back to de prayin' ground agin and got down on his knees. But there wasn't no big woods like it used to be. It had been all cleared off. He prayed and said, "Oh, Lawd, right here on dis spot ten years ago Ah ast you if Ah was called to preach and a voice tole me to go preach. Since dat time Ah been strugglin' in Yo' moral vineyard, but Ah ain't gathered no grapes. Now, if you really called me to preach Christ and Him crucified, please gimme another sign."

Sho nuff, jus' as soon as he said dat, de voice said, "Wanh-uh! Go preach! Go preach! Go preach!"

De man jumped up and says, "Ah knowed Ah been called. Dat's de same voice. Dis time Ah'm goin ter ast Him where *must* Ah go preach."

By dat time de voice come agin and he looked 'way off and seen a mule in de plantation lot wid his head all stuck out to bray agin, and he said, "Unh hunh, youse de very son of a gun dat called me to preach befo'."

So he went on off and got a job plowin'. Dat's whut he was called to do in de first place.

Armetta said, "A many a one been called to de plough and they run off and got up in de pulpit. Ah wish dese mules knowed how to take a pair of plow-lines and go to de church and ketch some of 'em like they go to de lot with a bridle and ketch mules."

SOURCE: Zora Neale Hurston, *Mules and Men*, 20–22.

Hurston's father was a preacher, and she chronicles his life and career in her first novel, Jonah's Gourd Vine. *John Pearson, the fictional stand-in for John Hurston, rises in the church hierarchy only to be thwarted by his adulterous liaisons. Ironically, his charisma works both for him and against him. Hurston writes about storytelling sessions on her family's front porch, with "very funny stories [told] at the expense of preachers and congregations." Tales such as the one above mock the delusional aspirations of those who (quite logically) hope to escape hard labor even as they engage in a critique of opportunistic clergymen.*

THE FARMER AND THE G.P.C.

One time dere was a man what was a farmer. One year he had a real good crop. But dis man was kinda lazy, and when it come time to gather de crop he tole ole lady dat he could not he'p gather de crop cause he felt de Lord was callin' him to go preach. He tole her to look up in de sky, and he pointed out de letters G P C, which he say meant, "Go Preach Christ" and he had to go.

But de old lady she was too much fer him. "Dose letters don' mean, 'Go Preach Christ,'" she said. "Dey mean, 'Go Pick Cotton.'"

SOURCE: Langston Hughes and Arna Bontemps, *Book of Negro Folklore*, 139–40.

JUMP ON MAMA'S LAP

Someone came to the door, and the little boy went to the door. His father asked him who was at the door, and he told him the Methodist Minister. So the father said, "Go hide all the liquor."

Then again, there was a knock on the door, and he asked him who was there. And he told him it was the Episcopalian Minister; so the father told him to go hide the food.

The next one came up was a Baptist, and he told him, say "Go jump in Mama's lap."

SOURCE: Daryl C. Dance, *Shuckin' and Jivin': Folklore from Contemporary Black Americans*, 59.

DEACON JONES' BOYS AND THE GREEDY PREACHER

Two of de faithfules' chu'ch membuhs Ah evuh seed, what git dat thing lack de Word say git hit, was Deacon Henry Jones an' his wife Sarah what b'long to de li'l' ole Baptis' chu'ch down to Wild Horse Slew. An' you talkin' 'bout a woman what could cook—dat was Sarah. She hab de reputation for bein' de bes' chicken fryer in de whole Bottoms; so de pastuh of de li'l' ole church what she b'long allus hab de vis'tin' preachuhs to eat Sunday dinnuh an' suppuh wid Deacon Jones, so Sarah kin fix 'em some of dem fine chicken dinnuhs de whole Bottom's talkin' 'bout.

Deacon Jones hab two li'l sebum-yeah-old boys what was twinses dat sho' was glad when de preachuhs comed to dey house for Sunday dinnuh, 'caze dey knows dey gonna git some good ole juicy drum sticks for dinnuh dat day. Sarah allus 'low dese li'l' ole boys to set at de table wid dey mammy an' pappy an' de preachuh, 'caze dey ack nice

"Jump on Mama's Lap," Daryl Cumber Dance, ed., *Shuckin' and Jivin': Folklore from Contemporary Black Americans*, 1978. Reprinted with permission of Indiana University Press. "Deacon Jones' Boys and the Greedy Preacher," from J. Mason Brewer, *The Word on the Brazos: Negro Preacher Tales from the Brazos Bottoms of Texas*. Copyright © 1953, renewed 1981. By permission of the University of Texas Press.

an' don' cut up. Dey's putty good li'l' ole boys an' don' raise no rukus lack lots of young-uns in de Bottoms when preachuhs comed to dey house to eat.

But Ah calls to min' one Sunday mawnin' when a big black preachuh comed from way somewhars to de chu'ch to preach, an' de pastuh sen's him to eat wid Deacon Jones an' Sarah, lack he allus been doin'. So when Sarah done put de victuals on de table, and de deacon done say de blessin's, dis big black preachuh rech ovah an' tuck de chicken plattuh an' pou'ed evuh las' piece of de chicken in his plate. De li'l' twinses, Bubbuh an' Bobby, was late gittin' to de table, 'caze dey hab to wash dey han's an' faces in de wash pan attuh de grown folks git thoo; so when dey come to de table an' set down an' looked at de chicken plattuh an' seed dat hit was empty, dey says, "What's de chicken, mammy?" But de preachuh don' gib Sarah time to ansuh. He stop chawnkin' on a good ole juicy drumstick, eye de li'l' boys rail mean lack, pints his finguh at de gravy bowl, an' say, "Eat gravy; gravy's good."

Dat ver' same Sunday attuh de chu'ch servuses dat night, de preachuh comed back to Deacon Jones' house for 'nothuh chicken dinnuh 'fo' he saddle his horse an' go way somewhat. Sarah hab a long red oil cloth table cloth on de table what hang all de way down to de flo' so far till you can't see unnerneaf hit to save yo' life; so while Sarah was cookin' a hoe-cake in de skillet in de kitchen an' Deacon Jones an' de preachuh was washin' dey han's an' faces on de back gall'ry, Bubbuh an' Bobby tuck de plattuh full of chicken Sarah hab on de table for suppah an' ca'ied hit under de table wid 'em an' et hit all up.

When de hoe-cake got done, Sarah tuck hit an' put hit on de table an' called Henry an' de preachuh to come to suppuh; so in dey comes 'dout lookin' on de table, an' say de blessin's. When dey gits thoo wid de blessin's, de preachuh looks down in de middle of de table what de chicken be at dinnuh time, but he don' see no chicken or plattuh neither, so he say, "Sister Sarah, what's de chicken?"

When he say dis, Bubuh an' Bobby sticks dey haids out from undah de table an' say, "Eat gravy, Elduh; gravy's good."

SOURCE: J. Mason Brewer, *The Word on the Brazos*, 108–9.

Recorded by the African American folklorist J. Mason Brewer in Brazos County, Texas, where the plantation culture of the old South flourished, this story can be read not only as a tale about a gluttonous preacher but also as a parable about outwitting those who amass goods, leaving little for others to enjoy. The two youngsters manage to turn the tables on the giant of a preacher, who wants everything for himself, and together they model the role of the trickster.

POPPA STOLE THE DEACON'S BULL

The reverend had a whole lot of kids, but the reverend didn't have any money, and so he could buy nothing to eat. Deacon had a bull, so the reverend went and stole the deacon's bull. He went and had people over to dinner; he even invited Deacon over. "Come over to my house on Sunday, 'cause right after church we're gonna have all kinds of beef." So Deacon said he'd come.

So he came over and sat down. You know how they do in the country, kids eat first and then the grown-ups. So the deacon sat down, and he said, "This is sure good food. *Um, um, um.* You know one thing, Rev?" He said, "What's that, Brother Deacon?" He said, "You know, somebody stole my bull." He said, "*Um,* ain't that something, people just going around taking other people's stuff." And at the same time he's the one that stole the bull.

So the kids were outside playing. The deacon went outside for a while to get some air after eating so much. And he stopped for a while to watch the kids playing. It sounded to him like the kids had made up a new game. They had each other by the hand, going around in a circle singing:

> *Oh, Poppa stole the deacon's bull,*
> *And all us children got a belly full.*

So the deacon walked over to them and said, "You know, if you sing that song again, I'll give each of you a nickel."

> *Oh, Poppa stole the deacon's bull,*
> *And all us children got a belly full.*

So he said, "How would you all like to make some more money, lots more?" They all said, "Yeah!" He said, "If all of you come to church next Sunday, I'll give you fifty cents apiece to sing that same song right there, just like the choir, because that song carries an important message."

So they were really excited now. They ran and told their mother that they were going to sing in church, and she was so glad to hear that the children were going to get a chance to sing that Sunday. Of course, she didn't know what they were going to sing about!

So the deacon went around to everybody's house and told them that Reverend Jones's kids were going to be in church that Sunday, singing. He told them of their beautiful voices and the great message of their songs. So everybody wanted to come down to hear it. They said, "The Lord sent these children to bring us this message." Pretty soon Deacon had gone all around the community spreading the word, and everyone got very excited.

So, finally, Sunday came. The children got all dressed up and cleaned up and went down to church. And they were clean and sparkly looking! Well, by the time they got there, the church was so packed that many people had to sit in the back of the church. So the reverend, their father, was so proud he told them, "Now, when you go up there, I want you to sing loud enough that everyone can hear what you're singing, because there are a lot of people in the back." So they said, "Yes, sir, Daddy, we'll sing very loud."

So you know how the preacher does before he brings on the gospel singers. He went to preaching, telling the congregation this and that, building up the people to a great excitement. But they mostly came to hear the song. Finally, the deacon stood up and said, "Ladies and gentlemen, you never know where the word is going to come from. Kids can carry a divine message if you learn how to listen to them." He said, "I want you to listen closely to this message that Reverend Jones's children are going to bring to you. Now, sing that song, children." They got up there and started singing away:

> *Oh, Poppa stole the deacon's bull,*
> *And all us children got a belly full.*

Now, there was so much noise set up when they started in, and the kids had such small voices, that their father couldn't hear them. So he said, "Sing up louder, now. Come on, you must sing louder so that I can really hear you." By that time the people down front are looking at him like he's crazy. So he wondered why they were looking at him. So they started singing again:

Oh, Poppa stole the deacon's bull,
And all us children got a belly full.

Now the reverend heard what they were singing. He just looked at them in the eyes, and started in, "Well, children—" he began,

When you told them that, you told your last,
Now when I get home I'm gonna kick your ass.

SOURCE: Roger D. Abrahams, *Deep Down in the Jungle*, 183–85.

Theft and the detection of a thief are the thematic drivers of this tale, with a deacon who is determined to have the truth come out in the most public way possible. "Child's song incriminates thief" is the folkloric designation for the story's chief trope, and in this case the children innocently boast about their feast, without being in the least aware of the consequences of the song. Many lines in this tale ("If you sing this song again, I'll give you a nickel") resonate with moments in the European story, "The Juniper Tree," in which a boy turns into a bird and is rewarded on multiple occasions for singing a song in which his parents' misdeeds are proclaimed.

THE HAUNTED CHURCH AND THE SERMON ON TITHING

Oncet down on de ole Washin'ton fawm dere was a Mefdis' preachuh by de name of Revun Logan what stay at de same charge for thirty yeah or mo'. He hol' de membership togedduh an' buil' de fuss chu'ch house in Eloise. Evuhbody in de Bottoms hab a good feelin' for Revun Logan, so when de new bishop dey 'lected hol' de annul

"The Haunted Church and the Sermon on Tithing," from J. Mason Brewer, *The Word on the Brazos: Negro Preacher Tales from the Brazos Bottoms of Texas*. Copyright © 1953, renewed 1981. By permission of the University of Texas Press.

conference down to Chilton one yeah, he change Revun Logan from de Wes' Texas Conference an' move 'im to de Texas Conference. Dis heah hurt Revun Logan's feelin's pow'ful bad, 'caze he bred an' bawn in de Bottoms, an' he ain't wanna trace his steps outen de Bottoms way dis late in life. He wropped up in de membuhship an' de settlement, but de new bishop lack de' pos'l' Paul dat de Word tell 'bout. He say don' none of dese things move 'im an' keep 'im from 'bidin' by de law what done been writ in de displin'.

Revun Logan all bowed down in sorrow an' his haa't moughty heaby wid de partin' from his chu'ch starin' 'im in de face; so de nex' mawnin' attuh he comed back from de conference de ole man what sweep up de ch'ch go by de li'l' pawsonage to pass de time of day wid 'im an' fin' 'im dead on the kitchen flo'. So dey buries 'im in de graveyard on de chu'ch groun's what he done hab de membuhship buy.

De nex' Sunday de preachuh what de bishop done sen' to teck Revun Logan's place come to preach his fuss sermon. De new preachuhs in dem days comin' up allus preach dey fuss sermon in de night time, so dis new preachuh gits up in de pulpit dat fuss night an' pray; den he raise his voice to lead a song; nex' he light out to preachin', but no sooner'n he staa't, de oil lamps all goes out an' ghostes staa'ts to comin' into de chu'ch house thoo de windows and de doors. Sump'n lack a gust of win' come thoo de whole chu'ch house. De pastuh, de membuhship, an' de chilluns all lights out from dere for de dirt road. De new preachuh saddle his hoss rail quick an' rides clear on outen de Bottoms, an' dey don' nevuh heah tell of 'im from dat day to dis one.

De bishop sen's 'bout fo' mo' preachuhs to pastuh de charge attuh dis, but lack as befo' de same thing happens an' dey saddles dey hosses an' lights outen de Bottoms, an' don' nevuh come back no mo'. De membuhship say dat dem ghostes was Revun Logan an' de ole pilluhs of de chu'ch what buried in de ch'ch graveyard comin' back, 'caze dey ain't pleased wid de fashion de bishop done treat Revun Logan.

Fin'ly, de bishop sen's a rail young preachuh what done finish up in a Mefdis' Preachuh school way somewhat. Dis his fuss charge an' he brung his wife wid 'im. De membuhship jes' know dis heah young preachuh gonna be scairt to deaf Sunday night when he staa't to preachin' an' de ghostes staa't to comin' in de windows, so dey meck hit up dat dey ain't narry one of 'em goin' in de chu'ch dat night; 'stid dey gonna all congugate on t'othuh side de dirt road 'cross from de ch'ch house an' crack dey sides laffin' when de young preachuh an' his wife come runnin' outen de chu'ch house when de lamps goes out an' de ghostes staa'ts to comin' in.

Dey lines up cross de road from de chu'ch house long 'fo' de young preachuh an' his wife goes into de chu'ch house dat night an' lights de lamps. But fin'ly de preachuh an' his wife shows up an' lights all de lamps in de pulpit an' 'roun' de walls. Den de preachuh tuck his Bible an' his hymn book out, turnt to a page in de hymn book an' raised a hymn. Den he put de hymn book down, open up his Bible, an' read a passage of scripture. When he done did dis, he offuh up a short prayer, den 'nounce his tex'. But de minnit he 'nounce his tex' de lamps goes out an' dee ghostes staa'ts comin' in thoo de windows lack ez befo'. But de preachuh an' his wife don' budge. He keep rat on wid his sermon lack nothin' ain't done happen an' de sperrits an' ghostes all teck seats in de pews till he finish his sermon. He preach a sermon 'bout tithin'—you gib one tent' of you' wages to de chu'ch, he say. So when he git thoo wid de sermon, he say to his wife, "Sistuh White, git de collection plate an' pass hit 'round so's de Brothuhs an' Sistuhs kin th'ow in de collection." An' when he say dis, de ghostes staa't flyin' outen de windows faster'n dey comed in, an' de lamps come to be lighted again.

When de membuhship see dis dey as staa't runnin' cross de road to de chu'ch house whar de young preachuh an' his wife was gittin' dey things togethuh to leave de chu'ch house. Dey rushes up to de new preachuh, shakes his han' an tells 'im de bishop sho' done sen' de rat preachuh to dis charge. Dey tells 'im he done broke de spell of de ghostes, an' dis must have been de truf, 'caze de ghostes ain't nevuh showed up no mo', from dat day to dis one.

SOURCE: J. Mason Brewer, *The Word on the Brazos*, 64–65.

> *Combining the preacher tale with stories about ghosts, this account of a haunted church gives us a preacher who is also a trickster. In a clever twist, the narrator claims that his tale is "de truf," on the grounds that ghosts have ceased to haunt the church.*

OLD BROTHER TRIES TO ENTER HEAVEN

Ole Brother have had he time in dis world. He have never done nothin' to ease de mind er a human, an' when he time come, he leff dis world wid a mighty cry an' struggle for de heavenly heights, an' wid he sly ways he manage to git to de top er de long hill. He hung 'round de gates er heaven for days, an' ole Peter recognize him an' run him off, but he kep' on comin' back.

He seed de Lord pass de gates one day an' stop Him an' plead wid Him, but it is mighty hard to fool de Lord an' de Lord 'fuse him an' tell him He feared to 'low him in, he record down below been so bad. He tell de Lord he have truly repent, an' de Lord tell him He know he is, but he ain' done it till too late. He tell him dey ain't no nuse to come wid all dis repentance ole as he is; date he ain' start it till he were lookin' right through de bars, an' he must be ain' like wuh he see in hell. He tell him He know he ain't repent for no love er Him, but kaze he wants to do he devilment wid pleasure an' ease; dat He b'lieve he jes tryin' to git into heaven kaze he think hell fire will be too distractin' an' he will be too busy payin' 'tention to de fire an' scorchin' to properly make other people miserable.

But de ole God have too much experience an' tell Ole Brother He wants him to git away from de gate. Ef he keep on hangin' 'round dere, it will gee heaven a bad reputa-tion. An' de Lord went back into heaven an' call He servants an' tell 'em He want 'em to run Ole Brother 'way from de gate. He tell 'em He done gee him notice, but dey must gee him a little time, an' atter dat dey must call all de dogs together an' put 'em outside de gate an' run Ole Brother spang into hell. He tell 'em don't trust no mistake. Ef dey go to de gate an' ain' see Ole Brother, put de dogs out anyhow an' see can't dey strike he trail, as he more'n apt to be dodgin' 'round some er de bush. You see God is sharp an' is mighty hard to change He mind.

But Ole Brother ain' guin up hope. He dodge 'round till he see Jesus. He know you kin do more wid chillun workin' on dey feelin's, an' he start workin' on Jesus. Axe Him to intercede wid He Pa for him. Well, he git hold er Jesus jes as de Lord's servants come out wid dem dog, an' Jesus, wid He lovin' kindness, was 'bout to let him go into heaven, but He Pa s'picion wuh were 'bout to happen—He been watchin'—so He come to de aid er He servants an' tell He Son not to interfere wid He commands, an' call Gab'el an' tell him to blow he horn an' git all de dogs together. He were so inter-rested in gitten Ole Brother 'way from dere, dat He stood out on de hill wid He hand over He eye shadin' it from de glare er de sun. He git so inter-rested till He climb up on a stump an' started whoopin' up dem dogs He Self. You could hear He voice ringin' all over de hill, an' I reckon it sound mighty nigh to hell. An' den de race commence.

De Lord is a sport when He has a mind to be, He gee dat Ole Brother a good start, but he were like a fox. Dey run him all over heaven hill. He struck out in a bee line for a cornder er heaven wey he heared dere were a hole in de fence, but de Lord done had dat crack stop up. He done have every hole repaired in He fence, but dat Ole Brother was hard to git shet er. He slip all 'round heaven—him an' dem dogs—an' angels was every wey whoopin' to de dogs. He run every wey—under brush an' through briar. He try every scheme known to a fox. He went over ditch an' through thicket, but dem dogs ain' never took dey nose off er he scent. You know Ole Brother got a scent, dat's one thing he can't git rid er.

Atter dey run around for over a hour, dey got him straighten out an' dem dogs was so hot to hind him, dat he leff de narrow path an' thicket an' token to de broad road wey dere ain' no obstruction an' headed he self for hell, den he done some runnin'. He runned like dere ain' no place but hell dat he wants to go to. He was guine at sech a rate till he was jes techin de road in spots, an' dem dogs was stretched like a string an' cryin' for God' sake sho' 'nough. But dat nigger done got all idea out er he head but one, an' dat was makin' hell 'fore dem dogs make him. He know he done wrong, dat de Lord done make up He mind an' ain' guh fool wid him now since He find out he try to corrupt He Son.

De devil knowed wha' was guine on an' he had de gates er hell closed, an' as dat nigger approach he sorter shy off a little bit as he seen de flames lickin' through de gates, but he look back an' see dem dogs an' seen a man on a pale white horse, an' he knowed everlastin' death was on he trail. Den he look at de gates one more time an' ain' pay no 'tention to de flame an' discount de groans he heared. He ain' hesitate no more, but went over de top an' enter de flames like a varmint guine to he den, an' de Lord like to kill He Self laughin'.

He say He ain' never waste much time on sports, but He has to take He mind off He regular business sometimes. He say He hound never has run better, an' it gee Him so much pleasure to think er how He outdone de devil. He say it ain' no nuse for de devil to be closin' he gates an' settin' he self up 'gainst Him. He say whenever He starts a sinner for hell, He moest generally puts him dere.

SOURCE: E. C. L. Adams, *Nigger to Nigger*, 214–17.

Dr. Edward Clarkson Leverett Adams published two volumes of folktales from South Carolina: Congaree Sketches *(1927) and* Nigger to Nigger *(1928). Adams set great store by the sermons he heard in black churches, where "the best poetry in America" flourished. In* Nigger to Nigger, *Tad, Scip, and others tell their stories to "Uncle Ned" in such a way that "We talkin' to we." These stories contain conversations about chain gangs and lynching as well as about social and moral injustices in general. "Any story of injustice or cruelty to the black people sets him afire," one journalist wrote about Adams, and his two collections try to transmit those stories to a broader audience. The tale about Old Brother trying to enter Heaven is irreverent in multiple ways, most obviously in its casual treatment of God and Jesus, less obviously in its mimicking of patrollers chasing down a runaway slave in the flight to hell scene. The story does not feature a preacher, but it stages a struggle that might easily have made it into a homily.*

PART XIV

FOLKLORIC COUSINS ABROAD: TALES FROM CARIBBEAN AND LATIN AMERICAN CULTURES

*C*reole is the term often used to characterize the rich mix of cultures that characterize Caribbean regions. While Europeans owned the estates that produced sugar, tobacco, and other agricultural products and served as colonial officials, African slaves labored in the fields and worked as servants. Thankfully, the capitalist model of exploitation and depletion did not operate in the sphere of folk culture, and the island inhabitants produced stories and song that shamelessly borrowed and combined elements to create culturally relevant narratives. The anthropologist Melville Herskovits wrote about syncretic creativity and its power to take bits and pieces from different cultures to make something new. Caribbean storytelling cultures show that process in action. The tales below have more than a touch of magic, and many illustrate the genius of a combinatory imagination that mingles tradition and innovation.

THE ORANGES

Once there was a little boy. His mother died on the day he was born, and his father took a second wife. This woman was wicked, and she made the boy work all day long. After sunset, when the day was over, she refused to give him anything to eat.

One day the boy discovered three oranges on the table. He was very hungry. They were round, ripe, yellow, and looked like three golden balls. He looked here. He looked there. He saw that no one was around. The oranges were shining brightly. He reached his hand out and took one. It was so sweet! He had never imagined oranges this sweet. They were very tiny. He looked at the other two oranges and thought of his stepmother. What would she say? How she would grumble! But hunger is stronger than shame. He ate another orange, then paused for just a moment before downing the last one.

When the stepmother returned from the garden, she noticed right away that her oranges were missing. She asked: "Where are the oranges I left on the table? Did you see my oranges? Whoever took my oranges had better get down on his knees and start praying, because I'm going to skin him alive."

The little boy was terrified when he heard those words. The other children in the house began crying because they were so hungry. The stepmother wouldn't give them any food at all.

"You have eaten my oranges and now you will see what I'm going to do about it."

The little boy was unable to sleep. The next day he went to his mother's grave and asked her to help him. While he was praying he noticed there was an orange seed on his pants. He brushed it off, and it landed on the ground. Suddenly two small roots sprouted from the seed and plunged into the ground. A small green shoot appeared. As the boy watched all this happening, he began to sing:

> Orange grow, grow my orange!
> Orange grow, grow my orange!
> Ay! My orange, ay! my orange!
> You are making me weep, my orange!

"The Oranges," from Suzanne Comhaire-Sylvain, "Creole Tales from Haiti," *Journal of American Folklore* 50 (1937): 229–32. Reprinted with permission of Indiana University Press.

The orange tree kept growing, and, as the boy sang, it grew faster.

My orange, flower, flower my orange!
My orange, flower, flower my orange!

Flowers began to blossom on every branch of the orange tree.

My orange, bear fruits, bear fruits my orange!
My orange, bear fruits, bear fruits my orange!

The flowers fell and turned the ground white. You could see a small green ball where the flowers had blossomed.

Orange, grow big, grow big my orange!
Orange, grow big, grow big my orange!

You could now see big green oranges in the tree.

Orange, ripen, ripen my orange!
Orange, ripen, ripen my orange!

The oranges turned yellow and looked as if they were made of gold.

Bend down branch, bend down my orange!
Bend down branch, bend down my orange!

A branch from the orange tree bent down. The child took an orange and ate it. Then he remembered the debt he owed. He took as many oranges as he could carry and returned to his stepmother's house.

"Look at this lazy boy! Where were you and what have you been up to? Hand over those oranges."

"I brought them for you, mother. Yesterday you scolded me about eating the oranges, and now I've found new ones to take their place."

The stepmother grabbed the oranges without a word of thanks. She did not peel them, but just bit into the orange and then swallowed it whole. "What delicious oranges! Show me where you got them." The boy pretended that he had not heard what she was saying. "If you don't show me the way, I'll crush you with the heel of my shoe."

The little boy took her over to the cemetery. She saw the orange tree and ran over to it. The boy sang:

> Orange, rise up, rise up my orange!
> Orange, rise up, rise up my orange!

The orange tree grew taller and taller, so tall that the stepmother looked tiny.

> Orange, break, break my orange!
> Orange, break, break my orange!

Suddenly there was a loud noise—thunder, boom, boom! The tree crashed right down on the woman, and her body landed on the graves in the cemetery. The boy returned home and found the children there. They were all hungry. He had killed their mother, and now it was his job to take care of them. He returned to the cemetery and asked the orange tree to grow so that he would have food for them.

From that day on, every morning, you could see a little boy going to town with a load of oranges. It is the little boy I have been talking about. After he picks the oranges, he always remembers to tell the tree to rise up. It rises up very high, and its trunk grows very small. That is why you cannot see it, and that is why even I have never seen it. But I know it is there.

SOURCE: Adapted from Suzanne Comhaire-Sylvain, *Creole Tales from Haiti*, 229–32.

> *Living out a worst-case scenario in a household where he is starved not only of food but also of love and affection, the hero manages to rescue himself. The striking contrast between the beauty and sweetness of the oranges from the tree at the mother's gravesite and the bitter depredations of the stepmother captures an opposition that serves as the motor of many fairy-tale plots. Luminous objects provide salvation, both aesthetic and spiritual, and have the power to crush the forces of evil.*

THE PRESIDENT WANTS NO MORE OF ANANSI

Anansi and all his smart ways irritated the President so much that the President told him one day: "Anansi, I'm tired of your foolishness. Don't you ever let me see your face again." So Anansi went away from the palace. And a few days later he saw the President coming down the street, so he quickly stuck his head into the open door of a limekiln.

Everyone on the street took off their hats when the President passed. When he came to the limekiln, he saw Anansi's behind sticking out. He became angry and said, "Qui bounda ça qui pas salué mwé?" (Whose behind is it that doesn't salute me?) Anansi took his head out of the limekiln and said, "C'est bounda 'Nansi qui pas salué ou." (It's Anansi's behind which doesn't salute you.)

The President said angrily, "Anansi, you don't respect me."

Anansi said: "President, I was just doing what you told me to do. You told me never to let you see my face."

The President said: "Anansi, I've had enough of your foolishness. I don't ever want to see you again, clothed or naked."

So Anansi went away. But the next day when he saw the President coming down the street he took his clothes off and put a fish net over his head. When the President saw him he shouted, "Anansi, didn't I tell you I never wanted to see you again clothed or naked?" And Anansi said, "My President, I respect what you tell me. I'm not clothed and I'm not naked."

This time the President told him, "Anansi, if I ever catch you again on Haitian soil I'll have you shot."

So Anansi boarded a boat and sailed to Jamaica. He bought a pair of heavy shoes and put sand in them. Then he put the shoes on his feet and took another boat back to Haiti. When he arrived at Port-au-Prince he found the President standing on the pier.

"Anansi," the President said sternly, "didn't I tell you that if I ever caught you on Haitian soil again I'd have you shot?"

"You told me that, Papa, and I respected what you said. I went to Jamaica and filled my shoes with sand. So I didn't disobey you because I'm now walking on English soil."

"The President Wants No More of Anansi," from Harold Courlander, ed., *The Drum and the Hoe*, 1960. Reprinted by permission of the Emma Courlander Trust.

With its playful puns, this Haitian tale about an encounter between the highest authority (the President, who is also known as "Papa") and irreverent Anansi enacts the slippage between the literal and the figurative in language. Anansi the Trickster wins each of the rounds by craftily taking advantage of the double register in language and turning it against the President.

THE NIGHT BEAUTY

There was once a girl so pretty that everyone called her the Night Beauty. Her brothers and sisters were jealous of her. They wished her dead, but no one knew how they felt. They kept their sister in the house all day long.

"You get sick so easily. It's better that we work double time in the fields than sit by your bedside when you become ill," they told her.

Whenever there was a dance or a wake in the neighborhood, the brothers and sisters said, "Just look at your face! You have dark circles under your eyes. One of us will stay home with you. Don't cry. We'll give you a full report on everything that happens."

One day, the girl was sitting quietly by the window, leaning on the sill and looking out at the butterflies, when the King's son happened to pass by. What a pretty girl! His heart leaped for joy. He returned in the afternoon, knocked on the door and spoke with everyone in the house. The next day he returned. He could not stay away, and he spent as much time as he could there. His love for her was wonderful.

He sent a huge bouquet of flowers to the Night Beauty. There were only roses in the bouquet. The eldest brother, the one who was the most jealous of his sister, threw the flowers on the ground, trampled them, and then strangled his sister. He carried the corpse as far away as he could. Then, after sunset, he dug a grave in a cornfield.

In the evening, the King's son came to visit and saw that everyone was in tears. "What has happened?" he asked. And the answer: "The Night Beauty is not here. She is nowhere to be found!"

A search took place, and everyone looked all over, by day and by night. Nothing! Three years passed by. The King's son married another woman, but he could not get

"The Night Beauty," from Suzanne Comhaire-Sylvain, "Creole Tales from Haiti," *Journal of American Folklore* 50 (1937): 215–17. Reprinted with permission of Indiana University Press.

the Night Beauty out of his mind. He gave some money to her relatives. They bought land, and the cornfield was part of the land they purchased.

One day they were digging, and a small bone leaped from a hole and landed in the road. The younger sister of Beauty was passing by and heard its song:

> Come over here, my dear sister.
> Dear sister of mine, come here.
> Come over here, my dear sister.
> Dear sister of mine, come here.
> Alas! The Night Beauty was killed
> Because of a bouquet of roses!

The girl was terrified, and she ran off to find her mother and older brother. When she took her mother over to the bone, it began to sing:

> Come over here, dear mother of mine.
> Dear mother of mine, come here.
> Come over here, dear mother of mine.
> Dear mother of mine, come here.
> Alas! The Night Beauty was killed
> Because of a bouquet of roses!

The woman was unable to move. The brother found them, and he heard:

> Come over here, you murderer.
> Murderer, come over here.
> Come over here, you murderer.
> Murderer, come over here.
> Alas! You killed the Night Beauty
> All because of a bouquet of roses!

He stopped up his ears to drown out the song and raced away. He ran through the town like a fish darting through water. Still running, he reached the country and the hills. He ran onward to another town and kept running until he reached some hills. Whenever he felt like he was about to drop dead, he would stop, catch his breath, and start running again. One day it was thundering, and he got lost in the woods, forever.

The mother returned home, but she was haunted by her daughter's death. It gnawed at her every moment of the day. Not even a month went by from the time that the bone began singing when they brought the woman to the cemetery.

SOURCE: Adapted from Suzanne Comhaire-Sylvain, *Creole Tales from Haiti*, 215–17.

Many Haitian fairy tales turn on sibling rivalry or intergenerational conflict, with lurid descriptions of violence. In this story, both brothers and sisters gang up on the beautiful heroine. Tales about "singing bones" that proclaim guilt can be found the world over, and, in this one, crime and punishment take center stage, leaving little room for the elaboration of courtship and romance.

MAN-CROW

Once there was a bird in the wood name Man-crow, an' the world was in darkness because of that bird.

So the King offer thousands of pounds to kill him to make the world in light again.

An' the King have t'ree daughter, an' he promise that, if anyone kill Man-crow, he will make them a very rich man an' give one of his daughter to marry.

So t'ousands of soldiers go in the wood to kill Man-crow. An' they found him on one of the tallest trees in the woods. An' no one could kill him, an' they come home back.

So there was a little yawzy[1] fellah call Soliday.

An' he say to his grandmother: "Gran'mother I am very poor. I am going in the wood to see if I can kill Man-crow."

An' the grandmother answer: "Tche, boy, you better go sleep a fireside than you go to the wood fe go dead."

"Gran'mother, I goin' to town fe buy six bow an' arrow."

So he went to Kingston an' bought them.

An' when him return home he ask his grandmother to get six Johnny-cake[2] roast, an' he put it in his namsack, an' he travel in the wood.

1 *yawzy:* Yaws is a disease in which ulcers form on the soles of feet.

2 *Johnny-cake:* cake made of flour and water and fried in lard

He s'arch until he find the spot a place where Man-crow is, an' he see Man-crow to the highest part of the tree.

An' he call to him with this song:

> Good mornin' to you, Man-crow,
> Good mornin' to you, Man-crow,
> Good mornin' to you, Man-crow,
> How are you this mornin'?

An' the bird answer:

> Good mornin' to you, Soliday,
> Good mornin' to you, Soliday,
> Good mornin' to you, Soliday,
> How are you this mornin'?

An' Soliday shot with his arrow at Man-crow an' two of his feather come out.
An' Man-crow come down to the second bough.
An' Soliday sing again:

> Good mornin' to you, Man-crow,
> Good mornin' to you, Man-crow
> Good mornin' to you, Man-crow,
> How are you this mornin'?

An' Man-crow answer as before:

> Good mornin' to you, Soliday,
> Good mornin' to you, Soliday,
> Good mornin' to you, Soliday,
> How are you this mornin'?

An' he fire after Man-crow an' two more feather fly out.
An' so the singing an' shooting go on.

At every song Man-crow come down one branch, an' Soliday fire an arrow an' knock out two feather, till five arrows gone.

So Brother Annancy was on a tree watching Soliday what he is doing.

An' the song sing for the sixth time, an' Man-crow jump down one more branch.

An' Soliday put his last arrow in the bow an' took good aim an' shot after Man-crow. So he killed him an' he drop off the tree.

An' Soliday go an' pick up the bird an' take out the golden tongue an' the golden teeth, an' shove it in a him pocket, an' Soliday come straight home to his grandmother.

An' Annancy come off the tree an' take up the bird, put ahm a him shoulder, cut through bush until he get to the King gate, an' he rakkle at the gate.

They ask: "Who come?"

He say: "Me, Mr. Annancy."

An' they say: "Come in."

An' the King said: "What do you want?"

"I am the man that kill Man-crow."

An' they take him in an' marry him to one of the King daughter an' make a very big table for him an' his family.

They put him in the middle of the table, but he refuse from sit there. He sit to the doorway to look when Soliday coming. (The King then do know that that fellah up to a trick.) An' directly Annancy see Soliday was coming, he stop eating, ask excuse, "I will soon be back." An' at the same time he gone outside into the kitchen.

An' Soliday knock at the gate.

An' someone answer him an' ask: "What do you want?"

"I am the boy that kill Man-crow."

An' they said: "No, impossible! Mr. Annancy kill Man-crow."

An' he take out the golden tongue an' teeth an' show it to the King, an' ask the question: "How can a bird live without teeth an' tongue?"

So they look in the bird mouth an' found it was true.

An' they call Annancy.

An' Annancy give answer: "I will soon be there."

An' they call him again.

An' he shut the kitchen door an' said: "Me no feel well."

3 *shame:* felt ashamed

All this time Brother Annancy shame,[3] take him own time fe make hole in the shingle get 'way.

They call him again, they no yerry[4] him, an' they shove the kitchen door.

Annancy lost in the shingle up to to-day.

An' the King marry Soliday to his daughter an' make him to be one of the richest man in the world.

Jack Mantora me no choose none.[5]

4 *yerry:* hear

5 *Jack Mantora me no choose none:* This standard way of closing a tale in Jamaica is connected with Jack Mantora, who stands at heaven's gate. The phrase could suggest an appeal to leave narrators blameless—after all it is Annancy who is at fault, not the storyteller.

SOURCE: Walter Jekyll, *Jamaican Song and Story*, 54–57.

Impostors are legion in folktales, and in this story Annancy tries to take credit for the feats of Soliday, a fellow with a mysterious name. The term Man-crow *suggests that the monster in the story is a hybrid of human and animal, a creature with the terrifying power to extinguish light and hope. Many Jamaican tales contain embedded songs, and the verses above can be imagined as melodies that can also migrate into other performative contexts.*

WORDS WITHOUT END

Once upon a time, there was a king who had only one daughter. The king said, "Any man who can give me a story without an end can marry the princess." Many tried but did not succeed. There was one last man who came in after everyone else was done. He was introduced to the king, and right away started into his story. He told the king: "One man had some corn. Some locusts gathered around this corn, and one locust came and took a grain. Another locust came and took a grain of corn. Then another locust came and took a grain of corn. Then another locust came and took a grain of corn." Soon the king grew tired. "I am sleepy. You can go and come back another time."

The man did so. And when he returned the following day, he started in: "And then another locust came and took a grain of corn. Another locust came and took a grain of corn. And then another locust came and took a grain of corn. And another locust came and took a grain of corn."

The king grew tired and he said to the man, "Your story has no end. Take the princess and marry her."

SOURCE: Roger D. Abrahams, *African American Folktales*, 2. Recorded in Tobago.

Anything to keep from being bored! The king in this tale poses a challenge that backfires in producing the exact opposite of the endless entertainment he desires. He becomes willing to do anything to end the drearily repetitious drumbeat about locusts and crop damage. Like the frame narrative in The Thousand and One Nights, *this tale also reflects on the activity of storytelling, although in a way that perversely (and comically) emphasizes its deadening effect rather than its power to animate and arouse curiosity. Many cultures have similar tales in which a task is repeated ad infinitum. In a Japanese version, one rat after another jumps ship; in an Irish variant, ants take one piece of grain at a time. Vance Randolph calls these "teaser yarns" the perfect bedtime story, for the tales are "drawled out in a deliberately sedative hypnotic monotone" (1955, 192).*

WHY PEOPLE DO NOT LIVE AGAIN AFTER DEATH

One day Cat met Dog, and they made conversation. They spoke of death, and Cat said, "Man is born, he dies, and when he dies he does not rise to lie again."

Dog said, "No, people die, they rise again."

They argued. Cat said, "Tomorrow let us go and see what God has to say about the matter." Dog said, "Yes, let us go."

But after Cat had left, Dog contrived to distract Cat on the journey. He placed bits of butter along the trail, thinking, "Cat will stop to eat some butter here, some butter there, and I will arrive at God's house first." Cat, on the other hand, placed fresh bones along the trail to distract Dog on the journey.

In the morning they set out. They came to where Dog had set out the butter, but

"Why People Do Not Live Again After Death," from Harold Courlander, ed., *A Treasury of Afro-American Folklore*, 1976. Reprinted by permission of the Emma Courlander Trust.

Cat did not stop. They came to the place where Cat had set out a bone, Dog stopped. He could not resist the bone. He gnawed at it, while Cat went on. Each time Cat came to the butter he merely looked ahead and kept on the trail. But each time that Dog found a bone he stopped and gnawed on it. So it was that Cat arrived at God's house first.

He asked God whether man died and remained dead, or whether he rose and lived again. God said, "What is your position on this matter?"

And Cat answered, "I contend that people die and do not arise from death, but remain dead." God replied, "Well, then let us leave it that way."

In time, Dog arrived. He put the same question to God. God said to him, "Well, the matter has been decided. Cat came. He contended that the dead should remain dead. I said 'Very well, that is the way it will be.' You, Dog, you are too late. Coming along the trail you did not keep your mind on your purpose. You stopped here and there, wherever you smelled something to eat. Therefore it shall be as Cat has said. People shall die and not live again."

SOURCE: Harold Courlander, *A Treasury of Afro-American Folklore*, 90–91. Told in Guadeloupe.

> *The twin themes of death and resurrection are presented in a lighthearted but weighty manner through the dialogue between Cat and Dog. God's momentous decision about whether to grant humans immortality ends up turning on a dog's distractability and unbridled appetite, thereby undermining the notion of divine wisdom and validating its capriciousness.*

THE MAN WHO TOOK A WATER MOTHER FOR HIS BRIDE

There was a poor man named Domingos living alone in his cabin in the countryside not far from the edge of a certain river. He had no family whatever, and as for his garden, it barely produced enough to keep him alive. No matter how much he cared for his corn, it would not flourish. The other farmers who lived near Domingos were also poor and wretched, but Domingos was the most unlucky of them all.

One morning Domingos wanted to pick a few ears of corn. As he walked from one stalk to the next, he noticed that some of the ears had already been picked, and he wondered who had been so heartless as to take the food from his mouth. The next day he returned to the field and saw that more ears had been picked. Anger rose up in him, and he swore to catch the thief and punish him.

That night he took his cane knife and went out and hid in the cornfield in a place where he could see intruders. He covered himself in grass and straw so that he was not visible. He waited while the night grew long, and the moon moved across the sky. He was beginning to fall asleep, and his eyes started closing. Just then, on the side of the field near the river, there was a rustling sound, as if someone was walking through the cornstalks. He was now awake! He grabbed his knife, thinking: "I'm going to kill the person who has been robbing me."

Domingos heard the person coming closer. Next came the sound of an ear being broken from its stalk. He heard another snap. He saw a shadow. Then he saw the person, and he ran out from his hiding place. What he saw surprised him, for the person taking his corn was a water woman who lived with others of her kind in the river. He grabbed her, shouting and threatening her, but he did not strike her. The moon was shining brightly, and he could see how beautiful she was. He asked: "Why do you steal from someone like me, who has barely enough to eat?"

The water woman answered, "I was hungry. I meant you no harm."

Domingos replied, "I should punish you." But she answered, "Let me go. I will return to the river. And from now on I will go elsewhere for food." Domingo's heart softened. It was warmed by the water woman's voice and her appearance. He said, "Why should I let you go?"

The woman replied, "What good would it do you to keep me?" And Domingos said, "Why, if I kept you, I would no longer be alone. I would have a wife like everyone else." She told him it was not possible. "When has a water person ever married a land person?"

But Domingos was captivated by the woman's voice and by her beauty. He asked her to stay. He pleaded with her. At last, moved by the warmth of his pleas, the water woman said, "We have been told by our elders that those who live on land and those who live in the water may not mix. Once long ago it happened that a young water woman was taken as a wife by a land person. At first things went well. But after a while the man began to beat her. He did not treat her as well as he had at first. And as time went on he began to ridicule her for her origins. He spoke contemptuously with her, 'What can I expect from someone who is a mere water woman?' And he spoke like that among the others living in the village. One night he beat her and said, 'Water woman! What are you doing living in my house among humans?'

"It was then that she left and returned to the river. The water people said, 'It has always been like this. We should never try to live with the land people.'"

Domingos said, "In my eyes you are not a water woman. You are just a woman. Why would I care where you came from? Stay here and come live in my house." And so the water woman stayed. She went to his house with him, and she became his wife. And because of that, Domingos' fortunes changed. The corn in his field grew large ears. His goats and cattle multiplied. People who lived nearby began to praise Domingos for his hard work. Once he had been too poor for anyone to pay attention to him. Now people listened respectfully when he spoke, because he was a man of substance.

Domingos built a new house. People came to him for help when they were in need. He had plenty of extra corn hanging from the branches of the large tree that provided shade for his house. But Domingos never stopped to think about why his fortune had changed. He became arrogant. And one evening after he had been drinking, he became abusive to his wife. He said, "Our children have bad manners. Why do you set such a bad example for them?" He added, "Why is it that I work hard in the field but you do nothing?" He went on, "The people who live nearby say bad things about you. Why are you so careless in your ways?" Domingos went on like that, accusing her of things and insulting her. She did not answer, and her silence angered Domingos all the more. He said, "Why don't you speak when you are spoken to?" And still his wife remained silent. At last Domingos shouted at her, "Water woman! You who came out of the river!"

When his wife heard those words, she got up from where she was sitting. She opened the door of the cabin and walked out. Domingos followed her, shouting curses at the water people. But something happened to Domingos. Suddenly he found that he was unable to walk because his feet were rooted to the ground. He saw his wife walk toward the river. One by one his children left the house and followed their mother. When the woman reached the edge of the river, she walked into the water and disappeared. Her children followed her. Domingos saw that his goats and cattle were also moving toward the water. One by one his cattle went into the water. They descended into the depths. They could no longer be seen. Domingos cried out. He tried to follow, but he could not move from where he was rooted. Then he watched as the ears of corn hanging in the tree by his house began to move. One by one the ears moved through the air as if they were flying. They flew toward the river, landed on the water, and then disappeared. After that, Domingos' house and everything in it began moving toward the river. Domingos cried out, "My house, my house!" But the house kept on moving and went into the river. The fences Domingos had built to hold his cattle began to move. Everything that had once belonged to Domingos left and followed the water woman into the river. Only then did Domingos' feet become unrooted. He ran back and forth, looking for all the things that had once belonged to him.

Everything was gone. Domingos had nothing. And he lived as the poorest of all men until the end of his days.

SOURCE: Adapted from Gilberto Freyre, *The Masters and the Slaves*, in *A Treasury of Afro-American Folklore*, ed. Harold Courlander, 246–48.

Marriages between mortals and mermaids, selkies, nymphs, birds, and water sprites are often the subject of folktales, and those unions rarely end well. Either the avian or amphibious creature longs for a return to the natural habitat (sometimes coming across by chance the skin or feathers they shed to take on human form) or they are devastated by the abusive behavior of a spouse and leave. This Afro-Brazilian tale uses the folktale about marriage to a mythical being as a cautionary tale about spousal abuse.

THE GIRL MADE OF BUTTER

Once was a time, a very good time,
Monkey chew tobacco and spit white lime.

There was a woman. She had a daughter who was made entirely of butter. Tom and William used to come courting her, and they didn't know this about her. So the woman never let those boys near her daughter, lest she melt with the heat. But, one day, she got so busy cooking for these two boys, the woman forgot to keep watch, and the boys saw their chance. They came and sat down next to the girl. The girl started singing while the woman was in the kitchen cooking, trying to remind her.

> Momma, come wash my skin,
> Momma, come wash my skin!
> Move off, Tom! move off, William!
> Till my momma has washed my skin.

The girl started melting because her mother wasn't there to wash her skin with cool water. She melted from her head down to her shoulders.

> Momma, come wash my skin,
> Momma, come wash my skin!
> Move off, Tom! move off, William!
> Till my momma has washed my skin.

She started melting more. She melted from her shoulder down to her waist. She started singing again:

> Momma, come wash my skin,
> Momma, come wash my skin!
> Move off, Tom! move off, William!
> Till my momma has washed my skin.

She melted from her waist down to her knees. All that time the woman was in the kitchen cooking, while her daughter was melting. The girl starting singing again:

> Momma, come wash my skin,
> Momma, come wash my skin!
> Move off, Tom! move off, William!
> Till my momma has washed my skin.

She melted from her knees down to her feet. When the woman did remember, she cried out, "Oh, my butter daughter! Oh, my butter baby!" She had forgotten all about her daughter. When she did go back in the house, she only found a pile of melted butter but no one else. Tom and William were gone.

The bow bended, my story ended.

SOURCE: Roger Abrahams, *Afro-American Folktales*, 167–69, adapted from Elsie Clews Parsons, *Folk-Tales of Andros Island, Bahamas*, 125–26.

Loss is the major theme sounded in this story that gives us the strange case of a melting girl. As suitors, Tom and William are bent on luring the girl from her oddly neglectful mother, but neither one is successful in the courtship. The tale begins with a traditional rhyme that marks a story as a fairy tale and ends with a line that aims to give closure to a tale so enigmatic that it is guaranteed to generate conversation.

TIGER SOFTENS HIS VOICE

Once upon a time a woman had one daughter, an' that daughter was the prettiest girl in an' around that country. Every man want the girl to marry, but the mother refuse them as they come. Tiger, too, wanted the girl, an' demands the girl, an' the mother says no. Tiger said if he don't get the girl he will kill her. So they remove from that part of the country and go to another part, into a thick wild wood where no one live. And she made a house with a hundred doors and a hundred windows[1] and a large staircase; and the house is an upstairs, an' there both of them live.

Tiger hear of it, always loafing aroun' the house to see if he can catch the girl, but the girl never come out. During the day, the mother went to her work, leaving the girl at home. When going out, the mother fasten all the doors an' windows; coming home in the evening, at a certain spot where she can see the house an' notice that all the windows an' doors are close as she leave it, then now she have a song to sing, go like this:

"Tom Jones, Tom Jones, Tom Jones![2]"

1 *a hundred doors and a hundred windows:* Excess and exaggeration are the mark of a fairy-tale style, and the mother relocates to a house that is seemingly inaccessible.

2 *Tom Jones:* A touch of humor comes in the use of a man's name to designate the "pretty girl."

(that's the name of the girl). Girl now—

"Deh lo, madame!"

Woman said to her now,

"Fare you well, fare you well, fare you well,
Fare you well, me dear; fare you well, me love!
A no Tiger, deh la, ho, deh la, ho?
Me jus' come, ho!"

Then the door open, so—

"Cheeky checky knock umbar,
Cheeky checky knock umbar,
Cheeky checky knock umbar."

The door don't open without that song now, and when it open, the mamma go into the house.

At that time, Tiger in the bush listening to the song. So one day while she was away, hear time for her to come home, Tiger approach the spot where she always sing. He now in a very coarse voice sings the song:

"Tom Jones, Tom Jones, Tom Jones!"

The girl look from the window, said, "Tiger, a who no know sa' a you!" So now Tiger go 'way an' hide till mamma come. When she come, he listen good. Next day, Tiger go to a blacksmith an' ask de blacksmith what he t'ink can give him, Tiger, a clear v'ice. De blacksmit' say he must hot a long iron an' when it hot, mus' take it push down his t'roat. An' de blacksmit' give him a bit of meat to eat after he burn the throat an' that will give him a clear v'ice. So Tiger go away eat de meat first an' den burn de t'roat after. Nex' day he went to the spot where the woman always sing from. An' that make his v'ice more coarser. He sing now:

"Tom Jones, Tom Jones, Tom Jones!"

The girl look thru the window an' say, "Cho! a who no know sa' a you!" So Tiger got vex' now, an' he went home, burn the throat first and afterward eat the meat, and that give him a clearer v'ice than the woman. The nex' day, when most time for the woman to come home from her work, Tiger went to the spot where he can see the house. He begin to sing:

"Tom Jones, Tom Jones, Tom Jones!"

The girl answer (tho't it was her mother now)—

"Deh la, madame!"

Then Tiger say,

"Fare you well, fare you well, fare you well,
Fare you well, me dear; fare you well, me love!
A no Tiger deh lo o-o-o
Me jus' come, h-o-o-o!"

The door commence to open now,—

"Cheeky checky checky knock umbar,
Cheeky cheeky checky knock umbar,
Cheeky checky cheeky knock umbar!"

And as the door open, Tiger step up an' caught the girl an' swallow her.

And when the mother coming home, reach to the spot and saw the doors and windows open, she throw down what she carry and run to the house. And she saw Tiger lay down. And the mother then went away an' get some strong men come an' tie Tiger, kill him, an' open de belly[3] an' take out de daughter. At that time, little life left in her an' they get

3 *open de belly:* In the Grimms' "Little Red Riding Hood," a huntsman cuts open the belly of the wolf. And in their "Wolf and the Seven Kids," it is the mother goat who cuts open the wolf's belly and liberates six of the seven children—the seventh managed to hide from the wolf.

back the life in her. The woman then leave the house an' go off away far into another country, and that is why you always fin' lot of old houses unoccupied that no one live in.

SOURCE: Martha Warren Beckwith, ed., *Jamaica Anansi Stories*, 117–18. Told by George Parkes of Mandeville.

Related to "Little Red Riding Hood" as well as "The Wolf and the Seven Young Kids," this story about a mother, a daughter, and Tiger is ostensibly a pourquoi tale, explaining why some houses remain unoccupied. In fact, it is far richer than that, telling a story about masquerade, deception, predation, and liberation.

A BOARHOG FOR A HUSBAND

Scalambay, scalambay[1]
Coops, scops, scalambay
See my lover coming there
Scoops, scops, scalamby.

Once upon a time—it was a very good time—Massa King[2] had an only daughter. And all the young fellows were constantly talking with each other about who was going to be able to marry her. They all came by to call on her, but none of them suited her. Each time one would come, her father would say "Now this is the one!" But she kept saying, "No, Daddy, this fellow here, I just don't like him." Or "No, Mommy, this one really doesn't please me." But the last one to come along was a handsome young fellow, and she fell in love with him right away. And of course, when she fell in love, it was deep and wide— she just lost her head altogether. What she didn't know was that she'd actually chosen a boarhog who had changed himself into a human to go courting.

Now the Massa King had another child, a little Old Witch Boy[3] who lived there and did all the nasty stuff around the palace. He was always dirty and smelly, you know, and no one liked to be around him, especially the King's beautiful daughter.

1 *Scalambay, scalambay:* The nonsense words have no particular relevance to the story, but they are encoded in the musical refrain to retard the action and also to animate the tale.

2 *Massa King:* Also known as Master King and Marster King in other stories, this patriarchal figure makes all the important decisions in the tale.

3 *little Old Witch Boy:* The brother is akin to the Cinderella figure, relegated to the hearth and forced to live in an abject state.

One day after work the young fellow came in to visit his bride, and the Old Witch Boy whispered, "Daddy, Daddy, did you know that the fellow my sister is going to marry is a boarhog?" "What? You better shut your mouth and get back under the bed where you belong." (That's where they made the Old Witch Boy stay, you see, because he was so dirty.)

Now when they got married, they moved way up on the mountain up where they plant all those good things to put in the pot, roots like dasheen, tania,[4] and all those provisions that hogs like to eat, too. One day, Massa King came up there and showed him a big piece of land he wanted his daughter and her husband to have for farming. The husband really liked that because he could raise lots of tanias—which is what boarhogs like to eat most.

4 dasheen, tania: root vegetables grown in the Caribbean

So one day he went up to work, early early in the morning. Now there was this little house up by the land where he could go and change his clothes before he went to work. He went into one side of the little house, and he started singing:

> Scalambay, scalambay
> Coops, scops, scalambay
> See my lover coming there
> Scoops, scops, scalamby.

And with each refrain he would take off one piece of clothing. And with every piece he took off he became more of a boarhog—first the head, then the feet, then the rest of the body.

> Scalambay, scalambay
> Coops, scops, scalambay
> See my lover coming there
> Scoops, scops, scalamby.

Well, about noon, when he thought the time was coming for lunch to arrive in the field, he went back into the house and put back on his clothes, took off the boarhog suit and put back on the ordinary suit he came in. And as he got dressed he sang the same little song to change himself back into a handsome man.

Scalambay, scalambay
Coops, scops, scalambay
See my lover coming there
Scoops, scops, scalamby.

After a while, the Old Witch Boy as usual came with the food, but this day he came early and saw what was going on, heard the singing, and saw the man changing. So he rushed home and told his father again, "Daddy, this fellow who married my sister up there really is a boarhog. It's true!" Massa King said, "Boy, shut your mouth," and his sister said, "Get back underneath the bed, you scamp you."

The next day, the Old Witch Boy got up very early and went up the mountain and heard the song again:

Scalambay, scalambay
Coops, scops, scalambay
See my lover coming there
Scoops, scops, scalamby.

All right, he thought, and he went down again, and he told his father what he had seen and heard. He even sang the song. Now Massa King didn't know what to think. But he knew he was missing a lot of tanias from his other fields, so he loaded up his gun and went to see what was going on up there in his fields. Mr. Boarhog was up there changing and didn't know he was being watched, but he thought he heard something so he kind of stopped. The Old Witch Boy started to sing, and Mr. Boarhog couldn't do anything but join in with him. And so there they both were, singing:

Scalambay, scalambay
Coops, scops, scalambay
See my lover coming there
Scoops, scops, scalamby.

And the man slowly changed into a boarhog. When the King saw this he couldn't believe his eyes. He took his gun and he let go, *pow!* And he killed Mr. Boarhog, and carried him down the mountain. The King's beautiful daughter couldn't believe what she saw and began to scream and cry, but Mass King told her what he had seen and what he had done, and then she had to believe it.

They cleaned Mr. Boarhog's body and had him quartered.[5]

5 *had him quartered:* The narrator comes in to report at the end: "And I was right there on the spot, and took one of the testicles and it gave me food for nearly a week!"

SOURCE: Roger Abrahams, *The Man-of-Words in the West Indies*, 171–72. From an informant in St. Vincent.

In tales about beauties and beasts, the plot turns on a redemptive transformation from animal to human. But in this story about a boarhog, the animal tricks the girl into marrying him by turning temporarily into an attractive man. What makes this tale unusual in addition is the role of the Old Witch Boy, who is consigned to the hearth to carry out all the dirty work, but who is wise beyond his years. Old Witch Boy has a deformed foot in some stories in which he appears, making him a grotesque male counterpart to the Cinderella figure.

PART XV

SOMETHING BORROWED, SOMETHING BLUE: FAIRY TALES

Fairy tales have more than a touch of magic and mystery. How do you explain a German story about a girl named Thousandfurs, who dresses up in pelts made from the coats of many different animals and takes up residence in a hollow tree? Why does a young man named Don Juan break ranks with his brothers and marry a monkey named Chonguita in a story told in the Philippines? What is that old woman doing in the Russian woods, living in a hut built on chicken legs surrounded by a fence with posts made from human skulls?

Churchill once spoke of "a riddle wrapped in a mystery inside an enigma" (he was referring to Russia), and that same phrase can be used to describe stories that are at their core deceptively simple and simply deceptive. We decode them not just while we are reading them, but also when we talk about them with others who have been shocked and startled by their content. Fairy tales, once told around the fire by adults to multigenerational audiences, were meant to start conversation and also to promote collective thinking about cultural values and hot-button social issues. They added to the store of communal wisdom in cultures where nothing was ever written down.

CINDERELLA

Po' little Cinderella was livin' with her auntie. De woman had two daughter of her own. An' she live in de fire-heart'. Wouldn' let her sleep in no bed no' not'in'. An' ev'y night her an' de two girls dress up des' as fine as dey could be, go out to de dance, big feas', havin' all kind of fun. Po' little Cinderella had to stay home in de ashes, nakin', an' havin' not'in' to eat. Ev'y time dey come home, dey huff up po' little Cinderella. Say she an't do what they leave her to do. De two girls d'ess up in robe in diamon's all ower, an' was goin' to de dance, goin' t'rough de woods. So de king an' de queen give a dance. An' de king inwited dem out. An' he had a gol' slippers (I think he was number two). An' dese fancy girls had wanted dem. An' de king said who de slipper fitted would be his wife dat night. De dove come an' bring some clothes fo' Cinderella. Den Cinderella gone out to de dance, an' dey didn' know her, dress so much. Dey was wonderin' what strange woman dat is. Den de king tryin' on de shoe on dey all feet. Some cut off deir

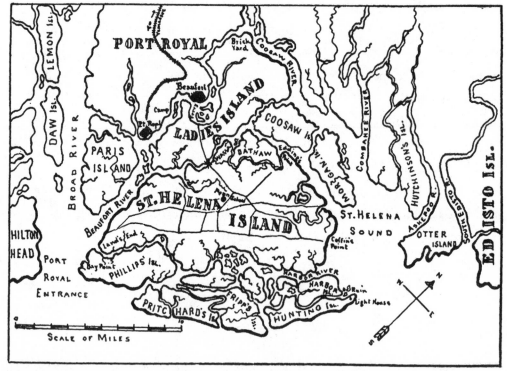

This hand-drawn map of the South Carolina Sea Islands was published in 1912 with the letters and diary of Laura M. Towne, a white teacher on St. Helena Island.

toe, tryin' to make de shoe fit dem. Some trim deir heels off, tryin' to make de shoe fit dem. After all, de shoes couldn' fit none of dem dat been dere. Den po' little Cinderella she come right on up in dat time, an' she grab de shoes. An' fit her right on de feet. Den she become de queen, married to de king, an' ride in de firs' chariot.

SOURCE: Elsie Clews Parsons, *Folk-Lore of the Sea Islands, South Carolina*, 120–21.

Told by James Murray and his wife, Pinky Murray, who were living on Hilton Head Island, this version of "Cinderella" is remarkably like the Grimms' tale in its unedited form, complete with hacked off heels and toes.

MR. BLUEBEARD

There was a man named Mr. Bluebeard. He got his wife in his house, an' he general catch people an' lock up into a room, an' he never let him wife see that room.

One day he went out to a dinner an' forgot his key on the door. An' his wife open the door an' find many dead people in the room. Those that were not dead said: "Thanky, Missis; Thanky Missis."

An' as soon as the live ones get away, an' she was to lock the door, the key drop in blood. She take it up an' wash it an' put it in the lock. It drop back into the blood.

An' Mr. Bluebeard was an old-witch an' know what was going on at home. An' as he sat at dinner, he called out to get his horse ready at once. An' they said to him: "Do, Mr. Bluebeard, have something to eat before you go."

"No! Get my horse ready."

So they bring it to him. Now he doesn't ride a four-footed beast, he ride a t'ree-foot horse.[1]

An' he get on his horse an' start off itty-itty-hap, itty-itty-hap,[2] until he get home.

Now Mrs. Bluebeard two brother was a hunter-man in the wood. One of them was old-witch, an' he said: "Brother, brother, something home wrong with me sister."

"Get 'way you little foolish fellah," said the biggest one.

1 *t'ree-foot horse:* The three-legged horse is thought to be a kind of phantom beast that rides only at night in the moonlight and can gallop faster than any other horse.

2 *itty-itty-hap:* an onomatopoeic phrase meant to capture the gait of the three-legged horse

But the other say again: "Brother, brother, something wrong at home. Just get me a white cup and a white saucer, and fill it with water, and put it in the sun, an' you will soon see what to do with the water."

Directly the water turn blood.

An' the eldest said: "Brother, it is truth, make we go."

An' Mrs. Bluebeard was afraid, because he knew[3] Mr. Bluebeard was coming fe kill him.[4] An' he was calling continually to the cook, Miss Anne: "Sister Anne, Sister Anne, Ah! You see anyone coming? Sister Anne, Sister Anne, Ah! You see anyone coming?"

An' Sister Anne answer: "Oh no, I see no one is coming but the dust that makes the grass so green."

An' as she sing done they hear Mr. Bluebeard coming, itty-itty-hap, itty-itty-hap.

Him jump straight off a him t'ree-foot beast an' go in a the house, and catch Mrs. Bluebeard by one of him plait-hair an' hold him by it, an' said: "This is the last day of you."

An' Mrs. Bluebeard said: "Do, Mr. Bluebeard, allow me to say my last prayer."

But Mr. Bluebeard still hold him by the hair while he sing: "Sister Anne, Sister Anne, Ah! You see anyone coming? Sister Anne, Sister Anne, Ah! You see anyone coming?"

Sister Anne answer this time: "Oh—yes! I see someone is coming, and the dust that makes the grass so green."

Then Mr. Bluebeard took his sword was to cut off him neck, an' his two brother appear, an' the eldest one going to shot after Mr. Bluebeard, an' he was afraid an' begin to run away. But the young one wasn't going to let him go so, an' him shot PUM and kill him 'tiff dead.

Jack Mantora me no choose none.[5]

SOURCE: Walter Jekyll, *Jamaican Song and Story: Annancy Stories, Digging Sings, Ring Tunes, and Dancing Tunes,* 35–37.

Mr. Bluebeard and Mrs. Bluebeard share much with their European counterparts, but Mrs. Bluebeard is not at all the curious, disobedient

---

3 *he knew:* she knew (*he* can refer to *he* or *she*)

4 *fe kill him:* to kill her (the masculine pronoun is often substituted for the feminine)

5 *Jack Mantora me no choose none:* In some Jamaican tales Jack appears as a listener, and the narrator closes with this phrase, which has been read to mean either "Don't blame me for the tale I've just told" or "I didn't have you in mind when I chose this tale." Louise Bennett, the Jamaican folklorist, writer, and actress, has another view. When she exchanged stories with friends, they had to say "Me no chose none," because "Annancy sometimes did very wicked things in his stories, and we had to let Jack Mantora, the doorman at heaven's door, know that we were not in favor of Annancy's wicked ways" (Jekyll 1966, ix).

figure found in French, German, British, and Italian variants of the story. And Mr. Bluebeard is no longer a wealthy aristocrat but instead a witch determined to murder his wives. The figure of Sister Anne appears in French versions of the tale.

THE CHOSEN SUITOR: THE FORBIDDEN ROOM

Is a boy name John. An' he had a sister. An' dis king was payin' dis boy sister mad-dress. Dis little boy was a witch, could tell whe' his sister goin' to get a good husban' or not. So when dis man come, his sister always put dis boy underneat' de step, an' put him to bed. So den dis little boy wake up an' tell his sister, "Sister, you married to de Debil." Sister slap him aroun' an' kick him, wouldn' listen de boy. So, sure enough, she married de man against de boy. Man kyarry his sister from dere an' kyarry him to his house, little over t'irty or fo'ty miles. So after kyarrin' dis woman summuch nights an' summuch days, dis boy know exaxly how dis man was treatin' his sister. One day de man han' his wife sewen key. An' he had sewen room in de house. But he show her de room, an' say, "Use de six room; but de seven room don' use it, don' go in dat room!" So one day his wife say to heself, "I got all de key. I wan' to see what is in dat room." He husban' been 'bout twenty-five mile from dere when she said dat. She wen' into de room, open de room. When she open de room, was nothin' but de wife dis man married, de skeleton hung up in de room. Dis one fall down, faint, right to de do'. Less dan half an hour she come to her sense. She lock de do' back. Gone, set down.

Husban' drive up to de do' at de time, an' tell um, "Dis night you will be in dat room."

Forty mile from her broder den. So her broder know dat his sister have a fas' horse. An' he took sewen needle wid him. He started fo' his sister den. He ritched his sister's place 'bout fo' o'clock. Sister was to put to deat' at fus' dark. When he see dat his broder-in-law come, he welcome him like any broder-in-law do, like not'in' goin' to be done.

Dis king ask him what his horse eat? He tol' him, "I feed my horse wid cotton-seed." Dis king den had to go half a mile from dis house to his nex' neighbor to get cotton-seed for his broder-in-law horse.

When he gone, he tell his sister, "Sister, take not'in', jump in de buggy!" Dey had fo'ty miles to go. When he get a half a mile from de house, he han' his sister dese sewen needle. He said, "Sister, he done hitch up his horse, he comin' after us." Drop one o' de needle, an' it become a swamp across de road. De king drive until he come to de swamp. He had to tu'n back home an' get a grubbin'-hoe an' axe to cut t'rough dere. All dat time John was goin' wid his sister.

De king was a witch himself. He cut um so quick, he was on dem again. She drop anoder needle. Den it become a ocean across de road. He had to sup up all dat water befo' he could star' again.

When dey was one mile of John house where his sister live, he tell his sister t'row all de needle out his han'. Dey become an ocean. Dey cross de oder side den. He drive down here. When he get to de ocean, he had to stop, couldn't get any furder. John an' his sister 'rive his ol' cabin why de king kyarry her from. An' dis sister gave de broder what she used to kick about lovin' praise. An' John save his sister life.

THE CHOSEN SUITOR: THE FORBIDDEN ROOM
(Second Version)

Once upon a time there was a man had one daughter. Every man come to marry her, she said, "No." So a man came, all over was gold. And she married him. He had a horse name Sixty-Miles, for every time he jump it was sixty miles. So they went. The more he goes, his gold was dropping. Mary Bell wanted to know why his gold was dropping. He said, "That is all right." They reached home soon. He gave her a big bunch of keys and take her around to all the room in the house. "You can open all the room except one room; for if you open it, I will kill you." She start to wonder why her husband didn't want her to open it. So one day she open it. It was great surprise. She saw heads of woman hanging up. She also saw a cast of blood. Her key dropped in the blood, and she couldn't get it off. So she began to mourn. The Devil daughter told her not to cry. She took three needles and gave it to her. "He is coming; but when you first drop one, there will be a large forest, and so on." She went and get Sixty-Miles, and she went. Now the Devil came from the wood. He had a rooster. He told his master, "Massa, massa, your pretty girl gone home this morning 'fore day. Massa, massa, your pretty girl gone home this morning 'fore day." The Devil look about the house for his wife, he didn't see her. So he went to get Sixty-Miles, and he couldn't find it. So he get Fifty-

Miles. Start after her. He spy her far down the road. He said, "Mary Bell, O Mary Bell! what harm I done you?"

> You done me no harm, but you done me good. Bang-a-lang!
> Hero, don't let your foot touch, bang-a-lang!
> Hero, don't let your foot touch!

The Devil catch at her. She drop a needle, and it became a large forest. He said, "Mary Bell, O Mary Bell! how shall I get through?"—"Well," said she, "go back home, get your axe and cut it out." And he did. He saw her again, and catch at her. She drop another needle, and a large brick wall stood in the way. He said, "Mary Bell, how shall I get through?"—"Go get your shovel and axe, and dig and pick your way." He done just the same way. And he get through all right. He spy her again. He said, "Mary Bell, what harm I done you?"

> You done me no harm, but you done me good. Bang-a-lang!
> Hero, don't let your foot touch.

He catch at her. She step into her father's house. The Devil get so mad, he carry half of the man's house.

> I step on a t'in', the t'in' bend.
> My story is end.

SOURCE: Elsie Clews Parsons, *Folk-Lore of the Sea Islands, South Carolina*, 47–49.

The first of the two chosen suitor stories recorded by Parsons was told by Jack Brown, a sixty-five-year-old boat builder living on Port Royal Island off the coast of South Carolina. It includes not only the wife's opening of a forbidden chamber but also a thrilling magical flight, thus emphasizing the twin themes of constraint and liberation.

The second version was told by Julius Jenkins, a pupil in Edding's Point School on the island of St. Helena off the coast of South Carolina.

THE SINGING BONES

Genuinely macabre is the legend of "The Singing Bones," which took place out in the bayou country.

A man, father of twenty-five children and unemployed, grew more and more morose. No matter how he tried he could not find work, and most nights his brood went to bed crying with hunger.

One day, after his usual exhaustive search for work, the father was amazed, as he dragged his lagging feet up on the porch of his home, to have the tantalizing aroma of roasting meat strike his nostrils. The family had had no meat for months. Rushing back to the kitchen he found his wife rending a large roast in the oven.

Immediately he demanded to know where the meat had come from, but his wife begged him not to ask questions, but to sit down and eat. Too tired and hungry to care anyway, he obeyed her like a child.

The next night and the next there was meat on the table, always the same delicious boneless pork-like meat, and the father and the children ate in unquestioning silence. Strangely, the mother never joined them, saying always that she had already eaten.

Soon after this he looked for a certain one of his children and couldn't find him. Asking his wife about him, she replied simply that she had sent several of the youngsters to her sister's for a few days.

But a week later he missed his favorite son.

"He's gone to my sister's, too," the wife said.

But weeks passed, then months, winter grew into spring, and one day, counting carefully, the father discovered that more than half of his offspring were missing. He was strangely saddened and depressed, but hesitated about questioning his wife, for she had developed a very bad temper lately and if any of the children were mentioned flew into a violent rage. Yet he knew something was wrong.

One afternoon, sitting out on his back steps to brood, he heard a faint humming sound from beneath the steps. The hum grew louder and louder. First he thought it was mosquitoes, but then with horror, he knew what he heard was the voices of children. They seemed to sing right into his ear:

> Our mother kills us,
> Our father eats us,
> We have no coffins,
> We are not in holy ground.

Leaping to his feet, the man stopped and lifted the concrete slabs that had served as steps. Beneath lay a pile of tiny human bones. Now he knew the ghastly truth behind the meat they had been eating, of what had become of his children.

He rushed into the house, strangled his wife, and beat her head to a pulp with an axe. Then he fetched a priest and had the bones of his murdered children properly buried. It is said that he was never able to eat meat again.

SOURCE: Lyle Saxon, Edward Dreyer, and Robert Tallant, eds., *Gumbo Ya-Ya*, 277–79.

THE SINGING BONES
(Second Version)

Once upon a time there lived a man and a woman who had twenty-five children. They were very poor; the man was good, the woman was bad. Every day when the husband returned from his work the wife served his dinner, but always meat without bones.

"How is it that this meat has no bones?"

"Because bones are heavy, and meat is cheaper without bones. They give more for the money."

The husband ate, and said nothing.

"How is it you don't eat meat?"

"You forget that I have no teeth. How do you expect me to eat meat without teeth?"

"That is true," said the husband, and he said nothing more, because he was afraid to grieve his wife, who was as wicked as she was ugly.

When you have twenty-five children you cannot think of them all the time, and, you do not notice if one or two are missing. One day, after his dinner, the husband asked for his children. When they were by him he counted them, and found only fifteen. He asked his wife where were the ten others. She answered that they were at their grandmother's, and every day she would send one more for them to get a change of air. That was true, every day there was one that was missing.

One day the husband was at the threshold of his house, in front of a large stone which was there. He was thinking of his children, and he wanted to go and get them at their grandmother's when he heard voices that were saying:

> Our mother killed us,
> Our father ate us.
> We are not in a coffin,
> We are not in the cemetery.

At first he did not understand what that meant, but he raised the stone, and saw a great quantity of bones, which began to sing again. He then understood that it was the bones of his children, whom his wife had killed, and whom he had eaten. Then he was so angry that he killed his wife; buried his children's bones in the cemetery, and stayed alone at his house. From that time he never ate meat, because he believed it would always be his children that he would eat.

SOURCE: Alcée Fortier, ed. *Louisiana Folktales: Lupin, Bouki, and Other Creole Stories in French Dialect and English Translation*, 61.

These stories are related to "The Juniper Tree," a European tale about a mother who kills her stepson and serves him up to his father in a stew. If the Grimms' version of that fairy tale turns on redemption through beauty (the boy turns into a bird that transforms the world with his song), these stories from Louisiana give us bleak, unforgiving violence driven by poverty and hunger.

THE MURDEROUS MOTHER

De little girl, he ma an' pa live in one house. An' de ma was complainin' fo' some time to eat an' kill de little girl fo' de moder eat. An' dey take up supper. An' de fader went to supper. An' de ol' man was eatin', an' he look aroun', an' ax de moder, "Where is little Mary?" An' de ol' woman was very frighten', but she didn' tell de ol' man. She say, "Oh, she is over to de auntie." De man eat on, worryin' 'bout de little girl. When he look aroun' to her again, ax about de little girl again, she says, "Is ower to he aunt." De man say, "You mus' bring um home, go fo' him!" She says, "No, she ain't comin' back to-night, she goin' to stay all night." De man eatin', but yet still was worry. Den de little spirit come right up to de man, an' sing,—

> Ol' Debil, ol' Debil,
> Don' you pull ma hair!
> My moder has killed me fo' t'ree green pear,
> My fader, my fader, don' you pull my hair!
> My moder has killed me, an' bury me there.
> My moder kill' me, my moder kill' me.
> My t'ree little sistuh get all my bone,
> Buried unduh de little white marble stone.

(When I hear dat song, you couldn' get me out o' door nohow. I been scared dat little song.)

SOURCE: Elsie Clews Parsons, *Folk-Lore of the Sea Islands, South Carolina*, 122–23. Told by Pinky Murray, a thirty-five-year-old woman from Savannah, Georgia.

THE STOLEN VOICE

An interesting conjure story, which I heard, involves the fate of a lost voice. A certain woman's lover was enticed away by another woman, who sang very sweetly, and who, the jilted one suspected, had told lies about her. Having decided upon the method of punishment for this wickedness, the injured woman watched the other closely, in order to find a suitable opportunity for carrying out her purpose; but in vain, for the fortunate one, knowing of her enmity, would never speak to her or remain near her.

One day the jilted woman plucked a red rose from her garden, and hid herself in the bushes near her rival's cabin. Very soon an old woman came by, who was accosted by the woman in hiding, and requested to hand the red rose to the woman of the house. The old woman, suspecting no evil, took the rose and approached the house, the other woman following her closely, but keeping herself always out of sight.

When the old woman, having reached the door and called out the mistress of the house, delivered the rose as requested, the recipient thanked the giver in a loud voice, knowing the old woman to be somewhat deaf. At the moment she spoke, the woman in hiding reached up and caught her rival's voice, and clasping it tightly in her right hand, escaped unseen, to her own cabin.

At the same instant the afflicted woman missed her voice, and felt a sharp pain shoot through her left arm, just below the elbow. She at first suspected the old woman of having tricked her through the medium of the red rose, but was subsequently informed by a conjure doctor that her voice had been stolen, and that the old woman was innocent. For the pain he gave her a bottle of medicine, of which nine drops were to be applied three times a day, and rubbed in with the first two fingers of the right hand, care being taken not to let any other part of the hand touch the arm, as this would render the medicine useless.

By the aid of a mirror, in which he called up her image, the conjure doctor ascertained who was the guilty person. He sought her out and charged her with the crime, which she promptly denied. Being pressed, however, she admitted her guilt. The doctor insisted upon immediate restitution. She expressed her willingness, and at the same time her inability to comply—she had taken the voice, but did not possess the power to restore it. The conjure doctor was obdurate and at once placed a spell upon her which is to remain until the lost voice is restored. The case is still pending, I understand; I shall sometime take steps to find out how it terminates.

How far a story like this is original, and how far a mere reflection of familiar wonder stories, is purely a matter of speculation. When the old mammies would tell the tales of Br'er Rabbit and Br'er Fox to the master's children, these in turn would no doubt repeat the fairy tales which they had read in books or heard from their parents' lips. The magic mirror is as old as literature. The inability to restore the stolen voice is foreshadowed in the *Arabian Nights*, when the "Open Sesame" is forgotten. The act of catching the voice has a simplicity which stamps it as original, the only analogy of which I can at present think being the story of later date, of the words which were frozen silent during the extreme cold of an Arctic winter, and became audible again the following summer when they had thawed out.

SOURCE: Charles W. Chesnutt, "Superstitions and Folk-Lore of the South," 159–60.

Charles Chesnutt (1858–1932) was a prominent and highly influential author whose short stories were widely read in the United States. Moving from North Carolina to New York City and finally to Cleveland, he took work as a legal stenographer and began publishing short stories in the Atlantic Monthly. *In 1899, he published* The Conjure Woman, *a collection of stories inspired by hoodoo beliefs and practices. The story above has a realistic setting but draws on a number of folkloric motifs, most notably stolen voices and magic mirrors. Chesnutt gives us in this story his characteristic blend of realism and fantasy, with a folkloristic commentary that reveals something about the social context of the tale.*

THE MERMAID

Before they had any steam, ships were sailing by sails, you know, across the Atlantic. The Atlantic was fifteen miles deep, and there were mermaids in those days. And if you called anybody's name on the ship, the mermaids would ask for it, say, "Give it to me." And if you didn't give it to them they would capsize the ship.

So the captain had to change the men's names to different objects—hatchet, ax, hammer, furniture. Whenever he wanted a man to do something, he had to call him, "Hammer, go on deck and look out." The mermaid would holler, "Give me hammer." So they threwed the hammer overboard to her, and the vessel would proceed on. The captain might say, "Ax, you go on down in the kindling room and start a fire in the boiler; it's going dead." Then the mermaid says, "Give me ax." So they have to throw her an iron ax. Next day he says, "Suit of furniture, go down in the stateroom and make

"The Mermaid," from *Negro Folktales in Michigan*, collected and edited by Richard M. Dorson. Cambridge, MA: Harvard University Press. Copyright © 1956 by the President and Fellows of Harvard College.

up those beds." And the mermaid yells, "Give me suit of furniture." So they had to throw a whole suit of furniture overboard.

One day he made a mistake and forgot and said, "Sam, go in the kitchen and cook supper." The mermaid right away calls, "Give me Sam." They didn't have anything on the ship that was named Sam; so they had to throw Sam overboard. Soon as Sam hit the water she grabbed him. Her hair was so long she could wrap him up—he didn't even get wet. And she's swimming so fast he could catch breath under the water. When she get him she goes in, unwraps Sam out of her hair, says, "Oooh, you sure do look nice. Do you like fish?" Sam says, "No, I won't even cook a fish."

"Well, we'll get married." So they were married. After a while Sam begin to step out with other mermaids. His girlfriend became jealous of him and his wife, and they had a fight over Sam. The wife whipped her, and told her, "You can't see Sam never again." She says, "I'll get even with you."

So one day Sam's girlfriend asked him, didn't he want to go back to his native home. He says yes. So she grabs him, wraps him in her hair, and swum the same fastness as his wife did when she was carrying him, so he could catch breath. When she come to land she put him onto the ground, on the bank. "Now if he can't do me no good he sure won't do her none." That was Sam's experience in the mermaid's home in the bottom of the sea.

Sam told the people the mermaid's house was built like the alligator's. He digs in the bank at water level; then he goes up—nature teaches him how high to go—then he digs down to water level again, and there he makes his home, in rooms ten to twenty feet long. The mermaid builds in the wall of the sea like the alligator. Sam stayed down there six years. If he hadn't got to courting he'd a been there yet, I guess.

SOURCE: Richard Dorson, *Negro Folktales in Michigan*, 147–48. Told by James Douglas Suggs.

Stories about seductive creatures, half animal, half human, are told the world over, and figure prominently in Celtic, Russian, and Scandinavian cultures. The mermaids in this story lure humans to their underwater homes, unlike Hans Christian Andersen's Little Mermaid, who strives to acquire a human soul through the love of a mortal.

THE BIG WORM[1]

"Once it was a time, a very good time
Monkey chewed tobacco, and he spit white lime.
It wasn't my time, it wasn't your time,
Was old folks time."

[1] *worm:* The term most likely refers to a reptilian creature, possibly a fire-breathing dragon.

[2] *Do i en e:* possibly remnants of an African chant or phrase

There was a man with two sons. They had no fire in the house. All they had to eat were raw potatoes. The man sent one of his sons to go fetch fire. The boy walked, and walked, and walked until finally he saw some smoke. When he found the fire, he discovered that it was coming from a worm. The boy said, "Give me some fire." The worm said, "I can't give you any. It's all mine." The worm said, "Come a little closer." *Good!* As soon as the boy had moved closer and was about to reach for the fire, the worm swallowed him up. The boy went down, way down, down inside the worm until he stopped. There he met all sorts of people that the worm had swallowed.

The man said to his other son, "I wonder where my boy has gone." The other son said, "Pa, I'm going to go look for him." He walked, and he walked, and he walked until he saw the big worm with fire in its mouth. The boy went over to it and said "Give me some fire!" The worm said, "Come and get it." The boy said, "Do i en e,[2] give me some fire." The worm said, "Come a little closer." Then it said, "Time to go home. Come and get the fire." When the boy went to get it, *pow*, the worm swallowed him down. The boy went down, down, so far down that he met his brother.

The boys' father said, "Now that my sons are gone, I may as well leave too." The man took a lance; it fairly glistened, it was so sharp. When he arrived at the place where the worm with fire in its mouth lived, the man said, "Give me some fire." The worm said, "You're too much for me." Then he said, "Come and get it." When the man went to get the fire, *pow*, the worm swallowed him up. The man took his lance, and, while he was falling down down down, he cut the worm's stomach until it was so wide open that all the people in there could climb out, and there were enough there to fill a big city.

SOURCE: Adapted from Charles L. Edwards, *Bahama Songs and Stories*, 72–73.

The father's rescue of the two sons from the belly of the worm is unusual in that, in fairy tales, most fathers leave their sons to their own devices, with the expectation that they will make their way through the world and survive its snares. Fetching fire has great symbolic importance and invites comparisons with myths about stealing fire or securing a flame in order to engage in activities ranging from the domestic to the inventive and creative.

THE TALKING EGGS

There was once a lady who had two daughters. They were called Rose and Blanche. Rose was bad, and Blanche was good. But the mother liked Rose better, even though she was bad, because she was her very picture. She would compel Blanche to do all the work, while Rose was seated in her rocking chair. One day she sent Blanche to the well to get some water in a bucket. When Blanche arrived at the well, she saw an old woman who said to her: "Pray, my little one, give me some water. I am very thirsty." "Yes, aunt," said Blanche, "here is some water." And Blanche rinsed her bucket and gave her good fresh water to drink. "Thank you, my child. You are a good girl. God will bless you."

A few days later, the mother was so bad to Blanche that she ran away into the woods. She cried and did not know where to go because she was afraid to return home. She saw the same old woman who was now walking in front of her. "Ah! My child, why are you crying? What is hurting you?" "Ah, aunt, mamma has beaten me, and I am afraid to return to the cabin." "Well, my child, come with me. I will give you supper and a bed. But you must promise me not to laugh at anything that you will see."

The old woman took Blanche's hand, and they began to walk into the woods. As they traveled, the bushes of thorns opened before them, and closed behind their backs. A little farther on, Blanche saw two axes that were fighting. She found that very strange, but said nothing. They walked farther and behold! Two arms were fighting. A little farther, two legs, and finally she saw two heads fighting with each other, and they said: "Blanche, good morning, my child. God will help you."

Finally they arrived at the old woman's cabin, and she said to Blanche: "Make some fire, my child, to cook supper." And she sat down near the fireplace and took off her head. She put it on her knees and began to louse herself. Blanche found that very strange. She was afraid, but she said nothing. The old woman put her head back in its place and gave Blanche a large bone to put on the fire for their supper. Blanche put the bone in the pot. Lo! In a moment the pot was full of good meat.

The old woman gave Blanche a grain of rice to pound with the pestle, and the mortar was soon full of rice. After they had eaten their supper, the old woman said to Blanche: "Pray, my child, scratch my back." Blanche scratched her back, but her hand soon had cuts on it, for the old woman's back was covered with broken glass. When the old woman saw that Blanche's hand was bleeding, she blew on it, and the cuts healed at once.

When Blanche got up the next morning, the old woman said to her: "You have to go home now, but since you are a good girl I want to make you a present of the talking eggs. Go over to the chicken-house. You must take all the eggs that say 'Take me.' You must not take the ones that say 'Do not take me.' Once you are on the road, throw the eggs behind you to break them."

While Blanche was walking home, she broke the eggs behind her. Many pretty things came out of those eggs—first diamonds, then gold, and finally a beautiful carriage and beautiful dresses. When she arrived at her mother's, she had so many fine things that the house could hold no more. And so her mother was very glad to see her. The next day she said to Rose: "You must go into the woods to look for the same woman. You must have fine dresses like Blanche."

Rose went into the woods, and she met the old woman, who told her to come into her cabin. But when Rose saw the axes, the arms, the legs, and the heads all fighting and then the old woman taking off her head to louse herself, she began to laugh and to ridicule everything she saw. The old woman said: "Ah! My child, you are not a good girl. God will punish you." The next day she said to Rose: "I don't want to send you back home with nothing. Go over to the chicken-house and take the eggs that say 'Take me.'"

Rose went to the chicken-house. All the eggs began to say: "Take me." "Don't take me." "Take me." "Don't take me." Rose was so bad that she said: "Ah, yes, you say 'Don't take me,' but you are precisely the ones I want." She took all the eggs that said "Don't take me," and she went off with them.

While she was walking, she broke the eggs, and out came a quantity of snakes, toads, and frogs. They began to run after her. There were even whips, and they whipped her. Rose shrieked and ran away. She reached her mother's so tired that she could not speak. When her mother saw all the beasts and the whips that were chasing after her, she was so angry that she sent her away like a dog and told her to go live in the woods.

SOURCE: Alcée Fortier, "Louisiana Nursery-Tales," 142–45.

A Creole variant of "The Kind and the Unkind Girls," this tale includes protagonists whose names point to French origins. The strong moral message about hard work and kindness is found in many nineteenth-century tales of virtue rewarded and vice punished.

RAMSTAMPELDAM

She was to marry to a king. An' de king said he would marry to her if she would spin a large room full of gold. An' while she was settin' down cryin',—she knew she couldn' do it,—a dwarf came an' put in an appearance, an' ask her what she would give him to do de tas' for her. She had a gol' ring, an' gi' him a gol' ring. An' jus' as soon dat room was full o' gol'. An' in de mornin', when de king come, fin' de room full o' gold. An' he was a greedy ol' feller, so he kyarry her in a large room, an' she mus' full dat too. Jus' as soon as she was lef' alone, her ol' friend come in again. So she tol' him, "I have the same task to do again."—"What will you gi' me now?"—"I ain't got but a gol' necklace." So she gave him dat necklace. Den in de mornin' de king came in again, an' foun' dat room full o' gol'. But he such a greedy feller, he gave her another task. She was settin' down cryin', but she didn' have nothin' to give dat ol' man again. Then he said to her, "I want you to promise me dat you will give me your first child." An' she said, "Yes, I'll do it. I'll give you my first child." An' when de king come in an' found de room all right again, den he married her. Den, after marriage a good little while, she had a beautiful child. But she forgot all her promise dat she made to de ol' man. She was too happy too. An' den on de birthday of de chil', de ol' man came up. He was in de crowd when dey had de birthday-party. Den she remembered her promise, an' she was awfully sorry den, because she had to part from her child.

Den de ol' man tell her, "I give you t'ree days to guess my name; an' if you guess my name in t'ree days, I won't take de chil', de chil' is yours." An' she commence to guess.

Every day he came, she guessed John, Jack, Peter; but de ol' man said, "No, none of dose are my name." 'Til dey arrive to de second day. After dat, de maid of de queen was walkin' along de road, an' came to a little hut. An' de ol' man didn' see her; an' he was stewin' an' jumpin' aroun' de pot, an' singin', "To-morrow I'll be de happiest man in de worl', because I'll have company. I'll have a little baby wid me. Nobody knows my name, dat I name Ramstampeldam." So de maid took de name to de queen, an' said she saw a funny little man, an' dat his name was Ramstampeldam. So de queen judge dat was de name she was tryin' to arrive at. So when de man came in dat day before de crowd an' deman' de chil', de queen said, "Ain't your name John? Ain't your name Peter? Ain't it Ramstampeldam?" Den de ol' man got so mad, he stamped his foot, went t'rough de floor, pop his laig off, ran off wid one laig.

SOURCE: Elsie Clews Parsons, *Folk-Lore of the Sea Islands, South Carolina*, 23–24.

Parsons recorded the story from an informant named James Miller, who was born in South Carolina and had worked as a slave on a plantation. According to her, the tale has "obviously a literary source," although she fails to mention explicitly "Rumpelstiltskin," a tale that may have moved from the written page in the Grimms' nineteenth-century German collection into oral storytelling cultures in the South.

KING PEACOCK

There was once a lady who was so pretty—so pretty that she never wanted to marry. She found something to criticize in all the suitors who presented themselves, saying of them: "Oh, you are too ugly." "You are too short." "Your mouth is too large."

One day a man arrived in a golden carriage drawn by eight horses. He asked the lady to marry him, but she refused. He threw a fit and then told her that in a year she would have a daughter that would be much prettier that she was. The lady felt nothing but contempt for him and sent him away.

A year later she gave birth to a pretty little girl. When she saw how pretty the girl was, she locked her up in a room at the far end of the house, with only a nurse to attend to her. The girl became more beautiful with each passing day. The nurse never allowed her to leave her room, or even to look out the window.

One day, while the old woman who was her nurse was sweeping the floor, she left the door open, and the young girl saw a large bird.

"Nurse," she said, "what is the name of that beautiful bird?"

The woman replied, "That is a peacock."

"If I ever marry," the girl said, "I want to marry King Peacock."

"May God hear you, my child."

That very day the mother appeared and went into a corner with the nurse. She drew a long knife from under her skirt and said, "I want you to kill my child. She has become prettier than I am."

The nurse began to cry and begged the lady to spare the poor child but it was no use. That evil heart could not be softened. When night fell, the nurse said to the girl, "My poor child. Your mother wants you to die, and I am supposed to kill you."

The girl was so good that she replied, "Well, kill me, nurse, if that's what my mother wants."

But the nurse said, "No, I don't have the heart to do any such thing. Here, take these three seeds and jump down into the well as if you were going to drown yourself. But before jumping in the well, swallow one of these seeds, and nothing will be able to harm you."

The girl thanked the nurse and walked down to the well to throw herself into it. But before touching the water she took one of the seeds and put it in her mouth. The seed fell into the water, and all at once the well became dry. The young lady was very sad to see that there was no water left in the well. She climbed out and walked into the woods, where she found a small house. She knocked at the door, and an old woman appeared. When she saw the pretty young girl, she said, "Oh! my child, why have you come here? Don't you know that my husband is an ogre? He will eat you up!"

The girl replied, "That's what I'm hoping for. My mother wants me to die."

The woman replied, "If that is the case, come in. But what a pity."

The girl sat down in a corner and began crying while she was waiting for the ogre. All at once they heard loud footsteps, and as soon as he opened the door, the ogre said, "Wife, I smell fresh meat in here." And he ran towards the girl. She looked at him with her big eyes, and he stopped himself, saying to his wife: "How can I possibly have a pretty girl like that for supper? She is so beautiful that all I want to do is look at her."

The girl said she was tired, and so the ogre took her to a beautiful room and ordered his wife to fan her with peacock feathers while she was sleeping.

The girl thought to herself: "It would be better for me to die now, since the ogre might change his mind by tomorrow and decide to have me for dinner." She put one of the seeds in her mouth and fell into a deep sleep. She slept and slept, and the ogre's wife continued fanning her the whole time. When three days had gone by and she was still not awake, the ogre looked at her and said: "What a pity, but I believe that she must be dead."

The ogre went to the town and brought home a coffin made of gold. He put the girl in it and set it on the river. Very far away, King Peacock was standing on the levee with his retinue, enjoying the cool breeze. He saw something bright and shiny floating on the river. He ordered his courtiers to see what it was. They took a skiff and could not believe their eyes. It was a coffin, and they brought it to the king. When he saw the pretty girl who seemed to be sleeping, he said, "Take her to my chambers." He was hoping that he would be able to wake her up. He moved her to a bed and rubbed her hands and face with cologne water, but to no avail. Then he opened her mouth to see what pretty teeth she had. He saw something red in her front teeth and tried to remove it with a golden pin. It was the seed, which fell on the floor. The girl awoke and said, "I am so glad to see you."

The king replied: "I am King Peacock and I want to marry you." The girl said, "Yes," and there was such a wedding that they sent me to tell the story everywhere, everywhere.

SOURCE: Alcée Fortier, *Louisiana Folk-Tales*, 57–61.

King Peacock has many of the motifs and tropes of "Snow White and the Seven Dwarfs"—a cruel mother, a benevolent servant, and a heroine revived by an adoring person of royal blood. The tale shifts into a female version of "Jack and the Beanstalk," in an unusual twist, with an ogress who uses brilliantly beautiful peacock feathers to fan the girl—with the feathers anticipating the name of the rescuer.

PREFACES TO
COLLECTIONS AND MANIFESTOS
ABOUT COLLECTING
AFRICAN AMERICAN LORE

William Owens, "Folklore of the Southern Negroes"

Lippincott's Magazine 20 (1877), 748–55

William Owens prefaced the nine examples of folktales he collected with observations about the importance of the tales as an index of "negro character," about which he deemed himself an "expert." Emphasizing the African origins of the tales, he also had much to say about belief systems (superstitious and religious).

1877

FOLKLORE OF THE SOUTHERN NEGROES
by William Owens

All tribes and peoples have their folk-lore, whether embodied in tales of daring adventure, as in our own doughty Jack the Giant-killer, or in stories of genii and magic, as in the *Arabian Nights*, or in legends of wraiths, witches, bogles and apparitions, as among the Scotch peasantry; and these fables are so strongly tinged with the peculiarities—or rather the idiosyncrasies—of the race among whom they originate as to furnish a fair index of its mental and moral characteristics, not only at the time of their origin, but so long as the people continue to narrate them or listen to them.

The folk-lore of Africo-Americans, as appearing in our Southern States, is a medley of fables, songs, sayings, incantations, charms and superstitious traditions brought from various tribes along the West African coast, and so far condensed into one mass in their American homes that often part of a story or tradition belonging to one tribe is grafted, without much regard to consistency, upon a part belonging to another people, while they are still further complicated by the frequent infusion into them of ideas evidently derived from communication with the white race.

Any one who will take the trouble to analyze the predominant traits of negro character, and to collate them with the predominant traits of African folk-lore, will discern the fitness of each to each. On every side he will discover evidences of a passion for music and dancing, for visiting and chatting, for fishing and snaring, indeed for any pleasure requiring little exertion of either mind or body; evidences also of a gentle, pliable and easy temper—of a quick and sincere sympathy with suffering wheresoever seen—of a very low standard of morals, combined with remarkable dexterity in satisfying themselves that it is right to do as they wish. Another trait, strong enough and universal enough to atone for many a dark one, is that, as a rule, there is nothing of the fierce and cruel in their nature, and it is scarcely possible for anything of this kind to be grafted permanently upon them.

Of their American-born superstitions, by far the greater part are interwoven with so-called religious beliefs, and go far to show their native faith in dreams and visions, which they are not slow to narrate, to embellish, and even to fabricate extemporaneously, to suit the ears of a credulous listener; also showing their natural tendency to rely upon outward observances, as if possessed of some *fetish*-like virtue, and in certain cases a horrible debasement of some of the highest and noblest doctrines of the Christian faith. These superstitions must of course be considered apart from the real character of those who are sincerely pious, and upon which they are so many blemishes. They are, in fact, the rank and morbid outgrowth of the peculiarities of religious denominations grafted upon the prolific soil of their native character.

Of the few which may be mentioned without fear of offence, since they belong to the negro rather than to his denomination, the following are examples: Tools to be used in digging a grave must never be carried through a house which any one inhabits, else they will soon be used for digging the grave of the dweller. Tools already used for such a purpose must not be carried directly home. This would bring the family too closely for safety into contact with the dead. They must be laid reverently beside the grave, and allowed to remain there all night. A superstition in respect to posture is by some very rigorously observed. It is, that religious people must never sit with their legs crossed. The only reason given—though we cannot help suspecting that there must be another kept in concealment—is, that *crossing the legs is the same as dancing, and dancing is a sin.*

These are fair samples of Americanized superstitions—puerile, it is true, but harmless. It is only when we come into contact with negroes of pure African descent that we discover evidences of a once prevalent and not wholly discarded demonolatry. The native religion of the West African, except where elevated by the influence of Mohammedanism, was not—and, travelers tell us, is not yet—a worship of God as such, nor even an attempt to know and honor Him, but a constant effort at self-protection. The true God, they say, calls for no worship; for, being good in and of himself, He will do all the good He can without being asked. But there are multitudes of malignant spirits whose delight is to mislead and to destroy. These must be propitiated by gifts and acts of worship, or rendered powerless by charms and incantations.

No one knows, or has the means of ascertaining, to what extent real devil-worship is practised in America, because it is always conducted in secret; but we have reason to believe that it has almost entirely ceased, being shamed out of existence by the loveliness of a purer and better faith, and a belief in the agency of evil spirits, and consequent dread of their malign powers, although still more or less dominant with the negroes, has also greatly declined.[1] To give a sample of this last: The time was—but it has nearly passed away, or else the writer has not been for many years in the way of hearing of it, as in the days of childhood—when one of the objects of greatest dread among our seaboard negroes was the "Jack-muh-lantern." This terrible creature—who on dark, damp nights would wander with his lantern through woods and marshes, seeking to mislead people to their destruction—was described by a negro who seemed perfectly familiar with his subject as a hideous little being, somewhat human in form, though covered with hair like a dog. It had great goggle eyes, and thick, sausage-like lips that opened from ear to ear. In height it seldom exceeded four or five feet, and it was quite slender in form, but such was its power of locomotion that no one on the swiftest horse could overtake it or escape from it, for it could leap like a grasshopper to almost any distance, and its strength was beyond all human resistance. No one ever

---

1 Of the terrible forms of superstition prevalent under the names of Obi, Voodooism, Evil-eye or Tricking, in which a trick-doctor or witch-doctor works against another person's life or health or plans, or seeks to neutralize the influence of another doctor, our subject leads us to say nothing.

heard of its victims being bitten or torn: they were only compelled to go with it into bogs and swamps and marshes, and there left to sink and die. There was only one mode of escape for those who were so unfortunate as to be met by one of these mischievous night-walkers, and that was by a charm; but that charm was easy and within everybody's reach. Whether met by marsh or roadside, the person had only to take off his coat or outer garment and put it on again inside out, and the foul fiend was instantly deprived of all power to harm.

Multifarious, however, as are the forms and aspects of folk-lore among this remarkable and in some respects highly interesting people, the chief bulk of it lies stored away among their fables, which are as purely African as are their faces or their own plaintive melodies. Travellers and missionaries tell us that the same sweet airs which are so often heard in religious meetings in America, set to Christian hymns, are to be recognized in the boats and palm-roofed houses of Africa, set to heathen words, and that the same wild stories of Buh Rabbit, Buh Wolf, and other *Buhs* that are so charming to the ears of American children, are to be heard to this day in Africa, differing only in the drapery necessary to the change of scene.

Almost without exception the actors in these fables are brute animals endowed with speech and reason, in whom mingle strangely, and with ludicrous incongruity, the human and brute characteristics. The *dramatis personae* are always honored with the title of *Buh*, which is generally supposed to be an abbreviation of the word "brother" (the *br* being sounded without the whir of the *r*), but it probably is a title of respect equivalent to our Mr. The animals which figure in the stories are chiefly Buh Rabbit, Buh Lion, Buh Wolf and Buh Deer, though sometimes we hear of Buh Elephant, Buh Fox, Buh Cooter and Buh Goose. As a rule each Buh sustains in every fable the same general character. Buh Deer is always a simpleton; Buh Wolf always rapacious and tricky; Buh Rabbit foppish, vain, quick-witted, though at times a great fool; Buh Elephant quiet, sensible and dignified.

JOEL CHANDLER HARRIS, INTRODUCTION TO *NIGHTS WITH UNCLE REMUS* (1883)

The volume containing an installment of thirty-four negro legends, which was given to the public three years ago, was accompanied by an apology for both the matter and the manner. Perhaps such an apology is more necessary now than it was then; but the warm reception given to the book on all sides—by literary critics, as well as by ethnologists and students of folk-lore, in this country and in Europe—has led the author to believe that a volume embodying everything, or nearly everything, of importance in the oral literature of the negroes of the Southern States, would be as heartily welcomed.

The thirty-four legends in the first volume were merely selections from the large body of plantation folk-lore familiar to the author from his childhood, and these selections were made less with an eye to their ethnological importance than with a view to presenting certain quaint and curious race characteristics, of which the world at large had had either vague or greatly exaggerated notions.

The first book, therefore, must be the excuse and apology for the present volume. Indeed, the first book made the second a necessity; for, immediately upon its appearance, letters and correspondence began to pour in upon the author from all parts of the South. Much of this correspondence was very valuable, for it embodied legends that had escaped the author's memory, and contained hints and suggestions that led to some very interesting discoveries. The result is, that the present volume is about as complete as it could be made under the circumstances, though there is no doubt of the existence of legends and myths, especially upon the rice plantations, and Sea Islands of the Georgia and Carolina seacoast, which, owing to the difficulties that stand in the way of those who attempt to gather them, are not included in this collection.

It is safe to say, however, that the best and most characteristic of the legends current on the rice plantations and Sea Islands, are also current on the cotton plantations. Indeed, this has been abundantly verified in the correspondence of those who kindly consented to aid the author in his efforts to secure stories told by the negroes on the seacoast. The great majority of legends and stories collected and forwarded by these generous collaborators had already been collected among the negroes on the cotton plantations and uplands of Georgia and other Southern States. This will account for the comparatively meagre contribution which Daddy Jack, the old African of the rice plantations, makes towards the entertainment of the little boy.

In the introduction to the first volume of "Uncle Remus" occurs this statement: "Curiously enough, I have found few negroes who will acknowledge to a stranger that they know anything of these legends; and yet to relate one is the surest road to their confidence and esteem."

This statement was scarcely emphatic enough. The thirty-four legends in the first volume were comparatively easy to verify, for the reason that they were the most popular among the negroes, and were easily remembered. This is also true of many stories in the present volume; but some of them appear to be known only to the negroes who have the gift of story-telling,—a gift that is as rare among the blacks as among the whites. There is good reason to suppose, too, that many of the negroes born near the close of the war or since, are unfamiliar with the great body of their own folk-lore. They have heard such legends as the "Tar-Baby" story and "The Moon in the Mill-Pond," and some others equally as graphic; but, in the tumult and confusion incident to their changed condition, they have had few opportunities to become acquainted with that wonderful collection of tales which their ancestors told in the kitchens and cabins of the Old Plantation. The older negroes are as fond of the legends as ever, but the occasion, or the excuse, for telling them becomes less frequent year by year.

With a fair knowledge of the negro character, and long familiarity with the manifold peculiarities of the negro mind and temperament, the writer has, nevertheless, found it a difficult task to verify such legends as he had not already heard in some shape or other. But, as their importance depended upon such verification, he has spared neither pains nor patience to make it complete. The difficulties in the way of this verification would undoubtedly have been fewer if the writer could have had an opportunity to pursue his investigations in the plantation districts of Middle Georgia; but circumstances prevented, and he has been compelled to depend upon such opportunities as casually or unexpectedly presented themselves.

One of these opportunities occurred in the summer of 1882, at Norcross, a little railroad station, twenty miles northeast of Atlanta. The writer was waiting to take the train to Atlanta, and this train, as it fortunately happened, was delayed. At the station were a number of negroes, who had been engaged in working on the railroad. It was night, and, with nothing better to do, they were waiting to see the train go by. Some were sitting in little groups up and down the platform of the station, and some were perched upon a pile of cross-ties. They seemed to be in great good-humor, and cracked jokes at each other's expense in the midst of boisterous shouts of laughter. The writer sat next to one of the liveliest talkers in the party; and, after listening and laughing awhile, told the "Tar Baby" story by way of a feeler; the excuse being that some one in the crowd mentioned "Ole Molly Har'." The story was told in a low tone, as if to avoid attracting attention, but the comments of the negro, who was a little past middle age, were loud and frequent "Dar now!" he would exclaim, or, "He's a honey, mon!" or, "Gentermens! git out de way, an' gin 'im room!"

These comments, and the peals of unrestrained and unrestrainable laughter that accompanied them, drew the attention of the other negroes, and before the climax of the story had been reached, where Brother Rabbit is cruelly thrown into the brier-patch, they had all gathered around and made themselves comfortable. Without waiting to see what the effect of the "Tar Baby" legend would be, the writer told the story of "Brother Rabbit and the Mosquitoes," and this had the effect of convulsing them. Two or three could hardly wait for the conclusion, so anxious were they to tell stories of their own. The result was that, for almost two hours, a crowd of thirty or more negroes vied with each other to see which could tell the most and the best stories. Some told them poorly, giving only meagre outlines, while others told them passing well; but one or two, if their language and their gestures could have been taken down, would have put Uncle Remus to shame. Some of the stories told had already been gathered and verified, and a few had been printed in the first volume; but the great majority were either new or had been entirely forgotten. It was night, and impossible to take notes; but that fact was not to be regretted. The darkness gave greater scope and freedom to the narratives of the negroes, and but for this friendly curtain, it is doubtful if the conditions would have been favorable to story-telling. But however favorable the conditions might have been, the appearance of a note-book and pencil would have dissipated them as utterly as if they had never existed. Moreover, it was comparatively an easy matter for the writer to take the stories away in his memory, since many of them gave point to a large collection of notes and unrelated fragments already in his possession.

In the introduction to the first volume of Uncle Remus, a lame apology was made for inflicting a book of dialect upon the public. Perhaps a similar apology should be made here; but the discriminating reader does not need to be told that it would be impossible to separate these stories from the idiom in which they have been recited for generations. The dialect is a part of the legends themselves, and to present them in any other way would be to rob them of everything that gives them vitality. The dialect of Daddy Jack, which is that of the negroes on the Sea Islands and the rice plantations, though it may seem at first glance to be more difficult than that of Uncle Remus, is, in reality, simpler and more direct. It is the negro dialect in its most primitive state— the "Gullah" talk of some of the negroes on the Sea Islands, being merely a confused and untranslatable mixture of English and African words. In the introductory notes to "Slave Songs of the United States" may be found an exposition of Daddy Jack's dialect as complete as any that can be given here. A key to the dialect may be given very briefly. The vocabulary is not an extensive one—more depending upon the manner, the form of expression, and the inflection, than upon the words employed. It is thus an admirable vehicle for story-telling. It recognizes no gender, and scorns the use of the plural number except accidentally. "'E" stands for "he" "she" or "it," and "dem" may allude to one thing, or may include a thousand. The dialect is laconic and yet rambling, full of repetitions, and abounding in curious elisions, that give an unexpected quaintness to the simplest statements. A glance at the following vocabulary will enable the reader to understand Daddy Jack's dialect perfectly, though allowance must be made for inversions and elisions.

B'er, brother.

Beer, bear.

Bittle, victuals.

Bret, breath.

Buckra, white man, overseer, boss.

Churrah, churray, spill, splash.

Da, the, that.

Dey-dey, here, down there, right here.

Dey, there.

Enty, ain't he? an exclamation of astonishment or assent.

Gwan, going.

Leaf, leave.

Lif, live.

Lil, lil-a, or *lilly,* little.

Lun, learn.

Mek, make.

Neat', or *nead,* underneath, beneath.

Oona, you, all of you.

Sem, same.

Shum, see them, saw them.

Tam, time.

'Tan', stand.

Tankee, thanks, thank you.

Tark, or *tahlk,* talk.

Teer, tear.

Tek, take.

T'ink, or *t'ought,* think, thought.

Titty, or *titter,* sissy, sister.

T'row, throw.

Trute, truth.

Turrer, or *tarrah,* the other.

Tusty, thirsty.

Urrer, other.

Wey, where.

Wun, when.

Wut, what.

Y'et or *ut*, earth.

Yeddy, or *yerry,* heard, hear.

Yent, ain't, isn't.

. . . It only remains to be said that none of the stories given in the present volume are "cooked." They are given in the simple but picturesque language of the negroes, just as the negroes tell them. The Ghost-story, in which the dead woman returns in search of the silver that had been placed upon her eyes, is undoubtedly of white origin; but Mr. Samuel L. Clemens (Mark Twain) heard it among the negroes of Florida, Missouri, where it was "The Woman with the Golden Arm." Fortunately, it was placed in the mouth of 'Tildy, the house-girl, who must be supposed to have heard her mistress tell it. But it has been negroized to such an extent that it may be classed as a negro legend; and it is possible that the white version is itself based upon a negro story. At any rate, it was told to the writer by different negroes; and he saw no reason to doubt its authenticity until after a large portion of the book was in type. His relations to the stories are simply those of editor and compiler. He has written them as they came to him, and he is responsible only for the setting. He has endeavored to project them upon the background and to give them the surroundings which they had in the old days that are no more; and it has been his purpose to give in their recital a glimpse of plantation life in the South before the war. If the reader, therefore, will exercise his imagination to the extent of believing that the stories are told to a little boy by a group of negroes on a plantation in Middle Georgia, before the war, he will need neither footnote nor explanation to guide him.

In the preparation of this volume the writer has been placed under obligations to many kind friends. But for the ready sympathy and encouragement of the proprietors of "The Atlanta Constitution"—but for their generosity, it may be said—the writer would never have found opportunity to verify the stories and prepare them for the press. He is also indebted to hundreds of kind correspondents in all parts of the Southern States, who have interested themselves in the work of collecting the legends. He is particularly indebted to Mrs. Helen S. Barclay, of Darien, to Mr. W. O. Tuggle, to Hon. Charles C. Jones, Jr., to the accomplished daughters of Mr. Griswold, of Clinton, Georgia, and to Mr. John Devereux, Jr., and Miss Devereux, of Raleigh, North Carolina.

J. C. H.

ATLANTA, GEORGIA.

ANONYMOUS, "WORD SHADOWS"

Atlantic Monthly 67 (1891), 143–44

The anonymous author of this article inadvertently captured the poetry of the folkloric imagination, and his many efforts to disparage and belittle black speech backfire when we look at the parade of examples that enliven and invigorate the English language.

WORD SHADOWS

(in "Contributors' Club")

If shadows of material objects are grotesque, even more so are the shadows cast by words from fairly educated lips into the minds of almost totally ignorant people. Display in utterance of these quaint word-shadows, if one may so call them, makes dialect.

This grotesquerie, this quaint transformation of something well known, real, and admirable into something queer, fanciful, and awkward, yet bearing resemblance to the fair formation it shadows, gives to dialect writing and to dialect speech that piquant flavor that all the world favors. Especially is this true of that lately full fashionable style of literary production, song and story, in negro dialect. The words of our language that enter the mind of the old-time negro have indeed found their way into a dusky realm. Here is with us a race which has wholly forgotten its own language, or whatever methods of communication it made use of in its African home. The language of an utterly diverse race it must perforce employ, since it has lost the tongue of its own people. Into the minds of the individuals of this race, a people hardly a century out of barbarism, the light of civilization shines with dazzling effect. The language they must use is the growth of centuries of civilization, its roots reaching to even older civilizations, its branches grafted with luxuriant word-growths of almost every nation on earth. It is little wonder that this language of ours assumes in these startled brains most fanciful shapes. To take down some of these shadowy effects, with our language for cause, would be to make a dialect dictionary, a glossary of plantation *patois*, a work for which, happily, there is now no need. But an effort to show a few of these vague, dusky shapes that our words take on may not be wholly uninteresting.

See, for instance, how our simple word "fertilizer" becomes on the tongue of an old darky gardener "pudlie." A giant is dubbed a "high-jinted man." A maid who will prove obedient to orders is described as an "orderly gal." A piece of ground that shows a bad yield of cotton or corn is called "failery lan'." Farming in the mouth of a negro laborer is "crapping." The favorite food of the cotton-field hand, the food he cannot live without, the strengthening bread made from corn meal, has its expressive name, "John Constant." Wheaten bread, a rare treat to the field hand, is "Billy Seldom." Bacon has its name, "Ole Ned." The best field laborer is the "lead hoe hand." To quit work for the day is to "lay by." To rise early to go to the field is "ter be in patch by hour by sun." An early breakfast is "a soon brekkus." Our word "accuse"—alas! One the negro often has occasion to use—is "'scuse." There are too few of the race who have not been, at some time or other, "'scuse of a pig," "'scuse of a cow," "'scuse of cotton-pickin' by night," "'scuse of a pa'r shoes," and so on down a long list of material and tempting articles.

The quaint technical phrases that the negroes make use of in their business talk are innumerable. To be ready to hire for a cook is to be "des on han' ter jump in de cook-pot." In ironing, to leave a cluster of wrinkles on the garment in hand is to put "cat-faces" on it. To wash only for visitors to a town or village is to "des only take in trans' washin'." To take day boarders is to take "transoms." To say that one is obliged to turn a hand to anything is to say, "Ever' little drug dere is, I hatter wag it."

A half-starved calf is a "calf dat's been whipped wid de churn-dasher." A good ploughman is a "noble plough han'." Rich land is "strong ground." To keep down grass is to "fight wid Gen'al Green."

To leave the technicalities for generalities, we find that any matter that is but ill adjusted is a matter "squowow"; ill adjusted in a lesser degree is "weewow." A well-arranged matter is pronounced all "commojious,"—a shadow of our word "commodious." A matter well accomplished is "essentially done"; as, for instance, "When she cooks, she des essentially cooks good." A person fit to adorn wealth is a "high-minded person," or "big-minded," or "great-minded." A wealthy person is one "stout in worldly goods." A proud person is an "umptious somebody." One who is only proud enough is "proud to de ikle." One who is slightly petted by good Dame Fortune is "des pettish." To be in trouble or distress is to "walk on de wearied line." To live easily and happily is to live "jobly and wid pleadjure." To be ill is to "have a misery." To be quite well is to be "des sorter tollerble." Entertaining conversation becomes in that shadow-language "mockin'-bird talk." A girl who loves to stay at home, what the poets would call "a home-keeping heart," becomes a "homely gal"; keeping for the word its English meaning, not its American perversion.

A queer gamut of color they run in their descriptions of their race: "a dark man," "a bright man," "a light gal," "a mustee 'oman," "a gingerbread boy," a "honey-colored lady."

Entering the mystic world, we find that a ghost is "a hant." Magic, black art, becomes "conjure"; the accent on the first syllable. Entering the world of song, we find that all lively lyrics are "sinner-songs," or "reels," or "corn-hollers," "jump-up-songs," or "chunes dat skip wid de banjo." Religious songs are "member-songs" or "hymn-chunes." Long chants are "spirituelles."

The dweller in the realm of negro religious beliefs and forms of worship endows our language with meanings entirely new to our experience. Not to be a church member is to be "settin' on de sinner-seat'," "still in de open fiel'," "drinkin' de cup er damnation," and many other such phrases. To enter the church is to "jine de band," to "take up de cup er salvation," to "git a seat wid de members," to "be gethered in," to "put on a shine-line gyarment," and so on *ad infinitum*.

SOURCE: Bruce Jackson, *The Negro and His Folklore in Nineteenth-Century Periodicals*, 25.

ALICE MABEL BACON, "FOLK-LORE AND ETHNOLOGY CIRCULAR LETTER" AND LETTERS IN RESPONSE TO THE CALL

To: Graduates of the Hampton Normal School and others who may be interested

Southern Workman 22 (1893), 179–81

Alice Mabel Bacon served as editor of the Hampton Institute's monthly magazine, the Southern Workman, *and launched a Folk-Lore and Ethnology Department in 1893. Below is Bacon's appeal for the value of folklore, followed by a set of letters lauding her initiative.*

FOLK-LORE AND ETHNOLOGY
CIRCULAR LETTER
To Graduates of the Hampton Normal School and others who may be interested.

Dear Friends:

The American Negroes are rising so rapidly from the condition of ignorance and poverty in which slavery left them, to a position among the cultivated and civilized people of the earth, that the time seems not far distant when they shall have cast off their past entirely, and stand an anomaly among civilized races, as a people having no distinct traditions, beliefs or ideas from which a history of their growth may be traced. If within the next few years care is not taken to collect and preserve all traditions and customs peculiar to the Negroes, there will be little to reward the search of the future historian who would trace the history of the African continent through the years of slavery to the position which they will hold a few generations hence. Even now the children are growing up with little knowledge of what their ancestors have thought, or felt, or suffered. The common-school system with its teachings is eradicating the old and planting the seeds of the new, and the transition period is likely to be a short one. The old people, however, still have their thoughts on the past, and believe and think and do much as they have for generations. From them and from the younger ones whose thoughts have been moulded by them in regions where the school is, as yet, imperfectly established, much may be gathered that will, when put together and printed, be of great value as material for history and ethnology.

But, if this material is to be obtained, it must be gathered soon and by many intelligent observers stationed in different places. It must be done by observers who enter into the homes and lives of the more ignorant colored people and who see in their beliefs and customs no occasion for scorn, or contempt, or laughter, but only the showing forth of the first child-like, but still reasoning philosophy of a race, reaching after some interpretation of its surroundings and its antecedents. To such observers, every custom, belief or superstition, foolish and empty to others, will be of value and will be worth careful preservation. The work cannot be done by white people, much as many of them would enjoy the opportunity of doing it, but must be done by the intelligent and educated colored people who are at work all through the South among the more ignorant of their own race, teaching, preaching, practising medicine, carrying on business of any kind that brings them into close contact with the simple, old-time ways of their own people. We want to get all such persons interested in this work, and to get them to note down their observations along certain lines and send them in to the Editor of the *Southern Workman*. We hope sooner or later to join all such contributors together into a Folk-Lore Society and to make our work of value to the whole world, but our beginning will be in a corner of the *Southern Workman* and we have liberty to establish there a department of Folk-lore and Ethnology.

Notes and observations on any or all of the following subjects will be welcomed.

1. Folk-tales—The animal tales about Brer. Fox and Brer. Rabbit and the others have been well told by many white writers as taken down from the lips of Negroes. Some of them have been already traced back to Africa; many are found existing, with slight variations among Negroes and Indians of South as well as North America. These, with other stories relating to deluges, the colors of different races and natural phenomena of various kinds, form an important body of Negro mythology. Any additions to those already written out and printed, or other variations on those already obtained would be of great value.

2. Customs, especially in connection with birth, marriage and death, that are different from those of the whites. Old customs cling longest about such occasions. The old nurse, who first takes the little baby in her arms, has [a] great store of old-fashioned

learning about what to do and what not to do, to start the child auspiciously upon the voyage of life. The bride receives many warnings and injunctions upon passing through the gates of matrimony, and the customs that follow death and burial tend to change but little from age to age. What was once regarded as an honor to the dead, or a propitiation of his spirit, must not be neglected lest the dead seem dishonored, or the spirit—about which we know so little after all—wander forlorn and lonely, or work us ill because we failed to do some little thing that was needful for its rest. And so the old ways linger on about those events of our lives, and through them we may trace back the thoughts and beliefs of our ancestors for generations.

3. Traditions of ancestry in Africa, or of transportation to America. Rev. Dr. Crummell, in his eulogy of Henry Highland Garnett, says of that great man, "He was born in slavery. His father before him was born in the same condition. His grandfather, however, was born a free man in Africa. He was a Mandingo chieftain and warrior, and, having been taken prisoner in a tribal fight, was sold to slave traders, and then brought as a slave to America." If this tradition was preserved for three generations, may there not be others that have been handed from father to son, or from mother to daughter through longer descents? The slavery system as it existed in the United States tended to obscure pedigrees and blot them out entirely by its brutal breaking up of all family ties, but even if only here and there such traditions are still found, they are worth preserving as tending to throw light upon the derivation of the American Negroes.

4. African words surviving in speech or song. Here and there some African words have crept into common use, as *goober* for peanut, which is manifestly the same as n'gooba, the universal African designation for the same article of food. Are there not other words less common which are African? Do not children sing songs, or count out in their games with words which we may have taken for nonsense, but which really form links in the chain that connects the American with the African Negro? Do not the old people when they tell stories use expressions that are not English and that you have passed over as nonsense? Are there songs sung by the fireside, at the camp-meeting, or at work, or play, that contain words, apparently nonsensical, that make a refrain or chorus? If there are, note them down, spelling them so as to give as nearly their exact sound as possible and send them in with a note of how they are used.

5. Ceremonies and superstitions—Under this head may be included all beliefs in regard to the influence of the moon or other heavenly bodies; superstitions in regard to animals of various kinds and their powers for good or evil, as well as all ideas about the medical or magical properties of different plants or stones. Here also may be noted all that can be learned about beliefs in ghosts, witches, hags, and how to overcome supernatural influences. How to cork up a hag in a bottle so that she cannot disturb your slumbers, how to keep her at work all night threading the meshes of a sifter hung up in the doorway and so escape her influence, how to detect or avoid conjuring, or magic in any form, how to escape the bad luck that must come if you turn back to get something you have forgotten, or if a crow flies over the house, or if your eye twitches, or if any of the thousand and one things occur which, in the minds of the ignorant and superstitious, will bring bad luck if the right thing is not done at once to avert the evil influence.

6. Proverbs and sayings—From the time of King Solomon until now there have always been embodied in proverbs many bits of sound wisdom that show the philosophy of the common people. The form that the proverbs and sayings take depends largely upon the habits and modes of thought of the people who make them. Thus a collection of the proverbs of any people shows their race characteristics and the circumstances of life which surround them. Joel Chandler Harris in his "Uncle Remus's Songs and Sayings" has given a series of Plantation Proverbs that show the quaint humor, the real philosophy and the homely surroundings of the plantation Negroes. A few specimens from his list may call attention to what we mean. "Better de gravy dan no grease 'tall." "Tattlin' 'oman can't make de bread rise." "Mighty po' bee dat don't make mo' honey dan' he want." "Rooster make mo' racket dan de hin w'at lay de aig." In Mr. Harris's book the Georgia Negro dialect is carefully preserved, but that is not necessary for our work, though adding to its value where it can be done well.

7. Songs, words or music or both. The Hampton School has been at some pains to note down and preserve many of the "spirituals" which are probably the best expression so far attained of the religious and musical feeling of the race, but there are innumerable songs of other kinds which have never been taken down here. One of the earliest methods of recording and preserving historical or other knowledge is

through the medium of rhythmic and musical utterance. The Illiad of Homer, the great historical psalms of the Hebrew poets, the Norse sagas, the Scotch, English and Spanish ballads were but the histories of the various races moulded into forms in which they could be sung and remembered by the people. In the absence of written records, or of a general knowledge of the art of reading, songs are the ordinary vehicle of popular knowledge. A few years ago, I was listening to the singing of some of our night students. The song was new to me, and at first seemed to consist mainly of dates, but I found as it went along and interpreted itself that it was a long and fully detailed account of the Charleston earthquake, in which the events of successive days were enumerated, the year being repeated with great fervency again and again in the chorus. Are there not other songs of a similar character that take up older events? Are there not old war songs that would be of permanent value? Are there not songs that take up the condition and events of slavery from other than the religious side? Are there any songs that go back to Africa, or the conditions of life there? What are your people singing about—for they are always singing—at their work or their play, by the fireside, or in social gatherings? Find out and write it down, for there must be much of their real life and thought in these as yet uncollected and unwritten songs.

There are many other lines along which observation would be of value for the purpose of gaining a thorough knowledge of the condition—past and present, of the American Negro. Are there any survivors of the later importations from Africa, or are there any Negroes who can say today, "My father or my mother was a native African?" If there are, talk with them, learn of them all they can tell you and note it down. Are there any families of Negroes, apparently of pure blood, characterized by straight or nearly straight hair? If there are, do they account for it in any way? What proportion of the colored people in the district where you live are of mixed blood? Give the number of pure and mixed blood. What proportion having white blood have kept any traditions of their white and Negro ancestry so that they know the exact proportion of white to Negro blood? How many have traditions of Indian ancestry? Reports on all these subjects would be in the line of our work.

And now, having shown as fully as is possible within the limits here set down what it is that the Hampton School desires to do through its graduates and all other intelligent Negroes who are interested in the history and origin of their own race, we would say, in closing, that we should be glad to enter into correspondence with any persons who wish to help in this work, and to receive contributions from all who have made or who can make, observations along the proposed lines of investigation. Correspondence with prominent men of both races leads us to believe that we have the possibility ahead of us of valuable scientific study, that in this age when it is hard to open up a new line of research, or add anything to the knowledge of men and manners and beliefs that the world already possesses we, if we labor earnestly and patiently, may contribute much that shall be of real and permanent value in spreading among men the understanding of their fellowmen as well as in furnishing material for the future historian of the American Negro. Is not this worth doing?

Correspondence in regard to this matter may be addressed to Miss A. M. Bacon, *Southern Workman* Office, Hampton, Va.

MORE LETTERS CONCERNING THE "FOLK-LORE MOVEMENT" AT HAMPTON

Since our last issue several pleasant letters have come to us, called out by the folk-lore movement.

From Mr. T. T. Fortune of the *N. Y. Age* the following response has been received.

Permit me to say that I enter fully and heartily into the spirit of your undertaking and shall have pleasure in giving you and it all the assistance possible in my sphere of activity.

From Rev. Alex Crummell, D.D. of Washington, comes the following letter.

You may judge of my interest in your letter from the fact that I myself have been endeavoring to secure interest in the same subject your letter suggests, in my circle in this city. I wished last year to enlist two or three friends of mine in the attempt to organize an "African Society" for the preservation of traditions, folk-lore, ancestral remembrances, etc., which may have come down from ancestral sources. But nothing came of it. The truth is that the dinning of the "colonization" cause into the ears of the colored people—the iteration of the idle dogma that Africa is THE home of the black race in this land; has served to prejudice the race against the very name of Africa. And this is a double folly:—the folly of the colonizationists, and the folly of the black man; i.e. to forget family ties and his duty to his kin over the water.

I, for my part, give my full adhesion to your plans. But I can do but little. The shades of evening are upon me. Age is fast relaxing my powers;—I am constantly up as it were to my eyelids in work and duty; but what assistance I can give I shall gladly render.

You are right in your reference to the ancestry of my dear friend Garnett and I have, myself, distinct remembrances of the African (tribal) home of my own father, of which he often told me.

I have the impression that wide and telling information will fall into the hands of persons interested in the project that you wish to undertake; and I shall look for your circular at an early day.

You give an admirable and orderly list of topics in your letter and my impression is that among the class you rely upon—students and graduates, full up to this day, of the remembrances of southern homes and parents, you will find a larger number of inquiring minds than among a more ambitious and pretentious class of our people.

I wish you great success; and I shall be glad to hear from you again.

Very truly yours,
ALEX CRUMMELL.

From Mrs. A. J. Cooper of Washington, author of that able little collection of essays entitled "A Voice from the South," comes this tribute to Gen. Armstrong's work combined with her approval of our new plan.

Your letter expresses a want that has been in my mind for a long time. In the first place the "Hampton idea" is one for which I have long entertained an enthusiastic regard and I have been sorry that my fate has not yet given me an opportunity of coming in contact with its work. I do not at all discourage the higher courses for those who are capable among my people, but I am heartily in favor of that broad work begun with so much thoroughness at Hampton. You have large views of things at Hampton and it must have been a large heart that inspired the movement and a wise, well-balanced head that conceived and developed the plan. General Armstrong is one of our national heroes, and his work is no whit inferior because it supplements and rounds off that begun by Lincoln and Grant.

As for your plan for collecting facts that disclose and interpret the inner life and customs of the American Negro, I believe such a work is calculated to give a stimulus to our national literature as characteristic as did the publication of Percy's Reliques to the English in the days of Scott and Wordsworth. It is what I have long wanted to take part in in some way and nothing would give me greater pleasure than to become a part of your plan. What you say is true. The black man is readily assimilated to his surroundings and the original simple and distinct type is in danger of being lost or outgrown. To my mind, the worst possibility yet is that the so-called educated Negro, under the shadow of this over powering Anglo-Saxon civilization, may become ashamed of his own distinctive features and aspire only to be an imitator of that which can not but impress him as the climax of human greatness, and so all originality, all sincerity, all *self*-assertion would be lost to him. What he needs is the inspiration of knowing that his racial inheritance is of interest to others and that when they come to seek his homely songs and sayings and doings, it is not to scoff and sneer, but to study reverently, as an original type of the Creator's handiwork.

Mr. Geo. W. Cable, whose name in literature occupies so assured a position that his approval is of the highest value, sends us the following:

I have just received your paper setting forth your plan for the study of Negro folklore and ethnology by the graduates of Hampton, and I must say to you at once that I consider it one of the most valuable plans yet proposed for the development of that literary utterance which I believe to be essential for the colored people to secure in order to work out a complete Emancipation. It is an attempt to enter into literature where literature begins. I believe that anyone on reflection will see that it is of grave and serious political value for a people whose development must depend so largely upon another people more fortunate and advanced, to make themselves interesting in literature. No American can overlook the value this has been and is still to the Indian. If you see any way in which I can be of service, I will be glad for you to let me know.

Yours truly,
GEO. W. CABLE

One extremely interesting phase of this new work is that it brings the worker into more agreeable contact with the best minds and broadest thinkers among the colored people, a contact that is certain to prove most helpful and encouraging to one who is interested in the present condition and future development of the race. The uniform courtesy and appreciative spirit of assurances received from members of the Afro-American press will furnish a chapter in itself for some further issue of the *Workman*. Suffice it to say that the *Workman* offers its heartiest thanks to all the editors who have responded so cordially to its new departure and will be glad in return to do what it can in any direction that they may suggest for the advancement of the Negro race.

WILLIAM WELLS NEWELL, "THE IMPORTANCE AND UTILITY OF THE COLLECTION OF NEGRO FOLK-LORE," AND ANNA J. COOPER, "PAPER"

Southern Workman 23 (1894), 131–33

William Wells Newell was an American folklorist who taught in the Philosophy Department at Harvard University and founded the American Folklore Society in 1888. He addressed the Folklore Conference held at the Hampton Normal School in May 1894. Anna Julia Cooper was born a slave and became an American educator who received her Ph.D. in History from the Sorbonne. The author of A Voice from the South: By a Woman from the South *(1892), she argued for the educational and spiritual progress of African American women as a means to improving the standing of the entire community.*

ADDRESS BY MR. WILLIAM WELLS NEWELL

"The Importance and Utility of the Collection of Negro Folk-Lore"

The subject of Folk-lore is one on which there would be no difficulty in expanding an address to any required length. This evening, however, I am not wound up to go, but to stop. I propose only to make some general remarks intended to explain the importance of gathering Negro Folk-lore and the future value of such collection; this accomplished, I shall resign the floor to members of your own society who will furnish you with practical illustrations of Negro Folk-lore.

It was for this purpose that I came from Cambridge, in the hope of forwarding an undertaking which appears to me most meritorious, and of promoting the work of the Negro Folk-lore societies, a movement which is significant in regard to the present intelligence and rapid progress of Southern Negroes. I shall, however, take away with me from Hampton far more than I can give you. I think that no one can attend a commencement of this Institution for the first time, without receiving a profound intellectual impression. The mighty problems to be worked out, the vast destinies of the United States, and of republican government, are brought to his attention in the most vivid manner, while hope, comfort, trust in the future, faith in the ultimate position of the Negro race, and of the prosperity and harmony of the section to which it chiefly belongs, are inspired by all that he feels and sees.

With regard to the plan of my discourse, I may be allowed to take an illustration from a jury service in which I have lately been engaged. When a good judge is endeavoring to cut short the irrelevant cross-examinations in which lawyers are prone to indulge, in the hope of something turning up to their advantage, he will ask: "How is that material?" On this, the examiner is bound to make it clear that he is "leading up" to some connection with the case unapparent to the listener. Now, if I seem to introduce remarks disconnected with my theme, I must ask you to suppose that I intend at a later point to make clear the materiality.

What is Negro Folk-lore? It is that body of songs, tales, old-fashioned religious beliefs, superstitions, customs, ways of expression, proverbs, and dialect, of American Negroes.

Lore means learning; folk, as I shall here use the word, means race.

The Folk-lore of Negroes in the United States then, is the learning or knowledge peculiar to the Negro race. It is that mass of information which they brought with them from Africa, and which has subsequently been increased, remodelled, and Anglicized by their contact with the whites.

All this body of thought belongs to the past. It is vanishing in proportion to the progress of Negro education; it fades away before the light of such institutions as Hampton; it is superseded by more advanced ideas, habits, morals, and theology.

If this be so, what is the use of concerning ourselves with these out-grown notions and usages? Is it not better to leave them to rapidly approaching oblivion? The living to the living, the dead to the dead? Of what use can any part of the matter indicated be to the future of Negroes in the South?

To answer this question, I must make a seeming digression. After the conclusion of your exercises, one of your Trustees, and a personal friend of my own, was almost disposed to lament that he himself had not been born a Negro. What a fine thing, he said, to belong, as you belong, to a race that has need of the heart and hand of every one of its members!

How excellent to do, as some of you who hear me are doing, or will do; to sacrifice something for the sake of one's race; to be willing to attend a poorer school, because you can not go to the better one without renouncing your racial ties, to abstain from a career of profit, because that is not the direction in which you can best aid and serve your race. Such a racial unity, where it exists, it makes life seem grand and simple.

My friend's remark set me to thinking. What race do I myself belong to? For my ancestors, I would have answered; they were English. But my state to-day, is not English. It is filled up with immigrants of many other nationalities, accustomed to speak other languages, and educated, so far as they are educated, in other literature. Irishmen, Germans, French, Canadians, Italians, Portuguese, Russians, Armenians, Polish Jews, have entered to fill up the void left by the progress and promotion of the English. These people, and their descendants, form a large majority of the city population, and are rapidly overrunning the country also. The children of the immigrants, however, are nothing if not Americans. They are willing to hear nothing of Ireland, Germany, Italy, or Portugal. They sing with confident enthusiasm "Sweet land of liberty ° ° ° ° land where my fathers died." The Frenchman Riviere or Dubois passes as Brooks or Wood, and when he returns to his native village, is apt still to retain that appellation as a matter of pride. The offspring of these people, in a few generations, will forget that their stock did not come over with the pilgrims. The Russian Jew speaks no Russian, but a dialect of German, a language which in all his wanderings, he has retained with obstinacy; but in America, he has cast aside its use, and adopted the English tone. The Jew retains his identity, only on account of his religion; but the children of the rest would be offended, if excluded from the American name and right. Yet I can hardly feel that I have any racial affinity with them. In the South the English stock has hitherto continued to occupy the field, and the white race, there, as a Virginian gentleman informed me, is synonymous with the English race; but this advantage, if it be one, does not affect the Northerner. Am I then without a race? No, there is still one kinship sufficiently wide to admit me,—the human race.

Now as to the "materiality" of these remarks. As I cannot claim alliance with any race less inclusive than humanity, so I desire to possess not Folk-lore, not the ideas or notions of a particular race. Each race has its distinctive customs, ideas, manners; civilization has but one set of customs and ideas for all races. The race is formed to be merged in the unity of races, as rivers flow to disappear in the ocean. There are not different kinds of botany, or astronomy, or art, or morality, or religion, for whites or negroes, any more than for European and American. The little brook is born on the mountain, it falls in a silvery cascade to the valley, it widens and deepens, and loses in the end its separate existence in the mighty sea.

Folk-lore, then, the mass of racial ideas and habits, is lost in this mental ocean; these special forms of life cease to have any continuing existence in fact. Should they therefore possess no further existence in memory? On the contrary. Man is memory; the more memory, the more humanity. This is true of not only pleasant recollections; cruel and unhappy memories also help to make up the mind; like the strings of a harp, when rightly sounded; not one but is capable of contributing to the music. The drops of material ocean may know nothing of their past history; but those of the human sea should be able to tell of the height to which they rose, the depth through which they have passed. I am speaking then, not with regards to the past, but the future, when I say that it is of consequence for the American Negro to retain the recollection of his African origin, and of his American servitude. For the sake of the honor of his race, he should have a clear picture of the mental condition out of which he has emerged: this picture is not now complete, nor will be made so without a record of song, tales, beliefs, which belongs to the stage of culture through which he has passed.

Let me now point this general theme by illustrations of particular fields included in Negro American Folk-lore.

Perhaps the most valuable distinctive property of the American Negro is his music. In newspaper controversy, a silly discussion has arisen as to whether the Negro really has any characteristic music, not borrowed from the whites. That such a debate could be carried on is evidence in itself of the necessity of Folk-lore societies, for the doubt is rendered possible only by the absence of any proper collection either of African or of American Negro folk music. In recommending such collection I am not proposing a work of simple curiosity. On the contrary, Negro music in Southern States is a treasure of which any race in the world might be proud. It is, or was, full of spirit, originality, melody, and suggestions. Unhappily, this quality is not sufficiently understood by the Negroes themselves. Too much in haste to appropriate the possessions of the whites, they are not aware that they are obtaining nothing as valuable as what they are surrendering. The power of original composition, by ear, belonging to a whole people, the ability on the part of a whole race to carry in its head a melody and harmony which has naturally grown out of a sentiment, is a precious gift, in which Northern whites are utterly deficient. It is indeed sad to observe that these touching and beautiful compositions, often breathing the very soul of music, are gradually being deserted in favor of the cheap, inartistic and nearly worthless music of the concert hall and songbook. It may be that Folk-lore societies, by diffusing a juster notion of the value of the Negro folk-music, can arrest its decay. If not, the record will still remain, as a perpetual boon to the musicians of the future.

The second kind of lore of which I shall speak is tales. One class of these have become pretty generally known as the tales of Uncle Remus. These are animal folk-tales, which in great part, make their hero the rabbit, celebrate the victory of skill over brute force. These compositions have their worth, of a somewhat different nature from that which I have claimed for the songs. In this case, the interest is in great part that of comparative study. These tales are by no means solely the possession of Negroes; on the contrary, a good many are nearly cosmopolitan. Proceeding from some common center, they have traveled about the world, and that by several different routes, meeting in America by the way of Africa, by that of Europe, and it may be, also by that of Asia. So extraordinary a phenomenon in itself excites curiosity to a high degree. Without attempting here to explain this relation, I shall only observe, that the universal diffusion of many tales constitutes a striking counterpart to the great diversity of racial customs. We have thus the most striking exhibition of the substantial mental unity of the human race, seeing that in the most primitive communities the same elements have recommended a story. That the mental variety of stocks is the result, not of original natural diversity, but of environment, is thus most strongly enforced, and in that doctrine might be found the strongest possible hope for the future of your own race, if it were not that such encouragement is now rendered unnecessary by the visible evidences every day before our eyes.

As to another highly interesting class of tales which relate to religious belief, to spirits and demons, and the like, I will only remark that the best way to correct superstitious notions is to collect and study them. When all are gathered and made to elucidate each other, what is false and absurd is at once seen to be false and absurd. Thus, in order to get rid of a disgraceful custom, or of ancient credulity, the best way is not to try to ignore its existence, but to face and find out what it is.

It is of the utmost consequence, as a possession of their former condition, to note the numerous customs, hitherto altogether unnoted, or imperfectly observed, that entered into this condition. The truer mental state of the race under slavery, entirely incomprehensible to those who looked on from the outside, will thus appear.

All this material will become lucid and full of picturesque and poetic interest, when we have full accounts of primitive African music, belief, and habits, when we have detailed accounts of the several tribes. It will doubtless be, also, that this tendency once introduced, it will become customary for American Negroes to attend to their genealogical record, and endeavor to discover, so far as they may, from what particular African source their own family was derived.

It is altogether probable that America, through the American Negro, is destined to exert a mighty influence in the continent of Africa. It is the opinion of one of the best qualified observers, not only that the Africans in their own land are in a certain degree in character similar, but that American Negroes still have a great affinity with the race from which they were derived. The United States is the star of hope to the African. What the Negro is becoming, as we hope, that the African and Africa must become. There will certainly be in the so-called Dark Continent Negro civilizations, the impulse of which will be derived from the educated Afro-American, who in becoming entirely an American will be no more ashamed of the continent of his origin, than the Anglo-American is ashamed of England. In promoting these mighty world movements, the advance of science will play a part. All political influence, of any sort, is foreign to the purposes of science; the Negro race, physically, will remain and wish to remain a separate race; and all the information which it can obtain relative to its antecedents, regarding its primitive and natural way of feeling, will be a weapon in his hand. We must know the truth about the plantation Negro, to deal with the plantation Negro; it is always the truth that makes free.

I have devoted my time, not to a discussion of Folk-lore, but to showing, as I trust I have succeeded in doing, that the study has its face towards the future, not towards the past. But I must not cease without a word for the sake of pure science. Science has no need to ask of any knowledge, whether it will be useful; for all knowledge is of necessity useful. It would seem hardly necessary to urge this of the study of popular traditions. If the English speaking world could obtain its pre-Christian Folk-lore, the ancient songs, tales, and beliefs of the English race, it would be willing to wipe out with a wet sponge, if necessary, all but the very greatest names in English literature. But you, more fortunate, have still the power of obtaining the traditions of your ancestors, and of preserving them with that pride that always should characterize every race in regard to its ancestral treasures.

Mrs. Cooper of Washington was next presented to the audience and read the following paper.

PAPER BY MRS. ANNA J. COOPER

In the direction of original productiveness, the American Negro is confronted by a peculiar danger. In the first place he is essentially imitative. This in itself is not a defect. The imitative instinct is the main spring of civilization and in this aptitude the Negro is linked with the most progressive nations of the world's history. The Phoenecians imitated the Egyptians, the Greeks borrowed from the Phoenecians, the Romans unblushingly appropriated from the Greeks whatever they could beg or steal. The Norman who became the brain and nerve of the Anglo Saxon race, who contributed the most vigorous and energetic elements in modern civilization, was above all men an imitator. "Whenever," says one, "his neighbor invented or possessed anything worthy of admiration, the sharp, inquisitive Norman poked his long aquiline nose," and the same writer adds, "wherever what we now call the march of intellect advanced, there was the sharp eager face of the Norman in the van." It is not then where or how a man or race gets his ideas but what use does he make of them that settles his claim to originality. "He has seen some of my work," said the great Michaelangelo of the young Raphael when he noticed an adroit appropriation of some of his own touches. But Raphael was no copyist. Shakespeare was a veritable freebooter in the realm of literature, but Shakespeare was no plagiarist.

I heard recently of a certain great painter, who before taking his brush always knelt down and prayed to be delivered from his model, and just here as it seems to me is the real need of deliverance for the American black man. His "model" is a civilization which to his childlike admiration must seem overpowering. Its stream servants thread the globe. It has put the harness on God's lightning which is now made to pull, push, pump, lift, write, talk, sing, light, kill, cure. It seems once more to have realized the possession of Aladdin's wonderful lamp for securing with magic speed and dexterity fabulous wealth, honor, ease, luxury, beauty, art, power. What more can be done? What more can be desired? And as the Queen of Sheba sunk under the stupendousness of Solomon's greatness, the children of Africa in America are in danger of paralysis before the splendor of Anglo Saxon achievements. Anglo Saxon ideas, Anglo Saxon standards, Anglo Saxon art, Anglo Saxon literature, Anglo Saxon music—surely this must be to him the measure of perfection. The whispered little longings of his own soul for utterance must be all a mistake. The simple little croonings that rocked his own cradle must be forgotten and outgrown and only the lullabies after the approved style affected. Nothing else is grammatical, nothing else is orthodox. To write as a white man, to sing as a white man, to swagger as a white man, to bully as a white man—this is achievement, this is success.

And, in all imitations that means mere copying, the ridiculous mannerisms and ugly defects of the model are appropriated more successfully than the life and inner spirit which alone gave beauty or meaning to the original. Emancipation from the model is what is needed. Servile copying foredooms mediocrity: it cuts the nerve of soul expression. The American Negro cannot produce an original utterance until he realizes the sanctity of his homely inheritance. It is the simple, common, everyday things of man that God has cleansed. And it is the untaught, spontaneous lispings of the child heart that are fullest of poetry and mystery.

Correggio once wandered from his little provincial home and found his way to Rome, where all the wonder of the great art world for the first time stood revealed before him. He drank deep and long of the rich inspiration and felt the quickening of his own self consciousness as he gazed on the marvellous canvasses of the masters.

"I too am a painter," he cried and the world has vindicated the assertion. Now it is just such a quickening as this that must come to the black man in America to stimulate his original activities. The creative instinct must be aroused by a wholesome respect for the thoughts that lie nearest. And this to my mind is the vital importance for him of the study of his own folk-lore. His songs, superstitions, customs, tales, are the legacy left from the imagery of the past. These must catch and hold and work up into the picture he paints. The poems of Homer are valued today chiefly because they are the simple unstudied view of the far away life of the Greeks—its homely custom and superstitions as well as its more heroic achievements and activities. The Canterbury Tales do the same thing for the England of the 14th century.

The Negro too is a painter. And he who can turn his camera on the fast receding views of this people and catch their simple truth and their sympathetic meaning before it is all too late will no less deserve the credit of having revealed a characteristic page in history and of having made an interesting study.

ZORA NEALE HURSTON, "HIGH JOHN DE CONQUER"

American Mercury (October 1943), 450–58

An African prince who was sold into slavery, John the Conqueror (or John de Conquer and John the Conker) is the high mythical counterpart to the humble John of the John and Old Master tales. The root of a plant called ipomoea jalapa *(related to the morning glory and sweet potato) is called John the Conquer root. Used in voodoo as one of the parts of a mojo bag, it was said to bestow power over others, grant good fortune in gambling, and cast sexual spells.*

Zora Neale Hurston's 1943 essay, "High John de Conquer," offers a glowing account of John's significance as the heroic embodiment of hope and the promise of freedom. High John begins as "a whisper" and becomes a real presence in the day-to-day lives of ordinary people, a bearer not just of hope, but also of the liberating power of song, story, and laughter. High John shares some traits with the protagonist of tales about John and Old Massa. If he is the infallible hero who leads and liberates, his lowly counterpart is an ordinary man gifted with the cunning of the mythical trickster. In those more earthy, realistic tales, we witness strategic victories, small and large, that emerged in the struggle for things ranging from the next meal to freedom.

One of Hurston's informants was at first reluctant to share her knowledge about John de Conquer. She feared that "smart colored folks" like Hurston were "shamed of the things that brought us through"—a stark reminder that education, for all its obvious advantages, inevitably led to the disavowal of a cultural heritage that had once formed the core of African American identity. The folklore of bondage was faced with the same challenges as was the case with what has been called "the wonderful music of bondage." Collecting tales kept them from disappearing, but it may also have diluted them, in part because the activity of preservation was carried out by those with a distance from antebellum slavery and with a "white man's education" (Sundquist 1992, 28).

Eric Sundquist has pointed out that Hurston captured African American vernacular at a critical moment, preserving narratives of subservience and rebellion encoded in a secret language that enabled slaves to communicate under the harshest of disciplinary regimes. She rewrote the foundational arts of a culture "in a modern idiom but left the reader—the white reader in particular, but perhaps the black as well—with an admonition: 'He can read my writing but he sho' can't read my mind' " (91). Hazel V. Carby sees in Mules and Men *an attempt to "make the unknown known and a nostalgic attempt to preserve a disappearing form of folk culture." In her view, Hurston ignores the migration of African Americans to cities and represents their culture as primarily rural and oral in an essentializing gesture that places the folk outside of history (1990, 80). But just how encrypted are the tales? Richard Wright once described a conversation in which he was accused by a social scientist from the West Indies of revealing "racial secrets to the white race." "Listen," he replied, "the only secret in Asia and Africa and among oppressed people as a whole is that there is no secret." His outraged interlocutor threw up his hands "in disgust" and declared, "You have now revealed the profoundest secret of all" (1957, 42–43). Tales of John de Conquer and John and Old Master reveal some of the open and not-so-open secrets of black communal history, giving us an insider's look at spirited forms of opposition to a disciplinary regime that worked hard to deny any kind of edge let alone a victory.*

Maybe, now, we used-to-be black African folks can be of some help to our brothers and sisters who have always been white. You will take another look at us and say that we are still black and ethnologically speaking, you will be right. But nationally and culturally, we are as white as the next one.[1] We have put our labor and our blood into the common cause for a long time. We have given the rest of the nation song and laughter. Maybe now, in this terrible struggle,[2] we can give something else—the source and soul of our laughter and song. We offer you our hope-bringer, High John de Conquer.

High John de Conquer came to be a man, and a mighty man at that. But he was not a natural man in the beginning. First off, he was a whisper, a will to hope, a wish to find something worthy of laughter and song. Then the whisper put on flesh. His footsteps sounded across the world in a low but musical rhythm as if the world he walked on was a singing-drum. The black folks had an irresistible impulse to laugh. High John de Conquer was a man in full, and had come to live and work on the plantations, and all the slave folks knew him in the flesh.[3]

The sign of this man was a laugh, and his singing-symbol was a drum-beat. No parading drum[4] shout like soldiers out for a show. It did not call to the feet of those who were fixed to hear it. It was an inside thing to live by. It was sure to be

[1] *nationally and culturally, we are as white as the next one:* Hurston courted controversy, and this particular statement reminds us of how contentious her sentiments can be.

[2] *in this terrible struggle:* Hurston is referring here to the unifying effects of World War II and intimating that High John can function as a universal hope-bringer, a move that some might consider a betrayal of her cultural heritage.

[3] *knew him in the flesh:* The word becomes flesh, and John becomes something more than human, a charismatic leader who incarnates hope in the midst of despair, a beacon of freedom that lights up the world of hard labor and promises liberation.

[4] *No parading drum:* Hurston draws a contrast between drums used for displays of military might and the singing-drum used for communal purposes. The "drum-beat" is an acoustical means of connecting with an ancestral heritage.

heard when and where the work was the hardest, and the lot the most cruel. It helped the slaves endure. They knew that something better was coming. So they laughed in the face of things and sang, "I'm so glad! Trouble don't last always." And the white people who heard them were struck dumb that they could laugh. In an outside way, this was Old Massa's fun, so what was Old Cuffy[5] laughing for?

Old Massa couldn't know, of course, but High John de Conquer was there walking his plantation like a natural man. He was trading the sweat-flavored clods of the plantation, crushing out his drum tunes, and giving out secret laughter. He walked on the winds and moved fast. Maybe he was in Texas when the lash fell on a slave in Alabama, but before the blood was dry on the back he was there. A faint pulsing of a drum like a goatskin stretched over a heart, that came nearer and closer, then somebody in the saddened quarters would feel like laughing, and say, "Now, High John de Conquer, Old Massa couldn't get the best of *him*.[6] That old John was a case!" Then everybody sat up and began to smile. Yes, yes, that was right. Old John, High John could beat the unbeatable. He was top-superior to the whole mess of sorrow. He could beat it all, and what made it so cool, finish it off with a laugh. So they pulled the covers up over their souls and kept them from all hurt, harm and danger and made them a laugh and a song.[7] Night time was a joke, because daybreak was on the way. Distance and the impossible had no power over High John de Conquer.

He had come from Africa. He came walking on the waves of sound. Then he took on flesh after he got here. The sea captains of ships knew that they brought slaves in their ships. They knew those black bodies huddled down there in the middle passage, being hauled across the waters to helplessness. High John de Conquer was walking the very winds that filled the sails of the ships. He followed over them like the albatross.

It is no accident that High John de Conquer has evaded the ears of white people. They were not supposed to know. You can't know what folks won't tell you. If they, the white people, heard some scraps, they could not understand because they had nothing to hear things like that with. They were not looking for any hope in those days, and it was not much of a strain for them to find something to laugh over. Old John would have been out of place for them.

Old Massa met our hope-bringer all right, but when old Massa met him, he was not

5 *Old Cuffy:* a generic slave's name

6 *Old Massa couldn't get the best of him:* High John de Conquer becomes the spiritual father of the many slaves who use their wits to lighten their labors by besting Old Massa.

7 *a laugh and a song:* For Hurston, redemption and liberation came through beauty, poetry, and song as much as through political action. Laughter enables the oppressed to rise up above their lot.

going by his right name. He was traveling, and touristing around the plantations as the laugh-provoking Brer Rabbit.[8] So Old Massa and Old Miss and their young ones laughed with and at Brer Rabbit and wished him well. And all the time, there was High John de Conquer laying his tricks of making a way out of no-way. Hitting a straight lick with a crooked stick. Winning the jackpot with no other stake but a laugh. Fighting a mighty battle without outside-showing force, and winning his war from within. Really winning in a permanent way, for he was winning with the soul of the black man whole and free. So he could use it afterwards. For what shall it profit a man if he gain the whole world, and lose his own soul? You would have nothing but a cruel, vengeful grasping monster come to power. High John de Conquer was a bottom-fish. He was deep. He had the wisdom tooth of the East in his head. Way over there, where the sun rises a day ahead of time, they say that Heaven arms with love and laughter those it does not wish to see destroyed. He who carries his heart in his sword must perish.[9] So says the ultimate law. High John de Conquer knew a lot of things like that. He who wins from within is in the "Be" class. *Be*-here when the ruthless man comes, and be here when he is gone.

8 *the laugh-provoking Brer Rabbit:* Among John's many trickster disguises is Brer Rabbit.

9 *He who carries his heart in his sword must perish:* The essay abounds with biblical allusions, among them: "They that take the sword shall perish with the sword" (Matthew 26:52).

Moreover, John knew that it is written where it cannot be erased, that nothing shall live on human flesh and prosper. Old Maker said that before He made any more sayings. Even a man-eating tiger and lion can teach a person that much. His flabby muscles and mangy hide can teach an emperor right from wrong. If the emperor would only listen.

II

There is no established picture of what sort of looking-man this John de Conquer was. To some, he was a big, physical-looking man like John Henry. To others, he was a little hammered-down, low-built man like the Devil's doll-baby. Some said that they never heard what he looked like. Nobody told them, but he lived on the plantation where their old folks were slaves. He is not so well known to the present generation of colored people in the same way that he was in slavery time. Like King Arthur of England, he has served his people, and gone back into mystery again. And, like King Arthur, he is not dead. He waits to return when his people shall call again. Symbolic of English power, Arthur came out of the water, and with Excalibur, went back into the water again. High John de Conquer went back to Africa,[10] but he left his power here and placed his American dwelling in the root of a certain plant. Only possess that root, and he can be summoned at any time.

"Of course, High John de Conquer got plenty power!" Aunt Shady Anne Sutton bristled at me when I asked her about him. She took her pipe out of her mouth and stared at me out of her deeply wrinkled face. "I hope you ain't one of these here smart colored folks that done got so they don't believe nothing, and come here questionizing me so you can have something to poke fun at. Done get shamed of the things that brought us through. Make out 'taint no such thing no more."

When I assured her that that was not the case, she went on.

"Sho John de Conquer means power. That's bound to be so. He come to teach and tell us. God don't leave nobody ignorant, you child. Don't care where He drops you down. He puts you on a notice. He don't want folks taken advantage of because they don't know. Now, back there in slavery time, us didn't have no power of protection, and God knowed it, and put us under watch-care. Rattlesnakes never bit no colored folks until four years after freedom was declared. That was to give us time to learn and to know. 'Course, I don't know nothing about slavery personal like. I wasn't born till two years after the Big Surrender.[11] Then I wasn't nothing but a infant baby when I was born, so I couldn't know nothing but what they told me. My mamma told me, and I know she wouldn't mislead me, how High John de Conquer helped us out. He had done teached the black folks so they knowed a hundred years ahead of time that freedom was coming. Long before the white folks knowed anything about it at all.

"These young Negroes reads they books and talk about the war freeing the Negroes, but Aye, Lord! A heap sees, but a few knows. 'Course, the war was a lot of help, but how come the war took place? They think they knows, but they don't. John de Conquer had done put it into the white folks to give us our freedom, that's what. Old Massa fought against it, but us could have told him that it wasn't no use. Freedom just *had* to come. The time set aside for it was there. That war was just a sign and symbol of the thing. That's the truth! If I tell the truth about everything as good as I do about that, I can go straight to Heaven without a prayer."

Aunt Shady Anne was giving the inside feeling and meaning to the outside laughs around John de Conquer. He romps, he clowns, and looks ridiculous, but if you will,

10 *went back to Africa:* Hurston presents John as an African cultural hero, a god connected to nature by the root that he leaves behind in his "American dwelling."

11 *the Big Surrender:* Aunt Shady Anne refers, not without a touch of irony (self-conscious or not), to the end of the Civil War as a time of "surrender" rather than victory.

you can read something deeper behind it all. He is loping on off from the Tar Baby with a laugh.

Take, for instance, those words he had with Old Massa about stealing pigs.

Old John was working in Old Massa's house that time, serving around the eating table. Old Massa loved roasted young pigs, and had them often for dinner. Old John loved them too, but Massa never allowed the slaves to eat any at all. Even put aside the left-over and ate it next time. John de Conquer got tired of that. He took to stopping by the pig pen when he had a strong taste for pig-meat, and getting himself one, and taking it on down to his cabin and cooking it.

Massa began to miss his pigs, and made up his mind to squat for who was taking them and give whoever it was a good hiding. So John kept on taking pigs, and one night Massa walked him down. He stood out there in the dark and saw John kill the pig and went on back to the "big house" and waited till he figured John had it dressed and cooking. Then he went on down to the quarters and knocked on John's door.

"Who dat?" John called out big and bold, because he never dreamed it was Massa rapping.

"It's me, John," Massa told him. "I want to come in."

"What you want, Massa, I'm coming right out."

"You needn't do that, John. I want to come in."

"Naw, naw, Massa. You don't want to come into no old slave cabin. Youse too fine a man for that. It would hurt my feelings to see you in a place like this here one."

"I tell you I want to come in, John!"

So John had to open the door and let Massa in. John had seasoned that pig *down*, and it was stinking pretty! John knowed Old Mass couldn't help but smell it. Massa talked on about the crops and hound dogs and one thing and another, and the pot with the pig in it was hanging over the fire in the chimney and kicking up. The smell got better and better.

Way after while, when that pig had done simbled down to a low gravy, Massa said, "John, what's that you cooking in that pot?"

"Nothing but a little old weasly possum, Massa. Sickliest little old possum I ever did see. But I thought I'd cook him anyhow."

"Get a plate and give me some of it, John. I'm hungry."

"Aw, naw, Massa, you ain't hungry."

"Now, John. I don't mean to argue with you another minute. You give me some of that in the pot, or I mean to have the hide off your back tomorrow morning. Give it to me!"

So John got up and went and got a plate and a fork and went to the pot. He lifted the lid and looked at Massa and told him, "Well, Massa, I put this thing in here a possum, but if it comes out a pig, it ain't no fault of mine."

Old Massa didn't want to laugh, but he did before he caught himself. He took the plate of brownded-down pig and ate it up. He never said nothing, but he gave John and all the other house servants roast pig at the big house after that.

III

John had numerous scrapes and tight squeezes, but he usually came out like Brer Rabbit. Pretty occasionally, though, Old Massa won the hand. The curious thing about this is, that there are no bitter tragic tales at all. When Old Massa won, the thing ended up in a laugh just the same. Laughter at the expense of the slave, but laughter right on. A sort of recognition that life is not one-sided. A sense of humor that said, "We are just as ridiculous as anybody else. We can be wrong, too."

There are many tales and variants of each, of how the Negro got his freedom through High John de Conquer. The best one deals with a plantation where the work was hard, and Old Massa mean. Even Old Miss used to pull her maids' ears with hot firetongs when they got her riled. So, naturally, Old John de Conquer was around that plantation a lot.

"What we need is a song," he told the people after he had figured the whole thing out. "It ain't here, and it ain't no place I know of as yet. Us better go hunt around. This has got to be a particular piece of singing."

But the slaves were scared to leave. They knew what Old Massa did for any slave caught running off.

"Oh, Old Massa don't need to know you gone from here. How? Just leave your old work-tired bodies[12] around for him to look at, and he'll never realize youse way off somewhere, going about your business."

12 *leave your old work-tired bodies:* What John proposes is similar to the practices of witches, who slip off their skins and go out riding in the night.

At first they wouldn't hear to John, that is, some of them. But, finally, the weak gave in to the strong, and John told them to get ready to go while he went off to get something for them to ride on. They were all gathered up under a big hickory nut tree. It was noon time and they were knocked off from chopping cotton to eat their dinner. And then that tree was right where Old Massa and Old Miss could see from the cool veranda[13] of the big house. And both of them were sitting out there to watch.

"Wait a minute, John. Where we going to get something to wear off like that? We can't go nowhere like you talking about dressed like we is."

"Oh, you got plenty things to wear. Just reach inside yourselves[14] and get out all those fine raiments you been toting around with you for the last longest. They is in there, all right. I know. Get 'em out, and put 'em on."

So the people began to dress. And then John hollered back for them to get out their musical instruments so they could play music on the way. They were right inside where they got their fine raiments from. So they began to get them out. Nobody remembered that Massa and Miss were setting up there on the veranda looking things over. So John went off for a minute. After that they all heard a big sing of wings. It was John come back, riding on a great black crow.[15] The crow was so big that one wing rested on the morning, while the other dusted off the evening star.

John lighted down and helped them, so they all mounted on, and the bird took out straight across the deep blue sea. But it was a pearly blue, like ten squillion big pearl jewels dissolved in running gold.[16] The shore around it was all grainy gold itself.

Like Jason in search of the golden fleece,[17] John and his party went to many places, and had numerous adventures. They stopped off in Hell where John, under the name of Jack, married the Devil's youngest daughter[18] and became a popular character. So much so, that when he and the Devil had some words because John turned the dampers down in old Original Hell and put some of the Devil's hogs to barbecue over the coals, John ran for High Chief Devil and won the election. The rest of his party was overjoyed at the pos-

13 *could see from the cool veranda:* With poetic economy of means, Hurston reveals the cruelties of slavery, with masters comfortably lounging in the shade, keeping an eye on weary laborers during a brief respite from "chopping cotton."

14 *reach inside yourselves:* Imagination produces garments and songs of superlative beauty, but always with the poignant reminder that reality will not be transformed.

15 *great black crow:* In Native American lore, Crow is the creature who brings daylight, and also the bird who, in bringing fire to humans, singes his shimmering rainbow feathers, turning "black as tar," and loses his melodious voice.

16 *a pearly blue, like ten squillion big pearl jewels dissolved in running gold:* Beauty is described with radiant luminosity, and *squillion*, which designates a large, indefinite number, enlarges and expands the visionary beauty of blues, gold, and pearly hues.

17 *golden fleece:* A symbol of royal power and authority, the golden fleece came from a winged ram held in Colchis. Jason and the Argonauts set out on a quest for the fleece on the orders of Pelias, King of Iolcus in Greek mythology.

18 *married the Devil's youngest daughter:* Among the many tales about John the Conquer is a variant of a tale type known to folklorists as "a girl helps the hero to flee." The story appears in its most popular form as the French "Jean, the Soldier, and Eulalie, the Devil's Daughter." Echoing the mythical account of Jason and Medea, it recounts tasks carried out by the hero with the help of a woman connected to the antagonist. John the Conquer and the Jack who marries the Devil's daughter are folkloric cousins who count the Argonaut Jason as a distant ancestor.

session of power and wanted to stay there. But John said no. He reminded them that they had come in search of a song. A song that would whip Old Massa's earlaps down. The song was not in Hell. They must go on.

The party escaped out of Hell behind the Devil's two fast horses. One of them was named Hallowed-Be-Thy-Name, and the other, Thy-Kingdom-Come. They made it to the mountain. Somebody told them that the Golden Stairs went up from there. John decided that since they were in the vicinity, they might as well visit Heaven.

They got there a little weary and timid. But the gates swung wide for them, and they went in. They were bathed, robed, and given new and shining instruments to play on. Guitars of gold, and drums, and cymbals and wind-singing instruments. They walked up Amen Avenue, and down Hallelujah Street, and found with delight that Amen Avenue was tuned to sing bass and alto. The west end was deep bass, and the east end alto. Hallelujah Street was tuned for tenor and soprano, and the two promenades met right in front of the throne and made harmony by themselves. You could make any tune you wanted to by the way you walked. John and his party had a very good time at that and other things. Finally, by the way they acted and did, Old Maker called them up before His great workbench, and made them a tune, and put it in their mouths. It had no words. It was a tune that you could bend and shape in most any way you wanted to fit the words and feelings that you had.[19] They learned it, and began to sing.

Just about that time a loud rough voice hollered, "You Tunk! You Judy! You Aunt Diskie!" Then heaven went black before their eyes and they couldn't see a thing until they saw the hickory nut tree over their heads again. There was everything just like they had left it, with Old Massa and Old Miss sitting on the veranda, and Massa was doing the hollering.

"You all are taking a mighty long time for dinner," Massa said. "Get up from there and get on back to the field. I mean for you to finish chopping that cotton today if it takes all night long. I got something else, harder than that, for you to do tomorrow. Get a move on you!"

They heard what Massa said, and they felt bad right off. But John de Conquer took and told them, saying, "Don't pay what he say no mind. You know where you got something finer than this plantation, and anything it's got on it, put away. Ain't that funny? Us got all that, and he don't know nothing at all about it. Don't tell him nothing.[20] Nobody

19 *fit the words and feelings that you had:* God's gift of music and improvisational song provides an expressive medium, an outlet for words and feelings that are not allowed to be made manifest in the world of slavery.

20 *Don't tell him nothing:* The exhortation to remain silent about what is in your mind had a powerful afterlife long after slavery came to an end.

don't have to know where us gets our pleasure from. Come on. Pick up your hoes and let's go."

They all began to laugh and grabbed up their hoes and started out.

"Ain't that funny?" Aunt Diskie laughed and hugged herself with secret laughter.[21] "Us got all the advantage, and Old Massa think he got us tied!"

The crowd broke out singing as they went off to work. The day didn't seem hot like it had before. Their gift song came back into their memories in pieces, and they sang about glittering new robes, and harps, and the work flew.[22]

21 *secret laughter:* Secret laughter may, of course, not go far toward undoing the harrowing physical effects of picking cotton from dawn to dusk under a hot sun.

22 *and the work flew:* The irony of the ending could not have escaped listeners, with work flying by but the slaves moored to the ground, laboring with their hoes.

IV

So after a while, freedom came. Therefore High John de Conquer has not walked the winds of America for seventy-five years now. His people had their freedom, their laugh and their song. They have traded it to the other Americans for things they could use like education and property, and acceptance. High John knew that that was the way it would be, so he could retire with his secret smile into the soil of the South and wait.

The thousands upon thousands of humble people who still believe in him, that is, in the power of love and laughter to win by their subtle power, do John reverence by getting the root of the plant in which he has taken up his secret dwelling, and "dressing" it with perfume, and keeping it on their person or in their houses in a secret place. It is there to help them overcome things they feel that they could not beat otherwise, and to bring them the laugh of the day. John will never forsake the weak and the helpless, nor fail to bring hope to the hopeless. That is why they believe, and so they do not worry. They go on and laugh and sing. Things are bound to come out right tomorrow. That is the secret of Negro song and laughter.

So the brother in black offers to these United States the source of courage that endures, and laughter. High John de Conquer. If the news from overseas reads bad, and the nation inside seems like it is stuck in the Tar Baby, listen hard, and you will hear John de Conquer treading on his singing-drum. You will know then, no matter how bad things look now, it will be worse for those who seek to oppress us. Even if your hair comes yellow, and your eyes are blue, John de Conquer will be working for you just the same. From his secret place, he is working for all America now. We are all his kinfolks. Just be sure our cause is right, and then you can lean back and say, "John de Conquer would know what to do in a case like this, and then he would finish it off with a laugh."

White America, take a laugh out of our black mouths, and win! We give you High John de Conquer.

STERLING A. BROWN, "NEGRO FOLK EXPRESSION"

Phylon 11.4 (1950), 318-27

Sterling A. Brown (1901–1989) was born in Washington, D.C., where his father, Sterling N. Brown, a former slave, worked as a minister and professor at Howard University. In 1932 Brown published his first book of poems, Southern Road, *a collection that focused on the lives of poor blacks living in rural regions. Considered a part of the Harlem Renaissance, even though he spent most of his life in Washington, D.C., Brown's students included Toni Morrison and Amiri Baraka. His rich repertoire of essays and poems meant that his literary influence extended well beyond the classroom.*

NEGRO FOLK EXPRESSION

For a long time Uncle Remus and his Brer Rabbit tales stood for the Negro folk and their lore. One thing made clear by the resurrection of Uncle Remus in Walt Disney's *Song of the South* is the degree to which he belonged to white people rather than to the Negro folk. A striking contrast to the favored house servant is such a folk character as Huddie Ledbetter, better known as Leadbelly, whose knowingness is stark rather than soft, and whose audience (certainly in his formative years) was his own kind of people, not the white quality. The bitter brew that Leadbelly concocted in the levee camps and jooks and prisons differs from the sugary potions that Remus and the other "uncles" dispensed. Both Uncle Remus and Leadbelly portray sides of the Negro folk, but to round out the portraiture Bessie Smith, Josh White, the Gospel Singing Two Keys, and such big old liars as those heard by E. C. L. Adams in the Congaree swamps and by Zora Neale Hurston in Central Florida are also needed. In any consideration of American Negro folk expression it is important to realize that even before Joel Chandler Harris revealed the antics of Brer Rabbit to America, John Henry was swinging his hammer in the Big Bend Tunnel on the C. & O. Road.

There is rich material on hand for a revaluation of the Negro folk. Out of penitentiaries in the deep South, John and Alan Lomax have brought the musical memories of singers with such names as Iron Head, Clear Rock, and Lightning. From what is more truly folk culture these men and others like John Hammond, Willis James, and John Work have brought hidden singers and songs. The Library of Congress Archives of Folk Music are crammed with solid stuff; the large recording companies are following the lead of small companies like Disc, Folkways and Circle in issuing albums of Negro folk music. Ten years after her tragic death in the Delta, Bessie Smith has been honored in a Town Hall Concert (even now I can hear her surprised cry: "Lord, Lord, Lord!"). And in Carnegie Hall Big Bill has sung blues from the sharecropping country, and Josh White has sung both mellow-blues and sardonic mockery, and Blind Sonny Terry has blown on his wild harmonica the joys of the fox hunt, of a high-balling train, and the wailing fear of a lost wanderer in a southern swamp. Folk singers of the spirituals, unknown yesterday, have their names placarded now; Harlemites pass around the name of Mahalia Jackson as they used to do that of Mamie Smith; and in the Harlem dance-halls where jazz bands "cut" each other on Saturday nights, spiritual singers battle each other on Sundays to cheering crowds. This commercializing will affect the genuineness of the stuff, but it is getting a hearing for folk material. And an audience for the authentic is growing.

All of this is part of the generally awakened interest in American folk culture, indicated by the diligence and popularity of collectors, anthologists, musicologists, and interpreters. Before its demise the WPA Federal Projects laid in a fine backlog of American folkstuff and World War II, of course, quickened interest in the American past. Though the furore may have something of the faddish about it, American folklore stands to gain more from enthusiasm and careful study than from the earlier disdain and neglect. The Negro creators of an important segment of American folklore should no longer be subjected to the condescension of the "oh so quaint," "so folksy," school. Looking on Negro lore as exotic *curiosa* becomes almost impossible if the body of available material is thoughtfully considered. Outmoded now are those collectors who could or would find only ingratiating aunties and uncles, most of whose lore consisted in telling how good their white folks were.

With the discarding of the old simplifications, the study of the Negro folk becomes complicated. The field of folklore in general is known to be a battle area, and the Negro front is one of the hottest sectors. One sharply contested point is the problem of definition of the folk; another that of origins. Allies are known to have fallen out and skirmished behind the lines over such minor matters as identifying John Hardy with John Henry. But this is not a battle piece. In general the vexed problems of origin are left for others, more competent in that area; strict delimitation of the concepts "folk," "folk literature" and "folk music" is not the purpose here. This essay aims instead to tell what the "folk Negro" (as most students understand the term)[1] has expressed in story and proverb and song. It is well known that folk culture among Negroes is breaking up. Some of the material (in discussing the blues, for instance) has been transplanted in the cities, but, though inexactly folk, it is used because its roots drew first sustenance from the folk culture.

I: FOLK TALES AND APHORISMS

Collectors, both scholarly and amateur, have long paid tribute to the richness of Negro folk expression. Enthusiasts like Roark Bradford and Zora Hurston overpraise Negro folk speech at the expense of the speech of white Americans. According to Bradford, "The most ignorant Negro can get more said with a half-dozen words than the average United States Senator can say in a two-hour speech."[2] But folk should be compared with folk; and considering the speech of white America to be barren and bleak does injustice to a large part of American folklore, to the gusto of the tall tale, for instance. The folk Negro's imaginativeness and pith can easily be recognized; they stand in no need of dubious comparisons.

In Africa the telling of tales is a time honored custom. The slaves brought the custom with them to the New World. According to the latest scholarship of Melville Herskovits, the body of tales they brought has been retained in relatively undisturbed fashion.[3] These tales were not dangerous; they were a way to ease the time; they could entertain the master class, especially the children. So they were not weeded out as were many of the practices of sorcery, or discouraged as were the tribal languages. In the African cycles the heroes were the jackal or fox, the hare, the tortoise, and the spider. The last, a sort of hairy tarantula, is little used in the lore of the southern Negro, but is hero of the Anansi tales of Jamaica. The African fox, more like our jackal, has become the American fox; the African hare, "Cunnie Rabbit," really a chevrotain, water deerlet, or gazelle, has become the American rabbit with the word cunnie Englished into cunning, and the African tortoise has become the American dry-land turtle or terrapin. In America, Brer Terrapin is a hero second only to Brer Rabbit whom he bests occasionally. Of the hero's victims the African hyena has become the American wolf, and the American fox and bear have joined the losing side. African animals—lions, leopards, tigers, and monkeys—are still in the cast of characters.

Close parallels to American Negro tales have been found extensively in Africa and the Caribbeans. Nevertheless, folklorists are wary of finding Africa the place of ultimate origin of all of the tales. Many of the basic plots are of great age and spread. Oddly enough, the three stories that Joel Chandler Harris considered unquestionably African, namely: "How the Rabbit Makes a Riding-horse of the Fox," "Why the Alligator's Back Is Rough," and "The Tar Baby Story," have close European counterparts, dating back hundreds of years. "The Tar Baby Story" has been traced to India through a study of nearly three hundred versions. According to Stith Thompson, it reached the Negroes and Indians of America by several paths, the main one being "from India to Africa, where it is a favorite and where it received some characteristic modifications before being taken by slaves to America."[4] In the Congo version a jackal is stuck to a tortoise covered with beeswax; among the Pueblo Indians a coyote catches a rabbit with a gum-covered wooden image.

To indicate the problems facing source-hunters, one of the most popular European stories might be considered here. In the Reynard cycle, and reappearing in Grimm's *Fairy Tales*, is the plot of the fox who played godfather in order to sneak away and eat food that he and the bear have stored in common. Asked the name of his godchildren (for he leaves three times) he answers Well Begun, Half Done and Done. Several collectors found the story in South Carolina, with Brer Rabbit cheating Brer Wolf, and the children variously named: "Fus' Beginnin'," "Half-Way" and "Scrapin' de Bottom," or "Buh Start-um," "Buh Half-um" and "Buh Done-Um." Easy attribution to American slaveowners, however, comes up sharp against the numerous African versions in one of which the rabbit fools his working partner, the antelope, with non-existent children named Uncompleted One, Half-completed One, and Completed One.

All of this illustrates the underlying unity of Old World culture. Africa then, is not the starting place of all the favorite Negro tales, but was a way-station where they had an extended stop-over. The long association with Asiatic Moslems in East Africa and the penetration of European powers into West Africa beginning with the slave trade affected the native tradition of tale telling. According to Stith Thompson, "The African finds enjoyment in nearly every kind of European folktale. He may do some queer things with them and change them around so that little more than a skeleton of the original remains and so that it takes the expert eye to discover that they are not actually native. On the other hand he may take the tale over completely with all its foreign trappings." Nevertheless Thompson believes that "the great majority of their [African] tales have certainly had their origin on the soil of central or southern Africa."[5] Regardless of original source, whether in Europe or Africa, American Negro fables have been so modified with new beasts and local color added, different themes, and different experiences, that an almost new, certainly a quite different thing results. Such is the way of written literature where authors took "their own where they found it," and such is even more the way of folktales.

"Den Br' Hoss, an' Br' Jack-ass, an' Br' Cow an' all dem, crowd close roun' Br' Dog, for dem was like yard-chillen, dey is peaceable an' sort o' scary. An' all de creeters what stan' up for Br' Gator scatter out wide away from dere, for dem was woods-chillen, rovin' an' wild."[6] Thus, according to a South Carolina tale, started the big row in the world between the tame and the wild creatures that is never going to stop.

This illustrates the process. The basic incident, the war between domestic and wild animals, is widely used in folktales, from the Orient to the Reynard cycle. But the details, the "entrimmins," according to Uncle Remus, the phrases "yard chillen," and "woods chillen," and the naming of their traits, give the flavor of the low country, where Samuel Stoney and Gertrude Shelby heard the above yarn.

Public recognition of the wealth of American Negro stories came in the late eighties with the appearance of Joel Chandler Harris's Uncle Remus Tales. A few animal tales had seen print earlier, but Harris was the first to give a substantial number. Soon he was besieged with correspondents who told him new tales or variants that they had heard from Negroes. Harris deserves the credit of a pioneer. He insisted that he gave the tales "uncooked," but there is too much evidence of his alterations to accept his word. The tales are not genuine folktales, in the sense of by the folk for the folk, for they are told by an old Uncle to entertain Young Marster. In line with literary trends of the time, Harris made them more sentimental and genteel and less racy than the folk tell them; he gives much about Negro life and character, valuable for purposes of local color but likely to be taken for granted by the folk; and he uses the devices of a skillful short story writer. Simpler and starker tales, with fewer alterations, have been taken from their native habitat by collectors such as C. C. Jones, Jr. (a contemporary of Harris), Ambrose Gonzales, Elsie Clews Parsons, Guy Johnson, and A. W. Eddins. Negro collectors are few and far between; Charles W. Chesnutt fashioned skillful short stories out of folk beliefs in *The Conjure Woman* (1889); and Thomas Talley, pioneer folk-collector, Arthur Huff Fauset, Zora Neale Hurston and J. Mason Brewer have published collections. Stella Brewer Brooks has written the best study of Joel Chandler Harris as folklorist. But educated Negroes by and large have not been greatly interested. From Harris's day to the present, collectors, being of different race or class or both, have been viewed by the folk with natural distrust.

Nevertheless, a considerable number of tales has been recorded. Many are animal tales; of these all are not strictly fables, which convey an ostensible moral, though some are. Whereas the more efficient Fox, crafty and cruel, hypocritical and scheming, amused the European peasantry, the American Negro slave took Brer Rabbit for hero. The harmless scary creature he invested with a second nature, and made him a practical joker with a streak of cruelty, a daring hunter of devilment, a braggart, a pert wit, a glutton, a lady's man, a wily trickster, knowing most of the answers, and retaining of his true characteristics only his speed on the getaway. Animals noted for greater strength and ferocity are his meat. Brer Fox has degenerated from crafty Reynard into something of a fool, though still a worthy opponent, but Brer Wolf and Brer Bear are numskulls. Commentators have long considered these tales of cunning overcoming strength, of the weakling out-smarting the bully, as a compensatory mechanism, a kind of oblique revenge, the wish fulfillment of an ironic people who could see few ways out of oppression.[7] It might be pointed out that none of the hero-animals in Africa are quite so helpless as the American rabbit. It is unlikely that the slaves did not see pertinence to their own experiences in these tales. Outsmarting was one of the few devices left them. So they made heroes out of the physically powerless who by good sense and quick wit overcame animals of brute strength who were not right bright. "You ain't got no cause to be bigger in de body, but you sho' is got cause to be bigger in de brain."

With his pardonable fondness for the creature, Joel Chandler Harris placed Brer Rabbit in the limelight. He is less focused on in other collections, though still the star performer. The theme of weakness overcoming strength through cunning remains uppermost. Brer Squirrel escapes from Brer Fox by reminding him to say grace; when the fox closes his eyes, the squirrel is treetop high. Brer Goat foils Brer Wolf, never trusting him from that day to this. Brer Rooster outeats Brer Elephant: "it ain't de man wid de bigges' belly what kin eat de longest." Animals and birds of everyday observation swell the company: the officious yard dog, the fierce bulldog, the hound, another fall-guy for the rabbit; the horse, the mule, the jackass, the bull, the stupid ox; the deer, the raccoon, possum and squirrel; the frog, the crawfish, and many kinds of snakes; the turkey buzzard, the partridge, the blue-jay, the marsh-hen; the mosquito, the hornet, the gnat.

Many tales drive home a point about mankind based on the animals' observed traits. The gnat, riding the bull's horn, says: "I gwine now. Ain't you glad you don't have to tote me puntop yo' horn no more?" The bull answers: "I never know when you come, and I ain't gonna miss you when you gone." The possum tells the raccoon that he can't fight because he is ticklish and has to laugh when in the clutch of his enemy, but the raccoon sees through the rationalization. With his belly full, running in the pasture, Brer Mule dreams that his father was a race-horse, but harnessed to a heavy cart and hungry, he recalls that his father was only a jackass. The ox rebukes the axle wheels for groaning; *he* is the one pulling the load, though he refuses to cry out. "Some men holler if briar scratch his foot, and some men lock their jaws if a knife is sticking in their heart."[8]

Ingenious explanations of animal characteristics and behavior occur in many tales. You never see a blue-jay on Friday because that is the day for his weekly trip to hell; the woodpecker's head is red because Noah caught him pecking holes in the ark and whipped his head with a hammer; the possum's tail is bare because, wanting music on the ark, Ham used the hairs to string a banjo; the alligator's mouth is all out of whack because the dog, God's apprentice helper, was either careless or cruel while wielding the knife in the week of creation, making the alligator and dog eternal foes; the porpoise's tail is set crossways because with his tail straight up and down the porpoise was too fast, he outsped the sun; Sis Nanny Goat, self sacrificing, allowed all of the other animals to get their tails first, hence, "Kind heart give Sis Nanny Goat a short tail"; the wasp is so short-patienced because he thinks everybody is laughing at his tiny stomach (he can't laugh himself because he would "bust spang in two").

Though performing other functions in the Old World, animal tales are often considered by American Negroes as "stories for the young uns." Animal stories were by no means the only stock, even in slavery. More realistic tales made direct use of unallegorized human experience. In coastal Georgia the folk still remember the tale of the Eboes who, hating slavery, marched singing into the tidal river and were drowned. The name of Ebo's Landing gives historic color to the tradition. The same folk tell also of the magic hoe that worked itself, and of the flying Africans who changed into birds and soared away to their homeland rather than take the overseer's whipping. Modelled on tales in African folklore, in the New World they take on the quality of dreams of escape.

More widespread in Negro folklore are the tales of the trickster Jack or John. In slavery days he outwits not only the devil but Ole Marster, Ole Miss, and the "patterollers." More recently his competitors have been the grasping landlord, the browbeating tough, and the highhanded sheriff, deputy, and policeman. Sometimes Jack, like Brer Rabbit, comes to grief himself, but oftener he outsmarts the opposition or makes his dare and is long gone. Jack schemes to get out of a whipping or to obtain freedom. Sometimes he is in cahoots with a sharp witted master to take advantage of gullible neighbors. Sometimes the repartee is sharp; a master tells that he dreamt of a heaven set aside for Negroes and found it to be run-down and generally messed-up; Jack retorts with his dream of white folk's heaven, all gleaming and glittering, with streets of gold, but without a solitary person in the place! The tellers aim at comedy, often richly satiric; the hardships of slavery are casually mentioned as if taken for granted by teller and audience; but Ole Marster and Ole Miss and the slaves themselves are ribbed with gusto, with toughminded humor. Pretentiousness and boasting ride for a fall; sentimentality is pricked; all the characters, white and black, master and slave, come "under the same gourd-vine," all are "made out of meat."

A favorite object of lampooning, familiar in general folklore, was the old maid, the master's sister. One of the fanciful plots has her turning into a squinch owl, her longdrawn wails voicing her yearning for a husband, but other tales satirize her bossiness and silliness in down-to-earth situations. The Irish were also satirized. Comparative newcomers with their own brogues and dirty jobs, the Irish were characterized as big dunces. Here, of course, the American Negro shares an Anglo-Saxon tradition. The "po' buckra," the "poor white trash," the "cracker," came in for contempt and hostility in Negro tales, but the stories about them were not often funny.

Exaggeration in the hearty tradition of American tall talk is pervasive. In Zora Hurston's recording, mosquitoes sing like alligators, eat up the cow and then ring the bell for the calf. The plague of the boll-weevil is graphically symbolized: "Old Man Boll Weevil whipped little Willie Boll Weevil 'cause he couldn't carry two rows at a time." Land is so rich that the next morning after a mule is buried, "he had done sprouted li'l jackasses"; it is so poor that "it took nine partridges to holler Bob White" or needed "ten sacks of fertilizer before a church congregation could raise a tune on it." A snail is sent for a doctor. After seven years his sick wife heard a scuffling at the door and cries out her relief. The snail says, "Don't try to rush me—ah' ain't gone yet." He had taken all that time to get to the door. Weather is so hot "till two cakes of ice left the icehouse and went down the streets and fainted."[9]

Quite common are the "why" stories; jocular explanation of the creation of the world, the position of woman, the origin of the races. One teller informed Zora Hurston: "And dats why de man makes and de woman takes. You men is still braggin' about yo' strength and de women is sitting on de keys [to kitchen, bedroom, and cradle] and lettin' you blow off 'til she git ready to put de bridle on you." But another informant explains why "de sister in black works harder than anybody else in the world. De white man tells de nigger to work and he takes and tells his wife."[10]

Mythological tales explain the origin of the ocean, where the hurricane comes from, why the wind and waters are at war, why the moon's face is smutty. Others enlarge material from the Bible. Ingenuity is especially exercised on filling in gaps in the creation story. Up in heaven a newcomer tells of the havoc of the Johnstown flood to a bored listener who turns out to be Noah. Peter is humanized more than the other apostles: famished, he brings a huge rock to the Lord to turn into bread and is nonplussed when he hears the pronouncement: "And upon this rock will I found my church." Religion is treated freely, even irreverently, but not to the degree of Roark Bradford's *Ol' Man Adam an' His Chillun,* which is synthetic, not genuine folk-stuff.

Tales about the origin of the races leave little room for chauvinism about a chosen people. The slaves knew at first hand that the black man had a hard road to travel and they tell of the mistakes of creation with sardonic fatalism. Uncle Remus tells how all men were once Negroes, "en 'cordin' ter all de counts w'at I years fokes 'uz gittin' long 'bout ez well in dem days as dey is now." One of Zora Hurston's informants told her that "God made de world and de white folks made work." Another said that the Negro outraced the white man and took the larger of two bundles that God had let down in the road. But the smaller bundle had a writing-pen and ink in it, while the larger bundle had a pick and shovel and hoe and plow and cop-axe in it. "So ever since then de nigger been out in de hot sun, usin' his tools and de white man been sittin' up figgerin', ought's a ought, figger's a figger; all for de white man, none for de nigger."[11]

Irony has been in the stories from the earliest recorded versions, but recent collectors have found it less veiled. Zora Hurston retells the yarn of the dogs' convention where a law was passed not to run rabbits any more. But Brer Rabbit stayed cautious: "All de dogs ain't been to no convention and anyhow some of dese fool dogs ain't got no better sense than to run all over dat law and break it up. De rabbit didn't go to school much and he didn't learn but three letters and that trust no mistake. Run every time de bush shake."[12] She tells another of the slave who saved his master's children from drowning. Old Master sets him free. As he walks off, old master calls to him: "John, de children love yuh." . . . "John, I love yuh." . . . "And Missy *like* yuh!" . . . "But 'member, John, youse a nigger." John kept right on stepping to Canada, answering his master "every time he called 'im, but he consumed on with his bag."

The age-old tale of the deceptive bargain gets added point down in the Brazos Bottom. Brer Rabbit, father of a large, hungry family, is sharecropping for Brer Bear who has him in his power. Brer Rabbit is forced to promise Brer Bear everything that grows above the ground. But that year he planted potatoes. The second year, Brer Bear settles for root crops, but Brer Rabbit planted oats. The third year, Brer Bear claimed both tops and roots, leaving Brer Rabbit only the middles. As a fine climax, Brer Rabbit planted corn. Another old tale of the goose that the fox threatened to kill for swimming on "his" lake, now ends with Sis Goose taking her just cause to court. "When dey got dere, de sheriff, he was a fox, and de judge, he was a fox, and de attorneys, dey was foxes, and all de jurymen, dey was foxes, too. An' dey tried ole sis goose, and dey convicted her and dey executed her, and dey picked her bones."[13]

There is similar edge in numerous jokes about sharecropping and the law. Landlords who "figure with a crooked pencil" are derided. One sharecropper held back a couple of bales from the reckoning. When told, after elaborate figuring, that he had come out even, he expressed his happiness that he could sell his extra bales. The landlord then cursed him to hell and back, telling him that he had to do all that hard figuring over again. When another sharecropper was told that his return was zero after making a bumper crop, he shut up like a clam. The landlord, distrusting his silence, insisted that he tell him what he was thinking. The sharecropper finally said: "I was just thinking, Mister Charlie, that the next time I say 'Giddap' to a mule again, he's gonna be setting on my lap." Yarnspinners weep in mimicry of the landlord who, in the early days of the New Deal, had to give government checks to his tenants, crying: "After all I've done for you, you so ungrateful that you cashed those checks."

Negroes borrow, of course, from the teeming storehouse of American jokes. Jokes about Negroes are of three types. The first includes those told by whites generally to whites (the kind collected by Irvin Cobb, for instance, and the stand-bys for after-dinner speakers, with such black face minstrelsy props as watermelon, chicken, razors, excessive fright, murder of the English language, etc.). Some of these may be found among Negroes who will belittle their own for a laugh as quickly as any other people will, but they are not the most popular. The white man's mark on a Negro joke often does not help it. A second type is told by Negroes to whites to gain a point. Sometimes verging on sarcasm, they use the license of the court fool. Then there are jokes strictly for a Negro audience, what John Dollard calls "part of the arsenal of reprisal against white people."[14]

Often too, the joke lays bare what the tellers consider a racial weakness and the outsider must not be let into the family secrets, as it were. Sometimes it pleads the racial cause. Jokes ridicule the myth of "separate but equal"; a Negro gets off free in traffic court by telling the judge that he saw whites drive on the green light so he knew the red light was for him. Hat-in-hand Negroes and workers too zealous on the job are satirized. During the war the jokes, or more truly anecdotes, took on a grimmer tone. One folk hero became the soldier who after being badgered on a bus, faced his tormentors and said, "Well, if I am going to die for democracy, I might as well die for some of it down here in Georgia." One repeated line concerned an epitaph: "Here lies a black man killed by a yellow man while fighting to save democracy for the white man." Many of these anecdotes are bitter; some, dealing with sadistic sheriffs and mobs are gruesome; yet they produce laughter, a sort of laughter out of hell. But they are shared by educated as well as uneducated and though passed along by word of mouth, they take us somewhat afield from the folk.

NOTES

1. That is, as a rural people, living in a kind of isolation, without easy contact with the outside world. Sometimes they are cut off from progress geographically (especially the sea-islanders or swamp dwellers or the people on back-county plantations). But even rural Negroes with better communication and transportation facilities are socially isolated by segregation and lack of educational and economic advantages. Unlettered, folk Negroes have a local culture transmitted orally rather than by the printed page.

2. Roark Bradford, *Ol' Man Adam an' His Chillun* (New York, 1928), p. xiv.

3. Melville Herskovits, *The Myth of the Negro Past* (New York, 1941), p. 275.

4. Stith Thompson, *The Folk Tale* (New York, 1947), pp. 225ff.

5. *Ibid.,* pp. 284–286.

6. Samuel Gaillard Stoney and Gertrude Mathews Shelby, *Black Genesis* (New York, 1930), p. 21.

7. For a very suggestive essay on this point, F. Bernard Wolfe, "Uncle Remus and the Malevolent Rabbit," in *Commentary,* July, 1949 (Vol. 8, No. 1), 31–41.

8. The quoted lines in the above paragraph are taken from Ambrose E. Gonzales, *With Æsop Along the Black Border* (Columbia [South Carolina]: The State Company, 1924), *passim.*

9. The quoted lines in the above paragraph are taken from Zora Neale Hurston, *Mules and Men* (Philadelphia, 1935), *passim.*

10. *Ibid., passim.*

11. *Ibid.,* pp. 101–102.

12. *Ibid.,* p. 147.

13. A. W. Eddins, "Brazos Bottom Philosophy," *Publications of the Texas Folk Lore Society,* No. II, 1923, edited by J. Frank Dobie. Austin, Texas: Texas Folk-Lore Society, pp. 50–51.

14. John Dollard, *Caste and Class in Southern Town* (New Haven, 1937), p. 308.

POETS AND PHILOSOPHERS REMEMBER STORIES

Meditations on African American Lore

There are two lasting gifts we can give our children—one is roots, the other is wings. —ANONYMOUS

Folklore is the boiled-down juice of human living. It does not belong to any special time, place, nor people. No country is so primitive that it has no lore, and no country has yet become so civilized that no folklore is being made within its boundaries.

ZORA NEALE HURSTON, *Go Gator and Muddy the Water: Writings by Zora Neale Hurston from the Federal Writers' Project* (New York: W. W. Norton, 1999), 69

We have been exiled in our own land and, as for our efforts at writing, we have been little better than silent because we have not been cunning. I find this rather astounding because I feel that Negro American folklore is very powerful, wonderful, and universal. And it became so by expressing a people who were assertive, eclectic, and irreverent before all the oral and written literature that came within its grasp. It took what it needed to express its sense of life and rejected what it could not use.

What we've achieved in folklore has seldom been achieved in the novel, the short story, or poetry. In the folklore we tell what Negro experience really is. We back away from the chaos of experience and from ourselves, and we depict the humor as well as the horror of living. We project Negro life in a metaphysical perspective and we have seen it with a complexity of vision that seldom gets into our writing.

RALPH ELLISON, "A Very Stern Discipline," *Harper's*, March 1967, 80.

I use folklore in my work not because I am Negro, but because writers like Eliot and Joyce made me conscious of the literary value of my folk inheritance. My cultural background, like that of most Americans, is dual (my middle name, sadly enough, is Waldo).

I knew the trickster Ulysses just as early as I knew the wily rabbit of Negro American lore, and I could easily imagine myself a pint-sized Ulysses but hardly a rabbit, no matter how human and resourceful or Negro. . . .

My point is that the Negro American writer is also an heir of the human experience which is literature, and this might well be more important to him than his living folk tradition. For me, at least, in the discontinuous, swiftly changing and diverse American culture, the stability of the Negro American folk tradition became precious as a result of an act of literary discovery.

RALPH ELLISON, "Change the Joke and Slip the Yoke," in
Shadow and Act (New York: Random House, 1964), 58

There are things that I try to incorporate into my fiction that are directly and deliberately related to what I regard as the major characteristics of Black art, wherever it is. One of which is the ability to be both print and oral literature: to combine those two aspects so that the stories can be read in silence, of course, but one should be able to hear them as well. It should try deliberately to make you stand up and make you feel something profoundly in the same way that a Black preacher requires his congregation to speak, to join him in the sermon, to behave in a certain way, to stand up and to weep and to cry and to accede or to change and to modify—to expand on the sermon that is being delivered.

TONI MORRISON, "Rootedness: The Ancestor as Foundation," in
Black Women Writers (1950–1980): A Critical Evaluation, ed. Mari
Evans (New York: Anchor Press, Doubleday, 1984), 340–41

A little boy read numerous stories in his children's books about various life and death struggles between a man and a lion. But no matter how ferociously the lion fought, each time the man emerged victorious. This puzzled the boy, so he asked his father, "Why is it, Daddy, that in all these stories the man always beats the lion, when everybody knows that the lion is the toughest cat in all the jungle?"

The father answered, "Son, these stories will always end that way until the lion learns how to write."

JOHN OLIVER, "Black Man's Burden," in *From My People: 400 Years of African American Folklore,* ed. Daryl Cumber Dance (New York: W. W. Norton, 2002), xxxiv

After his father died, and his mother went off to the north to find work, it was the old woman, pious and accepting, who had told him the old stories, raised him in the Church, and interpreted for him the ways of the world. He remembered her story of how God had put two boxes into the world, one big and the other small. The first Negro and the first white man had seen the boxes at the same time and run towards them, but the Negro arrived first and greedily appropriated for himself the larger box. Unfortunately this box contained a plough, a hoe, a cop-axe, and a mule, while the smaller box contained a pen, paper, and a ledger book. "An' thass why," the old woman would conclude, her face serious, "the Nigger been aworkin' evah since, an' the white man he reckon up the crop."

MIKE THELWELL, "Bright an' Mownin' Star," *The Massachusetts Review* 8 (1966), 6–7

The key to a tale is to be found in who tells it.

JAMES BALDWIN, *No Name in the Street* (New York: Random House, 1972), 45

People will argue that this anecdote has not been verified. But the fact that it has taken shape and survived through the years is an unmistakable indication that it addresses a tension, explicit or latent, but real. Its persistence underscores the fact that the black world subscribes to it. In other words, when a story survives in folklore, it expresses in some way a region of the "local soul."

FRANTZ FANON, *Black Skin, White Masks*, trans. Richard Philcox (New York: Grove Press, 2008), 45–46

These narratives from the southern states instruct us that talk functions in African American communities . . . as a means of having fun, getting serious, establishing credibility and consensus, securing identity, negotiating survival, keeping hope alive, suffering and celebrating the power language bestows.

JOHN EDGAR WIDEMAN, Foreword, Zora Neale Hurston, *Every Tongue Got to Confess* (New York: HarperCollins, 2002), xx

My lasting memories of my grandmother are of her telling me stories. I know that she told folktales and fairy tales from many parts of the world. I cried when she told Andersen's "Little Match Girl"—it was so beautiful and so sad. But my favorites, and I'm sure they were hers as well, were the Brer Rabbit stories. I howled with laughter

when Brer Rabbit asked the Tar Baby "and how does your symptoms seashuate?" . . .
Her mother had told her the stories and she told them to me with love and affection as
she sat in her favorite rocking chair in the middle of a large, old-fashioned kitchen. It
was a way for her to entertain me as she watched her cooking. . . . Small, helpless Brer
Rabbit always defeated his adversaries—the large animals—with his wit, humor, and
wisdom. In my smallness I related to the clever little hare who could always get out of
the most difficult situations with his sharp wit.

> AUGUSTA BAKER, Introduction, Julius Lester, *The Tales of Uncle Remus:*
> *The Adventures of Brer Rabbit* (New York: Dial Books, 1987), vii

It would be misleading, however, to leave the impression that all of the process of
writing was so solemn. For in fact there was a great deal of fun along the way. I knew
that I was composing a work of fiction, a work of literary art and one that would allow
me to take advantage of the novel's capacity for telling the truth while actually telling
a "lie," which is the Afro-American folk term for an improvised story. Having worked
in barbershops where that form of oral art flourished, I knew that I could draw upon
the rich culture of the folk tale as well as that of the novel, and that being uncertain of
my skill I would have to improvise upon my materials in the manner of a jazz musician
putting a musical theme through a wild star-burst of metamorphosis.

> RALPH ELLISON, *Invisible Man* (New York: Random House, 1952), xxii

Brer Wolf am might cunnin',
Brer Fox am mighty sly,
Brer Terrapin an' Possum—kinder small;
Brer Lion's mighty vicious,
Brer B'ar he's sorter 'spicious,
Brer Rabbit, you's de cutes' of 'em all.

> JAMES WELDON JOHNSON, *Fifty Years and*
> *Other Poems* (Boston: Cornhill, 1917), 7

My grandmother used to tell me Annancy stories every night. All the stories had songs
and she would sing a song over and over again, until I knew it and fell asleep singing

it to myself. These were my favorite lullabies. At school my friends and I would swap Annancy stories during recess and lunch time, but before telling a story, each child had to mash (kill) an ant, or else something terrible might happen to her mother: the poor woman might turn into a bankra-basket!

WALTER JEKYLL, ed., *Jamaican Song and Story: Annancy Stories, Digging Sings, Ring Tunes, and Dancing Tunes* (Mineola, NY: Dover, 1966), ix

My aunt Anna, my mother's sister, lived with us. She was as devoted to us children as was my mother herself, and we were equally devoted to her in return. She taught us our lessons while we were little. She and my mother used to entertain us by the hour with tales of life on the Georgia plantations, of hunting fox, deer, and wildcat; of the long-tailed driving horses, Boone and Crockett, and of the riding horses, one of which was named Buena Vista in a fit of patriotic exaltation during the Mexican War; and of the queer goings-on in the Negro quarters. She knew all the "Bre'r Rabbit" stories, and I was brought up on them. One of my uncles, Robert Roosevelt, was much struck with them, and took them down from her dictation, publishing them in *Harper's*, where they fell flat. This was a good many years before a genius arose who in "Uncle Remus" made the stories immortal.

THEODORE ROOSEVELT, *An Autobiography* (New York: Macmillan, 1913), 15

My mom died suddenly a few years back, and it kind of sent me on this journey of wanting to understand how I got to this place of writing all of these books and winning awards, and being recognized as "A Writer." You know, who got me here? How did I get here, given the various circumstances of my life? Once my mom died, I realized the people I loved were quickly becoming ancestors. They were dying, they were getting old, they were losing memory. And with them went these stories. Growing up African American, in a culture that's steeped in the tradition of telling stories orally, I knew that I had to speak to the people. I had to hear these stories.

JACQUELINE WOODSON, http:blogs.wsj.com/speakeasy/2014/11/21/
author-jacqueline-woodson-on-memories-verse-and-the-national-book-award/

In their opposing attitudes towards roots my father and my great-uncle made me aware of a conflict in which every educated American Negro, and some who are not educated, must somehow take sides. By implication at least, one group advocates embracing the riches of the folk heritage; their opposites demand a clean break with the past and all it represents. Had I not gone home summers and hobnobbed with folk-type Negroes, I would have finished college without knowing that any Negro other than Paul Laurence Dunbar ever wrote a poem. I would have come out imagining that the story of the Negro could be told in two short paragraphs: a statement about jungle people in Africa and an equally brief account of the slavery issue in American history. The reserves of human vitality that enabled the race to survive the worst of both these experiences while at the same time making contributions to western culture remained a dark secret with my teachers, if they considered the matter at all. I was given no inkling by them, and my white classmates who needed to know such things as much as I did if we were to maintain a healthy regard for each other, in the future, were similarly denied.

ARNA BONTEMPS, "Why I Returned," in *The Old South: "A Summer Tragedy" and Other Stories of the Thirties* (New York: Dodd, Mead, 1973), 73

As yet, the Negroes themselves do not fully appreciate these old slave songs. The educated classes are rather ashamed of them and prefer to sing hymns from books. This feeling is natural: they are still too close to the conditions under which the songs were produced: but the day will come when this slave music will be the most treasured heritage of the American Negro.

JAMES WELDON JOHNSON, *The Autobiography of an Ex–Colored Man* (Boston: Sherman, French & Co., 1912), 178

That old spontaneity out of which formerly there gushed an outpouring of the kind of stories which made Joel Chandler Harris famous seems to be lacking. There is a reticence and apology about telling stories of Rabbit and Fox which suggest sophistication and even shame. Only among children do these stories develop freely.

ARTHUR HUFF FAUSET, "Negro Folk Tales from the South (Alabama, Mississippi, Louisiana)," *Journal of American Folk-Lore* 40 (1927), 213

I heard the Dahomeyans singing. Instantly the idea flashed into my mind: "It is a heritage." . . . The Dahomeyan sings the music of his native Africa; the American negro spends this silver heritage of melody, but adds to it the bitter ring of grief for wrongs and adversities which only he has known. . . . If my hypothesis be correct, the man who asks where the negro got all those strange tunes of his songs is answered. They have been handed down to him from the matted jungles and sunburned deserts of Africa, from the reed huts of the Nile.

PAUL LAURENCE DUNBAR, *In His Own Voice: Dramatic and Other Uncollected Works* (Columbus: Ohio State University Press, 2002), 184

Finally, I acknowledge immense debt to the griots of Africa—where today it is rightly said that when a griot dies, it is as if a library has burned to the ground. The griots symbolize how all human ancestry goes back to some place, and some time, when there was no writing. Then, the memories and the mouths of ancient elders was the only way that early histories of mankind got passed along . . . for all of us today to know who we are.

ALEX HALEY, Acknowledgments, *Roots* (New York: Vanguard, 1974), viii

Storytelling—not just me telling stories, but exchanging them, learning other people's stories—is a way for me to get inside a culture. How people listen to my stories, too, is as important as the stories I collect from others; the questions they ask are clues to their thoughts, their culture . . . Storytelling, more than anything else, is a dialogue, and through dialogue you can discover what needs to be told. Minorities, especially, need to tell their stories, because if they're not heard, they're not part of the national consciousness. They don't exist.

KWAME DAWES, quoted in Pamela Petro, *Sitting Up with the Dead: A Storied Journey through the American South* (New York: HarperCollins, Flamingo, 2001), 133

The history of the American Negro is a most intimate part of American History. Through the very process of slavery came the building of the United States. Negro folklore, evolving within a larger culture which regarded it as inferior, was an especially courageous expression. It announced the Negro's willingness to trust his own experience, his own sensibilities as to the definition of reality, rather than allow his masters to define crucial matters for him. His experience is that of America and the West, and is as rich a body of experience as one would find anywhere. We can view it narrowly as something exotic, folksy, or "low down" or we may identify ourselves with it and recognize it as an important segment of the larger American experience—not lying at the bottom of it, but intertwined, diffused in its very texture.

RALPH ELLISON, "The Art of Fiction," *Paris Review* 8 (1955), 54

The need is great to perfect the art of storytelling, to keep alive this fund of stories that forms a body of learning of black culture and a tradition that is, truly, American. It is imperative to pass these gifts on as parts of a living heritage to those who are yet to come, for these will be the armor with which a seeker after truth may find roots, beauty, and a meaning to life. . . . "Please tell us a story from the book that's inside you."

I have said that these songs passed through a period when the front ranks of the Negro race would have been willing to let them die. Immediately following Emancipation those ranks revolted against everything connected with slavery, and among those things were the Spirituals. It became a sign of not being progressive or educated to sing them. This was a natural reaction, but, nevertheless, a sadly foolish one. It was left for the older generation to keep them alive by singing them at prayer meetings, class meetings, experience meetings, and revivals. . . . Today this is all changed. There is hardly a choir among the largest and richest colored churches that does not make a specialty of singing the Spirituals. This reawakening of the Negro to the value and beauty of the Spirituals was the beginning of an entirely new phase of race consciousness. It marked a change in the attitude of the Negro himself toward his own art material; the turning of his gaze inward upon his own cultural resource.

JAMES WELDON JOHNSON AND J. ROSAMOND JOHNSON, *The Book of American Negro Spirituals* (New York: Viking, 1954), 49

By ascribing actions to semi-mythical actors, Negroes were able to overcome the external and internal censorship that their hostile surroundings imposed upon them. The white master could believe that the rabbit stories his slaves told were mere figments of a childish imagination, that they were primarily humorous anecdotes depicting the "roaring comedy of animal life." Blacks knew better. The trickster's exploits, which overturned the neat hierarchy of the world in which he was forced to live, became their exploits; the justice he achieved, their justice; the strategies he employed, their strategies. From his adventures they obtained relief; from his triumphs they learned hope.

LAWRENCE W. LEVINE, *Black Culture and Black Consciousness: Afro-American Folk Thought from Slavery to Freedom* (Oxford: Oxford University Press, 1977), 113–14

Through their folklore, black slaves affirmed their humanity and left a lasting imprint on American culture. No study of the institutional aspects of American slavery can be complete, nor can the larger dimensions of slave personality and style be adequately explored, as long as historians continue to avoid the realm in which, as Du Bois has said, "the soul of the black slave spoke to man."

STERLING STUCKEY, "Through the Prism of Folklore: The Black Ethos in Slavery," in *Going through the Storm: The Influence of African American Art in History* (New York: Oxford University Press, 1994), 17

Close reading, so called, can become a bad habit, possibly a vice, where simple appreciation is concerned, but never does it start more quarrels than when the folk are involved. So let it be said quickly that Negro folklore, like almost any other kind, can be traced in its origins to a dim past when it drew on a common cultural heritage, which most of the folk of the world appear to have shared. In any case, the telling of tales is a time honored custom in Africa. By what steps the FABLES OF AESOP (Ethiop) became the animal stories of West Africa, of the West Indies, and of the slave states of the U.S.A. is a lively question but not to the point here. What does concern us is that the slaves brought with them to the New World their ancient habit of story telling as pastime, together with a rich bestiary.

ARNA BONTEMPS, Introduction, *Book of Negro Folklore* (New York: Dodd, Mead, 1958), viii

This book has to do with my early beginning. For it starts way back when, with my being the kind of child I was. I was the child who listened closely to grown-up women talking. To this day, I remember how my grandmother, my aunts and great-aunts and elder cousins looked when they talked. I've never forgotten how they moved their hands and gestured with their arms. The sounds of their voices and much of what they said stays with me.

When I was a child, I heard stories told by women. My mother told me the first tale I remember hearing. I didn't know it was a whimsy, a playful fancy, made upon the spot to comfort me.

. . . We'd sip hot cider, sassafras tea, and listen in wonder to the household tales. Of course, they were gentle reminders about nature's power, about ourselves in the world, where we came from, and who we were. I knew that one day I would make a book all about women like my mother, talkers, those tale tellers, and about whom tales were told.

VIRGINIA HAMILTON, *Her Stories: African American Folktales, Fairy Tales, and True Tales* (New York: Blue Sky Press, 1995), 105, 109

What the old men enjoyed most was telling jokes and stories. They told stories all the time, morning, noon and night, they were at it constantly. There were so many stories that it was often difficult to keep track of them, you got so muddled up. I always pretended to be listening, but to be honest, by the end it was all whirling round in my head. There were three or four African elders at Ariosa. There was a difference between the Africans and the Creoles. The various Africans understood each other, but the Creoles hardly ever understood the Africans. . . . I got on all right with them because I spent my whole life listening to them. They were fond of me, too.

ESTEBAN MONTEJO, *The Autobiography of a Runaway Slave* (London: Macmillan, 1968), 181

These stories are true, but one I am convinced is a fabrication because I never saw such a thing, and that is that some Negroes committed suicide. Before, when the Indians were in Cuba, suicide did happen. They did not want to become Christians, and they hanged themselves from trees. But the Negroes did not do that, they escaped by flying. They flew through the sky and returned to their own lands. The Musundi Congolese were the ones that flew the most; they disappeared by means of witchcraft. They did the same as the Canary Island witches, but without making a sound. There are those who say the Negroes threw themselves into rivers. This is untrue. The truth is they fastened a chain to their waists which was full of magic. That was where their power came from. I know all this intimately, and it is true beyond doubt.

ESTEBAN MONTEJO, *The Autobiography of a Runaway Slave* (London: Macmillan, 1968), 63–64

It is said that the first Africans upon the slave ships headed to the Americas sensed the coming of a great and lasting catastrophe. They knew that they needed something to protect and fortify them from the coming centuries of servitude and oppression, so they sent out an exalted wail beseeching God's mercy. God looked down on them and saw that they had nothing. They were naked and in chains. God, in His wisdom, took the very sound of their lamentation and turned it into their shield and their weapon and today we call that sound music. It is those majestic wails, that cry of despair, that music, in its ever-changing forms, that has nourished our people through the centuries.

ATTRIBUTED TO "SLEEPY WILLIE" BY HORACE MUNGIN, *The Devil Beats His Wife and Other Stories from the Lowcountry* (N.p.: n.p., 2004), viii

What would you think of whole groups of Negroes who had never heard of Brer Rabbit? Or of stories about Monkey and Baboon? Elephant, and all the other animals? Yet if you approach a Negro of Nova Scotia with the question, "Do you know the Brer Rabbit stories?" he is likely to look at you in wonderment, or even with a blank countenance, and shake his head and say, "Never heard any—what are they like?" Sometimes, after you have told him an Uncle Remus story, his face will light up a little, and he will say, "Oh, yes. I read one like that a long time ago in the Halifax Herald." After recovering from your chagrin, you say to him, "Don't you tell these stories around the fire?" He looks at you in astonishment and says, "Lord no, man, I never hears of 'em."

ARTHUR HUFF FAUSET, *Folklore from Nova Scotia* (New York: The American Folk-lore Society, G.E. Stechert, 1931), vii

"You know what I like about storytelling, are the unlimited possibilities," he asked-and-answered. "There aren't any rules. With folk music there are rules, unspoken ones. You can bend them pretty far, but once you break them you're in another genre. . . . Storytelling is different. You don't want to lie, if it's historical, you want to keep it true at the core, if you know what I mean, but you can be any first person character from the past that you like. I find that really liberating."

DAVID HOLT, quoted in Pamela Petro, *Sitting Up with the Dead: A Storied Journey through the American South* (New York: HarperCollins, Flamingo, 2001), 95

He likes the blacks' tales? That's natural. Who among us at his age didn't listen to them with pleasure? But for the rest, let's not kid ourselves. There is in these tales, aside from the dramatic interest, a malice that is often quite refined.

ALFRED MERCIER, *L'Habitation Saint-Ybars, ou Maîtres et Esclaves en Louisiane, récit social* (New Orleans: Imprimerie Franco-américaine, 1881), 109

Went to Florida and worked six months, back to New York for four months, weighed down by the thought that practically nothing had been done in Negro folklore when the greatest cultural wealth on the continent was disappearing without the world ever realizing that it had ever been. Money was found and I returned to the south and spent three years 1928–1931 studying and collecting (a) Negro folk tales (b) Negro secular songs (c) Religious expressions (d) Hoodoo practices.

> ZORA NEALE HURSTON, October 12, 1934, letter to Thomas E. Jones, President, Fisk University, in Carla Kaplan, *Zora Neale Hurston: A Life in Letters* (New York: Random House, Anchor, 2007), 315

We the darker ones come even now not altogether empty-handed: there are to-day no truer exponents of the pure human spirit of the Declaration of Independence than the American Negroes; there is no true American music but the wild sweet melodies of the Negro slave; the American fairy tales and folk-lore are Indian and African; and, all in all, we black men seem the sole oasis of simple faith and reverence in a dusty desert of dollars and smartness.

> W. E. B. DU BOIS, *The Souls of Black Folks* (Oxford: Oxford University Press, 2007), 7

Your country? How came it yours? Before the Pilgrims landed we were here. Here we have brought our three gifts and mingled them with yours: a gift of story and song— soft, stirring melody in an ill-harmonized and unmelodious land; the gift of sweat and brawn to beat back the wilderness, conquer the soil, and lay the foundations of this vast economic empire two hundred years earlier than your weak hands could have done it; the third, a gift of the Spirit. Around us the history of the land has centred for thrice a hundred years; out of the nation's heart we have called all that was best to throttle and subdue all that was worst; fire and blood, prayer and sacrifice, have billowed over this people, and they have found peace only in the altars of the God of Right. Nor has our gift of the Spirit been merely passive. Actively we have woven ourselves with the very warp and woof of this nation,—we fought their battles, shared their sorrow, mingled our blood with theirs, and generation after generation have pleaded with a headstrong, careless people to despise not Justice, Mercy, and Truth, lest the nation be smitten with a curse. Our song, our toil, our cheer, and warning have been given to this nation in blood-brotherhood. Are not these gifts worth the giving? Is not this work and striving? Would America have been America without her Negro people?

> W. E. B. DU BOIS, *The Souls of Black Folks* (Oxford: Oxford University Press, 2007), 167

Now for the great historic civilizations of Asia and Europe, it has been contended by some theorists that the mythopoeic imagination has been most profoundly stirred and has found its richest expression at three historic periods and in three specific areas, India, Greece, and Christian Europe of the Middle Ages. . . . On the basis of data obtained in the nineteenth and twentieth centuries concerning the unwritten literatures of aboriginal peoples, it is now quite clear that at certain points in their history, the mythopoeic imagination had been as vitally stirred and had expressed itself among them as richly and voluminously as was ever the case in Greece, India, and Christian medieval Europe.

> PAUL RADIN, Introduction, *African Folktales* (Princeton,
> NJ: Princeton University Press, 1952), 3

The cultural memory inscribed in the hegemonial "writing" of Western documents, imperial monuments, colonial rituals, trade records, and individual—fictional or autobiographical—recollections have as a general rule not contained the "words" of colonial or enslaved subjects; their visceral experiences, their memories of oppression and resistances have become left "behind" by Western historiography, prose, and poetry. Those "obscurities" now, in keeping with a continuing history of social and economic decolonization and cultural reorientation, need to be displaced by way of artistic recuperation of the colonial and imperial past from the point of view of those previously muted subjects. This recuperation is by necessity an artistic act and challenge, since in most cases, "chronicles" of the dates and facts of colonization—coherently figured from that subaltern perspective—do not exist. The pervasive ellipses of Western historiography will only be pointed out and filled by way of the (literary) imagination.

> SABINE BROCK, *White Amnesia—Black Memory? American
> Women's Writing and History* (Frankfurt: Peter Lang, 1999), 24

Though some writers have stressed European and Indian influences in Negro tales, there is little question of the retention of Africanisms. Materials of this kind are particularly susceptible to objective analysis, because of the many independent components which render assumptions of correspondence almost indisputable. A good example of how this operates is to be seen in the case of what is perhaps the best-known Negro story, *The Tar Baby*. . . .

The story is so characteristic of West Africa, that Africanists have themselves long used Joel Chandler Harris's version of this Negro tale from the United States as a point of comparative reference. There are some who maintain that the tale, as found both in this country and in Africa, originated in India; this is a matter of specialized and somewhat acrid controversy, which is so far from settled that it is still in the realm of conjecture and need not concern us here. The fact that such a complex series of incidents should have been combined into this plot sequence, both among African and among New World Negroes, brings the inescapable conclusion that, whatever its place of absolute origin, the tale as found in the New World represents a part of the cultural baggage brought by Africans to this hemisphere.

MELVILLE J. HERSKOVITS, *The Myth of the Negro Past* (Boston: Beacon Press, 1958), 272–73

If America is to grow as a nation built upon solid, shared, creolized "spiritual soil," Americans must open themselves to the African elements of the national culture, elements that have long been repressed in official histories. With such an opening, the nation might be able to draw in full upon Afro-Creole "gifts of the spirit" to accompany gifts of sweat, milk, blood, and knowledge that have long been accepted or appropriated without reservation. Such acknowledgment, such opening, must be accompanied by its double, meaningful acknowledgment of the haunting, warped, recurrently violent modes of being to which we all were bound in the founding of America.

KEITH CARTWRIGHT, *Reading Africa into American Literature: Epics, Fables, and Gothic Tales* (Lexington: University Press of Kentucky, 2002), 228

In their African setting these tales are called upon not just to deliver a specific message, but to initiate talk about that message. In other words, unlike most of the stories we are accustomed to encountering in books, these come from communities that continue to use stories as ways of pulling apart current subjects and piecing them together again, both through the story itself and . . . through the discussion and arguments that story engenders.

It is precisely the way that the storyteller "grabs your shirt" and thrusts you into the tale that isn't there in the folktales we read in literary collections such as those of the Brothers Grimm, where what we find on the whole is a record of stories as remembered by old people who no longer tell them actively. In contrast, the African stories here were recorded while still flourishing in social and cultural environments in which the artful employment of speech in all dimensions of community is encouraged and applauded. . . . For as the Mandingo say at the beginning of a story: "A really unique story has no end."

ROGER ABRAHAMS, *African Folktales* (New York: Random House, Pantheon Books, 1983), 10–14

We sat on the bank of the creek and ate our lunch. Afterward Dottle and Johno told stories, wonderful stories in which animals talk, and there are haunted houses and ghosts and demons, and old black preachers who believe in heaven and hell.

They always started off the same way. Dottle would say to Johno, "Mr. Bones, be seated."

Though I have heard some of these stories many, many times, Dottle and Johno never tell them exactly the same. They change their gestures; they vary their facial expressions and the pitch of their voices.

Dottle almost always tells the story about the black man who goes in a store in a small town in the South and asks for Muriel cigars. The white man who owns the store says (and here Johno becomes an outraged Southern white man), "Nigger, what's the matter with you? Don't you see that picture of that beautiful white woman on the front of this box? When you ask for them cigars, you say *Miss* Muriel cigars!"

ANN PETRY, *Miss Muriel and Other Stories* (New York: Houghton Mifflin, 1945), 33–34

Usually I think of myself as a storyteller. I would like for readers to look at a person telling the story from the first person point of view as someone actually telling them a story at the time. But when you are dealing with the omniscient point of view, you are not being told a story; you are reading a story, I feel. Now maybe what I need to do is sit in a chair on a stage and just tell people stories rather than try to write them. I wish I could do that. I wish I could be paid just to sit around and tell stories, and forget the writing stuff. But, unfortunately, I am a writer, and I must communicate with the written word.

JOHN LOWE, ed., *Conversations with Ernest Gaines* (Jackson: University of Mississippi, 1995), 88

In the books, there's always a happily ever after.
The ugly duckling grows into a swan, Pinocchio
becomes a boy.
The witch gets chucked into the oven by Gretel,
the Selfish Giant goes to heaven.
Even Winnie the Pooh seems to always get his honey.
Little Red Riding Hood's grandmother is freed
from the belly of the wolf.

When my sister reads to me, I wait for the moment
when the story moves faster—toward the happy ending
that I know is coming.

JACQUELINE WOODSON, *Brown Girl Dreaming* (New
York: Penguin, Nancy Paulsen Books, 2014), 207

SCIP: I come from wey de door is shet, an' I come to wey it still is closed. All I got is dreams, an' dey is drownded I ain' kin make my feelin's known. Laughin' ain' make no diff'ence now. God has overlooked me. I is not strong enuh I ain' kin make my feelin's known.

You axe me wuh I is an' I guh tell you. I is wuh I is. I isn't wuh I mought er been. To my lonesome self I ain' nothin' but a yellow bastard—augh, I ain' care—a yellow bastard wid no place—wid no place amongst de white folks an' a poorly place amongst de niggers.

De door is shet to me. Hemmed in on every side, I has nothin' but dreams. An' my thoughts is floatin' out, floatin' far above de tall tree tops, here an' dere, listenin' to de wind's soft tune above de tree tops an' de clouds. Across de stars dey wander for a lonely moment, an' den back again an' down, down, down into de mire. For de door is shet to me. Hemmed in, hemmed in on every side.

I ain' kin make my feelin's known, for I ain' nothin'—nothin' but a yellow bastard to white an' black alike. I is wuh I is—nothin' but a yellow bastard—an' I ain' kin make my feelin's known. Laugh, I ain' care.

TAD: I hear wuh you say. I ain' guy laugh an' I ain' guy cry. I ain' know wuh you is.

SCIP: Let's we finish move dis fertilizer.

E. C. L. ADAMS, *Nigger to Nigger* (London: Scribner's, 1928), 34–35

I was born in the South "fo' de wah," and as my parents were slave holders, I grew up among the negroes. To me they seemed vastly more interesting and more human than white folks. . . .

It was in . . . negro cabins that I first heard many of the folk-lore stories published by Joel Chandler Harris, and a lot more besides. . . . And it was in the long corn rows along the bottoms of the French-broad river that I heard from one of the old negroes these and many other stories that have now partly or entirely escaped my memory.

It is not strange that, under the circumstances, slavery seemed to me a natural and happy state of human existence.

Then came the civil war and after that the former slaves were taken in hand by political organizations and by the fishers in the muddy waters of the times. They were inveigled away from their former homes and friends, and finally left to the waves and winds of fate like so much flotsam and jetsam of the war.

Meanwhile I had been sent to school away from home. . . . I returned home for a short visit, and on inquiring about our former slaves I heard that Aunt Ellen lived about eight miles away, and that she had sent word to me to be sure to come to see her when I was at home for a visit. And of course I went.

I found Aunt Ellen in a state of poverty and wretchedness that went to my heart. . . . And I told her what I thought, or supposed I thought, in some such words as these: "Aunt Ellen, you were a lot better off as a slave than you are now. . . ."

And this is what Aunt Ellen replied: "De Lawd bless yo' soul, chile, dat's a fact; hit's jes lak you ben a sayin'. I knows I had mo' to eat an' mo' to wear, an' a better house to live in, an' all o' dem things, an' you all was mighty good to me; an' I didn' have none o' dese here doctah's bills to pay. But Law', honey, atter all, dah's de feelin's!"

From that day to this I have had no more to say in favor of human slavery.

JOHN CASPER BRANNER, "A Mere Matter of the Feelings,"
How and Why Stories (New York: Henry Holt, 1921), 3–7

The Creole Storyteller is a fine example of this paradoxical situation: the master knows of his tales and allows him to tell them, and sometimes even listens to them himself, so the Storyteller must take care to use language that is opaque, devious—its significance broken up into a thousand sibylline fragments. His narrative turns around long digressions that are humorous, erotic, often even esoteric. His dialogue with his audience is unceasing, punctuated with onomatopoeias and sound effects intended not only to hold his listeners' attention but also to help camouflage any dangerously subversive content. . . . The Storyteller's object is almost *to obscure as he reveals.* To form and inform through the hypnotic power of the voice, the mystery of the spoken word.

PATRICK CHAMOISEAU, *Creole Folktales* (New York: New Press, 1994), xiii

It is only in his music, which Americans are able to admire because a protective sentimentality limits their understanding of it, that the Negro in America has been able to tell his story. It is a story which otherwise has yet to be told and which no American is prepared to hear. As is the inevitable result of things unsaid, we find ourselves until today oppressed with a dangerous and reverberating silence; and the story is told, compulsively, in symbols and signs, in hieroglyphs; it is revealed in Negro speech and in that of the white majority and in their different frames of reference.

JAMES BALDWIN, *Notes of a Native Son* (Boston: Beacon, 1955), 24

As a form that emerged from a fluid, improvisatory tradition, the African-American tale helped forge a simultaneous sense of racial solidarity and American identity. Usually, the tales were told to exclusively African-American audiences. These storytelling performances created a community of speech, interpretation, and response among the slaves and, later on, among freemen and women. Ironically, the dehumanizing conditions of slavery, its prohibitions against literacy, against African language and ritual, reinforced the communal values of the oral tradition. Variations on the old African animal stories and the new American tales of Jack the slave and his master fed what Sterling Brown calls the "abiding deep well of Negro folk experience." At the same time there was a progressive, to-be-continued feeling about many of the tales, which opened the potential for action implied by the call-and-response pattern.

JOHN F. CALLAHAN, *In the African-American Grain: The Pursuit of Voice in Twentieth-Century Black Fiction* (Urbana: University of Illinois Press, 1988), 26

There is . . . a culture of the Negro which is his and has been addressed to him; a culture which has, for good or ill, helped to clarify his consciousness and create emotional attitudes which are conducive to action. This culture has stemmed mainly from two sources (1) the Negro church; and (2) the folklore of the Negro people. . . .

It was, however, in a folklore moulded out of rigorous and inhuman conditions of life that the Negro achieved his most indigenous and complete expression. Blues, spirituals, and folktales recounted from mouth to mouth; the whispered words of a black mother to her black daughter on the ways of men; the confidential wisdom of a black father to his black son; the swapping of sex experiences on street corners from boy to boy in the deepest vernacular; work songs sung under blazing suns—all these formed the channels through which the racial wisdom flowed.

One would have thought that Negro writers in the last century of striving at expression would have continued and deepened this folk tradition, would have tried to create a more intimate and yet a more profoundly social system of artistic communication between them and their people. But that illusion that they could escape through individual achievement the harsh lot of their race swung Negro writers away from any such path. Two separate cultures sprang up; one for the Negro masses, unwritten and unrecognized; and the other for the sons and daughters of a rising Negro bourgeoisie, parasitic and mannered. . . .

In the absence of fixed and nourishing forms of culture, the Negro has a folklore which embodies the memories and hopes of his struggle for freedom. Not yet caught in paint or stone, and as yet but feebly depicted in the poem and novel, the Negroes' most powerful images of hope and despair still remain in the fluid state of daily speech. How many John Henrys have lived and died on the lips of these black people? How many mythical heroes in embryo have been allowed to perish for lack of husbanding by alert intelligence?

Negro folklore contains, in a measure that puts to shame more deliberate forms of Negro expression, the collective sense of Negro life in America. Let those who shy at the nationalist implications of Negro life look at this body of folk-lore, living and powerful, which rose out of a unified sense of common life, and a common fate. Here are those vital beginnings of a recognition of value in life as it is *lived,* a recognition that marks the emergence of a new culture in the shell of the old. And at the moment this process starts, at the moment when a people begin to realize *a meaning* in their suffering, the civilization that engenders that suffering is doomed.

RICHARD WRIGHT, "Blueprint for Negro Writing,"
New Challenge 11 (1937), 270–71

I find that if I am going to write something, I can very often tell where it comes from, in terms of both the traditions of the particular literary form and the traditions of the people around me. Someone should pay some attention to how the folk stories which are told about Negroes in one meeting might be told about Jews in another. There is a basic unity of the experience, despite all the other stuff. The whole problem about whether there is a Negro culture might be cleared up if we said that there were many idioms of American culture, including, certainly, a Negro idiom of American culture in the South. We can trace it in many, many ways. We can trace it in terms of speech idioms, in terms of manners, in terms of dress, in terms of cuisine, and so on. But it is American, and it has existed a long time. It has refinements and crudities. It has all the aspects of a cultural reality.

RALPH ELLISON, "Remarks at the Academy of Arts and Sciences Conference on the Negro American, 1965," in Abraham Chapman, ed. *New Black Voices* (New York: New American Library, 1972), 404

My thesis, which rests on an examination of folk songs and tales, is that slaves were able to fashion a life style and set of values—an ethos—which prevented them from being imprisoned altogether by the definitions which the larger society sought to impose. The ethos was an amalgam of Africanisms and New World elements which helped slaves, in Guy Johnson's words, "feel their way along the course of American slavery, enabling them to endure. . . ." As Sterling Brown, that wise student of Afro-American culture, has remarked, the values expressed in folklore acted as a "wellspring to which slaves" trapped in the wasteland of American slavery "could return in times of doubt to be refreshed." In short, I shall contend that the process of dehumanization was not nearly as pervasive as Stanley Elkins would have us believe; that a very large number of slaves, guided by this ethos, were able to maintain their essential humanity. I make this contention because folklore, in its natural setting, is, of, by and for those who create and respond to it, depending for its survival upon the accuracy with which it speaks to needs and reflects sentiments. I therefore consider it safe to assume that the attitudes of a very large number of slaves are represented by the themes of folklore.

STERLING STUCKEY, *Going through the Storm: The Influence of African American Art in History* (Oxford: Oxford University Press, 1994), 4

In order for a people to develop a highly political and revolutionary consciousness, they must hold a high regard for themselves. They must know that they came from *somewhere*, in order to believe themselves capable of going somewhere; they must have a past before they can create a future for themselves. A people need legends, heroes, myths. Deny them these and you have won half the battle against them.

The French needed legendary figures like Joan of Arc in order to develop a national consciousness, without which any revolution is impossible. So we black folk need Saint Harriet of the Eastern Shore. We must build a literature of heroes, myths, and legends. The lives of Harriet Tubman, Frederick Douglass, Nat Turner, Sojourner Truth, are as formidable as George Washington's, and are based on a much more substantial reality. Our people, young and old, need such heroes desperately. Slavemasters Washington and Jefferson do not belong to *our* children. We need our own myths and legends to regain our lost self-esteem, our regard for each other as people capable of working together to move the mountains that stand before us. We need such a heritage in order to really believe that we shall prevail.

JOHN OLIVER KILLENS, *Black Man's Burden*
(New York: Trident Press, 1965), 45–46

Silhouette illustration from *The Tree Named John* by John Sale (1929).

IMAGE GALLERY A
Tale-Telling Sites:
At Home and in Common Spaces

Improvisation is the hallmark of expressive culture, and the scenes that follow capture sites of storytelling, in parlors and on porches, at markets and in festive spaces. What Trudier Harris has called the "power of the porch" enabled the passing on of wisdom through stories, with "good narrators" and "good listeners" participating in an interactive process. Good old lies provided the provocation for talk, and these images give us a sense of where and how community building took place, not just through the story but also through the "talk" generated by it. The images gathered here offer a partial view of the protected spaces where tales and talk circulated.

Nineteenth-century printed illustrations based on line drawings, such as "Sabbath" and "Coon Hunt," were produced in great numbers for magazines and newspapers with particular political positions, audience expectations, and technical requirements. The illustrators themselves were largely middle-class white artists relying on generic ideas about blacks and their activities. Photography, by contrast, coming into its own just when African Americans had become free citizens, seemed to offer special opportunities for authentic representation of black subjects. Frederick Douglass, who wrote extensively about photography, described its practitioners as engaging in a "wild scramble," with the rapid growth of commercial studios eager to create cabinet cards, stereoviews, and postcards for a growing market. The majority of the twentieth-century images included here were produced for the Farm Security Administration, originally the Resettlement Administration, a federal program established in the 1930s to combat rural poverty as part of Franklin Delano Roosevelt's New Deal. As freelancers working for the FSA Information Division, FSA photographers produced images documenting the conditions of agricultural and industrial workers in rural areas of the American South and West. This rich resource offers detailed, if limited, visual information about life in the United States in the first half of the twentieth century.

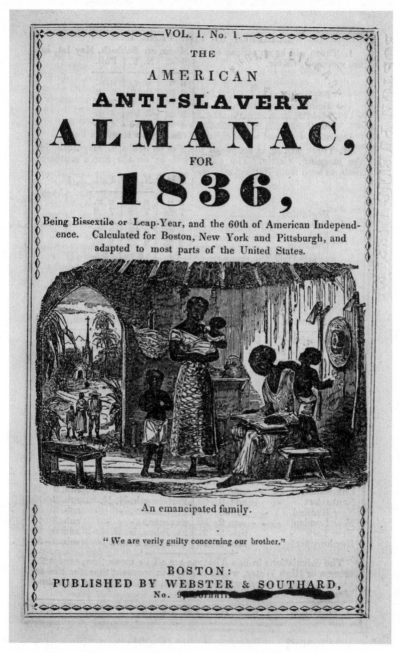

This cover illustration for *The American Anti-Slavery Almanac* shows an
emancipated family, with women and children reading from the Bible,
presumably a passage about Joseph and his brothers from Genesis 42:21, in
which the brothers reflect on their feelings of guilt about betraying Joseph.
The quotation might be relevant to the practice of slavery in general and
to the sense of remorse brought on by an inability to liberate enslaved
brethren. Reading from the Bible is a social practice that existed side by
side with storytelling, with sacred texts on the one hand and irreverent
improvisations on the other.

" *The Sabbath among Slaves.* "

Engravings by P. H. Reason were included in Henry Bibb's *Narrative of the Life and Adventures of Henry Bibb, an American Slave, Written by Himself*, 1849. "The Sabbath among Slaves" depicts various activities, ranging from napping to fistfights.

This scene of celebration on New Year's Day in Florida in 1886 shows the front porch as a festive site for making music for a multigenerational group. *Stereograph Cards, Prints and Photographs Division, Library of Congress.*

Plantation slave quarters in Port Royal, South Carolina (1862). *Civil War Glass Negative Collection, Prints and Photographs Division, Library of Congress.*

A Negro Cabin on the bank of the Tennessee.   [Page 542.]

In this illustration from a travelogue published in 1875, domestic animals roam the front yard to a cabin in the postbellum South, with the front porch as a site for what appears to be a woman with her grandchild. The woman's hand is raised in a classic gesture used in scenes of storytelling. *Edward King,* The Great South: A Record of Journeys *(Hartford, CT: American Publishing Company, 1875).*

This depiction of storytelling around the campfire after a hunt, published in *Harper's Weekly* in 1872, emphasizes the magnetic appeal of the tales—even the hounds seem to be hanging on the words of the teller.

THE 'COON HUNT—TELLING STORIES ROUND THE CAMP FIRE.—DRAWN BY R. N. BROOKE.—[SEE PAGE 974.]

Abolitionist Mary Livermore provided a detailed description of a "corn shucking" in her memoir about serving as a nurse during the Civil War, *My Story of the War*, published in 1897. Corn shucking bees signaled the beginning of the winter holiday season, when many enslaved plantation workers were permitted greater freedom than at other times of the year. Booker T. Washington remembered corn shucking as a festive event spanning a day and a night and attended by one or two hundred people, one of whom would lead the group in song.

Cabins at the Hermitage slave plantation in Savannah, Georgia, where slaves were raised for market. The homes were made of brick because there was a brickworks operation on the plantation (1903). *Stereograph Cards, Prints and Photographs Division, Library of Congress.*

Captioned "Cooking for the Family," this image was made in the latter part of the nineteenth century. *Robert N. Dennis Collection of Stereoscopic Views, The Miriam and Ira D. Wallach Division of Art, Prints and Photographs: Photography Collection, The New York Public Library.*

A log cabin with a covered porch is home to the women and children depicted (1890). *Yale Collection of American Literature, Beinecke Rare Book and Manuscript Library.*

The family of an African American lawyer gathers on the front porch of their home in Atlanta, Georgia (1899). *African American Photographs Assembled for 1900 Paris Exposition, Prints and Photographs Division Washington, Library of Congress.*

SLAVE QUARTER AT ROSEMOUNT

SLAVE CABIN AT THORN HILL

Carl Carmer's 1934 novel, *Stars Fell on Alabama,* illustrated by Cyrus Baldridge, was an unexpected bestseller. "Mostly a true book with some stretchers," it represented life in Alabama by blending social realism with folklore and enchantment, and with candid depictions of Southern racism.

A family gathers on the front porch of the Good Hope plantation in Mississippi (1939). *Farm Security Administration, Prints and Photographs Division, Library of Congress.*

An African American family poses on the front porch of their home on land near Wadesboro, North Carolina (1938). *Farm Security Administration, Prints and Photographs Division, Library of Congress.*

Nolan Pettway and some of his family members on their front porch in Gees Bend, Alabama (1939). *Farm Security Administration, Prints and Photographs Division, Library of Congress.*

A domestic scene from a tenant home on the Marcella plantation in Mileston, Mississippi (1939). *Farm Security Administration, Prints and Photographs Division, Library of Congress.*

A family on the porch of their home in Caswell, North Carolina (1940). *Farm Security Administration, Prints and Photographs Division, Library of Congress.*

Agricultural workers at a migratory labor camp in Florida on their improvised porch in front of a metal shelter (1941). *Farm Security Administration, Prints and Photographs Division, Library of Congress.*

A store near a cotton plantation in Mississippi where a porch provides a social space for men. Photographed by Marion Post Wolcott. *Farm Security Administration, Prints and Photographs Division, Library of Congress.*

A group of berry pickers near Independence, Louisiana, assemble around a stove to keep warm on a chilly day (1939). *Farm Security Administration, Prints and Photographs Division, Library of Congress.*

Rocks support the floor of a porch and unfinished timbers are used as pillars for this country store. Photographed by Dorothea Lange in Gordonton, North Carolina, in 1939. Ads for cigarettes, Coca-Cola, and scotch are reminders that the porch of the store is a site for leisure activities. *Farm Security Administration, Prints and Photographs Division, Library of Congress.*

Professional storyteller Liliane Louis tells Haitian folktales at a festival in Miami, Florida, in 1988. *State Archives of Florida / Saltzman.*

Augusta Braxston Baker, head of children's services at the New York Public Library from 1961 to 1974, began each storytelling session by lighting a candle and finished with one of the children blowing it out. *Photographed by Alexander Alland.*

The trio of men on the porch creates a conversational space animated further by the small dog at their feet and the child near the entrance to a store in Jeanerette, Louisiana, in 1938. *Farm Security Administration, Prints and Photographs Division, Library of Congress.*

IMAGE GALLERY B

Tale-Telling Sites: Places of Labor

Images showing scenes of labor cannot mask the stamina required to carry on, even when they show unclouded blue skies and verdant fields. In the interstices, the pauses that marked a respite from exertions, there was often time for conversational exchange, sometimes in the form of story. Scip and Tad, in E. C. L. Adams's *Nigger to Nigger*, for example, create poetry whenever they take a break, telling stories and expressing their innermost thoughts to each other.

Slaves working the sweet potato fields on a southern plantation make the work look effortless and serene, although all of the tasks involved required repetitive labors under what was often a blazing summer sun (1862). *Gladstone Collection of African American Photographs, Prints and Photographs Division, Library of Congress.*

Women work while a suited figure oversees their labors in a cotton field on the Retreat Plantation in Port Royal Island, South Carolina, in the 1860s. *Stereograph Cards, Prints and Photographs Division, Library of Congress.*

Agricultural workers take a break from their labors as a child playfully peeks out from a barrel that has been turned into a plaything (1868–1900). *Robert N. Dennis Collection of Stereoscopic Views, The Miriam and Ira D. Wallach Division of Art, Prints and Photographs: Photography Collection, The New York Public Library.*

Captioned "We'se done all dis's Mornin,'" this photograph is a heartbreaking depiction of youthful pride in carrying out labors (1868–1900; published 1905). *Robert N. Dennis Collection of Stereoscopic Views, The Miriam and Ira D. Wallach Division of Art, Prints and Photographs: Photography Collection, The New York Public Library.*

A well-dressed couple, most likely the owner of the plantation and his wife, stand before fields populated by agricultural workers, whose labors will produce the bales of cotton loaded on the wagon to be taken to market (1884). *Popular Graphic Arts, Prints and Photographs Division, Library of Congress.*

The cover illustration for Edward Clarkson Leverett Adams's *Nigger to Nigger* (1928) shows Scip and Tad in conversation, anticipating the exchanges that constitute the bulk of the sketches in the book.

The photographer Ben Shahn captured this scene of workers in Arkansas waiting for transport to the cotton fields. Note the size of the sacks slung over arms and shoulders (1941). *Farm Security Administration, Prints and Photographs Division, Library of Congress, LC-DIG-fsa-8a16196.*

Richard Wright's *12 Million Black Voices* included these two photographs showing well-dressed agricultural workers chopping cotton and picking it (circa 1930s; published in 1941).

Jacob Lawrence's *The Migration of the Negro* (1940–41) documented the flight of African Americans in the 1930s from the rural South to the industrial North in search of jobs and homes. In this third of sixty panels, the pyramid of human figures takes its inspiration from a flock of migratory birds. *The Phillips Collection, Washington, D.C. © 2017 The Jacob and Gwendolyn Knight Lawrence Foundation, Seattle / Artists Rights Society (ARS), New York.*

Allyn Cox (1896–1982) designed three corridors on the first floor of the U.S. Capitol building and painted wall and ceiling murals that depict portraits, historical scenes, and maps. Among those he designed was this scene of picking cotton in the postbellum era, one that creates an idyllic rural scene without any signs of the massive discomfort and pain of the labor involved. This painting was completed by EverGreene Painting Studios in 1993–1994. *Architect of the Capitol.*

SHARECROPPERS

A man and a mule are captured in Dorothea Lange's photograph of 1937. The sharecropper has one mule and the land he can cultivate with the plow. As part of the postbellum agrarian reform, slaves had been promised forty acres and a mule by Union general William T. Sherman in 1865. *Farm Security Administration, Prints and Photographs Division, Library of Congress.*

Thomas Hart Benton's *Cotton Pickers* (1945), despite its aestheticizing touches, reveals some of the heartrending aspects of labors in the field, with a child sleeping under a makeshift shade and backbreaking postures. © *T. H. Benton and R. P. Benton Testamentary Trusts / UMB Bank Trustee / Licensed by VAGA, New York, NY.*

John T. Biggers's *Cotton Pickers* (1947) preserves the beauty and dignity of the laborers even as it does not mask the depleting effects of the work they carry out. © *John T. Biggers Estate / Licensed by VAGA, New York, NY. Estate represented by Michael Rosenfeld Gallery.*

IMAGE GALLERY C

Illustrated Poems by
Paul Laurence Dunbar

Paul Laurence Dunbar was born in 1906 in Dayton, Ohio. He began writing at a young age and published his first poems as a teenager in *The Herald*, a newspaper published in Dayton. His first collection of poetry, *Oak and Ivy*, included poems in standard English as well as in dialect. He was working as an elevator operator at the time of the book's publication and sold copies of it to riders. By 1897 Dunbar had become well enough established to embark on a reading tour in England, and in the years that followed he wrote poetry, novels, and short stories. Dunbar was diagnosed with tuberculosis in 1900 and returned to Dayton in 1904 to live with his mother. He died in 1906 at age thirty-three. James Weldon Johnson praised him as "the first poet from the Negro race in the United States to show a combined mastery over poetic material and poetic technique."

Candle-Lightin' Time (1901) was the second in a series of six volumes, published by Dodd, Mead and Company and marketed as gift books, that combine Paul Laurence Dunbar's poems, photographic illustrations by the Hampton Institute Camera Club, and page decorations by Alice Morse, Margaret Armstrong, and other artists. It is likely that these publications were initiated by the Hampton Camera Club, an extracurricular group formed in 1893 that counted among its predominantly white members faculty and staff who were also active in the Hampton Folklore Society. Hampton Camera Club members produced over 450 images to illustrate dialect poems by Dunbar, and they also contributed photographs to the Folklore and Ethnology section of the *Southern Workman*, recording people, homes, and landscapes in the rural areas neighboring the Institute.

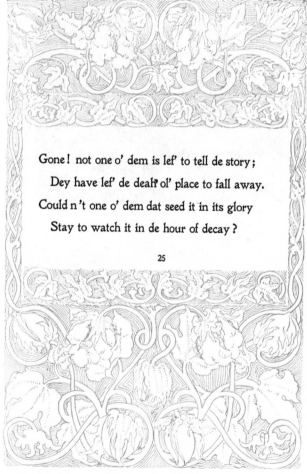

Gone! not one o' dem is lef' to tell de story;
   Dey have lef' de deah' ol' place to fall away.
Could n't one o' dem dat seed it in its glory
   Stay to watch it in de hour of decay?

25

In Dunbar's controversial poem "The Deserted Plantation," reprinted in the illustrated book
Poems of Cabin and Field (1900), a nostalgic black narrator laments the passing of plantation life,
including the departure of those who told stories.

" Fus' thing, hyeah come Mistah Rabbit ; don' you
    see him wo'k his eahs ?
Huh, uh ! dis mus' be a donkey, — look, how inner-
    cent he 'pears !
Dah 's de ole black swan a-swimmin' — ain't she got
    a' awful neck ?
Who 's dis feller dat 's a-comin' ?   Why, dat 's ole
    dog Tray, I 'spec' ! "

123

In the title poem of *Candle-Lightin' Time*, a father returns home at the end of the workday to regale his children with tales of Mistah Rabbit. The sequence of images depicts the storytelling scene minute-by-minute.

Dat's de way I run on, tryin' fu' to please 'em all
    I can;
Den I hollahs, "Now be keerful — dis hyeah las' 's
    de buga-man!"
An' dey runs an' hides dey faces; dey ain't skeered
    —dey's lettin' on:
But de play ain't raaly ovah twell dat buga-man is
    gone.

125

The photograph illustrating "A Cabin Tale: The Young Master Asks for a Story" in *Joggin' Erlong* (1906) employs the trope, used to memorable effect by Joel Chandler Harris, of the young white "master" soliciting tales from an elderly black man, who first protests and then complies. The photographs in *Joggin' Erlong* are attributed to Leigh Richmond Miner, a leading figure in the Hampton Camera Club.

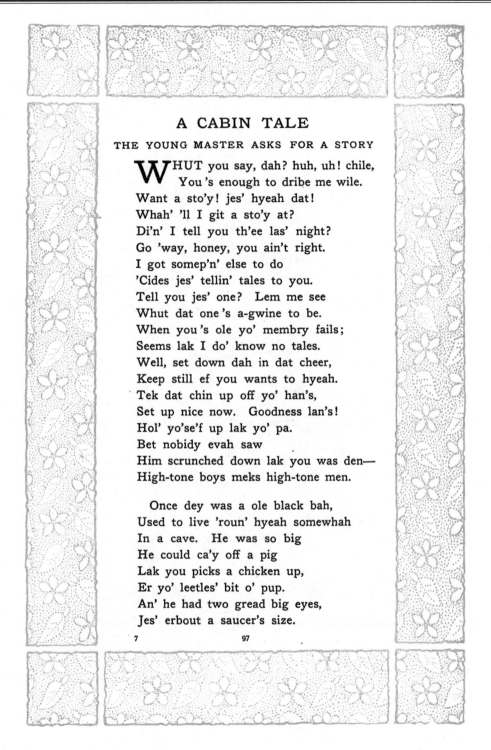

A CABIN TALE

THE YOUNG MASTER ASKS FOR A STORY

WHUT you say, dah? huh, uh! chile,
 You 's enough to dribe me wile.
Want a sto'y! jes' hyeah dat!
Whah' 'll I git a sto'y at?
Di'n' I tell you th'ee las' night?
Go 'way, honey, you ain't right.
I got somep'n' else to do
'Cides jes' tellin' tales to you.
Tell you jes' one? Lem me see
Whut dat one 's a-gwine to be.
When you 's ole yo' membry fails;
Seems lak I do' know no tales.
Well, set down dah in dat cheer,
Keep still ef you wants to hyeah.
Tek dat chin up off yo' han's,
Set up nice now. Goodness lan's!
Hol' yo'se'f up lak yo' pa.
Bet nobidy evah saw
Him scrunched down lak you was den—
High-tone boys meks high-tone men.

Once dey was a ole black bah,
Used to live 'roun' hyeah somewhah
In a cave. He was so big
He could ca'y off a pig
Lak you picks a chicken up,
Er yo' leetles' bit o' pup.
An' he had two gread big eyes,
Jes' erbout a saucer's size.

7   97

This image of two young men gathered around an older man appears in *Poems of Cabin and Field,* after the title page for the poem "Time to Tinker 'Roun'," which celebrates the leisure time afforded by a rainy day.

IMAGE GALLERY D

Joel Chandler Harris and the Uncle Remus Tales

Frederick Stuart Church (1842–1924) was an American illustrator. Born in Grand Rapids, Michigan, he served in the Union Army at age nineteen. He attended art school at the National Academy of Design and became a member of the Art Students League. His work appeared in *Harper's Bazaar*, *The Ladies' Home Journal*, and many other magazines. Specializing in depicting animals, both in their natural state and as anthropomorphized creatures, he illustrated *Aesop's Fables* as well as Chandler's Uncle Remus stories.

Frederick Stuart Church photographed by Napoleon Sarony. *Macbeth Gallery Records, Archives of American Art, Smithsonian Institution.*

James H. Moser (1854–1913) was born in Canada and moved to the United States at age ten. He studied at the Art Students League in New York City, and his work was published in *Harper's* and *The Atlantic Monthly*, among other magazines. He worked as art critic and illustrator for *The Washington Times*.

Portrait of James Henry Moser drawn by Joel Chandler Harris. *Collection of Samuel S. Fetherolf.*

Cover illustration for Joel Chandler Harris's *Uncle Remus, His Songs and His Sayings: The Folk-Lore of the Old Plantation*, 1880. The golden rabbit, smoking his pipe peacefully in a meadow, will be up to no good in the stories contained within the book.

UNCLE REMUS AND HIS DECEITFUL JUG.

UNCLE REMUS

HIS SONGS AND HIS SAYINGS

THE FOLK-LORE OF THE OLD PLANTATION

By JOEL CHANDLER HARRIS

WITH ILLUSTRATIONS BY FREDERICK S. CHURCH AND JAMES H. MOSER

NEW YORK
D. APPLETON AND COMPANY
1, 3, AND 5 BOND STREET
1887

The title page illustration for Harris's book won the author's approval as a "perfect" representation of Uncle Remus. F. S. Church made an engraving of the portrait executed by James Moser. In the frontispiece, Uncle Remus visits the editorial offices of "The Constitution" and brings along his "deceitful jug," a vessel that can look full even when it is empty.

For the first story in *Uncle Remus: His Songs and His Sayings* (1880), "Uncle Remus Initiates the Little Boy," F. S. Church integrated image and text, adding musical notes into the background to enliven what will become the first encounter between clever Brer Rabbit and treacherous Brer Fox.

For "Mr. Fox Is Again Victimized," the trio of Miss Meadows and the girls is painted in a Grecian style that contrasts sharply with the animal pair, the one dominating the other, who has been harnessed and subjugated.

Church's illustration for "The Wonderful Tar-Baby Story" turns the figure of the title into the Africanized image of a woman and offers contrasting stances, with the Tar Baby welcoming the pugilistic rabbit.

For "Miss Cow Falls a Victim to Mr. Rabbit," Church shows Brer Rabbit's wife and children grossly exploiting the trapped cow.

Brer Fox is outfoxed once again, this time by Brer Tarrypin, who takes advantage of reverse psychology in "Mr. Fox Tackles Old Man Tarrypin."

Mr. Terrapin and Brer Rabbit entertain Miss Meadows and the girls. Although Brer Rabbit appears to be holding court in his chair, it is Mr. Terrapin who has the attention of the ladies.

For "The Awful Fate of Mr. Wolf," Church pictured the horrific demise of Mr. Wolf and, for the multitude of rabbits surrounding the death trap, he displays the survival of the one with the quickest wits.

Terrapin outwits Brer Rabbit in a contest observed by Miss Meadows and the girls in this illustration for "Mr. Rabbit Finds His Match at Last."

"How Mr. Rabbit Saved His Meat" is illustrated with images of plenty and domestic contentment in Brer Rabbit's house and with endless labor on the part of Brer Wolf. Some might see these images as racially encoded, reflecting the divide between masters and slaves, with the one carrying out the work and the other enjoying the fruits of labor.

The buzzard, affiliated with death and destruction, is also, in the role of scavenger, associated with purification. Church's illustration reveals Brer Rabbit's deep vulnerability in the encounter found in "Mr. Rabbit Meets His Match Again."

Brer Rabbit peers at his two mortal enemies, whom he has succeeded in pitting against each other in "Mr. Rabbit and Mr. Bear."

Brer Bear is no match for Mr. Bull-Frog, who has taken a leaf from Brer Rabbit's book in "Mr. Bear Catches Old Mr. Bull-Frog" and engineers an escape by insisting that Brer Bear put him anywhere but on a flat rock.

Brer Rabbit ends up getting his choice of the ladies in a contest to see who can raise the most dust with a sledgehammer in "How Mr. Rabbit Succeeded in Raising a Dust."

Owls and bats, creatures of the night, surround the image of Uncle Remus carrying the little boy back home.

This illustration for "How Mr. Rabbit Lost His Fine Bushy Tail" offers a contrast between Brer Rabbit's foolishness, as he follows Brer Fox's advice about fishing, and the wisdom of the owl perched above him.

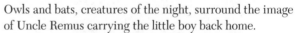

"The Corn-Shucking Song" was included in Harris's volume of Uncle Remus tales as an example of how chores were carried out to the rhythms of music and song, with lyrics that often contained tales embedded in them.

In this tableau, which accompanies "Plantation Play-Song," evenings are presented as an idyllic time of dancing and singing, with not a trace of exhaustion from the day's backbreaking work in the fields.

Harris's volume of Uncle Remus stories includes
several genre portraits by James H. Moser.

In "A Story of the War," we learn that Uncle Remus
"disremembered all 'bout freedom," and shot a Union soldier on
the "raw day" depicted in the illustration.

BROTHER RABBIT AND MISS MEADOWS.—p. 92

The incongruous pairing of Brother Rabbit with a human Miss Meadows in conversation with each other creates a platform for considering the relationship between Uncle Remus and the little boy. Brother Rabbit, who has a way with words, is wooing Miss Meadows, while Uncle Remus—as we know from the title of the first story in *Uncle Remus: His Songs and His Sayings*, "Uncle Remus Initiates the Little Boy"—is introducing the boy into the ways of the world.

NIGHTS

WITH

UNCLE REMUS

BY

JOEL CHANDLER HARRIS

AUTHOR OF "UNCLE REMUS."

(COPYRIGHT)

LONDON
GEORGE ROUTLEDGE AND SONS
BROADWAY, LUDGATE HILL
NEW YORK: 9 LAFAYETTE PLACE
1884

Portrait of Arthur Burdett Frost in his New Jersey studio, published in *The Independent* in 1905. Arthur Burdett Frost (1851–1928) was an American painter, illustrator, and graphic artist. One of the pillars of the "Golden Age of American Illustration," his work appeared in more than ninety books, among them hunting and gaming volumes as well as Joel Chandler Harris's books. A distant cousin of Robert Frost, he received his first break as an artist when he was asked to illustrate *Out of the Hurly Burly*, a volume of American humor by Charles Heber Clarke. Frost's illustrations for Joel Chandler Harris's work first appeared in *Century* magazine in 1884 for the short story "Free Joe and the Rest of the World." Frost subsequently went on to illustrate *Uncle Remus and His Friends* (1892), and Harris asked him to provide illustrations for a new and revised edition of *Uncle Remus: His Songs and His Sayings*. Harris was profoundly grateful to Frost for enlivening the volume with illustrations that he found beautifully suited to the tales

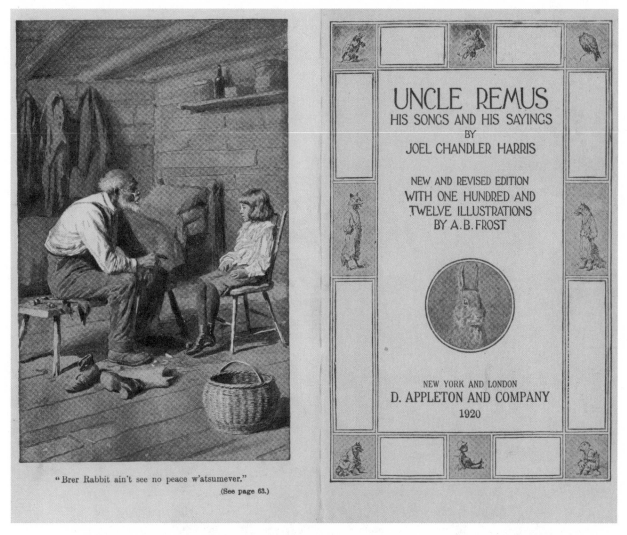

" Brer Rabbit ain't see no peace w'atsumever."

(See page 63.)

UNCLE REMUS
HIS SONGS AND HIS SAYINGS
BY
JOEL CHANDLER HARRIS

NEW AND REVISED EDITION
WITH ONE HUNDRED AND
TWELVE ILLUSTRATIONS
BY A.B.FROST

NEW YORK AND LONDON
D. APPLETON AND COMPANY
1920

of Uncle Remus. In a letter to Frost, he wrote, "Because you have taken it under your hand and made it yours. Because you have breathed the breath of life into these amiable brethren of wood and field. Because by a stroke here and a touch there, you have conveyed into their quaint antics the illumination of your inimitable humor, which is as true to our sun and soil as it is to the spirit and matter set forth. The book was mine, but now you have made it yours."

Joel Chandler Harris favored A. B. Frost's illustrations for his stories, in part because they were far less edgy than the ones executed by Frederick Church. For the frontispiece and title page of the volume illustrated by Frost, Uncle Remus's home and his possessions form a sharp contrast to the figure of the carefully coiffed boy, dressed like a little gentleman. Brer Rabbit's confrontational gaze captures the spirit of the stories, even if the antagonists portrayed in the vignettes seem charming and benign.

What follows are preliminary sketches and final images for the revised version of *Uncle Remus: His Songs and Sayings*.

Page decorations by Frost appear throughout
The Tar-Baby and Other Rhymes (1904).

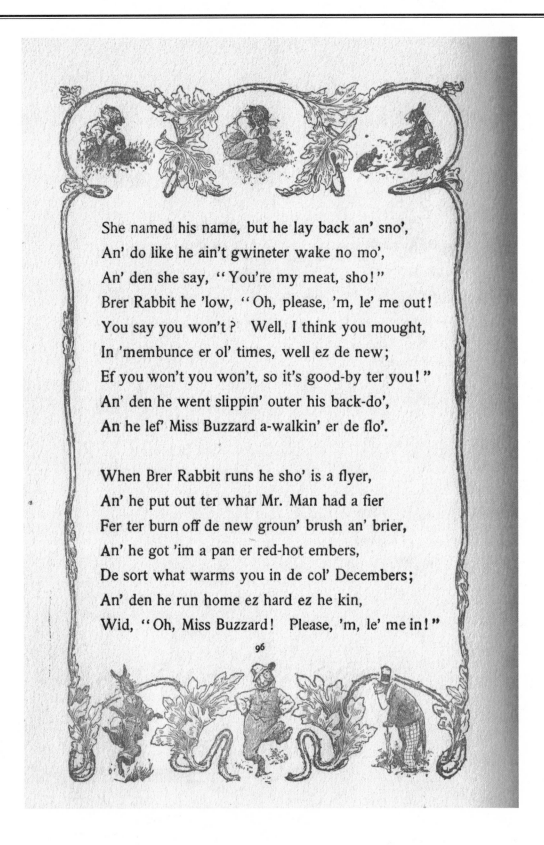

She named his name, but he lay back an' sno',
An' do like he ain't gwineter wake no mo',
An' den she say, ''You're my meat, sho!''
Brer Rabbit he 'low, ''Oh, please, 'm, le' me out!
You say you won't? Well, I think you mought,
In 'membunce er ol' times, well ez de new;
Ef you won't you won't, so it's good-by ter you!''
An' den he went slippin' outer his back-do',
An he lef' Miss Buzzard a-walkin' er de flo'.

When Brer Rabbit runs he sho' is a flyer,
An' he put out ter whar Mr. Man had a fier
Fer ter burn off de new groun' brush an' brier,
An' he got 'im a pan er red-hot embers,
De sort what warms you in de col' Decembers;
An' den he run home ez hard ez he kin,
Wid, ''Oh, Miss Buzzard! Please, 'm, le' me in!''

96

She flew'd right at 'im, wid wing an' claw,
An' he plunked de embers on her jaw!

An' on her neck! an' on her head!
An' in her house! an' on her bed!
An' dey scorched her so dat her eye got red!
An' she flung a flutter, an' she fetched a squall,
"Laws-a-massy, Brer Rabbit! you burnin' me
        bal'!"
An' fum dat day ter dis, bofe fur an' wide,
Whar de Buzzards had top-knots it's mos'ly hide!

97

Harris decided to set some of the stories in verse, in an effort to capture a more authentic oral style and perhaps also to capitalize on strong sales of his anthologies. Frost's decorative vignettes, delicate and whimsical, are included on each page of *The Tar-Baby and Other Rhymes* and made this volume particularly attractive as a collector's item.

In this 1921 cover illustration, Uncle Remus is surrounded by attentive figures from his tales as he gestures while telling stories to the little boy, transformed by his clothing into a twentieth-century figure.

In this frontispiece illustration for *Told by Uncle Remus: New Stories of the Old Plantation* (1905), all the animals, even those who do not populate forests, listen attentively to Brother Rabbit's description of his Laughing-Place, a site that he paints as filled with utopian pleasures.

UNCLE REMUS AND THE LITTLE BOY

In the frontispiece of this child-friendly version of *Nights with Uncle Remus,* Uncle Remus and the little boy seem to be sitting before a fire that casts an interesting shadow of Uncle Remus's hand. Note the broom and the hoe, signs of the daytime activities of the bespectacled old man, who is an animated teller of tales.

NIGHTS WITH UNCLE REMUS

BY

JOEL CHANDLER HARRIS

WITH ILLUSTRATIONS BY MILO WINTER

BOSTON AND NEW YORK
HOUGHTON MIFFLIN COMPANY
The Riverside Press Cambridge
1917

" *De dogs tuckin' der tails 'tween der legs, en dar wuz de Rabbit capperin 'roun' on a toomstone.*"—p. 157.

Front.

In the frontispiece for *Uncle Remus, or, Mr. Fox, Mr. Rabbit, and Mr. Terrapin* (1883), Brer Rabbit succeeds in frustrating the appetites of the hounds baying at him, while on the title page we see domestic ecstasy as Brer Rabbit's children await their next meal, more than likely a dish of Brer Wolf.

UNCLE REMUS

OR

MR. FOX, MR. RABBIT, AND MR. TERRAPIN

BY

JOEL CHANDLER HARRIS

WITH FIFTY ILLUSTRATIONS BY A. T. ELWES.

LONDON

GEORGE ROUTLEDGE AND SONS, Limited

BROADWAY HOUSE, 68-74 CARTER LANE, E.C.

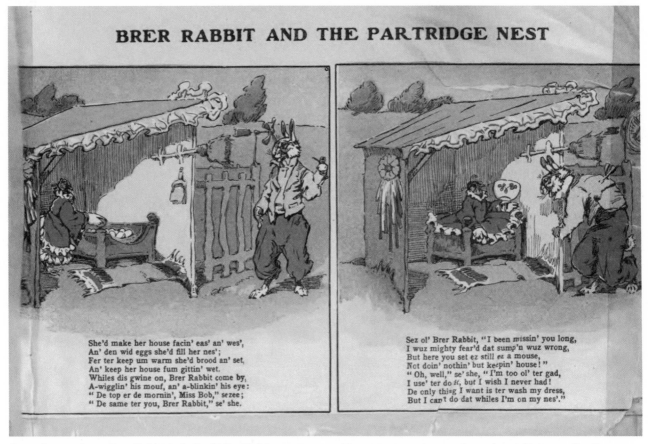

A cruel story about Brer Rabbit's theft of Miss Bob's eggs is turned into a *pourquoi* story about the nighttime calls of partridges in this illustrated collection titled *Uncle Remus and Brer Rabbit* (1907).

Editions of single stories were not uncommon, and Joel Chandler Harris's tale about a witch wolf is told to the little boy by Uncle Remus. The illustration shows a young man seeking advice about romance from "Jedge Rabbit." From *The Witch Wolf: An Uncle Remus Story*, illustrated by W. A. Dwiggins, 1921.

Silhouette illustration from *The Tree Named John* by John Sale (1929).

BIBLIOGRAPHY

Anthologies and Narrative Accounts

Abrahams, Roger D., ed. *African American Folktales: Stories from Black Traditions in the New World.* New York: Pantheon, 1985.

———, ed. *African Folktales: Traditional Stories of the Black World.* New York: Pantheon, 1983.

———. *Deep Down in the Jungle: Negro Narratives from the Streets of Philadelphia.* Chicago: Aldine, 1970.

———. *The Man-of-Words in the West Indies: Performance and the Emergence of Creole Culture.* Baltimore, MD: Johns Hopkins University Press, 1983.

Adams, E. C. L., ed. *Congaree Sketches, Scenes from Negro Life in the Swamps of the Congaree and Tales by Tad and Scip of Heaven and Hell with Other Miscellany.* Chapel Hill: University of North Carolina Press, 1927.

———, ed. *Nigger to Nigger.* New York: Scribner's, 1928.

———, ed. *Tales of the Congaree by Edward C. L. Adams.* Edited by Robert G. O'Meally. Chapel Hill: University of North Carolina Press, 1987.

Addo, Peter Eric Adotey. *Ghana Folk Tales.* New York: Exposition Press, 1968.

———. *How the Spider Became Bald: Folktales and Legends from West Africa.* Greensboro, NC: Morgan Reynolds, 1993.

Appiah, Peggy. *Ananse the Spider: Tales from an Ashanti Village.* New York: Pantheon Books, 1966.

———. *The Pineapple Child and Other Tales from Ashanti.* Illustrated by Mora Dickson. London: Andre Deutsche, 1969.

———. *Tales of an Ashanti Father.* Boston: Beacon Press, 1967.

Arbousset, T., and F. Daumas. *Narrative of an Exploratory Tour to the North-East of the Colony of the Cape of Good Hope.* Cape Town: C. Struik, 1968.

Armistead, S. G. "Notes & Queries: Two Brer Rabbit Stories from the Eastern Shore of Maryland." *Journal of American Folklore* 84 (1971): 442–44.

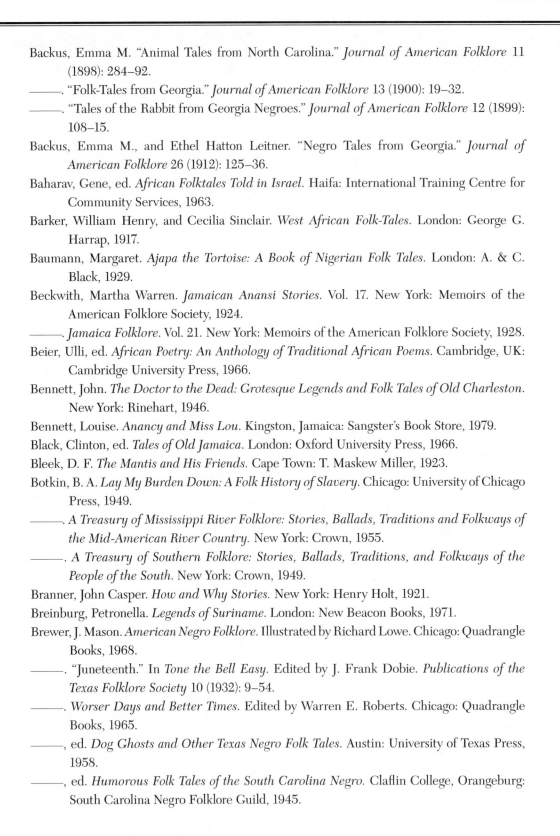

Backus, Emma M. "Animal Tales from North Carolina." *Journal of American Folklore* 11 (1898): 284–92.

——. "Folk-Tales from Georgia." *Journal of American Folklore* 13 (1900): 19–32.

——. "Tales of the Rabbit from Georgia Negroes." *Journal of American Folklore* 12 (1899): 108–15.

Backus, Emma M., and Ethel Hatton Leitner. "Negro Tales from Georgia." *Journal of American Folklore* 26 (1912): 125–36.

Baharav, Gene, ed. *African Folktales Told in Israel*. Haifa: International Training Centre for Community Services, 1963.

Barker, William Henry, and Cecilia Sinclair. *West African Folk-Tales*. London: George G. Harrap, 1917.

Baumann, Margaret. *Ajapa the Tortoise: A Book of Nigerian Folk Tales*. London: A. & C. Black, 1929.

Beckwith, Martha Warren. *Jamaican Anansi Stories*. Vol. 17. New York: Memoirs of the American Folklore Society, 1924.

——. *Jamaica Folklore*. Vol. 21. New York: Memoirs of the American Folklore Society, 1928.

Beier, Ulli, ed. *African Poetry: An Anthology of Traditional African Poems*. Cambridge, UK: Cambridge University Press, 1966.

Bennett, John. *The Doctor to the Dead: Grotesque Legends and Folk Tales of Old Charleston*. New York: Rinehart, 1946.

Bennett, Louise. *Anancy and Miss Lou*. Kingston, Jamaica: Sangster's Book Store, 1979.

Black, Clinton, ed. *Tales of Old Jamaica*. London: Oxford University Press, 1966.

Bleek, D. F. *The Mantis and His Friends*. Cape Town: T. Maskew Miller, 1923.

Botkin, B. A. *Lay My Burden Down: A Folk History of Slavery*. Chicago: University of Chicago Press, 1949.

——. *A Treasury of Mississippi River Folklore: Stories, Ballads, Traditions and Folkways of the Mid-American River Country*. New York: Crown, 1955.

——. *A Treasury of Southern Folklore: Stories, Ballads, Traditions, and Folkways of the People of the South*. New York: Crown, 1949.

Branner, John Casper. *How and Why Stories*. New York: Henry Holt, 1921.

Breinburg, Petronella. *Legends of Suriname*. London: New Beacon Books, 1971.

Brewer, J. Mason. *American Negro Folklore*. Illustrated by Richard Lowe. Chicago: Quadrangle Books, 1968.

——. "Juneteenth." In *Tone the Bell Easy*. Edited by J. Frank Dobie. *Publications of the Texas Folklore Society* 10 (1932): 9–54.

——. *Worser Days and Better Times*. Edited by Warren E. Roberts. Chicago: Quadrangle Books, 1965.

——, ed. *Dog Ghosts and Other Texas Negro Folk Tales*. Austin: University of Texas Press, 1958.

——, ed. *Humorous Folk Tales of the South Carolina Negro*. Claflin College, Orangeburg: South Carolina Negro Folklore Guild, 1945.

———, ed. *The Word on the Brazos: Negro Preacher Tales from the Brazos Bottoms of Texas.* Austin: University of Texas Press, 1953.

Brown, Sterling A., and Arthur P. Davis, and Ulysses Lee. *The Negro Caravan.* New York: Arno Press, 1969.

Browne, Ray B. "Negro Folktales from Alabama." *Southern Folklore Quarterly* 18 (1954): 129–34.

Burrison, John A., ed. *Storytellers: Folktales & Legends from the South.* Athens: University of Georgia Press, 1989.

Burton, W. F. P. *The Magic Drum: Tales from Central Africa.* London: Methuen & Co. Ltd., 1961.

Cabrera, Lydia. *Afro-Cuban Tales.* Translated by Alberto Hernández-Chiroldes and Lauren Yoder. Lincoln: University of Nebraska Press, 2004.

Callaway, Canon, ed. *Nursery Tales, Traditions, and Histories of the Zulus, in Their Own Words.* London: Trübner, 1868.

Cardinall, Allan Wolsey, ed. *Tales Told in Togoland.* Oxford: Oxford University Press, 1931.

Chamoiseau, Patrick. *Creole Folktales.* New York: New Press, 1988.

Chapman, Abraham. *New Black Voices: An Anthology of Contemporary Afro-American Literature.* New York: New American Library, 1972.

Chesnutt, Charles Waddell. *Collected Stories.* 1899. Edited by William L. Andrews. New York: Mentor, 1992.

Christensen, A. M. H. *Afro-American Folk Lore, Told Round Cabin Fires on the Sea Islands of South Carolina.* Boston: J. G. Cupples, 1892.

Clarke, W. R. E. *Some Folk Tales of Sierra Leone.* London: Macmillan, 1965.

Claudel, Calvin, and J.-M. Carrière. "The Tales from the French Folklore of Louisiana." *Journal of American Folklore* 56 (1943): 38–44.

Cocke, Sarah Johnson. *Bypaths in Dixie: Folktales of the South.* New York: E. P. Dutton, 1911.

Coffin, Tristram Potter, and Hennig Cohen. *Folklore in America: Tales, Songs, Superstitions, Proverbs, Riddles, Games, Folk Drama and Folk Festivals.* Garden City, NY: Doubleday, 1966.

Coggswell, Gladys Canes. *Stories from the Heart: Missouri's African American Heritage Collected and Told by Gladys Canes Coggswell.* Columbia: University of Missouri Press, 2009.

Comhaire-Sylvain, Suzanne. "Creole Tales from Haiti." *Journal of American Folklore* 50 (1937): 207–95.

Congdon, Kristin G. *Uncle Monday and Other Florida Tales.* Jackson: University Press of Mississippi, 2001.

Cotter, Joseph S. *Negro Tales.* New York: Cosmopolitan Press, 1912.

Courlander, Harold, ed. *The Drum and the Hoe: Life and Lore of the Haitian People.* Berkeley: University of California Press, 1960.

———, ed. *The Piece of Fire and Other Haitian Tales.* New York: Harcourt, Brace & World, 1964.

———, ed. *Terrapin's Pot of Sense*. New York: Holt and Rinehart, 1957.

———, ed. *A Treasury of Afro-American Folklore: The Oral Literature, Traditions, Recollections, Legends, Tales, Songs, Religious Beliefs, Customs, Sayings and Humor of People of African Descent in the Americas*. New York: Crown, 1976.

———, ed. *Uncle Bouqi of Haiti*. New York: Morrow, 1942.

Courlander, Harold, and George Herzog. *The Cow-Tail Switch and Other West African Stories*. New York: Henry Holt, 1947.

Courlander, Harold, and Wolf Leslau, eds. *The Fire on the Mountain and Other Stories from Ethiopia and Eritrea*. New York: Henry Holt, 1950.

Courlander, Harold, and Albert Kofi Prempeh, eds. *The Hat-Shaking Dance and other Ashanti Tales from Ghana*. New York: Harcourt Brace Jovanovich, 1957.

Crowley, Daniel J. *African Folklore in the New World*. Austin: University of Texas Press, 1977.

———. *I Could Talk Old-Story Good: Creativity in Bahamian Folklore*. Berkeley and Los Angeles: University of California Press, 1966.

Curtis, Natalie, ed. *Songs and Tales from the Dark Continent*. New York: G. Schirmer, 1920.

Dadié, Bernard Binlin. *The Black Cloth: A Collection of African Folktales*. Translated by Karen C. Hatch. Amherst: University of Massachusetts Press, 1987.

Dance, Daryl Cumber. *Folklore from Contemporary Jamaicans*. Knoxville: University of Tennessee Press, 1985.

———. *From My People: 400 Years of African American Folklore*. New York: W. W. Norton, 2002.

———, ed. *Shuckin' and Jivin'*. Bloomington: Indiana University Press, 1978.

Davis, Henry C. "Negro Folk-Lore in South Carolina." *Journal of American Folklore* 27 (1914): 241–54.

Dayrell, E. *Folk-Stories from Southern Nigeria, West Africa*. London: Longmans, Green, 1910.

Dobie, J. Frank. *Tone the Bell Easy: Publications of the Texas Folklore Society*. Vol. 10. Austin: Texas Folklore Society, 1932.

Dorson, Richard M. *African Folklore*. Bloomington: Indiana University Press, 1972.

———. *American Negro Folktales*. Greenwich, CT: Fawcett, 1967.

———. *Negro Tales from Pine Bluff, Arkansas, and Calvin, Michigan*. Bloomington: Indiana University Press, 1958.

———, ed. *Negro Folktales in Michigan*. Cambridge, MA: Harvard University Press, 1956.

Edwards, Charles L. *Bahama Songs and Stories: A Contribution to Folklore*. 1895. New York: G. E. Stechert, 1942.

Eells, Elsie. *Fairy Tales from Brazil*. New York: Dodd, Mead, 1917.

Elliot, Geraldine. *Where the Leopard Passes: A Book of African Folk Tales*. 1949. New York: Schocken, 1968.

Ellis, A. B. *The Ewe-Speaking Peoples of the Slave Coast of West Africa: Their Religion, Manners, Customs, Laws, Languages, etc.* London: Chapman and Hall, 1890.

——, *The Yoruba-Speaking Peoples of the Slave Coast of West Africa: Their Religion, Manners, Customs, Laws, Languages, etc.* London: Chapman and Hall, 1894.

Espinosa, Aurelio M. "A New Classification of the Fundamental Elements of the Tar-Baby Story on the Basis of Two Hundred and Sixty-Seven Versions." *Journal of American Folklore* 56 (1943): 31–37.

——. "Notes on the Origin and History of the Tar-Baby Story." *Journal of American Folk-Lore* 43 (1930): 129–209.

Fair, Ronald L. "Thank God It Snowed." *American Scholar* (1970): 105–8.

Faulkner, William J. *The Days When the Animals Talked: Black-American Folktales and How They Came to Be.* Illustrated by Troy Howell. Trenton, NJ: African World Press, 1993.

Fauset, Arthur Huff. *Black Gods of the Metropolis: Negro Religious Cults of the Urban North.* London: Oxford University Press, 1944.

——. *Folklore from Nova Scotia.* Vol. 24. New York: Memoirs of the American Folklore Society, 1931.

——. "Negro Folk Tales from the South (Alabama, Mississippi, Louisiana)." *Journal of American Folklore,* 40 (1927): 213–303.

Fortier, Alcée. *Louisiana Folk-Tales, in French Dialect and English Translation.* Boston: Houghton, Mifflin, 1895.

——. "Louisianan Nursery-Tales," *Journal of American Folklore* 1 (1888): 142–45.

Frazer, James G. "A South African Red Riding-Hood," *Folk-Lore Journal* 7 (1889): 167.

Frobenius, Leo. *Atlantis: Volksmärchen und Volksdichtungen Afrikas.* 12 vols. Düsseldorf: Eugen Diederichs Verlag, 1921.

Frobenius, Leo, and Douglas C. Fox. *African Genesis: The Folk Tales and Legends of the North African Berbers, the Sudanese, and the Southern Rhodesians.* New York: Benjamin Blom, 1966.

Fuja, Abayomi. *Fourteen Hundred Cowries: Traditional Stories of the Yoruba.* London: Oxford University Press, 1962.

Georgia Writers' Project. *Drums and Shadows: Survival Studies among the Georgia Coastal Negroes.* Athens: University of Georgia Press, 1940.

Gibbs, Laura, trans. *Aesop's Fables: A New Translation.* Oxford: Oxford University Press, 2002. http://mythfolklore.net/aesopica/index.

Gonzales, Ambrose. *The Black Border: Gullah Stories of the Carolina Coast.* Columbia, SC: The State Company, 1922.

Goss, Lina, and Marian Barnes, eds. *Talk That Talk: An Anthology of African-American Storytelling.* New York: Simon & Schuster, 1989.

Green, Thomas A., ed. *African American Folktales.* Westport, CT: Greenwood Press, 2009.

Hamilton, Virginia. *Her Stories: African American Folktales, Fairy Tales, and True Tales.* New York: Blue Sky Press, 1994.

——. *The People Could Fly: American Black Folktales.* Illustrated by Leo and Diane Dillon. New York: Knopf, 1985.

———. *A Ring of Tricksters*: *Animal Tales from America, the West Indies, and Africa*. Illustrated by Barry Moser. New York: Blue Sky Press, 1997.

Haskins, James. *The Headless Haunt and Other African-American Ghost Stories*. New York: HarperCollins, 1994.

Hendricks, William C., ed. *Bundle of Troubles, and Other Tarheel Tales, by Workers of the Writers' Program of the Work Projects Administration in the State of North Carolina*. Durham, NC: Duke University Press, 1943.

Herskovits, Melville J., and Frances S. Herskovits. *Suriname Folk-Lore*. New York: Columbia University Press, 1936.

Hughes, Langston, and Arna Bontemps. *The Book of Negro Folklore*. New York: Dodd, Mead, 1958.

Hutchison, Kwesi. *Folktales from Ashanti*. N.p., 1994.

Jackson, Bruce. *"Get Your Ass in the Water and Swim Like Me"*: *Narrative Poetry from the Black Oral Tradition*. Cambridge, MA: Harvard University Press, 1974.

Jacobs, Joseph. *Indian Fairy Tales*. London: David Nutt, 1892.

Jekyll, Walter, ed. *Jamaican Song and Story: Annancy Stories, Digging Sings, Ring Tunes, and Dancing Tunes*. Mineola, NY: Dover, 1966. First published 1907 by the Folk Lore Society.

Johnson, Guy B. *Folk Culture on St. Helena Island, South Carolina*. Chapel Hill: University of North Carolina Press, 1930.

Johnson, James Weldon, and J. Rosamond Johnson. *The Book of American Negro Spirituals*. New York: Viking, 1954.

Johnson, John H. "Folk-lore from Antigua, British West Indies." *Journal of American Folklore* 34 (1921): 40–88.

Jones, Charles G. *Negro Myths from the Georgia Coast: Told in the Vernacular*. Boston: Houghton Mifflin, 1888.

Jordan, A. C., trans. *Tales from Southern Africa*. Berkeley: University of California Press, 1973.

Katz, William Loren. *Black Indians: A Hidden Heritage*. New York: Atheneum, 1986.

Kennedy, R. Emmet. *Gritny People*. New York: Dodd Mead, 1927.

Leeming, David, and Jake Page. *Myths, Legends, and Folktales of America: An Anthology*. New York: Oxford University Press, 1999.

Lester, Julius. *Black Folktales*. New York: Grove Press, 1969.

Lindahl, Carl, ed. *American Folktales from the Collections of the Library of Congress*. London and New York: Routledge, 2004.

Louis, Liliane Nérette. *When Night Falls, Kric! Krac!: Haitian Folktales*. Edited by Fred J. Hay. Englewood, CO: Libraries Unlimited, 1999.

Lomax, John A., and Alan Lomax. *American Ballads and Folksongs*. New York, Macmillan, 1934.

Lyons, Mary E., ed. *Raw Head, Bloody Bones: African-American Tales of the Supernatural*. New York: Scribner's, 1991.

McCarthy, William Bernard. *Cinderella in America: A Book of Folk and Fairy Tales*. Jackson: University of Mississippi Press, 2007.

McDonogh, Gary W., ed. *The Florida Negro: A Federal Writers' Project Legacy*. Jackson: University Press of Mississippi, 1993.

McPherson, Ethel L. *Native Fairy Tales of South Africa*. Illustrated by Helen Jacobs. London: Harrap, 1919.

Mooney, James. *Myths of the Cherokee*. Washington, DC: Government Printing Office, 1902.

Mungin, Horace. *The Devil Beats His Wife and Other Stories from the Lowcountry*. N.p.: n.p., 2004.

Nassau, Robert H. *Where Animals Talk: West African Folk Lore Tales*. Boston: Richard G. Badger, 1912.

Nicholls, David G. *Conjuring the Folk: Forms of Modernity in African America*. Ann Arbor: University of Michigan Press, 2000.

Nickels, Cameron C. "An Early Version of the 'Tar Baby' Story." *Journal of American Folklore* 94 (1981): 364–69.

Odum, Howard W. "Folk-Song and Folk-Poetry as Found in the Secular Songs of the Southern Negroes." *Journal of American Folklore* 24 (1911): 255–94.

———. "Folk-Song and Folk-Poetry as Found in the Secular Songs of the Southern Negroes (Concluded)." *Journal of American Folklore* 24 (1911): 351–96.

Okeke, Uche. *Tales of Land of Death: Igbo Folktales*. New York: Zenith Books, 1971.

O'Meally, Robert G. *Tales of the Congaree*. Chapel Hill: University of North Carolina Press, 1987.

Owen, Mary Alicia, ed. *Voodoo Tales as Told Among the Negroes of the Southwest*. New York: G. P. Putnam's Sons, 1893.

Owens, William. "Folk-Lore of the Southern Negroes." *Lippincott's Magazine of Popular Literature and Science* 20 (1877): 748–55.

Parsons, Elsie Clews. *Folk-Lore of the Antilles, French and English*. New York: Memoirs of the American Folk-lore Society, 1943.

———. *Folk-Lore of the Sea Islands, South Carolina*. New York: American Folk-lore Society, 1923.

———. *Folk-Tales of Andros Island, Bahamas*. Lancaster, PA: American Folk-Lore Society, 1918.

Peck, Catherine, ed. *A Treasury of North American Folk-Tales*. New York: W. W. Norton, 1998.

Peterkin, Julia. *Roll, Jordan, Roll*. New York: R. O. Ballou, 1933.

Petro, Pamela. *Sitting Up with the Dead: A Storied Journey through the American South*. New York: Flamingo, 2001.

Radin, Paul. *African Folktales*. Princeton, NJ: Bollingen Series, Princeton University Press, 1952.

Randolph, Vance. *The Devil's Pretty Daughter*. New York: Columbia University Press, 1955.

———. *The Talking Turtle and Other Ozark Folk Tales*. New York: Columbia University Press, 1957.

Rattray, R. Sutherland. *Akan-Ashanti Folk-Tales*. Oxford: Clarendon Press, 1930.

————. *Hausa Folk-Lore, Customs, Proverbs, etc.* 2 vols. Oxford: Clarendon 1913.

Sale, John B. *The Tree Named John.* Chapel Hill: University of North Carolina Press, 1929.

Sanfield, Steve. *The Adventures of High John the Conqueror.* Illustrated by John Ward. New York: Orchard Books, 1989.

Saxon, Lyle, Edward Dreyer, and Robert Tallant, eds. *Gumbo Ya-Ya.* Boston: Houghton Mifflin, 1945.

Sherlock, Philip M. *Anansi the Spider Man: Jamaican Folk Tales Told by Philip M. Sherlock.* New York: Thomas Y. Cowell, 1954.

Sidahome, Joseph E. *Stories of the Benin Empire.* London: Oxford University Press, 1964.

Simpson, George Eaton. "Traditional Tales from Northern Haiti." *Journal of American Folklore* 56 (1943): 255–65.

Skinner, Neil. *Hausa Tales and Traditions.* 3 vols. London: Frank Cass & Co., 1969.

Smiley, Portia. "Folk-Lore from Virginia, South Carolina, Georgia, Alabama, and Florida." *Journal of American Folklore* 32 (1919): 357–83.

Smith, Alexander McCall. *The Girl Who Married a Lion and Other Tales from Africa.* New York: Pantheon, 2004.

Spears, Richard, ed. *West African Folktales.* Translated by Jack Berry. Evanston, IL: Northwestern University Press, 1991.

Stanley, Henry M. *My Dark Companions and Their Strange Stories.* London: Sampson Low, Marston, 1893.

Stoney, Samuel Galliard, and Gertrude Mathews Shelby. *Black Genesis.* New York: Macmillan, 1930.

"The Story of Demane and Demazana." *The Cape Monthly Magazine* 9 (1874): 248–49.

Talley, Thomas W. *The Negro Traditions.* Edited by Charles K. Wolfe and Laura C. Jarmon. Knoxville: University of Tennessee Press, 1930.

————. *Thomas W. Talley's Negro Folk Rhymes.* 1922. Edited by Charles K. Wolfe. Knoxville: University of Tennessee Press, 1991.

Tanna, Laura. *Jamaican Folk Tales and Oral Histories.* Kingston, Jamaica: Institute of Jamaican Publications, 1984.

Theal, George McCall. *Kaffir Folk-Lore.* London: S. Sonnenschein, Le Bas & Lowrey, 1886.

Tracey, Hugh. *The Lion on the Path and Other African Stories.* London: Routledge and Kegan Paul, 1967.

Vernon-Jackson, Hugh. *West African Folk Tales.* Mineola, NY: Dover, 2003.

Watkins, Mel, ed. *African American Humor: The Best Black Comedy from Slavery to Today.* Chicago: Lawrence Hill Books, 2002.

Weeks, John H. *Congo Life and Folklore.* London: Religious Tract Society, 1911.

Woodson, Carter Godwin. *African Myths Together with Proverbs.* Washington, DC: Associated Publishers, Inc., 1928.

Writers' Program of the Work Projects Administration in the State of South Carolina. *South Carolina Folk Tales: Stories of Animals and Supernatural Beings.* Columbia: University of South Carolina, 1973.

Young, Richard Alan, and Judy Dockrey Young. *African-American Folktales for Young Readers*. Atlanta, GA: August House, 1993.

Zenani, Nongenile Masithathu. *The World and the Word: Tales and Observations from the Xhosa Oral Tradition*. Edited by Harold Scheub. Madison: University of Wisconsin Press, 1992.

Picture Books

Aardema, Verna, ed. *Half-a-Ball-of-Kenki: An Ashanti Tale Retold*. Illustrated by Diane Stanley Zuromskis. New York: Frederick Warne, 1979.

Kantor, Susan. *Illustrated Treasury of African American Read-Aloud Stories*. New York: Black Dog & Leventhal, 2003.

———. *One-Hundred-and-One African-American Read-Aloud Stories*. New York: Black Dog & Leventhal, 1998.

Keats, Ezra Jack. *John Henry: An American Legend*. Illustrated by Jerry Pinkney. New York: Pantheon, 1965.

Lester, Julius. *John Henry*. New York: Dial, 1994.

Musgrove, Margaret. *Ashanti to Zulu: African Traditions*. Illustrated by Leo Dillon and Diane Dillon. New York: Puffin, 1992.

Small, Terry. *The Legend of John Henry*. New York: Doubleday, 1994.

Thomas, Joyce Carol. *The Six Fools*. Collected by Zora Neale Hurston. Illustrated by Faith Ringgold. New York: HarperCollins, 2006.

———. *The Three Witches*. Collected by Zora Neale Hurston. Illustrated by Faith Ringgold. New York: HarperCollins, 2006.

Secondary Literature

Abrahams, Roger D. *The Man-of-Words in the West Indies: Performance and the Emergence of Creole Culture*. Baltimore, MD: Johns Hopkins University Press, 1983.

An Abstract of the Evidence Delivered before a Select Committee of the House of Commons in the Years 1790 and 1791, on the Part of the Petitioners for the Abolition of the Slave Trade. Cincinnati: American Reform Tract and Book Society, 1855, 53–54.

Appiah, Kwame Anthony. *In My Father's House: Africa in the Philosophy of Culture*. New York: Oxford University Press, 1992.

Ashe, Bertram D. *From Within the Frame: Storytelling in African-American Fiction*. New York: Routledge, 2002.

Asim, Jabari. *The N Word: Who Can Say It, Who Shouldn't, and Why*. New York: Houghton Mifflin, 2007.

Baker, Houston A., Jr. *Blues, Ideology and Afro-American Literature*. Chicago: University of Chicago Press, 1987.

———. *Long Black Song: Essays in Black American Literature and Culture*. Charlottesville: University of Virginia Press, 1990.

Bascom, William. *African Dilemma Tales*. The Hague: Mouton, 1975.

———. *African Folktales in the New World*. Bloomington: Indiana University Press, 1992.

———. "Cinderella in Africa," *Journal of the Folklore Institute* 9 (1972): 54–70.

———. *Ifa Divination: Communication between Gods and Man in West Africa*. Bloomington: Indiana University Press, 1969.

Beamon, Tanika J. "A History of African American Folklore Scholarship." PhD diss. University of California, Berkeley, 2001.

Ben-Amos, Dan. *Sweet Words: Storytelling Events in Benin*. Philadelphia: Institute for the Study of Human Issues, 1975.

Benjamin, Shanna Greene. "A Trickster in Transition: Nineteenth-Century Representations of Aunt Nancy." In *Loopholes and Retreats: African American Writers and the Nineteenth Century*, edited by John Cullen Gruesser and Hanna Wallinger, 43–57. Wien: LIT Verlag, 2009.

Bernstein, Robin. *Racial Innocence: Performing American Childhood from Slavery to Civil Rights*. New York: New York University Press, 2011.

Bicknel, Jeanette. "Reflections on 'John Henry': Ethical Issues in Singing Performance." *Journal of Aesthetics and Art Criticism* 67 (2009): 173–80.

Blake, Susan L. "Folklore and Community in *Song of Solomon*." *Melus* 7 (1980): 77–82.

Bogle, Donald. *Toms, Coons, Mulattoes, Mammies, and Bucks: An Interpretive History of Blacks in American Films*. 4th ed. New York: Bloomsbury Academic, 2001.

Bone, Robert. *Down Home: A History of Afro-American Short Fiction from Its Beginnings to the End of the Harlem Renaissance*. New York: G. P. Putnam's Sons, 1975.

Bontemps, Arna. "Why I Returned." *Harper's Magazine* (April 1965): 177–82.

Brennan, Jonathan. *When Brer Rabbit Met Coyote: African-Native American Literature*. Urbana: University of Illinois Press, 2003.

Bronner, Simon J. *Folk Nation: Folklore in the Creation of American Tradition*. Wilmington, DE: Scholarly Resources, 2002.

Brown, Cecil. "Frankie and Albert/Johnny." In *Greenwood Encyclopedia of African American Folklore*. Vol. I, edited by Anand Prahlad, 462–66. Westport, CT: Greenwood, 2006.

———. *Stagolee Shot Billy*. Cambridge, MA: Harvard University Press, 2003.

Brown, Sterling A. "Negro Folk Expression," *Phylon* 11.4 (1950), 318–27.

Brown, Norman. "The Stickfast Motif in the Tar-Baby Story." In *India and Indology: Selected Articles by W. Norman Brown*, edited by Rosane Rocher. Delhi: Motilal Banarsida, 1978.

Brunvand, Jan Harold, ed. *American Folklore: An Encyclopedia*. New York: Garland, 1996.

Bryant, Jerry H. *"Born in a Mighty Bad Land": The Violent Man in African American Folklore and Culture*. Bloomington: Indiana University Press, 2003.

Calame-Griaule, Genevieve. "The Oral Tradition as an Art Form in African Culture." *Presence Africaine* 19 (1963): 197–214.

Callahan, John F. *In the African-American Grain: The Pursuit of Voice in Twentieth-Century Black Fiction*. Urbana: University of Illinois Press, 1988.

Campbell, Jane. *Mythic Black Fiction: The Transformation of History*. Knoxville: University of Tennessee Press, 1986.

Carpio, Glenda. *Laughing Fit to Kill: Black Humor in the Fictions of Slavery.* Oxford: Oxford University Press, 2008.

Cartwright, Keith. *Reading Africa into American Literature: Epics, Fables, and Gothic Tales.* Lexington: University Press of Kentucky, 2002.

———. *Sacral Groves, Limbo Gateways: Travels in Deep Southern Time, Circum-Caribbean Space, Afro-Creole Authority.* Athens: University of Georgia Press, 2013.

Chappell, Louis W. *John Henry: A Folk-Lore Study.* Jena, Germany: Frommannsche Verlag, 1933.

Chiji, Akoma. *Folklore in New World Black Fiction: Writing and the Oral Traditional Aesthetics.* Columbus: Ohio State University Press, 2007.

Chireau, Yvonne P. *Black Magic: Religion and the African American Conjuring Tradition.* Berkeley: University of California Press, 2006.

Clifford, Carrie W. "Our Children." *Crisis* 14.6 (October 1917): 306–7.

Cohen, Karl F. *Forbidden Animation: Censored Cartoons and Blacklisted Animators in America.* Jefferson, NC: McFarland & Co., 1997.

Courlander, Harold. *The Drum and the Hoe: Life and Lore of the Haitian People.* Berkeley: University of California Press, 1960.

Cox, Karen L. *Dreaming of Dixie: How the South Was Created in American Popular Culture.* Chapel Hill: University of North Carolina Press, 2011.

Cox, Marian Roalfe. *Cinderella: Three Hundred and Forty-five Variants of Cinderella, Catskin and Cap O' Rushes, Abstracted and Tabulated with a Discussion of Medieval Analogues and Notes.* London: David Nutt, 1893.

Cronise, Florence M., and Henry W. Ward. *Cunnie Rabbit, Mr. Spider and the Other Beef.* London: Swan Sonnenschein, 1903.

Cunard, Nancy, and Hugh Ford, eds. *Negro: An Anthology.* New York: Continuum, 1996.

Dance, Daryl. "In the Beginning: A New View of Black American Etiological Tales." *Southern Folklore Quarterly* 40 (1977): 53–64.

DeVoto, Bernard. *Mark Twain's America.* New York: Houghton Mifflin, 1932.

Dickson, Bruce D., Jr. "The 'John and Old Master' Stories and the World of Slavery: A Study in Folktales and History." *Phylon* 35 (1974): 418–29.

———. *Violence and Culture in the Antebellum South.* Austin: University of Texas Press, 1979.

Dorson, Richard M., ed. *African Folklore.* Bloomington: Indiana University Press, 1972.

———. *American Folklore.* Chicago: University of Chicago Press, 1959.

———. *Negro Tales from Pine Bluff, Arkansas, and Calvin, Michigan.* Bloomington: Indiana University Press, 1958.

Du Bois, W. E. B. *The Souls of Black Folks.* Chicago: A. C. McClurg, 1903.

Dundes, Alan, ed. "African Tales among the North American Indians." *Southern Folklore Quarterly* 29 (1965): 207–19.

———. *Cinderella: A Casebook.* Madison: University of Wisconsin Press, 1988.

———. *Mother Wit from the Laughing Barrel: Readings in the Interpretation of Afro-American Folklore.* Jackson: University Press of Mississippi, 1990.

Edwards, Jay. *The Afro-American Trickster Tale: A Structural Analysis.* Bloomington: Monographs of the Folklore Institute, Indiana University, 1978.

Ellis, A. B. "Evolution in Folklore: Some West African Prototypes of the 'Uncle Remus' Stories." *Popular Science Monthly* 48 (1896): 93–103.

Ervin, Hazel Arnett, and Hilary Hollady. *Ann Petry's Short Fiction: Critical Essays.* Westport, CT: Praeger, 2004.

Faraclas, Nicholas, Ronald Severing, Christa Weijer, Elisabeth Echteld, and Marsha Hinds-Layne, eds. *Anansi's Defiant Webs: Contact, Continuity, Convergence, and Complexity in the Languages, Literatures and Cultures of the Greater Caribbean.* Proceedings of the ECICC Conference, Guyana 2010. Vol. 2. Curaçao/Puerto Rico: Fundashon pa Planifikashon di Idioma and University of the Netherlands, Antilles, 2011.

Finnegan, Ruth. *Oral Literature in Africa.* Cambridge, UK: Open Book Publishers, 2012.

Fisher, Dexter, and Robert B. Stepto. *Afro-American Literature: The Reconstruction of Instruction.* New York: Modern Language Association, 1979.

Fishkin, Shelley Fisher. *Lighting Out for the Territory: Reflections on Mark Twain and American Culture.* New York: Oxford University Press, 1997.

Ford, Clyde W. *The Hero with an African Face: Mythic Wisdom of Traditional Africa.* New York: Bantam, 1999.

Gates, Henry Louis, Jr. *Figures in Black: Words, Signs, and the "Racial" Self.* New York: Oxford University Press, 1987.

———. *The Signifying Monkey: A Theory of African-American Literary Criticism.* New York: Oxford University Press, 1988.

Gayle, Addison, Jr., ed. *The Black Aesthetic.* New York: Doubleday, 1971.

Gomez, Michael A. *Exchanging Our Country Marks: The Transformation of African Identities in the Colonial and Antebellum South.* Chapel Hill: University of North Carolina Press, 1998.

Goodwine, Marquetta L., and the Clarity Press Gullah Project. *The Legacy of Ibo Landing: Gullah Roots of African American Culture.* Atlanta, GA: Clarity, 1998.

Hakutani, Toshinobu. "Richard Wright, Toni Morrison and the African Primal Outlook upon Life." *Southern Quarterly* 40 (Fall 2001): 39–53.

Hale, Thomas A. *Griots and Griottes: Masters of Words and Music.* Bloomington: Indiana University Press, 1998.

Harper, Michael S., and Robert B. Stepto. *Chant of Saints: A Gathering of Afro-American Literature, Art, and Scholarship.* Urbana: University of Illinois Press, 1979.

Harris, Trudier. *Martin Luther King Jr., Heroism, and African American Literature.* Tuscaloosa: University of Alabama Press, 2014.

Herskovits, Melville J. *The Myth of the Negro Past.* Boston: Beacon Press, 1941.

———. *Rebel Destiny: Among the Bush Negroes of Dutch Guiana.* New York: Whittlesey House, 1934.

Higgins, Therese E. *Religiosity, Cosmology, and Folklore: The African Influence in the Novels of Toni Morrison*. New York: Routledge, 2001.

Hill, Donald R. *Caribbean Folklore: A Handbook*. Westport, CT: Greenwood Press, 2007.

Hughes, Langston. *The Collected Works of Langston Hughes*. Vol. 9. Columbia: University of Missouri Press, 1956.

Hynes, William J., and William G. Doty, eds. *Mythical Trickster Figures: Contours, Contexts, and Criticisms*. Tuscaloosa: University of Alabama Press, 1993.

Jackson, Bruce. *The Negro and His Folklore in Nineteenth-Century Periodicals*. Vol. 18. New York: American Folklore Society, 1967.

Jarmon, Laura C. *Wishbone: Reference and Interpretation in Black Folk Narrative*. Knoxville: University of Tennessee Press, 2003.

Johnson, James Weldon, and J. Rosamond Johnson. *The Books of American Negro Spirituals*. New York: Viking, 1954.

Johnson, Yvonne. *The Voices of African American Women: The Use of Narrative and Authorial Voice in the Work of Harriet Jacobs, Zora Neale Hurston, and Alice Walker*. New York: Peter Lang, 1998.

Jones, Charles G. *Negro Myths from the Georgia Coast: Told in the Vernacular*. Boston: Houghton, Mifflin, 1888.

Jones, Gayl. *Liberating Voices: Oral Tradition in African American Literature*. Cambridge, MA: Harvard University Press, 1991.

Jordan, A. C., trans. *Tales from Southern Africa*. Berkeley: University of California Press, 1973.

Joyner, Charles. *Down by the Riverside: A South Carolina Slave Community*. Champaign: University of Illinois Press, 1985.

———. *Shared Traditions: Southern History and Folk Culture*. Urbana: University of Illinois Press, 1999.

Katz, William Loren. *Black Indians: A Hidden Heritage*. New York: Atheneum, 1986.

Ladd, Barbara. *Resisting History: Gender, Modernity, and Authorship in William Faulkner, Zora Neale Hurston, and Eudora Welty*. Baton Rouge: Louisiana State University Press, 2007.

Lemke, Sieglinde. *The Vernacular Matters of American Literature*. New York: Palgrave Macmillan, 2009.

Levine, Lawrence W. *Black Culture and Black Consciousness: Afro-American Folk Thought from Slavery to Freedom*. Oxford: Oxford University Press, 1977.

Lévi-Strauss, Claude. *From Ashes to Honey*. New York: Harper & Row, 1973.

Light, Kathleen. "Uncle Remus and the Folklorists." *Southern Literary Journal*, 7 (1975): 88–104.

Litwack, Leon. *Been in the Storm So Long: The Aftermath of Slavery*. New York: Vintage Books, 1980.

Locke, Alain. *The New Negro: Voices of the Harlem Renaissance*. 1925. New York: Atheneum, 1992.

Lomax, John A. "Stories of an African Prince: Yoruba Tales." *Journal of the American Folklore Society* 26 (1913): 1–12.

Lott, Eric. *Love and Theft: Blackface Minstrelsy and the American Working Class.* New York: Oxford University Press, 1995.

Major, Clarence, ed. *Juba to Jive: A Dictionary of African-American Slang.* New York: Viking, 1994.

Manning, Patrick. *The African Diaspora: A History through Culture.* New York: Columbia University Press, 2009.

Marcus, Greil. *Mystery Train: Images of America in Rock 'n' Roll Music.* 5th ed. New York: Plume, 2008.

Marks-Tarlow, Terry. *Psyche's Veil: Psychotherapy, Fractals, and Complexity.* London: Routledge, 2008.

Marshall, Emily Zobel. "Anansi, Eshu, and Legba: Slave Resistance and the West African Trickster." In *Human Bondage in the Cultural Contact Zone: Transdisciplinary Perspectives on Slavery and Its Discourses*, edited by Raphael Hörmann and Gesa Mackenthun, 170–86. Münster: Waxmann, 2010.

May, Kathryn E. *Who Needs Light?* Bloomington, IN: Authorhouse, 2011.

McDaniel, Lorna. *The Big Drum Ritual of Carriacou: Praisesongs in Rememory of Flight.* Gainesville: University of Florida Press, 1998.

McKay, Nellie Y. *Critical Essays on Toni Morrison.* Boston: G. K. Hall, 1988.

McWhorter, John. "'Tar Baby' Isn't Actually a Racist Slur." *The New Republic* (August 3, 2011).

Meek, Charles Kingsley. *Law and Authority in a Nigerian Tribe: A Study in Indirect Rule.* New York: Barnes & Noble, 1970.

Messenger, J. C. "Anang Proverb-Riddles." *Journal of American Folklore* 73 (1960): 225–35.

Minton, John. *"Big 'Fraid and Little 'Fraid." An Afro-American Folktale.* Helsinki: Soumalainen Tiedeakatemia / Academia Scientiarum Fennica, 1993.

Mobley, Marilyn Sanders. *Folk Roots and Mythic Wings in Sarah Orne Jewett and Toni Morrison.* Baton Rouge: Louisiana State University Press, 1991.

Moody-Turner, Shirley. *Black Folklore and the Politics of Racial Representation.* Jackson: University of Mississippi Press, 2013.

Moody, Shirley C. "Anna Julia Cooper, Charles Chesnutt, and the Hampton Folklore Society: Constructing a Black Folk Aesthetic through Folklore and Memory." In *New Essays on the African American Novel: From Hurston and Ellison to Morrison and Whitehead*, edited by L. King and Linda F. Selzer, 13–32. New York: Palgrave Macmillan, 2008.

Moon, Bucklin, ed. *Primer for White Folks: An Anthology By and About Negroes from Slavery Days to Today's Struggle for a Share in American Democracy.* Garden City, NY: Doubleday, Doran, 1945.

Morgan, Winifred. "Signifying: The African-American Trickster and the Humor of the Old Southwest." In *The Enduring Legacy of Old Southwest Humor*, edited by Edward J. Piacentino, 210–26. Baton Rouge: Louisiana State University Press, 2006.

———. *The Trickster Figure in American Literature.* New York: Palgrave Macmillan, 2013.

Nelson, Scott Reynolds. *Steel Drivin' Man: John Henry. The Untold Story of an American Legend.* Oxford: Oxford University Press, 2006.

Nickels, Cameron C. "An Early Version of the 'Tar Baby' Story." *Journal of American Folklore* 94 (1981): 364–69.

Nikola-Lisa, W. "John Henry: Then and Now." *African American Review* 32 (1998): 51–56.

Ogundipe, Ayodele. *Esu Elegbara: Change, Chance, Uncertainty in Yoruba Mythology.* Ilorin, Kwara State: Kwara State University Press, 2012.

———. *Esu Elegbara, the Yoruba God of Chance and Uncertainty: A Study in Yoruba Mythology.* 2 vols. PhD diss. Bloomington: Indiana University Press, 1978.

Olmsted, Frederick Law. *The Cotton Kingdom: A Traveller's Observations on Cotton and Slavery in the American Slave States, 1853–1861.* New York: DaCapo, 1996.

Opoku-Agyemang, N. J. "'A Girl Marries a Monkey': The Folktale as an Expression of Value and Change in Society." In *Arms Akimbo: Africana Women in Contemporary Literature,* edited by Janice Lee Liddell and Yakini Belinda Kemp, 230–38. Gainesville: University Press of Florida, 1999.

Oster, Harry. "John and Old Marster." *Journal of the Folklore Institute* 5 (1968): 42–57.

Page, Thomas Nelson. *Social Life in Old Virginia before the War.* Freeport, NY: Books for Libraries Press, 1897.

Parr, Michelann, and Terry Campbell. *Balanced Literary Essentials.* Markham, Ontario: Pembroke, 2012.

Pelton, Robert D. *The Trickster in West Africa: A Study of Mythic Irony and Sacred Delight.* Berkeley: University of California Press, 1980.

Peterson, Christopher. "Slavery's Bestiary: Joel Chandler Harris's *Uncle Remus Tales.*" In *Bestial Traces: Race, Sexuality, Animality.* New York: Fordham University Press, 2013.

Piersen, William D. "White Cannibals, Black Martyrs: Fear, Desperation, and Religious Faith as Causes of Suicide among New Slaves." *Journal of Negro History* 62 (1977): 147–60.

Propp, Vladimir. *Morphology of the Folktale.* Austin: University of Texas Press, 1968.

Puckett, Newbell Niles. *Folk Beliefs of the Southern Negro.* Chapel Hill: University of North Carolina Press, 1926.

Rabaka, Reiland. "Preachers." In *The Greenwood Encyclopedia of African American Folklore.* 3 vols. Vol. II, edited by Anand Prahlad, 1013–16. Westport CT: Greenwood, 2005.

Radin, Paul. *The Trickster: A Study in American Indian Mythology.* New York: Philosophical Library, 1956.

Rice, Alan. *Radical Narratives of the Black Atlantic.* London: Continuum, 2003.

Rickels, Patricia K. "Martin Luther King as a Folk Hero." *Xavier Review* 1.1–2 (1980–81): 65–74.

Rico, Patricia San José. "Flying Away: Voluntary Diaspora and the Spaces of Trauma in the African-American Short Story." *Revista de Estudios Norteamericanos* 13 (2008): 63–75.

Roberts, John W. "The African American Animal Trickster as Hero." In *Redefining American Literary History,* edited by LaVonne Brown Ruoff and Jerry W. Ward Jr., 97–114. New York: Modern Language Association, 1990.

———. "'Railroad Bill' and the American Outlaw Tradition." *Western Folklore* 40 (1981): 315–28.

———. "Stackolee and the Development of a Black Heroic Idea." *Western Folklore* 42 (1983): 179–90.

———. *From Trickster to Badman: The Black Folk Hero in Slavery and Freedom.* Philadelphia: University of Pennsylvania Press, 1989.

Rocher, Rosane, ed. *India and Indology: Selected Articles by W. Norman Brown.* Delhi: Motilal Banarsida, 1978.

Rogin, Michael. *Blackface, White Noise.* Berkeley: University of California Press, 1996.

Ross, Joe. "Hags Out of Their Skins." *Journal of American Folklore* 93 (1980): 183–86.

Ruas, Charles. *Conversations with American Writers.* New York: Knopf, 1985.

Scheub, Harold. *African Oral Narratives: Proverbs, Riddles, Poetry and Song.* Boston: G. K. Hall, 1977.

———. *The African Storyteller: Stories from African Oral Traditions.* Dubuque, IA: Kendall Hunt, 1999.

———. *The Tongue Is Fire: South African Storytellers and Apartheid.* Madison: University of Wisconsin Press, 1996.

———. *Trickster and Hero: Two Characters in the Oral and Written Traditions of the World.* Madison: University of Wisconsin Press, 2012.

Schmidt, Gary D., and Donald R. Hettinga, eds. *Sitting at the Feet of the Past: Retelling the North American Folktale for Children.* Contributions to the Study of World Literature No. 45. Westport, CT: Greenwood Press, 1992.

Schuler, Monica. *"Alas, Alas, Kongo": A Social History of Indentured African Immigration into Jamaica, 1841–65.* Baltimore, MD: Johns Hopkins University Press, 1980.

Smith Storey, Olivia. "Flying Words: Contests of Orality and Literacy in the Trope of Flying Africans." *Journal of Colonialism and Colonial History* 5 (2004). *Project MUSE*, https://muse.jhu.edu/.

Smitherman, Geneva. *Black Talk: Words and Phrases from the Hood to the Amen Corner.* Boston: Houghton Mifflin, 1994.

Snead, James. *White Screens. Black Images.* Edited by Colin MacCabe and Cornel West. New York: Routledge, 1994.

Southern, Eileen, and Josephine Wright. *Iconography of Music in African-American Culture (1770s–1920s).* Vol. I: *Music in African-American Culture.* Garland Reference Library of the Humanities, Vol. 2089. New York: Garland, 2000.

Spalding, Henry D., ed. *Encyclopedia of Black Folklore and Humor.* New York: Jonathan David, 1972.

Spencer, Onah L. "Stackalee." *Direction* 4 (1941): 14–17.

Sperb, Jason. *Disney's Most Notorious Film: Race, Convergence, and the Hidden Histories of Song of the South.* Austin: University of Texas Press, 2012.

Spillers, Hortense. "Mama's Baby, Papa's Maybe: An American Grammar Book." *Diacritics* 17 (1987): 65–81.

Spinks, C. W., ed. *Trickster and Ambivalence: The Dance of Differentiation*. Madison, WI: Atwood, 2001.

Stewart, Marian. *Jamaican Anansi Stories and West African Oral Literature: A Comparative Introduction*. Kingston: African-Caribbean Institute of Jamaica, 1982.

Stuckey, Sterling. "Through the Prism of Folklore: The Black Ethos in Slavery." In *Going through the Storm: The Influence of African American Art in History*, 3–18. New York: Oxford University Press, 1994.

Sundquist, Eric J. *The Hammers of Creation: Folk Culture in Modern African-American Fiction*. Athens: University of Georgia Press, 1992.

———. *To Wake the Nations: Race in the Making of American Literature*. Cambridge, MA: Harvard University Press, 1993.

Taylor, Diane. *The Archive and the Repertoire: Performing Cultural Memory in the Americas*. Durham, NC: Duke University Press, 2003.

Taylor, Yuval. *Darkest America: Black Minstrelsy from Slavery to Hip-Hop*. New York: W. W. Norton, 2012.

Taylor-Guthrie, Danille K. *Conversations with Toni Morrison*. Jackson: University Press of Mississippi, 1994.

Thomas, H. Nigel. *From Folklore to Fiction: A Study of Folk Heroes and Rituals in the Black American Novel*. New York: Greenwood, 1988.

Toll, Robert C. *Blacking Up: The Minstrel Show in Nineteenth-Century America*. New York: Oxford University Press, 1974.

Turner, Patricia A. *I Heard It through the Grapevine: Rumor in African-American Culture*. Berkeley: University of California Press, 1993.

Uther, Hans-Jörg. *The Types of International Folktales*. 3 vols. Helsinki: Suomalainen Tiedeakatemia, Academia Scientiarium Fennica, 2004.

Varty, Kenneth. "The Fox and the Wolf in the Well: The Metamorphoses of a Comic Motif." In *Reynard the Fox: Social Engagement and Cultural Metamorphoses in the Beast Epic from the Middle Ages to the Present*, edited by Kenneth Varty, 245–67. New York: Berghahn Books, 2000.

Wagner, Bryan. *The Tar Baby: A Global History*. Princeton, NJ: Princeton University Press, 2017.

Washington, Robert E. *The Ideologies of African American Literature: From the Harlem Renaissance to the Black Nationalist Revolt*. Lanham, MD: Rowman & Littlefield, 2001.

Waters, Wendy W. "'One of Dese Mornings Bright and Fair, / Take My Wings and Cleave De Air': The Legend of the Flying Africans and Diasporic Consciousness." *Melus* 22 (1997): 3–29.

Watkins, Mel. "Talk with Toni Morrison." *New York Times Book Review*. September 11, 1977, 48, 50.

Wilentz, Gay. "If You Surrender to the Air: Folk Legends of Flight and Resistance in African American Literature." *Melus* 16 (1989–90): 21–32.

Wolfe, Bernard. "Uncle Remus and the Malevolent Rabbit." *Commentary* 8 (1949): 31–41.

Wright, Richard. *12 Million Black Voices: A Folk History of the Negro in the United States.* New York: Viking, 1941.

———. *White Man, Listen!* New York: Doubleday, 1957.

Yenika-Agbaw, Ruth McKoy Lowery, and Laretta Henderson. *Fairy Tales with a Black Consciousness: Essays on Adaptations of Familiar Stories.* Jefferson, NC: McFarland, 2013.

Joel Chandler Harris

WRITINGS

Harris, Joel Chandler. *The Complete Tales of Joel Chandler Harris.* Edited by Richard Chase. Boston: Houghton Mifflin, 1955.

———. *Daddy Jake the Runaway and Short Stories Told after Dark.* New York: Century, 1889.

———. *Free Joe and Other Georgian Sketches.* New York: Scribner's, 1887.

———. *Nights with Uncle Remus: Myths and Legends of the Old Plantation.* Boston: Houghton Mifflin, 1883.

———. "The Old Plantation." *The Daily Constitution,* December 9, 1877, 2.

———. Review. *Atlanta Constitution,* November 21, 1877, 2.

———. *Uncle Remus and His Friends.* Boston: Houghton Mifflin, 1892.

———. *Uncle Remus: His Songs and His Sayings. The Folk-Lore of the Old Plantation.* New York: D. Appleton, 1880.

———. *Wally Walderoon and His Story-Telling Machine.* New York: McClure, Philips, 1903.

SECONDARY LITERATURE

Baer, Florence E. *Sources and Analogues of the Uncle Remus Tales.* Helsinki: Suomalainen Tiedeakatemia Academia, Scientiarum Fennica, 1980.

Bickley, R. Bruce, Jr. *Joel Chandler Harris.* Boston: Twayne, 1978.

———. *Joel Chandler Harris: A Reference Guide.* Boston: G. K. Hall, 1978.

———, ed. *Critical Essays on Joel Chandler Harris.* Boston: G. K. Hall, 1981.

———, and Hugh T. Keenan. *Joel Chandler Harris: An Annotated Bibliography of Criticism, 1977–1996. With Supplement, 1892–1976.* Westport, CT: Greenwood, 1997.

Bone, Robert A. *A History of Afro-American Short Fiction from Its Beginnings to the End of the Harlem Renaissance.* New York: G. P. Putnam's Sons, 1975.

Brasch, Walter M. *Brer Rabbit, Uncle Remus, and the "Cornfield Journalist": The Tale of Joel Chandler Harris.* Macon, GA: Mercer University Press, 2000.

Brookes, Stella Brewer. *Joel Chandler Harris—Folklorist.* Athens: University of Georgia Press, 1950.

Chase, Richard, comp. *The Complete Tales of Joel Chandler Harris.* Boston: Houghton Mifflin, 1955.

Cochran, Robert. "Black Father: The Subversive Achievement of Joel Chandler Harris." *African American Review* 38 (2004): 21–34.

Cousins, Paul M. *Joel Chandler Harris: A Biography*. Baton Rouge: Louisiana State University Press, 1968.

David, Beverly R. "Visions of the South: Joel Chandler Harris and His Illustrators." *American Literary Realism, 1870–1910* 9 (1976): 189–206.

Evan, Robert C. "Tricksters in *Uncle Remus: His Songs and His Sayings*." In *The Trickster*, edited by Harold Bloom, 219–28. New York: Chelsea House, 2010.

Gerber, A. "Uncle Remus Traced to the Old World." *Journal of American Folklore* 23 (1893): 245–57.

Harris, Julia Collier. *The Life and Letters of Joel Chandler Harris*. Boston: Houghton Mifflin, 1918.

Hedin, Raymond. "Uncle Remus: Puttin' on Old Massa's Son." *Southern Literary Journal* 15 (1982): 83–90.

Hemenway, Robert. Introduction. *Uncle Remus: His Songs and His Sayings*. New York: Penguin, 1982.

Ives, Sumner. *The Phonology of the Uncle Remus Tales*. Gainesville: American Dialect Society, 1954.

Lester, Julius. *Further Tales of Uncle Remus*. New York: Dial, 1990.

———. *The Last Tales of Uncle Remus*. New York: Dial 1994.

———. *More Tales of Uncle Remus*. New York: Dial, 1988.

———. "The Storyteller's Voice: Reflections on the Rewriting of *Uncle Remus*." In *The Voice of the Narrator in Children's Literature: Insights from Writers and Critics*, 69–73. New York: Greenwood, 1989.

———. *The Tales of Uncle Remus*. New York: Dial, 1987.

Malinowski, Bronislaw. *Coral Gardens and Their Magic*. London: Allen & Unwin, 1935.

Mixon, Wayne. "The Ultimate Irrelevance of Race: Joel Chandler Harris and Uncle Remus in Their Time." *Journal of Southern History* 56 (1990): 457–80.

Peterson, Christopher. *Bestial Traces: Race, Sexuality, Animality*. New York: Fordham University Press, 2013.

Rubin, Louis D., Jr. "Uncle Remus and the Ubiquitous Rabbit." *Southern Review* (1974): 784–804.

Sanders, Mark A., ed. *A Son's Return: Selected Essays of Sterling A. Brown*. Boston: Northeastern University Press, 1996.

Stafford, John. "Patterns of Meaning in *Nights with Uncle Remus*." *American Literature* 18 (1946): 89–108.

Turner, Darwin T. "Daddy Joel Harris and His Old-Time Darkies." *Southern Literary Journal* 1 (1968): 20–41.

Walker, Alice. "The Dummy in the Window: Joel Chandler Harris and the Invention of Uncle Remus." In *Living by the Word*, 18–32. San Diego: Harcourt Brace Jovanovich, 1981.

———. "Uncle Remus: No Friend of Mine." *Southern Exposure* (Summer 1981): 29–31.

Wolfe, Bernard. "Uncle Remus and the Malevolent Rabbit." *Commentary* (July 1949): 31–41.

SONG OF THE SOUTH

Cripps, Thomas. *Making Movies Black: The Hollywood Message Movie from World War II to the Civil Rights Era.* New York: Oxford University Press, 1993.

Crowther, Bosley. "Spanking Disney." *New York Times,* December 8, 1946, section 2, 5.

Frost, Jennifer. *Hedda Hopper's Hollywood: Celebrity Gossip and American Conservatism.* New York: New York University Press, 2011.

Gabler, Neal. *Walt Disney: The Triumph of the American Imagination.* New York: Vintage, 2007.

Keenan, Hugh T. "Twisted Tales: Propaganda in the Tar-Baby Stories." *Southern Quarterly* 22 (1984): 54–69.

Korkis, Jim. *Who's Afraid of the Song of the South? And Other Forbidden Disney Stories.* Orlando, FL: Theme Park Press, 2012.

Rapf, Maurice. *Back Lot: Growing Up with the Movies.* Lanham, MD: Scarecrow Press, 1999.

Russo, Peggy A. "Uncle Walt's Uncle Remus: Disney's Distortion of Harris's Hero." *Southern Literary Journal* 25 (1992): 19–32.

Thomas, Inge M. "Walt Disney's *Song of the South* and the Politics of Animation." *Journal of American Culture* 35 (2012): 219–30.

Turner, Patricia A. *Ceramic Uncles and Celluloid Mammies: Black Images and Their Influence on Culture.* Charlottesville: University of Virginia Press, 2002.

Washington, Fredi. "Fredi Says," *People's Voice,* November 30, 1946.

Watts, Steven. *The Magic Kingdom: Walt Disney and the American Way of Life.* Boston: Houghton Mifflin, 1997.

Zora Neale Hurston

WRITINGS

Hurston, Zora Neale. *Dust Tracks on a Road.* Philadelphia: J. P. Lippincott, 1942; New York: Harper Perennial, 1996.

———. *Folklore, Memoirs, and Other Writings.* Edited by Cheryl A. Wall. New York: Library of America, 1995.

———. *Jonah's Gourd Vine.* Philadelphia: J. P. Lippincott, 1934; New York: Harper Perennial, 1990.

———. *Moses, Man of the Mountain.* Philadelphia: J. P. Lippincott, 1939; New York: Harper Perennial, 1991.

———. *Mules and Men.* Philadelphia: J. P. Lippincott, 1935; New York: Harper Perennial, 1990.

———. *Novels and Stories.* Edited by Cheryl A. Wall. New York: Library of America, 2004.

———. *The Sanctified Church: The Folklore Writings of Zora Neale Hurston.* Berkeley, CA: Turtle Island, 1981.

———. *Seraph on the Sewanee.* New York: Scribner's, 1948; New York: Harper Perennial, 1991.

———. *Tell My Horse*. Philadelphia: J. P. Lippincott, 1938; New York: Harper Perennial, 1990.

———. *Their Eyes Were Watching God*. Philadelphia: J. P. Lippincott, 1937; New York: Harper Perennial, 1990.

SECONDARY LITERATURE

Blake, Susan L. "Folklore and Community in *Song of Solomon*." *Melus* 7 (1980): 77–82.

Bloom, Harold, ed. *Zora Neale Hurston: Modern Critical Views*. New York: Chelsea House, 1986.

Boyd, Valerie. *Wrapped in Rainbows: The Life of Zora Neale Hurston*. New York: Scribner's, 2003.

Carby, Hazel V. "The Politics of Fiction, Anthropology, and the Folk: Zora Neale Hurston." In *New Essays on* Their Eyes Were Watching God," 71–93. Cambridge, UK: Cambridge University Press, 1990.

Croft, Robert W. *A Zora Neale Hurston Companion*. Westport, CT: Greenwood Press, 2002.

Cronin, Gloria, ed. *Critical Essays on Zora Neale Hurston*. Boston: G. K. Hall, 1998.

Davis, Cynthia. *Zora Neale Hurston: An Annotated Bibliography of Works and Criticism*. Lanham, MD: Scarecrow Press, 2013.

Faulkner, Howard J. "*Mules and Men*: Fiction as Folklore." *CLA Journal* 34 (1991): 331–39.

Gandal, Keith. "A Shameful Look at Zora Neale Hurston." In *Class Representation in Modern Fiction and Film*, 45–91. New York: Palgrave Macmillan, 2007.

Gates, Henry Louis, Jr., and Kwame Anthony Appiah, eds. *Zora Neale Hurston: Critical Perspectives Past and Present*. New York: Amistad, 1987.

Glassman, Steve, and Kathryn Lee Seidel, eds. *Zora in Florida*. Orlando: University of Central Florida Press, 1991.

Grant, Nathan. *Toomer, Hurston, Black Writing, and Modernity*. Columbia: University of Missouri Press, 2004.

Harris, Trudier. "Africanizing the Audience: Hurston's Transformation of White Folks in *Mules and Men*." *Zora Neale Hurston Forum* 8 (1993): 43–58.

———. *The Power of the Porch: The Storyteller's Craft in Zora Neale Hurston, Gloria Naylor, and Randall Kenan*. Athens: University of Georgia Press, 1996.

Hemenway, Robert. *Zora Neale Hurston: A Literary Biography*. Chicago and Urbana: University of Illinois Press, 1980.

Hinnov, Emily M. *Encountering Choran Community: Literary Modernism, Visual Culture, and Political Aesthetics in the Interwar Years*. Selinsgrove, PA: Susquehanna University Press, 2009.

Howard, Lillie P. *Zora Neale Hurston*. Boston: Twayne, 1980.

Hurston, Lucy Anne. *Speak, So You Can Speak Again: The Life of Zora Neale Hurston*. New York: Doubleday, 2004.

Jennings, La Vinia Delois. *Zora Neale Hurston, Haiti, and Their Eyes Were Watching God*. Evanston, IL: Northwestern University Press, 2013.

Jones, Sharon L. *Critical Companion to Zora Neale Hurston: A Literary Reference to Her Life and Work.* New York: Facts on File, 2009.

Kaplan, Carla. Introduction. *Every Tongue Got to Confess.* Edited by John Wideman. New York: Harper Perennial, 2001.

———. *Zora Neale Hurston: A Life in Letters.* New York: Doubleday, 2002.

Karanja, Ayana I. *Zora Neale Hurston: The Breath of Her Voice.* New York: Peter Lang, 1999.

King, Lovalerie. *The Cambridge Introduction to Zora Neale Hurston.* Cambridge, UK: Cambridge University Press, 2008.

Ladd, Barbara. *Resisting History: Gender, Modernity, and Authorship in William Faulkner, Zora Neale Hurston, and Eudora Welty.* Baton Rouge: Louisiana State University Press, 2007.

Lawless, Elaine J. "What Zora Knew: A Crossroads, a Bargain with the Devil, and a Late Witness." *Journal of American Folklore* 126 (2013): 152–73.

LeClair, Thomas. "The Language Must Not Sweat." *The New Republic,* March 21, 1981.

McKay, Nellie Y. *Critical Essays on Toni Morrison.* Boston: G. K. Hall, 1988.

Peters, Pearlie Mae Fisher. *The Assertive Woman in Zora Neal Hurston's Fiction, Folklore, and Drama.* New York: Garland, 1998.

Plant, Deborah. *Every Tub Must Sit on Its Own Bottom: The Philosophy and Politics of Zora Neale Hurston.* Urbana: University of Illinois Press, 1995.

West, M. Genevieve. *Zora Neale Hurston and American Literary Culture.* Gainesville: University of Florida Press, 2005.

Yitah, Helen. "Rethinking the African American Great Migration Narrative: Reading Zora Neale Hurston's *Jonah's Gourd Vine.*" *Southern Quarterly* 49 (2011): 10–29.

Fiction, Autobiographies, and Essays

Baldwin, James. *Notes of a Native Son.* Boston: Beacon Press, 1955.

Brodhead, Richard H., ed. *The Journals of Charles W. Chesnutt.* Durham, NC: Duke University Press, 1993.

Brown, Sterling. *Negro Poetry and Drama, and The Negro in American Fiction.* New York: Atheneum, 1969.

———. *A Son's Return: Selected Essays of Sterling A. Brown.* Edited by Mark Sanders. Boston: Northeastern University Press, 1996.

———. *Sterling A. Brown's A Negro Looks at the South.* Edited by John Edgar Tidwell and Mark A. Sanders. Oxford: Oxford University Press, 2007.

Carmer, Carl. *Stars Fell on Alabama.* New York: Farrar & Rinehart, 1934.

Chesnutt, Charles W. *The Conjure Woman.* New York: Houghton Mifflin, 1899.

Douglass, Frederick. *Life and Times of Frederick Douglass Written by Himself.* Hartford, CT.: Park Publishing Co., 1882.

Dunbar, Paul Laurence. *The Complete Stories of Paul Laurence Dunbar.* Athens: Ohio University Press, 2006.

Ellison, Ralph. *Flying Home and Other Stories.* New York: Random House, 1996.

———. *Going to the Territory.* New York: Random House, 1986.

————. *Invisible Man.* New York: Random House, 1952.

————. *Shadow and Act.* New York: Random House, 1995.

Hamilton, Virginia. *The Magical Adventures of Pretty Pearl.* New York: Harper & Row, 1983.

Haley, Alex. *Roots.* Garden City, NY: Doubleday, 1976.

Hughes, Langston. *Essays on Art, Race, Politics, and World Affairs.* Edited by Christopher C. De Santis. Columbia: University of Missouri Press, 2002.

Kennedy, R. Emmet. *Black Cameos.* New York: Albert & Charles Boni, 1924.

Killens, John Oliver. *Black Man's Burden.* New York: Trident, 1965.

Marshall, Paule. *Praisesong for the Widow.* New York: G. P. Putnam's Sons, 1983.

Montejo, Esteban. *The Autobiography of a Runaway Slave.* Edited by Miguel Barnet. Translated by Jocasta Innes. London: Bodley Head, 1968.

Morrison, Toni. *Playing in the Dark: Whiteness and the Literary Imagination.* New York: Vintage, 1993.

————. "Rootedness: The Ancestor as Foundation." In *Black Women Writers (1950–1980): A Critical Evaluation,* edited by Mari Evans, 339–45. New York: Anchor Press, 1984.

————. *Song of Solomon.* New York: Knopf, 1977.

————. *Tar Baby.* New York: Vintage, 1981.

O'Neill, Eugene. *All God's Chillun Got Wings.* In *Plays.* New York: Horace Liveright, 1925.

Perry, Richard. *Montgomery's Children.* New York: Harcourt Brace Jovanovich, 1984.

Reed, Ishmael. *Flight to Canada.* New York: Avon, 1975.

Twain, Mark. *The Adventures of Huckleberry Finn.* New York: Harper & Brothers, 1912.

Online Resources

Smithsonian National Museum of African American History and Culture
http://nmaahc.si.edu/

Library of Congress Digital Collections
https://www.loc.gov/collections/

Farm Security Administration/Office of War Information Black-and-White Negatives
http://www.loc.gov/pictures/collection/fsa/

Carnegie Survey of the Architecture of the South
https://www.loc.gov/collections/carnegie-survey-architecture-of-the-south/about-this-collection/

American English Dialect Recordings: The Center for Applied Linguistics Collection
https://www.loc.gov/collections/american-english-dialect-recordings-from-the-center-for
-applied-linguistics/

Florida Folklife from the WPA Collections, 1937 to 1942
(includes recordings of Zora Neale Hurston)
https://www.loc.gov/collections/florida-folklife-from-the-works-progress-administration/
about-this-collection/

Tending the Commons: Folklife and Landscape in Southern West Virginia
https://www.loc.gov/collections/folklife-and-landscape-in-southern-west-virginia/

Traditional Music and Spoken Word Catalog
https://memory.loc.gov/diglib/ihas/html/afccards-home.html

Voices from the Dust Bowl: The Charles L. Todd and Robert Sonkin Migrant Worker Collection,
    1940 to 1941
https://www.loc.gov/collections/todd-and-sonkin-migrant-workers-from-1940-to-1941/
    about-this-collection/

Lomax Collection
https://www.loc.gov/collections/lomax/about-this-collection/

Southern Mosaic: The John and Ruby Lomax 1939 Southern States Recording Trip
https://www.loc.gov/collections/john-and-ruby-lomax/about-this-collection/

W. E. B. Du Bois
https://www.loc.gov/rr/program/bib/dubois/

African American Photographs Assembled for 1900 Paris Exposition
http://www.loc.gov/pictures/collection/anedub/dubois.html

New York Public Library, Schomburg Center for Research in Black Culture
http://www.nypl.org/locations/schomburg

Schomburg Center Prints and Photographs Division
http://digitalcollections.nypl.org/divisions/schomburg-center-for-research-in-black-culture
    -photographs-and-prints-division

Yale University, African American Studies at Beinecke Library
http://beinecke.library.yale.edu/about/blogs/african-american-studies-beinecke-library

Richard Wright Papers
http://hdl.handle.net/10079/fa/beinecke.wright

Randolph Linsly Simpson African-American Collection
http://hdl.handle.net/10079/fa/beinecke.pubsim
http://brbl-dl.library.yale.edu/vufind/Search/Results?lookfor=JWJ_MSS_54&type=CallNumber

National Association of Black Storytellers
http://www.nabsinc.org/

American Antiquarian Society
http://www.americanantiquarian.org/african-american-resources

American Folklore Society, Folklore Collections Database

http://www.folklorecollections.org/

University of North Carolina at Chapel Hill Wilson Library, Southern Folklife Collection
http://library.unc.edu/wilson/sfc/

Documenting the American South
http://docsouth.unc.edu

Southern Sources: Exploring the Southern Historical Collection blog
http://blogs.lib.unc.edu/shc

State Library and Archives of Florida
https://www.floridamemory.com/

Valdosta State University, South Georgia FolkLife Collection
http://archives.valdosta.edu/folklife/

Michigan State University, African Oral Narratives
http://www.aodl.org/oralnarratives/

Harvard University, Hutchins Center
Image of the Black Archive and Library
http://hutchinscenter.fas.harvard.edu/image-of-the-black-archive-library

Blvck Vrchives
http://www.blvckvrchives.com/

American South: The Front Porch
http://www.blvckvrchives.com/american-south

Black Past
http://www.blackpast.org/

Zora Neale Hurston Florida Memory Blog
http://www.floridamemory.com/blog/2014/10/13/zora-neale-hurston/